WE, THE ACCUSED

Ernest Raymond
Born in 1888, Ernest Raymond came to fame with his 1922 novel, *Tell England, A Study in a Generation*, set during the First World War. His next big success was *We, The Accused* (1935). A third novel, *The Chalice and the Sword* (1952), found a wide readership.

Raymond's autobiography, *Please You, Draw Near*, was published in 1969. He was awarded an OBE in 1972, and died in 1974.

Clive Stafford Smith [illegible] a formidable reputation on both sides of the Atlantic as a campaigner against the death penalty. A lawyer specialising in civil rights, Stafford Smith's book *Bad Men* tells of his experiences working on behalf of detainees at Guantánamo Bay. He lives in England, where he is director of Reprieve.

We, The Accused

We, The Accused

Ernest Raymond

FOREWORD BY CLIVE STAFFORD SMITH

CAPUCHIN CLASSICS

CAPUCHIN CLASSICS
LONDON

We, The Accused

First published 1983
This edition published by Capuchin Classics 2009

2 4 6 8 0 9 7 5 3 1

Capuchin Classics
128 Kensington Church Street, London W8 4BH
Telephone: +44 (0)20 7221 7166
Fax: +44 (0)20 7792 9288
E-mail: info@capuchin-classics.co.uk
www.capuchin-classics.co.uk

Châtelaine of Capuchin Classics: Emma Howard

ISBN: 978-0-9559602-5-3

Foreword

For the past 25 years, the death penalty has been a part of my daily work. I am very grateful that the overwhelming majority of the people I have represented have avoided the execution chamber, but my mind can rarely avoid memories of the six men who have died.

One was Nick Ingram. He and I were born in the same hospital – a maternity ward in Cambridge – but we only met on his arrival on Georgia's Death Row. We became close friends over the twelve years that I tried to stave off his execution and as I close my eyes, I still see the images, seared into my brain like black and white negatives: Nick dying in the electric chair.

While I wish others would read about capital punishment – and be inspired to do something about ending it – reading about the condemned is not the way I generally spend my leisure time (which is precious to me!). I am not quite sure why I agreed to consider writing a brief foreword to *We, The Accused* by Ernest Raymond.

I am very glad that I did, because it is a magnificent read, and certainly enriches the canon on the subject of capital punishment, in line with the goals of the Capuchin series – reviving unjustly forgotten works. While the book has been out of print, the film world saw the potential in Raymond's tale of murder-in-marriage: Alfred Hitchcock considered it for production (but was deterred by its 'downbeat' nature) and the BBC created a series starring Ian Holm in 1980. But it as a novel that this story is most powerfully told, as it is Raymond's precise and thoughtful prose that makes the narrative so mesmerizing.

It is easy to explain a miscarriage of justice or a crime of passion – but when your chief protagonist is accused of premeditated murder, the reader's empathy is always going to be hard won. This is the challenge that Raymond set himself, and I admire his achievement. The second half of a capital trial in America involves a similar challenge; the issue of guilt has already been decided, and we lawyers have to present the life and circumstances of the defendant in a way that enables the jurors to reject death as the appropriate punishment.

Evoking empathy is the key – empathy rather than sympathy, as pity tends to dehumanise its subject. The challenge is to persuade the jurors to see parallels between their own experiences and the prisoner's. It is a terrible responsibility.

I came to care deeply for the chief protagonist in *We, The Accused* – a human nonentity, Paul Arthur Presset, who is accused of poisoning his wife. The book is a series of character studies – of victim, of killer, of policeman, of lawyer, of judge, of prison warder, of executioner, and of husband, wife and lover. There is little sense of any absolute of good and evil. Everyone is a shade of grey, as all human beings are wont to be.

'I daresay some of 'em weren't such bad fellows after all,' suggests one guard, speaking of the prisoners facing execution. The guard is swinging his pickaxe, digging a six-foot grave for a prisoner who still lives within the gaol, in the fullest of health, destined soon to die.

'They're never so bad when you know them,' replies the other. 'And no one can say what brought them to it. Happen there was more to it than any of us knows. Happen they didn't have much chance.'

These words foreshadow the mantra of Sister Helen Prejean (famous as the feisty nun portrayed in the film *Dead Man Walking*) that 'everyone is more than his worst fifteen minutes.' She should know. We used to run into each other periodically at Louisiana's Death Row.

Ernest Raymond makes sure that his central character Paul Presset is more than his worst moments. The author weaves a dense relationship where few will doubt that Presset was the kinder partner in his marriage to Elinor. At the same time there are moments of insight into Elinor's character that make her murder seem even more tragic.

We, The Accused rings true to my experience on many levels. Another of the desperately unfortunate prisoners who died on my watch was Edward Earl Johnson, whose hope and despair leading up to his 1987 execution in the Gas Chamber was captured in the BBC documentary, *Fourteen Days In May*. The kindest people in the last days of Edward's life at Mississippi State Penitentiary were the guards, with Warden Don Cabana the most humane of all. Don was a stereotype of a Deep Southern corrections man, drawling directions to his staff. But he got to know Edward and treated him as a human being in his final days and hours, serving him that final meal of shrimp, and ensuring that his family was there to hug him towards the end.

As *We, The Accused* runs towards its denouement, it is uncertain whether clemency will save Presset: clearly he should be saved, but who will be his salvation? Meanwhile, the prison Governor, a retired army colonel, approaches his task with regimented prejudices in perfect order. But on visiting the man in his care,

> he was struck with surprise, as the two warders came to attention and the prisoner nervously copied them, to see a small, sad-eyed, and apparently harmless man. A few minutes of conversation, and he was surprised to find him courteous, considerate, and uncomplaining. And with the days, this surprise became distress, a distress that could find relief only in little services to him.

This book is held to have contributed to the ultimate demise of capital punishment in Britain; more than three quarters of a century on the Americans are still executing each other. Raymond sums up what to me has always been the most potent argument against the death penalty in the simple description of a man counting down towards death:

> These wasting hours, how to fill them? Take a man in perfect health, keep him with the utmost care in perfect health so that

> he can really suffer, remove the future from him – cut out, that is to say, all aspiration, all hope of achievement, all necessity to earn, all desire to make the body fine and the mind strong, all pleasure in creative work – and how will he spent the hours? Drift from one unrecoverable minute to the next.

We can debate various issues about the death penalty: Does it deter other crimes? Does it save society the cost of incarcerating the prisoner for life? Can we be sure that the condemned is guilty? Can a capital trial ever truly be fair? And thus, on and on.

For me, these questions have always been beside the point. As I have come out of the witness room, the execution completed, I have always looked up at the waiting stars – it is always around midnight, for we rarely perform these dark deeds in daylight. We have just methodically put a fellow human being to death and I ask myself: Has the world become a better place?

While an earnest minister may appear in the pages of his book, Ernest Raymond does not preach at his audience. Nevertheless, it is clear that all those years ago he gave an eloquent and profound answer to my question. I only hope that one day our society – 'We, The Accused' – can plead 'not guilty' to Raymond's ultimate charge.

Clive Stafford Smith
Cambridge, March 2009

Clive Stafford Smith is the director of Reprieve, the UK legal action charity that uses the law to enforce the human rights of prisoners, from death row to Guantánamo Bay. For more information and to support this work, see www.reprieve.org.uk, or contact Reprieve, PO Box 52742, London EC4P 4WS. Telephone: +44 (0)20 7353 4640, e-mail: info@reprieve.org.uk.

A Note on the Places and Time of this Tale

The police stations and prisons in the last part of this story are composite pictures, and their inhabitants fictitious. In the same way the story's date must be considered as composite; that is to say, I have conceived it as happening on the whole, in a time when gold coins were in use and money had earlier values and prison officers were called warders, but pursuing essential rather than mere factual truth I have allowed one or two modern improvements in prison and police methods to appear as if in existence then, and, for descriptive value have used 'warder' and 'officer' interchangeably and called all prison rooms 'cells'. In a word I have here and there taken a dramatist's liberty with chronology and picked the best from different years, to try to build for you the truest story I can.

E. R.

PART I

Chapter One

Daylight, coming on duty with gradual step, took over London from the night. As a regiment relieves another, secretly and in a great quiet, the daylight crossed the highways and the side-streets, dropping its platoons at their posts of duty. Only the late and the early workers saw it come, for it was a September morning and the sun rose at half-past five: the watchman watched it over his dying brazier and the hole in the road; the strolling policeman saw it across a yawn, as he waited for *his* relief; the drivers of market carts or brewers' drays saw it over their horses' cruppers, and the milkman over his churn and cans; the labourers, walking to their work past the shuttered windows or crossing the main roads so unusually empty, brushed shoulders with it; sad-eyed women pulled up their blinds to it; and captives in prison, as it struck their cell walls, woke to its message and to memory. And far away – always far away – dogs barked a greeting to it.

In a moment or two, like an Arabian jinnie, it had created a city out of darkness and nothing. It had made the long blocks of houses and the isolated buildings solid and four-square and whole. It had washed colour on to the façades and given depth to the long ravines of the roads. It had thrown shadows beyond the lampposts and the masts of ships, and lit up a network of wires over the huddled and straggling assembly, as the dew and the sun, between them, light up the cobwebs over the undergrowth. It had created anew a few of man's finest achievements and more of his mistakes.

Perhaps we may account Islington Vale, in the north of London, as one of the mistakes. But not the worst of them: there was, in these days, much worse stuff between the Vale and the City's heart, for here were the courts and alleys where the poorest lived, and the criminals ran to the earth that bred them. Islington Vale came back to life as a congregation of 'residential', if decaying, roads and crescents and squares that stood linked together where the Caledonian, Camden and Holloway Roads run to meet near the road named after the Seven Sisters. Indeed, these three great rivers of traffic and business may be said to have created the 'residential' district of Islington Vale as the Euphrates and Tigris created Mesopotamia.

But we account it a mistake, since men should do better than build such narrow and pretentious houses on fields that once were lovely. We can but remember the beauty that lies slain and buried beneath them. It was of Islington Vale that Fitzstephen, friend of Thomas à Becket, wrote, 'On the north of London are fields for pasture, and open meadows, very pleasant, into which the river waters do flow, and mills are turned about with a delightful noise. Beyond them an immense forest extends itself, beautified with woods and groves, and full of the lairs and coverts of beasts and game.' That was in Becket's day; and for many centuries afterwards these northern fields were the playground of London. Fine gentlemen with hawks on their wrists came this way for a day of falconry among the partridge and the heron. Meaner citizens with their dogs came laughing to chase the hare. Here is a body of sportsmen, gentle and boorish both, with Harry the King at its head, trooping out with old yew bows and long arrows to practise at the butts which stud the fields, and to scorn a shot which is less than twelve dozen yards. Here is Elizabeth herself, with her gentlemen in swords and ruffs, riding out by Aldersgate Bars to find the same refreshing air. Here come the jolly citizens and braw lads (Shakespeare among them, perhaps) to find the cream and syllabubs at the dairies and pleasure gardens, and to hunt the ducks in the ponds or the milkmaids behind the wall:

'Where's dame, quoth son of shop,
She's gone her cake in milk to sop.
Ho, ho! to Islington! Enough!
Fetch Job, my son, and our dog, Ruff,
For there in pond, through mire and muck,
We'll cry, Hay, duck! There, Ruff! Hay, duck!'

And here, in the next two centuries, come the literary men and the artists and the wits, boarding the sixpenny stage that plies every hour between the city and Canonbury, to find the same quiet country air. Here's Oliver Goldsmith, bringing his friends to Islington for a roaring Irish jaunt. He has breakfasted them at his Temple Chambers, and brings them forth by the City Road. They stroll through the fields and order dinner at Highbury Barn. Then on through the pleasant places for tea in a milkmaid's garden, and supper and song at an eating house in Canonbury, and so we all come roaring home to London.

And now all that is left of these dear northern fields is the narrow patches of garden behind the stucco houses; beautiful only in May, before the smoke dust falls on the leaves.

The Caledonian Road runs up the middle of Islington Vale; and Elm Tree Road (what famous tree of the old pleasure gardens did the name celebrate, and did Goldsmith know it and sit beneath it with the milkmaid or the serving wench?) Elm Tree Road breaks from the Caledonian Road and runs east-north-east towards the Camden Road; so it is easy to see that the shafts of sunlight this morning quickly visited the houses on its northern side and peeped in at the life behind. These houses on the north side were all alike: squarish houses built in pairs, with walls of grey brick and roofs of Welsh slate, and worth about fifty pounds a year. Each had a narrow front garden fenced from the road by the pretentious business of a dwarf wall, an iron railing, and brick piers with cement caps by the gate. Some of these piers, unable to sustain their ill-founded dignity, were already listing a little mournfully; but others were still very prim and upright and clean. From the gate a flagged path went to a flight of fully eleven York stone steps, which mounted to a heavy stucco porch and a broad, if blistered, hall door.

Now, the steps were flanked with brick piers and a low wall, and one of the houses went so far as to have a small grey urn on either pier. Postmen and dustmen and errand boys would designate this house 'the house with the urns' at the time of which we are writing; and they did so for long afterwards, for by then the house had a story. This particular morning it was obviously inhabited: the front garden was cared for, the venetian blinds were neatly down, and the milk can stood on the doorstep. But in later years, thanks to its story, it stood empty, its garden overgrown, its windows cracked and grimed, and the same old venetian blinds askew; and people came up the street on purpose to take covert glances at it. Errand boys, not the least bit covert, stood and stared at it, their frank mouths open. Most people gave their longest look to the steps, thinking of those who had gone up them, and those who had hurried down them, especially for the last time. What emotions of joy and exultation, of alarm and terror and despair, those steps had known! One glanced again at the worn places in their treads, before passing on. Then Time mantled the house in the mercy of forgetfulness, and people lived and laughed in it once more.

A venetian blind slatted up in the window next the front door, and an exceedingly rosy face looked out. Such a face, with its full cheeks and happy eyes, could not have been in the world for much more than sixteen years. If the cheeks were rosy and full, the forehead was white and broad, with brown hair about it, and a flat maid-servant's cap above. A pair of plump round arms, issuing from rolled-up pink sleeves, pushed up the window sash, and dusted the sill with a soft brush. Then face and arms turned away, and one saw a pink cotton back disappearing.

Annie Mavis was having a sweep and a dust-round in the dining-room, before either master or mistress was awake. Like her face, her figure was short and plump and round; and her pink print dress, her plain apron, her black stockings and square shoes did nothing to lessen the general roundness. The busy hands were dirty from raking out the kitchen grate, and the brown hair, quickly thrown up, had fallen into some disarray; but because she was sixteen and fresh and lively, it was all quite pleasant to look upon. Where in the grey Islington roads she fetched her rosy colour it would be difficult to say; perhaps she was a daughter of the milkmaids, and still flew their flag in her cheeks.

A marble clock on the marble mantelpiece struck seven, and Annie laid down her dust-pan and brush, and ran buoyantly up the stairs to a door on the first floor. Here she knocked once and knocked again.

'It's seven o'clock, sir.'

'What?' said a voice within; plainly the voice of a waker. 'Yes, what?' It sounded a little frightened, as if its owner had wakened too suddenly.

'It's gone seven o'clock, sir.'

'Pardon? . . . Oh, yes, it's you, is it, Annie. Oh, thank you, Annie.' There was something kind, even affectionate, in the repetition of her name; and in the attempt at facetiousness that followed. 'Seven o'clock, is it? Well, really! Upon my word!'

'Yes, sir.'

'Well, this won't do at all, will it, Annie? By the way, don't wake Mrs Presset.'

'No, sir.'

'No. She was rather poorly last night, she said; and I think you'd better take her up some breakfast on a tray . . . if you don't mind. Just a little.'

'I see, sir.'

'Yes. . .' and the voice added apologetically, 'She's not really very well. Thank you so much, if you will, Annie.'

'All right, sir.' And Annie came away from the door and ran down the stairs, but not without a sniff and a pout.

Inside the room the master lay in bed for one minute – two minutes – longer. He had to slough off the terror of a dream. In the dream he had been a child again in his father's little stationer's shop at Petfield. It was some dread hour between midnight and dawn, and he had slipped guiltily down the stairs to steal a book from the stock of Sunday School prizes. In the shadowed dark the little shop with its counter, its glass cabinets, and its shelves piled high with stock, was a menacing place, and nowhere could he find the book he wanted, and he must find it before something happened – or something came nearer – and his head ached with frustration and defeat. He climbed on the shop ladder, and rummaged on the high shelves, till the cardboard boxes of envelopes and the brown-paper parcels of notepaper came down upon him in a cataract, starting alarm in his heart and tears in his eyes. He searched frantically among ledgers and cash books and hymn books, and then came the foot on the stairs! Someone was coming down to find him. He dashed through the dark parlour to the shed at the back where the printing press and the ink-slab stood black and gloomy in the dark, and the imposing surface shone like a lake of metal. He hid among the machines, and knew that his father was coming down the stairs in his braided coat, with a stick in his hand. Already Winnie, his sister, was peeping at him to see what would happen; and his mother had appeared from somewhere, frightened, vexed and irritable. 'Aren't we poor enough without your doing this?' she asked as he slunk by the machines. 'Haven't I worries enough without your provoking your father? God knows what'll come to you, shifty as you are! Your father's going to take a stick to you, and make no mistake about it! He's coming now.' And they heard his footsteps nearer. The boy was frantic. To get out – to get free – to escape from this shed with its terrible machines – out into the daylight where there was a radiance – an especial radiance for him, which was somehow sweet to the taste and exhilarating like wine! To get to it and be free and happy beyond words – but he could not move; his feet were clamped to the floor like the column on the inkslab; there was only darkness and faces about him, though some other part of his mind could see the radiance outside and far away, like a golden cloud. And the step came nearer, and someone knocked on the door. 'What? . . . Pardon? . . .'

'It's seven o'clock, sir.'

Oh, the relief to wake and to find oneself no longer that frightened child but Mr Paul Arthur Presset, fifty years old, ten years married, and master of his own house. And to know that the knocker was only little Annie. And that inaccessible radiance in his dream: he identified it at once with a joy that had come into his life. Only a few months ago, and he had felt his life to be rather dull and dismal – though not, to be sure, as dark and disturbing as that shed in the dream – and now this joy! This incredible joy!

He got up and stood on the frayed carpet, a spare and thin little man in a night-shirt. He pushed his feet into slippers, picked up a book from the bedside table, and went quickly across the landing to the bathroom. It was such a bathroom as thousands more of his class must be shaving in that morning: its walls papered with an imitation of dutch tiles, and its window with an imitation of stained glass; its bath boxed in by a kind of mahogany sarcophagus; a framed mirror hanging over the wash-basin, and a framed picture from a Christmas

Annual over the bath. He began by turning on the cold tap to fill the bath, but this was done only for the ear of Annie in the kitchen, or of Mrs Presset, if awake, in the bedroom nearby. An occasional cold bath was the proper thing for a man; and he let them suppose that he took and enjoyed one. But he had no intention of plunging into anything so chill and heart-arresting. When the time came he would do as others before him – splash the water first with one foot and then with the other, so as to leave wet footprints on the floor. Meantime he let the tap run with a lively noise.

He laid the book open on the window shelf beside him, so that he could study it as he shaved. It was a key to Stone's 'French Prose Composition', and he intended to study the page till he almost knew it by heart, so that he shouldn't teach his boys anything wrong this morning, but, rather, should exhibit before them a remarkable facility. Ever anxious to retain his job, he had recently allowed his headmaster to suppose that his knowledge of French was larger than it was; just as, on applying for the job, he had pretended to slightly more Latin than he knew.

He began to lather his cheek, and, as he did so, gazing into the mirror, he was shocked and disappointed by the face that he saw: that dishevelled hair, that lined forehead, those tired eyes, those undeniable grey bristles in the stubble, and, most disheartening of all, that weak, resentful and obstinate chin – how could she love him in the way she did? How could anyone love a face like that? And yet she did. Women must be very different from men, and care little for sensuous beauty. He liked neatness and tidiness; and it was shocking, the difference between himself when untidy from bed and himself when brushed and spruced for school. She must never see him like this. Never.

The razor scraped through the bristles, and the stiffness of his beard pleased him. He was proud of having a strong beard: it was compensation for his short, thin, knobbly body. And, washing his hands, he was happier again because he was proud of them too; and indeed they were beautiful, or would have been beautiful on a taller man, with their long oval palms and long sensitive fingers tapering to pointed nails. He forgot his disappointments, and remembered only the radiance. By four o'clock he would be walking to meet it, and by five he would be in its heart. Diffidence changed to confidence. After all there was a better side to his character, as there was a better side to his looks. In the past he had been a trifle shifty sometimes, but he would try not to be so now – at least, not more than was quite unavoidable. He would try to be worthy of her. He hated his own timidity and shiftiness, really; and as a first step towards conquering it, he suddenly decided to get into the cold bath. Not to convince Annie or his wife, but to convince himself that he was better than he thought. He forced himself into it – right up to the neck, with no shirking – and the cold shock forced him as quickly out. He rubbed himself with the towel, while his body glowed and his conscience glowed. Then back to his bedroom across the dark landing, book in hand, going quietly past the room where the door was shut.

Soon he was entering the dining-room, just as Annie brought in his egg, and he laughed with her, rubbing his hands, 'That's right, Annie. Put it down. I've got an appetite this morning! The water was a bit colder than usual, but there's nothing like it to give you an appetite. Absolutely nothing. Have you got something nice for Mrs Presset?'

'Yes, sir.'

'Good,' said he, spreading the French book open by his place. 'You don't mind, do you? We must do what we can for her when she's a little below par. We can't all be as bonny as you, you know! Or me, either! I'm never ill from one year's end to the other. So run up and take her a nice breakfast.'

Annie gave him a bright, grateful glance, and withdrew.

And Mr Presset sat down cheerily, drawing his chair under him. As he chipped his egg and conned his French, he was little aware of the room around him, which seemed the permanent furnishing of his life; but it had its significance. The wallpaper was red with a silken stripe, and surmounted by a frieze depicting a woodland sunset – or twenty-five woodland sunsets – which frieze was the only thing in the room selected by himself, and expressed something deep in his nature. The window was draped with long lace curtains from bamboo rod to floor, and behind the curtains, as nearly horizontal as might be, were the venetian blinds which we have seen Annie pulling up. Against the red walls were a mahogany sideboard with several heavy cruets upon it, a brown bookcase with a cupboard beneath, and a suite of saddle-bag chairs and sofa. From a brass picture rail hung some engravings of stags and other game, a study of a shy elopement in Regency cloaks, and, far more striking than these, a greatly enlarged photograph of Mrs Presset, which showed her, face and bust, in a velvet evening dress, a pearl necklace, and a coiffure of many years before. This photograph of Elinor Presset, big and plump and prosperous, seemed to preside over the room, as well it might, for all this heavy furniture had been hers when she was the wife of a more successful man than Mr Presset; and both felt that it was hers still.

There was a letter by his plate, but he did not open it. He had no sooner recognised the writing than he resolved not to open it, lest it worried him and spoiled his day; and, suddenly glancing at it over the French book, he seized it and thrust it into his jacket pocket.

He went on eating and reading, till he heard Annie go by with a jingling tray and felt moved again to show his fondness for her by a jocosity. 'Now be careful, Annie! Be careful!' he called; and Annie laughed with that excessive appreciation which servants accord to the jokes of their masters. Soon he heard her feet treading the room above him, and a bed creaking, and voices.

After eight. He rose. Now he must go up to the bedroom and say goodbye to Elinor. But not yet. He would not go there yet.

Like a child he would run for a while from the thing that hurt. Truth to tell, though he was not without some affection for Elinor, he would have preferred to get out of the house without saying goodbye to her at all; but that would be too unkind. No, he would go first into the back garden and look at the new buds on the chrysanthemums or pull up a weed or two from the paths. For this was to escape from a pain that he dreaded into a peace that he loved.

Stone steps with an iron railing led him down on to the gravel of the back garden; and immediately he felt the touch of healing. The woodland sunset in the dining-room and this garden behind the house were two expressions of the same desire in Mr Presset. His desire, as he liked to put it, 'was to the green things of the earth', and if he loved one instrument more than another, it was the little trowel in the tool shed, for, with this in his hand and a day's work done, he would fossick and finick among the beds, or scrape the moss from the paths, and be wholly serene. The garden was the usual oblong patch, bounded on three sides by grey-brick walls with ivy-hung trellises above them, and on the fourth by the flat grey back of the house. Beneath the two side walls were beds of black London soil, furnished with shrubs of privet, euonymus and laurel; and against the far wall was a rockery whose component parts were chunks of concrete and blackened brickwork and one or two huge white shells. This rockery was well draped with ivy, fern, and creeping jenny; and a big sycamore brooded above it. The centre of the garden was a square of grass and flower beds, bounded by the gravel paths. For trees there were the big sycamore, a row of three pollarded limes, and a slender lilac that was the pride of its owner's heart when its leaves were fresh in the youth of the year.

He walked along the gravel paths, drawing at a cigarette and gazing at the shrubs and flowers. Not the best time of the year, really. In late September the twigs of the shrubs in a London garden were black as the trunks of the trees, and the leaves were dusty and wilting, and the golden privet was gold no more. Spring was the time – spring when the leaves were as fresh and soft as any in the hedgerows, and the privets were really golden, and the lilac was hung with blossom; when the beds were yellow with jonquils and daffodils, and arabis was white on the rockery. Everywhere then the spears of the iris shot up from the beds, flat and green and tall, and he waited for their flags to fly. Every spring he brought new primroses and cowslips from his country walks, and planted them with the trowel; they were not often successful, but it was good to come out each morning and sit on his heels to study their condition. It was astonishing the pleasure he drew from sitting on his heels and considering the advance of green things. He would examine the growth of tiny new blades of grass as a man might watch his daughters, with anxious pride. The primroses fetched from the country we may call, perhaps, his adopted daughters; but he watched them with an even greater solicitude, because they were delicate and ailing.

This autumn morning he halted in his walk to pick a dead branch from among the michaelmas daisies. The chrysanthemums were not doing too well; and, after a glance at his watch, he yielded to temptation and hurried to the dark tool shed for the trowel. Bringing it back, he allowed himself a minute or so of breaking up the earth and raking it into comeliness. Sitting on his heels, he noticed tufts of grass and gatherings of moss on the gravel path; and he rooted up the one and scraped away the other. This surgery exposed the black soil beneath the gravel; so he rose and picked up all the small stones he could see on beds or grass, and sprinkled them over the wounds, and trod them in with his heel. He would have liked to give the whole morning to this pleasant, finicking occupation, but it could not be; so he brushed his hands together to scatter the dust, and replaced the trowel in the tool shed. Then, with a resigned 'Well. . .' he went into the house and up the stairs to say his goodbye to Elinor.

Not a soul in the world, and certainly not Elinor herself, knew how she hurt him. If the pleasure he drew from gazing at grass blades was out of all proportion to its flimsy cause, so were the stabs that certain aspects of Elinor gave him. The cause was simple and common enough, really: just the difference between his dream of a mate and the reality; and his experience differed only from the usual one in degree and in intensity of pain. Most men and women have to make this adjustment between a dream and the reality, and they do it by easy stages till the price is paid and all is well; but Paul Presset could never adjust; the difference was too large, and he shivered and suffered. Presently we shall tell what combination of circumstances, and what weaknesses and vanities in himself, caused him to marry, late in life, a woman older than he and so little like his desire; but for the moment this was the situation, that he could not look at her without sooner or later taking a sharp – an incredibly sharp – pain. That was why he usually wanted to run, rather than go and kiss her goodbye.

The world's view of Elinor Presset was one thing, and Paul's another, because Paul's alone was coloured by a deep emotional disappointment. In the eyes of the world she was a large, well-dressed, not unprepossessing woman, something dull and heavy in hand, perhaps, but a pleasant enough neighbour as neighbours went. All were ready to enjoy a gossip with her at a tea-party or in the street; but only one, Mrs Bessie Furle, to make a close friend of her: probably they scented in her, without knowing it, a certain hardness, a certain dullness, and an odd kind of abstracted preoccupation with herself. But they liked her well enough, and exchanged the time of day with her very pleasantly. In the eyes of Paul, when he dared to let them fall on her – well, she was the emphasis on his loss; and her lank, grey hair hurt him; her veined complexion and her large, unshapely form hurt him, destroying all desire; the hardness in her eyes hurt him, and the corresponding hardness in her words; her slackness and untidiness in the home (for she dressed and smartened herself only for others) hurt him; and the fact that she was something of an invalid, or studied to be, so that his desire, had it arisen, could not have been satisfied, was a permanent nagging sore.

Except in his periods of irascibility, he was always kind to her, for it was not in his nature to be unkind; and the world of Islington Vale supposed that Paul and Elinor Presset were as happy as most married couples. Elinor supposed it too. She was not a woman to look towards any far horizons, and so was tolerably content with her life, and imagined her husband to be the same. She did not know that she was the negation of all his hopes. She did not know that when he came to bid her goodbye each morning, the sight of her, blowsy, dishevelled, and hard-eyed, on her disordered bed was a lash across the face of a very hungry man.

He took the lash as he entered today. She was sitting up with the breakfast tray at her side; a dressing-jacket, not too clean, over her big-boned shoulders, and her white nightdress showing the creased and chickeny skin of her throat. The eyes that she lifted to him were opaque and dull; not hostile or unkind, but no affection sparkled in them, no particular interest, and certainly no gaiety. On a chair by the bed her day-clothes were thrown in a careless heap. At once he remembered with bitterness that it was only for others that she made herself smart, and his eyes swung to her dressing-table, which was the theatre of this fraud. Here she built up the Elinor that the world saw. Everything on it chafed him: the rings on the branched ringstand, the combings in the hair-tidy hanging by the mirror, the pin-curls, the hair-pads, the hair-net rolled up and secured by a hair-pin in the frame of the mirror, the face cream, and the dust of face powder over everything – mirror, table-top, drawers, and floor. 'If I had ever loved her, I suppose I should have accepted all that,' he thought. 'Now, if it were *she*' – and again he saw the radiance, like a glow behind a fog.

But in kindness to Elinor he must hide all these thoughts, so he said, 'Well, goodbye, dear.'

'Oh, are you off now? Well, goodbye.'

'How do you feel this morning?'

'All right. I'm not ill. Just obeying Dr Waterhall, and taking it easy; that's all. Were there any letters?'

'Letters? Yes. Yes, there was a letter. One.'

'Well, who was it from? What are you making a mystery about?'

'I'm *not* making any mystery. I don't make mysteries. It was from Mother.'

Elinor made a sound of irritation behind her teeth. 'I suppose she wants money as usual.'

Instantly he was angry with her. He had been angry with his mother for writing again, and now he was angry with Elinor for being angry with her. Always he was angry when he suspected that Elinor despised his people, and therefore him. 'I don't know what she wants,' he snapped. 'I haven't read it yet.'

'Well, for goodness sake don't give her any more. She must learn to stop this badgering. Doesn't she realise you've got some duties to me?'

'I shall give her what I like. I shall certainly give her some more if I decide to. And she doesn't badger. Please don't say she badgers. I don't care for it, really. She thinks we're better off than we are; that's all. And illness is illness, all said and done. Father's had a nasty turn, and they've little enough between them. Though I don't think I *shall* send them any more,' he added, hastily. 'Not, as a matter of fact.'

'No, of course not. You've given them quite enough. You'll be back to tea, I suppose?'

'Pardon?' A cleverer woman might have perceived that he was gaining time; that his eyes were looking straight into hers with that excess of shiftiness which will not allow the glance to shift away. 'Tea?. . . No. No, I shan't be back to tea. . . In fact, I may be quite late. Yes, I'm taking some of the boys in extra work. I shouldn't expect me back before supper. Not really.'

'I hope that Heasman man's paying you extra for all this overtime. Is he? I'll be sure he isn't!'

'He's not, as a matter of fact,' said Paul, with the hauteur and aggressiveness of the insecure. 'Not a penny, if you want to know.'

'I thought so! And why you give him a moment's extra work without extra pay, *I* can't see. He pays you little enough, goodness knows. You let yourself be put upon—'

'I *never* let myself be put upon!' She had pricked too sharply the vanity of a small, thin man with a weak chin and meagre limbs. 'That's a thing I flatter myself I've never let happen. I've never let anyone put upon me yet. Not anyone in this world. If you can't distinguish between loving one's work enough not to think of money first, foremost and all the time and being put upon, I can't help it. I don't happen to be one who regards money as the first and only thing in the world.'

'It's absurd,' said Elinor, hardly aware of what she said.

'Well, that's your view; and mine's mine; and there's an end,' announced Paul.

'Love your work! It's the first time I've heard you say you love it. You grumble enough about it at times.'

'Well, perhaps "love" is hardly the word. But one can be conscientious about it.'

'Well then, all I can say is that that Heasman man trades on your conscientiousness.'

'That may be. That may very well be,' agreed Paul, by no means displeased with this new reading. 'I think it quite possible that I give him more than other men would, because I happen to take a pride in my work and like to see it well done. But I understand him when he says that a school like his simply *can't* pay very high – er – remunerations. And anyhow, as I always say, a man who goes into the scholastic profession with a view to making a fortune is rather more of a fool than I flatter myself I am. It's all a question of values. Values,' he repeated impressively.

'Yes, well. . .' murmured Elinor, consentingly, for she never quite knew what Paul was talking about when he began upon 'values'.

'Yes, well. . .' echoed Paul musingly, and decided that this would be an amicable moment in which to part. 'Well, goodbye.'

'Goodbye, Paul. Then we'll expect you back to supper?'

'Yes. By suppertime. And possibly a little before then,' he added as a last peace offering. 'Goodbye.'

He kissed her. He did it quickly, because he had to do it against the recoil. Then he hurried from the room, like a child hurrying from the stick. And on the dark landing he told himself, 'It's my fault. There's no getting away from it, it's my fault. I married her for her money, just as she married me for her own convenience, and now I'm paying for it. I don't see that I can blame her particularly, I don't really. She only did exactly what I did, and if it doesn't happen to hurt her now like it hurts me, well, that's – that's no fault of hers. God, I wouldn't have believed anything could hurt so much!'

Still, he was much happier outside the room. So wonderfully relieved that at the foot of the stairs he called, 'Well, goodbye, Annie.'

And Annie appeared at the dining-room door with a crumb scoop in her hand. 'Goodbye, sir.'

'Look after the house while I'm gone.'

'Yes, sir,' smiled Annie.

'And not too much dreaming about a certain young clodhopper we know!'

'No, sir,' agreed Annie, blushing rosily, and giving him a delighted pout.

'He isn't worth all that, you know. Not really. We none of us are.'

'No, sir,' answered Annie, automatically.

'Good. Glad you understand that. Goodbye.'

'Goodbye, sir.'

And now he was outside the house and had closed the door. And if he was relieved outside the bedroom upstairs, he was still more relieved outside the house. It was as though he shut something from his life when he pulled the hall-door to. And ahead of him, at the day's end, there was the radiance, the joy!

He ran down the hearthstoned steps and turned on to the pavement of Elm Tree Road; a small figure in a well-brushed black suit, bowler hat, and square-toed shoes, with a bag in his right hand and an umbrella hooked over the left arm; walking briskly towards the rumbling traffic of the Caledonian Road, and destined to a fame as wide as half the world.

Chapter Two

Mr Presset turned from his quiet street into the Caledonian Road. He became one of the many people streaming along its pavements towards their work in or around the City of London. For half a mile or so he would walk among them, and then turn out of the racket into the peace of Bishop Abercorn Square. This half mile was never a pleasant stretch of his walk. The litter in the gutters offended his craving for tidiness; the squalid streets to the right of him stirred his dread of poverty; the little struggling shops reminded him of a little stationer's in Petfield and how it had failed; and the people who were not hurrying towards the City – old and slow-footed women, muttering to themselves as they dragged to the shops, loafing and workless men at the corner, and bedraggled young wives with their babies and their bags of purchases – all reminded him that he was fifty and his worth in the market was daily leaking away. And as for the hurrying workers, they gave him sometimes a moment of vision (for there was always incipient vision behind his thoughtful eyes): he saw that he and they were only so much tossed spume, created and driven by unseen winds, and that this was a position lacking in human dignity: one should not be driven along by a momentum other than one's own; one should create, and not be created.

Oh, if he were not so insecure! If he had, say, four pounds a week of his own! Then he would escape into the radiance and dwell with it for ever, in a cottage among green things. He would live a life of his own. But no, he couldn't be so unkind to Elinor. What was he to do then? He wasn't going to give up the radiance – no, no; that was equally impossible – unimaginable – his heart died within him at the thought. What then? He didn't know. He couldn't see at all what would happen. He just drifted along with his dilemma, leaving its solution to the future.

And then a smell of apples – he was passing a fruiterer's – wafted him straight away to the apple-loft above the stationer's shop at Petfield. He was a child again and saw the village High Street and the shop-front of Presset's the stationer's, with its door in the middle and its two round bay windows, all on its own brick terrace at the top of six hollowed steps. Standing in the shop door he saw his dapper little father, in his braided velvet coat, twisting his long moustaches or smoothing his pointed beard. His father leapt to memory first – before his kind, worried mother – before his pale sister Winnie – because his father had frightened him. Not that he was an unkind little man or a bully – he was nothing of the sort – he was just a vain, flamboyant creature, full of dreams and schemes for himself, and for his children too, since they must surely have brilliance, and their advancement would be glory for him. He laughed and joked with them for most of the day, but he could be moody and peevish when anxieties beset him, and he was the kind of man who says, 'I am master in my house. When I order my children to do a thing, it is done,' so, believing in the stick for a boy, he used it too easily and too often on his son.

Mr Aubrey Presset, in brief, was too big for his shop. He was too big for Jane Presset, his wife. He was too big for the whole village of Petfield, up to and including the rector. In his secret thoughts he was too big for the whole of rural Sussex and for the fringe of most of its towns. He was a man of ideas, wasted in this threepenny village, among a lot of old cabbageheads. He was designed for a larger sphere, and should certainly have married a more brilliant mate. A gentleman and a genius, in fact: hence the braided velvet coat, the silky pointed brown beard, and the long moustaches which he curled as he stood on the narrow terrace between his shop door and his six white steps. He would stand there, gazing down the High Street and dreaming his dreams. A little Alexander, in a world too small.

And when his children were about twelve and thirteen, he had the misfortune to dream of the *Petfield and District Courier*. Unable to see anything done without thinking he could do it better himself, unable to hear of another man's achievement without being faintly jealous, he read one morning of a stationer in a neighbouring county who had started a local paper with some success, and six minutes later, he conceived the idea of the *Petfield Courier*. It was but a glimmer at first as he stood at his shop door; but by the evening it was a furnace in his head. Splendidly sanguine, he strolled up and down the parlour behind the shop, descanting to Jane and his gaping children on a widening circulation, an increasing advertisement revenue, a gradual conquest (by sheer merit) of the whole county and finally of London, and the birth of a whole spawn of lesser journals.

'I shall write the editorials myself; I shall mould opinion, my girl!' said he, flushed and radiant and taking a seat by the fire. 'I shall begin quite modestly. I shall concentrate on Petfield first – on the nobility and the gentry and all the local idiocy generally. I shall mention everyone of them by name in this connection or that, and they'll all buy the paper to see themselves in print. That you can gamble on. I flatter myself I understand human nature, especially in a moth-eaten spot like this, and I know how to trade on its weaknesses. Trust *me*. And the moment it begins to go – that same moment, Jane my girl! – I give up this trumpery shop and devote myself to pushing it like – like the deuce. I shall turn this place into the *Courier* offices. Yes, those two bow windows'd look very well, emptied of notepaper and Sunday School prizes, and all that Methody muck, and with just some neat curtains, and "Courier Offices" on the glass. Heavens! I'd get a satisfaction from kicking out all that stuff! And we'll do it. Given an ounce of luck, there's a fortune in it, I believe.'

Jane Presset, a commonplace little woman, with a bag of mending on her lap and a bag of anxieties under her hair, stared at him. 'But won't it be very expensive to print?'

'Of *course* it'll be expensive to print!' he retorted, hurt, as always, by opposition and distrust. 'Because I can assure you it's going to be done properly. I'm not going to be associated with anything cheap and hasty.'

'But how are you going to do it without capital?'

'Good God, how have other men done it? What other men have done I reckon *I* can do. Yes, I should think so.' And he stroked a moustache, moving his lips forward and back, and meditating. But he did not say how he would do it.

'Well, you'll do it whatever *I* say,' murmured Jane, looking for a new reel of cotton.

'Yes, yes,' he answered, not listening, and still hurt. If he'd had any doubts of success, this timidity of Jane's would have squashed them. She didn't believe in him, as he wanted to be believed in. She never realised what a man she had married. Empty of enterprise, that's what she was, like all women. 'Heavens!' he exclaimed at last, so that the children jumped. 'Great and merciful heavens, what an Idea! Of course! I shall print it myself. I shall set up my own presses. And we can run a printing works as well. We shall rake in additional revenue from that. We'll print the Rector's dam-fool tea-meetings and that sawney Slocombe's sales, and every penny of profit – every penny, Jane, my child, and Paul, and Winnie! – we'll put back into the paper, to establish it properly. By the lord Harry, I'll go into the question of a press tomorrow.'

'But won't a printing press be terribly dear?'

'And are there no such things as second-hand machines? Is there such a thing as credit? Is there such an arrangement as buying by instalments, or is there not? I seem to have heard of such things somewhere. It's faith that's wanted; that's all. Faith and drive. And I've no reason to suppose I lack the last. Yes, I shouldn't at all mind having a big printing works as well. It'd be something worth while to hand on to the boy when I put my old harness aside.'

'But won't you have to employ a man to set up the print, like? Who's going to do that?'

Aubrey thought. 'If necessary, I shall set it up myself.'

'But you don't know how.'

'One can learn, can't one? I don't mind what I turn my hand to, so long as it's worth doing, and not selling penholders to a lot of old women. Yes, I daresay I'll do it myself at first, and until we begin to make money. Most great businesses have begun like that. "Who shall despise the day of small things?" '

'Ah, well,' sighed Jane. 'You'll do it if you want to, whatever *I* say.'

'Certainly. And in five years' time you'll know I was right. The shed. The shed at the back, Janie! There you are! There's the very place.' He was thinking of a large shed where his predecessor, the corn and seed merchant, had stored his sacks and cartons. Eager as a child, he exclaimed, 'Why, it's absolutely made for it. It's plenty large enough and it's properly built. Magnificent! Where old Seed-pod stacked his corn and his meal and his birdseed, we'll raise something better. We'll raise opinion there, and taste, and – and things that'll one day reverberate through the country. Printing presses instead of dog biscuits, eh? A good smell of ink instead of dust and bran. "Presset's Printing Works"; or "Aubrey Presset and Son", eh, Paul? You're the Son, and don't forget it. Or better perhaps, "The Petfield Courier Printing Works . . . Aubrey Presset and Son for all press work" – why, the very name's an omen!'

And as the fire dimmed and Jane lit the lamp, he talked of silks for her in the near future, and luxury and comfort in her old age, with a couple of girls to wait on her. 'I shall never want more. What more we've got we'll give to travel, old lady. I've always wanted to see the romantic places of the world. One of my ancestors must have been a great explorer, I fancy, in good Queen Bess's days. And Paul shall go to a good school and to Oxford and have everything that I didn't have. And Winnie shall have a dowry worthy of a Presset. Come on, let's celebrate! Let's be cheerful about it. Paul, run to the nincompoop, Dorking's, and ask for a bottle of his best Madeira. We'll drink to "Aubrey Presset and Son".'

'Oh, but ought we to afford it?' protested Jane, ever worried by expenditure.

'Yes, surely, surely. This is a great day. You're in at the birth of something big. "Aubrey Presset and Son, Printers and Publishers, Petfield, Sussex".'

And Paul, hurrying along the Caledonian Road, remembered with pity how his little father swept out the shed the very next morning and whitewashed its walls to make it beautiful for his presses. He remembered the day when the presses were due to arrive, and his father's excitement, which drove him a hundred times to the shop door and turned his eyes up the High Street towards London, while his long nervous fingers stroked his moustaches. They came, two of them; and Aubrey, a little pale, escorted them into the 'Works'. One was a huge unwieldy thing that frightened Jane even more than Paul. It was old-fashioned even then, but sturdy and powerful, and ready to print for a century yet – for just so long, in fact, as men could be found to love it, and feed its bearings with oil, and its bed with sheets of paper. Its maker's love and pride was moulded on the metal everywhere. An iron eagle with outstretched wings surmounted the high back; and on the surface below a dolphin curled and reared its head. A brass name-plate, plumb in its breast, said proudly, 'Columbian Press, Invented by George Cheyney, Manufactory, Aldersgate Street, 1848'. The other was a much smaller one, not above a child's height; and Jane found herself wishing that Aubrey had contented himself with this one alone. Its nameplate was a small retiring thing, and said only, 'Hopkins Albion Press, 1856'. An ink-slab was placed by the side of each. After the presses came case-frames, a cutting machine, an imposing surface (that is to say, a table of highly polished metal on which the type would be imposed into chases) and an old wooden bookbinder's press, solid as a scaffold, which Aubrey had been quite unable to resist. 'We may go in for binding too,' he explained. 'I may even publish in a small way. Little books on the district and such like. "The *Courier* Series".' And when the last of this furniture and equipment was in, and the men had gone away with a drink inside them, Aubrey walked proudly among his machines, turning their handles, pulling their levers, and saying, 'Now we'll see.'

But it was the presses that slew them. Aubrey Presset as a man of business – aye, and Aubrey Presset as a maker of dreams – perished on his machines. In little Petfield there was not a public large enough to buy his news-sheet or to fill his presses with work; and the *Courier* obstinately failed to conquer the country around. Ill-printed and carelessly written (for it is far easier to dream world-shaking articles at your shop door than to sit down to the drudgery of writing them) the *Courier* began to fade, even as its type faded after the hundredth sheet had been pulled. Aubrey kept it alive long after he should have allowed it to die. It appeared on his shop counter long after Fred Barton, the compositor whom he had employed in his bright opening days, had taken his last wages and gone. Every Thursday morning he 'went to press'; which is to say that he went alone into the shed and shut the door on himself, and, sadly turning the handle and working the lever, pulled a hundred copies of the *Courier*.

It was not that he loved it. It was that he loved himself, and pride forced him to postpone the day when he admitted defeat to the cabbage-heads of Petfield, to the old fool of a rector, and – to Jane, his wife.

To admit it to Jane was perhaps the most difficult of all. To the end of her days she would think that she had been right. But she hadn't been, really. If he had had a few hundreds of capital, or if he had had a public of any intelligence about him, or if he had had a brilliant wife to inspire him, he would have won through. No doubt he had not written its copy as well as he might; but without an audience, what artist had ever been able to give of his best?

And then came the final blow. At Hillgarth, two miles away, a little upstart town which had been increasing in size since the Brighton and South Coast Railway dropped its station there, Paterson's, a firm of stationers and steam printers – *printers*, if you please! – set up in business, with capital behind them and practical men, not artists, at their head. But there was a blessing in the blow: it enabled Aubrey Presset to salvage his pride. He threw up the fight and declared to all, 'I have been beaten by money. Yes, I know when to surrender. But I think I may say I retire defeated but not disgraced. If I'd had money I'd have fought 'em. It's money that talks in this world all the time. Money, money, money. Mere brains alone can achieve little. And then there are those steps. I shall always say that those six steps and the narrow terrace in front of my shop have helped to ruin me. No one comes up steps and balances on a terrace to look in a shop window, unless they've got to. A little money, and I'd have altered the whole shop front. I've always had the ideas, but never the money.' To Jane he often spoke of those six damned steps as a contributory cause of his failure; because he could not speak to her of a third cause, a good but inadequate wife, who was empty of faith and ideas.

So he filed his petition and waited for the end. And here, forty years later, his son, on a London pavement, was moved almost to tears, as he pictured his father wandering silent among his silent machines, and sometimes pulling a lever or giving them a drop of oil.

They sold him up as a bankrupt. The new firm at Hillgarth stepped in and bought him, of course: and Presset's of Petfield became Paterson's of Hillgarth. They were generous to him, when they had decided that generosity might be the best policy. They made him manager of the Petfield branch, with a salary of two pounds a week, plus a commission on increase of business. So Aubrey Presset continued to stand in his braided coat at his shop door, twisting his moustaches with long nervous fingers and thinking about himself. But he no longer thought of himself as a success. He saw himself as of calibre too fine to succeed in a vulgar world. He would battle no more: it was so much more pleasant to dream. 'Give me a roof, a fire, and a book, Jane, old dear, and I shall ask no more.' And he fed the lamp of his vanity, by reading and discussing books which he was sure that nobody else in Petfield could understand – certainly not the old fool of a rector. Thus he was able to be a genius still.

But meanwhile Jane Presset had become obsessed with a dream. Much thought was going on within her small fair head and behind her worried eyes. Her husband's head filled with grandiose schemes which he was not big enough to fill; Jane Presset's smaller head was busy with a simple ambition which she was safe to achieve. She was looking down twenty-five or thirty years, and seeing their old age together. She was seeing it very clearly. Hers was a peasant mind, with its one great dread: destitution in old age. And, correspondingly, one great hope: a cottage in Petfield, a fire in its grate, and a sure pound a week to free the heart from care. Rest at the last, and comfort and security. Jane Presset began to save. And she could do it well. Aubrey, in his new mood, had decided to hand over his weekly stipend to her. 'You take the money, Jane, old lady, and do the best you can with it. I'm a failure. Yes, a failure: beaten by money and six damned steps. I begin to think I'm the artist type, which can create the ideas, but must hand them over to more practical people to carry out. You're a practical person, so take the money: it's better so. Give me a shilling or so for a smoke; that's all I ask.'

So Jane took the weekly wage, and her brain worked busily. You might often have seen her doing little sums on paper with a pencil she drew from her pale hair. If she could save five shillings a week, that was twelve pounds or so a year. Two hundred and fifty pounds in twenty years. Well over three hundred in twenty-five. And surely such a sum would buy an annuity on two old lives. A pound a week, and then rest in a cottage, and warmth and security! Steadily, week after week, she put by her crown piece, and sometimes a shilling or two more. The game became master of her thoughts. You may call her mean, you may even dub her a miser, but she was not this. She was just a woman eager to be generous but dogged by fear of the future. There is not much room in the menaced life of the poor for the more expansive virtues. Jane had seen expansiveness in her husband, and she had known that terror in the heart when disaster raps at the door. And now she believed that she alone could save the future, and that she must do it for both their sakes.

So in secret she put the money by. At first it went in a low drawer, but one day the lady in the Petfield Post Office told her all about the Post Office Savings Banks which Mr Gladstone had established a dozen years before, and how they held your capital for you as safe as the Bank of England, and paid you interest on it. She might deposit up to £200 in all, said the lady in the post office, and if she saved more than that, they would invest it for her in Government stock up to £300. Three hundred pounds of Government stock! That became her distant goal, her celestial city on the hills. She told no one, but some of the happiest hours in her life were when she took her pencil from her hair and, with much sucking of its point, played games with figures to see what her capital would look like next week, next month and next year. She would tell Aubrey one day, but not yet. And the years went by, and it became more difficult to tell. And lo! that which had been a delight in her heart was now a skeleton in the cupboard. The lie accumulated as the sum accumulated; and the greater both grew, the greater grew her fear of telling. The deceit and the sum together seemed to have built themselves up into a crime.

Supposing Aubrey came to hear of it! And what on earth would he say when the time came to tell him of her years of deceit? What would young Paul say?

Paul. She felt very guilty about Paul. They had not really been fair to him. When the shop foundered, they had taken him away from Pearsall College and put him out to work. Pearsall College was a large 'gentlemen's school' in a town not six miles from Petfield, 'almost a public school'; and Aubrey, when he set up as Editor, Newspaper Proprietor, and Publisher, had suddenly decided that this was the only school for a son of his. He took Paul from the little stone school by the church, and sent him to Pearsall. Three terms Paul spent at Pearsall, and then his father, having failed in the eyes of the world, became an artist above such vulgar measurement, and very ready for his children to turn their unpretentious penny in the simple labours of the poor. Winnie went to stitch in a milliner's at Hillgarth, and Paul became the errand boy of the shop at home. But Jane was never at ease about this. She knew of the sum in the drawer; she knew that Paul was unconsciously contributing his mite towards its growth; and she wondered if they 'didn't ought to have done better by the lad'.

She did not know that Paul, son of Aubrey and son of Jane, was dreaming, too. He loathed, loathed, *loathed* his job of errand boy. Respect for worldly position and wealth had soaked into him from father, mother, and school. In his earliest years his father had been all for gentility, and when that gentleman cast away the vulgar measurements of the world, he still contrived to believe that he had excellent blood in his veins and all the tastes of an aristocrat; his mother, from first to last, never abandoned her peasant respect for gentility and money; and as for Pearsall College, it was a chicken-yard of lads who simply didn't know that there were people who measured life differently. So Paul, with his basket on his arm, suffered such shame as only a child can know – why, some of the boys of Pearsall had seen him with the basket and jeered! He suffered whenever he set forth on his errands. He ran down streets if he saw someone coming who would despise him, and hid in stable yards. At night he dreamed that the boys had found him with his basket of shame and had danced in mockery around him, and he started awake with a failing heart. He, who was by nature affectionate and lively, became resentful, secretive and grudging. And his mother, when anxious and irritable, snapped at him; and his father, when morose, beat him. The beatings added timidity to the anxiety he inherited from his mother. He turned into himself and lived his own life. He stole books from the shop and read them in secret places; sometimes he read them as he walked along with his basket. On holidays he went off on long, lonely walks, feeling happier and easier the farther he got from the steep High Street of Petfield. And gradually he knew that a great ambition was wandering with him everywhere, or sitting at his side. It accompanied him across the meadows around Petfield, and sat with him in the woods. It climbed with him on his favourite journey of all, up to the top of the high downs above Brighton or Lewes. It set his cheeks aglow, like the sea-wind up there, as he walked on and on, into new, hidden places.

He would run away to London, as all the story books suggested. Unknown there, he would find employment, no matter what; and out of his wages he would buy books, and out of his spare time attend evening classes, and work and work and work till he had passed a big London examination – had he not read of Livingstone studying his Latin book as he worked at his loom? And when he had passed his examination he would enter upon one of the professions, and write to announce his achievement to the people at home. How pleasant their admiration, their amazement, and their pride! Winnie – how much bigger he was than she! – Winnie would sit amazed.

Of course the beatings, the basket, and a thinness in his limbs had built this need for bigness; but it was not wholly self-centred. The old affection had a place in its make-up too. Always he saw himself sending large cheques to help his parents, or to advance the unsuccessful Winnie into more genteel spheres.

If a dream is masterful enough, it is bound to create itself as fact. As Aubrey had raised his presses in the shed, as Jane was creating her capital in the post office, so Paul one day went out from Petfield and made his way to London. He found employment as a clerk in the back of an ironmonger's shop, and every night he worked at his books or attended the evening classes. He told the old people nothing of his aim, desiring to burst it on them as an accomplished fact. Three times he sat for the London Matriculation, and the third time he passed.

Passed! He was a Member of London University! More, he had a sum of money all ready to send to his mother, along with the tale of his success.

And there was astonishment in the stationer's shop, and much pride. Such pride as Paul ('so disappointing' of late) had never stirred before. 'I'm damned!' exclaimed Aubrey. 'The boy would appear to have brains! And if only he has a little luck he may go anywhere. He's got staying-power too. That was always *my* weakness. Not much luck, very little staying-power, and six damned steps. But young Paul may go anywhere. He may—' and the ever sanguine little man, taking his pipe from his mouth as they sat by the fire, sketched out to Jane the dazzling possibilities that lay before his son. The Bar, perhaps. The Bench. Or Trade. 'If he cares to give his mind to it, he might succeed where I failed. I could always imagine the plan of campaign, but could never slog away at the detailed staff-work. It was never my *forte* to serve tables. *He* may be different. Jane, we may see great things. Perhaps he may lift the name of Presset where I tried to lift it. . . . Well, there's no reason why he shouldn't have brains,' concluded Aubrey, though he had always supposed there was *one* reason; but he couldn't very well mention it to his wife. After a few minutes of restlessness in his fireside chair, he got up, fetched his hat, and went down the High Street to tell the cabbage-heads of Petfield that his son was a Member of London University.

Jane stayed in the parlour and, suddenly seeing her son in a new light as a man of affairs, much cleverer than herself, weighed the question, Should she take him into her confidence and tell him about the awful sum in the bank? It would be such a relief to tell someone, if only he didn't rebuke her for 'the wrong they done him'. Perhaps, now that he was a successful man, he would readily forgive.

Once again an idea was masterful enough to create itself quickly. Jane begged her brilliant son to come and see her, as she had much to tell him and wanted his advice. And he, flattered, came down in his best suit and smartest linen. And a very flattering sensation it was, to hear his mother, who used to chide him, speaking as if he were far cleverer than she.

'You've always been so good, Paul. I'm sure that, ever since your father's failure, you've been no cost to us at all. And now without any help that a lad ought to have, you've done this. It's wonderful, my boy. I feel I've someone strong to lean on now. Your father, good though he is, was never quite a one to lean on, as you might say. I've been so worried and beside myself sometimes in the past years. Now let me tell you all that's on my mind.'

And she told him her tale, apologizing that she had 'meant it all for the best'.

To her surprise Paul proffered no censure but only praise. As a matter of fact, he did not know whether he was more astonished by her revelation or touched by her humility. And he could not bear that she should feel guilty and stand in shame before her son. She had done wonders, he declared, absolute wonders; and of course she had been perfectly right to keep it dark from father. 'You know what father is. He'd fill up immediately with some hare-brained scheme, and the whole sum'd go down the gutters in a year.'

'Yes, that's what *I* thought,' said Jane, with a strange desire to cry.

'Good heavens! To think of your having amassed all that! I tell you what, mother. I shall hope to get well-paid employment now, and I'll send you what I can from time to time, to add to your savings. Then, if you like, you can say that we both had a hand in preparing this glorious surprise for him, and it won't seem as if it was all made up of money he had earned. Would that be any help?'

'Oh, Paul, that'll be wonderful! That's taken an immense load off my mind. I knew you'd think of something. I knew I was doing right to ask you. Oh, isn't it wonderful that you should have turned out like this, with never a proper chance at all? I've at least been fortunate in my son.'

But, back in London, Paul soon learned that matriculation was not the beginning of wealth. It didn't seem to open many doors. Too fine to be a shop-clerk any longer, he saw but one alley open to him: schoolmastering. And because this sounded better than other things to a poor boy out of a shop, he turned into it. He secured resident posts at the cheaper private schools, but even this he could not do without lies. He represented himself as an Editor's son who had been educated at Pearsall College. He said that his father had always intended to send him to Oxford, but recent losses had prevented him doing so. And the cheaper schools, which never look too closely at qualifications, took him on, for he was then a soft-voiced, welmannered, willing youth, if rather small. To his parents he represented the schools as much better than they were, for he did not want to step down from the pedestal on which they had placed him. And partly because he liked the feeling of being the well-to-do son who helped them, partly because he did not wish to appear to be earning little, he scraped together a few pounds to send them at the end of each term.

So ten or fifteen years went by, and with the approach of the forties came fright. The old timidity and anxiety leapt into life. Once he was middle-aged he would not be wanted in the resident posts any more. He would have to sink into some non-resident post at a grey and dubious academy. Perhaps not even that . . . He began to lie about his age.

Then he met Elinor. He had just become a non-resident master at Bishop Abercorn College, Islington, with a stipend of £150 a year, and was living for want of any other home, at the Misses Forsters' boarding-house off the Caledonian Road. Among the paying guests in this establishment – most of them 'ladies in reduced circumstances' – was Elinor Pope. But she was only spending an interval in her life with the Misses Forster. She had just lost her husband, a man who had climbed from a subordinate rank to a high position in the Life and Universal Assurance Company; and though he had left her with a pleasant little income of £250 a year, it was quite insufficient to keep up their house in Camden Crescent, so she had 'got it off her hands', warehoused the furniture, and was now sitting in the Islington boarding-house, while she deliberated what to do. She was then forty-five, and Paul forty-two; and both were very lonely; and soon a boarding-house friendship sprang up between them. She liked the quiet little schoolmaster who listened so courteously to her difficulties and then gave her his solemn advice, or took her so trustingly into his confidence and enlarged on aspirations of his own. He seemed so ready to like and be liked; and he had a merry humour too, at times. There was a softness and a studied courtliness in his manner that marked him off from louder men; and she always felt as if on cushions in his company. The child of a lower middle-class home, she was secretely impressed by the spangles of scholarship with which he always decorated his talk, and by his easy admissions, made without a hint of bragging, that he was an Old Pearsalian, and that his father, if 'in somewhat reduced circumstances' now, had been by profession an Editor, Journalist, and Publisher.

A new thought swam in among the meditations of Mrs Pope. Why not, she thought, why not? She was lonely, she wanted companionship, she was forty-five and could hardly expect to do much better than this little man, his hundred-and-fifty added to her two-fifty would enable them to run a larger house that would hold her furniture, and together they should be able to live on a couple of hundred or so (she had an odd aversion to spending more of her two-fifty than she needed) and, when the last word was said, one would never meet a kinder man – so why not?

A thought like this is bound to shoot across from one mind to the other. It passed easily into Paul's head, and its appearance there was not at all unpleasant. He took it with him on the daily walk from the boarding-house to the school. So far he had been too poor to marry; but he was forty-two and would like to have a home of his own. Between them they would have £400 a year, and that sounded like wealth to the son of Jane Presset. They would have a comfortable house, all the furniture of which she spoke so much, and a servant. Almost grandeur, to Paul. And, above all, Security. Yesterday he had been so anxious about the future that he dared not think of it; now – the old sanguine dreamer leapt up: why, with a large house and furniture, he might take a few private pupils and add a few hundreds to his income! He might even start a flourishing school of his own!

But perhaps there was a stronger motive than any of these. It would be something big to tell his parents. It would be good to write and say, 'Elinor and I will be quite well off, so I expect I shall be able to send you a little more.' By 'marrying well' he would live up to their view of him as the family success; and of late the thought that had saddened him most was the thought of sinking into poverty before his parents' eyes. Without his knowing it, his father's stick and his mother's chiding still worked in him; and he had to stay on his pedestal.

Aubrey and Jane Presset were nearing seventy now; and Winnie, poor pale Winnie, was dead these ten years. The old couple had done with the stationer's shop and lived in a cottage higher up the road. Jane Presset, at least, had created her dream to the full. She had a cottage, a fire, and a pound a week. And the anxious hour when she told her husband of her savings was far in the past. It had been less alarming than she had feared. At first he had been indignant and sulky. 'It's not nice to be distrusted, I *must* say. And it was my money, after all. Some of it Paul's? – well, it's not very nice to think of you and him conspiring against his father – just as if he couldn't be trusted. When I think what we might have done with a little capital – but that's a woman all over: no courage: no adventure: never risk a penny to make a pound. They care for nothing but security, while a man's all for a little enterprise.' But as the cloud passed over, he saw that the day was really very sunny indeed. Intoxicatingly so. Jane and he were now people of means. Work and worry were gone from their lives for ever. The exuberant Aubrey could be angry no more. 'Oh, well, old girl, I daresay you were right. I expect you're really the better man of the two. I was ever lavish and wild, and it doesn't answer in this world. Come, give us a kiss, mother; and write and tell Paul I'm proud of my boy.' Whereupon he put his hat on his head and went down the High Street to the Arms where he could boast in the bar that he had now an income of his own; not much, but enough to put some cheese on his bread till the end of his days.

So Elinor and Paul married and moved her furniture into the house in Elm Tree Road. In the first days, their life together, if not a love affair, was a very comfortable friendliness. They were seeing their new house, new garden, new neighbours and new interests rather than each other. But all too quickly the illusions faded out. Private pupils were few, and paid little; and, moreover, the taking of pupils was against the terms of Paul's employment, so that, when Mr Heasman, his headmaster, heard of it, he professed himself astonished at such deception and told Paul that he could honour his agreement or leave the school; words which cut Paul deeply and sent him humiliated into the street. Elinor developed some slight trouble of the heart, and this ended all thought of starting a school of his own. And gradually, living opposite her day by day, he saw the real Elinor. He saw that she had really married him just because it suited her. He saw that her real interests were herself, her house and her furniture, and that he was only a piece of that furniture, and a piece full of flaws which, if they couldn't be mended, might at least be pointed out. His keen and thoughtful eyes pierced through to the resentments festering in her. She resented that the furniture was hers, that their income was largely hers, that his profession which had sounded so grand had proved so grey, and that if only she had chosen a successful man, she might have been comfortable and well-to-do. In the first happy days, longing for friendship and understanding, he had told her all about his father and his schooling and his early troubles; and she, who had welcomed his deceit about the private pupils since it brought more money into the house, now used the fact that he had deceived her about his education, and the fact that he had been poor, as sticks to strike him with. She would let him see that she thought she had married beneath her. And sometimes she seemed driven to look for faults in his table manners and for vulgarisms in his speech. And if you look for such things with a morbid fear, you will surely find them. Elinor, in such a mood, saw them everywhere, and they looked larger than life in her eyes; and then Paul was irascible indeed.

And the strange thing was that, with it all, she was tolerably happy. She enjoyed her house, her furniture, her heart trouble, and her resentments.

Not so Paul, as we have seen. He managed to suffer quite astonishing aches. Still, he had bought with it all his measure of security, and if the ache was at its worst, he would quiet it with the thought, 'Well, it's every bit as much my fault as hers. I've made my bed, and I must lie on it. So keep smiling, Paul my boy; you're not quite dead yet.' He was thinking this, as he turned out of the racket of the Caledonian Road into the tranquillity of Bishop Abercorn Square.

Chapter Three

In Bishop Abercorn Square the houses were of a pattern similar to his own; and they stood in pairs about a railed-in rectangle of shrubs and grass. Because they were large most of them had been converted into two maisonettes; but one pair – the pair he was approaching – had met the opposite fate and been knocked into a single large house. The privet hedge which divided the two gardens, back and front, had been removed; and thus this house stood as a big square mansion with a garden all round. And exactly over the centre of its front railings, rising above the laurel and the euonymus, was a board on two poles. It said:

> Bishop Abercorn College
>
> Headmaster: Mr A. Heasman, B.A. (Math. Hons. Clare Coll. Cambridge)
>
> assisted by a staff of fully qualified resident and visiting masters
>
> Next term begins ....

Paul turned in at the gate; and a din of young voices reached him from the house. He entered by a side door, marked 'Scholars' Entrance', and passed into a large basement room at the back. Its floor was covered with a linoleum most of whose pattern had perished beneath the visiting feet; and on this shiny surface, clean as a hospital floor, a few napless rugs swam lazily. Three wicker armchairs stood about the fireplace, and six mahogany chairs about a large dining table in the centre of the room. Against the wall opposite the fireplace was a cupboard whose door had swung open, to reveal the caps and gowns of the masters. The windows looked out upon the back garden, four feet above the basement level – if garden it could be called after being asphalted over to make a large playground from wall to wall. As Paul came in, the ceiling was a-tremble with the feet of scurrying boys. He was in the Common Room.

Paul had, in fact, entered upon what was behind the board. What was behind the board was a school built by Mr Heasman, B.A., on that snobbery of the lower middle classes which will not send its child to a government school, but insists on being able to say, at the cheapest possible price, 'I paid for my boy's education.' Mr Heasman had not started out with the idea of building such a school. Like Paul and his father before him, he had started out with a sunlit dream. But soon he found that he had a partner, Necessity, and that this partner was stronger than he. It forced his prices and his catering down. It bade him cater for the many parents in Islington Vale who elected to pay a trifling sum for the shadow of education rather than pursue its substance for nothing at all. Such people liked the word 'College', and if ever they questioned the reality behind the word, they anointed their doubt with 'B.A. Math. Hons. Clare Coll. Cambridge'. Necessity had come early into partnership, and Mr Heasman had never been able to afford his M.A. He was now a grey and tired man, struggling on with some eighty boys who paid £4 a term (or less, by private arrangement), and a few doubtful boarders in the house next door. If his staff of resident and visiting masters was fully qualified, they had got their qualification by experience rather than by academic distinction. There were three of them. Mr Presset, whose career we have sketched; Mr Leonard Inglewood, a merry clown of thirty-five, as heavy in build as he was light in heart, whose one ambition, so he said, was 'to be done with this footling schoomastering and to start a good honest pub'; and young Norman Sandys, who was new this term. Mr Sandys had been to Oxford for a couple of terms, it is true, but he had also come down from Oxford in a way one didn't inquire into, and was now profoundly contemptuous of the school in which he had temporarily secured a job at '£60 a year, resident' and of his two colleagues, Presset and Inglewood. There was also a visiting mistress for the little boys, at '£30 a year, non-resident', a Miss Bawne who had been pretty once but was now thirty and reserved and fading. Music was taught by Mr Heasman himself, who 'took' a few boys on the piano in his own drawing room, and thereby made a little extra money.

This music in Bishop Abercorn College should be heeded carefully and paid the tribute of respect. It may sound monotonous and melancholy sometimes, as the children worry it out in the distant drawing-room, but it tells us of the best in Mr Heasman. Mr Heasman had gone forth into life with a real love of music, and it had come to this! One's partner, Necessity, cared nothing for the slow movement in Beethoven's Fourth Symphony, nor for some exquisite passages in his Violin Concerto which could carry Mr Heasman far away from Islington Vale and make him whole and fine and sweet again. But sometimes, when school was over and the partner was gone, Mr Heasman would play these passages in the empty drawing-room, and his wife and the few boarders upstairs would know, if they had the wit, that he had gone, too, into regions where no one could follow him.

He was not an ill-natured man, and he shut his ears when the same coarse partner whispered that Mr Presset and Mr Inglewood were of use because, being middle-aged and without degrees, they had no chance of getting anything better, and one could work them as one would: and that young Sandys was of use because, though merely a pup and a conceited pup, too, one could mention to the parents that he was an Oxford man. Miss Bawne was of no moment one way or the other. She could stay or go: there were ten thousand more in the market exactly the same as she.

Paul hung his bowler hat and his umbrella in the cupboard and put on his 'scholar's' gown. He came to the table and laid the French book there, and opened it for a last glance. But no good. There were heavy steps outside, a voice shouting lively salutations to the boys, and Mr Inglewood rolled boisterously in. His walk was always a kind of roll, as if he were keeping his heavy thighs from rubbing together. He rolled in, and stopped abruptly as he saw Paul.

'Hallo, my darling!' said he. 'Hallo, my lovely one!'

And he stood stock still, blinking his little eyes as if to accustom them to the dazzling enigma of a Mr Presset gowned and studious five minutes before time. His round open face, freckled about the flattish nose as one might expect after a glance at his ginger hair, was such a theatre as lent itself well to a round-eyed, flabbergasted stare. In his crumpled blue suit, with the heavy legs apart, his thick hands on his hips, he stood there, blinking bedazzled eyes.

'Good morning,' acknowledged Paul, and dropped his eyes to the book again.

'Not cheery?' inquired Inglewood. 'Not gay? Strange! A beautiful morning and a fine opportunity before you of doing noble work. Come, come! I'm full of beans myself, and in a most attractive mood.' And with that he abandoned the stare and walked towards the cupboard. 'Where's the lad?'

'I neither know nor care,' said Paul.

'Snappy,' commented Inglewood to the cupboard. 'I'm afraid you don't like him. You should try to be understanding like me. You should remember the difficult position he finds himself in.

After all – I mean to say! – he's a gent and we're not, Bertrand. No, no, we're common. He's been to Oxford.'

'He's also come down from Oxford.'

'Catty. Distinctly catty. Still, even if he came down in something of a hurry, he did once go *up* to Oxford; and that makes all the difference between him and you and me. Surely you can see that. Bertie dear, be reasonable. That means he's a gent. Obviously.'

'He's a puppy,' said Paul.

'Oh, granted. Granted a thousand times. But such a thoroughbred one, such a blood puppy, if I may say so – hark at the darlings! How we love them!' He glanced up at the ceiling, which shook and rattled with the horseplay above. 'I think it's decent of him to associate with us at all,' he continued, drawing on his gown.

'Well, if it comes to Oxford, he's no more a member of Oxford University than I am of London, then.'

'Yes, but *London*! London, my boy! *What* is London? Where is it? How can you expect an Oxford man to take London seriously? I mean, be fair. A London degree is almost a badge of shame. It's really better to have no association with the place at all, like me. And then, of course, there's Cheltenham. Don't forget: he was at Cheltenham before Oxford.'

'Well, *I* was at Pearsall.'

'Yes, but, once again, Cheltenham's Cheltenham, and Pearsall's Pearsall. You're dull this morning, Bertrand. *Cheltenham*, mark you! I don't wonder he makes us remember we're a cut below him. It's only natural. I mean, I'm trying to understand him, and I don't see what else he could do.'

'He's what I should call a callow adolescent.'

'Oh, *yes*. Yes, every time. Underdone. A very underdone young man, but that's why you shouldn't judge him till he's been basted a little more. I'm sure I do my best to – but, *ahem*!' Inglewood coughed warningly, and turned and looked out of the window. 'Did j'ever see a lovelier morning? Sun on the asphalt, bird on the wing—'

Norman Sandys entered. Not only in his slimness and youth, but in his attire, he was remarkably different from the other two. They were in dark suits and black shoes; he wore a light brown sports coat with patch pockets and leather buttons, grey flannel trousers, fawn socks and brown brogue shoes.

Inglewood, turning from the window, jerked back his head and dropped it to one side that he might study from an advantageous angle this agreeable picture.

'How fresh and young he looks, Bertrand,' said he.

'Don't be more of an ass than you can help, Inglewood,' retorted Sandys.

'Why? Don't you want a companion this morning?'

'I don't think that's very funny,' said Sandys, who did not seem in the best of tempers.

'There you are!' sighed Inglewood, spreading a hand in despair. 'They're neither of them in their happiest vein this morning. They're down. It's a pity . . . a pity . . .' And, thrusting back his gown, he drove both hands into his trouser pockets, to jingle his money and watch them.

Paul had turned away the minute Sandys came into sight. Sandys said not a word of greeting to him, and there was a heavy silence in the room.

'Now don't you two start getting chatty together,' begged Inglewood.

'You really are the perfect ass,' said Sandys with a grin.

'But you haven't said good morning to each other. You really haven't, you know. Now say it nicely my lambs.'

'Did I not? Well, good morning, Presset.'

Automatically, as Paul looked up at the young man, his hand shot to the nape of his neck and stayed there. It was a characteristic action with him. Always he put his hand to his neck when he felt an inferiority, or feared he had said, or was likely to say, something wrong. He did it when he spoke to Mr Heasman, who was his employer, or to Norman Sandys who was an Oxford man and despised his breeding. He did it if he asked a favour of a friend, or sought directions from a policeman. He did it when he was telling a lie to Elinor. It was a habit that had come out of his childhood when he excused himself to his father. 'Good morning,' he said; and slowly the hand came away.

'That's right,' said Inglewood, encouragingly; and to maintain the friendly atmosphere, he continued, 'Who's got the blessed task of taking the boys to their football this afternoon?'

'I have,' announced Paul.

'But how's that? I thought you always took the juniors?'

'Mr Heasman said he wanted Mr Sandys to take the juniors for a bit.'

Sandys shivered. He shivered because Presset said '*Mr* Heasman' and '*Mr* Sandys'. The little words, so placed, revealed the whole of Presset's background. In Sandys' own circle anyone would have said, 'Heasman wants Sandys to take the juniors', but Presset always put the handle to the name: '*Mr* Sandys', '*Mr* Inglewood'. And he spoke of his wife as '*Mrs* Presset' instead of as 'Elinor' or 'my wife'; and he said, 'Pardon?' and 'Pleased to have met you, I'm sure.' And whenever he said these things, Sandys almost hated him. Sore about the school in which he found himself, he focused his hate on Paul. Heasman had at least been a gentleman once; Inglewood was too frankly and jovially vulgar to dislike; Miss Bawne was a mere governess, like any other; but this little Presset, straining to be refined and committing every social blunder, seemed to symbolise the tenth-rate school. So that already, although only a few days of the term had gone, he was beginning to hate him. He hated his black coat, square-toed shoes, and collar slightly out of date; he hated his mannerisms, such as blowing his nose with both hands and swinging his handkerchief round before replacing it in his pocket; he hated to hear him speak of his 'Latin Class' ('Where did *he* learn any Latin, I should like to know'); he hated his phrases; and, for the life of him, he could not help looking for these vulgarisms, waiting for them, and then lifting his nostrils and curling his lip when they disgusted him. Once or twice they had fretted him so unbearably that he had snubbed the offender.

'Well, if you take my advice,' continued Inglewood, 'you'll get the game started, and then run about because it looks well, but think your own thoughts, or say over your French verbs for tomorrow, or compose poetry or something all the time; and now and then, for form's sake, give a hell of a blow on the whistle. It'll be quite safe to do that: someone'll be sure to be doing something wrong, and the others'll know what it was. By the way, have you glanced through those essays for me?'

'Yes. Here they are, and that's the order I put 'em in.'

'Well now, that's real kind of you, Bertrand,' Inglewood took a sheaf of papers from Paul. 'Bertrand really does know something about English Composition. Damned if I do. I'm never quite sure whether it ought to be "me" or "I". And as for "was" and "were" life isn't worth living with two such little swine about. Thank you, Bertie; you're a gent.'

'Don't mention it. You're welcome, I'm sure.'

Again Sandys shivered. His lips framed the awful words, 'You're welcome, I'm sure'; they squared with the pain of them; and suddenly, as if fearful of what he might do or say, he went from the room.

Paul noticed that shivering exit. 'What happened?' he asked.

'I dunno.'

'Did I say something wrong?'

'I dunno. I can't make the fellow out.'

'If I did, and he – God! who does he think he is? Who's he to stand there, thinking himself superior and shivering when I speak? God damn him – I—'

'Don't worry about him, old chap.' Inglewood was no longer the clown, but a friendly comforter – though the clown in him could never stay long below ground. 'He's not worth it. He can think what he likes about *me*, and I hope it disagrees with him vilely. It won't trouble *me*. I know what I think about him, and I know what I think about you, old horse. And I'll tell you, if you like. You're worth a hundred of him, any old day of the week, Sunday included. But not Bank Holidays. I've an idea you're pretty insufferable on Bank Holidays.'

'He's no better than you or me. He's a puppy, that's what he is, a dirty, stinking little puppy. Because his father had sixpence more money than yours or mine, that doesn't make him a shade better than you or me. I'll guarantee I've as good a brain as his; I'll guarantee I'm as well educated as he; I'll guarantee I've read books he'll never read if he lives to be a hundred – with his loafing about, and his grey flannel trousers, and his sports coat. Stupid little puppy, without an idea in his head worth having! And he – *he* to presume to stand there and look supercilious, and walk off, as if he couldn't stand us any longer! And to try to snub me – he tries to snub me sometimes! Christ! There'll be trouble sooner or later, unless he changes his manners quite a deal. Sometimes he makes me feel as if I could kill him.'

'I should,' said Inglewood. 'I certainly should, if I were you. And now come to prayers. Come along.' A gong had sounded in the distance, followed by a rush of feet overhead. 'Come and pray. And let me tell you one thing.' Inglewood touched him on the lapel of his coat, like a confiding counsellor. 'If you're going to pray, *pray*. Let there be no half measures about it. *Are* you going to pray?'

'I doubt it,' said Paul with a grin, his passion fading.

'Well, I think I shall today. Just for a change. Someone ought to.' And he rolled out of the room in front of Paul.

Chapter Four

Paul sat at his table in his classroom with twenty boys at their desks in front of him. One of the many Pauls that made up the total Mr Presset was certainly an artist, wounded by any want of fitness between a place and its present function; and such unfitness was here. Here was a lofty room with a handsome marble mantelpiece, a handsome door, expensive wallpaper, and a large bay window overlooking the back garden; a room obviously designed for large and prosperous living; and it was filled with three rows of ink-stained desks, a blackboard, and a case of littered bookshelves. In the desks sat twenty boys, some in Norfolk suits and knickerbockers, some in blue suits shiny at the elbows, and one or two in long-trousered pepper-and-salt suits with high collars. Of these lads some were adolescent and pimply, some were still beautiful with the bloom of childhood, and some were pale and weedy and lank. And the fine room all around them seemed aware that it filled its use so ill; it looked empty and depressed, so that no man, with a sense of perfections, could be wholly at ease in it.

Still, his hours in his classroom were far from unhappy. He was popular with the boys. Always wanting to be liked, he was quick to show kindness to the boys who showed fondness for him; and this affection bred affection; and since schoolboys move as a herd, it was soon the fashion to like Old Presset. One might have thought that this desire to be liked would have meant a weakness of discipline, but it was not so: he was too short-tempered for that. Also, when the subject appealed to him, he interested them. As a solitary man, he had become something of a bookworm, and of late his books had stirred the inchoate artist in him, so that, excited and flattered by his new ideas, he burned to give them out to somebody (Elinor being no use) and here was his class, an audience to his hand. He poured the bubbling thoughts over his pupils, with enthusiastic words, eager gestures, and brightening eyes, and quite often with jokes that were well on their level; and the boys, content to sit back and listen, found his instruction much more savoury fare than the conventional meat of Mr Heasman and Mr Sandys. (What happened in Mr Inglewood's class no one quite knew.) The idea that Presset was an authority on Literature was held enthusiastically by Mr Inglewood and less enthusiastically, but for business purposes, by Mr Heasman (Mr Sandys did not hold it at all); and this morsel of reputation was very pleasant to Paul, who straightaway studied in his books to justify and increase it. And he was seldom so happy as when dazzling the boys with the ideas the last book had given him, and seeing their sustained interest and admiration. He was a cribber, of course; he could not have found the ideas without the aid of the books; but at least he loved them when he saw them and caught alight at their flame.

It was English Composition this morning. English Composition was quite a feature in Bishop Abercorn College where the curriculum, to quote Mr Heasman's prospectus, aimed at 'a good commercial education'. Whether Mr Presset's doctrine this morning was of commercial value is a question. He was hot from a book called 'Rebel Art'. In his view, had he read it earlier, it might have changed the whole course of his life. He was inflated with it, distended with it; and he must vent on someone the crowding ideas, vaguely seen but surely felt, that the book had given him.

'Let's see, boys, it's English Composition this morning, isn't it?'

'Yes, sir. . . . Hurray! . . . Oh, good egg!'

That 'hurray!' was sweet in the ears of the master.

'Well, the subject of the essay today will be "Art is Rebellion".'

Art is Rebellion! Art is – the boys frowned in their effort to understand. And since the subject sounded unfairly abstruse, some felt moved to murmur, 'Phew!' and 'I *say*!' Others dropped their jaws in a pretended collapse, or fanned themselves to bring about a recovery. One of the elder ones fitted the appropriate words to his injury. 'What on earth does that mean, sir?'

'Well, that's what I'm going to tell you, aren't I?'

'Of, of course.' The boy, as one who has just seen the truth, admitted that his question was unnecessary, and apologised. 'Sorry, sir.'

'But first, is there any lad bright enough to have the slightest perception what the words mean?'

To judge by the silence, no. A few frowned again in an effort to encompass some meaning: one saw by their lips that they were repeating, 'Art is Rebellion. Art is—' as if by reiteration they could make it into sense. The rest seemed quite unworried by their lack of brightness. They sat back, free from strain, and awaiting a better man's interpretation.

'No,' said Mr Presset. He was not surprised. A week ago he didn't know himself what the words meant, but there was no need to tell the boys that. 'Very well, then.'

He rose. It was business now to instruct and catechise the boys, for three-quarters of an hour, on the essay's theme, while they took notes or asked questions, with a view to writing the essay (generally an exact reproduction of the notes and the answers) in the course of the week at home. 'Right. I'll try and explain.' And, walking up and down, with his eyes on the floor or swinging round upon his class, he spluttered out what he meant.

First, Art was a rebellion against nature itself: against the formlessness and the disorder and the chaos . . . and the untidiness. It was Form . . . Pattern . . . Order . . . Harmony . . . Perfection. Yes, it was an effort to shape the disorderly uprush of life into patterns – exquisite patterns – patterns in sound, in line and mass and colour, and in words. But if in this sense it was a rebellion against nature, they must remember that it was also itself a part of nature, and nature's finest blossoming. Perhaps it was an earnest of the larger and broader perfections to which nature would one day rise through the agency of the spirit of man.

Paul was speaking with feeling – and all the more because, as he spoke, he was seeing the weeds on his garden path, the dinginess of the passage from his bedroom to the bathroom, the shiftless drift of his daily thought, and all the muddle, discord and dilemma that was life for most people today. He spoke warmly and with lit eyes, because a starved and undeveloped side of him was struggling into words. He felt hot and nervously stimulated, and excited with admiration of himself.

Secondly, the artist tended always to appear anti-social. He was a creature of sympathy and vision – otherwise he wouldn't be an artist but a financial magnate or something crude like that – and, as a moth flew to the flame, so his eye must fly to wherever there was injustice and stupidity, and the sight would move him to some creative act. If his medium were words, then his writing would really be a very dangerous form of rebellion, since it wielded the power of the *word*, the terrible armament of the new idea. Words were more powerful than anything else. 'I care not who make's a nation's laws, so long as I can write its songs.' So to stagnant minds in the places of authority, he must always appear anti-social, while really being one of the most pro-social beings in the state. The stinging critic of the established institution was the very health of the state, and the pioneering heretic was its principle of growth and its only hope of development.

Then again, the artist was usually in rebellion against all the sordid values of the ordinary money-making man. (Good commercial education, this!) The artist measured life qualitatively, not quantitatively. He drew his delight from the quality of his experience, not from the quantity of his gain. That was why he was always in greater sympathy with the tramp or the monk than with the money-making merchant or the social climber. Indeed, it would be safe to say that in every artist there lurked either a tramp or a monk. Secretly he longed to be free from the tyranny of property and praise, and to live, either as a tramp for himself, or as a monk for others. 'I'm sure there's one or the other in me!' laughed Paul, forgetting that in these words he was identifying himself with an artist. 'I wouldn't give you a thank-you for a vast business or a huge palace. Give me a small house, and a chance to roam the country and hear the birds sing, and a few very dear people for friends, and a book to read – let me be done with slavery to money and the good opinion of a lot of silly people – and I mean: that's what I mean by measuring life qualitatively as the artist does – if you understand what I mean—'

His eloquence had broken up, because his ideas had burst the limits of his utterance. And suddenly he felt tired. It was a difficult subject, and the strain of trying to express what he could only feel had given him a slight headache. And in his excitement he had gone on beyond his three-quarters of an hour. He knew this by a din of shrill voices on the asphalt under the window; the kindergarten boys had come out for their 'break', and there was Miss Bawne standing guardian over their play. Standing there with her back to the house, she looked the very symbol of the drudgery in their trade. Her slim back which ought to have belonged to a sprightly young woman, was neat enough in shirt-blouse and skirt, but somehow looked listless and defeated; the movements of her arm, as she directed their game, were perfunctory and effortful, as if her conscience worked them, and not her heart; and at times she most obviously lost sight of the little boys and fell into dreaming. Paul turned from the window.

Strictly he should begin on the French Prose now, but the thought of it repelled him. French offered too many resistances to a man with a headache. And he wanted to sink into thought. Let him have at least a quarter of an hour of rest.

'Well, boys,' said he, pausing at his table, 'that's been rather a difficult subject. I think I'll let you have fifteen minutes or so, to start shaping your essay now. Yes, before you forget it all. You can begin on it at once. That'll lessen your homework for you a bit, won't it?'

'Oh, thank you, sir; thank you,' said the boys.

'Don't mention it,' said Paul. 'You're welcome, I'm sure.'

And there was a rattling of books and paper, followed by a scratching of pens. Bent over their desks, the boys were grappling with the subject, with their tongues out. And Paul sat his own body behind his table, but his mind flew far away. It flew over the background of his life, examining it. Why was one so different from all that one could see? Why could the intellect see the truth, but the man as a whole stay incapable of following it? So far from being the brave, free, generous rebel whose likeness he had been sketching for the boys, he was timid and slavish and mean – really. That letter in his pocket! He had shied from reading it lest it contained a request for money, and he didn't want to give money away. Mean. . . . No, it wasn't really meanness; it was just financial timidity, fear of the future; if he had plenty of money, he'd like to give largely to all, and especially to his mother. . . . But the fine rebel artist wouldn't be bound by this need for security. He'd measure the present moment for what it was worth, scorning the future; and he'd make it good and joyous by giving generously.

Bah! he wouldn't be timid; he'd be what he could see. And the very fact that he could see all these things showed that he was a fine fellow in some ways. He pulled the letter from his coat pocket, cut the envelope, and read:

'My dearest Boy (Boy at fifty!) – What a long time since we heard anything of you! Father and me long to hear of all your doings and all your successes. Father was saying only yesterday in one of his moods you know we never hear now, he's gone ahead of us. And I said how can you father when he's always been so good to us, but you know he doesn't mean it. Really he's awfully proud of you. I hear him talking to people about your works and your fashionable marriage as he calls it. Poor father he's still rather poorly after his illness and looks so run down that I have had to get him some pick-me-ups and things and what with the doctor's bills and one thing and another I've properly run into debt. I suppose you couldn't help me a little. I hate asking you again, sending us money so often as you have during father's illness, but I have no one else to turn to, you are the successful one of the family. And if I can once get straight again I can then keep well within the money. But don't if it's difficult. On the whole it's wonderful how well we are, seeing that Aubrey's 74 and me 71. I am sure I don't feel it, and on the whole old age is a happy time, no more cares, no more terrible days like those in the shop when you were a boy, just quietness and rest. I think your dad feels this too and is happier than he has ever been. He always said luck was against him except in one thing, he had success with his boy. I wish I could make him see religion as I have done of late. It's a great comfort to me to feel God in everything but I can't get your dad to see it. He only scoffs, he's too proud of his brain really and you can only see these things by becoming as a little child. I tell him I am glad I never had a brain like his and yours because so often these things are hid from the wise and prudent and revealed unto babes. If you could manage to send a pound or two I should be glad as winter will be here soon and I want to get in some coal and I really must pay off one set of bills before starting another. But don't if you can't, I never want to be a burden on you but just your loving old Mother.'

Paul folded the letter once, let his hand fall to the table, and surveyed the conflict within him. One side of him was saying, 'Give. Give generously. Give five whole pounds, and think of her joy and yours. Give courageously, trusting the future.' But the other side said, 'Keep your money. You sent a pound only the other day. You can't go on like this. And you've spent a terrible lot lately on *her*, and it's difficult enough to explain to Elinor where *that* money goes. And in a few years now you may not be earning anything at all. And if you got ill. . . .'

But he had no doubt which was the grander side, and he began to warm with a glow of happiness as he knew that he would indulge it. Granted that a voice whispered, 'You are only doing it because you are vain of their pride in you, and want to appear wealthy to them'; but he answered it, 'No, that motive is there, I know, but there's a desire to be good to them too. And I want to be more like what I can see. And I'm *going* to do it; I'm *going* to. Now. This moment. It's no good seeing these things if one doesn't act on them.'

He pulled a cheque-book from his pocket, spread it open, took his desk-pen, and began to write. He felt splendid, triumphant, as he penned the words, 'Pay Mrs Aubrey Presset—'

And that moment the handle of the door turned. Only one person in the school would turn that handle without knocking: Mr Heasman. Paul looked up. Alarm started his heart pounding like an engine. Here was he, attending to his own work in school hours. Impossible to slip away the cheque-book, because the boys would see the quick, guilty action, and despise him. No guilty boy, fearing capture and the cane, could sit more chained by terror to his seat, with eyes fixed on an opening door.

Yes, Mr Heasman, with his greying hair, dull, tired, eyes and rounding figure in the ancient B.A. gown, was coming in and shutting the door behind his back, as he glanced over the twenty boys writing so quietly at their desks. Paul rose; his hand went to the nape of his neck; and he stepped towards the headmaster to prevent him coming near the table and seeing the private letter and the open cheque-book. But even as he did so, he saw that Mr Heasman had perceived a guiltiness in the movement. Mr Heasman approached slowly, and stood near the table, his body half-turned towards the boys.

'What are these lads doing now, Mr Presset?'

'They are – they are writing an essay. Yes, I had given them rather a difficult subject, so I thought they might just start on it.' Impossible to lie in front of the boys. 'I was just going to glance over their work and see that it was on the right lines, you see.'

'I see.' Mr Heasman directed his eyes to the master's table and saw the letter and the cheque-book. 'Normally they would be doing French at this time, would they not?'

'Yes. Normally it's their French hour. Certainly. But I felt it wiser to start them on this particular essay. It – it's more than usually difficult.'

'Yes.' Mr Heasman had heart enough not to humiliate a master before his class; but his eyes strayed to the cheque-book again. 'Well, what I really came about was to ask you to be so good as to take one or two of my boys along with yours to football this afternoon. I am called away.'

'Certainly I will. Yes, I can easily manage them,' said Mr Presset, eager to be obliging and to recover lost ground. 'Yes, that'll be quite all right.'

'Thank you.' He went to the nearest boy's desk and picked up his essay to look at it. 'Art is Rebellion? What does that mean, Mr Presset?'

'Pardon?' inquired Paul nervously.

But Mr Heasman did not answer: he was reading in the round schoolboy hand, 'Art is a sort of rebellion against nature because it can't stand at any price the disorder and cahos and untidiness everywhere, so it feels it must make patterns and harmonies of its own. Music for instance is like an escape. . . .' And then Mr Heasman, reading no more, was remembering the opening of Tchaikovsky's Concerto No. 1, where the piano came riding in on waves of orchestral sound, gloriously united with them, yet fighting and mastering them, till it left the soaring waves behind, to weave delicate patterns of its own like tracery on a silence . . . and then the song of the violin in the opening of the second movement, wistful yet confident and happy, and soon to be repeated among the reeds, like an echo down in the grass: a pure, untrammelled thing, wandering free over the surface of the world, of whose cares and assoilings it knew nothing, though maybe born of them. He remembered playing these patterns to himself in the drawing-room, with the door shut, that he might be alone with them, and escape.

'Well, well,' he said, dropping the essay with a smile. 'I suppose there's some truth in it. But I don't think they're old enough to understand. . . . Thank you, Mr Presset; that's all, I think.'

And absent-mindedly he drifted from the room, shutting the door quietly after him.

And Paul? Paul returned to his desk shaken. Did Mr Heasman really see the guilt in his face and movements? And had the boys noticed it? Had they seen him as a shrinking hypocrite? And oh God, this sudden entry of the headmaster, just when he was feeling so triumphant, had shown the real, unconquerable Paul, frightened and furtive. Unconquerable? No, perhaps not unconquerable, but for how long?

He sat at his table, as disheartened as a man may be. The unfinished cheque lay before him. Drawing it towards him, he filled it up with a shaking hand, determined not to be completely defeated.

Chapter Five

Canonbury Fields lie in the east of Islington Vale. They are three green playgrounds which the long regiments of houses have never been allowed to invade. Tall lime trees stand around them, like a line of sentinels; and behind these an inner row of plane trees; and a ribbon of asphalt path runs between the two rows of trees. Shrubberies border the asphalt, and at intervals there is a seat for old men holding their pipes or foot-weary women holding the handles of their prams. The rest is the three broad plats of grass, where the children play, except where the hurdles are up, to enable the turf to recover. The streets are obliged to run round the Fields; and they are some of the oldest streets in the Vale, built when Canonbury was a charming village for citizens of London who wanted to escape into the country. Rows and crescents of eighteenth-century houses look down upon this green common; and very beautiful they appear, in their simple dignity, when seen behind the trees.

Organised games are, or used to be, allowed upon the grass for those who had a permit from the County Council of London; and Bishop Abercorn College possessed such a permit. So here this afternoon were some thirty of the Abercorn boys playing 'soccer' between the goal-posts, and Mr Presset in his black suit running hither and thither with the flow of the game, and occasionally blowing his whistle and pointing out an error with his arm. It was four o'clock and the shadows of the plane trees had begun to lengthen on the grass. The old houses beyond the trees stood in a blue mist. Here and there on the seats an old man sat with his pipe, now watching the game and now forgetting it. On the grass, at a distance from the players, one or two workless men reclined at full length, sleeping in the last of the sun. And at the edges of the grass, where it was thin beneath the trees, sparrows hopped and pecked, and starlings and fat pigeons waddled around. The only sounds were the muted roar of traffic from the highroads; and against this constant background the shouts of the Abercorn lads and the whistle of their master, Mr Presset.

They did not think, as they played, that this green common, and a few others like it among the huddled houses of Islington, were all that was left of those old northern fields, once the vast playground of London; nor that themselves were the inheritors of the City schoolboys who came out here with their teachers in Plantagenet days and opened their games of ball, while the staider citizens sat astride their horses and looked on. Nor did Mr Presset, running up and down with his whistle, and often (it must be confessed) thinking his own thoughts, know that he was not very far from a retreat to which Goldsmith and the mad poet, Kit Smart, would repair, to think their own thoughts and turn them into poetry. But so the people come to the still places and go, and each is the centre of his own world which no one else has ever visited or seen.

He was very happy just now, because it was four o'clock and the radiance of the evening was very near. At half-past four he could dismiss the boys and wander off alone to it. Again and again he looked at his watch, and as it worked towards the half hour, his anticipation was like a thirst.

'Half-past four. We must stop now, boys. You can go home now. Okely and Ellwood' – he turned to the only two boarders – 'you'll take the ball back to the school, won't you? I shan't be coming back myself.'

'Right you are, sir!'

The panting boys went to their jackets, and, drawing them on, walked south and westward home; but Mr Presset, after patting his brow with a handkerchief and swinging it round before replacing it in his pocket, turned towards the east.

He walked along the asphalt path to the other end of the fields. It matched well with his mood that a glamorous evening should be throwing sunlight and shadow in patches of apricot and blue. His pipe lit and puffing blue smoke that exactly answered the smoke from a distant bonfire of dead leaves, he crossed the sunlight and shadow, till he came to the chestnut trees that stand about the Highbury entrance to the Fields. Between these he passed out into the streets of Highbury. He was going farther and farther from his home into parts where no one knew him. Leaving the main street, he turned into Kelross Road, a neat little avenue of small red-brick houses standing behind pollarded planes. It always pleased him rather, this quiet and polite little road, with its notice 'Street Cries Prohibited' and its trim gardens; it met and fitted, perhaps, some inexpressible need in him. Kelross Road bent round and finished in a mere passage between two grey garden walls, capped with broken glass, over which poplars and sycamores branched. This leafy passage opened into the fine thoroughfare of Highbury New Park Road, which he crossed at once, so as to enter the side street immediately in front of him. Most aptly – at least when Mr Presset passed through on his present business – this side street was called Paradise Road; after he had passed through, this aptness, we suggest, fell to the ground and perished on the hard pavement; for there was little of Paradise there, really. It led into quite the most inaptly named highway in London, Green Lanes, which for the most part is houses, shops, crowded pavements, screaming trams and tearing motor cars. But let the name stand, because it is full of the past.

Dodging the trams and the buses and the motor vans, he crossed this road, and came to the entrance gates of Clissold Park.

If you have not yet visited Clissold Park, go and look at it. It might be a corner of Kew Gardens dropped down in the midst of the grey North London streets. In May it is an expanse of fresh green grass, studded with daisies, while a white mist rises from it; and within its borders can be found almost all the trees that stand at Kew; for it was once a rich man's pleasance. In May the chestnuts are alight with blossom, and their pink and white flowers lie in drifts along the paths; and the scent of a hundred other blossoms sails along the warm, spring air. There is the song and chatter of many birds, and the scream of the peacock, because, if you walk right on you will pass an aviary. You will also pass deer – deer in North London! – and see the children feeding them with bread-crumbs and green food. An artificial stream curves through it, called the New River, and the pink and white blossom from the chestnuts floats on the still, green water. The banks of this river, between the railings and the water, are ribbons of pure country, a-blow with high grasses and sedges, yellow with buttercups and white with cow-parsley. It was because Mr Presset had discovered it in May that he made it his trysting place in late September. It had wilted a little, of course, and the rusty leaves strewed the edges of the New River instead of the pink blossom; but it seemed to carry still, like a ghostly overtone, the glory of its spring.

He walked a little way along the path, and turned on to the grass towards the first great chestnut, and sat on a seat placed on the worn ground beneath its spread. From this seat, by sitting sideways with his arm along its back, he could command the entrance gates. The next tree was an ancient thorn, centuries old, but green in patches still. Some of its heavy limbs were supported on poles, and a railing went all round it, to preserve its old age in peace. Probably, in the centuries and in the days of the rich man's park, it had looked upon too many quaint happenings to be other than cynical (as became a thorn tree) about that which was to happen now.

Paul waited, his eyes on the gates. The evening was very still. Over the grass and beyond the park railings he could see the people passing, but they were too far away for him to hear their voices or their feet. He could see the scintillating of the trams as they carried their colour past the railings, but here, where he sat, their clatter and clang was little more than a murmur. Sparrows dropped from the branches and pecked near by; and a pair of dogs, chasing each other over the grass, broke off their gambols to come and sniff at his legs. He bent sideways to pat their heads – but suddenly left them and stood up.

She had come through the gates and was approaching up the path, with an incipient smile. A very great joy rose in Paul that she should care to come thus to find him. Dressed in a neat blue coat and skirt, white shirt-blouse and large hat, and with her slim figure and dawning smile, she looked very pretty from here, where one could not see the lines on her face. Not that Paul minded those lines any longer: it had seemed so wonderful that a girl only thirty, and thus twenty years younger than he, should be ready to love him in the way she did, that he would have poured his waiting love upon her, had she been far less pretty than she was. Though he would not have put it so crudely, he had been 'in no position to pick and choose'. And indeed she must have been exceedingly pretty once, with her large clouded eyes, before the sorrow filled them, and with her full lips, before they set so easily into sadness. Her hair was beau-tiful still, brown and abundant, and shot with gold. And now, as he walked towards her, the smile peeped at her lips, as it always did on seeing him, before she reorganised her face into seemlier behaviour.

'Good evening, Mr Presset,' she said, as if they were on no better terms than this.

And he answered her in the same vein. 'Good evening, Miss Bawne.'

'I trust you have not been waiting long.'

'No, Miss Bawne, I have not. And I trust you left Mr Heasman well, and all his brats.'

She made a gesture of impatience. 'Ach' – there is no other way to write her characteristic expression of disdain – 'don't talk about them. I've come to be happy.'

'Then come, my dear.'

And that, for the present, was all they said. He linked his fingers in hers, and drew her away behind the old thorn, where he took her in his arms and kissed her. The pressure of her kiss was as eager as his, as if she too had known what it was to starve for this. He lifted his face and said, 'Ah, bless you, Myra'; and she, looking up with eyes that opened and closed again, said simply, 'I love you, Paul.' Ecstasy was the only word for his happiness then.

He led her to a secluded seat they had long discovered, in a curving path between shrubbery and high plane trees, with the old village church of Stoke Newington hiding behind the leaves.

Here he sat with only his arm about her shoulder, ready to draw it away, should anyone come by. He felt lively and facetious, and, staring at her, said, 'Myra, it gets me beat.'

'What does?'

'This.'

'This being what, exactly?'

'Why, that you should really *want* to come and be with me. I can't grasp it.'

'And why, pray?'

'I can't understand why you should care for me at all. It seems very poor taste. I was looking at my face only this morning, and thinking, how on earth can she love a mug like that?'

'I think it's a very nice "mug".'

'But ugly, Myra; old and ugly.'

'Do you think you're ugly?'

'Most disturbingly so.'

'Well, I don't. And, anyway, if you were, it wouldn't matter. Do you think ugliness ever matters with women?'

'I can only conclude that it doesn't.'

'And if it comes to beauty, I'm no longer very much. My dear, I was thirty-one last birthday!'

'And I was fifty!'

'Well, then, we're a couple of faded beauties, if you ask me. Let's be content with that.'

'No. I want to get to the bottom of this. What is it that matters with women? What is it that they are ready to love?'

'Oh, the expression, I suppose—'

'What sort of expression?' interrupted Paul, much interested, since a compliment seemed to be hovering near.

'Oh, I don't know; kindness and humour and—'

'But can you see those things in my face?'

'Oh, *yes*.' She seemed confident about it. 'Yes, my angel! You've the kindest eyes . . . and smile too. . . .'

'Well now!' smiled he.

'At least, you always look like that when you're with me.'

'Ah, perhaps!'

'And not only when you're with me – now I come to think of it. Do you suppose I didn't notice all these things about you, long before we – long before you – long before this—'

He kissed her mouth to put an end to her difficulty, and she smiled and continued, 'Exactly. Long before that sort of thing. Why, it was your kindness and natural courtesy that made me like you at first. And the other people like you too, I know. Don't have such a poor opinion of yourself. The boys like you, and Mr Inglewood likes you—'

'And Mr Sandys hates me—'

'Ach, that's a compliment. *That* conceited little worm!' Myra could put plenty of hate into her tone. 'And just remember; since then – why' – she drew his hand on to her lap – 'you have given me back a faith that there's goodness in men. You have, really! You *know* you have. And I think I value that more than anything else. It was awful – *awful* – when I had lost all faith in it. It was so terribly dark, and then you came, and I began to think that perhaps I had been wrong. I suppose I'm not the sort that likes to believe in no one. It hurts too much.'

'Why did you despair so?'

The bitterness, the hate, almost crept back into her tone. 'I don't see that Life's let me do much else. It's so brutal. Oh, do you know, Paul, they *terrify* me, some of those streets that I come through to get here. They bring that darkness near me again; and I feel that, if I lost you, I should sink back into it. They – they're brutal.'

'Myra, what do you mean?'

'Oh, it's as father used to say. A few men are kind as individuals, but when they get together, they form something so soulless. They're no longer "He" and "they"; they become a huge "IT". That's what he used to say; and that huge "It" finished him off, as it finishes off everyone who isn't strong enough to beat it. It built those nasty, soulless streets, and it's busy beating everyone in them.'

He let her run on. And she spoke of her father, who had been a clerk in a firm of caterers and had served them well, but when illness had weakened him and he was no further use to them, they had cast him off and left him to die. He was human wastage, that was all. And now her mother scraped together a living by letting rooms to poor, work-worn people, but she too, like him, would be so much wastage soon. And there had been Martin – Martin who had been content with her for his 'girl' while her father lived, but had cooled off when he died and her mother took to letting rooms. Cooled off, and went, and was married a year later! He had taken the best of her years, she said: years when she still had some looks, and might have found other lovers. In fact, she had always believed that the fading of her looks was another reason why he sneaked away from her. She had had a year or two of abject misery which 'completed the ruin of her looks' (as she put it, while Paul squeezed her hand in protest, for truly it was a ridiculous remark), and then Paul came with his 'infinite tenderness'. Also his need of her. 'It's funny,' she added, smiling, 'you have a gift for laughter and fun, and yet behind it a steady sadness. I used to wonder what caused it. I used to look at you quite a lot, you know! And now that I understand, I find it so marvellous that I can do something to heal and comfort you. I so want to be of use to someone.'

'Of use!' laughed Paul. 'Why, you're the whole of my happiness. The only time I'm perfectly at rest is when I'm with you, my darling.'

'Ah, yes, but there's no hope. Nothing can come of it . . . ever. . . .'

'I don't know. . . . If I had the courage to break free . . .'

'Ach, no! Don't talk of it . . . don't talk of it. . . . Besides, it wouldn't be of any use. I couldn't take you, unless you came to me without – without hurting anyone. I just know I couldn't. She's sick – and oh! It's the way I was brought up, I suppose; the church, and all that. Mother was always tremendously pious, and is still; I can't think how she manages it. I seem to have lost most of my faith now, but I know I could never be happy if I thought I'd done anyone such a wrong.

'And instead you would chain me to misery?'

'Oh, it's no good arguing, Paul dear. I just can't see it in any other way. I don't seem to mind as long as your – as long as *she* knows nothing, because then there's nothing to hurt her. But I'm terrified when I think, supposing – supposing one day we're seen?'

'That's where I'm more selfish than you. I sometimes wish something desperate would happen so that we should be forced to take each other.'

'No, no; don't speak of it.'

The trees had been spangled with light from the west, when they began their talk; but now, with the sinking of the sun, the light had gone out. Silence sat between them for a little while;

and then it began to be dark between the high trees. Abruptly, and with a shiver, Myra rose. 'I must go.'

'No, don't, he pleaded. 'It's so wonderful to have you.'

'Oh, I must! I'm so afraid. I'm so afraid of someone finding out. Supposing the Heasmans got to know?'

'Stay a little longer. Just a little.'

'I can't. I mustn't.'

'Yes, *please*.' And he pulled her back to the seat, and gathered her into his arms.

She let her head rest on his shoulder. 'Only for a few minutes, please,' she said. 'I would rather it were so.'

And they sat thus without speaking while Paul tried to find words for something he wanted to say. Time and again the words got to his lips, but no farther. It was only when she moved to break from his arms that he held her tight and spoke.

'Listen, Myra. Will you – will you one day give me more? Why not? It's as you say, if no one knows but you and me, no one will be hurt. *Will* you?'

Myra kept her head on his shoulder without answering. Then she said, 'No, my dear, let us stay like this. I feel less guilty like this. . . .'

'Very well,' said he, resignedly; and ever so slightly his embrace slackened around her.

But at this she looked up, and saw the sadness in his face, so, touching his hand, she begged, 'Don't look sad. It doesn't mean that I don't love you with all my heart and soul. . . . You know I *want* you, but. . . .'

'I know,' he said. 'I understand.'

Her quick break-away, and her looking at her feet, suggested that, after thought, she was going to say more; and he waited. But instead she rose and said, 'Come. We must go now. She will be wondering where you are. It's nearly seven o'clock.'

Paul rose too, and took a long kiss, for here they would part and go home by different ways. And something in his embrace seemed so silent and sad that she lifted her eyes to his, and began, 'Paul. . . .'

'Yes, Myra?'

'About what you said just now – it's so difficult for me, brought up as I've been, but – but – I may get used to the idea . . . and perhaps one day . . . you do understand, don't you?'

'My dear!' he whispered, dazed with happiness and gratitude. '*Oh, my dear*!'

Chapter Six

Paul walked home through the darkening streets. Unknown to him, his lower lip was thrust obstinately forward. He was not going to feel afraid of Elinor. Not for a moment, thank you. No one should ever say of him that he was a hen-pecked husband. If he wanted to be half an hour late, he'd *be* half an hour late. He was working himself up into a little temper so as to be ready for any quarrel.

As he turned into Elm Tree Road, however, and saw his house, he recoiled from the prospect of ill-feeling and a quarrel. Oh, how wonderful it would be to come home to a house he loved, and to embrace in the hall a woman who ran to welcome him! To hold Myra in his arms as the mistress of his house and the partner of his life! This thought, by saddening him, softened him; and he felt a desire to be kind. Yes, he'd try to be patient with Elinor.

Passing through his gate, he walked up the flagstones to the steps. As always, each tiny flaw in the little front garden wounded him. One day he must find a little money for putting it in order. Somehow it would ease his sore, if he could make this garden perfect: the cracked flagstones replaced by whole ones, the gravel round the oval flower bed clean and shining, and the earth in the bed hoed and weedless. And the garden at the back too: he'd like to spend a pound or two on that.

He let himself in; and as he did so, the clock in the dining-room struck eight. That meant that the time was only a quarter to – but still, he was three-quarters of an hour late. He hung his hat and umbrella on a single peg on the hat-stand and went into the dining-room, where Elinor was certain to be, because the evening was cold and, unless there was company, she never allowed a fire in the drawing-room.

She was there, sitting in an easy chair by the fire. She looked a very different Elinor from the one he had left in bed that morning. Evidently she had been visiting her friends: her hair was well done, her face powdered, gold chains rested on her large bosom, and her white blouse had a high, whaleboned collar that seemed to brace up and smarten her whole figure. A "severe" style in blouses always suited this large woman, correcting her looseness. Tonight, with her ordered grey hair, she looked almost handsome.

'Well, dear?' he began, remembering the resolve to be kind.

'Where *have* you been?' she demanded. 'I thought you were never coming.'

'Well, I told you I should be a little late.'

'You call this "a little late!" Why, it's eight o'clock!'

He felt himself firing up, and the resolve melting in the heat. 'It's not. It's only a quarter to, by rights.'

'Well, supper's at seven; and you know it.'

'I know my supper'll be when I want it. I said I should be late, didn't I? I said I should be late.' Angrily, he dragged a chair from the table, and pulling his blue felt slippers from under a chair, began to unlace his shoes.

'Well, I think it's most inconsiderate to Annie,' persisted Elinor, whose wrath had plainly been gathering for many minutes before he came in. 'If you never think of me, you might think of her. I don't want her washing up all hours of the night.'

This was to touch him on a raw place, because, if he prided himself on anything, it was on his consideration for Annie.

'I don't think *I'm* inconsiderate to Annie. I go out of my way to help her always. Everybody knows that. Ask *her*. Let's have her up and ask her, shall we?' And, with a slipper half on, he shuffled along to push the bell by the mantelpiece.

'Don't be ridiculous. Where have you been all this time?'

'I have been to Bishop Abercorn College where I have an appointment as a master.'

'I suppose you think that's amusing. You've been there till half-past seven, I suppose?'

'I had to stay with some of the boys who wanted help. And then I had a bit of a headache and went for a walk with Mr Inglewood.'

'Oh, *that* man.' There was always contempt in her voice when she spoke of Inglewood. Where two people strain to keep up an appearance of good companionship, the strain may sometimes produce a kind of buried hostility which drives each into a faint dislike of what the other likes. Paul felt a secret dislike for most of her friends, and she a more open dislike for his.

'Yes, *that* man. I haven't many friends left, and I think him one of the best; and I may tell you I've every intention of keeping him.'

'Keep him as long as you like, but don't ask me to know him, that's all. He's just about as vulgar as anyone I've ever met. How he comes to be a schoolmaster passes my comprehension.'

'Well, at any rate, he's as good as I am.'

Elinor tossed her head: this was difficult to answer. 'Well, I refuse to admit that he's as good as *I* am. I've not been accustomed to associating with men of his type, and I'll thank you not to ask me to do so now.'

'Pooh!' Paul laughed sarcastically. 'I warrant you he wouldn't come near the house if you paid him. He knows where he's welcome and where he isn't. You generally make that clear to most people, and especially to my friends. And as I'm not likely to see him here, I'll go for a walk with him sometimes; and that's the end of that. Perhaps we could now have supper.' And he sat himself emphatically before the cold meat on the table.

Elinor, without a word, touched the bell near her chair, and, rising, came to the table. Very soon Annie was pushing open the door with the corner of her tray, on which the vegetable dishes jingled.

'Well, Annie,' Paul greeted her. 'I'm sorry I'm late. I got held up.'

'That's all right, sir.'

'No, it isn't. You mustn't be up all night washing up. Mrs Presset and I'll eat just as quickly as possible. We'll *bolt* our food, see? Come on, Mrs Presset, put it away.'

'That's all right, sir. I've nothing much to do this evening.'

'Still, it isn't fair to have you working all hours of the night. So we'll finish up the whole boiling lot by half-past eight. That's a wager, is it? And if we're a minute later than half-past eight, I'll come down and do the washing up myself.'

Annie, not knowing how to answer this before the mistress, blushed and went out smiling.

'I suppose you talked to her like that on purpose to annoy me,' said Elinor.

'I wasn't aware of it,' said Paul.

'You know I dislike familiarity with servants. I've told you so often enough. It doesn't make them any easier to manage, and they don't respect you any the more for it.'

'Perhaps you'll leave me to be the judge of that. If that was familiarity, I shall go on being as familiar with Annie as long as I like. I am very fond of Annie, and I may tell you she's fond of me too.'

Elinor plied her knife and fork very delicately, while the aggrievement rankled within. Soon it *had* to vent itself in a wounding word.

'I'd like you to remember that she's my maid, and I pay for her.'

Paul slammed his knife and fork on the table. 'Oh, for God's sake, don't keep reminding me that it's mostly *your* money and *your* furniture! We know it by now. You've got two-fifty and I've got a hundred and fifty. That's that. We know it. If you like, I'll have it printed as a sign, and we'll hang it up in this room, where I can see it every day. And then you won't need to remind me of it. Shall we do that? You've got two-fifty from your late husband, and I've got a hundred and fifty from my screw. He did everything for you, and I've done nothing: we'll shove that up too, in big type. It keeps us all in our proper places. I vastly improved my position by marrying you, and you sacrificed everything – mine was all gain, and yours was all loss – and let me tell you I don't believe a word of it! I believe you were quite glad to marry me. At the time you thought it would suit you very well, whatever you may have thought since. I see what I see, and I know what I know. God damn it, I'm not quite a fool!'

The light in Elinor's eye was now as angry as his. 'You forget you wilfully deceived me in a lot of things. Lies about your father and mother. Lies about your education—'

'Leave my father and mother out of this, please. They're poor; but *you* didn't begin in too rosy a way, either, and you kept pretty dark about it. *You* weren't in too big a way when he was only an insurance agent, for all your high-and-mightiness since. And as for education, God help us all, the less you say about it, the better! I may not have been to good schools, but at least I've educated myself, and I read books that you couldn't understand the first word of. As long as you read nothing but sixpenny novels, you can ill afford to talk about education. At least, that's *my* view.'

His words had fanned her wrath into a savagery that cared not what it said. 'Perhaps you don't know,' she began, 'that, when I married you, every friend I'd got assured me that I was—'

'Throwing yourself away,' supplied Paul. 'Well, for pity's sake, if you feel like that, why don't you break with me? I lived alone before, and I daresay I can go on doing so. I might even find someone to love me, and someone I could make happy. There are those who *can* love me.' He burned to tell her that he was loved; that someone only that evening had said, 'You gave me back faith in the goodness of men'. Oh, if ever she did find out about Myra, how one side of him would triumph! 'I never used to quarrel with people,' he continued, more gently, 'and there have been those who have liked me. I shall be able to find happiness for myself, I fancy.'

'We may as well talk sense,' said Elinor, somewhat quietened too. 'We're married, and we must put up with it.'

'Well, then, don't go throwing your money and your furniture in my face. I don't like it.'

For a time there was silence again. Paul got on with his cold meat and mashed potatoes, working his fork rapidly and vigorously. It is a convention that a fork shall be used only one way up; but convention, in this instance, is empty of sense; and the sanity of the common people has always used a fork, when necessary, as a spoon. Paul had done so for forty years before meeting Elinor, and was quite incapable of losing the habit now; especially in angry and forgetful moments. Vigorously tonight he swept the mashed potatoes into the hollow of the fork. Elinor watched. She was the completely conventional person; and her nerves were on edge; so on edge that she was driven to seek her torture by watching the action, though she had to bite her lip as she did so. To watch was to make the irritation fester and fester till it could know no assuagement but in speech.

'I wish you'd get out of that disgusting habit – using your fork as a spoon.'

He drove back his chair and jumped up. He hurled his napkin to the table. 'Oh, Christ! Will you leave my manners alone? I won't be taught manners at my time of life. Especially by one who's got a hell of a lot to learn herself. I tell you I simply bloody well won't stand it. Do you understand?' His eyes were aflame with rage.

Elinor rose. 'If you're going to use words to me like those, I'll leave you.'

'Well, thank God for that. That's the first agreeable word you've said to me this evening.'

'You are very, very wicked, I think. You know that Dr Waterhall said I wasn't to be excited. You know he said that he wouldn't answer for the consequences if I was unduly excited. I'll go to my room. You can tell Annie that I'm not feeling very well.' She sailed to the door.

'All right. I'll tell her I made you ill with my manners. . . . Good night,' he called after her. 'Now perhaps I can have my meal in peace.'

Sitting down again, he pushed away his plate and snatched at some cheese. After eating this angrily, and before the last mouthful was finished, he got up, pushed the bell, and bent down to stir the fire.

Annie entered with her tray; and immediately he felt that goodwill towards her because she was fond of him.

'Come on, Annie,' said he, approaching the table. 'I'll give you a lift with it. You're late, and it's all my fault. Now then! Willing hands make light work.'

'It's all right, sir. Don't you trouble, sir.'

'Annie, don't argue. Put down the tray and do what you're told.'

Her eyes brightened; and, much pleased by her grateful look, he whipped the crockery together and piled it on the tray; got the crumb scoop out of the sideboard drawer and scooped up the crumbs; took one end of the long white tablecloth and helped her to fold it up; and, finally, since they had loaded the tray heavily, carried it down to the kitchen for her.

Then he came back to his chair and his gloom. He stretched his slippered feet on to the fender, lit his pipe, and took up a book. But he couldn't read. Resentment was storming in his head, throwing up arguments and pithy replies and stinging sentences for Elinor; and soon he laid the book on his knees and stared into the fire. He let his thoughts run to the place where they rested in a warm, glowing happiness: Myra.

If only he were free! Let him think of ways by which he could get free.

Divorce? No. That would finish him in his profession. And even if it didn't, Elinor, who could be vindictive enough, might see that other things did. She knew how he had fibbed to the school about his parenthood, his education, and his age, and, if he left her for another woman, she would surely see to it that this deceit and his adultery damaged him as much as possible. No, divorce was not possible: it made an end of his earning power.

What else? Only one other thing, her death. She might die with that dicky heart of hers. And if she died – resist it though he might, he felt a joy swelling in him and quickening his heart. These thoughts were very wrong, but how could one help them? One's brain *would* think; it *would* examine possibilities. He didn't *want* her to die – no, that would be too selfish, but if by chance she did, everything would be solved: he would be free, he would have money and furniture, he would be independent of his profession, and his future would be safe.

But no, no: it was not for the sake of her money and goods that he wanted her to die – he was not as bad as that – it was only that he might be free again. He'd rather the money wasn't there; it gave an added selfishness to these thoughts. And what was he saying? He didn't want her to die. No; oh, no. Poor Elinor . . . if there was any other way he could be free, he'd wish her all the happiness in the world with another man. Still, when one thought it over, perhaps this feeling of guilt was excessive: was there any great harm in dreaming that her heart had carried her off, and the money was there and must be used? Was there any harm in imagining his first steps . . . and his words to Myra? . . .

With his feet on the fender, and his hands in his pockets, he dreamed on till the fire died.

Chapter Seven

That was a typical day for Paul Presset, except that he could not always meet Myra, and that Elinor and he did not usually quarrel in the evenings. Usually they kept their smoudering hostility well damped down; for their own comfort they did not allow it to flare up, but directed their talk to matters of common interest. And, in truth, they did not see very much of each other. Paul was up early, breakfasted alone, walked about his garden with the trowel, went up and got his goodbye over with a formal kiss, and quickly escaped into a restfulness with Inglewood who liked him, and into a flattered satisfaction with his boys, since in their eyes he was a person of authority and learning. He came home in the evening and sat quietly with a book, seldom lifting his eyes to Elinor for fear of the stab her untidiness, her veined skin, or her dull eyes could give him. And she went to bed early after giving him a formal kiss.

He knew that she did not expect him in her room, because such a thing had not happened for years; her desires had never been strong, and now she regarded her illness as having 'finished that sort of thing for ever'. This annoyed him, not because he had any desire for her – indeed the idea repelled him – but because she should think it of no importance that his wife had failed him. 'What does she think a man's made of?' he would grumble to himself. 'A man finds someone else. . . . A man isn't made of stone, even if some women are. . . . A man pretty soon looks elsewhere, and I don't see how you can blame him. Serve her right if she knew!' Ah, if only she could know, somehow, that Myra had said, 'You know I *want* you,' and promised, 'Perhaps one day. . . .'

Elinor's day was as remote from him. She got up soon after he had gone, and dressed at her dressing-table, often chatting to Annie as she did so. Annie would stand near the chest of drawers with her dust-pan and brush suspended in her hand, listening and saying, 'Yes, mum,' 'Really, mum?' and perhaps, 'Lord, mum!' Elinor liked to tell this girl how very well off she had been in Mr Pope's time, and how they had had a large house and entertained on quite a big scale; and how much better off Mr Presset ought to have been, if his father, the Newspaper Proprietor, hadn't lost his money speculating. 'He went to a good school, of course, but he ought to have gone on to Oxford, when he'd have made much more money in his profession,' she would explain, fixing a pin-curl and patting it into place. 'You can never really climb to the highest positions without an Oxford degree'; and Annie, interested, inquired 'No, mum?' 'No,' Elinor confirmed; 'and it's a pity because he might have gone far. He's got ability.' To which Annie replied, 'I'm sure he has, mum'; and Elinor concluded, 'Yes, I hear he's a very fine teacher. Especially of Literature.'

The only times when she was not chatty and friendly with Annie were after the coal or gas bill had come, or Annie had reported a breakage in the kitchen. Then, though she did not berate the girl, for fear of losing her, she walked about the house, silent, sullen and testy, with her monetary loss for a nagging companion; and Annie, redder than ever, bustled about the kitchen, banging down the saucepans on the stove, slamming the cupboard doors, declining to 'hear' the front door bell, and muttering, 'I don't want any of *her* looks, thank you. I'm not going to have her come the heavy over me. She needn't think!'

After some light housework, Elinor did her shopping in the Caledonian Road where things were cheap; then she had dinner, if it could be so called, since she was usually 'content with a mere peck'; and after dinner, feeling lonely, she would take up her novel to read of happier women. She liked only happy stories, declaring (for she used every hack phrase) that there was sorrow enough in life without reading about it in fiction. But herein she was unwise, because the tale of happy love would stir her discontent, so that often she would abandon the book and decide to go out and see her friends. Of these she had many, because she was a good gossiper, and other home-keeping women welcomed her visits; but the chief of them, and her only real confidante, was Bessie Furle. She loved to sit by the hour in Bessie's drawing-room on the other side of Elm Tree Road, and tell her the real truth about Paul. And little Bessie Furle, as small and compact as Elinor was large and full-bodied, loved to sit still and hear it all.

The drawing-room of Mrs Furle differed from the other drawing-rooms in this better-class district of the Vale only in the number of oriental souvenirs around. An Indian carpet covered the floor, and an Indian tablecloth overhung the small, upright piano; an elephant hewn out of a single tree-trunk formed the support for a tray of Indian brass; Burmese garments hung in a glass-fronted cabinet; models of the Pyramids and of Hindu gods stood upon the mantelpiece; and pictures of the De Lesseps statue at Port Said, the Elephanta Caves at Bombay, and a large two-funnelled liner had the places of honour on the walls. It did not need a very quick wit to guess that Bessie Furle was the widow of a sailor. And a glance at the printing under the picture of the liner showed that he had been a captain in the P. & O. He had died at Port Tewfik of malaria; and now Bessie sat on her sofa among the other souvenirs he had collected and housed in Islington Vale.

On the afternoon following the quarrel Elinor felt a longing to talk to Bessie, and was soon sitting in her drawing-room, with the elephant tea-tray between herself and her hostess. And in this congenial room she not only seemed a very different person from the irritated woman of the previous night, but she was so. Our character can take its shape from those we sit with; and we are at our best with those who like and admire us. This woman, sitting with the sympathetic Bessie, was now, and without hypocrisy, companionable, kind and well-meaning.

'Oh, my dear,' she said, 'do let us talk. Can you bear with me if I pour out my woes? It's what I've come for, I'm afraid.'

'Of course, my dear; of course!' urged Bessie, two motives driving her: a real desire to help her friend, and an eager desire to hear the woes.

'You can't think what a comfort it is to have you to talk to.'

'I know, I know,' said Bessie understandingly. 'One must have at least one person to whom one can speak confidentially. Life wouldn't be bearable otherwise. Now tell me all about it.'

'Oh, we had such a row. Last night. I'm all shaken by it still. I don't know whether I'm wrong, but he seems more irritable of late, as if he had some secret. He fires up at the least little thing.'

'Poor Paul. He's worried, I expect. What was it about?'

'I don't see what he has to worry him. He has a much more comfortable home with me than he could possibly afford himself. It was about – I don't know what it was about. I said something about his being a little late, and he turned and rent me. Sometimes I'm afraid he'll do something violent.'

'Oh, no, dear. Not Paul. He's not that sort.'

'Well, last night he gave me a look as if he hated me.' Elinor drew her handkerchief from her bag, feeling that the tears were near. 'There's one fundamental fact, and it's no good shutting one's eyes to it: we're not really suited to one another. Among other things – I wouldn't say this to anyone but you – but he's not my class, and that's insuperable . . . He told me lies, you know, when he married me. Oh, yes, he did. One can't forget that. His people are nothing, really. Oh, my dear, I wouldn't say this to a single soul in the world but you – you know I wouldn't – you know I'm always loyal to him – and I beg you not to let it go a yard farther, but he's rather a climber, really, and I see now that he never really loved me' – she patted her eyes – 'he only married me for my money and the position.'

'Oh, no, Elinor. No. You mustn't think that.'

'But I do think it, Bessie. What else can I think?' Her mouth was working against the tears, and she rolled the handkerchief into a tight ball. 'And if I hadn't the money, I believe he'd leave me tomorrow. I do, really. He almost said so, last night.'

'Nonsense dear. Where would he go to? What would he do?'

'He regrets it now – he regrets having married me. And what he doesn't seem to understand is that I could have married others. It's not every woman who can bring two hundred and fifty a year and a houseful of beautiful furniture into a home. He had nothing himself. But I was ready to give it all to him; but I didn't think he would turn against me.' Under Bessie's warm sympathy, Elinor was fast filling with tears. The sympathy acted on her like wine, releasing her tongue and slackening her grasp of truth. She poured out words to justify herself and to make her story as good and complete as possible. 'I'm sure I've done everything I could – always – for him, and to be treated like this! He used words! Terrible words. A navvy's words – and to me who's given him everything! I made my will in his favour. Long ago I did that. I said to him, I've nobody else, and anything may happen to me at any time. You'd think that in his own interests he wouldn't go out of his way to insult me. One can alter a will – but who else have I got, since mother died? I shan't alter it, but – oh, I can't see that he has done so badly by marrying me. He owes any comfort he's got to me, and all hope for the future. I *do* think he might be kinder. I *do* think so.'

Bessie came to her side to take her hand and soothe her and, unconsciously, to flatter her. She mustn't make too much of it; she mustn't take on so about it; she was too sensitive and highly strung; she'd be much happier with a slightly thicker skin like hers, Bessie's; all married people had these tiffs and said terrible things in their tempers; she remembered more than one unpleasant scene between Captain Furle and herself, yes, when he so far forgot himself as to use sailor's words to her, and she thought she would never get over it; and yet no one could say they weren't a happy couple on the whole, and she was sure she was heartbroken when he died.

Elinor came home comforted after all such talks. And in the evening she would be quite glad when Paul came home, even though he didn't speak much. Men were like that, sinking into their pipes and their books; and it was companionship to feel them about. And no doubt, as Bessie had said, she'd be very upset if he died. The house would seem empty, and she would not know what to do. The world could be a very lonely place for women.

It was as we have said: Elinor, despite her outpourings to Bessie Furle, was far from unhappy in the house in Elm Tree Road. Had she been a cleverer woman, with insight into herself, she would have seen that her occasional disagreements with Paul were a part of the comfortable furniture of her life, and her opportunities of reminding him that her connections were better than his, and her money larger, and his table manners inferior, were not the least of her satisfactions. Paul was torn – torn between Myra on the one hand and Security and Kindness on the other. Elinor was not torn at all.

So they spent their days, drifting along with circumstances that did not change. The introduction of some new factor would be necessary to turn the drift into direction; but such a new factor did not appear. Elinor was not likely to take any drastic step; Paul had neither the courage nor the cruelty to break away and go to Myra, even if she would have taken him on such terms; and Myra, as yet, had neither the courage nor the cruelty to give him up. Paul was always hoping that some new thing would happen, and believing that it must, since his mind wouldn't hold the idea that his destiny wasn't entwined with Myra's; but what that new thing would be he could not imagine; it lay beyond the dark.

So they drifted along, hiding their secrets and presenting a very fair face to the world of Islington Vale, which thought of them, and spoke of them, as "very nice people".

Chapter Eight

Paul looked from the window of the train as it crossed a bridge over the Thames. It was a morning of St. Luke's summer: a pale blue sky arched over London, and a low sun lit the silken river and turned the buildings on the northern side into the palaces of an enchanted city. Spires and towers and domes, and tall chimneys even, stood wrapped in colour drawn from mother-of-pearl; and these colours found an answer in the tints on the fringes of fleecy cloud. Where the tide was he did not know, but the broad river seemed as still as the sky, so that the traffic on the embankment moved between the stillness below and the stillness above. The tiny lorries and vans and taxicabs, and the slower pedestrians, looked like the movement of men across the stillness of eternity. By a miracle of light London was corrected of every flaw and made perfect at last. What was the mischief of the gods, that they gave to men these moments, when their hunger for perfection was satisfied? Did the gift mean anything? Did it promise anything? Or was it, like the brief blooming of a flower, its own justification, and no more?

Whatever the answer, Paul was very happy today, as the train drew him from this glimpse of a London transfigured into the midst of the swarming houses. He was going to spend half this October Sunday with his parents, and the late afternoon with Myra who, unknown to them, was coming out to the country to join him. With his parents, as with his pupils, he was always happy, because they looked up to him as a success, and his mother at least listened to him as to one who spoke with authority. He liked to expound to them the ideas he had drawn from his last book and to give a slightly exaggerated picture of his life in London. And after this pleasant occupation, Myra would be alone with him in the beauty of the country; and the day was going to be good to them, sunny and warm. And if he was likely to brag to his parents, he intended to do the opposite with Myra. He was going to tell her the truth about his childhood. As sentimental as most men, he longed for one person in his life 'from whom he had no secrets', with whom he need not lie, and in whose perfect understanding there was peace. And if she knew all, and if – if something happened to set him free, what joy, what sweetness, to take her down to Petfield and present her to the old people there!

Warm in the woods. An idea was with him that kept his eyes from newspaper or books and dimmed the vision from the window. An idea so potent, so gripping, that he wanted to dwell with it all the way from London to Hillgarth, while his eyes gazed before him, unseeing. At times it made him restless, so that he shifted his position in his seat and braced back his shoulders. 'Perhaps one day . . .' she had said. Supposing today in the seclusion of the woods he knew! His breath halted and quickened. Starved too long, he could not think this thought without a failure of his breath, a pounding of the heart, and a hunger in the throat that was almost a sickness. It seemed to heighten his life-power. He felt young and powerful and thirstily exultant; and when he lit his pipe to quiet this surge of life, it shook the hand that held the match. He was obliged to force himself to his newspaper that he might think the thought no more.

He left the train at Hillgarth and got into the old horse bus for Petfield. The road from the little modern town of Hillgarth to the old village of Petfield runs along a watershed ridge in the midst of Sussex, so that the views to the north stretch right away to the forests of Ashdown and St. Leonards, and those to the south, though these are interrupted by foliage and upward slopes, to the grey and undulating sweep of the South Downs. Today the meadows on the north were a full green; and the beeches stood upon them in clumps of red and gold. Enough of their leaves had fallen to unveil their silver trunks and ashy branches whose lines were so taut and strong that they looked like arms straining upward to the sky. The power of this upward strain! The power of upthrusting life! The domes of the horse-chestnuts were crimson and amber and green like the cheeks of ripened apples, and their nuts littered the grass beneath them. And the tangled hedge that ran with the road was bright with the scarlet berries of dog-rose and thorn, and the blue-black fruit of bramble and privet. Everywhere the prodigal plenitude of this strong, upthrusting life.

The bus stopped by the corner of Petfield High Street, and Paul jumped down and walked up the hill with a swinging stride. Its brick pavements wound up from the Drake's Head and the church, past houses of which hardly any two were alike: some gabled, some hip-roofed, some grey-brick and some weather-tiled. Here on its narrow terrace, with its two bow windows, was the old stationer's shop; but Jane and Aubrey Presset had not been there for many a year. Their cottage was out of sight, far away on the very crown of the hill, facing Bannister Green, where the High Street of Petfield became the high road to London.

Paul came quickly to the Green. It was a triangle of grass, bordered on the east by a quickset hedge behind which a few tiled cottages stood among their fruit trees, and the west by a row of lime trees and the London Road. Jane Presset's cottage stood on the London Road. It was one of two built together and the other was really the prettier, with its receding roof and two dormer windows; Jane's was taller and narrower, with a hipped roof, and it had a wooden porch with the parlour window at the side and the bedroom window above. A small garden lay about three sides of it, and evidently Aubrey had found much pleasure in pottering here with a trowel: its beds foamed with michaelmas daisies and marguerites, the tall sunflowers nodding above them; and the manifold stars of the dahlias made packets of colour everywhere.

Paul went up to the porch and rattled on the door. Immediately he heard a happy voice within, and hurried steps; and the door opened, revealing his mother, now a typical old cottage woman, small and heavy-shouldered and lumbering, but with a healthy skin, bright little eyes, and thin white hair.

'Paul, my darling!' she exclaimed, and embraced him. 'Father, here he is! He's come!'

A chair creaked in the parlour, steps creaked on the floor, and Aubrey Presset appeared. Aubrey in his seventies was probably handsomer than he had ever been. Though a short man, and dressed only in a countryman's Sunday best – black coat, black tie, stiff collar and stiff cuffs – yet his fine pointed beard and curly moustaches, now quite white, and the abundance of silky white hair on his crown and above his ears, gave him a dignity and character all his own. Throughout his life he had imagined himself an interesting person, well above ordinary men; and whether or not he was this, he certainly looked it; just as certainly as Jane looked a perfectly ordinary old cottage woman.

'Well, Paul,' said he, with a freedom from excitement proper to a superior person, 'how is it? Come in, old man. Come along in. We're poor, proud, and pretty, but we're glad to see you. Your mother's been like a kettle on the boil all the morning. Come in and "tell the old man of all your greatness in Egypt". You see, I know the Bible, even though the old lady thinks I'm sadly irreligious. Just because I won't go to her God-box down the road.'

'Yes, come along, dear,' echoed his mother; 'and don't listen to his nonsense. I wonder he isn't afraid something'll happen to him, talking like that.'

So they all went into the parlour where Jane sat down on a hard chair with her hands on her knees that she might stare at her successful son, and Aubrey motioned Paul into one easy chair and sank himself into the other.

They inquired after Elinor, and why she never came to see them; and Paul explained that she was never very well; but Jane, without a trace of malice and perhaps a trace of pride, suggested that the real reason was that they were not good enough for her; and instantly Aubrey affirmed that he was good enough for anybody. Paul told them all about the school and how he was now taking the top form in Latin – boys of sixteen and seventeen! – and that the English Composition of the whole school had been entrusted to him; and Jane's immediate comment was, 'I suppose they'll be giving you a rise.' But Paul questioned this, expounding that it was no good expecting much money in the scholastic profession: it was like Art; you must either do it because you loved it, or leave it alone; there was no great money to be got out of it. And Aubrey endorsed this enthusiastically, declaring that it was the way *he* had always looked at life: it hadn't got him anywhere, but by the lord Harry, he'd done what he wanted to and thought worthwhile; he'd never measured success as the idiot world measured it. This prompted Paul to pour over them, with brightening eyes, all the ideas he'd drawn from 'Rebel Art', while his mother listened admiringly and uncomprehendingly, and Aubrey endorsed it all, as he grasped it, with high enthusiasm, slapping his hand on his knee. 'Absolutely right! I've always said it! I've always said it! But I could never make the pumpkins here understand. I'm glad Paul sees it so clearly. Live splendidly in the moment; risk all; and damn the future!' And he contrived to leave the impression that it was because he had always lived gallantly, and in the sign of Art, that he had not been a worldly success and now lived in a cottage on a pound a week. Paul, much encouraged by this approval, gave them most of the lecture he had recently given to his lecture class; and it certainly sounded very well, the words being long and sonorous and scholarly. 'Isn't it wonderful to listen to him?' said Jane. 'It's as good as an education, I declare! Isn't it, father?' But Aubrey's assent to this was somewhat grudging, as if he didn't like the suggestion that he needed an education, and as if he was thinking, deep within himself, that he too was a stimulating person to talk to.

Then his mother said, 'Now you stay here and talk to your dad, while I see to the dinner'; but Paul replied, No, he was coming to help her, and laughingly repelled her insistence that it would spoil his lovely clothes and that he wasn't accustomed to such kitchen work, he with his servants and all! And in the kitchen he was touched to watch her chatting away, while she drew the steaming saucepans from the range and the dishes from the oven, sometimes putting back a wisp of her white hair. So obviously had she prepared the best meal she could imagine to welcome her son: roast beef, roast potatoes, Yorkshire pudding, horse-radish, cauliflower, and apple tart with cream! She enjoyed dishing it up, and she enjoyed the chatting. She put the potatoes round the beef, and deplored her husband's lack of religion, and his tendency to scoff which seemed so wrong. 'He's proud of his great brain, of course, and I should be the last to deny he'd got one, and that you've inherited it from him, but it seems like Pride, and the wisdom of this world is foolishness with God. Pass me them dishes, will you, dearie?' She put the other potatoes and the cauliflower into their dishes, and declared that old age was really the happiest time of one's life. 'No more worries and cares; your children well placed – poor Winnie! I wonder what she'd 'a done – no more work bar keeping your house decent; and your house the home in which you're settled forever. Take the vegetables, will you, dearie? You'll know what I mean in another twenty years or so. Here we are, father. You carve, won't you? Sit here, Paul; and I tell you what: as soon as we've finished, which won't be above half an hour, I'm going to bundle all this in the kitchen, to wash it up this evening, and you and me and dad'll go for a walk down the High Street. I want to show you off. People are always arstin' after you, and I expect we shall meet a lot of them, being Sunday and so warm and dry. What a pity you've got to get that early train home. What time was it?'

'It's the three-fifteen to London,' said Paul, dropping his eyes, and wishing he had not got to lie to them.

'Well, there's a shame! Can't you possibly stay a little longer?'

'No, I'm afraid not. I must take that one. Yes.' And the thought of Myra, and his hope of what might happen today, played fast and loose with his breath. Filial love was there, but it was helpless against passion.

'But how are you going to get to Hillgarth? There's no bus at that time, not on Sundays.'

'I shall walk it.'

'Yes, you was ever a one for that game. But' – she put her head on one side to think – 'Oh, well, it's not too bad. We can be finished by half-past one – hurry on, Dad – and we can have a walk round for the best part of an hour.'

'Of course we can!' He was happy to yield himself up to his Mother's pride; and he was not lightly touched when, walking up and down the High Street – their walk, thanks to the artful old lady, was little more than a coming and going between the church at the bottom and Bannister Green at the top – she slowed her step at the sight of friends, that she might be able to present to them her son from London.

But at last the clock at the corner of the Hillgarth Road marked half-past two; and he bade farewell to them there, she clinging to him and begging him to come again soon and watching him till he was out of sight beneath the fall of the road.

Out of sight he quickened his pace, and in less than half an hour was standing in Hillgarth, near the old wall of the cattle market, where he could both watch the London train as it rolled in on its high embankment and command the steps of the old grey station house, down which Myra must come. Since he might be recognised in Hillgarth, it was his plan, directly she appeared, to walk off towards the farmlands on the north, while she followed at a distance, to join him behind the trees.

Here came the train; also a minute of dismay when she did not immediately appear; and then the sight of her on the station steps. Always when seen at a little distance like this, her figure, slender and frail, seemed that of a fresh young girl. He saw the usual smile begin on her lips, as she perceived him, and the abrupt reorganisation of her face into something seemlier. Delighting in the apparent youth of her, and breathless with his hope, he turned and led the way. Leaving the road, he took a footpath that wound over the meadows and up the hills towards Petfield. He crossed a stile and a streamlet, and, seeing in the next field people lolling in the afternoon sun, passed on behind an old farm house till he came to a little dip under two spreading oaks. Here he waited for her. As she approached, the smile peeped and retired in disgrace again; and he noticed the pains she had given to her dress and the undoubted touch of colour she had added to her cheeks and mouth. Probably only he knew that Myra, the modest and retiring schoolmistress, had a solicitude about her looks as keen as the next woman's and a secret hunger in her body that was probably stronger because more starved. Sometimes he believed that it was this aching hunger which had enabled her to take him, just as his had rendered him indifferent to any fading in her. This afternoon, as he took her narrow body into his embrace, she responded passionately; and his happiness distended the heart.

'Come along, Miss Bawne! This path mounts higher and higher, till at last it brings you to the top of the world, where you sit down and have your reward, a view of the South Downs.'

'What a lovely day it is!'

'What a bright remark!'

'Oh, well, we can't always be dazzling. And it's too hot, anyway. What are you looking at?'

'Look!' he exclaimed, pointing upwards. 'Martins! Martins still here, though the swallows have gone!'

'I don't know how you can tell one from the other.'

'And look! See!' Pleased with her admiration, he was eager to justify it. 'A kestrel. D'you see it? Hanging up there in the air, almost stationary. That's a kestrel, or "windhover" as it's called in these parts.'

'How on earth do you know all these things?'

'You forget I was a country lad. I always had a passion for the birds,' he bragged. 'And that reminds me: I'm going to tell you something today.'

'How very interesting! What is it?'

'Wait.'

They were now climbing the slope of a meadow: two figures in their dark London clothes, and of a like size; for, though Myra was not tall, she was as tall as he, and though spare, not so much sparer. They had left the streamlet behind, but if they turned their heads they could see its course by the deeper green of the grass and the ribbon of rushes. The red Sussex cattle moved slowly towards it and lowered their muzzles amid the rushes where it lay. Only silence seemed possible, and Paul and Myra walked up and up, over stiles and through hazel woods, ever higher and higher, till at length they reached the level fields of the crown, and looking backward, saw Hillgarth in a hollow on their left and Petfield near at hand on their right, with woods and hills between them, and the grey downs behind.

'Let's sit here,' suggested Paul, and flung himself down beneath a hedge.

'What was it you were going to tell me?'

He pointed to Petfield. 'That's where I used to live.'

'Thank you, my angel,' laughed Myra. 'I knew that.'

'Yes, but you didn't know all.' And he told her all about his childhood and his errand-boy days; and how he had suppressed this ever since, and how happy it made him to confess to her. But even so, even before Myra, habit took command, and compelled him to paint these things as rather better than they were. He waited for her comment. It did not come, and he glanced at her averted face.

'Oh, I'm so glad!' she said.

'Glad? Why glad?'

'Because I think it brings you nearer to me. I'm really rather a diffident person, I suppose; and I've always felt I was just a little beneath you.' She turned gleefully towards him. 'Oh, I'm glad we're neither of us anything very much.'

'But what about the lies?'

'Ach, but we all do a little of that, don't we? When I was thirty I always implied that I was twenty-seven; and now that I'm thirty-one, I shall probably say I'm twenty-eight. And I'm sure I'm the most ignorant kindergarten mistress in London, but I didn't tell Mr Heasman that, poor dear. I let him think that I was rather well-informed.'

He picked up her hand and took it on his lap. 'You're wonderful.'

'Well, that's the first time I've ever heard *that*!'

'You are. You're so full of understanding.'

'I don't think it's that at all. It's just that I've much less conscience than you. In fact, I'm not certain that I've any at all.'

'Conscience! Conscience! And yet' – he pressed her hand tight – 'your conscience won't let you do what I want.'

'Which is—'

'You know. Your conscience won't let you give yourself to me.'

'Oh, but I mean in little things. That's so big.'

'Are you going to do it, Myra?'

She looked down at the grass, and picked a blade and played with it. 'Perhaps . . . one day. . . .'

After that they did not speak but gazed ahead of them. The farthest woods were purple, save where the falling sun hit them and showed them yellow. A beech before them spread a branch with a few bronze leaves against this purple background, like Chinese lacquer. And from the woods below came a wild call: a young pheasant defying the challenge of an older bird.

Paul brought over his other hand, and stroked her wrist. 'This is happiness, isn't it?'

'Perfect.'

'Let's talk about what we'd do, if . . .'

'No. No, don't do that. It makes me feel mean and guilty.'

'But perhaps it's only a dream. There can be no harm in dreaming. Or let's say what we'd have done if we'd been free when we first met. I've often worked it all out, Myra: the things that really matter; the simple, natural things, I mean. First, there's cover and warmth, and that means a small house somewhere, and fuel for the fire; then plenty of good food, because eating's one of the greatest pleasures of the day, whatever you may say; then the sight and smell of green things, which means a garden and the country near at hand; then what else? – some work that is congenial – building a shed or digging the garden; then a few people whom you really care about; and books; and lastly, the most comfortable bed that money can buy, because there's nothing quite so perfect as falling asleep. That's all I want.'

'Oh, yes! yes!' cried Myra. 'The country for me, too! Quietness and peace. I no longer like a lot of people. I seem to have got afraid of them. Whenever I'm with strangers I always feel strained and headachy – do you? I want just one or two, with whom I'm perfectly at ease and happy. And to be done with teaching a lot of children whom one ought to love but unfortunately doesn't! Sometimes I have a fancy to do what my auntie did, where I used to go as a child.'

'To the Lakes?'

'Yes! The lovely, adorable lakes! The mountains and the fells! Scafell and the Gable and Glaramara! I know them as you know your beloved downs, because I spent nearly every holiday there. They seemed like paradise to a child from Brixton, and I sometimes see myself doing as auntie did, if I had a few pounds of my own, starting a little guest house somewhere by one of the Lakes, with a mountain just behind the cabbages in the back garden. I wouldn't see the people more than I could help; I'd stay in the background and do the housekeeping, and you (if you were there) could potter among the cabbages and feel the donkey's legs, and so on; and whenever possible we'd walk along the high fells and over the passes. They're worth fifty of this stupid place. Downs, indeed, when you can have Fells!'

'Strange that you call a thing that goes up "a down" and a thing that rises "a fell",' said Paul, idiotically.

'Really!' objected Myra. 'My sweetheart!'

They ate the 'tea' she had brought – jam sandwiches and cake and bottled milk – and then, as the sun was low, she suggested, 'I suppose we'd better be going back now'; and a sharp disappointment pierced him, that her thought had not run with his; but he had not the courage to tell her what his thought had been; so he stood up and made ready to return. Together they went down the hill, with linked fingers but not speaking at all, because he was occupied with his thought, his heart shaking and pounding, and it is possible that now the thought had crossed to her. They came to the tilt of a meadow, where the track went down to a wood of hazel and ash. It was steep, and they footed their way delicately; and as the path brought them under the trees, he suddenly drew on her fingers and led her aside into the deeps. She feigned to laugh and asked, 'Where are we off to now?' but her voice trembled, and he answered only, 'Come, dear. Let's be alone together a little longer. There's not too much happiness in the world'; and they bent their heads to pass under the branches of the hazel shrubs and between the tall young sapling ashes, which sprouted from ancient and knotted boles almost flush with the ground. The floor of dead leaves, old twigs and creeping mercury was flecked by the low sunlight; and he led her deeper and deeper till the path seemed far away. Then, sinking to a bed of old leaves, he drew her down to sit within his arm, and she came willingly. Her head rested on his shoulder, and while he stroked her cheek and neck, she kept her eyes closed and her lips slightly smiling; but when he felt for her breast, she drooped away from him, and murmured, 'Oh, Paul. No!' He persisted gently; and about her drooping, and her soft gasps, 'Paul!' there was something that suggested she both loved his touch and feared it, wanted it and did not want it; once or twice she gave him the glance of a frightened deer, but, none the less, she stroked his hair; and at last life had its way with her: she turned to him passionately, abruptly, and drew him down, with her eyes closed again and the faint smile back on her lips, welcoming him.

Chapter Nine

Round the first corner in Elm Tree Road was Morton Avenue, a very quiet little curving road. Nine times out of ten, if you came to its corner, you saw it stretching away, with nothing on its pavements except the alternating gas lamps and the line of coal-holes. Its houses, being of a later date, were smaller and more ornate than those in Elm Tree Road. Built of a paler grey brick, they had elaborate architraves to the windows and a sort of balcony, balustraded but quite inaccessible, over the bay window of the front room. No basements here; their ground floor rooms were really on the ground floor, and you did not approach the front door up an imposing flight of steps, but along a tiled path, and between a railing and a neat little garden of privet and laurels.

In one of these lived Dr Waterhall. The glow of his round red lamp was one of the first things you noticed in the fall of a winter evening. Beneath it, fixed to his little front railing, was his brass plate, with 'Dr Waterhall' in the centre and his surgery hours in the bottom left-hand corner. A keen-eyed woman, coming to visit him in one of the surgery hours, would first have remarked that the little garden had no flowers in it like its neighbours, but only a bed of ferns; and, on being admitted by a comfortable fat housekeeper and shown into a small dining-room, would have guessed at once that there was no mistress in this home. This little room was very clean: the brown linoleum shone with wax, the little sideboard smelt of furniture polish, and the bronze and china ornaments stood at orderly intervals on the mantelpiece; but it was comfortless; it was made for a meal designed by a housekeeper, and nothing more. If conducted, not to the consulting room at the back, but up the narrow staircase to the doctor's study, she would have got exactly the same impression: the brass rods shone in the light from the fan of the front door, and the banister-rail was almost tacky with polish, but the carpet and the wallpaper were of dark, old-fashioned designs, and the window on the landing had a quite insufferable plant on the sill. They were the stairs of a man who did not notice such things.

Very different the study: there was no feminine taste here, but all the comfort in the world. An immense easy chair, with a footstool prostrated before it, was clearly the monarch of the room. The large roll-top desk, littered with novels, magazines, cigar-boxes and ash-trays, was no more than a corpulent gentleman-in-waiting. And everything else was courtier to it: the fire blazing its comfortable flattery; the coal-box waiting with the coal and kicking the slippers behind it; the paper-rack, the boxes of cigars, and the matchbox-holders of grotesque patterns which were always empty because the doctor had put the matches in his pocket. Manifestly the pictures were there to fill up bare places on the walls, and for no other purpose; they were large coloured photographs of places the doctor had visited on lonely holidays – Venice and Rome and Interlaken – and a few coloured pictures of men playing games, with a joke printed beneath, which joke had pleased the doctor to the extent of compelling purchase, but would sicken him now if he saw it, which, however, he never did. Cigar smoke filled the room: if it was not present as an actual cloud, it was present as a ghost, in a strong, stale smell.

And all that a perceptive woman could have read in the house, she could have read in the doctor himself. A short, pot-bellied man of sixty-five, he was something of a dandy, but there were spots on his lapels that a wife would have removed; usually he wore spats, but, whatever the colour of his suit, he was content with thick blue socks, a mistake which a wife would have quickly corrected; his talk to women was garnished with those exaggerated gallantries – the "fair sex", "your charming sex, Madam", "it is the right of beauty to command" – that a woman would have laughed out of him; and if the woman was still young and attractive, she heard his unsatisfied desire speaking in the gallantries and peeping in the friendly, twinkling eyes. Some people saw in him a likeness to the late Edward VII; though less rotund, he had the same fine nose, they said, and the full chaps and the receding grey beard. The beard was pointed, and red under the lip where it was not grey. Undoubtedly Dr Waterhall was among those who saw this likeness, for he was inclined to dress like his late sovereign, wearing a grey suit to match his silvering hair, a white waistcoat-slip, and a brown Homburg hat. He had even a feather in the ribbon of the hat, which would have looked very fine in Central Europe, but seemed inappropriate on the pavements of Islington.

Much character showed in the Homburg hat. He cocked it always slightly to one side; and a hat worn to one side is sure proof of a certain self-satisfaction, generally unconscious, because, if it becomes conscious, the man is ashamed of revealing it, and puts his hat straight again. Dr Waterhall was a lonely man, and quite free from introspection, and therefore a busybody. Without perceiving it he allowed this meddlesomeness to get the better of his natural benevolence. No more conceited than his neighbour, but hard up for something to do, he liked to cock his hat on one side and go off to a committee meeting of the hospital, or vestry meeting of the church, and there get a matron sacked or a curate reprimanded. Walking along the Caledonian Road, he would see the sprightly but unseemly postcards in the windows of the cheap stationers, and, drawn to them as surely as a nib to a magnet, he would, after studious examination of them, decide that it was his duty to write to the police about continental obscenity in the London streets. Though savouring very heartily a clubroom jest with his friends, he would not tolerate it in the pages of a novel (much as it interested him there) but wrote straight off to its publishers that he would never read another book from their house. Few things gave him more gratification than to find a mistake in his newspaper, especially in the subjects of which he held himself a master, for then he would hurry to his desk and address a letter to the editor. He much enjoyed his power and authority at inquests, where he would put up his pince-nez with a trembling hand (for he was getting old) and deliver a carefully prepared speech. And one of the best days of his life was when he was called as expert evidence in a nullity suit, and was able to satisfy the court that a husband could be impotent with his wife and potent with other women. Many sides of his nature were satisfied that afternoon.

He was too lively and sociable to have many enemies, but his meddlesomeness had made him one or two. And these were never the poor people, with whom he was always benignant, but generally the powerful ones like the chairmen of committees or the vicars of churches (Dr Waterhall had hawked his devotions round to several churches in Islington Vale, not being easily satisfied with the payment of respect they offered). Liking him at first, as all did, but soon tiring of his well-meant officiousness, they haply said something impatient behind his back; and, hearing of this, he disliked everything about them and condemned it everywhere. Let them offend him in one point, and he fell foul of them in every other: he allowed no good of their attainments or their work, their furniture, their faces, or their children. He put on the Homburg hat to sally forth and condemn them in this house and the next. He was a genial and affectionate friend, and an irreconcilable enemy.

Nevertheless, most people were inclined to speak of Dr Waterhall as 'rather an old dear' and the wittier women, seeing him pass their windows at eight o'clock of an evening, with the hat aslant and his cane under his arm, would feel an almost maternal affection and exclaim, 'Poor old darling! He's like a lonely boy trying to find someone to play with.' In which words they put their finger straight on the truth. Seldom an evening went by but he would toss his newspaper on to the desk, having read every article in it, and most of the advertisements, and his own letter to the editor (if there was one) three times, and, sighing in his loneliness, fetch down the hat and set off along Morton Avenue in search of someone to talk to. He would go from door to door, beseeching the householder not to let him in if he was likely to be a nuisance, till he found one where he felt welcome, when he would sink into a chair and argue for the rest of the night. He liked all people (except those he had quarrelled with) so he had a large district to visit; but as often as not he rounded the corner into Elm Tree Road and fetched up in the sitting-room of Paul and Elinor Presset. Paul had never the heart to make him other than welcome; and the doctor liked as well as anything else to smoke his cigar with Presset and to talk his gallantries to Elinor.

The two men argued vigorously, the doctor all for discipline and authority, Paul for more liberal views; but they avoided a quarrel. Secretly Paul thought his brain a much finer instrument than the doctor's, but with his natural gentleness and desire to be liked, he would oil and ease his arguments if he saw the doctor getting heated. And Dr Waterhall could get astonishingly heated on questions of discipline and authority. Astonishing how in old men of his type such beaming goodwill can partner with such an unconscious passion for violence and cruelty! Hotly he would advocate a dose of grape-shot for Indian and Egyptian mobs, a machine-gun for the Irish, the lethal chamber for imbeciles and criminals, and the birch, and plenty of it, for young children. He inveighed against doles for the unemployed – 'if a man will not work, neither shall he eat' – and the modern pampering of prisoners – 'a little more of the treadmill and the cat, and we shouldn't hear of so much crime, my dear Presset.' He loved the subject of the compulsory sterilisation of the unfit; only with him 'the unfit' covered a wider population than usual. As was to be expected from one of his kind, a mere questioning of blood-sports or capital punishment, deprived him of reason: he became a bung of emotional vehemence. In a single evening he would defend these noble sports, and declare that flogging was the proper punishment for those who were cruel to animals. And as most of these topics could inflame Paul quite as much as his guest, but on the opposite side of the fence, it was sometimes by the narrowest margin that the argument didn't flare up into the final conflagration.

One evening Dr Waterhall drew a light grey raincoat over his blue suit and set the Homburg hat at the correct angle on his head and started off for the Presset's house in Elm Tree Road. Elinor had invited him to dinner. A new dentist, Mr Worksop, had just come into the neighbourhood, and Elinor, always socially active, had soon left cards on the Worksops and was now giving them a little dinner; and who more suitable to meet a dentist and his wife than the doctor? So here was Dr Waterhall coming through a dark clear night and casting his eyes up to the lighted windows of the Pressets' home. He was quite looking foward to the evening. Or course a dentist was not the equal of a doctor, but he was no snob! Why, some of his best pals in the Vale were mere commercial travellers or bank clerks or equivocal people like the Pressets – and this young Worksop would certainly look up to him this evening and listen respectfully to his talk, as a dentist should with a doctor or a new resident with an old-established one. Mrs Worksop would listen flatteringly too; and while both would probably be embarrassed in a strange room, he would be perfectly at ease, bantering Paul and teasing Elinor. In fact, he would be, as you might say, the guest of the evening.

Annie, rosy from the chaff he had given her in the hall, showed him into the drawing-room, and he swept his eye round a semi-circle of people, all looking somewhat strained and artificial, as happens in the few minutes before a meal.

At first the little room seemed very full, but the company quickly dwindled into focus as five people: Elinor looking very large and fine in a foamy and flouncy dress of green silk; little Presset; Worksop and his "fair lady"; and that perky little captain's widow, Bessie Furle. He was slightly disconcerted to see the women dolled up as they were, and little Presset in evening dress, or in his idea of it – an old dinner-jacket suit with a watch-chain stretched from vest-pocket to vest-pocket, a stiff shirt-front with a brass stud in its centre, a clean linen handkerchief thrust into his breast pocket for decoration only, and grey socks crumping down over highly polished but ordinary walking shoes. Young Worksop, on the other hand, a long, clean-shaven and apparently mild young man in the thirties, was perfectly dressed, with a pearl stud, silk socks, and patent-leather shoes – a shade too perfectly, the doctor thought. 'Just like these Pressets to dress up for a little do like this' he told himself for his comfort. 'Straining after gentility, that's what it is.' And immediately he felt, not ashamed, but distinguished, in his neat and unpretentious blue suit.

'Well, my dear,' said he to Elinor. 'How's Elinor? . . . Well, Mrs Furle, no need to ask you whether *you're* feeling bonny. I shall never make a living out of *you* . . . How do you do, ma'am? How do you do, sir?' – he bowed to the Worksops – 'You've just come to these parts I hear? . . . How do, Paul, old boy! Shift along there, and make room for me. No, don't disturb yourself, fair lady;' and he sat himself between Paul and Worksop and began to show the company how to be hearty and unembarrassed instead of artificial and strained. That the three men had got together didn't worry him; unknown to himself, he was being driven to show his superiority to a dentist by talking to the company generally or to Paul, his old friend, and letting some time elapse before, in his graciousness, he turned and talked to Worksop.

Soon Paul and the doctor were in hearty talk, Paul shifting excitedly in his chair, and the doctor sometimes touching him on the knee, with a 'No, my dear boy.'

Elinor watched, irritated with both, but more with her husband. A guest can be forgiven, but not a husband. Why hadn't he any social sense? There was poor Mr Worksop left to talk, or rather, to listen, to Bessie. If he'd any sense, he'd be trying to make him feel at home, instead of talking his dull politics to Dr Waterhall. She hardly listened to Mrs Worksop, fascinated to watch his gaucherie. Also, as hostess, she was anxious about the meal. Mrs Briscoll, the charwoman, was helping Annie, and all should go right; but it was time that Annie came in and announced, as she had been instructed, 'Dinner is ready, madam.' Elinor was looking forward to the word, 'dinner'. As a rule, unable to call it dinner, she avoided mentioning it to strangers or called it 'our evening meal'; never 'supper'. Why didn't Annie come? And Paul was still rattling away to the doctor. Would he never say a word to poor young Mr Worksop, who must be bored to distraction by Bessie's chatter – was that Annie's step? No. While paying polite attention to Mrs Worksop, she found herself repeating Annie's words, 'Dinner is ready, madam.' Would she never come?

And just then the lively argument between Paul and the doctor perished; and Paul in the best of spirits turned round, looked at Elinor, and inquired, 'Is there any reason why we shouldn't go in to supper?'

Supper! The little idiot had given the whole show away. Flushed with anger, she snapped: 'It'll be ready when it's ready.'

The flush flew over to his cheekbones; but the doctor, unaware of these winged hostilities, was jocose. 'Quite right Elinor! Don't let him be greedy. You wait till you're told to go in, old boy. What have *you* done to deserve your supper?'

Supper! She could have cried: and Annie's entry at that very moment seemed pompous and ludicrous. 'Dinner is ready, madam.'

'Oh, *dinner*! I see,' exclaimed Paul, savage with his wife and determined to hit back. 'I see. We've gone up in the world. Dinner's ready. Come, Bessie, I'll escort you in.'

'Thank you,' giggled Bessie, a little gushing.

'Don't mention it,' begged Paul. 'Charmed, I'm sure.'

Elinor felt like killing him. They filed into the dining-room; and here, taking the head of the table, he was fussy. 'Here you are, Bessie,' said he, pointing gaily with a knife. 'You sit on my right. Doctor, you go on Bessie's right. Hurry up! March! Mr Worksop, you go on Mrs Presset's left, and Mrs Worksop, you come here, will you? That's right isn't it? *Seniores priores*.'

'Of course it's right!' snapped Elinor. The man was still betraying his ill-breeding: those who knew what was right didn't talk about it like this. Worksop for the first time noticed her tone and looked uncomfortably away. Paul's mouth set in an ugly line.

'You can serve the soup, Annie,' said Elinor.

There can be few torments to equal those of a snobbish woman who has persuaded herself that her husband is vulgar and will reveal his vulgarity to their friends. The woodland frieze of the dining-room looked down that evening on a considerable piece of human suffering amid the mahogany. Elinor found herself listening in agony for Paul's self-revelations in his chatter, and then lifting her voice to talk him down, that some of the company might be protected from hearing him. She found herself correcting his statements so as to show the company that they did not really hold the views of the vulgar. 'Oh, no, we don't, Paul,' she would assert. 'We don't really think that.' And

Paul, having no intention of being thought a henpecked husband by these new people would retort, 'Well, I do, at any rate. You can think what you like, my dear. That's what *I* think.' And the doctor, much amused, exclaimed, 'Hello, hell! He's getting saucy, isn't he, Elinor? . . . Mrs Worksop, do you put up with that from *him*?' – indicating young Worksop. ' 'Pon my soul, it's the age of rebellious husbands. What's the world coming to? *I'd* have got married, if I'd thought I'd be allowed to answer back!'

Matters improved when the soup gave place to the fish. Paul, suddenly ashamed of this public sniping and deciding that his guests mustn't be let down, addressed himself to entertaining Bessie Furle and Mrs Worksop; and Elinor enjoyed a period of peace while she talked to the doctor and the dentist. But the peace was shattered, and her head nearly split open, by a call from Paul, 'Fill up the doctor's wine glass, Elinor. And you can fill up mine too, if you like. It's a good drink, that. Where did you get it?' She affected not to hear, since she had got it from the grocer's, and not from her wine merchant, as in her late husband's time; and, anyhow, this exasperating betrayal that he was surprised by a bottle of wine on the table was immediately capped by his plain statement of the fact, in an effort to be funny. 'My golly, I wish you came every night of the week, Mrs Worksop. It's only when we have company that we get wine like this. Fill it up, Elinor.'

Have company! Oh, my heaven! In the odious phrase his shopkeeping parents stood revealed. One can be sorry for Elinor, since all suffering, whether worthy or unworthy, is pitiable.

The wine was undoubtedly enlivening the doctor, and Paul too, who was unaccustomed to it. The doctor loved a wordy combat, and, when warmed by a meal, would do his best to provoke it: he would toss on to the table some political or religious squib that was sure to ignite little Presset, and then the jolly argument would begin. He did this now: he affirmed his belief in martial law to bring railway strikers to their senses, and at once the battle was joined: hot, impatient advocacy shot across the bosom of Mrs Worksop who sat between the combatants. Worksop said nothing. Not yet at his ease, and anxious to offend neither doctor nor host, he kept his views to himself. Bessie Furle was equally out of it: she who could talk so fluently on persons and things was quite uninterested in large, general questions: and she just ate her food delicately and in silence. Elinor bit her lip and tried to catch Paul's eye with an instructive glance. But what use, what use? What was the good of trying to teach behaviour to a man of fifty?

Now, if it is torment to a wife to see her husband vulgar, it is infuriating to a husband to perceive her shame. Paul caught her glance, and his blood rushed up. He to be despised by *her* – he who taught Latin and read books beyond her comprehension! And to be rebuked, and glanced at, before people – hell! After they'd gone tonight, he'd tell her a thing or two, he'd say, 'I won't put up with it, d'yer see?' And in the meantime he'd give her what she looked for. He'd be gaily and defiantly vulgar. He'd show his independence, and his refusal to be glanced at, by referring to the potatoes as 'spuds', the gravy as 'the juice, Doc', and the wine as 'the liquor'. All of which he did; and the odd thing was that this jocosity saved the evening. The Worksops found it happy and sufficiently amusing, and only Elinor knew that it was directed like pistol shots at her. Though perhaps Bessie Furle, watching in silence, knew it too.

The sweet was gone; and the dessert; and Elinor began to wonder when would be a good opportunity to rise and shepherd the ladies into the drawing-room. Leaning forward with her hands apart on the table's edge, as one who was about to rise, she looked from speaker to speaker, waiting for a suitable pause in their talk. And in time the talk stopped; a tiny silence held the room; her lips moved for utterance, but – Paul spoke first. 'Well, folks,' said he, also resting both hands on the table. 'if we've all done, we may as well get into the parlour, eh?'

Oh, sick and impotent misery! Never was Elinor nearer to an hysterical outburst than then. He had spoiled all. He had ruined everything. And *parlour*! So often, when warmed with anger or excitement, he brought up this terrible word from his childhood.

Fury in her heart, but cold dignity in her voice, she explained, 'You men will have your coffee in here. Come, Bessie. . . . Will you come into the drawing-room, Mrs Workson, and have some coffee?'

'Coffee? Oh, is there coffee?' said Paul.

Ah! She got the women from the room.

And Paul, perceiving that he had done something wrong again, watched her departure with a fury larger than hers. 'I won't have it, I won't have it. I'll have one or two things to say to you tonight, my good lady. I'll put an end to this sort of thing, once and for all: see if I don't. No one shall despise *me*, and get away with it.'

Chapter Ten

The days narrowed and darkened into winter. Along the edge of the path in Canonbury Fields the leaves were down from tired and empty trees. The football pitch of the Abercorn boys was churned into mud. There were many fogs that November; and Paul, on his way to the school, moved like a shadow through the grey haze; and when he arrived in the basement Common Room, he saw that the boys were barely visible on the asphalt playground. They lit the gas early in the classrooms on these days, and it burned yellow with a halo around it. When the fogs rolled away, they left thundery skies, yellow and threateningly alight. Then came gusty days of December, when Paul's umbrella was not hooked over his arm, but up against the driving rain and blown about like a sail; and in the evening the lamplight lay on the hard wet road like a riding-light on the sea. But occasionally there was a day of opalescent beauty, such as winter can give to London, when the pale amber of the sunlight rested on the upper faces of the long blocks of houses, and bathed the camber of the road; and buildings in the far distance were blue like country hills.

Now that the woods offered their hospitality no more, it was difficult to meet and be with Myra. How in winter can one be with one's mistress, if one cannot spend the night from home? He was forced into uneasy stratagems, compassed about with lies. He would take her to cheap Bloomsbury hotels for a few hours of an afternoon, and explain to Elinor that he was spending the time with Inglewood. At the reception bureaux he lied poorly. In his nervousness and guilt, he could not bring himself to say other than 'Mr and Mrs Presset' – one lie, that this woman was his wife, was sufficient. And it was a nervous business, explaining to the clerk that he and his wife wanted the room only for an hour or so, as they were but passing through London and needed somewhere to rest. His discomfort betrayed him; and when he had gone up the stairs with Myra, the reception clerks would look at each other and say, 'The wicked old man! Does he really think he gets it past us? And she's his little piece, is she? Well, he's easily pleased, I must say.' 'Yes, but what about *her*?' asked another. 'Oh, *her. She's* got to take what she can get. Though she doesn't look that sort, I must say; but you can never tell what's in 'em, really. I remember a girl who looked like a Sunday School teacher . . .' and so on. 'And "Presset!" ' they laughed. ' "Presset", mind you! How did he think of that, the sly old dog!' And since the reception clerks and many of the hotels were acquainted with one another, and sometimes exchanged their views on the pageant of life that passed before their plate-glass windows, this interesting couple, 'Mr and Mrs Presset', became quite well known in Bloomsbury.

At first Myra was terrified of the hotel vestibules, the long lobbies, and the hostile rooms. Her real tendency was to fly from life, not to run and grasp it like this; and the same tendency was in Paul, not to be overcome without strain and heat: he might over-persuade her, and reassure her, and try to provide strength for both, but his heart palpitated, and the moisture stood on his brow as he went with his tale to the reception bureau or guided Myra along the carpeted corridor, at the heels of a bell-boy in buttons. He was not a facile sinner.

This unkindly winter laid many old people in their graves, and among them Myra's mother. Then Paul, though distressed at her distress, was happy in fussing about her, advising her, and acting as her man of business. He helped her sell the house and furniture, and when she had found a room and put a few pieces in it, he induced her to accept a weekly remittance of a few shillings from him. 'You've *got* to let me help you, my dear. How can you possibly live on the little you've got now? I won't let you do it. D'you hear, my girl? I won't have it. It's pure selfishness on my part; I'm not going to be miserable, watching you starve, and you, who've got quite nice parts really, aren't going to be so selfish as to ask me to suffer like this. Just to please your pride! What's your pride compared with my misery? Myra, this is final: a few more shillings'll make all the difference to you, and either you take it from me and make me inordinately happy, or I shan't believe you love me.' And it was true that her acceptance of it made him happy. 'Curious,' thought he. 'I love mother and dad, but I find it a real effort to send them money, whereas it's no effort to give it to Myra, but only joy.'

At first he was exercised as to how to pay over the money with the least injury to her pride. Possessed by an odd idea that paper was less offensive than metal, he would buy a postal order and slide it surreptitiously into her bag, or humorously under the skin of her glove; and her long kiss of gratitude was a great delight. That a banker's order would be the simplest and easiest way he saw very clearly, but he did not like to write the order, for fear of what the bank might think. Of Elinor he had no fear: a completely unsuspicious person, whatever her other faults, she had not looked into the passbook of his separate account once in their married life. But the bank clerks? – would they suspect anything? Why? 'M. Bawne' might be a poor relation or an old retainer or anything. And at last his obstinacy asserted itself: he was going to do what he liked with his own money; if he wanted to help a colleague who was poor, he'd damned well do it, and bank clerks, and anyone else who pried into his affairs, could think that they liked. He went into the bank that very day and wrote the order.

They had one happy time when Myra was able to come to him in Elm Tree Road. Elinor had gone away. Bessie Furle, declaring that the winter had done her no good, had begged her to come for a weekend to Bournemouth; and Elinor, bored in her echoing house, had been very willing to go. There was a difficulty about leaving Annie and Paul in the house alone: 'It doesn't seem quite nice,' said Elinor, 'though Annie would be as safe with Paul as with the Bishop of London. Paul isn't that sort at all. But somebody'll have to look after him.'

'Let her come in the morning and go home at nights,' suggested Bessie. 'Paul's a man and won't mind being in the house alone.'

'We might arrange that,' Elinor agreed.

And they arranged it so, Paul offering no objection, but even encouragement. Elinor went; and when she was gone, Paul suddenly told Annie that he had been visited by an idea: he would go to see his parents in the country from Saturday afternoon till late on Sunday night, and that would give *her* a bit of a holiday, too. He was sure she deserved it. She could have her Saturday afternoon off, and not come again till seven on Monday morning. How would she like that? Wouldn't that be rather jolly?

'Oh, yes, *thank* you, sir,' said Annie. 'Thank you very, very much.'

'And look here: I'm going to give you something to spend. I want you to be happy.'

'Oh, *thank* you, sir.'

'Don't mention it,' said Paul. 'You're welcome, I'm sure.'

Then he had the task of persuading Myra to come and be with him from late on the Saturday night till very early on the Monday morning. It was a difficult task. 'Oh, no, no,' she persisted, shuddering from unsheathed life as from an unsheathed sword. 'No, I shouldn't like to do *that*.' 'Oh, yes, yes,' he countered. 'It's a chance in a thousand. And "nothing venture, nothing win," my dear. If you want happiness badly, you've got to pay a price for it. It's on the other side of effort and danger –

I'm coming to see that more and more. I see what I've missed in the past, because I've hugged on to safety. I don't intend to do it any longer in the little time I've got. You'll come, won't you?'

'But it seems so mean, going to her house. It seems different.'

'That's nonsense. The place where things are done is nothing: it's the thing itself that matters. And we've accepted that. And I can have you so seldom, my darling, and time passes. . . . It alarms me, the way it runs by. . . . Do come. . . . No courage, no happiness.'

'But supposing I were seen?'

'No, I've no fear of that. It's very dark at night, and dark in the mornings, too. You could leave while it is still dark and no one is awake. It'll be an adventure, dear. And never before shall I have had you for so long. Nearly thirty-six hours! Do do it. A little courage and effort, that's all.'

And Myra, unable to refuse him anything if he looked disappointed and sad, came. No one saw her come or go. And very happy was their long hidden time behind the walls of that house with its merry cooking and picnicking together, its hush-hush, whispering movements up the stairs, and its silent sitting in the dark by the flame of the fire; it was like the secret and perilous game of two children. She slipped away unseen in the dark of Monday morning. And nothing tangible or visible was left of her visit. Paul himself, after she had gone and before Annie arrived, walked into every room to make sure of this. In the kitchen where they had cooked and joked, into the dining-room where they had sat, into the bedroom where they had slept. Not a trace anywhere. Nothing to be seen, after the most careful peering, on floor or dressing-table, bed or chair. No – his eye was satisfied – the room was as if Myra had never been there.

And his eye had served him well, but the eye is not all. When Annie was making his bed, supposing him to have returned from his parents' home late last night, she suddenly stopped as she lifted a sheet off the chair to spread it. She brought it close to her face. Parma violet! 'Chrimes!' Quickly she lifted the pillow and sniffed at it. 'Good gawd!' Around Annie's head played the fragrance of powder and scent, with which Myra had sought to make her faded looks as charming as might be, for her lover.

She stood there, amazed. What could it mean? The meaning that seemed so plain she refused to accept: no, not of Mr Presset; Mr Presset wasn't that sort at all; good gawd, no! It must have some other and simpler explanation. And she went on with her work, pausing at times to reconsider the mystery. She considered it often in the following days.

But Paul went to and fro between home and school, ignorant of the gossip of reception clerks and the recurring wonder of Annie. He walked with other thoughts. Having tasted the completion of union with Myra, he thought always: how to get free to have her for ever, for the thought of parting was now intol-erable; how to break through to Myra and yet retain his only possible profession and the salary that would keep her; how to go from Elinor without hurting her, without feeling too much the stings of conscience, without shocking and wounding Myra, without stirring Elinor's vindictiveness so that she told the world the dangerous things she knew. His eyes turned inward on the problem, as he hurried along the Caledonian Road, bumping into people with eager apologies, dodging from vans whose drivers hurled their curses after him, and even at times missing his turning into Bishop Abercorn Square. How to get free? It wasn't possible. Flight wasn't possible. Divorce wasn't possible. He was tied to Elinor for as long as she lived – and these people with delicate hearts often lived to a good age. Besides, he didn't want her to die – at least, he wasn't going to allow himself to want it: that would be *too* selfish. No, no, Elinor must live her life, poor dear; and he – but the thought of losing Myra was no longer supportable. What then? 'God knows!'

In the company of the problem he turned one morning into the Masters' Common Room to hear Inglewood saying to Sandys, 'My dear fellow, the point isn't, Did she do it? but, Was it *proved* that she did it? I think she did do it, and very sensible of her too; but I still maintain, and I will go to my grave maintaining, that if people can be hanged on evidence like that, then we're none of us safe.'

'I don't care a damn about that,' retorted Sandys. 'If she did it, that's good enough for me, and I hope she swings.'

'But it's the precedent, my dear ass! I'm not thinking of her so much, as of you and me – and Bertrand here – good morning, Bertrand. It's not her I want to protect from such a damned dangerous verdict, but us. *You*. Now p'raps you see my point.'

'I don't. Such questions aren't likely to arise about you and me.'

Paul noticed that young Sandys, with his usual hostility, tried to keep the reference of the talk to Inglewood and himself.

'Don't you believe it!' cried Inglewood. 'That's my whole point. Given evidence like that, and any of us may be swinging before we know what we've done. Look here, Bertrand, aren't I right? You've read the Luigiani case, I suppose, haven't you?'

'No,' said Paul, going to the cupboard with his hat, umbrella and coat. It was a brown and overcast morning, with a brown light in the room. The gas was on, Inglewood, already in his disreputable gown, stood with hands in pockets, gown pushed back, and his burly legs apart. Sandys, long and slight, stood opposite him, in his grey flannel trousers and sports coat, with his gown over his arm. One flame leapt, flickered, and died, in the sluggish fire; and the large, bare room touched Paul with a chill embrace. Overhead, the horseplay of the boys shook the ceiling like thunder. 'Luigiani? Who's he?'

'He's a she. Don't you read your papers, man?'

'I've not looked at one for days.'

'Galumpus! He must be in love! Well, listen: Mrs Luigiani, as she now is, was yesterday sentenced to death for doing her antique husband in. An old Mr Brewer, and serve him right—'

'Oh, yes, I remember something about it a month or so ago.'

' '*Course* you do. Well, I've no doubt she did it, and I'm very pleased she did: the old bounder obviously married her for one thing only, bad old man! because he was wealthy and a swell, and she was only a little black-eyed Italian shop-girl, bless her sweet, pretty face and lustrous eyes. And there was a handsome young Italiano ruffian of her own age and class, waiting for her, with the promise of a cosy little pasta shop in Soho, and happiness and life and ice-cream and all that. So she did the really sporting thing, and helped old Brewer to be gathered to his fathers. That's the tale, isn't it, Sandys?'

'That's it,' Sandys agreed.

'Good. She did the deed, mind you, but that isn't the point: the point is, have they proved it? I say, No. Not within a thousand miles. Sandys says that it doesn't matter. I say it matters like hell.'

'Why?'

'God in his abounding mercy! Why am I inflicted with mental defectives for my colleagues? Don't you see, Bertrand, that if it is enough to show that the lady wanted to marry someone else, and that there was weed-killer in the house, and the old man most conveniently died of a colic, and like a good but commonplace husband he had left a will providing for his wife – if *that's* all you've got to prove, well, we're none of us safe any more. The shadow of the gallows is over us all.'

'But I suppose the doctors found poison in the body, didn't they? They called expert evidence, I imagine.'

'Doctors! Experts! Heaven save us from experts! One set of experts always says one thing, and the other set says the opposite; and both are probably wrong. Isn't everything that the doctors thought a century ago proved absolutely wrong now? And yet we hang someone on their beastly dogmatic assertions, every third week or so! Of course they dug the old bird up, and having done that, of course they found arsenic in his body. Have they ever done anything else? And why the devil they're always digging for trouble, I don't know. I should have thought there was quite enough on the surface without digging down for it. And they always find it! In this case they'd only got to find two grains of arsenic in the body to hang the poor little Luigiani, with her wicked, black eyes; and you bet your life they found it! And a pompous expert had only to go into the witness-box and say so, for a British jury to gape at him like a row of codfish on the fishmonger's stall, and consider the case proved. But is it? *Is* it? I believe it is true to say that you can get arsenic in your body from wallpaper and artificial flowers and textiles and beer and jam, and I daresay, for all the experts know, from a lot of other things – and certainly from patent medicines. And these colicky invalids are always patent-medicine cranks. And that's absolutely all that they've got against poor little Mrs Luigiani, but it was ample, *ample*, and she's for it.'

'But it sounds pretty black against her,' said Paul, now in his cap and gown, and standing listening.

Inglewood sighed, and sat on the table. 'Really, Bertrand, you're not very intelligent. I'm *saying* that it sounds black against her, but I'm also saying that that isn't enough. Listen: old Brewer died of gastro-enteritis, which is little more than a jolly name for dyspepsia; and it chances that the symptoms of arsenic poisoning are exactly the same as those of gastroenteritis. Have you got that? Very good. Now everybody's got a husband, haven't they? and everybody's got a house; and if their house is in London, they've got flies; and if they've got flies, they need fly-paper, and arsenic can quite easily be extracted from fly-paper; or if they've a house in the country, they've got a garden; and if they've got a garden, the garden has paths, and the only way to keep the paths clean is to get weed-killer which is fifty per cent arsenic – so roughly you may say that a vast majority of people have got arsenic in their house, sooner or later. Good. Then the husband dies of stomach trouble as is the case with thousands; and his will is shown to have provided for his wife, as is the case with all husbands, because all husbands are gents; the wife promptly marries again, being utterly miserable in an empty house – and immediately some damned mischief-maker says she probably did him in, so as to have his money and marry the new man. Scotland Yard hears of it and says, "Gastroenteritis! Hello, hello! Suspicious this!" and they out with their shovels and dig like fury. Their precious experts put on their spectacles and find two grains of arsenic in the body, which might have got there any old how – and that's the lot: my lady goes down the drop with the hell of a swing.'

Paul shook his head. 'I can't think it'd happen as easily as that.'

'No, that's your trouble: you can't think. But try. Just try to. It might happen to Sally Heasman here.' Inglewood always referred to his headmaster's wife as Sally: her name was Winifred. 'In fact, it probably will. I hope it does. She's got a husband – you can't deny that, can you? She's got Bill Heasman. And she must be sick to death of him – nobody can deny that, either. She'd be much happier with the hundred or so he'll leave her and without this fatuous school, and without Sandys. I mean, Bertrand: you must remember Sandys.'

Sandys sighed languidly and looked out of the window. 'You're desperately un-funny, sometimes, Inglewood,' said he.

'I'm not talking to you, Babe. I'm talking to Bertrand, my boy friend. Sally has also a garden: you may observe it through the window there. In the front part there are gravel paths and grass, I think; I seem to have seen a jobbing gardener at work upon them. Bill Heasman dies with a bellyache and is buried. Sally, feeling lonely, suddenly thinks better of Sandys and marries him, a fine, upstanding young man, after all; and very comfortable they are with the nice little sum old Heasman left in his will. Now it all turns on whether she marries him in three years or six months. If she waits three years, she's safe; if she does it in six months, they dig up Bill and find their two grains of arsenic, which she's quite innocent of having put there. Two grains. Excellent! Goodbye, Sally.'

'Sounds convincing enough,' laughed Paul.

'Absolutely. And the moral is, that it really doesn't matter whether she's done it or not: she gets away with it, or swings, just the same. So if she's really tired of Bill, she may as well do it, so long as she's got the sense to wait two or three years before marrying Sandys. What doctor's going to suspect that the dyspepsia before him is a case of wilful poisoning? He'd no more suspect it than he'd think of a million dollars being left to him: such a thing doesn't happen to one's self. So he signs the death certificate, "Gastro-enteritis" and goes home to supper. I wouldn't mind betting that fifty per cent of the coves who've died of gastric trouble were helped on by their wives—'

'Oh, drat it, Inglewood!' objected Sandys. 'What rubbish!'

'Well, thirty per cent. I'll be moderate. I'll be really conservative. Say thirty per cent. But that's another reason why I thank heaven I'm unmarried: it's too dangerous. Let it alone, Sandys dear. Don't marry Sally when Bill dies, which God grant may be soon. And confound it, there's the gong.'

Chapter Eleven

Paul was happy that winter. In some ways it was at once the most tormented and the happiest time of his life. His problem might rack him, but one horn of the dilemma was piercingly sweet; though fifty, he was knowing love for the first time. If he walked with a nagging problem, he walked with a silent ecstasy, too. He loved, and was loved; he was needed; he was a support for one who leaned against him. And the dark and windy January days went by with such a glamour upon them as no days of his life had carried, before. The Lent term began at Bishop Abercorn College and even this, the dullest term of the year, had the light upon it.

And then, the term being but three days old, at half-past nine one morning, the door-handle of Mr Presset's classroom turned, no knock having preceded it, and Mr Presset's heart jumped in alarm, as it always did, when he knew the headmaster was coming in. Not that he need feel a guiltiness this morning, because, as the handle turned, he was seated at his table, correcting the homework of a boy who stood at his side. Indeed, once the heart-leap was over, he felt pleased that Mr Heasman should see him so conscientiously engaged.

But Mr Heasman looked distressed and uneasy; he coughed apologetically, he hesitated for a second, keeping hold of the handle after he had shut the door, and, as he came towards the table, his eyes went to the window rather than to Paul.

Paul gently pushed the boy back that he might hear what his headmaster had to say.

'Oh, Mr Presset – no, please sit down – I – er – I only came to say, could you give me a word before you go home this evening?'

Paul's hand shot to the nape of his neck. 'Yes, certainly Mr Heasman. Certainly.'

'Yes – er – there's something I want to say to you. It's – well, I'll expect you at half-past four, then, over at the house?'

'Yes. Quite. Yes. Certainly, Mr Heasman. . . .'

'Right.' Mr Heasman seemed relieved to have got it over. 'Well, how are these boys going on? Are you satisfied with them?'

'Oh, quite. Very. . . . Yes, I think so.'

'Good.' But Mr Heasman did not seem really to have listened. 'Very well, then: I'll expect you at half-past four?'

'Yes.'

'Thank you. Thank you very much. Good morning.'

'Good morning.'

Now what did that mean? What was in the wind? Mr Heasman had seemed unhappy, as if he had some awkward tale to tell at half-past four. Had he, Paul, done something wrong? The question, like a presence in the room, like an inspector who sits watching a school teacher with his class but gives no inkling of his thoughts, sat in Paul's head all that day, without hope of answer; and if he was nervous when he could hurry across to the house next door where Mr and Mrs Heasman lived with their boarders, he was also a little thrilled, for the eyes of danger are bright to us all. He went through the open front door, and walked along the passage to the door of Mr Heasman's study. He went towards the music of a piano, gently played, and did not know that it was the *adagio* of a Bach Concerto. But he knew that it was the fingers of Mr Heasman creating it a little wistfully, for his compensation. When he knocked, the music stopped.

'Come in,' called Mr Heasman's voice; and Paul heard him cough.

He entered. It was a small room, and rather depressing with its college groups on the walls showing that Mr Heasman, grey and dispirited, had been an athlete once; with its marble busts of Beethoven and Mozart and Bach, to show where his real interests lay; and with its two shields at the sides of the over-mantel, one bearing the arms of Clare College and the other those of the University, to speak of larger and livelier days than these present ones, of which the worn leather chairs, and the threadbare carpet told so much. The old upright piano, with its yellowing keys and tattered music on top, stood in the heart of the room, like the citadel it was, for the garrison to retire to, and be safe.

'Oh, yes . . . Presset. . . . Yes.' Mr Heasman rose from the piano stool. 'Do sit down.'

Paul obeyed; but Mr Heasman only walked up and down slowly. More than ever Paul felt convinced that this was the discomfort of a man, not unkind, who did not like what he was about to do. He watched him with frightened eyes.

Mr Heasman cleared his throat. 'I must confess, Presset, that I don't at all like what I have to say. I – er – I'll take you frankly into my confidence. You must have noticed, haven't you, that things are not too good just now. I've had a very anxious time lately; very anxious indeed, I may say—'

What is coming, thought Paul, silent, terrified. Can I bear it—?

'It's exceedingly difficult to make ends meet. The coal alone for these two houses – and the rates – and bad debts – and the boarders, we find, hardly pay for their keep – I'm sure my wife slaves herself to the bone with them—' he halted in his walk and looked at Paul for sympathy.

'Yes,' agreed Paul, but his voice came huskily.

'And the long and the short of it is that I've got to go very carefully into my budget. I've got to trim my sails. It's a question of cutting somewhere, or giving up altogether. Now you must see that the biggest item of all is the stipends of the two non-resident masters. I pay you a hundred and fifty pounds, don't I? Well, it's obvious to me that I could get some young lad like

Sandys for about sixty resident, and that would work out much cheaper, you see, because the food and service is already there for the boarders and his keep would cost practically nothing – but I confess I don't like it – I don't like it at all – you've served the school well and loyally—'

Paul wanted to ask what precisely he was suggesting, but he did not dare to, for fear of the answer: he sat silent and staring.

And Mr Heasman threw forth his underlip; it was true that he was unhappy at what he was doing, first because he was a good natured man, and secondly because he doubted not that little Presset would be more useful to him, more safe, more fearful of losing his job than some bumptious and rackety youth. 'And – er—' he beat the fingers of one hand on the back of the other – 'I'm afraid I've only one course, Presset, and that is to give the usual notice, or ask you to accept a stipend of a hundred pounds. I very much hope it will be the latter,' he hastily added, 'even though it'll cost me more. What do you say?'

But Paul only looked up at him, white and shaken. He had been quite unprepared for this.

'Perhaps you'd like to think it over?'

'I don't think I could accept a hundred pounds,' said Paul, his pride struggling up. 'No, I don't think I could accept that. I think I must say that I must look out for another post—' but, as he said this, his heart sank; he would never get another post – he would be dependent on Elinor – he would be unable to help Myra – God!

'Well, if you feel that . . .' began Mr Heasman.

'Let me think it over,' Paul interrupted quickly, and his hand went to his neck. 'I should be very sorry to leave the boys. I've got fond of them. . . . I like the work. . .'

'I very much hope you'll decide to stay,' encouraged Mr Heasman. 'Very much.'

'I must think it over,' said Paul, musingly; and suddenly asked. 'What about Mr Inglewood?'

'I shall have to put the same proposition before him.'

'I see.' Paul was relieved. It was selfish, but he was relieved, because he had feared that Mr Heasman thought *his* hundred and fifty less well spent than Inglewood's. 'Well, there's nothing to do but think it over. I—' but suddenly he could say no more. He rose, nodding at his own thoughts like an old man; he must get away, for he had learned that, though he was fifty, the tears could still mass in his throat and spring very near to his eyes. He smiled rather stupidly at Mr Heasman and moved towards the door. Mumbling a goodbye and a thank you, he went from the room, his head a little in advance of his body, as if he walked through a haze.

In the passage he blew his nose, and pushed on. He hurried across to the Common Room, dodging Inglewood and even Myra; and, having snatched his hat, coat, and umbrella, escaped into the Square and the Caledonian Road. 'I won't accept it! I won't! It's humiliating.' But he would have to accept it. It was a choice between a hundred a year and nothing at all. He must have *some* money of his own, so as to be able to continue the little subsidy to Myra and to pay now and then for the chance of her company. Yes, he would have to accept. That was definite – final – and it was good to have found a decision.

And now he'd got to tell Elinor. He wasn't frightened of telling her – not he! Frightened of Elinor? Pooh – but he disliked the prospect of unpleasantness; that was all. And if she used her tongue on him, he'd be rude; he was in no mood to be bullied.

'Elinor dear,' called he, at the foot of the stairs. 'Could you come down for a minute?'

He knew from her 'What?' and her quick descent that she was alarmed at his tone. Together they went into the dining-room where she dropped on to a chair, a little breathless as one whose heart was not too sound, and he went and stood facing the window with his hands behind his back and his eyes on the front gardens of Elm Tree Road. In this attitude he told her all.

She gasped. 'What? It's disgraceful. I never heard anything so disgraceful in all my born days. It's an insolent offer. Of course you won't accept it. You won't dream of accepting it.'

'I've no course but to accept it.'

'Have you no pride? I never heard the like of it. You'd put up with an insult like that?'

'I don't know that it's an insult. He can't make money if he can't. But whether it is or not, I can no longer afford to be proud.'

'Don't talk such nonsense. Tell him tomorrow that you'll get another job.'

'But I can't get another job. That's the point. I know my market value, and you don't; so please don't lecture me. I've thought it all over, and I've decided to accept.'

'And what about *me*? What about me, pray? I find it hard enough to make ends meet, as it is. Fifty pounds a year'll make all the difference. I won't put up with it.'

He shrugged. 'Seems to me you'll have to put up with it.'

'You needn't adopt *that* tone, *please*. You've no cause to talk to me like that. If you'll give a moment's thought to me, you'll tell the man what you think of him, and set to and do something else.'

'And do what, pray?'

'I don't know. How should I know? What do men do?'

'It's very obvious you don't know. I can never get another job, and I can't change my profession at fifty. One just can't; one gets set. I can't turn to business; I never had an ounce of business sense. All my life I've cared for books, and things like that.'

'Then you shouldn't have married and taken on responsibilities. Can't you get pupils or something? Other men put their backs into things—'

'I can't *make* pupils. I've tried, haven't I?' He turned on her sharply. 'See here: I'll tell him tomorrow that I wouldn't touch his offer with a barge-pole, if you like to run the risk of having me penniless on your hands.'

The shot found its mark. Elinor stared at him, momentarily defeated. That unconquerable dislike of spending a penny of her income on anyone but herself rose up to bid her take care. Take care what she was saying. Better Paul with only a hundred than with nothing at all. She tossed her head; and then asked more quietly, 'Well, what do you suggest? Say you accept this disgraceful offer, how do you suggest we shall manage? I must have a house for my furniture. I must have some help in the house, my heart being what it is. I must pay my doctor's bills, and Dr Waterhall insists that I ought to live in reasonable comfort. And I ought to be able to, having money of my own—'

Paul swung round: he had fired up like a magnesium flash. 'Oh, yes, I know! Say it! Say it! Say how much better off you'd have been if you'd stayed single. Go on! I don't mind. I like to hear it!'

Always a little frightened of him when he took fire like this and glared at her with such wild eyes, she only turned her face away and gave herself to thought. If they must do with fifty pounds less a year, what had they best save on? The house? No, they couldn't get rid of it for a long time. Their food? Hardly; she had already cut the food bills as low as possible. Coal and gas? But how could she scrape a penny more from the coal and gas bills? Annie? Ah, here perhaps there was something. Yes, this way they might even save more than they lost. . . . 'The only thing I can suggest,' said she, 'is that we get rid of Annie. We might make do with regular visits from Mrs Briscoll. We should have to divide the extra work, of course. I can do the light work upstairs, dusting and sweeping and making the beds, but I can't possibly do any heavy work, standing at the kitchen range and dragging in coals and emptying dust bins. But Mrs Briscoll'd do most of it. And I might have a small gas-stove put upstairs, so that I could cook myself a meal, and give you something hot now and again, when you come home. Yes, we might part with Annie. . . .'

'And who's going to get my breakfast. I've got a long day's work in front of me, I'd have you remember.'

'Other men get their own quite cheerfully. That's all nonsense. You do plenty of violent work in the garden when you fancy it, and surely you can cook yourself an egg. Lots of people are managing with only a charwoman these days. If you feel you can turn to and help with the work downstairs, we might manage.'

Paul looked grumblingly at the window. But he knew that he was in no position to grumble. Always he had given Elinor two pounds a week towards the housekeeping, and kept a pound for his own expenses; and if by this new arrangement, he could still keep fifteen shillings or so for himself, and have money for Myra, he must agree to it. 'Well, if you think that's best,' said he.

So it was that, quite soon after the fragrance of Myra in the bedroom had set Annie wondering, the master, distressed at the thought of losing her, and distrustful of Elinor lest she bungled and hurt the child, came into the kitchen and said, 'Well, Annie, has the mistress spoken to you yet? I'm afraid we're going to have to lose you.'

Annie turned to him, wide-eyed, but quite undismayed, as servants are, when they receive their warning.

'We've had monetary losses, you see, and we can no longer afford a maid. Can't be helped. We've got to make do with Mrs Briscoll coming once in a while. I'm really sorry, though: we've got on well, haven't we? And you'll get a very nice place somewhere – perhaps a much better one than this – because the mistress and I'll say all we can for you. Nobody could have served us better, and I wish you could have stayed with us always.'

'But who's going to get your breakfast sir, and do the heavy work when Mrs Briscoll isn't here?'

'Oh, I dare say I shall give a lift with that. I shan't mind. And I tell you what: you must come and see us sometimes. I don't want to lose all touch with you. Will you come and tell us how you're getting along?'

'Of course I will, sir.'

'You've been happy here, I hope?'

'Oh, yes, sir. I'm sure you've been that kind to me, I shouldn't have been in a hurry to go myself at all, I shouldn't.'

'Well, now you must do better for yourself than we can, Annie.'

'Yes, sir.'

And the same day Elinor, feeling a little guilty and wondering what Annie would think when she heard that Mr Presset was going to do housework, got into talk with the girl and, driven on by the feeling of guilt, told her a very definite lie. 'Yes, it's a pity, Annie, but he's had some losses and we must rub along as best we can. The master says he can manage his own breakfast, and of course Mrs Briscoll'll be coming in pretty regularly. I don't quite like the idea of the master working in the kitchen, but he seems quite to fancy it. In fact it was all rather his suggestion; and we can but see how it works.' To which Annie listened with no more comment than 'Yes, mum' and 'no, mum', but took leave to wonder if this were really the truth.

And then her time came to bid them goodbye; and Elinor and Paul lived alone in a house that seemed very large and empty. Mrs Briscoll came two or three times a week for a 'general turn out and clean up'; otherwise they shared the work. Elinor easily persuaded herself that her share was as large as her husband's; and she certainly busied herself with many things on the first landing, even if she seldom came down to the kitchen. She made the beds, dusted the bedrooms, put gloves on to clean the brass taps in the bathroom, washed most of her own clothes and many of Paul's – as, to be sure, she had always done, the desire to save money overcoming the desire to save her hands – and at midday cooked a light meal for herself. Like many large and heavy women, she was a small eater: usually she boiled herself an egg or made some beef tea and toast. She liked to keep the afternoon free for visiting, but in the evening she returned to her gas stove and 'prepared a little something' for Paul. Her estimate of a meal for a thin but vigorous man in middle life was the same as that for a large and delicate woman, and the 'little something' was generally an egg and some cocoa, or a herring and some tea.

For his part, Paul took Annie's alarm clock up to his bedroom and set it for half-past six. It rasped off his sleep like a file; and he got up, put on dressing-gown and slippers, and went down into the dark morning to get in the coal from the backyard and the milk from the front step. He polished the brass of the front door (thinking of Myra), cleaned the boots and, taking some hot water, went up the stairs again to shave and dress. This done quickly, he came down again to the kitchen and boiled a couple of eggs or fried four rashers of bacon. He rather enjoyed it all: in part he was satisfying some real, original Paul, the son of Jane Presset; in part he drew from all cleaning processes a strange healing. Hating dust and rust and stains, just as he hated weeds in the garden, he drew a delight, a peace, from polishing the knives on the knifeboard, black-leading the kitchen range, and rubbing its steel bars or its fender with emery paper. Sometimes he would look forward all day to cleaning the stove in the evening. When the eggs and the tea were ready, he laid a tray and carried it up to Elinor, who said guiltily, 'Thank you, Paul. Perhaps Dr Waterhall will let me do more soon. But you do the breakfast, and I'll do the supper. That's fair, isn't it?' 'That's all right,' he answered cheerily, and went down again to the kitchen to take his breakfast alone. Breakfast over, he strolled with his pipe into the garden, to look at the buds breaking on the shrubs in the premature warmth, and to bend down and consider the tulips peeping above the beds or the crocuses spearing through the grass. Often he was tempted to fetch the trowel and do a little hoeing and scraping, for the air was scented with the promise of spring.

Chapter Twelve

It began in Egyptian Bazaars. Travelling faster than the fastest ship on the sea, and faster than a rumour over Arabia, it swept across to India and mastered the East. Six million died in India; and how many more in China, Japan, and the islands of the Pacific, no man has ever known. And those that died were but a small portion of those that it struck down. Majestic as it was terrible, the great pandemic, even while mowing down the crowded millions of the East, began its march to Europe and the West. It came like a conquering army, passing through frontier defences as if they were not there, boarding the west-bound ships and using them for its transport, and flying with the winds and the birds. With unerring skill, it found the weakest places, occupied them, and radiated its destruction from there. Whenever there were streets of narrow houses, crowded with ill-fed and ill-clad people, it marched in; and soon all the industrial wens of Europe went down before it. Setting out from India in January it was all over Europe before the month was over, and ranging along the waterfronts of Britain. In Britain it found no better soil than beneath a damp and smoke-laden pall over London. It went up the river and invaded the dwellings and tenements on either shore. It ran looking for the slums everywhere, and in due time found those squalid side-streets on the northern stretches that so depressed Mr Presset when he walked to his work along the Caldeonian Road. Capturing these freely, it advanced its attack on the better-class district farther on. And soon it was sounding the defences of Elm Tree Road.

For such a great pandemic Influenza seems too homely a word. And yet it was no more than this common and periodic disease that, attaining exceptional virulence, was scourging the world.

And one evening Paul came home to find Elinor in bed, her hair tossed into untidiness on the pillow, her face red and flushed, and the bed-clothes worried into disarray. He took the accustomed lash, even as she moaned, 'Oh, I feel so bad. It's got *me* now. I've been shivering so, I've been shivering so, I've been doubled up with it. And there was no one in the house.'

He comforted her. 'Oh, my dear, I'm so sorry. But there's nothing to worry about, if you take proper care. Keep warm and I'll fetch the doctor. This bad time only lasts a day or two.'

And he lit her a fire, got her a drink, and went out into the road again. The road was wet, and down its curving vista the gas lamps threw broken bars of light, like lamps at the margin of a motionless stream. Round the corner of Morton Avenue he saw the single red lamp above Dr Waterhall's gate, casting a red flush on the pavement below. The twin lights of a car stood immediately beside the flush, staring at Paul like two eyes. Otherwise the little avenue was empty as usual; and the gas lamps, bathing it at intervals, seemed as lonely as any in London. From a steeple in the background a single bell was calling to evensong.

The doctor was in. He himself pulled the door open almost before Paul had rung the bell; and there he was, standing in his hall and talking to his housekeeper, with his hat on his head at a happy angle. Apparently he was in the best of spirits. 'What? Elinor now? Well, that's nothing, old boy. Keep her warm. *She's* in no danger; it's the poor it's killing off like flies. I'll come round when I can, but God knows when that'll be. I've never had such a time, old chap; I'm being literally worked off my feet. I'm on the go from eight in the morning till twelve at night. Ask Mrs Westall here. Why, I've had to hire a car, and permanently – waiting for me at every hour of the day or the night! Only way I can get through the work. I'm just off now to about twenty patients, some of whom are at death's door.' Obviously he was as happy as ever in his life. And because happy, healthy; there was a brightness in his twinkling eyes, a briskness in his manner, a trimness in his receding grey beard, grey suit, white waistcoat slip, and stiff cuffs. Here was a busy and important man. Surely for a lonely old gentleman who is at once goodhearted and a busybody, there is no profession like a doctor's in an epidemic. 'Yes, shift along, old boy, I must be off now. Tell Elinor not to be anxious. It isn't affecting people of her age at all badly. It likes the young and the old, not the forties and the fifties. I might be afraid myself, only nothing ever touches me. Tell her she's feeling a damn-sight worse than she is. And *I'll* be round.'

He was round about eight. He spent five minutes with Elinor in the bedroom, and then came down to explain her condition to Paul in the dining-room. This he enjoyed immensely. He enjoyed it so much that he found it difficult to leave talking and step out to his car. Was he not the expert speaking with authority to the ignoramus? Walking up and down in his enthusiasm, he took out, cut, and lit a cigar. 'First cigar I've had today! As a rule I don't allow myself to smoke till I've finished my rounds. Don't like to take the smell of tobacco into sick rooms, but I simply couldn't keep *this* pace up without a whiff now and again. I suppose I've seen fifty patients today. I've had to snatch my meals when and how I could, but I don't seem to feel it. I'm still pretty tough, even if I'm getting on for seventy. And I've been an active man all my life. She's not got it badly. Funny business, this 'Flu. You see, it's a disease for which we really haven't discovered the micro-organism responsible, so we can't arrive at an efficient prophylaxis. No.' Paul saw that he loved using the learned and fine-sounding terms that were probably unintelligible to a layman. 'Actually there's an epidemic every thirty weeks or so, but it only materialises properly if its period of incidence is in the winter. But there's never been an epidemic quite so lively as this one. Usually the mortality rate is only about three per cent, but this time – whew! It isn't dangerous in itself, you see. It's the complications.'

'What complications?'

'Inflammation of the lungs. Pneumonia. Bronchitis. It's followed by a good deal of debility, you see, and the body hasn't its usual resistance. So we must take every care, that's all. Keep her room at an even temperature, and look to the draughts. She'll probably have a period of acute depression, but there'll be nothing in it. All perfectly normal. Just keep her free from worry and strain, because her heart is funny. How old is she?'

'Fifty-four.'

'*Is* she? Oh, well, that's only a chicken after all. Now, who's going to stay and look after her?'

'That's what I was wondering. This *would* come just when Annie hasn't been gone above a week.'

'Somebody ought to stay with her,' mused the doctor aloud. 'What about that perky little Captain's widow, Bessie Furle. She's an active and fussy little body.'

'Bessie. Yes, Bessie'd come when I'm not here, I'm sure. It'll be only for two days after all, because I shall be here on Saturday and Sunday.'

'Fine! Well, get Bessie; only tell her for the sake of the Lord in His Heaven not to talk too much. Tell her I said so. Tell her to shut up, 'tenny-rate till the fever's down. She won't be able to hold out longer than that, and it wouldn't be fair to ask her, ha, ha, ha! You know what these women are: they're all at sea if they're not talking.'

And Dr Waterhall, still talking, put on his hat at a prouder angle than usual, since he was a man with a permanent car and a chauffeur, and went down the steps to these luxuries.

For the present Paul had little time to think. He went to the cellar, got coal, made up the fire in Elinor's room, returned to the kitchen and prepared a dish of soup, and then went round to Bessie's with the news and his request.

Bessie, opening to him, scented alarm from his face, heard his story, and was delighted. She might say, with grave looks and a lowered voice, 'Oh, my dear Paul! Of course, of *course*, I'll come along;' but her tingling delight was revealed in her race upstairs, her breathless donning of her hat, and her quick, happy search for anything that might be of use. Drama had entered her quiet and empty life. She was invited at last to play a leading role, and a very attractive one too, that of a Lady Samaritan. 'Yes, I'll just come and have a look at her now, Paul. I'll just see that she's all right for the night, and then I'll be back first thing in the morning. And don't you worry about anything. Afraid? No, I'm not in the least afraid. Poor, poor Elinor.'

When, about an hour later, he had chivvied Bessie from the house, Paul went down to the kitchen to make himself a basin of beef tea and a slice of toast to dip into it. And sitting at the kitchen table with his basin and his bread, he gave play at last to his thoughts. Chewing the toast, he came face to face with a thought which hitherto he had pushed aside. It was so wrong, but he had best have a look at it, if only to knock it out of the way. When he had come home and heard she was ill, he had been conscious at first of nothing but a great hope. The hope had lit up his mind with a sudden glow. He had doused the flame at once, but when later the doctor spoke of her tricky heart, it had leapt up again. It was wicked – wicked to wish that she would die of it, but how could one help these thoughts? How could a prisoner help hoping for his release? Was he being over-conscientious, and did all people have such thoughts occasionally? Release! Oh, the great hope had a free riot now, as he drank from his spoon. Was he going to be set free? And be left enough money to live on till the end? Was it his destiny after all to be happy with Myra? If it were – oh, if it were, he'd try to take her such a love-story as passed her dreams. She had not had much happiness, and henceforward she should be one of those few who achieved perfect happiness with their mates. He had made every mistake in marriage, but he had learned his lessons and would treat a new wife very differently.

So sweet these pictures that he spent an hour with them, sitting humped over the table; and since all such luxuriating gradually enervates the will to withdraw from it, he allowed the thought to pass on to a still more terrible one. If he liked, he could make his hope sure. How simple it would be. Beware of draughts, the doctor had said. He was alone in the house, and he might open her window and door while she slept. He might let out the fire and lower the temperature of the room. Then the complications would set in, and immediately like a devoted husband, he would send for the trained nurses, but the complications would have their way, with a heart like hers. No one would question anything: she would be merely one of the thousands who had died in the epidemic. So simple. His prison walls were of cardboard, which he could break with a touch. And beyond the walls was an open country more gracious than any he had hoped to know.

But no, no. It was wicked even to play with such thoughts. He stood up abruptly, and the action was a symbol of his withdrawal from, and extinction of all such thoughts. He went straight upstairs and knocked at her door. 'Are you all right, Elinor?' No answer. Good; she was sleeping; and he stepped in on tip-toe and put the screen round the bed to guard her from draughts, and mended the fire.

Before her time in the morning Bessie arrived, like one whose impatience drives her early to her pleasures. He could go off to his college, she said, with nothing to worry him; let him leave all to her; whatever the doctor had said, she would do. And Paul hurried to the school and entered the Common

Room, not without pride in his heart, and a suitable gloom on his face, so that Inglewood said to Sandys, 'Glum, isn't he, Norman? Hush, hush! He's got to attend the inquest today.'

'No,' answered Paul gloomily. 'I've got my wife very ill.'

Immediately Inglewood shed the motley and put on the garment of a friend. 'Oh, I say, old boy, I'm so sorry.'

'Yes.' Paul shook his head. 'I've got *her* down with it now.'

And even Sandys murmured his sympathy.

Paul hurried away to find Mr Heasman; and Mr Heasman asked him if he'd like to return home, but he answered with some feeling of heroism, 'No, no. It's very kind of you, but I can manage quite all right. I have left her in good hands.' He met Myra in a corner of the passage, and told her; and she replied, 'Oh, I'm so sorry'; but her eyes looked with an exaggerated straightness into his, so as to give sincerity to her words. 'It's – it's not dangerous, is it?'

'Oh, no,' he said.

'Oh, I'm so glad!'

But he knew that, in spite of herself, the great hope had lifted in her. And he did not blame her for this: how could one control such thoughts?

'No, nothing dangerous,' he repeated; and for a moment thought of adding, 'There's always a danger of complications, of course'; but he didn't. Why?

'Oh, I'm *glad*,' repeated Myra.

'It only means that I shan't be able to meet you tonight, and may not be able to for a few days.'

'Ah, of course not! You must be with her.'

The morning and the afternoon held him at the school, and it was nearly five o'clock before he set off with a quick step for home. Passing the fruiterer's in the Caledonian Road, he saw some flowers, and he went in and bought a bunch of them. It would be pleasant to enter Elinor's bedroom with these in his hand. He ran up his steps and opened the door with his latch key; but he had not closed it before Bessie came running down the stairs.

'Oh, I'm so glad you've come back,' were her first words.

'Why?'

'She's not been at all well. Really at one time I didn't like things at all. I was worried.'

'What's happened?'

'She's had a lot of sickness and a lot of pain. She can keep nothing down. I don't know what it is.'

'Great lord! Have you told the doctor?'

'No, he came quite early this morning, and it hadn't developed then.'

'But she's better now, you say?'

'Yes, she's distinctly better. She's had a little weak tea.'

'Well, I'll look after her now; and if she gets any worse, I'll send for him, see? You get back home, Bessie, and thank you very, very much. You must be tired out.'

'I'll stay if I can be of any use. I'll stay all night if you like.'

'No, I insist on your getting some rest. Go back and get a comfortable night's sleep. I shall quite enjoy being nurse for a change. Come back in the morning, if you'll be so good.'

'Certainly I'll come back; and if you want me in the night, send for me.'

'Yes, yes,' said he, smilingly but a little impatiently. She did fuss so.

Bessie, a quick-eyed little woman, noticed the slight impatience and deliberated whether to be offended. But, deciding like a woman of sense, that they were all naturally 'a bit put about', she got her things together and went home.

The rest was a weary, lonely, and unhappy night. Elinor seemed to get worse as the night deepened. She tossed with fever, she complained of severe pains, and often she was sick. And Paul, his mind a battlefield between the excited and glowing hope and his distressed dislike of so cruel a thought, his eyes seeing a glimmer of unbelievable happiness on the horizon and his conscience driving the eyes from it, ministered to her as tenderly as any nurse; because, in doing so, he was ministering conviction to himself that his better side was master. And Elinor murmured her thanks again and again; and he felt ashamed. When he was not attending to her, he sat glumly in a chair by her window, or wandered aimlessly about the passages and up and down the stairs, more aware of loneliness than he had ever been, in that large, dark, empty house, with thoughts that no one, not even Myra, must ever learn. He saw loneliness as an intense, complete, and ultimate thing, shutting off a man and his thoughts from every other soul in the world, even the best beloved of all. Wandering into the chilly dining-room, he sat thinking about it, with his elbows on his knees.

When Bessie came at breakfast time, she found him white and haggard, and she listened with thrilled eyes, as he said, 'She's been worse, if anything, in the night. I've been up with her since about twelve.'

'Did you send for the doctor?'

'No, I thought I'd wait till the morning, especially as she seemed easier in the small hours. He's had such a rotten time, so he was telling me, that it seemed a shame to drag him out of bed.'

'Oh, I don't know,' argued Bessie, who didn't like to see good drama cancelled so easily. 'Doctors must expect that sort of thing.'

'Well, I'll nip round to him now. And I think I'd better tell the school I can't come, hadn't I?' Unknown to himself he had sunk back at that moment into a bewildered boy, asking counsel of a mother.

'Yes, I quite think so. Yes, certainly . . .' agreed Bessie, welcoming this small addition to the drama. 'Yes, run round to the doctor and the post office, and I'll go up to Elinor.'

So Paul hurried round to Morton Avenue and left his message with the doctor's housekeeper, and then to the post office in the

Caledonian Road. Here he was going to send a telegram to Mr Heasman. He might have telephoned, but he was unfamiliar with the instrument, and oddly afraid of it; besides, a telegram appealed to his dramatic sense. He wrote on the form, 'Wife rather worse hope return Monday'; and felt an interesting person as he handed it to the woman behind the counter. But she, after prodding at each word with her pencil, said only, 'Sixpence, please'; and put the pencil back behind her ear, without any larger emotion.

On his return he found Dr Waterhall with Bessie in the dining-room.

'Ah!' exclaimed the doctor. 'Come on. It's nothing, old boy – at least, I don't think so. All very ordinary. The whole system is upset, and the digestive apparatus gets infected with the rest. She probably had a dickens of a temperature in the night, and that's what frightened you, but it's down this morning. Gastritis; that's what it is; acute gastritis.'

Gastritis? Who was using that word only a little while ago? Or some word very like it? Oh yes: he saw the basement Common Room in the brown light of a winter morning, and Inglewood sitting on the table, hands in pockets and gown thrown back, as he talked to Sandys and himself. Curious, how soon a word which has been used in talk, crops up again! What was it Inglewood had been saying? If your wife died of gastrenteritis, you could quite easily be hanged. Good God!

'Is that the same as gastroenteritis?' he asked.

'What do *you* know about gastroenteritis?' laughed the doctor. 'Getting learned, aren't you? Yes, very much the same, only we generally suspect some definite irritant in the case of gastro-enteritis, like food poisoning of some sort or other. Now my only anxiety with Elinor is this: if the sickness is severe, it sometimes produces a certain amount of collapse see?' and, buttonholing Paul, he gave him a learned discourse on symptoms and treatment, decorating his talk with the most erudite terms he could find – and he could find a great many, because he had lately read up on his subject again, in view of the epidemic. And he went down the steps to his car with a chain of these scintillating phrases behind him, like the tail of a kite.

That evening, after Bessie had gone, Paul sat in Elinor's room by the side of her bed. It was six o'clock, and getting dark. The single bell from the neighbouring steeple had just finished its monotonous call to weekday evensong. The old-fashioned brass bed had a canopy over it, like a baldachin; and a single flame, dancing on the fire, set the shadow of the baldachin dancing on the ceiling. But the canopy itself, and its drapery, were completely motionless; and beneath its staid indifference, the bed-clothes lay tossed and tumbled with Elinor's sighing and impatient movements. She was exceedingly depressed, sometimes weeping to herself, and always, when she spoke to Paul, letting the tears well up in her eyes, as if, in her extreme weakness, she had lost all control of them. She had been silent for some time when, of a sudden, she said 'Paul.'

'Yes, dear?'

'I've been thinking a lot as I've lain here, and I want to say that, if I die—'

'Don't talk so stupidly,' he interrupted cheerily. '*You're* not going to die. Why, you're ever so much better already. Anybody can see that.'

'Well, you never can say. Some people have gone off quickly enough, and I'm not one of the strongest.' The very words were enough to draw up her tears. 'But what I wanted to ask you was this: it may seem stupid, but I've got a desire to be buried along with mother in Trusted churchyard. I think I've always fancied it, since I buried her there myself, one lovely spring day, before I knew you. It seemed such a peaceful spot, on its little hill, and with the lovely old church on one side and the tall trees on the other, and all the lovely country around. I remember I said at the time, "I want nowhere better to lay than this, myself." And I keep on seeing that grave as I've been laying here. Mother was awfully fond of me, you see. She was the only person, I sometimes think, who ever really loved me. I haven't managed to inspire much love in my life.'

'Now, now, don't work yourself up,' soothed Paul. '*That's* all right! We just shan't bury you in Trusted or anywhere else – not for twenty years yet.'

But though he spoke gaily, he was saddened by this glimpse of a hidden Elinor, disappointed and wistful and utterly solitary as he.

'No, but if anything happens, promise me you'll do this for me. The grave is deep enough. I don't think I ever told you, but when I chose the site and thought it the most beautiful I could find, I ordered them to make it big enough for another: you see, I hadn't met you then, and – well, I didn't feel about Brian, somehow, that I'd rather be in his grave than in Mother's – just as – curious, isn't it? – Mother evidently had no great desire to be buried with Dad. I sometimes wonder if we were like each other, and didn't make a great success as wives—'

'Now then!' rebuked Paul, with a bedside smile. 'Don't talk like that.'

'Oh, but I know. I haven't been all that you thought when you married me, any more than – however, I daresay it was partly my fault, though, when you're never very well, you can't help but be a bit trying, I daresay. But I've always felt that I should like to go back to mother. She so loved Trusted Church, after she went to live there, and she set her heart, as she put it, on sleeping under its shadow. She'd like me to come and join her, I fancy—' but here the words put a pause to speech.

'Now then, now then!' was all Paul could say, as soothingly as possible.

'But you *will* promise me that you'll – oh dear, oh dear, this pillow is hard, and the bed's like iron – thank you, Paul; I'm sorry to be such a nuisance – you *will* promise to do this for me, won't you?'

'Of course I'll promise to do anything and everything you ask; but don't worry! It'll be you that'll put me underground, not I you! Women always live longer than men, don't they now?'

'But I keep on *seeing* that grave. Does that mean anything, do you think?'

'It means that you're run down and depressed, as Dr Waterhall said you would be, just before you began to get better. It really means that you're beginning to get better. Think of that. It's all over now!'

'Do you really think so? But I feel so tired. I feel so tired. I think I'll try and sleep.'

'Yes, try and sleep.'

The fever rose again that night, so that she was very restless; and he sat with her a great while, ministering to her. And as he sat there, in the periods of silence, he thought much on her words. He seemed to be seeing farther into her, and into himself. Poor Elinor. She was a woman without the gift of loving; self-sufficient. As a child she had loved her mother; but as she grew up, she had developed selfishness, which destroyed the power to love. She hadn't really loved her first husband, or him. He too was selfish; but one part of his selfishness had taken the form of a craving to be loved, and this craving had forced him to go out and search and find, and love.

When he came to her in the morning, she lay very quiet. Had she not opened her eyes as he moved about, he would have thought her in a coma. Dr Waterhall arrived early; and after a few minutes with Elinor, came down to Paul in the dining-room. He was not jocular this morning; he looked grave. He fixed his eyes on Paul, as if wondering how he would take his words. None the less, in the quiet words he paraded, because he could not help it, a good section of his learning. Sometimes in a malignant type of the disease, he said, the poison spreads rapidly and powerfully, and there was always danger of heart-failure. Elinor's heartbeat was very rapid, and her exhaustion after any movement suggested some injury to the nerves or muscles of the heart. She must be kept very quiet indeed. By the evening he hoped to be able to say pretty definitely if she was weathering the storm: 'if not' – he shrugged his shoulders – 'you're in for trouble, old man; you're in, maybe, for a long illness, with what issue I wouldn't like to say. I'll look in more than once in the course of the day – though I've over fifty patients to see – and I think I ought to be able to give you definite news tonight.'

At his midday visit he looked graver still. The man in him, as distinct from the doctor, had a taste for alarm; and quite often the alarmist got the better of the doctor. It did so now. He found it difficult to resist a dramatic shaking of his head, as he spoke to Paul in the passage by the hall door. 'I don't altogether like the look of things, old chap. I don't. I shouldn't be fair to you, if I said less. She's weaker this morning; definitely weaker. But it may be just extreme debility. We can only wait and see. I can do nothing for the present, so I'll get on to my other patients – I've still about thirty or forty to see – and I'll be back again this evening. Cheerio, old man; keep your spirits up. It may all be perfectly natural. Where's that chauffeur-feller? Is he there? I'm not half giving him a run-round these days. Ah, yes; there we are.'

Weaker. Alone in the kitchen Paul sat clenching his fists and driving the nails into his hands, to fight the great hope that *would* rise. It rose attacking his throat with an emptiness like the anticipation of a great delight; an exquisite and tingling emptiness. He made tasks for himself that he might forget the thought – lose sight of it – slip away from it – but never was it far from him. It shook his hands as he worked. In a score of ways he ministered to the sick woman upstairs, but the hope walked with him round her bed. Restlessly he shut windows, adjusted the screen and poked the fire, but often as he did so, he forgot what he was doing, because he was thinking of something else. Awful, awful, but he seemed to be looking forward to the doctor's evening visit as one looks forward to a visitor who will bring one joy. He found himself looking at the clock, and counting the hours before he came. Ah no! it was too inexpressibly selfish and wicked, but what could one do? Some thoughts are autonomous; they think themselves; they live of their own will, and defy control. Four o'clock; five o'clock; six o'clock; and he might come any time now. Was it possible – was fate really going to be so good to him, as to give him all? – but stay! stop it! what was he saying? To defeat his own evil desire he found himself praying, 'O God, make her recover. O God, grant that she may get well. . . .'

A knock at the front door. He had come. Well, whether one desired or conquered desire, one would know soon now. The fact would just *be*, regardless of his emotions. He watched the doctor ascend to her room, and then returned to the kitchen and sat down on a hard chair by the table, trying, if it were possible, to empty himself of any thought whatsoever. He said one last prayer, 'O God, grant that he says she will get better'; and then, clenching the fists, looked at the dish-covers on the shelf over the range, and the plates on the dresser, and the view of the garden framed in the window, so as to keep his thought, if thought there must be, in innocent places. But let you once start wool-gathering, and, before you know it, a dominant hope will be sovereign and all-pervading in your mind. The pity, which he forced, fell away; the hope, which was natural and spontaneous, spread over and possessed the field. Was it possible that all he had ever wanted was going to be granted to him? Did a life of perfect sweetness, such as was given to few, stretch before him? Freedom to marry whom he would – money for his few needs – an end of daily drudgery in a classroom – some country place with Myra. He did not know it, but there was a smile on his face, as he sat there, gazing at so sweet a future, and welcoming it.

A door had shut. Dr Waterhall was coming down. Paul's heart raced, as he left the kitchen, to meet the doctor at the stairs' foot. Conscience was suspended; there was just a momentary pause in time, a narrow gulf between one life and another. The Fact was to be announced. He did not even speak; his eyes alone addressed their inquiry.

Dr Waterhall smiled. 'It's all right, old man. I'm glad to say I don't think there's anything to fear. She's going to get better.'

'I see,' said Paul. 'That's good.'

Chapter Thirteen

Then Myra moved.

It was not till March was over London, with pale blue skies and a misty sunlight, and the warm breath of spring was in the air, that he was able to meet her again and walk with her alone. But at length, in the last hour before sunset one day, he stood near the ancient thorn in Clissold Park, and looked towards the gate for her coming. The day was bright, if not warm; above him the sky stretched in a luminous emptiness that was nearer white than blue; and along the northern line, where the trees of the park closed his view, it shaded into grey; while southward over the tops of the houses and near where the diffident sun was going down, it brightened into a ribbon of transparent light. The parkland grass was the grey-green of March, and stretched away to bare trees still mauve with winter. From a shrubbery where gardeners were at work a smell of stable manure came blowing across to him; and it quickened his breath with happiness, because it seemed to bring the Shires into the midst of London. He felt suddenly exhilarated, expectant, and alive.

And here was Myra coming through the gate from Green Lanes, and recognising him with the breaking smile that peeped and went home again ashamed. But it seemed to go home more quickly than usual today, and a presentiment of coming pain touched him like a breath. He gave a shake of his head, to throw it from him. This evening at least he was going to be happy; and as Myra came up, he took the fingers of one of her hands and led her along the path towards the shrubberies and the bridge over the New River.

'And she's really getting much better?' asked Myra.

'Yes,' said he, looking straight ahead of him. 'The doctor says that there's no reason now why she shouldn't live another twenty years, if she's put to no undue strain.'

'Oh, I'm glad!' exclaimed Myra. 'I'm so glad.'

'Yes,' agreed Paul.

A faint warmth, heavy with the scent of greenery, rested on his cheek, like the warmth in a glass-house. 'My God!' he exclaimed excitedly; 'It'll be spring again in a few weeks'; and he squeezed her hand. 'And the daffodils will be all out along here; and all the trees and shrubs will put on that wonderful first green.'

'Yes,' said Myra, and let fall a sigh.

He heard the sigh, and again the foretaste of pain touched him, but he would not endure it. 'There's nothing quite like the first spring days,' he went on enthusiastically, 'when the thorn trees are all dusted with a young green, and the early leaves of the chestnuts hang down like puppies' ears – have you ever noticed *that*? – and the lime trees are all gay with pink buds, and the blackbird – "the blackbird has but a boxwood flute, but I love him the best of all". And the mowers are out on the grass for the first time. . . .'

Myra did not answer.

'Sad?' he asked, turning and looking at her.

'Yes . . . very,' she admitted.

'Why?'

'I've done a lot of thinking in the last week or two. I've *had* to.'

Again his heart was falling, in dread of what he might hear; but he affected liveliness. 'Well, why has it made you sad?'

She looked to one side of her, staring over the grass, without an attempt to answer for a long time. Then, brightening and even giving a little skip, she said, 'Wait till we're sitting down somewhere, and then I'll tell you all.'

'As you will,' he conceded, somewhat grandly.

They crossed the bridge over the stream, and took the

deserted paths behind the old house. And passing down the avenue of shrubs and high trees, with the spire of old Stoke Newington church behind the tracery of leaves, they saw the secluded seat where they had always been accustomed to sit. It was the sight of this that forced Myra to speak.

'We've got to end it, Paul.'

'End what?' he exclaimed in alarm. 'What do you mean?'

'We must part. I know it now. I've known it for a long time, of course, but I've only just *let* myself know it. I simply can't stand it. I'm not nearly big enough for this sort of thing, and that's the plain truth of it. I have such awful thoughts, sometimes. Paul dear: I wanted her to die! I hoped she would – isn't it *too* awful? I tried my hardest to fight down the hope, but I just couldn't. And I – yes, I was disappointed when I heard she was getting better. Oh, it's all too wicked. I shiver whenever I think of it. It comes, I suppose, from playing with sin.' She shook her head sadly. 'There's no getting away from it, Paul dear: your duty is with her, and mine is to go away and leave you alone. I've gone over and over and over it, again and again and again – I've told myself a thousand times all that you said about it's not being wrong so long as no one is hurt – but I can't believe it. I can only see perfectly clearly what I've got to do. It's my upbringing, I suppose: I can't shake it off. . . .'

He had been listening with blank face, dropped jaw, and anguished eyes that never moved from the vista before him. When she paused, he said nothing; and they passed the familiar seat, since it seemed pointless to sit there any more. So protracted was his silence that she looked up to his eyes for an answer.

'It isn't possible,' he said.

'Why?'

'I can no longer live without you. I'll die, I think. You're absolutely the only happiness I've got in life.'

'No, it only seems like that,' she said, to comfort him. 'But it's not really so bad. You'll get used to doing without me. We all do. After all, there's death; everyone has to accept the death of those they love, and go on living. And they do.'

'But I shall be seeing you every day at the school. It'll be unbearable.'

'That won't be for long. The term is nearly over, and I am going at the end of the term.'

'*What?*'

'Yes. I have already told Mr Heasman. And he can get plenty more like me, and I know that *I* can get some other job.'

He dropped a sigh heavier than hers had been. Then, because he *must* put off the final hour, and *must* hope, he asked, 'But I shall be able to see you now and again, before the terms ends. It isn't goodbye today, is it?'

'Yes. . . .' she said, looking away. 'Yes, please. I'd rather get it over quickly.'

'Very well.' There is a despair that will not argue. 'And you are going out of my life for ever?'

'Yes. . . . Yes, my dear. . . . There's no hope of anything else.'

'I think I shall kill myself,' said he, suddenly.

'No, you won't. You're not selfish like that. You wouldn't do that, I know, if only for my sake. And there's your mother too – you're fond of her.'

'But I can't bear it, Myra!'

'But you *will* be able to. If I can, you can. I prayed for hours about it last night. I haven't prayed for ages partly because I seemed to have lost all my old faith, and partly because I couldn't, going with you as I did – and *living* with you – but last night I was able to, because I only wanted to find out what was right. And suddenly I seemed to see it all clearly, and get strength. She is ill, my dear; and your duty is with her. You must take it up and bear it. We're meant to have burdens. I saw it clearly last night: we're meant to have very difficult tasks so that we may develop strength and courage – and some sort of grandeur.' She felt for his hand, and pressed it firmly between both of hers. 'Try to love her and bear with her, and be good to her.'

'I always try to be good to her as far as I can, but I can't love her. You can't force love. I – I hate her; and she hates me. I see it in flashes of her eyes; and we bear it because it's easier than to break with it. You're asking me to do something impossible. I could endure, and be kind, as long as I had a little joy with you. I only want a little joy, and I don't believe that's wrong. I *can't* believe it. God meant us to have some joy, as well as the burdens, else why – why did he send the spring into the world? He meant us to have both. . . . Myra, don't go from me.'

'I must. You may see it one way; but I can only see it the other. And I know what was the truth for me last night.'

'It's not the truth at all. It's just that you've always wanted to run away from life, and now you've found an excuse for doing it. You've always been afraid of the big things, and now, without knowing it, it's almost a relief to you to be able to call your fear "duty" and "religion". That's all it is.'

'Well, if that's *me*, that's *me*,' she smiled. 'I can't be other than I am. And it's the only truth for me. I *know* it.'

'Ah, well. . . .' His despair enabled him to take Myra's decision as a fanatic draws a knife into himself. 'Let it be then. Let it be. . . .'

'It'll get easier to bear every day, my dear.'

'Perhaps . . . perhaps. Will you wait for me in case – if anything happened?'

Myra thought; and they had reached the end of a path, and turned back upon their tracks, before she replied, 'No, I'm not going to say that. I think I must go right out of your life. I don't want you to be hoping that' – and she paused, rather than utter the hope. 'And I don't want to hope it either. In that way I should still be holding you.'

'And would you marry someone else?'

'Ach, don't let's talk about that. I shan't be ready for that for years, and I don't know who'll want me then,' said she with something of the old laughter. 'But I suppose if anyone were fool enough to ask me, and I cared for him enough, I might say, Yes, and try to do my best by him.'

'All right . . . and I wish I could say, "I hope he'll come along for your sake"; but I can't; I don't want it. I'm too selfish for that. I want you to care for nobody but me for ever and ever.'

'I shall care for nobody in the same way, if that's a comfort to you. Of that I'm sure.' And again she pressed his hand as if to press the certainty into him. 'Paul, I seemed to see such a lot last night. We've had our happy times, and must be grateful for them. Perhaps nothing is meant to last. Happiness justifies itself by existing for its moment, and that's all – like the roses, as you've always said.'

'But Myra, let me get used to it. Let me see you off and on, just till the end of the term?'

'No, please, *please*. I shall go to pieces if we do that. Don't you understand: I *must* get it over quickly.'

'Very well.'

'Paul, you *do* understand?'

'Oh, yes, yes. . . . I understand. . . . All I ask is that you'll still let me help you. Give me that consolation—'

'No, no; I can't take anything from you any more. No; that'd be impossible. You must see it.'

'But how are you going to live?'

'I shall manage. At my age one can always get some sort of work.'

'Very well,' sighed he, pushing the knife further home. 'Let it be. Let it be.' And in this mood of self-torture he stopped in the path. 'Myra, let's do it now. What's gained by waiting? I can't bear this, and I feel I'd rather be alone. I want to begin getting used to it. You'll give me a kiss?'

'Yes.'

They walked to where a curve in the path led to shelter behind the trees. And here he took her into his arms and held her in a last tight embrace. And despite all that she had said, her love, and the old passionate hunger that would never be satisfied any more, flared up beneath his kiss, so that she too drew him as if she would draw him into herself, and murmured, 'My love! My darling!'

Inflamed by her grasp and her words, hope sprang up in him again. Looking into her eyes, he begged, 'Myra, stay with me.'

'No.'

'Yes, my dearest. Let's shake off everything. Let's run. Let's *go*! I'll find work somewhere. I'd rather tramp from workhouse to workhouse with you than go on living without you.'

'No, dear . . . please . . . we shouldn't be happy, because I at least should be feeling guilty all the time. No, give me one more kiss.'

One more kiss, he holding her tight in unreleasing arms. It was she who, putting her palms against his breast and shaking her head, gradually pushed herself from him. She held both his hands, pressing them for a long minute; then abruptly dropped them, and turned and went. He followed her slowly as far as the bend of the path, but she went on without turning her face. She ran round the little headland of trees; and Paul stood alone.

Chapter Fourteen

Myra had been Paul's happiness, self-respect, youth and charm. We are at ease and happy, our minds are healthy and our souls as good as may be, when we walk with those who like and believe in us. They are our healing and our grace; giving us back our vigour and vitality; our trust in ourselves, and our portion of goodness. But with those who despise us we are disabled once more, diffident and clumsy and inert; and grace and goodness fall away. Myra, in her womanly fashion, had often called him 'sweet', and had not been wholly amiss. He was sweet with her, but at home, feeling himself despised, he was sour. Especially now that she was gone. Wounded like the rest of us, he had found a healing in her. Remove the healing, and the sickness starts afresh: the buried conflicts, unable to converge any more on the point of harmony, are active again, draining all energy away. Hidden from sight, they short-circuit the battery, and the light goes out.

Paul dragged himself to the school, drove himself through the lessons, and wandered aimlessly home. At home he, whom Myra had called 'sweet', could be rash and violent with Elinor, blazing up into rudeness at a breath of criticism. 'I don't choose to be catechised,' he would say. 'I'll spend my time where and how I like'; and he would go out and slam the door.

Slamming the door on mornings of the Easter holidays when he had nothing to do, his bowler hat set thunderously on his head and his umbrella hung on his arm like a weapon of offence, he would fare forth on a stroll – but where to he didn't know. He strolled towards all that was left of his healing, and that is to say that he strolled towards self-torture. Sometimes he would walk along the street where she had lived and glance up to her window. Gone. Those were not her curtains. She had gone quickly as she said she would. Or he found his feet taking him along the familiar track from Canonbury Fields to Kelross Road, with its neat little red houses, its pollarded plane trees and its quiet; and through the quaintly named Paradise Road and Green Lanes, into Clissold Park. That it was spring in the park fitted well with his melancholy. The wide stretch of grass under the giant chestnuts was green as the grass at a freshet's verge; and everywhere it was speckled with daisies. A dust of green lay on the antique thorn, and the chestnuts hard by were breaking into full leaf. The domes of the oaks were powdered with brown buds, while the ash trees beside them were still bare and cindery as in winter. From the lime trees came a chatter of sparrows; and a burble of pigeons from behind the shrubberies. He crossed the bridge and walked around the curve of the New River; and here, along that ribbon of natural country between the railings and the water, under its procession of trees, he saw the daffodils and forget-me-nots; and cuckoo-pint, celandines and daisies. It was a long strip of pure meadow; and if he walked with his eyes on it, and away from the ordered parkland on his right, he walked in the Shires. In a month from now it would be yellow with buttercups and white with cow-parsley; and the pink and white chestnut blossom would float on the stagnant water as it lay dark and green beneath the trees.

One morning he left the banks of the stream and sat glumly under a tree to think. For days past a thousand and one things he would like to say to Myra had been pullulating in his brain – pretty and sentimental things, and passionate and heroic things – and now they danced in his head like hothouse flowers. He wanted to sit humpily, and pick and finger them.

All emotion, and especially when its power is heightened by constriction, creates words and phrases easily; and as these sprang into his mind, the undeveloped artist in him savoured what he imagined to be their high literary quality. As a matter of fact, though some of them were apt and moving, most were the stock phrases of the lover, and others were pompous and stilted; but he thought them equally beautiful, and craved the one audience for them. Full-charged at last, he knew that he would at least have to write them down if he was to be rid of them and know peace. He would write them in the form of a letter to Myra; whether the letter would ever be sent, since he had no address, was another matter. Even to write to her in imagination would be relief; and if by chance he were able to send the letter, the peace, though fugitive, would take the name of happiness.

He jumped up, resolved to begin the letter as soon as possible, and to know relief. He hurried homeward along the pavements, with the phrases springing up all the time; till at last, his head a buzzing hive of them, he had to stop, snatch from his pocket an old envelope and a pencil, and jot down memoranda. He went back along Kelross Road and through Canonbury Fields, halting every twenty or thirty paces to pencil a few more words. He halted and wrote many times in the Caledonian Road, with the pedestrians swirling by him, and the traffic roaring past.

At home he went straight to the drawing-room where there was a little feminine writing table of black-painted wood. He felt secure in the drawing-room which was seldom visited. There was no fire there this morning, but he didn't mind: he was too occupied with his thoughts to notice the temperature of a room; and anyhow, some of the spring warmth was coming in from the garden. He shut the door. It was nearly dinner time, but he must start, he must start! Let him sip at least the first sweets of relief.

'My dearest Myra,' he began, and what joy it was to write her name! 'Forgive me if I do wrong in writing to you, but I feel I cannot endure the agony and the heartache another day without some such alleviation as this. Women, I fancy, are more heroic than men; and I, at any rate, am no hero; so you must allow me this little modicum of heartsease. I do not want to be selfish and to buy my relief at the cost of your pain, but, in the bottom of my heart I do not think that this will be so; I believe that it will be some balm to your grief to know that I am thinking of you every moment of the day. It is almost like happiness again to be sitting down and writing to you. When to a middle-aged and loveless man there comes anyone as dear and sweet as you and gives him all that the most sanguine could desire and far more than most men achieve, the loneliness that follows her departure is terrible indeed: it is the darker for the unwonted brightness that went before.' His pen raced on, the sentences burgeoning as luxuriant and unrestrained as the spring blossoms; and the richer they were, the greater was his relief. 'I had little happiness in my life till you came; but then all was sunshine. I never knew such bliss was possible as I have known in your arms. Be sure of this: it is worth having lived to have given a solitary man such happiness. I think often of the words of that beautiful song, the Rosary: "The hours I spent with you, dear heart, are as a string of pearls to me", and at other times I say over and over again, "It is better to have loved and lost than never to have loved at all". I live only with memories now – memories of that evening in the woods at Petfield, and of happy, happy times in dull little rooms that we know, and of one blissful weekend when we kept house together and I could think of you as my wife. And then on a March day, like a bolt from the blue, came your decision to leave me, and all the sunshine went out of my life. Myra, my beloved, I shall get used to it, I know; one day I shall even be able to pray that you may learn to love another man better than you loved me, and so find the peace you deserve. . . .'

So the phrases came: each new idea giving birth to others, till they were such a multitude on his nib that only a few could hope to force their way on to his paper, and the rest must go back into oblivion again.

And while he was writing them, Elinor called him into dinner. 'Yes, yes,' he answered impatiently; 'I shan't be a moment'; and hastily he added a few more sentences, and scribbled a few notes on a spare sheet of paper, and then hid everything under the litter of a drawer. 'Just coming!' he called, to strengthen Elinor in her endurance.

And he went into the dining-room and sat at the table by her side and pretended to eat the cold meat and potatoes which she had spread. But as he chewed, his mind was shaping more sentences, so that he knew nothing of what he ate, and was hardly conscious of Elinor at the table's head.

'What have you been doing?' she asked suddenly.

'Pardon?' he inquired, coming out of his abstraction.

'What have you been doing so mysteriously in the drawing-room?'

He parried the question with sarcasm. 'I wasn't aware that I had been doing anything mysteriously in the drawing-room.'

'Yes, you go in there and shut yourself in, and I don't hear a sound from you.'

'I have been writing a letter, if you want to know.'

'Who to?'

'To His Majesty the King.'

Elinor muttered her impatience, so he explained further, 'Perhaps I don't choose to tell all my letters.'

'How absurd! Why try to make a mystery of it?'

'Mystery? What is there mysterious about it? Has it ever occurred to you that some of my friends may have entrusted me with their confidence?'

'That Inglewood, I suppose?'

'That Inglewood perhaps. And yet again, perhaps not.'

'Really you're too stupid sometimes,' said Elinor. 'I've no patience with you.'

And they spoke no more till the end of the meal, when Elinor, assembling the plates and dishes, said, 'If you'll take these to the kitchen, I'll go and lie down. I'm a little tired.'

'Righto!' he replied cheerfully, glad to make amends for his rudeness, and exceedingly glad that she was retiring to sleep and would leave him to his engrossing creation. 'I'll wash 'em up. Righto! Leave it to me.'

He piled the plates in the kitchen, returned and paused at the staircase foot till he heard the creaking of Elinor's bed, and then went into the drawing-room and shut the door on himself. He went quickly to the desk and resumed the writing. He wrote on and on, piling page upon page, and all the house was silent, if he lifted his ear to listen – completely silent, except for the complaining shudder of a window, somewhere on the top floor. An hour passed over the heads of Elinor resting and Paul writing; the clock in the dining-room rang three and half-past three, both tinklings unnoticed by Elinor above and Paul across the passage; the drawing-room chilled as the April day clouded over and its early brightness gave place to a premature dusk; the window upstairs began to complain more regularly; and then a knock rattled on the front door.

'His Majesty King Chance,' said Frederick the Great, 'does three-quarters of the business of this miserable universe.' It was not the single knock of a tradesman, nor the double knock of a postman, but a quadruple ratta-tat-tat, at once firm in its demand for admittance and ingratiating in its apology. It must have awakened Elinor if she slept, and it certainly lifted Paul's head from his work. He muttered annoyance and waited; and the knock came again, courteous, masterful, and refusing to be denied. Paul put down his pen, and went to the door.

On the top of the steps stood a most perfectly dressed man, tall, neat-waisted, smiling and thirty, with a large black bag in his hand. His was no face that Paul knew, but his happy smile as if his final ambition had been attained in this vision of the householder, and the slight *salaam* which he accorded him, suggested some exquisite shop-walker in one of the more expensive stores. His manner was neither grandeur nor obsequiousness, but a most elegant bastard, born from both.

'You are' – and he glanced at a paper – 'Mr Presset, are you not, sir?'

'That's right,' agreed Paul, mystified.

The gentleman removed his gloves, folded them together, smoothed them between two fingers, and, bending them over, put them on the balustrade of the steps.

'I have reason to believe that you are a master in a well-known school here, are you not, sir?'

'That's right,' said Paul.

'Yes. . . .' The stranger was gratified; and now his voice was lubricated with goodwill. 'Well, I have something here that I feel sure will interest you. I mean, it's being taken up by all the most progressive in the scholastic profession. I mean, I could show you a list of those who have ordered it, but I won't take up your time with that, you being a busy man, I'm *very* certain. And parents too, who have their children's interests at heart. They're one and all—'

'I'm afraid I haven't time just now,' began Paul.

'Just one minute sir. *Just* one minute.' A teacher instructing a child to swim could not have been more encouraging. 'Give me sixty seconds of your time, Mr Presset, and I'll undertake to have you interested. Many people have thanked me for being a little – er – importunate, shall I say? That is my card. I represent the Modern Era Book Publishing Company. Yes. Now, sir, let me show you—'

'I'm sorry, but you really must excuse me—'

'Just *half* a minute, sir. Just half a minute, Mr Presset. I assure you I won't detain you a second longer if you prove to be uninterested. I mean, I don't believe in doing that; but I think I can promise to interest you, if you have the welfare of your pupils at heart, as I am very sure you have.' All these words were covering a pause while he opened the black bag and produced a large and handsome volume. 'There, sir. You are married and have children of your own, perhaps, have you, sir?'

'No. I have no children.'

'No. Well. Well, there's a lot to be said for having no children.' He said it as if he would have Mr Presset look always on the bright side. 'I have two boys myself – fine little chaps – and I speak from experience when I say that I've never known anything like this method for teaching the young mind. I mean, there never *has* been anything like it, I mean. So you see I'm one of those who believes enough in my own wares to use them myself. Believe in them? I should just think I did! I regard this as an absolute revolution in the methods of teaching, and I'm not alone in thinking this, neither, I may tell you! I hold that in twenty-five years nobody'll teach in any other way, not those with any vision, if I may so put it. Twenty-five? Five, sir, five! Five years'll see this system conquer the world; and if you arst me, sir, you'll get in on the ground floor. I'm saying it because I want you to have the chahn'st—'

'You really must excuse me,' repeated Paul, edging back into the house. 'I know I shan't order anything, so it isn't fair to take up your time.'

'Just one-tenth of a minute, sir. Not a second more if it doesn't interest you. I never was one to stay and pester people. It doesn't do any good – never. This is the book I want you to take just one glance at. Just one. Now look here—'

'But I am very busy just now—'

'Glance at it, sir, glance at it. You see it's a method of teaching Litera-cher, Hist'ry, Jography, Composition – in fact, almost the whole range of learning apart from Mathematics and Foreign Languages – in one systematised and wholly enjoyable way. The nippers – the kiddies, I should say – lap it up like cream. Simply lap it up, sir. So far from driving them to their studies, you can't keep 'em away from it, I promise you. I know, because I've two chaps of my own – fine little chaps – and they've learnt more from this – look, sir, look!'

Rather than hurt his feelings, for his eyes were so enthusiastic and his smile so triumphant, Paul went forward on to the step, took the book, and glanced through the pages, his visitor meanwhile standing at his side and expounding everything with a restless forefinger, a spate of words, and a faint smell of cheese and beer. The pages revealed a well-organised system of teaching everything by means of Literature. The 'World's Greatest Stories' were arranged in a chronological sequence, from 'Ben Hur' through 'Harold' and 'Ivanhoe' and 'Peveril' to 'Barnaby Rudge' and 'Jane Eyre', and for each tale was provided a history with gorgeous illustrations called 'The Time', and a geography with maps called 'The Place', and so on.

'Fascinating, isn't it?' demanded the enthusiast, over Paul's shoulder. 'Did y'ever see anything like it? Irresistible. The kiddies can hardly get hold of it, because the grown-ups are monopolising it all the time. You see, the hist'ries connect up, and by the time the kiddies have read the last tale, there's nothing they don't know. Absolutely nothing at all; not about Hist'ry, that is. And Command of Language! Think of that. You see the Composition Lessons, don't you? Personally I've found them the most fascinating of all. And if I've got any command of my own language – and it sounds as if I had, ha, ha, ha! It sounds as if I had, don't it? – it's entirely owing to these books that I speak like I do. It's an amazing system. Literally amazing. It's one of those inspirations of genius that are as simple as they are profound. And seven volumes covers it all. Seven volumes at three pound, thirteen and six the set. The whole of knowledge for three, thirteen, six: I mean, that isn't dear. Actually, it can hardly be done at the figure: it's only because we believe that we've got something of great public utility that we are quoting it at that price and pushing it so exten – if "pushing" is quite the word – I don't know; I only know that I myself wouldn't handle the work if I didn't feel that I was bringing a real good into the houses of the people. I've sometimes been offered a line that I didn't like handling at all – I'm not going to tell a lie about it. I *have*. We all have to compromise with our consciences once in a while if we're to live, is it not so, Mr Presset? But I've never done it with any real enthusiasm; not like this. This is a line which it is an absolute privilege to be associated with, and I'm saying God's truth when I say that my conscience is in this. I've seen what it can do with my own nippers—'

'Now wait a minute,' said Paul. Two qualities in him were delaying him on the door step: his courtesy, which would not allow him to send a stranger rudely away, and his vanity, which did not like the stranger to think that he could teach *him* how to teach or that he had a gullible fool to deal with. 'Now, come, come; you can't get away with all that, you know! You and I are sane men, and know perfectly well that your firm isn't pushing these books from altruistic motives—'

'From what, sir?' The stranger's command of language had not advanced to this word.

'They're not doing it as public philanthropists, but for profit. And I've nothing against that, particularly; they're perfectly entitled to get a profit on a good thing. But they're doing it for a profit, and you're doing it for a commission, eh?'

'Oh, quite sir. Oh, absolutely. You're perfectly right. We all have to live, and I'm not going to lie about *that*. But there's such a thing as cutting profits to the bone. You'll allow there's such a thing as cutting profits to the bone, sir?' He appealed as one reasonable soul to another.

'But only with a view to making more money in the end, Mr – I didn't catch your name.' He smile disarmingly. 'You haven't a fool to deal with, you know.'

'Oh *no*, sir. I can see *that*, sir. I never thought *that*, sir. On the contrary, I knew directly I saw you, that I could only get you by putting over the *true* stuff. And if I may say so, sir, it was because I knew I was up against an intelligent man that I felt so sure that you, at least, would give me an order.'

Paul shook his head. 'You've really come to the wrong house, old man. I'm a master myself, as you know; I am – er – the Head of the English Department at my school – and that means firstly, that I could get a copy of such a book at trade prices, and secondly, that I've long ago formed my own methods and am vain enough to think them the best possible. All masters are vain, you know!' He handed back the book. 'My dear chap, all that you are showing me here I have been doing in my own way for the last twenty years.'

'But then consider, sir, what handmaidens to your work these books would be – I mean—'

'No,' said Paul firmly. 'I'm sorry, but I must really go now. I was in the midst of most important work when you came—'

'You wouldn't like them on appro. to show your Headmaster?'

'*I* am the head of the English Department. No, there's nothing in it, old chap; you're wasting your time. I wish you all the luck in the world, but they're not for me. I'm sure they'd be excellent for some people.'

'Very good, sir.' The stranger was as smooth and unabashed in retreat as in attack. He packed the books carefully, closed the bag, picked up his gloves, and turned with a goodbye and a smile down the steps. Paul hadn't the heart to close the door till he had passed through the gate.

King Chance. If a casual peddler, crossing from door to door, had not come up the steps of that house in Elm Tree Road, there would have been a different story to tell of the householder who opened the door to him and then delayed on the steps because he was both courteous and vain. Elinor, lying upstairs had been unable to sleep for some time. She could only lie and think. And soon she was wondering what had been in the letter that Paul had been writing. No suspicion of an amorous intrigue crossed her mind; whatever else Paul was, he was not that sort. Could it be a business letter? Was he secretly gambling in stocks and shares? Or was he, perhaps, sending money to his parents, unknown to her? Or had he, perhaps, lent money to that Inglewood, who had got into difficulties? It would be just like him to throw money away on a bounder like that. What *could* it be? . . . So thinking and questioning she fell into sleep.

A knock at the door awoke her; a confident and rattity knock such as gentlefolk give. She raised her head from the pillow and listened. The knock came a second time, and she heard the drawing-room door open, and Paul hurry along the passage. The front door opened, and she strained her ears. A man's voice, fluent and smoothly argumentative . . a movement of boots on the steps . . . Paul's voice . . . the man again. Who could it be?

Curiosity impelled her from her bed. She went to her window but she could not get a view of the visitor from there. She pushed her feet into slippers, and went softly down the stairs, as far as the half-way landing. Here she listened again, and in a pause in the doorstep talk called, 'Who is it, Paul?'

He did not answer.

'Who is it, Paul?'

He couldn't hear her, because the hall door had nearly closed behind him. Curiosity sent her further down, that she might see and hear better; and at the foot of the stairs she saw through the drawing-room door her little black writing table with a pile of manuscript upon it. Ah, that letter! And the length of it! Whom could he be writing to at such length? Not a woman in a thousand could have resisted the call to curiosity; and Elinor needed no more weakness than most to foot it softly to her great opportunity. Just the name and the first few lines: that was all she wanted to know. She glanced towards the leaded glass of the front door and saw the shadows of Paul and a taller man in earnest colloquy; and the next second she was stepping across the drawing-room carpet to the desk. She looked down on the pile of paper.

'My dearest Myra'! . . . 'When to a loveless man there comes anyone as dear and sweet as you and gives him all that the most sanguine can desire. . . . I never knew such bliss was possible as I have known in your arms . . . one blissful weekend when we kept house together and I could think of you as my wife. . . . Myra, my beloved. . . .'

'Oh!' Elinor's closed hand had gone to her heart. She swayed and caught hold of the back of a chair. She felt sick . . . stunned . . . it was a dazing blow for which she had been quite unprepared. 'Myra . . . mornings when my classroom was irradiated by a sight of you in the garden. . . .' It was that little governess at the school . . . yes, Myra Bawne was her name. 'Oh, oh, oh!' She swayed and moaned. Then a mad rage came to strengthen her. A mad rage against him – he to have been carrying on like this when for all practical purposes she was keeping him – he to dare to sit at her desk and write to his mistress! – but a madder rage against her. How they had tricked her! The poor fool the creature must have thought her! Oh, it was unbearable when you thought of it. They carrying on in each other's arms while she was left at home in the dark! 'A weekend together' – when, when, *when?* It could only have been when she was away with Bessie that time – *in her own house!* Oh, the shameless creature! Come, oh, come, Paul – finish talking to that man that I may talk to *you*. Come and let me speak, or my mind will go mad!

The hall door shut; and, shaking in every limb, she waited. He came quietly back to the room – and saw her there. He stopped, white as the paper on which he had written, but no whiter than she.

Her knuckles rested on the black writing table, as an accuser's hand might rest on an indictment. His palm went to the nape of his neck, as he prepared a lie, if happily she had not read the letter; but even as he thought this, he knew that she knew, and he withdrew the palm.

'Well?' said she, as if to demand an explanation.

He could not speak; he was collecting his wits.

'I have seen this letter. Well? What have you to say, pray?'

His wits came together; his eyes lit angrily. 'That you have got what you deserved. If you come prying into my correspondence—'

'I didn't pry into it. . . . My eye chanced to fall on it and at once I knew that I was justified in reading on.'

'Well, now you know all,' said he, feeling that a bright unconcern would hurt her most.

'Yes, I know . . .' and she produced *her* weapons. 'I know you as I've never known you before. You sickening little hypocrite. You to have lied to me all this time, and to have presented a moral face to the world, and set up as a schoolmaster, and all the time to have been carrying on with a loose woman—'

'Wait—' said Paul threateningly.

But Elinor didn't listen. She had sharpened her stilettos while she waited, and she was going to use them. 'You – *you* to be a Don Juan! Pooh, it's laughable. If you could see yourself standing there – faugh! – and then ask people to think of you as a likely lover! You, old enough to be her father, and you suppose she's doing it because she loves you! Thank you, I know women too well. She's been doing it for what she can get out of you – and of *my* money too – and for all I know, she's got other infatuated fools who're ready to provide for her when *your* back is turned. And she comes to *this* house! She dares to! And you and she have been talking about me together, I expect. Oh! It's plain she's utterly unscrupulous – and she teaching young children! If I can find out where she's gone to, I'll see that they know what she is, and that pretty soon! She's no better than a woman of the streets.'

Paul stepped forward, his fists clenched at his sides, his lower teeth showing like a dog's. 'You shall not speak of her like that. She's the only thing in this world that I love—'

'*Love!*' sneered Elinor.

'Yes: love with all my heart and soul – *and* she loves me!' Through the rage a sense of triumph began to glow: he was exultant; this was an hour for which he had hoped. '*You* never gave me any love, so, thank you, I turned somewhere else for it; and I may say that the first woman I turned to gave me all that I could desire. *She* found something in me that she could love. She even said once that I'd given her back faith in the goodness of men. I had a long task to make her consent to come and be the bit of sweetness and comfort that every man needs, but do you think I hesitated? Not after I'd weighed up the life you proposed for me at home. Oh, no! You may be content to live without affection, but I'm not. What the hell do you think I've been made of all this time? Have you ever given a moment's thought to whether I needed the ordinary life of a man? Not a bit of it: you didn't need that sort of thing yourself, and you've never really thought of anybody else's needs in all your born life. Very good. If that's the position, we soon know where we are. A man doesn't consent to starve for ever. No, thank you. He finds his mate elsewhere.'

'You mean that you admit that you've lived with her as your mistress?'

'Of course I do! What else do you think I'm saying? And let me tell you she did it out of her goodness, not out of her badness. I persuaded her that I couldn't live without her. Nor am I the least ashamed of it. I bless the day when I decided to live my own life. It's been the most perfect thing that has ever happened to me. And if I haven't told you before, it was only because I didn't want to hurt you. Otherwise I've rather longed to tell you, just to bring you to your senses. Time and again I've been on the point of letting you have it, but I've forborne. And upon my soul, I'm glad you've found out at last.' He lifted his shoulders and protruded his under lip. 'It does me good.'

'You stand there and tell me to my face that, while I've been sick and ill, you've been living with her, and that, while I went away to recuperate, you brought her to this, *my* house. No doubt when I was nearly dying that time, you had her here.'

'Oh, no, I didn't. I didn't do *that*. I'm only an ordinary man, but I'm not a cad.'

'Not a cad? Then perhaps you'll tell me what caddishness is, for I confess I'm at a loss to know. Such things have always been called caddishness in any circles *I've* moved in. I suppose it's that Inglewood and the society you keep. And your parents think you so fine! If they knew! Me to be treated as a poor fool who didn't matter – oh, it's unbearable! It's killing me. Let me sit down.' She pressed her hand to her heart, and went to a chair and sat there panting. 'My heart feels funny. You know Dr Waterhall said I wasn't to be put to any strain like this. . . .'

'It's all over now,' said Paul, a little frightened for her. 'She's left me. As a matter of fact she left me, because she couldn't bear to think of your suffering.'

'And you think I believe that?' panted Elinor, looking up at him. 'Do you think I believe anything a woman like that says? You men are easy dupes, aren't you? If she's left you, it's because she's tired of you. She's probably found someone she liked better. Someone a few years younger.'

'My God!' began Paul – but paused: one could not hit out at a woman whose breast was palpitating like that. 'Well, think what you like. I happen to *know*. If it's any comfort to you, think that. There's been suffering enough in this matter, and it's all over now.'

'It's not over. It'll never be over as long as I live. The memory of it will haunt me always.'

'Well, have it your own way,' said Paul, with his maddening acquiescence. 'I daresay you're right. And certainly the insults you've heaped on the one I love will remain with me for ever.'

'Nothing can ever be the same again,' said Elinor, getting up to go. 'How can I ever trust you again? Oh, I don't know what to do or think. I must go and be by myself. I must try to get used to it. And at the moment I can't stand the sight of you there.'

'All right,' said Paul. 'And if when you've thought it over, you'd like me to go out of your life, let me know. It won't break my heart. I've suffered enough in this house.'

'*You!*' scoffed Elinor, with one last stab of her eyes as she went through the door.

Chapter Fifteen

For weeks they spoke to each other and saw each other no more than was necessary. They were polite; and passed. Their life in the echoing house made this separation easy. Paul rose at the call of his alarm clock, went down to the kitchen, put some breakfast on a tray, and carried it up to her room, for which she murmured an uncomfortable thank you. After his own breakfast he went from the house very quietly, shutting the door behind him with the politest care. On his return in the evening he found a dish prepared for him in the kitchen; and he warmed it up, ate it, and went out into the garden, where the spring now walked in its pride. He touched and tended his plants, and all the time he tended his grievance too. With the fall of dark, and when he knew that Elinor was shut in her bedroom, he put the tools away but brought the grievance back into the house; and he and it shared a book and the lamplight together, till ten o'clock, when they climbed the stairs in silence to his bedroom and shut the door on themselves. Elinor busied herself about the empty house, cooking a dish on the gas-stove and at the same time stirring the cauldron of her wrath, savouring its bitterness, and often bringing it to the boil. She kept the wrath to herself for a day or two, but then could dwell alone with it no more. She put on her hat, took her parasol, and set off for the house of Bessie Furle.

Bessie herself came to the door.

'Oh, my dear, I'm in such trouble,' said Elinor. 'I'm worn out with worry.'

'But what is it? My dear, come in and tell me. There's nobody in, so we shall be perfectly alone. Come up at once.' Bessie's words rang with sympathy, and the sympathy was as real as it was pleasurable, but for the present the only expression in her little black eyes was a piercing curiosity. 'Now then, my dear, do tell me. Sit down. Sit down there.' She arranged a cushion on the sofa, and herself took a chair opposite. 'Why, you look worried to death.'

'I am. So far I've told no one. I've been too ashamed to. But this afternoon I felt that I must share it with someone or go mad.'

'Of course you must. Isn't that what friends are for?'

'I go over it and over it,' said Elinor.

'But what is it?'

'It's Paul; he's—' but here she broke down in tears.

'Has he been getting irritable again?'

'Oh, no, it's much worse than that. He's – oh, it's too ridiculous – he's been carrying on with a young woman.'

'*No!*' Bessie's astonishment was the ultimate thing: she had been guessing at many causes of Elinor's distress, but never this.

'Yes, it is so. I chanced to go into a room where he had been writing, and I saw a letter beginning, "Myra, my beloved," or something like that. The shock was so great that I read on without knowing what I was doing. You never saw such a passionate love letter. If it were not so serious, it would be laughable – absolutely laughable. Did you ever know anything more ludicrous in a man of fifty? He wrote like a silly boy who thinks nobody but him has ever been in love before. It was the most maudlin stuff—'

'But who is she?'

'She's that governess at the school. A little nonentity, as I've always heard, without a word to say for herself: about thirty. She's no lady, of course: that goes without saying, or she wouldn't have behaved like this. As a matter of fact, I know it for a surety that her mother let lodgings. And he's gone all crazy about her, and she, of course, hadn't let the grass grow under her feet. *That's* evident.'

'But what did you do?' Bessie sat forward in her chair to hear.

'I had it out with him then and there.'

'Much better,' agreed Bessie, nodding her head in approval and tightening her lips in conviction. 'Much better.'

'And he didn't attempt to deny it. Indeed he almost gloried in it. Threw it in my face that it had been going on for a year.' Elinor clenched her fist on her knee. 'Oh, when I think of that woman, I could kill her.'

'But is it – has it come to—'

'Of course it has! He made no bones about it. I tell you he *gloried* in it.'

'Oh!' Bessie's indignation was as great as her astonishment. 'And you've been such a good wife to him! How *can* he?'

This sympathy was the only touch needed to quicken the hysteria. Elinor's head went from side to side; her mouth worked in its losing battle with her tears; she abandoned the battle and let the tears gush forth. It was for this defeat that she had come.

'There, there!' soothed Bessie, touching her knee.

Meanwhile Paul was as woodenly unhappy as man could be. Hostility filled his home, and a blankness stared at him in the world outside. Despair blocked every road of escape that thought could explore. Like a desert sky it spread over and around him to the ring of the horizon; menacing, stationary, permanent. His cheeks grew thin and hollow, his eyes large and bright, and his look bewildered and vacant. Permanent, because there was no hope of seeing Myra again, and no prospect of a reconciliation with Elinor. Certainly not the latter: this resolution was his best comfort. He was never going to forgive her; never! Some insults were not to be forgiven. '*You* a Don Juan! . . . She did it for what she could get out of you. . . . She left you because she was tired of you, and because she's found someone younger. . . . She's no better than a woman of the streets.' Thank you, madam; those words were final.

Luckily he found some periods of forgetfulness, and almost of well-being when his hands were occupied in the garden.

The May glory was in the garden now. Once in the year the whole of grey Islington Vale, its long straight roads, its terraces, crescents, squares, and gardens, put on this beauty, before the dust of London withered the leaves. The cracked house-fronts were hidden behind the full and fresh young green of their garden trees, and from some of them the wisteria hung in clusters like grapes of a lavender tint; the globes of the trees were overspread with the pink and white of May, or draped with the mauve of lilac, the pink of chestnut, and the yellow of laburnum; the golden privets along the railings were really gold; and strange sweet fragrances came down the pavements or lingered in the gardens, resting on the warm air.

But this approach to perfection in his garden made more undesirable than ever the weeds in the beds or the moss on the paths. He hoed with the trowel, and for a while was at peace. He did not perceive that when a man cannot solve a larger problem, he may turn for alleviation to solving a smaller one, easy and near at hand. He knew only that the glow as he bent over the beds, his back aching and his sweat dropping to the earth, was akin to the glow that comes when an ache is stilled. There was pleasure in the bite of the trowel into the earth, in the feel of powdery, dry soil on his hands, in the touch of the breeze on his damp brow, and in the sense of tingling health in his limbs and his breathing. The smell of the turned earth was good, and of the bonfire crackling in the corner, which he would poke and regulate and enlarge for hours. It was good to tread like a countryman on loose soil in heavy boots, and at the end of the day to scrape the caked earth from their soles.

He finished the beds first, and then turned to the less delightful, but still soothing task of rooting up the grass-tufts and scraping the moss from the gravel. But, unfortunately, to disturb the gravel thus was to uncover the dark London soil beneath, and he seemed to be making the paths more spotted and unsightly than before. Also they were so far deteriorated that there was hardly a square inch but needed his surgery, and the spring and the summer would be gone before he had cleaned them all with a trowel. And one Saturday afternoon, when the warm air was drawing his sweat from every pore and touching it with delight, he rose from his seat on his heels, straightened his aching back, and shook his head. He knew that he was beaten.

Just then Mrs Briscoll, the charwoman, came out with some refuse and saw him. She tossed her sweepings into the dust-bin and, returning to the kitchen door, paused there, a round woman in a blue apron, with the strained and steamy face of the daily house-scourer.

'You should arst Mr Briscoll to give you a hand with that, sir,' said she. 'He'd clean up all that for you in no time, if you was to arst him.'

'He would, would he?' laughed Paul, for it was always his tendency to be jocular and pleasant with those who served him.

'Yurse,' answered Mrs Briscoll, with unruffled seriousness. 'It's his job. I meanter say, he's doing it every day of the week.'

'Does he? I'd forgotten that.'

'Yurse, he works for Mr Clifton, the nurseryman. It wouldn't take him half an hour, it wouldn't. He could come round one evening after his work's done, now that the days are getting all that longer. I'll arst 'im to step round, shell I? What I meanter say is, he'd do it to oblige, I'm shore.'

'Oh, but I should want to pay him for his time. "The labourer is worthy of his hire," you know.'

'Well, I daresay a shillin' wouldn't hurt you. It wouldn't cost above a shillin', I'm shore. And it'd be better than bendin' like that and breaking your back. He's got proper stuff to do it with; jest mixes it up and spreads it down, and it kills off everything.'

'Expensive stuff, is it?'

'Oh, he wouldn't worry you about that, sir. Nah' – she contemplated the paths and felt convinced in her estimate – 'It wouldn't want all that lot. He'd bring a bit round from the shop, I expect. Not enough to worry about, it wouldn't be; and he wouldn't arst you nothin' for it.'

'Well, it's very kind of you to suggest it, Mrs Briscoll. This *is* breaking my back, as you say.' He threw back his elbows to straighten and ease his back. 'Getting old, Mrs Briscoll, getting old!'

'Go on, sir!' laughed Mrs Briscoll, disposed for the first time to joke, now that the serious business was over. 'You ain't as old as all that. Not by a long way. Though we're none of us new bread from the baker's, as you might say. Still, what we've lost in our faces we've gained in our heads, I make no manner of doubt. I'll arst 'im to step round then, shell I? He'd like to oblige you, I'm shore.'

Mr Briscoll stepped round the next evening. Like Dr Waterhall, like Mr Presset himself, indeed like all men, he enjoyed stepping into the position of the expert who speaks with learning and authority. Alfred Briscoll may have been a lean and weather-beaten figure, underfed as a child and therefore short, bandy-legged and round-shouldered now, but he had his self-esteem. In his collarless shirt, open waistcoat, and rolled-up shirt-sleeves, he stood on the path, nodding his head and pushing his mouth into a corner, like a doctor taking a first view of a patient spread below. He did not speak at once. He maintained the silence of a man whose brain was giving all its knowledge and acumen to the case before him. He walked along the paths, kicking at grass-tufts with the toe of his heavy boot, or scraping off the moss with his hob-nails. In passing, he glanced at the scars left by Mr Presset's trowel, and smiled tolerantly. He finished the course and came back to the place from which he had started; and all the time

Mr Presset followed one step behind him, like a humble learner. After this impressive examination, he pushed his mouth up into a corner again, nodded his head, and gave forth a considered opinion. He pronounced his diagnosis.

'Tidy mess,' he said.

'Yes,' Paul confessed, somewhat ashamed.

Alfred Briscoll looked up at the sky, full blue, cloudless and warm with the May evening. The best of doctors will sometimes emphasise their difficulties that their cures may shine forth the brighter, and Alfred Briscoll shook his head at the sky. It was not really the right time of the year, he said; 'not relly'.

'No?' asked Paul.

'Too dry. For putting down weed-killer, you didn't ought to have it too wet or too dry. If it's too dry, it doesn't soak in properly – at least, so I reckon meself; and if it's wet, it's like to wash away.'

'Well, what do you suggest?'

'Oh, I'll put it down, and we'll 'ope for a tidy shower. Better too dry than too wet. I might even step round and give it a sprinkle with the waterin' can. I'd like to make a good job of it.'

'When will you do it?'

'Oh, I've got the stuff here. I set it down by the kitchen door I found enough in the bottom of an old tin to do all you'll need here, sir. It needn't cost you nothing.'

'Oh, thank you very much.'

'Yurse . . . it was just some I had by me. I intended to throw it away, but thought it might come in handy. And now it has, hasn't it?' He wandered back towards the kitchen door. 'If you can let me have a bucket and some water and the can, that's all I shall want.' It was the voice of a specialist, well versed in his mystery, and asking for this and that in the invalid's room.

'That's easy,' said Paul, and, much interested, he hurried into the scullery, and produced a pail at the kitchen door. 'That's your article, isn't it?' he asked enthusiastically.

Alfred Briscoll looked at the pail without excitement. He picked up from the ground a cylindrical tin, gazed thoughtfully at its contents, and, coming to some conclusion about them, went to a tap and added water to them, measuring the fall of the water with a sidelong, steady, and learned gaze.

Paul watched the operation with that interest which most of us give to the skilled labour of others; and Briscoll, glad to have an admiring spectator, explained, 'You add roughly three parts of water to one of powder, you see, and that gives you your solution. Then you add the proper amount of water to the solution, and thet's all. I wish most of my jobs was as simple as this.' He stirred his mixture with a stick, and tipped a rose-coloured transparent liquid into the pail. 'Now for the water, sir, and we'll soon be giving them weeds a picnic.'

'Ugly looking stuff,' said Paul, for there was something sinister in the rose-coloured tint.

'You're right there, sir. 'Tain't drinking water, exactly. The powder's sixty per cent arsenic. Sixty per cent arsenic, that's what it is; thet's why it don't leave nothing alive on the paths. You'll have a pleasant job sweeping up the dead worms the next day or two.'

'But look here! The birds won't get it, will they? I don't want the birds hurt. I've induced quite a few to visit this garden.'

'It won't do them no good if they get at it,' said Briscoll mercilessly, because he was proud of his powder. 'But they're pretty cute, is birds.'

'Well, I only hope so. Sixty per cent arsenic. Good lord! When that tin's full, there must be enough to kill half London?'

'Pretty near, I reckon,' said Briscoll proudly. 'Yes, properly distributed, it ought to make a tidy mess of London.'

'But aren't you afraid of it? Getting it on your fingers, and that? What's a fatal dose?'

'I don't right know. Something very small.'

'It's two grains.' An old conversation with Inglewood and Sandys had jumped into memory. 'Yes, I know it is. Two grains – but that means less than four grains of that powder, doesn't it?'

'Something like that, sir. I know that it only wants a pinch of it in a cup 'a tea, and the party's done for. Half a teaspoonful's more than enough to poison a bottle of beer, I'm told.'

'Good lord!' said Paul. 'For God's sake take care of yourself!'

If less than half a teaspoonful poisoned a bottle of beer, then a good deal less than half a teaspoonful must be enough for a cup of tea – a mere pinch – but heavens! What was he thinking about? No, that was nothing; the thought had just flitted on to his mind; and one simply couldn't help one's brain thinking curious thoughts sometimes. Probably every soul in the world was visited sometimes by thoughts that must never be told. But these other people weren't frightened by them. Why was he always so frightened by one particular thought. Why did he forever twirl and feel and bend it, as a man tried a drawn sword? Enough: he was worrying again; and there was no sense in it.

Briscoll had now made one pailful of the mixture and tipped the best part of it into the watering can. He brought the can to the paths and began to spray them. He walked along, swinging the fine plume of spray from left to right, and Paul followed, watching. It was good to see it falling on the weeds and draining down to their roots, and to know that every second now was bringing nearer the clean, yellow paths.

Briscoll emptied the last canful on the last yard of path. 'Thet's all, sir. Not a very serious job, is it?'

'No,' agreed Paul; and added, 'Well, thank you very much. Quite interesting to watch. Now we'll see what we'll see. And by the way, "the labourer is worthy . . " you know . . .' and he pushed a shilling into Briscoll's hand.

'*Thet's* all right, sir. Only too pleased to be of 'elp to yer,' demurred Biscoll, but pocketing the shilling, none the less. 'Pleased to do what I can at any time.'

He put the pail in the scullery, and the can in the garden shed, and the old tin, after a glance to make sure that it was empty, on the dust-bin. And he pulled on the jacket which he had brought on his arm, and straightened his cap.

'Well, good evening, sir.'

'Good evening. Have a cigarette?'

'Thenk you, sir. I don't mind if I do.'

Always friendly, Paul accompanied him to the front gate; and then turned to walk round the house into the back garden and look again at the paths. And as he strolled along the gravel, he thought, 'If the merest pinch is enough for a cup of tea, then there's enough in solution on the bottom and round the sides of that tin. . . And nobody would ever know that I had possessed the stuff. There would be no record of my having bought it, and Briscoll would swear that he had emptied the tin and thrown it away. . . . Damn! Why does fate deliberately thrust an opportunity in one's way? Strange . . . rather frightening. . . . Though I suppose it's natural enough, really. As Inglewood said, once the idea is in your head you'll come across arsenic soon enough. Frightening? What silly and morbid nonsense! These are only thoughts that my brain *will* think; and I'm quite happy and unworried about them. They're academic, that's all' – he rather liked the word – 'and I am only thinking how easy it would be to do, if I were a different person. And anyhow the tin is thrown away and will be taken by the dustmen tomorrow. Tomorrow is the dustmen's day.'

Thus thinking, and whistling comfortably, he returned into the kitchen, and nearly bumped into Elinor. She was bustling there with a kettle and a teapot. . . . He shivered. It had been a shock to see her large body, active and apparently vigorous, immediately after his idle thoughts.

As usual, after a supper punctuated by the fewest possible

remarks, and these inordinately polite, Elinor retired to her bedroom, and Paul sank into his easy chair. He settled his shoulder so that the gaslight fell on his book; he rested his feet on the fender. But he could not get on with the book: something got between his brain and the meaning of its sentences; it was the large cylindrical tin resting on the top of the dustbin.

Was it really empty? He knew that his mind could not settle into calm until he had answered this question. Why this should be so, he would not inquire: it simply *was* so. Had he not better go and look? After all, it wouldn't really be safe to leave dangerous stuff like that about. It was almost his duty to go and look into the matter. But, duty or not, he'd got to: something was driving him. He jumped up and went out to the back-yard and picked out the tin. He brought it into the light of the kitchen gas. Briscoll had replaced the lid before tossing the tin on the refuse; and Paul twisted it off. Just as he had thought: a tiny little pool of the rosy solution had drained to the bottom of the tin, and there was even some of the untouched powder at the lips and upper sides – so little water had Briscoll used in making his mixture. No fault of his that his brain insisted on saying, 'A quarter of a teaspoonful.' H'm! Good job he had looked at it: surely one oughtn't to leave stuff like that lying about. . . . He waited – what would he do? He would put it in the shed – in a far corner where it could do no harm to anyone. Who knew? He might even want to use it again, if some of the weeds declined to die. So he dipped his head under the low lintel of the shed, and stowed the tin in a far corner out of sight.

Then he came back to his chair and picked up his book again, feeling strangely easier. Once or twice that evening he paused in his reading to consider putting the tin back on the dustbin; but he did not do it, and took up his book instead.

Chapter Sixteen

Now, each morning, he had the deep interest of hurrying out to the back garden to walk along the paths and see the moss rusting away and the grass-tufts greying with death. He sat on his haunches to see how much 'deader' they were than yesterday. Or he fetched the trowel to pick up the dead worms that lay about the gravel like casualties on a battlefield, and to bury them deep under the earth that the birds might not partake of their death. When in a day or two the moss was a rust-red carpet and the grass-tufts were like the grey lifeless hair of an ancient man, he swept at them with the broom or scraped at them with the trowel, and lo! the paths were clean. Now, morning and evening, it was his peculiar peace to walk with pipe in mouth and hands in pockets around a garden that for once in its story was perfect, its beds rich and raked, its paths neat and glistening.

The evening after his work with the can Alfred Briscoll had come back for his tin, thinking that perhaps it was unwise to leave so dangerous a thing on a dustbin, but Paul, who was in the garden at the time, laughed and said, 'You're too late. The dustmen took it away this morning'; and he was glad that Briscoll had come back and learned that his tin had gone to the incinerator within a dozen hours of his leaving it – but there! He was thinking that ridiculous thought again. Stop it.

By slow and cumulative means, by a little more speech today and an inquiry tomorrow, Elinor and Paul rebuilt the façade of their life together. In his heart Paul grudged even this pretence of reconciliation, because it implied the old imprisonment again, which was tolerable for her but intolerable for him; but he played his part in it, pity preventing him from humiliating her by a rejection of her advances. He was even more courteous than before.

But all the time, behind smiling or genial eyes, he was occupied with but one thought: 'Something will happen; something must be going to happen; what it will be I do not know; I know only – I feel it in my blood and bones – that Myra and I are not destined to be parted forever like this. Our souls are blent together, and our lives must blend soon. Only wait, and it will happen.'

The hope that it would happen, whatever it might be, made tolerable the months of summer. One must give it time. One couldn't expect it to happen within two months, or three, or four of Myra's going. Probably, in the wisdom of fate, they were being given this absence to endure that their love might be strengthened and their reunion and life together be all the more wonderful. So the sun of that year lifted its arc before the windows of Islington Vale, and lowered it; and Paul saved himself from despair by walking with a hope and a dream.

But, time passing, doubt stirred and raised an anxious face. Things were going on the same as ever, and the months were building up into a year. Every day that passed set the likelihood of happiness farther away. Every day brought nearer the time when he would no longer be able to make a move: when habit and custom would hold him fettered to his place. 'Full soon thy soul shall have her earthly freight And custom lie upon thee with a weight Heavy as frost and deep almost as life.' And every day was making easier Myra's adaptation to her new life. She herself had said, 'One accepts; one adjusts oneself; one can lose anybody, because one has to.' And she was right. Always more sensible and realistic than he, she had spoken the hard truth. It was the saddest thing in the world that one could so adjust oneself to loss. After a period of pain one accepted the final loss, and was happy again. 'She will forget me – that is to say, I shall pass often from her thoughts. She even said, "If anyone is fool enough to ask me, I may marry." And I shall forget *her* – No, I will *not*. I will not let it happen. . . . But she is younger; she has most of her life and experience before her. And there is her wonderful compassionate nature. Some man will trade upon that. Oh, what can I do? Nothing. Nothing. I've been over the question again and again, and the answer is, Nothing.'

For a moment he saw that old cylindrical tin lying hidden in a dark corner of his garden shed. But quickly he put the picture from him. No. No, *no*. He even made a step towards the back garden and the shed that he might get rid of the tin forever – but he did not make the second step. He turned back into the room. It would be absurd, melodramatic, to throw it away; he wasn't afraid of it; he would never really be tempted to use it.

But once – one dark evening – his thoughts had been quite different. He had gone into the shed to find his birch broom, and his eye, disobeying his will, had strayed to the cylindrical shape in the dark corner. And at once his conscience had cried, 'Quick! Now! Throw it away!' and he had moved towards it; but the sudden realisation that it would mean the certain loss of Myra and a lifelong despair, had inhibited his arm . . . and he had come out again into the sunlight.

It had been summer then; but all too soon summer's face was wet with the kiss of autumn. The rain slanted across the dark trees, with the leaves in its hands. It beat into the gross richness of his nasturtiums, and bent his chrysanthemums and michaelmas daisies to the earth. The leaves of his pollarded limes lay on the beds, and the weeds and moss reappeared on the paths. Each morning as he looked from his window at the yellow in the trees, and the beds strewn with slain blossoms and dead leaves, the words formed on his lips, 'Too late soon. . . . Too late soon. . . .' The strain of holding his sham smile before the world and forcing up his insincere kindnesses to Elinor began to sit like a permanent ache in his head. He would wake fresh in the morning, and then, at the first thought of his frustration, the headache would wake too; and from that time it stayed all day. From that time the feeling of exhaustion began: the buried conflict quickly draining off the energy accumulated in sleep. Everything seemed to require too great an effort: letters, shopping, teaching, and even talking; and he just drifted from hour to hour.

He could ease the headache in one way only: by indulging in a dream of success. Then all the stream of his being converged into one channel, and flowed full and tranquil and free. He would be at home: supper would be over; Elinor would be out of sight; and he would have sunk into the comfort of his chair. And he lowered the newspaper or the book to his knees, and let the thoughts run free.

'Just supposing – let's encourage the picture for a change – perhaps if I don't repress it, I will get free of it.' And oh, the happiness that came as he thrust normality aside and thought whatever he liked! It would be simplicity itself: the tiniest pinch flicked into a cup of tea. The means was there. Strange that it should have come to him, who would never have had the courage to go and find it. Was that the Devil's hand? Was there, then, really a Devil?

Who would ever suspect? Didn't he remember Inglewood joking about it? 'It's a thousand to one chance against the doctor or anyone else suspecting anything. He can't imagine such things happening to *him*.' And 'most husbands are gents and leave something to their wives.' Her *will*! He started up in his chair, his body shaking and his brow moistening as he tasted fear. She had made a will in his favour: would that be enough to start suspicion? Suspicion! *God!* 'Only start the suspicion,' Inglewood had said, 'and they'll twist everything you've ever done into proof of your guilt.'

But no, how stupid! He sank back into his chair. As Inglewood had said, it was perfectly natural for a wife to leave everything to her husband. There was not a speck of danger in her will; only his guilty imagination had seen it there. If he took fright at a ridiculous idea like this, he'd never do anything. It was like a horse backing at a wisp of paper in his path. He must have courage. Besides, didn't she threaten to alter her will after we had that row? 'Well, I rather hope she did. Yes, I think I do. And not because it would remove a cause of suspicion, but simply because I don't want to do it for *that*. I'd rather not have the money. I only want freedom. If the money chances to be there, it can't be helped, of course; and one would be a fool not to use it. But we could have managed without it. I could have earned for another ten years or so, and Myra could have earned a little, and we could have put by a sum to start that little guest-house in the Lakes among the mountains she loves. Yes, I'd as soon Elinor's money wasn't there; I would, really. But *has* she altered her will? I don't know, and I can't ask. I don't know, and I'm glad I don't, because it'll be proof positive to myself, that I didn't do it for that—'

But what was he saying? Only indulging in a dream to heal his headache, which was now fully gone. He took up his book again.

Chapter Seventeen

Paul had come to a resolve.

He was going to see Myra again; if only from a distance, he was going to see her again. He was going to find out where she worked and snatch a glimpse of her. It would be torment, no doubt; but somehow the torment would be a relief. God knew what would happen afterwards; but he didn't care; he felt driven to do this, as a madman is driven towards action of which his broken sanity can still see the peril.

Where had she gone? How was she living? There was a way to find out. His brain, always a scheming one, worked rapidly now because all his being was concentrated on the one desire. A letter. A letter that had been brought to the school for Miss Myra Bawne, and put into his hand because it was too important to trust to the chances of being forwarded. With this in his hand he would knock up the woman in whose house she had lived and demand Miss Bawne's address that he might convey it to her personally. A Mrs Bohntree, wasn't it? She had never seen him, because the need for secrecy and Myra's timidity had forbidden him to visit the house. Knowing nothing about him, she would suspect nothing. 'Just some good-natured master from that school,' she would say.

So one Friday evening he hurried from Bishop Abercorn Square to Myra's street and, heedless of the quick protests of his heart, ascended the steps of the house and rang the bell. A pause, soon becoming pregnant with disappointment; and then, just as it was at its heaviest, slippered feet approached the door. It opened to show a heavy, peering, short-sighted woman;

Mrs Bohntree, beyond a doubt; and Paul, with a stuttering voice and an uncontrollable rush of blood to the cheeks, asked, 'There was a Miss Bawne who lived here, was there not?' He glanced at an envelope in his hand. 'Miss Myra Bawne.'

'That's right. But she's been gawn a long time now.'

'Yes, I know. .' he stuttered, and confound it! He could not meet her eyes but looked away, while perfectly aware that the woman was staring in some surprise at his discomfort. 'I – er – someone brought this letter to the school because it was too important to trust to the post, and I said I'd deliver it personally. Could you oblige me with her address?'

'Oh, but let me forward it,' said Mrs Bohntree, putting out her hand. 'You're never going all that way?'

'N-no. I practically promised to deliver it myself. Yes, I definitely promised. She's in London, isn't she?'

'Oh, yes. She's in London all right.'

'Yes; exactly; and I don't want anything to go wrong with it.'

'Nothing's likely to go wrong with it,' objected Mrs Bohntree, somewhat offended. 'But if you're so set on taking it yourself—' and she told him Myra's address. Miss Bawne lived in a street off the Chiswick High Road. Yes. She had gawn and got a job in some millinery and gown shop in the High Road, and she lived with a family in a street near her work.

'Thank you. And you don't, I suppose, know anything about her working hours? I mean, I should have liked to give her this in her free time. I mean, it wouldn't be altogether nice to take it into the shop.'

'Her working hours is the same as anyone else's. It's a one-man business – or a one-woman business, perhaps I should say, because his wife seems to do all the work – and that was how she got it without having served any apprenticeship. I expect she got it on her manner – not that she was all that pretty, mind you, but she was very quiet and ladylike and well-spoken, as you know.' Unaware of the sweet pain she was giving to her listener, Mrs Bohntree rambled on. 'And she was old enough not to be skittish any longer. You felt you knew where you were with her, which is what they look for in a business like that, where a gurl has to serve lady customers – they've not so much use for them flighty ones, really. But you was asking her hours. As far as I can remember, there's only her and a young apprentice in the shop, so she doesn't get any too much time. She works from nine to seven on most days, and she's lucky if she gets off before five o'clock on Thursday.'

'Nine to seven,' repeated Paul aloud.

'Yes, but not on Fridays. Today's Friday, isn't it? Friday's their busiest day apart from Saturday, if you understand.'

'Well, what time does she get off on a Friday?'

'I should say about eight o'clock. You see, the men get their wages on a Friday, mostly, and the women come buying. I used to do it myself, when Mr Bohntree was alive.'

'I see. Then I might find her at home sometime after eight o'clock?'

'I dessay. . . .' But Mrs Bohntree smiled knowingly. 'Unless, of course, there's a young man about. You never can say.'

Paul's face showed nothing of the knife-stab he had received. He even laughed in tune with Mrs Bohntree, saying, 'Well, I daresay that's quite probable. . . . Thank you. Thank you very much. Goodbye, Mrs Bohntree.'

And Mrs Bohntree shut her door on him and stood for a space in her passage, thinking, 'Now I wonder if that was the man. There was a man behind it somewhere, I've always believed. It's only about a man that you can get as low as all that; and I always suspected that it was one of them masters; and he had my name off pat enough. But surely not one as old as that! Why, he's old enough to be her father. Still, you can never say with them girls, especially the quiet ones like her.'

And Paul went on towards Chiswick. He was impatient to see

the outside of her shop and to take the first sip of pain; too impatient to mind that he must delay near it for two hours before she would emerge, and he could drink the full draught. He had no intention, of course, of 'finding her at home', as he had pretended to Mrs Bohntree, but only of standing at a distance and watching her pass. Mrs Bohntree? Had she guessed anything from his ridiculous blush and stutter? But what did it matter if she had? He would never see or hear of her again. Stop this worrying. It was only because he was sick in mind that he saw danger in every shadow.

The evening had been dry when he came out from the school, though a quilt of grey cloud had overlaid the sky and darkened the hour. But now, as he mounted the stairway of a bus crowded within, he glanced at the sky to make sure that it was safe to ride on the unsheltered deck. Damn! A heavy grey blanket was coming up from the west; and, even as he sat down, the first raindrops fell and the wind moved. It was going to pour – and pour all night. God curse it! With the passionate anger of a child his tears could have spurted at the perversity of fate; now for two hours outside Myra's shop he would have to walk up and down, or huddle for shelter, beneath a shattering rain. But never mind: he didn't care if he got wet through; he didn't care if he died; it would solve a lot if he died. Nevertheless, he unhooked the waterproof apron and pulled it over his knees; and, as well as he could, he put up his umbrella and drew it close over his crouching shoulders.

The rain was in full force when he dismounted from a second bus at the beginning of Chiswick High Road; and the shop fronts were already alight, in the darkness of the evening. But he didn't care. He was going to walk now, lest a bus carried him past her shop. So, huddling high-shouldered beneath his umbrella, he strode rapidly along the south-side pavement, his eye examining every shop on the opposite side where 'Purcells,

Millinery and Gowns' was to be found. The damp penetrated to his knees and shins, and trickled down his arm when he changed his umbrella hand, but for the present he did not feel it: his excitement was an anaesthetic, and his mind apprehended nothing but the hunt in hand.

He stopped. There it was! 'Purcells, Millinery and Gowns'. Oh, Myra, Myra! So near; only a plate glass window between them! He looked at his watch: twenty-past six. Best part of two hours to wait, with a heart trembling with sweetness and pain. He looked up the street for somewhere to stand in shelter. If only there was an eating house where he could sit by the window and keep watch on Purcells! But there was no such place. He could not obstruct the doorways of shops: must he walk up and down, up and down, in the beating rain? A gust of wind tore at his umbrella, and he muttered miserably. He walked on, twenty yards, thirty yards, forty yards, and then, just as he felt he must turn round again, he saw he was opposite a bank that of course was closed. With a gasp of relief, he stepped into its vestibule, lowered his umbrella, and tilted away the rain that had collected in the rim of his bowler hat. From here his eye could enfilade the high road and fix on the doorway of Purcells. With quivering and clumsy hands he lit himself a pipe, while his eye lifted above the flame to its duty along the road.

For two hours he waited. The trams grating across his line of vision maddened him. So did the buses halting and blocking his view, and a cart ambling by just as he had seen a back that might be hers, and a man and a woman standing to chatter immediately in front of him. They provoked him almost to tears. His eyes watered with the strain of staring over such a distance and dodging the people and the traffic and refusing to be dazzled by the variegated lights of the shops and the spluttering arc lamps on their stands and the brilliant windows of trams and buses, across which the rain slanted in glistening needles. His body shivered as his trousers, wet from knee to ankle, blew against his legs; his head ached; his limbs and back wearied with standing so long, but it was only in odd minutes, when the excitement receded, that he noticed these pains. A clock near-by struck the quarters, and every quarter was an hour long. A policeman passed him, and returned with an examining eye; and Paul pulled out his watch, to let the fellow imagine he was waiting in shelter till someone should come to meet him.

Eight. The clock was striking. Now. Any minute now. His heart racing, his body weak from anticipation, his head one massive ache, he strained his gaze on the doorway of Purcells. After six months he was going to see her figure again. Perhaps a quarter of an hour he was held thus, and then – was it she? – ah, yes! Unmistakable! That was her walk. She was hurrying into a little run because of the rain. All the love in him surged up as never before; it was torment to see her there, and yet the torment was sweetness. She was coming into nearer view; and he drew into his shelter in a sudden terror of being seen. She passed; and his eyes followed her. He must run to her and speak – yes, what did anything matter? – he was mad with love of her – oh, the overwhelming pain of this love and the terrible joy of it! He left his shelter to hurry after her; he twisted across the road, through cars and vans and trams; he was on her pavement fifty yards behind her; he was running towards her back – and then, at a corner, a young man came from the other side and greeted her with a doffed hat and a smile.

Paul stopped as if a stone had blinded him. She was talking with the young man, while her foot dangled merrily; she was smiling and laughing with him – and oh, God, no! – he touched her elbow, tossing his head towards the rain, and together they went up the side road out of view.

With an anguish only bearable because it was too much to suffer at once, Paul walked to the corner and gazed up the side road after them. They were running from the rain with laughter, the young man still touching her elbow. The street curved, and they were gone from view once more.

Paul's mouth dropped. His heart turned to sickness in his breast. His hand, which had shot to the nape of his neck as if fearing a blow, had come slowly, despairingly away, that his fingers might play stupidly along his mouth. The shiver, which he had hardly noticed a few minutes ago, now shook and worried his body and limbs. He had been tormented before, but there had been a sweetness of confidence and tender melancholy in the heart of the torment; and now this was taken from him. It had been, in a second, expunged.

Dizzied, he turned round and walked homeward. He saw a Hammersmith bus, and mechanically got inside it. Numbly he sat down and bought a ticket. Then he rested both hands on the hook of his umbrella, and stared vacantly, and thought.

Thought allayed the sharpest pain. It had to. It had to rebuild his belief in Myra's loyalty, if he was to endure; but, even as he perceived this compulsion, his whole being rose in a tide of assurance that his belief was true. 'She loved me. If ever I've known anything clearly in this world, I've known that. She could not have turned to another. Not yet. Not so soon. I am being silly. He likes her, but she has nothing beyond friendship to give him. She likes a little admiration, naturally. Is she never to see a man, poor child? What more natural than that he should put a hand on her elbow, to hurry her out of the rain? He was but seeing her home, and she likes the admiration (she always did); but she would drop him tomorrow if I came to her. I know it; I know it with everything in me. Oh, Myra, wait a little longer. How can I get to you? . . .'

All the way home his thoughts went milling round, in buses, in tube trains, and on foot along the Caledonian Road. He pieced together the reassuring arguments and went over them as he hurried through the rain. He was busy with one as he turned the key in his door. At sight of the dark passage, he shut the door slowly, and despair gathered round him again, while his brain said, 'Too late.' If two years or ten years hence he were freed from this prison in which he was now shutting himself, it would be too late. What was the good of reassuring himself that Myra was loyal? Every day that went by brought nearer the time when she would find comfort with another man. Men were able to love her; and perhaps more now that he had taught her so much more of love. With her sympathy, her need, and her certainty that Paul was forever lost, she would gradually yield to some other man. Was it not her sympathy which had first brought her to love *him*? What had happened before would happen again. This man would hold her at last in his arms; and she would enjoy his body and grow to love him.

He bolted the door, and went round the ground-floor rooms shutting the windows against the driving rain. It was half-past nine; and he would go to the comfort of his bed and there think and think in the darkness. Slowly as an aged man, but weighted with thought rather than with years, he climbed step by step up the stairs. Sighing, he crossed the landing and was about to open his door when Elinor's voice called, 'Paul, Paul.' And, turning, he saw a ribbon of light beneath her bedroom door.

He went in.

'Where have you been?' she demanded, with a note of exasperation that had been absent from her sparse words for many a day. 'You've been away since eight o'clock this morning. It's nearly ten now.' He saw that she had been waiting for hours for this chance to release a gathered anger; that she had kept the gas alight so as to be awake when he came in; and that she had a hundred punishing sentences rehearsed and ready. Oh, he knew Elinor. She had risen on her arm beneath the baldachin of the bed's canopy; and her hair was in disorder about her face; her skin, robbed of its powder, was red and veined; and her eyes, staring at him, were hard and unloving. He took the familiar lash, but tonight its sting was sharper than usual.

If only he could run from it to his room, and shut the door on himself!

'I've been unwell ever since tea time,' she pursued. 'Something disagreed with me. I was sick and faint, and not a soul in the house! I had to lie down, and I wanted someone to go and get me some medicine or some brandy. I was afraid I was going to be like I was before. And I might have died here, and no one would have been any the wiser. It's wicked to leave a sick woman alone in a house like this for fourteen hours.'

'I'm sorry. I didn't know you were ill. Shall I get you something now?'

'It's too late now. I've felt better since I laid down,' said she sulkily; and he saw that she didn't want a reconciliation till she had emptied over him the accumulation of her wrath. 'Where *have* you been?'

'I've been out on business.'

'What business can you have at ten o'clock at night? And on a night like this! Look, you're wet through. Where have you been to get like that?'

'I have had some important business of my own.'

'What business?'

'I don't choose to account for my every step. I'm not a child.'

She looked hard at him. 'You haven't been meeting that woman, I suppose?'

'What woman?'

'Don't be absurd. You know who I mean – the creature you took up with.'

'I don't know to whom you are referring. I've never associated with "creatures". If you mean a woman I loved once and who loved me—'

Elinor made a sound of contempt behind her lips.

'And don't sneer at her, please,' said Paul, his mouth taking an ugly set. 'I shall not stay to hear her abused.'

'If I thought you'd been taking up with her again – and me

lying sick and ill here – *Have* you been seeing her again?'

'You're talking rubbish. You know we parted months ago.'

'I know that you *said* you did. But how can you expect me ever to trust you again?'

'Well, don't trust me. And if you don't there's an end of it. I can do no more than say the truth. And you seem to forget' – he threw back his head and barked a single short laugh– 'that you were good enough to suggest that she'd left me because she'd found someone better. It seems that you never really thought so. I'm glad to see that.'

For a moment this disorganised Elinor's attack. She recovered position by saying, 'I shouldn't trust her an inch. When she said she'd only left you because your duty was to me, I wasn't taken in. I thought, if it suits her book to come back, she will – and I think so still.'

'Well, think what you like; but please keep your thoughts to yourself. I can put up with a good deal, but I won't hear *her* abused by any soul on this earth!'

'Think what I like, may I? But perhaps I may not be content with just thinking. There are ways of finding out.'

'I don't know what that means.'

'*I* do. *I* know the ways.'

'Well, *take* them!' shouted Paul, his temper suddenly flaring. 'Take them, for all I care. Have me followed by detectives if you like—'

'Please don't shout at me. I'm not at all well, and you know you've no right to leave me alone for fourteen hours.'

'I leave you alone for about nine hours every day I go to school.'

'Yes, but I know where to get hold of you then.'

His temper sank down into a still dark tarn of sulks. '*I* didn't know you were ill. How was I to know you were going to get ill?'

'You knew that I was in a delicate state. I turned very sick indeed at about four o'clock. I think it was some raw tomatoes I had had. And when I'm ill like that, it affects my heart. I was at my wit's end where to turn.'

Some sympathy mingled with his sulks. 'I'm sorry for that. It was just an accident that it happened while I was out for some time. I may tell you I had worries of my own too. I do what I can as a rule—'

But she destroyed his sympathy by a scoff behind her lips, and immediately his anger flamed higher than before. His eyes glared, and his voice rose. 'Well, am I never to go out at all? Am I to ask permission every time I want a walk? Am I to come home and give you an account of everywhere I've been. No, thank you. I took my life into my own hands at fifteen, and I'm not going back to apron strings at fifty! I shall lead my own life in my own way; and the sooner you grasp that, the better!'

Elinor, mad all day to vent her fury, let it storm up and take command of her. 'You will not lead it with that woman and stay with me. It's my house and my furniture and my money, and I'm not going to provide a hotel for you while you go gallivanting with a woman whose best place would be on the streets—'

His eyes flashed. In that moment they looked like a madman's eyes, and she recoiled from them. 'You say that again, and I'll – my Christ! I won't answer for myself. I've given her up, but I won't hear her insulted. I won't, I tell you, and I mean it! She was good. She knew what sympathy and unselfishness were in a way you never will. Say that again, and I'll – but my God, I'd better get out – I'd better get out!'

And he ran from the room, on to the dark landing, where he stood still with his hand to the back of his head. By force of habit he went slowly down the stairs to the dining-room, where he walked up and down.

His misery was complete. It was an intolerable, sick despair. His temples beat, his limbs shook, his heart played tricks, and his wild eyes rested on objects without seeing them. The one sustaining hope that sooner or later he would get to Myra had deserted him. The time approached with every day when she would marry and be lost to him. And that meant that he must live to the end in this home. He couldn't do it. Drag on with this life day after day, when his hatred of it drained him of all energy and split his head? Daily despair and inertia? It was impossible. But what else? Nothing. He felt as if his brain must give away.

Suicide. Very lovely seemed the white emptiness, the forgetful sleep, that lay beyond death. But no, he couldn't inflict such suffering on Myra. He was not going to spoil Myra's life foever. No, not that. In his passionate misery he found himself breaking into extravagant and tearful heroics, and sipping a faint compensation from them. 'No, I will endure anything for you, my dear. You may desert me, but I shall never, never do anything that can injure you. I loved you too well. . . .'

Drink? Ah! Other men had found some peace this way. And his mind and body were craving an opiate. Should he go out and get relief? It would be a new experience for him whom hitherto drink had not tempted at all, if only because his thrift had held him back from the experiments of livelier and lavisher men. But now, by all the devils! let him try it. He cared nothing for thrift tonight.

He went softly to the door, his secretiveness captaining him even in this mutiny of emotions. He put on his overcoat and buttoned it round his throat, for the wind had mounted. As he opened the hall door, the wind drove at him, almost as if it would buffet him back; and, going out, he had to pull the door strongly against the force of its protest. The door shut with a bang. On his top step the rain beat and stung his cheeks as if it would say, 'Go back!' But he went on down the steps. The gate whined, as he and the wind together opened it. He turned on to the pavement, and now both wind and rain were driving at his back as if they would say, 'Well, go on if you will. . . . Go on. . . .' And the flood-water in the gutter ran at his side down the road, like a strange companion eager to learn what his business might be. Some dead leaves flew ahead of him, like mischievous spirits of the night.

His business took him to the brightly lit door of a public house in the Caledonian Road. He pushed it open; and at once the saloon bar struck close and warm after the driving cold without. Not many men were here on such a squally night, though the voices of a group in high argument came from the public bar beyond the screen. A man with his bowler pushed back leaned against the counter talking to a fat and flaxen barmaid of forty. This man turned as the door swung behind Paul, and greeted him. 'Welcome, mate. Come in, but leave the wind behind. Not much of a night, is it?'

'No,' agreed Paul, and could think of no more to say.

'No,' repeated the man. 'It's better to have the wet inside you than outside you on a night like this, eh, miss?'

'You're right,' agreed the barmaid, and then inquired of Paul, 'Yes, sir?'

'Whisky, please,' ordered Paul, sitting himself on a high stool by the counter, dumpily, like a labourer whose work has exhausted him.

'That's the stuff!' endorsed the humorist, beside him.

'Water or splash?' asked the barmaid, after she had measured his whisky.

'Pardon?' demanded Paul, not immediately understanding. 'Oh, yes. . . . Water please.'

She pushed a jug along the counter to him, and Paul lifted it with a hand that shook like an octogenarian's.

'Eh, you're cold?' said the man who had been watching him from the side of his eye.

'I am, a bit,' agreed Paul, pouring out the very smallest measure of water, since custom seemed to demand it. And the man, perceiving that he did not want to be talkative, returned to his gossip with the barmaid.

Paul took a long sip of the whisky, and another, and another.

It ran hot and comforting down his body; and as quickly as might be, he emptied the glass. On a head unaccustomed to neat spirit its effect was rapid. He felt better; almost hopeful again.

'I'll have another please, miss,' he said diffidently; but neither barmaid nor her confidant showed any surprise.

He emptied the next glass as quickly; and as it permeated his being, he felt more than hopeful; he felt enlarged, sanguine, grandiose. He felt confident that everything he desired was coming to him, and he felt 'big' – one of the big men who take their destiny in their own hands and create it, instead of being created by it. He ordered another glass – 'I think I'll have one more, miss. I've got a bit of a chill. Yes' – and he drank from it; and the glow of assurance brightened; the old timorous caution faded out so that he wondered how he had ever been at its mercy; the restless conscience seemed to have struck its tent and gone from his life, so that he could see it only in the distance; and the idea came to him, as he twirled his glass.

If only she died of this illness as she so nearly did before! And he could make sure that she did. So simply – and he would never really know if she would have died in any case, or not. Less than a quarter of a teaspoonful dropped into a glass – just to make sure – and the future, instead of being desperate, would be exquisitely lovely. Only a flip of the finger – careless almost – and he could go forward to happiness. And think! think! never had such an opportunity been his as tonight! Why, she had got ill while he had been out; she had got ill at four o'clock, and he had been out of the house from eight in the morning till ten at night! She had only to get a little worse and . . . collapse. And she had had precisely the same illness before, so it would all seem so natural. But – the 'but' came from the far away conscience, and he strengthened himself against it: don't lose your courage; don't go back into timidity . . . In what? What drink could he offer late at night? Brandy. The doctor had recommended sips of brandy and water last time; so he might well suggest that now when she was so much easier a good glass of brandy and water was the obvious thing. And later he would substitute another glass for the one from which she had drunk. . . .

Two men had come in while he meditated, and they were in lively colloquy with the humorist who had first addressed him. They exchanged their coarse banter, and did not know what the stranger on the stool, one pace to their left, was thinking and planning, as he twirled his glass. They barely heard him as he asked, 'Could you let me have a little brandy to take home, miss?'

'Yes, sir. How much would you like?'

'Oh, I shan't need much. How do you sell it?'

'You can have a quartern. That's about *so* much.'

'Thank you. Yes, I'll have that. Thank you; that'll do nicely. And have you a bottle I could have?'

'Yes, we've got bottles for it.'

And the barmaid put the brandy in a small flat bottle like a flask, knowing nothing of the part she was playing.

Paul, watching her fill the bottle, told himself that it didn't mean he had decided anything; it was only that he was going to take it home in case. . . .

The barmaid passed the bottle across the counter and swept his money into the till where it jingled among more innocent coins.

And Paul sat there humpily, though the chamber of his head was still brilliantly lit, and he felt equal to anything. But he had decided nothing, he told himself, so there was no harm done. He didn't know what he was going to do; he was just thinking, that was all. And he was entitled to think, wasn't he?

'Time, gentlemen, please.'

The landlord had appeared from a back room.

There was a finishing of glasses; and a general movement to the door.

'What?' said Paul.

'Time,' explained the landlord, brightly.

'Oh, yes,' assented Paul; and, murmuring to himself, 'I din't know,' he put the bottle into his pocket and went out with the others into the night.

'Good night, George . . . Good night, Jeff . . . Good night, Charlie,' said they, as they took their separate ways. The humorist looked at the rain, its slanting needles silvered by the light from the door. 'That's nice stuff to walk home through,' said he to Paul. 'I wish I were one of the homeless, by crikey, I do!'

'Why?'

'Because then I should be already there! Ha, ha, ha! Good night, sir.'

'Good night.'

Good night. Was there a hideous inaptness in that 'good night', thought Paul, as the humorist took his laugh and his footsteps down the pavement into the night, and he himself turned towards Elm Tree Road. But it was so difficult to think clearly. Other people passed him, going about the simple business of their lives. Was he alone flying from simplicity for a night? The wind and rain beat in his face on this return journey, but he did not notice them; his mind, aglow with confidence and hope, was yet occupied with the submissions of his conscience, though the conscience seemed oddly fuddled and confused. Here was his house. With a thumping heart he passed through the gate and up the steps, staring at his door. At the top step he halted, as if waiting to see whether his conscience would recover. But it seemed in a catalepsy. Only furtiveness was moving in him: before he turned the key he looked back at the houses on the opposite side of the road to make sure that no one was watching a criminal entry. Their blinds were down like lids over eyes that will not look. And nothing was in the street, between house-front and house-front, except the one-way traffic of wind and rain.

He went in and shut the door softly behind him. In the hall he stood hesitating, with knees trembling, but with the same sense of exultation, courage, and 'bigness' in his head.

Should he? Yes, he knew he was going to. He hardly knew any longer why he was going to, but he knew he was going to. He just felt impotent to turn back, as though something stronger than himself were driving him. He just couldn't turn back now, and lose happiness for ever. Not without this simple lift of his hand. He would put the glass of brandy beside her bed, and leave the rest to chance. If she took it, well and good. . . .

He went almost mechanically to the back door, and, bending low under the rain, crossed the dark path towards the low black ark that was his garden shed. Only the backs of sleeping houses, and the wind-thrashed trees, looked down upon his movements. These, and the clouds scudding above him. He went to the far dark corner of the shed and found with his searching fingers the cylindrical tin.

A few minutes later, for one hurries nervously over such business, he knocked fearfully at Elinor's door, beneath which the ribbon of light was still showing. 'Are you awake?'

'Yes.'

He went in. As he saw the large room, the canopied bed, the littered dressing-table, and the dishevelled figure on the bed – all of which had stabbed him so terribly in the past – many strange thoughts struggled to birth, but could not live: something was denying them life. It was the driving determination to go on; he couldn't turn back now. 'I've brought you some brandy and water, in case you feel bad in the night. It'll ease you. You remember the doctor prescribed it last time.'

She seemed surprised – perhaps touched – by this kind action after the quarrel. 'Oh, thank you,' said she, rising on her arm. 'But I don't think I shall need it now. I feel rather better.'

He was amazed at the depth of his disappointment. 'Oh well, just as you like,' said he, putting it on her bedside table.

She perceived his disappointment, and construed it in the ordinary way. 'But it was kind of you to go out and get it on a night like this. Can you stop the windows rattling? And there's one upstairs, too. I tried to sleep, but couldn't with this noise; and the wind depresses me at any time. And there's something going drip-drip from the roof; it's driving me mad. If only the rain'd stop!'

Was he not going to put up a fight? Was he going to be beaten at the first barrier? No. 'The rain's lessening now,' said he, going to the window and looking round the blind, 'and the wind isn't what it was. If you drink this, it would help you to sleep.'

'Do you think so?'

'Yes, I do.' Oh, this accursed aptness and inaptness of ordinary words!

Touched, she felt she must not disappoint him. 'Well, if you make it hot, I think I might like it like that. It was kind of you to have thought of it.'

'All right, I'll hot it up for you, and put some lemon and sugar in it, shall I?'

'Thank you. It's very kind of you.'

With the glass in his unsteady hand, he went down to the kitchen again. 'What am I doing?' he asked. But whether or not he could say what he was doing, he could not stop. Like an automaton he pursued his tasks in the kitchen and returned up the stairs. Like an automaton – but he could hardly breathe as he carried the glass to Elinor's side. 'There.'

'Thank you,' said she, rising on her arm again. 'I think I shall enjoy this.'

And she sipped it.

He watched narrowly. Was there any taste in the drink . . . any burning? He did not know.

No, apparently not. She drank again, sighed, and pressed both hands round the comforting warmth of the glass. Then drank again. And after several such short drinks she took a long one, and emptied the glass. 'Yes,' said she, satisfied. 'That was comforting,' and she lay down again.

Done! He had really done it! Nothing could undo it now. Strange how simple it was when you came to do it. He even tried to stir up guilt and horror, but he could not. Tonight he could almost wonder what it was that people made such a fuss about. It seemed a terrible thing to read about, but a very natural thing to do. He gazed down at her; and behind his unworried gaze a glimmer of excited hope was ready to blaze up into an overpowering exultation.

She was speaking; quite naturally as if nothing remarkable had been done in the last minute. 'You go to bed now. I shall be all right.' And her voice was kinder than it had been for many long days.

He went, taking the glass from which she had drunk. In the kitchen he hid it away, and soiled another with new brandy and new water.

Then went to his bedroom, where he partly undressed and lay down to wait. He lay with his eyes open, thinking. Astonishing this feeling of ease and health! He had not felt quite such a peace for twenty years. It was as though some discord in his life had been resolved; as though a jumbled kaleidoscope had been given the correct turn, and the harmonious pattern that had then jumped into being had meant serenity and calm. He was reminded of times when he had hungered for an expensive thing – his guinea fountain pen, for instance, or his three-guinea overcoat – and, after doing battle for months with his parsimony, he had gone out on a sudden impulse and bought the thing, to find such immediate satisfaction and rest that he had never given a thought to the expense again.

Outside the wind seemed to be dropping, and the rain to have ceased. A little while ago the gutters had been overflowing on to the path, but now the flow had become a steady drip such as Elinor had noticed; and gradually the interval between the drips lengthened. Soon the drips were so far apart that one forgot them. The night was passing. A whistle from the railway, the rumble of a lorry in the Caledonian Road, the far-away hoot of a motor car seemed to make audible the silence that enveloped his house. And within its walls nothing seemed about to happen; the silence was as complete. Was the poison going to fail after all? Had it perhaps lost its virtue during its long incarceration in the shed? He really knew very little about it: perhaps exposure and evaporation had a neutralising effect on it, and it had long been powerless. To his surprise he had a momentary feeling that if this were so, he would be glad. Some burden, not yet shouldered, would never have to be borne. But the next moment that dull conscienceless automaton that had taken control of him cancelled the feeling. No, to the end of his life he would have to remember that he had done this thing, and he might as well have the reward for which he had paid the purchase price.

And while he was thinking this he heard a sound that stopped his heart and jerked him into a sitting position to listen. Yes, Elinor's voice calling, 'Paul, Paul . . . Oh, Paul!'

It was an agonised cry; and, all thought suspended, he rushed into her room.

She was sitting doubled up in her bed, her face contorted with pain. And the eyes that glanced at him were opaque with misery. 'Oh, I feel so bad again. I've been so terribly ill. It's like what it was that time before. Oh, Paul, it does hurt so!'

She spoke like a child; and Paul's compassion in that minute was an agony, too. 'Oh, my dear, what can I do?' he said; and his thoughts ran, 'I didn't mean it to hurt so much. I didn't! God knows I didn't! Oh, God don't make it hurt like that.'

'Oh, Paul, I can't bear it.'

He felt mad with distress: he had not known it would hurt like that; on his honour he had not known! 'I'll run for the doctor. He'll give you something to stop it. He must.'

'Oh, anything, anything!' begged Elinor, gasping. 'It's – it's unbearable. And it's affecting my heart, I feel as if I was suffocating.'

'Well, only wait. I won't be gone above a minute. I'll run all the way. Will you be all right alone for a minute?'

'Yes, I feel a little better now – just a little,' and she lay down again, and groaned.

Paul ran from the groan. He hurried on an overcoat and slippers and rushed from the house. He ran to Dr Waterhall's door and pushed the night bell. No answer at first, and the delay maddened him. He banged on the knocker, repeating all the time, 'Oh, God, don't make it hurt so much. I didn't mean it to hurt like that. Tell me it would have hurt, in any case . . . even if . . .' Steps within stayed his muttering, and Dr Waterhall himself came to the door in a dressing-gown, his silver hair and red-grey beard ravelled by the pillow, and his eyes blinking with sleepiness.

'Oh, Doctor, you must come at once. Elinor's terribly ill. She felt terribly ill this afternoon, and now it's got much worse. It's just what it was before, only worse . . . I don't like the look of her at all.'

Annoyance showed in the doctor's eyes: plainly he thought it a needless alarm and did not want to come out at this time of night. He suggested a treatment. He spoke of hot-water bottles applied to the stomach, sips of brandy and water, and a couple of opium pills that he would give to Paul. But Paul protested, 'No, no; you must come. I mean it. She's in pain, man; she's in terrible pain, I tell you. If you could see her, you would come. Oh, please, please.'

Dr Waterhall, looking at his white face, shrugged his shoulders desperately. 'Oh, all right. Very well. I'll be round as soon as I can.'

'Thank you. And, oh, Doctor, bring something that'll stop the pain. It's terrible to see her suffering like that.'

'Yes, yes,' agreed the doctor petulantly. 'I can soon stop that.'

Paul ran home, stunned from thought. He hurried up to the room, and found Elinor lying back, very weak. 'I think I'm dying,' she said.

'No, no,' he comforted. 'Dr Waterhall will be round any second now.' And he arranged the clothes over her, and sat at her side, holding her hand to comfort her, and occasionally resting his palm on her brow. Doing this, he was conscious of no hypocrisy, because he was incapable of clear thought. He was just an elemental human being, stabbed by sight of pain. And somewhere behind his mind the consoling thought was stirring 'It might have been like this in any case. It may have nothing to do with me. After all, it was just like this last time. Perhaps it's not my fault.'

The gate whined, and feet sounded on the steps. He gave her hand one last encouraging pat, and went down to meet the doctor.

'How is she?' asked the doctor, wiping his boots.

'She's easier. Yes, I think she's easier. Thank God.'

Dr Waterhall nodded, as one who would say, 'I thought so. A wholly unnecessary alarm,' and without another word went up the stairs; while Paul turned into the dining-room.

There he waited, listening to the steps and voices overhead, and still incapable of clear thought. He seemed to be just existing, not thinking; and in a very short time the door opened upstairs. He went out into the passage to meet the doctor coming down; and his eyes, not his voice besought the verdict. They stood opposite each other at the foot of the stairs.

Dr Waterhall looked at him sympathetically and nodded to himself, his lower lip pushing at the upper, while he thought. The doctor was a man of genial parts, but had he had all the geniality in the world, he must still have been pleased with an alarm, and especially one that gave him a leading part to play. 'You're right, old man,' he said. 'She's very ill; very ill indeed.

We shall have to get a nurse to her. I'll go straight away and get Nurse Owen.'

'But Doctor, is she – do you mean that she may die?'

'I won't conceal from you that it's very serious, old chap. More so, I'm afraid, than last time.'

'But, Doctor, she was perfectly well when I left her. She was well up to four o'clock. What can have caused it?' His eyes played over the doctor's face.

'Oh, it's simple enough, but I mustn't stay talking now; I must go and – you see, it's like this.' Even in this urgency, even as he hastily buttoned up his overcoat and pushed on his hat, he could not resist his desire to stand before Presset as the expert, the learned authority, with a bagful of medical terms to toss into a layman's eyes. 'You patients are all the same: you never take our orders seriously till the pain begins. I tell her to go carefully with her food, but she's too lazy to prepare herself a proper meal, and eats a lunch of cheese and tomatoes' – and he was away on an exposition of fermentation, pressure on the stomach, resultant pressure on a dilated heart, and the possibility, that must not be overlooked, of collapse.

Paul listened with eyes fixed on the lecturer. 'I see,' he kept saying. 'I see'; and in the first pause, he asked, 'But have you stopped her pain?'

'Oh, yes, yes,' said the doctor, brushing the interruption aside. 'I've given her a couple of opium pills that'll —'

'And you think that it was that meal that caused it?'

'Oh, no doubt, no doubt,' repled the doctor, impatiently, unheedingly, unaware that Paul had seized the words to himself for a balm, eager only to continue the exposition as they walked to the door. He was now explaining compensated heart, aortic valves, and mitral disease. Elinor's condition, he said, was common enough among women. He himself in his long experience had known only too many cases where death had been caused by heart failure following gastric-enteritis – 'but we'll hope it won't come to the worst,' he concluded, on the door-step. 'Now you go and sit with her. That'll ease her. Give her brandy in sips if she needs it; and I'll have the nurse round in two two's. So-long for the present, old man. We'll hope for the best.'

Slowly Paul mounted the stairs and went into the room. Elinor turned her eyes towards the door as it opened.

'How do you feel now?' he asked.

'Very drowsy. I shall be asleep in a minute. I think it must be the pills he gave me.'

'No pain?'

'Not at the moment.'

'Thank God. Well, shut your eyes and try to sleep. It'll do you good, and I'll be here.' She shut her eyes as if she had not the will to hold them open. And Paul drew up a chair and sat at the bed's side, looking down upon her. His conscience was still numb. Now that her pain was over, he felt the same woodenness of emotion as before. He could think, but he could not feel. And his thoughts were activities of his reason, and of no other part of him. His reason was telling him, as he sat there, a mere watcher and waiter, that old Dr Waterhall had suspected nothing; that Fate had played into his hands by giving her an attack of gastric trouble a few months ago and showing her to the doctor then in a stage of collapse. Now precisely the same thing had happened so that it all looked simple and straight-forward. So natural that there was nothing to suspect anywhere, and he could hardly suspect himself. She might have died in any case. Yes, that first attack had come without any aid, and it was quite possible that her illness of tonight had followed the normal course, and that his act had played no part in it. Quite likely, since that stuff in the tin, for all he knew, might well have lost its potency. Yes, it might be that he had had nothing to do with it at all, and anyhow, he could always think so.

His thoughts were wandering on, when Elinor lifted her head and looked at him. With an effort she brought her hand from under the clothes and touched him.

'Yes?' he asked, taking the hand.

'I'm going, I think, Paul,' she said, her hand gripping his convulsively.

'No; you'll be all right,' he protested.

'Oh, but . . . I feel so bad . . . my heart . . . it can't last, I'm sure. Paul, if I'm dying, I'd like to say something . . . I'm . . I'm sorry if ever I've been unkind to you, but I was never very well—'

'Oh, no, no! Don't say that,' he begged, a shaft of shame piercing him. 'It's I who've often been unkind. And I'm sorry, I'm sorry.'

'No, you've been a good husband . . . very patient with me, I'm sure . . . You'll bury me with mother, won't you? I'd like to lie in Trusted churchyard. I've always wanted to. It's so peaceful there . . .'

'You're not going to die,' he said, trying to sound cheerful and patting her hand. 'Not a bit of it!'

But she shook her head. 'I think so . . . I feel like it. Give me a kiss, Paul.'

He stooped and kissed her on the forehead, and with her weak hand, she turned his face round that she might kiss his cheek. 'I'm going to try to sleep,' she said. 'Stay with me, won't you?'

'Why, of course. I shall be with you all the time.'

'And let me keep your hand. I shan't feel so lonely then.'

'Of course, my dear.'

She did not shut her eyes, but stared at the ceiling. At first her respirations were like sighs, and then like gasps, and Paul watching, believed that, though her eyes were open, she was lapsing into unconsciousness. Why did not the doctor come with the nurse? Had he had some difficulty in finding her? She was breathing still, but very strangely, and he was sure that she was unconscious. 'Elinor,' he whispered; and 'Elinor' again, more loudly; but her eyelids did not flicker, nor her hand in his give any answering sign.

Soon she was breathing no more.

Dead! Elinor was dead. He rose and walked to the window and back again. He stopped: and stood still as a statue, the only living person in that house. Over the bed with its rumpled clothes and recumbent, open-eyed figure, the canopy stretched, tidy, orderly, indifferent; and the bed looked like a catafalque. The house, as if in reverence, had put on the perfect silence. And Paul stood there, thinking. And suddenly he knew that he was looking at the future, not at the past. What now? Useless to pretend that his heart wasn't astir, so as to be ready, when he should let it, to bound with relief and joy. Useless to pretend that a white light of exultation wasn't ready to rise in his head. Useless to pretend that a thought, like a glorious visitor, wasn't knocking to come in and cry, 'You are free! You are well-to-do, because you've known all along that Elinor never touched her will! You are well-to-do – *you* who have never had a penny of your own! Your future is secure; all anxiety and doubt are over; and you can go to Myra when you will! She will have you, beyond the shadow of a doubt. All, all that you ever dreamed is coming to you. . . . Is it possible? . . . Life, intolerable yesterday, is now an ecstasy. . . .'

He turned back to the window, and looked out. The dawn was grey over the house-tops. And his lips, independent of his will, whispered to the world of freedom, 'Myra . . . Oh, Myra, my dear . . .'

PART II

Chapter One

A year or two after the young Paul Presset set off from Petfield in Sussex to attempt his fortune in London, another young man of Wildean in Hertfordshire came slowly up a rutted cart-track, chewing the stem of a long javelin of grass and contemplating a similar errand. Only, since he was in some ways a very different young man, the fortune he proposed to build in town was very different. At the top of the farm-road was a moss-green gate, and here he came to rest, with an elbow on the gatepost. He looked up and down the lane on to which the farm-road issued, and, ascertaining that he was alone in a green world, gave himself up to a term of dreams. Behind and below him in the hollow could be seen the buildings of Handip Farm where he worked; and this, perhaps, was a symbol. He was a tall young man with wide shoulders and thick limbs, and for the present he lacked grace; there was still something of the countryman's lumber in his movement and heaviness in his stance, and one could not have sworn that his legs, in their breeches and gaiters, were not a trifle bowed. His face was round and frank, with thick but pleasant features. Not much of his character was written as yet on that bare and open sheet, but certainly the butcher's curl, allowed to flower into the world from under the peak of his cap, suggested the usual measure of vanity. His hands, lifted now from the twin pockets of his breeches, were large and squab, with bitten nails; and from this one might have deduced that he was given to times of discontent and secret thinking; as was the young Paul Presset before him; as youth should be. In one of his hands was a twopenny cherry-wood pipe, which he now lit with pride and self-satisfaction; evidently he had not been a smoker long. The sun-touched evening air is a stimulant for any man; and Jack Boltro felt healthy, vigorous, potent and sanguine; as his own creation, the blue smoke, rose and drifted away. 'I shall not go on with it,' he said to himself; and later, 'No, I shall not go on with it.'

He meant that he would not work for his father any more. His mind's eye saw old Sam Boltro, content to be a small and struggling tenant-farmer, with a fringe of grey beard round his chin, and a suit of broad-cloth for chapel on Sundays, and, unlike his brother farmers, a round condemnation of tobacco and dances and beer. Jack Boltro felt a proper duty to, and a proper liking for, his father, because there was something quite simple about the lad, but he felt also that he was built for larger and livelier things than his present labour. He despised the tranquil country and longed for the speed and excitement of London. He saw no reason why he should not make a name in London; had he not taken prizes in the Sunday school? Was he not an adept at all sports on the green, and did not the girls cast eyes at him? 'Yes, I shall do it,' he said; and later, 'Yes, I reckon I'm as good as the others, and better than most.'

After this grandiloquent utterance it may seem strange that the desire of his heart was to become a policeman. But it was so. Ever since he and the other boys of the village read in a lurid weekly about the exploits of the old Bow Street Runners, and promptly organised themselves into a squad of officers who chased a fugitive every evening over five miles of country and clenched their teeth with sadistic delight as they snapped the shackles on him, he had longed to be a real policeman and chase real fugitives. He longed to achieve dazzling feats of detection and capture; to snap the bracelets round this criminal's wrists and twist the cuff of that one's jacket, and march them both off to gaol (he had no knowledge of any difference between police station and gaol); to get his name into all the papers, break all records in the matter of early promotion, and return to an admiring village in the beauty of an Inspector's uniform. He and Eddie Brast, his crony and confidant who shared the ambition, used to have long talks about it behind a gorse-brake on the common, or in their secret wood. It was from Eddie that he learned that they had just formed, up in London, a new department of the police, a body of specially picked men who spent all their time in the detection and chasing of prisoners. And they got special allowances and special rates of pay, these men! But neither Eddie with the excited lips nor Jack with the gazing eyes knew that these specially picked officers wore no uniform but went about looking exactly like other men, a fact which would have shocked and disappointed them both. The London police, Eddie explained, preferred the country lad, because he was so much bigger and stronger; and Jack Boltro, listening, unwittingly braced back his good shoulders; and neither knew that, while it was true that the Metropolitan Police preferred the recruit from the country, their reason was less because his body was big than because his brain was empty; it was much easier to fill the countryman's brain with their own goods when the London lad's brain was already so full of cunning and sauciness. Further, said Eddie, the London police were paid better than the county constabulary, and were certain of pensions, and had ten times the opportunities of getting to the top; it was a fact, an absolute fact, that the first thing they told you on joining was that you could rise, if you had the brains and the gumption, to the top ranks of all, excepting only that of Commissioner, which was always filled by a swell. The Force was quite different from the Army, where you had the devil's own job to get above the rank of sergeant-major; every constable with the brains and the gumption might hope to be a Superintendent, which was as good as a colonel (said Eddie), or at least an Inspector, which was pretty much the same as a major. And John Boltro, listening, had not the least doubt that he possessed the brains and the gumption.

He did not doubt it now, as he smoked by the gate, some time after Eddie had gone off and, apprenticed himself to a hairdresser. 'I will do it,' he said.

So John Boltro came up to London, as Paul Presset had a few years before him. He had little difficulty in getting accepted as a constable. The medical examination he walked through as through tissue paper, and the educational examination in those days was only a little more than nothing. There being no Police Training School as yet, he was merely given a few weeks' drill with other recruits in the yards of Wellington Barracks – while the guardsmen, to whom the barracks belonged, stood around and laughed. Roared with laughter, till the healthy cheeks of country lads were redder than ever with blushes. From this drill John Boltro emerged somewhat flattened beneath the impression that his duty as a policeman was, not to think and act for himself, but to obey, and that on the hop. No one had ever spoken to him so before. After this instruction he was duly sworn in. He swore that he would well and truly serve the Queen in the office of constable; that he would act as a constable for preserving the peace, and for preventing crimes and offences, and for apprehending offenders against the peace; and that, while he continued to hold the said office, he would discharge the duties thereof to the best of his skill and knowledge, faithfully, according to law, without fear, favour, affection, malice or ill-will.

He was now a constable, if a gaping and anxious one.

His trim new uniform was a comfort – a very distinct comfort – and in this he was sent on to his first beat in the charge of an old bearded constable, who was to show him the ropes. It was in the M Division, and the beat was a Southwark beat; and this was the old constable's instruction, as they patrolled the grey and garbage-strewn streets. ' 'It 'em first,' he said. ' 'It 'em first before they 'it you. I know they've told you not to draw your truncheon till you've kerried persuasion as fur as it'll go; well, that's all right, but I've always found that the best persuasion in these parts is me fist or me knee, with the truncheon to follow, if the other arguments fail. The people round here understand that sort of talk, and respect it too, what's more. Patience may be all right in the A Division, where everyone's respectable, except round about Great Peter Street; but they laugh at it down here; what they like is for you to 'it 'em first. At least, so I've always found.'

'I see,' said John; and in his naive enthusiasm he began to pour out his hopes of early advancement.

The old policeman laughed. And laughed a second time, after they had turned a corner. 'Gahn! It's only the lucky ones that bring that orf! You've got to get promoted to Sergeant in a certain time, or never at all; and it isn't easy if you haven't had the education. Yuss. Miss the last train, and you stay on the platform for ever. Look at me. Twenty-seven years in the service, and still where I was when I started! Thank God that in a year's time I can get me maximum pension and clear out. Of course you may have more book-learning than you look to have, but you don't strike me as the kind they make a sergeant of easily. Still, keep 'oping. Keep 'oping. It never 'urt the Christmas goose yet.'

Then, in what seemed a very few days, he found himself patrolling his beat alone. And, so doing, he felt abnormally conscious of his appearance. As he walked along he was seeing all the time a tall, wide-shouldered, youthful figure in a helmet (which felt extraordinarily high), a blue tunic with metal number and letter on the collar, a belt with a truncheon of crocus wood slung behind, and shining regulation boots. But he also felt very proud. He felt that the whole authority of the State spoke in his words, and he was eager for an opportunity to exercise it. If nervousness rose, his swelling self-confidence rose with it and shouldered it away: he was of a different metal from that old disgruntled P.C., and soon, quite soon, he would be famous for his vigorous actions and smart arrests.

This conceit suffered more blows in a month than in his whole life before. Patrolling his beat with fine conscientiousness at two and a half miles an hour, he soon learned that, down certain streets, his uniform inspired, not awe, but fun; that his word of authority provoked, not apologies and quick retreats, but jeers and brickbats and laughter; and that his fresh, round, country face below the helmet, and his tall, beefy figure in the new and spotless uniform, so far from being a source of admiration and envy to the slum-dwellers of London, was apparently the richest mine of jests they'd struck for many a day. Few experiences could be more embarrassing than to walk along a street, at two and a half miles an hour, while the wags called from windows and doors, ' 'Ave you got the hay in yet, Jack?' or 'How's the potato crop doin' in this weather, Mr Boltro?' or 'Gahn, he's sulky! They wouldn't let him take the bull to the cow.' One night, and its memory made him blush for twenty years after, he saw a crowd of men quarrelling outside a tavern, and, anxious to show his power, told them to stop their fighting and move on, or he'd take their names and addresses; and they, after one look at his rawness, forbore to quarrel with one another any more but hustled him all together, tripped him up, trampled on him, and escaped with his lantern and helmet as souvenirs.

It was almost as bad at the station. His fellow constables made fun of his rustic words, his rolling ploughboy walk and his astounding ignorance of this London of theirs. They would greet his entry with 'Heave up, boys!' and 'Whoa, now!' as if they thought his proper place was behind a plough; and when he was sent on an errand into another sub-division, they would call after him, 'If you can't find your way back, Jacky, ask a policeman.' Hard drinkers, many of them, they would take him, in their leisure hours, to distant pubs and there try to make him drunk, with much laughter at his timidity and his manifest desire to escape. The Inspector sometimes roared at him, as if he thought him a bumpkin; and more than once placed him 'on the report'. Very early he learned that he was not all he thought himself as he stood by the gate above Handip Farm. He lodged in these first weeks with a married policeman; and there was a time when a Metropolitan police constable with '321 M' on his tunic, in the privacy of his lodging, cried.

His ambition, however, was a powerful enough horse to carry him passionately through the obstacles. These early discouragements must either break him or make him; and, thanks to the ambition, they made him. They mixed a new and very secret humility with the conceit. 'I'm not what I thought myself, that's plain; but I damned well *will* be. Life's not going to be so easy as I imagined, but it's not going to beat me. We shall see!'

His heart was set on being transferred to 'the Department' (as the Criminal Investigation Department was always known) where he need wear a uniform no more. His colleagues would have laughed, had he told them of his hope, but he resolved that, if it meant a change in his walk and his talk, and a vast addition to his learning, well, he would work these miracles. He kept his eyes (which were small) wide open, so as to learn all he could from the bearing and behaviour of successful officers; and especially he modelled himself on Second Class Sergeant Winser, standing like him, bearing his shoulders like him, and walking like him. His back straightened, the roll went from his walk, and if ever there had been an ellipse between his legs, it was visible no more. He kept his ears (which were large) wide open, listening to the vocabulary and accent of impressive inspectors and station sergeants, and he remembered the one and practised the other. He noted well every rusticity at which townsmen laughed, and, though the laughter hurt him, he corrected its cause. When inspectors rebuked him, he bit his lip and reined in his spurred temper and was properly subservient to them, waiting for the day when *he* should be an inspector and put others on the report. He read and studied in his spare time, tingling with pleasure at the thought that, while others were drinking, he was reading, and slowly, secretly, passing them by. He trudged along his beat, working it well to time but dreaming all the way of some spectacular deed which should overthrow the old legend of his stupidity and start a new one of his brilliance; for policemen, he perceived, were no less like sheep than other men and would all say together what the bell-wether said. So his eyes whisked hither and thither over the road as he saw himself surprising three burglars at their work, or charging into a gang of toughs who were committing robbery with violence, or, best of all, discovering a dead body and catching the assailant unaided. In all these scenes he quickly 'knocked off the criminals and took them to the nick'; to be publicly commended by the Police Court magistrate the next day, and later rewarded by the Commissioner.

But the distinction halted in its approach. His vanity was pleased when he brought in a few drunks, or moved on itinerant musicians and obstructing crowds, or spoke severely to the prostitutes (who interested him very much) or ordered the slaughter and removal of an injured horse; but, whenever he had a share in a violent and important arrest, the glory seemed always to go to the sergeant or the inspector. Both his vanity and his kindliness were pleased when he helped the old and the blind across the road or took fatherly charge of a strayed child, or stopped a hawker being cruel to his moke, or, on his night duty, knocked up the early risers (at a fee of sixpence a week); but these things added nothing to his career, and at last he resolved, since glory lay not in his path, to go out and look for it.

Within another beat of his section were situated those streets which the station called the Death Alleys. You saw them beyond the dark railway arches at the ends of Connecticut Street and Strawberry Lane, for they lay in the triangular space between two brick viaducts that converged towards the river. The arches, low and long as corridors and hung with smoke-black lichen, were a fitting gateway to the paved alleys of low, flat-fronted houses, with their broken windows and tottering chimney stacks and roofs of black fluted tiles. The police were instructed never to visit these lanes except in couples; but it was accepted by all, from inspectors down, that they did not visit them at all. Here were kip-houses notorious as the meeting-places of gangs; here were yards where the van-lifters met; here were chalked messages on the viaduct walls, 'The next flatty (policeman) that comes this way gets the same as the last'; here were doorways and double-bedded rooms to which the sailors from Rotherhithe were lured by women to the koshes of their men, who laid them out, emptied their pockets and carried their bodies through the unpoliced streets to the entrance of the arches. It was no uncommon thing for the police to see the bodies of sailors, nearly dead, lying under the arches in the light of early morning. 'No, we don't go down there,' they said to P.C. Boltro. 'We get someone to "come copper" and then go in force and collect our man. If you want promotion, that's your spot, but it's promotion to heaven and more glory than most of us want.'

John Boltro got himself posted to this beat. Ambition was stronger than fear; and at four o'clock one morning, when he was yawning along Connecticut Street and thinking that in two more hours now he could report off duty at the station, he saw a woman cross the light of a dingy gas-lamp and turn under the railway arch, with a man one pace behind her. He stopped. He knew the woman, for he had shadowed her as far as the arches before. She had not seen him because the winter night was like pitch and his bull's-eye lantern, after a fashion of those days, was inside his great-coat to keep him warm. Had his opportunity come? For hours the streets on this side of the arches and the alleys on the other had been silent as if everyone slept; never before at so late, or so early, an hour had he seen the victim brought home; if he followed them and saw violence or murder done, he might be able to knock off the criminal while no one was covering the deed, and before the woman could raise the neighbourhood.

Securing the strap of his truncheon round his wrist, he followed. He crept along the tunnel of the archway, fear hammering at his heart, and his conscience rebuking him for hoping the man was 'for it', but what would you? Ambition, stronger than fear, is also stronger than pity. The alley beyond the arch was empty, and the houses quiet; there were lights behind some of the blinds, but the sole purpose of these might be to fight the vermin in walls and floors. The woman and the man turned the first corner, and John Boltro quickened his pace to lessen the interval between them. But no sooner was he at the corner than he saw, thirty paces on, a scuffling in the dark, and the man's body felled to the stone flags. Then another man stooped over him, while the woman stood by. On tiptoe, wondering if his last minute had come, John Boltro ran forward; the man, who had handed a watch to the woman with the words, ' 'Ere, take the kettle for Christ's sake!' turned at his step; and immediately, before the man could bring his cosh into play, John swung his truncheon, not on to arm or elbow as usually instructed to do, but down on to the back of his neck to make sure. The woman screamed and screamed, and, terrified, John rushed and dragged his prisoner, half silly from the blow, round the corner and towards the archway. He was a little wizened fellow and powerless in John's hands, even if his senses had been fully about him. Screaming, the woman ran after them, which doubtless helped matters, for she, like them, was soon away from her friends and in the healthier neighbourhood of Connecticut Street. Here John whipped out his whistle and blew three short blasts, as if his life depended on it. The sound split and shivered the silent fabric of the night, and soon the nearest constable was racing wide-eyed towards it. John bade him get help for the victim in the alley and continued to drag his catch to the station. The woman had run.

It is a fact, regrettable but natural, since one's own life is always so much more important than anyone else's, that he was hoping the victim would be found to be dead, and he to have captured a murderer, so that the noise of it might echo proportionately far. Thus was John Boltro, an ordinary goodhearted lad, prepared to see two people die, to the greater glory of John Boltro. The victim was not found to be dead but John got his lighter ration of glory. Certainly, at the station, after he had told his tale at the Charge Room desk, the Station Officer said, 'Bloody young fool! Trying to show off!' but at court the magistrate commended him very cordially, and in due time the Commissioner rewarded him with five shillings. His colleagues chaffed him; but there was something of admiration in their chaff. The new and better legend had begun.

Pleased with the new reputation, he laboured to build it up; and soon his need of self-esteem compelled him to believe it bigger than it was! So that he took a shock when, seeing a notice in *Police Orders* asking for volunteers for the C.I.D., he put in his application, only to be told by the Local Detective-Inspector that 'his education was nothing near good enough'. Somewhat sour at this, he went off in rebellious mood, but again the grim determination shut his fist and threw out his chin; he told himself that nothing would be gained by sauce – there was no sense in quarrelling with his bread and butter or in cutting off his nose to spite his face – and he would serve himself best by being pleasant and amenable to the old fool of a Detective-Inspector. He would use the old fool as a stepping-stone. And thereafter he was a model of smart obedience at the station; and, on his beat, he was a machine for memorising the facts he would have to know if he was to pass his exams, and spelling over and over again the long words that had tripped him up. And in time there appeared a new order for police constables to be transferred to the C.I.D., and the local Detective Inspector, pleased with his willingness and quiet efficiency, and anxious to display his own power, asked him, 'Do you still want to go to the Department, Boltro?'

'Yes, sir,' said John.

'Well, shoot in your application. I think I can work it for you now.'

'Thank you, sir. Thank you very much.'

A week later the notice appeared that he was transferred on probation to the C.I.D. He wrote home at once to explain what an honour this was. Only the most trusted, he told his parents, were selected for this difficult and responsible work. He was now Detective Boltro. And he let them understand that there was danger in the detective's life; he *had* to tell his parents this, because, like other men consumed with the desire for glory, he could not, for the life of him, prefer his parent's ease to his own renown.

The rest is the story of the irresistible advance of a single-track mind. Detective Boltro began with a very ordinary brain, but a human brain of any order is a remarkable instrument, if its every power is directed to one end. And John Boltro was determined that, if industry could do it, he would be Superintendent Boltro before he died. All his colleagues assured him that memory was the detective's best tool, and he knew that he had an excellent memory – indeed, an uncreative brain nearly always implies a tenacious memory. He studied

Informations and the *Police Gazette*, memorising the faces of wanted persons or old lags; he explored the *Modus Operandi* list, conning the methods and habits of specialising criminals, as a hagiographer might con the lives of the Saints; he sucked the brains of old detectives and mentally pigeon-holed all that seemed of use; he cultivated informants (criminals prepared to 'come copper', that is) like a gardener cultivating orchids, till he could boast that he knew of every criminal in the division, every thief, fence, pimp, crimp, coiner, load-carrier and putter-down. Money didn't matter: he gave far more to his informants than he asked to have refunded. Sleep didn't matter; he was out and shadowing for twenty-five hours (as they sometimes put it) out of the twenty-four. Marriage didn't matter; he was satisfied that for the present a wife and kids would hinder him in his career.

And every rogue for miles around knew him. There is an odd camaraderie, a certain mutual respect that sometimes approaches affection, between the police and the criminals with whom they do battle. Out of business hours, so to speak, each exchanges the time of day and a joke, as they pass in the street. 'Bully Boltro' they called him, sometimes in admiration, and sometimes in annoyance after he had handled them roughly, away from Authority's eyes – if, say, he had used his truncheon or his fist in ways which they knew as well as he were against the regulations. They knew him as a big, determined, but not unkindly young man, of six years' service in the force, splendidly self-confident, fighting fit, and five times more powerful than loose-living toughs like themselves. And if he knocked them off, they understood that it was his job, just as roguery was theirs, and were more likely to blame the narks than him.

And all this time he was watching other successful men, noticing their language and deportment, and correcting and adapting his own; and all the time he was studying books that would help him in his trade, with the result that quite a deal of education filtered into him, as a kind of waste-product from his real work. He was astonishingly different in manners, mien and eye from the self-sufficient young oaf who had rolled up from Hertfordshire several years before. All agreed that he was marked down for success, and consequently many thought him over-rated.

He was not too squeamish. 'In the Force it was a case of everyone for himself,' he would say. So sometimes he kept good information to himself till he could handle it, since it wasn't the stamping out of crime that interested him so much as the advancement of John Boltro. And when after three years he was promoted to Third Class Detective-Sergeant and transferred to the North Central Division, he was not above collecting the credit for work done by younger detective officers; after all, this game had been played on him. Out of Authority's sight his methods, as we have seen, were not always according to the rules: he would trap suspects into incriminating themselves before he cautioned them, and he would frighten their wives by saying, 'Of course, you may get into trouble yourself if you don't tell us all you know;' which was quite untrue. But, as he said, his job was to make an arrest, and a little of the blind eye and the Nelson touch was sometimes needed. He would trump up a case against a man he wanted to get, or touch up the evidence against one who was surely guilty. It was his business to get a conviction, he said, and to put dangerous people into clink, and if sentimentalists and armchair critics had his job to do for a month, they'd soon get shut of some of their nicety.

On the other hand he delighted in his kindness to his prisoners when he'd got them, and his tact in handling them. When bringing them from a distance he would buy them food and fags and newspapers, and talk to them as men. 'I can do anything with them by a little humouring,' he would boast. 'Why, some of 'em have said to me, "It's all right, Mr Boltro; we shan't do the dirty on you, because you always treat us like gentlemen." I don't know how many birds I've brought in in my time, but I don't suppose I've used the bracelets a dozen times.' He could be kind to their families, too. Distress might reach his imagination slowly, but when it lay beneath his eyes, it stirred him always; and many more times than once he had put his hand into his pocket to help a starving family whose man he had taken for theft.

For some years he was Local Detective-Inspector in the R Division, and then – the farm-lad's dream-picture was nearly created now – they appointed him a chief inspector and transferred him to the Yard. As exhilarated as a schoolboy who has got into his First XI, he sat at his desk in a room at Scotland Yard, and felt himself one of the big men of the land. Truly astonishing the difference between this large, hearty, hard, egotistical, but not ill-natured man and the young John Boltro who loafed by the gate nearly thirty years before. If the child is father to the man, environment is the mother from whose womb the child gets him. Let that environment be made up of success, praise, the obedience of subordinates, the sycophancy of prisoners, power over the telephone, power with A.S. (All Stations) messages, a steady (and secretly surprising) rise in one's scale of living and style of dress, and young John Boltro will certainly father Chief Inspector Boltro, sitting in his room at Scotland Yard. His hair, now grey, is short and crisp and well-ordered; his eyes, if small and rather hard, can twinkle with laughter and friendliness; his mouth is a grim, thin-lipped, straight line which some would call strong but others merely truculent; only his nose is unchanged: a little thick and coarse, it suggests the farm-road down which he came. This is the face of a man fairly competent at his job, and very unimaginative about it. The rarer thoughts of finer minds do not trouble him; it has never occurred to him, for example, that crime and sin are not necessarily synonymous terms; and when he writes his reminiscences (as he certainly will, for all chief inspectors do) he will be quite unaware that he is revealing in every line, not only the fine detective whom he likes to see in his mirror, but also the slightly ridiculous (bless his heart!) egotist and braggart whom he will never see at all. He is well-dressed always; and when he has to attend a ceremony, he wears a white waistcoat slip and a pearl pin in his black silk tie.

It is an idea of Scotland Yard detectives that no one would know them for what they are; and it is true that their disguises are often remarkable; but when they are in their ordinary civilian kit, the original burly, uniformed constable will sometimes shine through. This was so with Chief Inspector Boltro. At first sight you might not have suggested that he was a detective; but once you have been told this, you would have cried. 'Why, yes, he looks like it! That face and figure belonged certainly to a blue uniform once upon a time.'

He was a hale and vigorous man, because successful and happy. He was married now, and had four children, three girls and a young knicker-bockered detective, all of whom delighted his heart. He had many friends because he was good company and could be thoroughly sentimental about the pals who had worked with him on jobs, the Chiefs under whom he had served, and the bright lads who had served under him. He had enemies too – those who swore he went into the witness-box and collared the credit for their work, or that he didn't stand by them when they were in trouble for fear of his own skin – but what successful man is without his traducers?

One thing only he needed to complete his happiness. He longed to be put in charge of a murder case whose notoriety would sweep his name to the farthest cottages in the land. But such a piece of luck was rare as a lottery prize. Murder was as one in a hundred, or less, compared with burglaries, warehouse robberies, jewel thefts, forgeries and confidence tricks; and of the thirty or forty murders a year only one or two achieved the real resounding notoriety, and why should one of these plums fall to him? But it might; and he waited and hoped, and waited and hoped. One got a little tired of this daily unadvertised drudgery on lesser crimes.

And then one morning his Chief, the Assistant Commissioner, summoned him to his room. 'See here, Jack,' he began, lifting some foolscap sheets from his wide mahogany writing table, and pointing with his other hand to a leather easy-chair, 'but first take that pew.'

The Assistant Commissioner of that day was one of the most popular the Force had known. Though his neat, slim figure, fine face, and silver hair, to say nothing of his title, proclaimed him to his subordinates as a highly educated swell who moved in the best circles, yet, liking and valuing the breezy informality of the London police, he would play his part in it and, dispensing with the 'Mister', greet superintendents and chief inspectors by their Christian names.

'See here, Jack; this is a job for you. It's on your old ground, in the North Central Division, down Islington way; and I suggest you take Sergeant Doyle with you, as he knows the division so well. It looks to me as pretty a case of murder as you could want, and I'm not sure that there aren't a couple of them mixed up with it, a young woman as well as the man.'

Chapter Two

Six months before that happened, Paul had heard the young clergyman's voice: 'Forasmuch as it hath pleased Almighty God, of this great mercy, to take unto himself the soul of our dear sister here departed, we therefore commit her body to the ground. . . .'

The young clergyman, his surplice blowing in the October wind, stood at the foot of the open grave and tossed with one hand a sprinkling of earth into its depths, while with the other he tried to hold his violet stole from flying out like a pennon. On the north brink of the grave stood the mourners: Bessie Furle, Mrs Worksop, some strange relatives of Elinor, and Dr Waterhall, because, as he had said, 'I was fond of Elinor.' A step in front of them, since in their delicacy they had allowed him pride of place, stood Paul, in a black overcoat, with his black bowler hat held unconsciously against his breast, and his sparse hair at play with the wind. A little way behind this group, most ostentatious of all in his delicacy, stood the exquisitely dressed young undertaker, his keen, clean-shaven face a perfect professional blend of sorrow, reverence, and sympathy. His men, pretending to no such interest but quiet nonetheless, stood at a little distance among the ancient tombs, in their worn frock coats and chafed silk hats.

There was another figure looking down upon the grave: a figure in Sicilian marble and standing on marble steps, at the grave's head, though rolled back a few feet by the stonemasons today; the figure of an angel with a basket of flowers on her left arm and her right hand extended to scatter blooms on the dead.

This right hand, if you could not see the marble flowers in its fingers, seemed to be pointing for all time to the grave. And the angel was the one conspicuous thing among the tombs of Trusted churchyard. Massive, flamboyant, the only piece of florid Victorian sculpture in that ancient quiet, it stood white and incongruous among the tilting headstones of a bygone day, the few wooden crosses weathered and mossy, and the low green mounds which had no memorial.

Paul looked at this figure. Strange revelation of Elinor's character! Elinor, parsimonious, undemonstrative, self-sufficient, seemingly unaffectionate, had raised in her love and tastelessness this monument to her mother, and spent, he could see, a large sum upon it; and on its marble step she had inscribed, 'In memory of Ada Morse, my beloved mother who fell asleep. . . . "Peace, perfect peace." ' Poor lonely Elinor had one affection in her life and clung to it as to a rock. The child lives in us to the end, and now Elinor, large and heavy with middle age, lay once more in her mother's lap.

She lay in the middle of a green acre that sloped downward from the south wall of the church to a row of ancient limes. Not a little church, though Trusted was a thinly populated and somnolent village now, bestirring itself only on market days, but a noble pile, built in the great days of the cutlers, with high castellated walls, proud buttresses and pinnacles, and a spire that proclaimed to the green miles of Essex the old glory and the old pride of the cutlers. The south porch, with its priest's chamber above it, looked down upon the undulating slope of the churchyard; and one might wonder, as one stood among the tombs, what coloured processions of master cutlers, guildsmen and brotherhoods had passed beneath that porch, before the glory went north with the trade from Trusted. The pride of mediaeval Christianity was here, and the mercy too; for within the embrace of the churchyard wall were some thatched white almhouses, that the living might share God's closeness with the dead.

The dead. Unshepherded thoughts wandered through Paul's mind. Had any other of these ancient dead come to their graves as Elinor came? They had lain here for a hundred years, and no one would know now. '. . . it hath pleased Almighty God to take unto himself . . .' but *had* it pleased him to take her, or had she been sent to him? The young priest, rather new to his task, Paul suspected, and rather pleased with his voice and his expressive reading, never thought for a moment that unusual meanings might have crept into his words today. 'He cometh up and is cut down like a flower. . . . In the midst of life we are in death; of whom may we seek for succour but of thee, O Lord, who for our sins art justly displeased. . . . Thou knowest, Lord, the secrets of our hearts. . . .'

And then: 'I heard a voice from Heaven saying unto me, *Write*. . . .' The young priest had raised his voice as he said this, and for a trice Paul's left hand flew to the nape of his neck.

Now the priest, lifting his eyes to a wrack of clouds, was offering some prayers, while Paul's thoughts rambled over the last few days. Everything had assured him that he was perfectly safe. Everything had established his security. Dr Waterhall had not hesitated to sign a death certificate, and his friendliness and helpfulness had been proof that no hint of doubt had entered his mind. Bessie Furle had said with tears, 'I always expected something like this. I was afraid she'd go suddenly like this.' His parents had expressed no surprise, his mother offering to come up at once and 'see after him until he could get someone'. At the school Heasman, Inglewood and Sandys were equally sympathetic and empty of surprise. So too Mr Nevern, the lawyer. Driven by an excitement that his better parts disliked but which was probably inseparable from one who had been poor all his life, Paul had gone to Mr Nevern, a little quiet old man, ostensibly to learn if Elinor's will expressed any particular wishes. And when Mr Nevern was gone to find the will, Paul had thought, 'If it is altered, good. At least I shan't have done it for *that*. And if it is not altered, good also'; but with all his heart he was wishing only one thing. Mr Nevern returned and they read that Elinor had bequeathed all her real and personal estate to her husband absolutely.

The undertaker had been no less sympathetic. Indeed he had been the very oil of sympathy. He had been the distilled essence of courtesy, understanding and consideration. He had come on soft feet into the house, never speaking above a whisper to his men, and sometimes laying one palm in the other as a priest does in his pulpit. 'Leave all to me, sir,' he had said. 'We will take all off your hands'; and in answer to any wish expressed by Paul, 'I quite understand, sir. I perfectly understand. Naturally, sir . . . we shall do exactly as you wish.' Before seeing the undertaker, Paul had given great thought to cremation. His brain, ceaselessly working in his lonely house, had not been likely to overlook the idea of cremation. But whenever he had said to himself, 'Yes, that's what I'll do,' he had heard Elinor's words, 'Bury me with my mother in Trusted churchyard,' and they pierced to his pity. The idea of cremation would have horrified her, and oh, he wanted to grant her her last wish. He had wronged her enough already . . . if of course he *had* hurried on her death, which was by no means certain. . . . All the kindness in him recoiled from the cruelty of denying her last wish. He *could* not do it. Funny! Funny that it should be impossible to do her this unkindness, and yet possible to . . . mix that drink. Funny, too, that for the present he could feel no remorse: it was as if his conscience, active elsewhere, had been injured at this point and made insensitive. And when he had put tentative questions to the undertaker about cremation, and learned of new forms that would have to be filled up and a new doctor who would have to be called in, his desire to be kind had been reinforced by caution. Caution, not fear. He didn't believe that there was a thousandth chance of suspicion ever stirring against him. An exhumation? Such things simply didn't happen to oneself; they happened to the millionth person, like death in a railway accident or the prize in a lottery. No, he had felt strangely 'big' and strong in the last few days, and free from the old exaggerated fears; and he had given Elinor her wish. So it was that his kindness, his vanity, his caution and his sense of perfect safety had shaped together his decision to lay Elinor in Trusted churchyard.

And now, as he gazed down upon her lying where she longed to be, in this peaceful and lonely churchyard, where no one surely would worry her any more, he felt glad that the memory of a kindness should be later than the memory of a wrong.

The priest, apparently a High Churchman, was now extending his warm living hand over the grave, much as the angel spread a hand of stone, and saying, 'Eternal rest grant her, O Lord, and let light perpetual shine upon her. May she rest in peace.'

And that seemed to be all. He mumbled the Grace, took off his violet stole and kissed the cross at its neck, and walked towards the church.

Paul walked a little way among the tombs. Reading their dimmed inscriptions, he remembered that the undertaker, when begging that all arrangements might be left to him, had asked him what words he would like inscribed on the base of the headstone; and he, Paul, had temporised, saying he must have time to think. Well, what was he going to put on? 'In loving memory'? But he revolted from the insincerity of it. 'Who died. . . .'? 'Who fell asleep. . . .'? 'Who passed away. . . .'? He wandered on among the graves, looking at other men's inscriptions; and gradually his decision formed. And here was the obsequious undertaker approaching, doubtless to ask if all had been as he wished and if he were ready to return to the carriage. Paul turned towards him.

'I have decided on that inscription,' he said. 'Yes. . . . Personally I prefer reticence. Absolute reticence and restraint, see? I don't care for all this flowery stuff.'

'Absolutely, sir,' said the undertaker with great emphasis, his nod implying that he counted Paul among the few elect who saw this truth. 'I agree with you every time.'

'Yes . . . so I'd like you just to put on it, "Elinor Presset, wife of Paul Arthur Presset. Died . . ." and the date.'

'I quite see, sir. I'll instruct the stonemason accordingly. And any text beneath?'

'Yes. . . . Yes, I've chosen that. . . . I'd like you to put just. . . just "Grant her Thy peace." '

* * * * *

If he had had any fear of exposure, it diminished with every day. And finally it died. Not in a living face anywhere could he see a trace of doubt or questioning. And October deepened into November, and already it was a month since that midnight and grey morning which he had shut away in a locked cupboard of memory. Or rather, it was, as it were, a dead spot in his memory: if it quivered with life for an instant, he would quickly tell himself, 'She would have died very soon in any case, from all the doctor said about her heart. And quite likely her illness was developing along its normal course that night. I've a strong fancy that there was nothing much wrong with that brandy except its quantity, as the doctor suggested.' And the place in memory was dead again.

He lived alone in the house because he could not immediately get rid of the lease. Mrs Briscoll came in morning and evening to 'do' for him. Daily he set off to his school and taught his boys English and Latin and French, and ran up and down with them at their football in Canonbury Fields. And in the evening he walked home, surprisingly happy. He would not have believed that the farther side of such an experience could be so quiet and unremarkable. The one memory anaesthetised, all was amazingly peaceful. Dreams spent the evening with him, and hope walked always at his side, a dear and flattering companion.

He lived on a few shillings a week. Not that there was any scarcity of money, but because it gave him a keen pleasure to reduce his expenditure to a minimum and so accumulate money for Myra.

Daily he hoped to hear from Myra. When she heard of Elinor's death, surely she would write such sympathy as was possible. Each morning as he came downstairs he looked on the doormat for her letter. But the letter was never there. Either she had not heard, or, if she had, her modesty and decency insisted that *she* must not take the first step. Yes, he must take it; but modesty and decency told him that he must first let a little time pass. Say three months. And in the meantime he might hope to meet her by accident, which would be the best solution of all. He took to wandering in Clissold Park on Saturday and Sunday afternoons, on the chance that she too might revisit the old scenes.

Autumn was nearing its end, but, turning to goodness before death, it gave to London some lovely days of pale blue and paler gold. It dressed Clissold Park in a beauty almost equal to that of her spring. The great solitary trees on the parkland grass were decked in their red and russet and yellow. The limes were empty, but the beeches spread their branches of copper-brown and apple-yellow leaves against the faint blue arras of the sky. Some of the larches were a sighing yellow, but others were on fire against the dark firs. And here and there a fir stood dark amidst a crowd of yellowing trees – dark and heavy and stern, but splendidly constant. Paul walked on; and on either side of him, the long black ribbon of the asphalt path was bordered with yellow leaves. He crossed the bridge and, wandering round the curve of the New River, saw that here also the yellow leaves lay under its rural banks, at rest on the staid green water. If he turned his eyes to the water and away from the women with the prams, the running children, and the old men on the park seats, he might have been strolling in Petfield woods.

But he never found Myra here. And soon anxiety stirred. That young man who had met her! Had he – no, Paul shook his head: he believed, nay, *knew* that she belonged to him, at least for some years yet. Still, however he might deny the anxiety, he was soon gripped by an impatient hunger for reassurance. Let only two months have passed, and he would go and look for her. He must not let her escape him now. Yes, two months. Always a little superstitious, he kept to the exact date; and on the evening which closed the second month after Elinor's funeral, he set off for the Chiswick High Road.

His heart was a-tremble with excitement and nervousness, but also high with hope. It was a Monday, and she should be out soon after seven. As last time he made of the bank's vestibule a watch-box and there waited, dodging his eyes between the traffic to stay them on the door of her shop. The shop-fronts were ablaze with lights and illuminations, and the pavements were awash with people, because the Christmas shopping was on patrol in the Chiswick High Road. In the past the holly and tinsel and fairy lamps of the Christmas decorations had always saddened him, but tonight, in the clear, frosty air, they sorted well with a burgeoning festivity in his heart. Fifty he may have been, but he felt no different from a youth standing beneath the lattice of his first beloved.

There was a time between seven and half-past when he feared lest she had quitted this place of business, but even as he argued with the fear, he saw her stepping on to the pavement. He did not hesitate; he went across the road and faced her.

'Myra.'

'Oh!' She stared, frowned, gasped 'Oh!' again, and trembled.

'I came on purpose to find you. I found out where you lived from Mrs Bohntree—'

'Oh, but you shouldn't have done that—'

'Yes, but wait. Let me walk a little way with you. I've a lot to tell you.'

'Oh, ought we to?' she objected, her thinking disorganised.

'Yes. That's all right. Please . . .'

They walked on together, and from the side of his eye he could see how her arm was shaking.

'Did you know about Elinor?'

'No.' She turned to him abruptly.

'She – she died a little over two months ago.'

'Oh, my dear!' Myra laid her finger on his hand. 'I'm so sorry. Poor Elinor.'

'Yes, it was the same trouble that attacked her about a year ago. You remember . . .'

'And what are you doing now?'

'Waiting for you,' he said with a sad little smile; and as she turned from this, added, 'I'm living alone for the time being. I just go back and forth to the old school, and Mrs Briscoll looks after me. Myra, that's why I wanted to see you. You see, such a lot depends on what you say now – all my next steps. Myra, are you still free?'

She answered in a low voice. 'Of course.'

'And' – he could scarcely strengthen himself to ask the question, for fear of what he might hear – 'do you still feel the same?'

Again, in the same low voice, she answered, 'Of course.'

He felt for her hand and pressed it. 'I knew it! I didn't really doubt for a moment. My darling!' And, still holding her hand, he asked almost merrily, 'Hasn't anyone been making love to you?'

'No.'

'Sure?'

'Oh, well, there was one youth who seemed to want to make a fool of himself. He was quite a nice boy, but I wouldn't let it be more than friendship. I – I *couldn't*.'

'Bless you . . . But don't hurt him too much . . . One can suffer so abominably over it.'

Myra smiled. 'Oh, I don't think he's in danger of dying over it. It was never a very serious attack.'

'I'm glad. Well now . . . you see, dear, if I thought you would marry me in about a year's time, I should know what to do now. Will you?'

She stayed silent.

'Will you?'

'Yes. Oh, yes.'

Her low-breathed conviction was a shaft of incredible happiness: it seemed impossible that to him, Paul Presset, such a shaft could have come. 'Myra!' he murmured; and then, pressing her fingers, suggested, 'And we'll go and live in the country and never worry about anything any more?'

'Oh, it can't be Paul! It's too good to be true.'

'It *shall* be. Perhaps we'll go to Sussex, and perhaps to your Lakes. Perhaps to the Downs, and perhaps to the Fells.'

'Oh, Paul! . . . But I think we ought to wait more than a year.'

'My dear, I can't wait for you. I'm not as young as I was.'

'Still . . . I don't think . . .'

'I don't mind waiting, so long as we meet sometimes. Only do let me see you, and as often as possible. I'm so terribly lonely. I really haven't a close friend in the world. Couldn't we meet sometimes – far away from anyone we know?'

'Oh, but ought we to? So soon?'

'Yes . . . Life is so short. We needn't be seen; it's just a matter for you and me alone, and what the hell does the world matter? You want to, don't you?'

'You know I do.'

'Then we will.'

'But it's winter now.'

'We'll go far away to the seaside where there's sunlight and we are unknown and "no one can track us to our hurt". Oh, we'll be so happy! Myra, come somewhere where I can give you a kiss.

I've been hungering for you so long. Where's the nearest green place to this disgusting highway?'

'Acton Green.' The old laughter sparkled for a second in her eyes.

'And where's that?'

'It's round here. It's not much of a place. Not a Clissold Park.'

'But it has a high concealing shrubbery somewhere, I doubt not?'

'I really forget,' said Myra.

As they walked along, he asked her about her job, and she explained with little amused skips that 'he gave it to me because he said I was ladylike! I hope you think so, too'; and 'I get a pound a week and a commission of threepence in the pound!' Live on it? Certainly she could. She lived with a *most* respectable working-class family, paying fifteen shillings a week and sharing a room with the daughter. Oh, yes, she got quite tired sometimes, since her hours were from nine to seven on most days, and she never got away before eight on Fridays and nine on Saturdays. But Thursdays were the great days: she got off at five o'clock then! Five o'clock, my sweetheart!

'Looks as if Thursdays and Sundays are going to be our only possible days,' grumbled Paul.

'M'm,' she nodded. ' 'Fraid so, my angel!'

They were now at Acton Green, and he led her towards a hidden place, where he took her in his arms and kissed her. She brushed her lips on his again and again, passionately at first, and then sighing, 'Oh, we've no right to be so happy. Not yet.'

'Yes, yes . . . my beloved.'

'It's not very wrong, is it? It seems so cruel.'

'It's right. All love is always right.'

So they resumed their meetings and wove anew the texture of happiness that had been so roughly torn. But now, as before, they were hindered and handicapped by the difficulty of a secret and satisfying meeting in winter. It was not difficult to spend Sundays together. If the weather was fine and crisp, they converged by separate roads on to green and unfrequented places, and there wandered in the lanes and woods; if it was wet and blustery, they took different trains to seaside resorts where at least there were picture houses and tea rooms and catering for such as they. But on the weekday evenings they could do but little. Paul tried to persuade her that one could hide oneself in parts of London better than in the loneliest village, but she would not listen. She had a horror of being seen with him so soon after Elinor's death, and was not happy unless the green miles stretched between her and Islington.

And soon these infrequent and fettered meetings were not enough. They wanted more of each other. They longed for a room to themselves, a warm fire, and a locked door. And on their Sunday walks they discussed how they might achieve these. Yes, how? They could hardly hire a room for a few short hours on a Thursday evening. He could not come to her house, nor she to his. On a Saturday night, it would be difficult to go to an hotel when she could not join him till ten o'clock. And anyhow, every hotel in London, it seemed to her, was too close to Islington. Still, this last was the only thing to do, if sometimes they were to have long hours alone together. 'I have it!' exclaimed Paul. 'Let's go to a hotel whose very expensiveness will mean that no one who knows us is likely to be there. Why not? I have the money, and if we were married, I should be spending it on you. There'll be no danger; not the slightest. We shall arrive at night when it's pretty quiet; you can come veiled and pass straight through, and I shan't delay at the reception bureau, you can be sure. Besides, good heavens, who's going to know *me* in a hotel like the Great South Western? We get over-anxious, you know. We both do. I'm pretty good at it, though I'm getting much better of it lately; but you're a double-dyed panicker, *you* are! And I'm not going to let panic hold us back from our happiness. Life's too short, and I'm too old. Just once a week, my dear. Shall we do this?'

She consented to do it, and they put the plan into practice. They would go as 'Mr Preston and wife' to the Great South Western or other of the more expensive railway hotels, Myra passing quickly through the entrance hall, and Paul lingering not a moment longer than he need at the reception office. They would stay hidden in their room, and leave early in the morning if it were a Monday, or late at night if it were Sunday evening when Paul, prospecting ahead of her, reported that the entrance hall was deserted and the dark street empty and still. 'You go first,' he would say, 'and I'll pay the piper and follow.' So she slipped out and wandered guiltily along the pavement, anxious to be past the hotel windows, while he stuttered and fumbled at the window of the reception office, more nervous that he would have liked her to know, and, gathering up his change or perchance forgetting it, followed after her with heated cheeks. And they hastened along the lamp-lit street, glad when they had turned a corner and were out of view of the hotel.

But there was no need for this fear. They were not seen in a hotel.

Chapter Three

Mr Worksop, the dentist, like his neighbour, Mr Presset, prided himself on a feeling for nature. It was, to tell the truth, a new feeling in him, and it had been inserted by Mr Presset; but, now that his instruction was complete, he equalled his master in enthusiasm. He now felt a pity and some small contempt for those who spent their leisure in the drab London streets instead of going forth to find the loveliness that was England.

Encouraged by this enthusiasm in his disciple, Mr Presset had founded a walking club. A few of them were men of Mr Worksop's age, in the late thirties; but more were contemporaries of Mr Presset, in the forties or early fifties. They were thus of all shapes and sizes, some stout and lively, others thin, be-spectacled and earnest, and others neither thin nor stout but small and nondescript and probably fussy. They admitted no ladies, for a pretty humour ran in the club, and they were wont to say to their wives, 'No, my dear, no ladies. The whole point of the club is that we get out of the racket and tramp in search of peace.' They were not afraid of 'a bit of weather' – a hardihood which they published proudly to lesser men – and this had inspired their founder to give them a name. It was a name that seemed very amusing to him and them, but caused embarrassment to those whose conception of humour was different: they called themselves, 'The Antique Weather Tiles.' Gaff Ellison, a solicitor's clerk and one of the stout and lively, had wanted to call them 'The Twelve Apostles', chiefly, said he, because there were forty of them; but the stricter ones thought this rather profane. Like most local clubs it had started with a flourish, enrolling a membership of forty zealots, which quickly dwindled to fifteen.

But these fifteen were enthusiasts. As many of them as could fared forth on Sunday mornings, let the weather be what it might. They assembled at a chosen house in most appropriate kit; thick boots or shoes on their feet, mackintoshes over their shoulders, satchels angular with sandwich tins slung at their hips, stout ash sticks (with spikes) in their hands, and dogs (one or two) at the ends of leashes. With their ordnance maps in their hands or in their pockets, they streamed off. Burnham Beeches knew the little company well; Epping Forest saw them pass; the North Downs heard their voices; and Windsor Great Park, when the rust was on the bracken; and Virginia Water, and Hainault Forest, and, best favoured of all, the Lower Greensand Hills.

In the club's first months of life Mr Presset had usually been the leader, and a very good leader too, if a little inclined to show off his country lore and pose as a naturalist. He would lead them among the bracken and pine of the greenland hills, picking for their instruction bell-heather and ling and bilberry and thyme. He would expound the geological formation that caused this outcrop of sandhills between the chalk of the North Downs and the clay of the weald. He spoke so often of 'the lower greensand' that 'The Lower Greensand Hills' became a standing joke of the club as well as their favourite destination. He even induced them once, in the club's most vigorous days, to come to the Lower Greensand Hills before dawn on a Sunday morning of spring, that they might hear the opening chorus of the birds and strive to identify their songs. And there they had stood beneath the pines, with their coat-collars turned up and their hands thrust deep in their pockets, while he announced the names of the soloists as they piped up one by one: the skylark first; then the cuckoo far away; then the thrush, the robin and the blackbird, till all voices were woven into one luxuriant tapestry of song.

But in the months before his wife's death he had seemed too anxious, or too preoccupied, to come often with them, and in the months after her death he had neglected them altogether; but this had seemed very natural, and they followed Mr Worksop instead. 'We mustn't worry little Presset,' they affirmed good-naturedly. 'The wound'll heal up in time, and then he'll come walking again.'

One Sunday of fine frost fully twelve of them crowded into Mrs Worksop's sitting-room. Beside Worksop himself, long, cleanshaven and earnest, the little company included George Buckwell, a brother dentist, John Henderson, a traveller in leather goods, Steve Condon, a chartered accountant, young Brentwood, a bank clerk, Percy Linyard, a music teacher who played the French horn in small theatre orchestras, and Gaff Ellison, the stout and lively old solicitor's clerk, whose voice we have already heard; and Tosh Johnson.

Tosh Johnson, so called by the others because he always signed his Christian name 'Thos.', was a very thin and active little man of sixty, a retired hosier with fussiness and self-importance written in his every movement. His walk was a hurrying stride, the body swaying forward at each springy step, the head peaking and peering as if he were resolved to be 'in' everything and hoped always for a chance of being informative and helpful, and the high shoulders, when he slowed his pace and swung his stick, taking on a self-satisfied and consequential swing. A busy-body like Dr Waterhall, but without the doctor's jollity, he had insinuated himself into a dozen committees in Islington Vale and was the most restless sidesman at his parish church. It was inevitable that such a bustling little old man should become first lieutenant to Worksop.

And now Mrs Worksop's room ran with that noisy jocosity which seems peculiar to the male on holiday, the female showing no signs of it.

'How is it you're not at church, George? Sorry to see this!'

'Well, if Tosh Johnson can swing the lead, *I* can, can't I? Tosh is a blooming sidesman and goes round with a bag; he's almost as good as the bible-puncher himself, you might say.'

'Yes, it's a bad example he's setting us.'

'Pastor Greenfields for me today,' said Tosh Johnson sententiously.

'Pastor Greensand, you mean,' corrected Gaff Ellison. 'Ha, ha, ha!'

'Mrs Worksop'll represent us all at church,' suggested her husband in his quieter voice.

'Fine. That'll be swell,' said Percy Linyard, the music teacher. 'And you'll pray for us, won't you, Mrs Worksop? Especially for young Jim Brentwood here; he needs it. Most of the rest of us are past praying for. Too far gone in sin.'

'Speak for yourself!' shouted Gaff Ellison. 'I'm a saintly man. I'm going to say my psalm on the hillside. What's more I'm going to sing a hymn.'

'Angels and ministers of grace defend us!' muttered Percy Linyard.

'Yes, I am – and that was Shakespeare by the way, Percy. I'm going to sing "Oh, happy band of pilgrims"; and I wish you'd brought your French horn.'

'Not that old cap again!' protested John Henderson to Steve Condon. 'Steve's got the same old cap. I'm sick of the sight of it.'

'Don't you listen to him, Steve,' cried Gaff Ellison. 'No walk is complete without Steve's cap. It's our mascot, you might say. Personally I shouldn't go with you at all if he didn't bring it along. And I may say I don't usually associate with such company.'

'What I'm thinking,' said Steve, who was a wag of the long and languid pattern, 'is that all men look fools in knicker-bockers, but I don't really know which looks the worst, the thin ones or the fat ones. For my part I'm inclined to give the palm to the thin ones, but – I don't know – when I look at Gaff—'

But Gaff Ellison was shouting, 'Gentlemen. Gentlemen. I'll ask you all to observe George Buckwell's boots. Those, gentlemen, are what all the best walkers wear.'

'Well, I've come to do some walking, I have!' retorted George Buckwell, hoping that he was keeping up the level of wit.

'I haven't!' declared Gaff. 'Not really. I shall wait for you fellows at the local hostelry.'

'You seem to do more talking than walking, all of you,' laughed Mrs Worksop.

'That's what I say,' agreed Gaff. 'Let's get off, Worksop. We'll take him off your hands for a bit, Mrs Worksop. He's trying in the home, I'm sure.'

'Ah, be off with you!' laughed the lady.

'Now will you only listen to that?' begged Gaff of the company. 'There's a way to talk to a man old enough to be her brother, ha, ha, ha! Push off, boys. We're not wanted here. Lead on, Tosh, my little sunshine.'

'Whither are we bound, Gaff?'

'Why, to the Lower Greensand Hills. Where else?'

They flowed out of the house, but so ample was Gaff Ellison's jocosity that he had to look back when they were all on the pavement and leave a last offering with Mrs Worksop. 'We'll see that he behaves himself, Mrs Worksop. You know what these grass-widowers are.'

'That's right. Have a good time.'

'And mind you behave yourself too, while we're gone.'

The little company turned into the Caledonian Road, and mounted a tram, while the ruder urchins of the gutters shouted their good wishes for the journey.

An hour or so later they were on the far and southern side of the Hackhurst Downs, and here they found a thick white mist between the chalk hills and the sand. Great was their joviality then. Boys, what a mist! They bent their backs to the bracken-covered slopes, those in the rear calling out to those in the van, who were Worksop and Tosh Johnson of course, 'Hey! Go slow, folks. Keep together, lads, or we'll be lost. There's a mist way back here, whatever you may be getting into up there.' And as they climbed on, their voices sang through the fog.

'Say, boys, but it's a lovely view, isn't it? Look, I can see a pine tree ten yards away! Anybody seen Tosh! Is he still in sight? Hold back, Tosh, we're not as young as you, you know; and I'm not as thin as I was' – this was Gaff Ellison – 'Hey, Captain! Ask Tosh to get out his map and tell us where the blazes we are. Are we up in the clouds?'

For Tosh Johnson loved them to be lost in the woods so that he could open out his ordnance map, put on his spectacles, and trace wise lines on it with his forefinger. As they got higher, blither spirits, feeling that they were lost on a cloud-capped mountain, began to yodel, and the cynics begged them to desist.

'What we want is Mr Presset here, to point out the birds,' said Gaff, intending a joke, since no one could see anything ten yards' distance from his eyes. 'That there is a swallow, and the other's a corn bunting.'

'No, I reckon it's a mercy we can't see anything,' said one of the cynics. 'We don't have to look at the trees and the birds and the flowers, and be told their blasted names. This is what I call a proper walk: nothing to see and therefore no blasted education.'

'I suppose we're going all right,' called another. 'I seem to be going up hill; is that in order? Are you sure we're not going back towards London?'

'You leave it to Tosh,' recommended Gaff Ellison. 'I'm following Tosh. Though I wish to God he'd go slower. He don't weigh what I do.'

'Oh, Tosh is no good,' shouted Linyard, for Tosh to hear. 'That ruddy map of his is all wrong.'

And from up the height came Tosh's voice, to justify his reputation, 'We're on the northern slope of Pitch Hill.'

'Are we?' retorted Linyard. 'Well, it's extraordinarily like Baker Street in a fog.'

At the lunch hour they sat down in the dead bracken and under the bare dwarf oaks, and complained that they could not see their sandwiches or what Mr Worksop was drinking, way over there in the mist. They were witty at the expense of Tosh Johnson's pipe, begging him to take the foul thing to the window. They ordered young Brentwood to make up a fire and burn their litter; and when he very readily started upon this game, searching around for dry fir-cones or twigs, they jumped up and joined him in it, as engrossed as boys at play in the garden. They poked its poor smoulder with their sticks; they stood around it watching its brief history, till the last ember died; and then they stamped its ashes into the ground, and called, 'Fall in! There's dirty weather to wind'ard, but what does a brave Tar care? Lead on, old salt.'

Then up and up, their boots snapping the twigs and trampling the cones and dead leaves, while dark firs and slender birches loomed on either side of them like shadows in the white fog.

'Tell that poultry in front to go slower,' begged Gaff, seriously tiring.

'Are we anywhere near the top, Tosh?' called the one he addressed.

'Ought to be, I think,' Tosh called back, rather doubtfully.

'Go on! He doesn't know where we are. But push on. We are bound to get to the top of somewhere at this rate.'

Sometimes one of them burst into a suitable song: 'Beware the pine tree's withered branch, Beware the awful avalanche. . . . Excelsior!' or 'They climbed the steep ascent of Heaven, mid peril, toil and pain; O God, to us may grace be given, To follow in their train. Amen'; and so onward and up, in a straggling line, the lean one vigorous still, the stout ones tiring and lagging. And then, of a sudden, the mist was flushed through with light; and the voices of Worksop and Johnson, at the head of the line, exclaimed, 'Great Heavens!' And all of them, one by one, emerged from the mist into a brilliant sunlight as a man comes up from water; they rose out of a damp cold into a dry Alpine warmth. Above the blanket of mist the sun was hot as a summer's day, just as it is above the snow line in Switzerland.

'Holy saveloys!' ejaculated Gaff, as he panted up into the brilliance.

'Well, that's the first time I've been above the clouds,' said Linyard.

'I've done it in Switzerland,' said Tosh, obviously proud to display his knowledge of foreign parts.

They saw now that they were on a littered path that ran up through a wood of tall larches and Scotch pines. Their feet crunched on pine needles and bark, brittle twigs and dry turf, as they paddled through the sunlight and shade. On either side of this red path the sunlight striped the boles of the trees and lay in discs and spangles on the undergrowth. That the summit of the hill was just before them they could tell by the unbroken blue of the sky that stretched behind the last tall pines. And very soon they saw that Worksop and Johnson were halted and standing at gaze like climbers who can get no farther. They stood by the seat called "The Judge's Seat" because a famous judge placed it here to command one of the most famous views in England. Quickly the others came abreast of them; and all gasped in astonishment and admiration. Never, probably, had the judge foreseen a view like this.

A vast sea of white cloud stretched from the cap of the hill over the whole weald to the South Downs. And only the higher summits of the South Downs showed above it, like blue islands far away. This vast white sea, with the sun blazing on it, was still and yet stormy: some of the clouds seemed to rear back and roll over like huge breaking waves. And the sunlight glistened on their crests. To the right the summits of Highdown and Telegraph Hill rose like nearer and wooded islands, and to their left the other brows of the greensand range abutted like headlands into the dead white sea. And over the whole glistening cloudscape the dome of sky was stainless blue.

It silenced their levity. They stood before the wonder in a trance.

'Who could have believed that we'd have found this up here?' said Worksop. 'It shows that it pays to come out in all weathers.'

'You wouldn't believe that it was England,' said Tosh Johnson. 'I've never seen anything better in Switzerland.'

'And to think that there's a whole world at the bottom of that sea, villages and pubs and churches and schools!' murmured Steve Condon.

'And probably a parson praying for fine weather,' suggested Gaff, recovering from the seriousness.

'It's easily the finest sight I've ever seen,' began another—

But just then Worksop touched Johnson on the arm. 'Look!' he exclaimed. 'Good *night*!' And he pointed to a couple sitting farther down the slope of the hill, in the attitude of lovers, and staring before them at the dazzling spectacle. Apparently the tired company had approached the hill-top and spoken too quietly for those two down there to hear. 'Keep back. I'll eat my hat if that isn't Mr Presset.'

'Who? Where?' exclaimed the others.

'Don't let him see you. Keep back a little. It wouldn't be fair to let him think he's watched. See? There. It *is* him, isn't it?'

'Well, I'm damned!' muttered Gaff. 'Yes, that's Presset. My golly! He hasn't been long in finding consolation, has he? And she doesn't look much more than a girl!'

'Now we know why he hasn't wanted to come with *us*,' laughed another.

'I never knew he was a ladies' man,' said Condon.

'He's been a damned dark horse, if he is,' said Linyard.'

'Shh! Don't let him see us. That'd be a bit too embarrassing for us all,' said Worksop. 'Let's walk along to a farther brow where they won't see us. . . . Well, if that doesn't take the cake: Mr Presset and a young lady! Finding consolation so soon!'

'Well, why shouldn't he, if he wants to?' demanded Gaff. 'Good luck to him, I say.'

Now, walking on, they had a new topic for their wit.

'Well, worth climbing for, that,' said Gaff. 'Two marvellous views: a blooming ocean of clouds, and old Presset with a girl.'

'Enjoying the view, eh?' said another. 'Gum, he'd have had a good view behind him, as well as in front, if he'd turned round and seen Tosh standing there!'

'It only shows what you'll find on the other side of the mist,' suggested a third. 'If the real truth were known about Tosh, for instance. . . .'

'Yes, and I wouldn't answer for Percy either.'

'Oh, but I never suspected any good of Percy. But little Presset! That's another story.'

'He's formed a new club, that's all; with a membership limited to two.'

'But with power to add to their number what?'

'Now then, Gaff! That'll do; that'll do!'

Chapter Four

Not in all their lives had Paul and Myra been so happy as in these first months of the new year.

Paul seemed permanently possessed by an exhilaration whose physical effect was like the delicious well-being and thirst that follow a long day's labour in the hayfield. Fear lest the past should lift its face and call to him troubled him hardly at all: if sometimes he gave a thought to that millionth possibility, he would quickly be done with it, telling himself that it was but a momentary spasm of an old timidity, whose power was fast leaving him. Getting into bed, he would think that another day – one more day – had added its little stone to the mounting cairn that buried the past. He was twenty-four hours securer than yesterday.

In Myra's happiness there was not even this tiny flaw. She, though friendless and poor and, as she insisted, *passée*, was loved by a man who seemed kindness itself, who had no idea but to serve her, who needed her, who rejoiced in her existence, who not only forgave but loved and delighted in her weaknesses and vanities, with whom she was always at her best, wise, witty and gay, and to whom she so obviously ministered refreshment and recreation by her embrace. All that was empty mother in her joined the woman who had starved so long, and she knew no happiness like feeling that she had given him ecstasy and comfort and filled him with peace. Her own body enjoyed his caresses, but her heart enjoyed still more the knowledge that she was the medium of his bliss. It is possible that there is no love sweeter than that of two 'faded' persons, who missed it in the freshness of youth.

How they enjoyed talking over their plans! In the coming autumn they would be quietly married; or in the following spring, at the latest. For a while they would take a smaller house in London – ever so small, Myra begged – and he would continue in his present work, saving money against the sunny retirement. They had both been poor enough to enjoy adding up the sum they might save if he worked for another three years. 'A man can honestly retire at fifty-five, can't he, Myra?'

'I should think he could retire whenever he likes,' she laughed.

'Oh, no,' said Paul, whose conscience was as ordinary as ever, save only in one dead spot; 'a man ought to do a job of work in the world – at least till fifty-five.'

'But I've no such feeling of duty to the world, my precious,' said Myra. 'It can go and stew in its own juice, for all I care.'

'Ah, but then you're an unscrupulous woman,' he retorted, and kissed her. 'I've noticed it.'

More immediate were their plans for their next meetings. It was still in winter, and they were still faced by the old difficulty of meeting often enough in a room behind a closed door. They argued and argued three plans. The first was that she should give up her work and live a free life in a room of her own at his expense. But Myra hated this, both because she had all his happy interest in the accumulation of savings, and because she fled from the thought of taking his money before they were married. The second was that she should get new work in a new district as 'Mrs Thomas', whose husband was a traveller who could return to her only occasionally; but she was frightened of this – frightened of the lies which she could never sustain and frightened of exposure; but he was so persistent, so enthusiastic, and she so incapable of refusing him anything when he looked disappointed, that she consented to do this, but 'not for a little while yet; not till she'd got more used to the idea'. So the third plan came into view: that in the meantime she should come sometimes to his empty house, under cover of the winter dark. Just once or twice. There alone could they have all the time to themselves without fear of the eyes of landladies or the too-marked indifference of reception clerks; without need of making false entries in hotel books or scanning the faces in restaurants. There too, and this was a point never far from the minds of either, they could save their money for the great days ahead.

She would not have been Myra if at first she had not shaken her head very dubiously over this. Once she was behind his door she would not mind, she said; but how was she to approach the door? Someone would be sure to see her from across the street; someone would see her leaving in the early morning; she had suffered agonies that last time, when she slipped from his house. Oh, why wouldn't the world let people be happy together?

Paul, feeling stronger and bigger than she, and proud of his courage and venturesomeness, argued that there could be no full living without risk, and that an element of danger always doubled the joy. 'Don't be so timid, my dear. No perfect thing can be created except at a price.' Let her risk it once or twice. No one in the road knew her by sight; and if she did not come too often, she might pass for a mere inquirer, or even for the charwoman! That was if anybody saw her in the dark, which was unlikely enough. People were not as interested in them as all that.

And in the end she came. He had the waiting house prepared for her, flowers in the room at the back, a bright fire burning up its chimney, and a table laid with the chocolates and the soft drinks that she liked. And she came: she chose her moment when the dark street was empty, and came quickly along the pavement, veiled but trembling, though not a blind moved in the windows of the houses. As she ran round to the back door, her heart pounded against her breast like the fist of a terrified man pounding against a door that held him trapped. Paul opened to her; and she stood, pale and breathless, in the passage. He shut the door behind her, and took her into his arms.

Chapter Five

Dr Waterhall was still lonely in the evenings. And lively too. The completion of a day's work always involved for him an onset of high spirits; and it was sad to have to sink himself and this fine zest into an easy chair of an empty room. Good spirits cry to be shared with someone. He wearied of turning the pages of his paper over and over, even if it contained a letter from him to the Editor; he grew bored with his novel; he began to sicken of the pictures round his study wall, the coloured photographs of Venice and Rome and Interlaken, and the sporting pictures with their stale jokes beneath; he hated the sight of his roll-top desk, littered with books and magazines and dusty letters. He was bored, and he dropped his hand over the arm of his chair till his fingers touched the ground. He felt no different from a boy who longs to go out and find someone to play with.

And usually he went out. He put the Homburg hat at an angle on his head, lit a new cigar, buttoned high the collar of his overcoat, and went out into the illuminated night. Sometimes he went to a theatre or a cinema, but more often to the door of this friend or that, where he apologised for disturbing him and declared he wouldn't come in if he was likely to be a nuisance. Of necessity the people, invited him in, and he entered, vowing that he would not stay long. And he sat down by their fire, and stayed there for the rest of the evening, arguing politics or religion or blood sports with the man, while the cigar danced at his lips.

When Elinor Presset died, it occurred to him that Paul would now be lonely. It must be gloomy, indeed, living without so much as a housekeeper in that large, grey house, and it was certainly his duty to go round sometimes and give the man his company. So, as soon as delicacy allowed, he made a habit of coming, once or twice a week, round his corner into Elm Tree Road, and taking the glimmer of his cigar up Paul Presset's front steps. Sometimes Paul came to the door and nodded him in very pleasantly, but on other evenings his knock and his persistent ringing drew no answer, and he wondered where the devil Presset go to – till he was completely satisfied, nay, exuberantly sympathetic, when Paul confessed that very often he couldn't stand the loneliness a minute longer and went off to a music hall or a cinema.

At first Paul was alarmed by this obstinate sociability of the doctor. Supposing he turned up one evening when Myra was there! But, as in other alarms, he quickly saw that there was little in it. The doctor came so often when he was in, and the house empty, that his visits, to be sure, were almost a good thing, as a preventive of suspicion. And if by the remotest chance he did turn up when Myra was there, well, he just wouldn't open the door to him. Of course it was well within the doctor's habit to wander round the house to the back, in search of a lighted window and a good friend, but he wouldn't be made suspicious by the light behind the blind of a back room, because Paul had told him that, if he went off to a cinema, he always left one light burning to admonish marauders. This careful explanation had been a necessary precaution on Paul's part, since the doctor was quite capable, on seeing a light in the empty house, of deeming it his duty to pick the lock, or raise the neighbourhood, or call up the police, in the interests of his friend. Indeed, there was nothing he would have enjoyed more.

Often the arguments over the doctor's cigar and Paul's pipe were heated enough; in the first place, because a mischief in the doctor prompted him to say provocative things so that he could enjoy a hot argument, and in the second place, because both were conceited men, Paul considering himself better read and more modern than this old reactionary, and Dr Waterhall never forgetting that he had enjoyed a university education and stood in a better social position than this little pedagogue, and each being exceedingly intolerant of the other's kindly tolerance of his stupidity.

But both had good humour enough to cool down later in the night, and to outbid each other in generous acknowledgment that viewpoints could differ, and to part the best of friends on the door-step.

Until their great argument on everlasting punishment; though even on this heated occasion they saved the argument from flaming into a manifest quarrel. But seldom had the vanity of each been so pricked. The doctor, while conceding that the material fire of hell was an outworn notion, swore by everlasting punishment; Paul, whose vision, if dim and frowning, flashed to places far beyond the doctor's sight, would have none of it. Dr Waterhall, raising his voice to overlay his host's, declared that the issue was definite enough; either we believed the Bible and Jesus Christ or we didn't, and he, for his part, was a Christian and did. Paul, lifting his voice from under the doctor's, retorted that it wasn't anything like as simple as that: he had read some Higher Criticism and knew that the Greek word *aionios*, which the translators had rendered 'everlasting' really meant 'for an aeon, or an epoch', or, perhaps, 'for many aeons'. The doctor, exasperated, not by the argument which he didn't intend to listen to, but by the false quantities which Presset had given to *aionios*, raised his impatient voice and said, '*I* know that. Good God, I know all about *aionios*. I've *done* Greek, man! I've done it in the original. You can't be a doctor without knowing Greek. You forget I've been some years at the University.'

'University!' scoffed Paul, with the traditional answer of one who had not enjoyed that advantage. 'University! I don't know that *that* proves anything. Mind you, I don't say that you didn't learn anything there, but I do know that a pass degree can be nothing more than a receipt for money.'

'If you think you can be a doctor by just paying money—' began Dr Waterhall.

'And it isn't only *aionios*,' continued Paul, giving no more heed to his opponent's points than his opponent did to his; 'there's *kolasis*, too. It doesn't mean punishment in the sense of vengeance, but in the sense of correction. I'm not quoting myself. It's all as old as the hills. It was Dean Farrar—'

'I don't care if it was the Pope who said so,' interrupted the doctor. 'If anybody tells me that Christ didn't mean what he said in the parable of the Last Judgment, I simply don't believe him, and that's all. It's all an attempt to dodge the sterner side of Christianity. I've no use for a flabby, sentimental Christianity. I believe in discipline, and plenty of it; and punishment where punishment is due. God isn't a softy' – (No, he thinks God's rather like Dr Waterhall, thought the angry Paul) – 'and people'll pull up their socks again when they really believe that God is to be feared—'

'And then their morality won't be worth a halfpenny!'

'Don't be so ridiculous, man! We have to punish children, don't we, in order to train 'em?'

'Yes, but not *eternally*. On and on and on. Good God, you can't have brought a ha'porth of imagination to bear upon it. It's – it's—' he paused for want of words.

'I've as good an imagination as you,' said the doctor. 'I think I've every bit as good an imagination as you. I've thought quite as much about this question of eternal punishment, and I find I can imagine it quite well.' And indeed he could.

'Then I'm sorry for you,' said Paul.

'Sorry! Keep your sorrow to yourself. I don't want anyone to be sorry for *me*.'

'If God is like that,' pursued Paul, staring at the wall, unseeing, 'he's simply no gentleman, but a dirty cad. Man's more merciful than He, in that case, and may well snap his fingers in His Almighty face when He sentences him to hell. You don't *really* believe it. You know you don't. You can't!'

Dr Waterhall pressed on the arms of his chair as if about to rise and go. But he sank back again with a 'Tch!' of irritation. 'I *do* believe it, and that's enough. You schoolmasters always imagine that nobody's got any brain or any knowledge but yourselves. I can tell you, imagination is needed in *our* work.'

'What maddens me,' said Paul, who had followed out his own thoughts instead of listening, 'is that this hell of yours must always be for the other fellow. No man would believe in it for himself; and that's what makes those who support it seem so disgustingly self-righteous.'

'Well, if I'm disgusting—' began the doctor, moving in his chair.

'I believe in the same hell for myself as for the other fellow. I am pretty sure that I shall deserve punishment, but I shall hope that God will make it as merciful as he can. You, I imagine, think you are going straight to an everlasting heaven?'

'I don't know that I think that. I've no doubt that there are many better men than I, but I've tried to lead a decent life. I've not injured my neighbours. It's the *cruel* brutes for whom hell isn't bad enough.'

'Pah!' scoffed Paul, and stood up; then abruptly turned towards the doctor. 'Have *you* never been cruel?'

'I hope not.'

'Well, I think you have.' Paul's eyes flashed. 'To be unimaginative is to be cruel. It's cruel to go about urging the punishment of strikers and rebellious Indians and criminals and all the rest of the underdogs, without the least attempt to grasp their position.' He stamped about the room, in the struggle for words. 'You make no attempt to understand their environment. You don't know what it is, never to have had a chance. Some understanding, that's all I ask for! Imagination. And now you want to torture everlastingly those who've made a mess of their lives, and whose souls have grown all twisted and awry in the infernal undergrowth of this world. And you say you're not cruel!' This time the doctor reached his feet in his determination to go; and Paul, seeing him, quieted down. 'No, don't go. I'm sorry if I've been rude. But really we oughtn't to argue. We just don't deal in the same coin. I believe in mercy. With all my soul I believe in mercy.'

The doctor consented to be soothed, and sat down again: the night was still young, and his fireless study didn't attract him. 'You're a sentimentalist,' he said quite pleasantly. 'No doctor is ever a sentimentalist.'

'And that's a word that's never worried me in the least. In arguments like these it never means more than that you're riled by the fellow who's prepared to be a shade more humane than you. Only you should have put "maudlin" with it. "Maudlin sentimentality," that's the hack phrase—'

'I never use hack phrases!'

'No, no; no, no, no. Don't let us get excited again. All I'm saying is that if to believe in love and infinite understanding and forgiveness is to be a maudlin sentimentalist, then I'm quite content to be called one.'

And there it ended. They turned to other subjects and tried to recapture good humour. But the savage interchanges had left a crack in their friendship. A coolness and something perfunctory spoiled their courtesies and laughter on the doorstep. And the doctor took an aggrievement, which revived in the night air, along the pavement and round the corner of Morton Avenue.

He rehearsed all that Presset had said, and every recollection inflamed his self-love the more. *Aionios,* indeed; and with a false quantity at that! Throwing Greek at him who had really done Greek. A pass degree a mere receipt for money! Great Powers, did he dare to think *him* a dull type? 'I'm sorry for you!' Damn the man! 'Unimaginative and cruel!' A score of retorts danced in his head as he went through his gate. So good were they that he planned to go back one evening and open up the argument again. When one was inflamed as this, one needed a hotter quarrel for one's healing.

The wound was much better the next morning, and it healed during the day, while he had no time to think of it. By the evening, after supper, his natural good humour was in its seat again, and he began to wonder how he had managed to work up such a heat. What had it all been about? What had made him so excited? Simply that Presset had obviously revealed that he thought himself a better intellect than him – God blast the man! He dared to, did he? 'Dean Farrar said it.' Dean Hell!

The wound had opened again – Better not to think of it. It exasperated him so. Last night in bed it had been real pain. It was like torture to think that Presset despised his imagination and his intellect. *Presset!*

Rather than the wound should suppurate afresh, he decided to go out. That was the worst of leading a lonely life: one thought too much. Yes, he couldn't stay in his study tonight, so he walked to where his hat was tossed on to a chair. He would go out and find someone to talk to, because the only way to heal this sort of thing was to work off the indignation, either on the offender or on somebody else. To go and knock Presset up two nights running would be impossible, so he'd have to go to somebody else and talk about him. To whom? He was on the tiled path between his door and his gate before he had answered this. Worksop? No, he had visited Worksop only last Wednesday. Tosh Johnson? Tosh was a fussy little idiot, but by the same token he would be an excellent audience, safe for sympathy, and sympathy was what his sickness needed more than sense. Granted that he was only a retired hosier, but a man in the doctoring trade couldn't afford to be snobbish. Yes, he flattered himself he'd get a good reception at Tosh's, who was an appalling little snob, if ever there was one.

So Dr Waterhall followed his long cigar in the direction of Johnson's house in Heathfield Crescent.

The maid showed him into a brown and green dining-room where Johnson sat in an armchair reading a newspaper.

'Don't get up,' begged the doctor. 'What a time of the night to call! Your dear lady gone to bed?'

'Hardly. It's only nine o'clock. She's away at her sister's.'

'Ah, well.' Dr Waterhall sank into the easy chair opposite, thinking that this was by no means bad news. 'But I really mustn't stop. I expect you're busy.'

'Not at all. Do I look like it? Stay as long as you like and have a chat. You've not been to see us for a long time.'

'No, I won't stop long. Have a cigar. It's a good honest-to-God Havannah.'

'Thank you; I don't mind if I do. . . . Yes, thank you very much,' said little Johnson, drawing a cigar rather gingerly from the case which his visitor extended 'Thank you.'

And very soon they were seated opposite each other, with gossip and smoke drifting between them, and the firelight playing on the fender which upheld their feet. It was Dr Waterhall's business to bring the conversation round to Presset, but this was not easy to do, because Johnson was as big a talker as he. However, he waited his opportunity, behind his cigar; and at last, through a discussion on the need for discipline in the world, he arrived at the story of his argument with Presset last night.

Tosh Johnson listened, leaning forward in his chair, knocking the ash off his unfamiliar cigar, and nodding. 'Yes, yes,' he kept saying; and then, when the doctor had finished, he surprised him by the statement, 'Yes, I heard all about that.'

'You've heard all about it already?'

'Yes – but wait a minute. I suppose you know all about Presset? You know he's found his consolation? Hasn't been long about it, has he?'

'What the devil do you mean?'

'He's in love again, it would seem.' And Tosh Johnson, his eyes alight and knowing, as an old man's can be when the talk is of amorous matters, and his thin body leaning forward that he might make his points with the butt end of his cigar, told him of all that they had seen by the Judge's Seat on the crown of Pitch Hill. 'Yes, it was Mr Presset all right. His arm was round her waist, and her head was on his shoulder, just like a couple of seventeen-year-olds on a Saturday night. It's so! As Gaff Ellison said, we had two remarkable views that day.'

'Ha, ha, ha! Well, I'm damned!' The doctor laughed heartily to hear of Presset on an amorous adventure. This was excellent; this was better healing than he had expected from Johnson, to be able to see Presset in a ridiculous light and to enjoy a laugh at his expense. 'Ha, ha, ha! So he's turned into a ladies' man, has he, now that he's free? Holy Moses! Well, we live and learn. Thank you, Johnson; thank you for that story. I wouldn't have missed that for anything. Presset! It takes some swallowing, doesn't it? Ha, ha, ha! Presset above the clouds with a his arm round the lady! Presset up in the clouds with a vengeance, *n'est-ce pas*?' It made him feel very much better, and he wiped his eyes with his handkerchief. 'But you were saying that you'd heard about our famous argument. How was that?'

'I met him this morning in the Caledonian Road, and I very soon gathered that you were both a little sore. He let off to me about it, outside Willis's, the stationer's.'

'Did he? Well, well, he's got his consolation, as you say; which is more than I have. I'm sure she'll stroke his cheek for him – fact, she's probably doing it now, somewhere, ha, ha! Ha ha, ha!'

'Yes,' said Johnson, and his eyes took on that keen but guilty hardness more often seen in old women when they are about to throw the mischief into the broth; 'and it may interest you to know that he thinks you a second-class brain.'

'*What!*'

'That's what he said. He said that all that dull unimaginativeness, as he called it, was the sure sign of a second-class brain.'

The doctor stared – gaped – while his brain resettled after the shock.

'That's right. That's just what he said,' nodded Tosh. 'How d'you like that? I've no doubt he thinks exactly the same of me. Anyone who can still believe in old-fashioned notions he's content to dub a second-class brain.'

The doctor was still speechless. He had come to Tosh Johnson's door for healing, but he was not after all, to find it. On the contrary, he had found such aggravation of his wound that it was now a staccato stabbing and a burning. It was a bigger thing now than talk or laughter could cure. He talked, he vented his indignation, he exposed all the doubts that had ever come into his mind about Presset; but he knew that he wanted to be out in the street, back in his study, alone with this sickening insult. Tosh's inadequate and commonplace assents were no balm for this. And soon he picked up his hat, buttoned his coat with a shaking hand, and got himself out of the house. And on the pavements, under the stars, storming along with his mouth a thin straight line, he vowed that he would never speak to that bumptious little outsider again.

'A second-class brain.' It was a light word of Paul's tossed down carelessly enough to Johnson, outside Willis's, the stationer's. But of all the words he ever uttered, it was probably the one that had better been left unspoken. It festered in the doctor's mind – festered for days and weeks – waiting, though it knew it not, for something that was travelling along a tortuous path to find it and to settle in it, as in a goal. This something was a rumour sinister indeed.

Chapter Six

The path of the rumour was tortuous. The whisper ran and leapt like a little spluttering flame along a fuse that twisted in and out; but the train of combustible stuff had been well and safely, if unwittingly, laid by Elinor before her death. Few men can resist the temptation to give off another man's joke as their own, and eleven men told eleven wives that, high above the mist on Pitch Hill, they had come upon two remarkable views. The wives were more shocked than the men, who treated the tale with levity; but, for the present, they saw in it no more than 'execrable taste' on the part of Mr Presset.

Mrs Worksop took the story to Bessie Furle, with whom Elinor had so kindly made her acquainted. And Bessie, listening on the sofa in her drawing-room, with a stocking and a darning needle dropped to her lap, exclaimed, 'Well, I never! It must be the same woman as before. Well, I – a slim, youngish girl, you say? Yes, it's her, I'll be bound!' And when Mrs Worksop asked to whom she referred, Bessie, looking down upon her stocking and twisting her mouth and putting her head to one side before she spoke, explained how Elinor had told her some time before her death that Paul was carrying on with the governess at his school. 'She made me vow never to tell a soul, she was that ashamed; and I don't think I ever have; but it can't hurt her now, poor soul. She's at rest now' – and Bessie began to darn – 'but it was serious enough then. It had gone as far as – yes, it had gone as far as that;' and she nodded significantly, but kept her eye on the darning. 'She must be an indecent creature,' she added, after nodding again at Mrs Worksop's astonishment, 'with Elinor hardly cold in her grave. Of course, it may be another: my opinion of Paul changed completely when I heard about the governess, but I expect it's the same. They were supposed to have broken it off, but he was still writing to her. And such letters too! Elinor saw one. Funny how any man in the fifties seems likely to make a fool of himself. Poor Elinor. I hope she's spared this.'

Straightaway Mrs Worksop carried this new and illuminating information to her friends, one of whom, a rather frivolous young woman, testified with delighted eyes to having seen Mr Presset on Waterloo Station saying an affectionate goodbye to a young person whom she had supposed to be his niece or something – 'and that was a long time before – oh, yes, a long time before they saw him from Pitch Hill!' 'Well, really!' was the universal comment; but though all disapproved, they stopped at that. The creeping rumour, however, made suspicious the sight of Myra, late one evening, going through the gate of Mr Presset's house, which otherwise might have excited no comment. It enabled Mrs Webster, who lived opposite, to see something guilty in the girl's quick run round towards the back door. She watched to see if she came out again, but she did not, and in due time, the lights of the house went out.

When this news circulated among Mrs Worksop and her friends, disappointment with Mr Presset approached dismay. Then that was why he continued to live alone in that strange way, when he could well afford a housekeeper! The woman must be quite shameless. True she had been seen only once, but who would be likely to see her on dark nights, unless they chanced to be at their windows? You could be sure it wasn't limited to once. People were cold to Mr Presset now, if they met him, or they spoke only formal courtesies; and meanwhile the rumour, creeping and leaping along, carried the hint that there were goings-on in that dark house where Mr Presset lived alone.

It returned, thus laden, to Bessie; and Bessie bethought herself of Mrs Briscoll who, recommended by Elinor, came twice a week to her house. Mrs Briscoll was still 'doing' for Paul, and should surely have an idea as to whether there was any truth in these tales. So the next day, when Mrs Briscoll, standing on the stairs with the dust-pan and brush, mentioned that she couldn't come, not on Thursday she couldn't, because she was obliging Mr Presset a little longer that day, Bessie saw the door of opportunity open, and walked through.

'Pity Mr Presset has lost all his friends by his extraordinary behaviour,' she said.

'What behaviour, mum?'

'Why, his carrying on with that woman.'

'Woman, mum?'

'Yes. . . .' If one has spoken ill of a man, one is apt to justify oneself by making the ill as convincing as possible; and Bessie continued, 'He's always about with a woman. It's been going on for months. Ever since poor Mrs Presset died, in fact.'

'You don't say so! Oh, it's wrong, that's what it is!'

'Yes, and quite a young woman, too.'

'Oh, he shouldn't ought to. I can't say as I liked Mrs Presset – not as you'd say, really *liked* her, but he shouldn't ought to behave like that. It's hardly decent.'

'She's been seen going to his house late at night. I should have thought you'd have met her.'

'No, *that* I haven't. She's never been there, not while I've been in the house. Well, I never! You can't trust any of 'em, can you? . . . Such a quiet and nice-spoken gentleman. . . . But do you really believe it, mum?'

'I *know* it,' affirmed Bessie, who had to complete her justification. 'I know that he was carrying on with her before Mrs Presset died. I knew all about it, but my lips were sealed in her lifetime.'

'Is that so? In her lifetime! . . . Come to think of it, I remember young Annie Mavis – I told her at the time, I said, "Annie, you ought to be ashamed to say such things!" but perhaps she was right, after all.'

'What was that?'

'It was when poor Mrs Presset went away with – with *you*, wasn't it, mum? – and Mr Presset lived there alone, Annie going home at nights; and one morning she come and was doing the bedroom, when she swore she smelt scent and powder and such like. I told her she could get summonsed for saying a thing like that. I never believed it for a second, myself I didn't; but supposing it was true! Will you only think of it?'

'Goodness gracious!' said Bessie. 'That's the first time I've ever heard of that.' And immediately she saw herself carrying this pungent new morsel to her interested friends. She was impatient to be off with it.

And if Bessie Furle was eager to tell, so was Mrs Briscoll. Alfred Briscoll was hardly home and settled to his tea before she was telling him all. And Alfred, like the men above him, roared with laughter. Being a peaky, undergrown, weather-beaten Cockney, he was, by natural order, a humorist. He threw back his head, laughed long and loud, and drank deep from his cup to send the joke down well.

'I don't see that you've no call to laugh,' rebuked his wife, standing above him with her arms akimbo, as full-fleshed as he was lean, but certainly not his master, since Alfred had long ago vowed that no one should ever come it over him. 'It's indecent, I think.'

'Well, he's proper put the blinkers on us all, 'asn't he? I'll lay there's not a man anywhere that'd have suspected it of him. And she? What can she see in a little ole cockolorum like that? Gaw, if he can get away with it, it makes me wonder what I've been doing with my time!'

'Elfred, don't talk so! A clean-living man like you!'

'*Still!*' protested Alfred, as if it were asking a deal of a man to forgo such opportunities as this. 'But if I tried to do it, I should be copped in no time. Gaw, how do they do it? He's been a subtle one, hasn't he? It makes me wonder – yuss, strike me, but I wouldn't mind betting he put his ole woman where he could find her, so that he could get off with the gurl.'

'Elfred, don't *say* such things!'

'Oh, it wouldn't surprise me, neither!' laughed Alfred, with a sideways nod, as he chewed vigorously his mouthful of herring and bread and washed it down with a draught of tea. 'If he could'a deceived us so properly abaht the one thing, why not abaht the other? Eh? What 'jer say to that, Lil?'

'He's not like that.'

'So I'd've said a minute ago. But I'm not so sure nah. Nah, I'm not at all so sure. These quiet coves are often the artful ones. Yes, I bet he done it,' decided Alfred, cheerfully.

'Hush! Supposing anyone should hear you!'

'But he might'a done it!' submitted Alfred in self-defence.

'He might'a put a spot of something in her tea. Others'a done it. And they lived all alone, didn't they? And' – suddenly he laughed noisily – 'she died of indigestion, didn't she? Yes, you bet he put a spot of – Crikey! – Gawd in Heaven!—'

'What? What is it?' demanded Mrs Briscoll, her eyes starting.

'Gawd – fetch – me – home! D'you think he *did* do it, mother? Nah, he couldn't'a done. Pass over the loaf.'

'What are you thinking of?'

'I'm thinking of a tin of weed-killer I took him.'

'Oh, be quiet, Elfred!'

'Well, you arst me, didn't yer? Of course it's only a coincidence, but. . . . Yuss, I took that tin of Whittaker's Weed Killer to his paths and – God's love, Lil! – we had a hell of a talk as to how much was wanted to kill a person. We did, gawspel truth! He walked with me round the paths, arstin' how much you'd 'ave to put in a cuppa tea. Straight he did! Yuss, and now I come to remember, I lef' the little ole tin on the dustbin and when I went back in the morning, it was gawn with the rest of the muck. At least so he told me.'

'How you can sit there and say such things!'

'Well, I'm only jokin', aren't I?' he objected, seeing that she was really shocked. 'But don't forget, Lil – don't forget that she was ill once before.'

'Yes, but that was before you done his garden for him.'

'That's right. That's right,' he agreed, perhaps sorry that his humorous little tale had a flaw in it. 'But still, his mind was runnin' on poisons, wasn't it? Perhaps the first one didn't work, ha, ha, ha! and he was after another! Don't forget he inherited all her brass. Yes, don't forget that. So he gone on till he found one that worked, and then everything in the garden was lovely.'

'I won't listen to such talk. It don't seem right, even in fun. And any'ow, the doctor would have known if there was anything wrong.'

'I don't know that that goes for much,' said Alfred, ruminating. 'They generally get it past the doctors. It's the big men in Scotland Yard they can't get it past. Nah, they can't get it past them in a hurry. And wouldn't they like to nab a gentleman like Mr Presset! Crikey, the papers wouldn't be big enough to hold it! Whereas poor folks like you and me don't get 'em any fame worth speaking of. A wash-out, we are. If ever you do me in, I'll be surprised if you get more than a paragraph to yourself, ole gurl.'

'Oh, be *quiet*, Elfred!'

Alfred Briscoll, liking the flavour of his grim little jest, gave it freely to his friends. And of these some found it equally palatable and passed it on in the same merry mood, but others, less humorous and preferring a dark tale, forgot that it had been a joke and passed it on as a suspicion. The rumour, continuing along its path, darkened.

Now Dr Waterhall, like his neighbours, had an oblong patch

of garden behind his house in Morton Avenue, and Paul and Elinor had once asked him why, instead of letting it go to rack and ruin, he didn't get Alfred Briscoll to come round of an evening and tidy it up. And Dr Waterhall, too little interested to work in it himself, now employed Briscoll for an hour or so once a week. And when he heard the gate click and Briscoll's steps going round to the back, he would think that here was someone to whom a bored and lonely man might go out for a gossip. So, putting on his hat, for, like many doctors and many bachelors, he was excessively careful of his health, he wandered round to where Briscoll was busy with the birch broom. He came round on an evening ten days after the conversation between Mr and Mrs Briscoll.

'Good evening, Briscoll.'

'Evening, sir.'

'Have a cigarette?'

'Thank you, sir. I don't mind if I do.'

And Briscoll took the cigarette from the case, put it behind his ear, and continued sweeping with the broom. The doctor followed, chatting pleasantly, till they came to a corner that was permanently in the shade, the bluff promontory of his kitchen and the similar promontory of next door's kitchen shutting it from the sun for all twelve months of the year. Alfred Briscoll looked upon this corner and shook his head. With that professional gloom about a garden, its soil, its sunlight, its previous treatment and its future prospects, which the jobbing gardener brings through a gate, he shook his head despondently and said, 'You'll never do much with this corner, sir.'

'No?' inquired the doctor, who was unaware of a desire to do anything with it.

'Nah.' Alfred was convinced. 'It lies that damp, yer see, and gets no sun nor wind.'

'I suppose not.'

Alfred gazed at it, sucked his teeth, and nodded several times. This was the position he liked to be in: for a space he was the learned doctor with the patient beneath his eyes, and Dr Waterhall was no more than the uninitiated layman standing by.

'Pity to do nothing with it,' he said at last. 'I might start a fern rockery like that Mr Presset's got at the foot of his garden. Yes, I could fork up the ground well, and mix some brick rubble with the subsoil to drain it, and work in a nice lot of leaf mould' – he enjoyed detailing the treatment in professional terms, exactly as Dr Waterhall did – 'and then we could plant a few ferns under the rocks – mind you, decent ferns, not the stuff that Mr Presset brings home from the woods, which are no better than weeds, to my way of thinking.'

At this second mention of Mr Presset he was reminded of the conversation with his wife.

'Well, do that if you like,' said the doctor. 'It won't cost too much, will it?'

'Nah, it won't break you. It won't cost all that much. A half sov'rin'd go a tidy way to covering it. Then we might put in some Solomon's Seal and some creeping jenny and some bluebells. Mr Presset has managed to make his bluebells grow. Pity there's all this talk about Mr Presset, isn't it, sir?'

'Talk? What talk?'

'Well, there's those that are going so far as to say that it wasn't all as it should be about Mrs Presset's death.' If Briscoll had looked up, he would have seen a keen, staring interest in the doctor's eyes; but instead he put his broom against the wall. Taking the rake, he began to work along the beds, the doctor following him, cigar in mouth and hat at an angle. 'But what I says is, if *you* was satisfied, that's all there is to it. I say to 'em, "The doctor knows; we don't." '

'I was perfectly satisfied,' the doctor announced emphatically, his self-love fearing suddenly that these gossipers had been casting their aspersions on *him*. 'But how on earth did such an idea get about?'

'Well, you know what people are, sir. First they hear that he'd been kerryin' on with a young lady, having her to his house and all that—'

'Oh, I knew all about that,' interrupted the doctor, liking to appear knowledgeable, though, in fact, the later details had not yet reached him.

'Of course.' Briscoll associated himself with the implied contempt of the gossipers. 'It's all my eye, no doubt, but there y'are! They hear that he was kerrying on with her for long before his wife died; and from that it's not as far as across the road to say he put his missus where he could find her, especially as she had the money and he stood to get it if she went off. I admit I said it in jest myself to Mrs Briscoll. I said, Come to think of it, I remember his talking about arsenic when I put down that there weed-killer for him.'

'*What*? What was that? Arsenic?'

At first the doctor's reaction to Briscoll's talk had been no more than the happiness which comes to us all when we hear that a man we dislike is being spoken of badly. But as Briscoll, raking the beds and drawing the doctor after him, rattled on about the weed-killer tin and the discussion on fatal doses, an unforeseen doubt looked the doctor in the eyes. Unforeseen and disturbing, but oddly fascinating. After a second's thought he pushed it from him as ridiculous; but it came and looked at him again. 'It's within the bounds of possibility,' he thought, to encourage himself, because he wanted to make friends with the doubt. 'There's no question that it's within the bounds of possibility. But no! . . . Still . . . you never can tell. . . .' Of late he had run down Presset heavily to his friends, and the more he had run him down, the worse, by auto-intoxication, he had believed him. And now he felt an imperious desire to escape from Briscoll's chatter, and be alone in his study with a thought.

He made his excuse and walked upstairs to his room, thinking all the way, 'Good God, could it have been? . . . No. . . .But . . . there's no denying she had all the symptoms of arsenical poisoning. . . .' He entered the room and dropped into his chair to think. He got up, and walked up and down to think. And memory, which captures everything and stores everything, though our conscious minds may perceive only the larger pieces in its store, suddenly threw up two remarks of Pressets on the night of Elinor's death: 'I've not been feeling very well myself,' and '*She* told you that.'

Now, why did Presset say that he had not been feeling very well himself? Had he forgotten that Elinor was supposed to have eaten the irritant substance while he was away from the house? Was it a slip? He had emphasised so strongly that her illness had begun at about four o'clock during his absence. When told that it had been unwise to give her so much brandy, he had insisted, 'But the sickness began long before that. *She* told you that.' Why that emphasis on 'she'? Did he fear his own words would be suspected? *Had* there been a guilty anxiety in his manner that night – a fussy eagerness to exculpate himself? Great God, but what were these thoughts? Was he sane to ask himself such questions about Presset? Presset who declared his hatred of cruelty. . . . Presset who had called him unimaginative and cruel because – 'Unimaginative and cruel' – blast him! The doctor, his wound burning at the first touch of memory, now felt that he would like to believe this wickedness of Presset. There was no doubt that the whole story fell perfectly into pattern; the other woman, the nagging and unwanted wife, the will, the lonely life together, the arsenic in the tin, the exact symptoms . . . *and that previous illness*! Great Saints! Precisely the same symptoms then! The doctor stopped his walk with a jerk. 'My God, I begin to believe he did do it.'

But no! It was too appalling an accusation. He was losing his head. His vindictiveness against the little man was running away with him. He went to his chair, and deliberately picked up a book to read, and forget for a while.

But he couldn't. He couldn't get the fascinating question out of his head. Was it possible? After all, the fact that he was the last person you'd expect it of had been true of all such murderers. And, by the lord, another point: why did he get rid of that servant girl, Annie Someone, when they could well have afforded a maid? And – point after point – that first illness occurred within a week or two of Annie's departure! *Good Pities!* Did he do it? *Did* he? By now Dr Waterhall felt that he could know no rest again till this thrilling question was answered. And there was only one way it could be answered. 'And it ought to be done. At least the matter ought to be inquired into further. I'm not necessarily accusing him of murder; I want it done, if you like, to rid him of a terrible suspicion – and there's no doubt, as Briscoll said, that the suspicion *is* going around. Yes, I begin to think I have a duty, either to Society or to him.'

He felt delighted to be convincing himself; and at the same instant came the strongest argument of all, one that jerked him forward in the chair, with both hands gripping its arms. 'If he did it, I suppose he thought he could easily get it past an old fool of a doctor like me. He thinks I'm a fool – he as good as said so: 'a second-class brain' – my Christ, I'll show him he doesn't get past *me* like that – that I'm not the fool I look.'

But what would his position be? He lay back in the chair to think it out. Would he damage himself? Because he wasn't going to sacrifice one tittle of his reputation in the interest of abstract justice. But there was no question of such damage. On the contrary, he would appear an interesting and very honourable figure before the world. He would say, 'I was satisfied at the time, but subsequent events have caused me to doubt, and I've felt it my public duty to come forward. . . . Even though Mr Presset had once been a personal friend of mine, I could not let that stand in the way of my duty to Society. . . .

And I had my duty to the dead as well as the living' – yes, a good phrase, that – 'She was my patient.' And the judge would commend him for his public spirit; and thereafter he would be a famous figure in the Islington streets, people pointing him out and whispering together after he had passed.

The turbulent argument was now settling into a vaguely formulated but very satisfying dream. Lying back in his chair with his feet on the footstool, and turning up his face ever and anon to blow smoke into the air, he saw himself walking up the steps of Scotland Yard (the inside of which he had often wanted to see), being taken along the corridors to some high official's room (because, after all, he was a man of position), telling his story in admirable phrases ('I make no accusations, sir. I simply feel that there are grounds for further inquiries'), being an authoritative and trusted expert in the subsequent proceedings (which, though gruesome in one event, he was quite eager to see and share in, such was his everyday boredom), being photographed and written about in the papers, and achieving a universal fame at last. Sorry for Presset? Not if he'd really done it. No sympathy for him then. If he'd really done it, he could suffer the full penalty of the law; and he, for his part, would be glad to have had a share in bringing him to justice.

A dream so engrossing and so flattering was bound to issue as action. Two evenings later Dr Waterhall, having nothing to do, put on his most impressive suit and his Homburg hat and, not lightly excited, walked out into Morton Avenue. A man of average kindliness, but lacking any insight into his motives, he did not know that one of the strongest of them was the desire to punish a man who had called him a 'second-class brain'. He walked on, actually passing the gate of Presset's house, and not sure even now that he would walk up the steps of Scotland Yard – and yet quite sure, for the rumour, spitting and spluttering along its serpentine fuse, had found at last its blasting charge.

Chapter Seven

So it happened that Chief Inspector Boltro answered a summons from the Assistant Commissioner and, the following day, paced up and down the office of the Divisional Detective Inspector at the North Central Police Station, the head station of the division. At the broad desk, littered with reports and statements, sat Divisional-Inspector Osley. Sitting in that seat of authority, though younger, slighter and quieter than the big man pacing up and down, one might have supposed him the senior; but he simply sat here by right, as head of the detective force in his division and lord of his 'manor'. In his neat lounge suit he would have looked a smart young manager of a business house, if the room hadn't been bare of all luxury, brown, ill-lit, and as indifferently equipped as most offices in London police stations. Frank Osley was a very different type from John Boltro. John Boltro was fond of saying 'I'm one of the old school', by which he meant that he had had to fight his way up from the bottom, with devil an advantage at all, and twice as many kicks as halfpence. Osley had come up from the bottom too, as every policeman must, but they were getting better educated recruits when he joined and stiffening up the examinations, and they picked a lean young winner in Frank. He was the youngest D.D.I. in the force, recently promoted from the H. Division where his operations against the criminals of Whitechapel had made him the most famous of the younger school. He listened quietly to the Chief Inspector today, some-times making a note on his blotting pad; and he appeared to be very respectful; but, like every new appointment – like a new headmaster, new band-conductor, new hospital matron, new vicar – his opinion was not high of the men who had preceded him.

At the side of the desk, with legs crossed and pencil and notebook in his hands, sat Detective-Sergeant Doyle. He also was of the newer type, a product, indeed, of the new Police Training School: lean, spruce, quiet, well-spoken, and with very little smell of the blue uniform about him.

'It's going to be a big thing, Frank,' said Boltro, pleased to feel he was showing to young Osley the same geniality that the Assistant Commissioner had shown to him. 'It looks to me he's a clever and cunning rogue. We're not dealing with a common little killer, but with a highly educated man. This bird's a clever criminal: poisoners always are – up to a point, but only up to a point. I'm glad because I shall like to pit my brains against his, but we shall have to proceed carefully against him – very carefully, my boy.' Like all romantics, Chief Inspector Boltro preferred things to be in the superlative mood.

'If he's done it, sir,' corrected Osley.

'If he's done it, of course. If he's done it; naturally. But I shall be very surprised if he hasn't. I've seldom seen everything fit in so neatly; and the Chief thought so, too. And anyhow, we're making inquiries on the assumption he has, aren't we? No one else is suspected. If he didn't, of course, so much the better for him,' and he very nearly added, 'and so much the worse for us!'

'Quite,' agreed Osley, knocking with the butt of his pencil on the desktop.

'Well, what I think is – and I don't mind telling you. I've given quite a lot of thought to this – we've got to make a few preliminary inquiries quickly and then pounce. Pounce on him and the girl simultaneously, before they can have primed themselves up with any lies. What I mean is, it's going to be all over the place once we start. This Mrs Furle'll be running around to tell all her friends, and this Annie Somebody'll just walk out and inform the whole of her street. It'll be round to Presset and the girl before we are. F'rall I know, he's already got wind of the gossiping.'

'I shouldn't think he has, sir,' Osley suggested, but very politely, not wishing to expose to Boltro how much clearer was his own brain. 'It seems he's living alone with no friends at all, and it's not quite the sort of gossip you report to a man, unless you're a friend warning him. They're suggesting murder, mind you. No, I should think we've a clear run of a day or two.'

'I don't know. I don't feel at all sure of that.' Boltro shook his head, preferring to believe in his difficulties and in the necessity of pouncing. 'Anyway, I'm not risking too much. What I mean is, he's certain to have destroyed all real evidence, so I propose we pounce on him and the girl at the same time in their different places, before they know what's afoot. Because don't forget, Frank, old man, there's always the possibility that she knows all about it, too. In fact, I think it looks very much like it; and the Chief was inclined to think so, too. Very much like it. So look: I'll go and see him as soon as I've got enough information to frighten him into speaking the truth, while you're seeing her—'

Osley, doubtful, compressed his lips. 'Is that all in order—'

'Absolutely. Absolutely. I mean: we shan't be having it in our minds to arrest either him or her, before we've *seen* 'em, shall we? Of course not! *You* trust *me*: I shall know when to slip in the caution all right. I know exactly the right moment to do these things, I reckon. Yes, I'm a pretty old hand at this sort of thing. And as for *her*, there's nothing to stop you doing what you like with her. After all, she's not his wife, is she? . . . Eh? That's so, isn't it?' he demanded stubbornly, since Osley didn't answer. 'She's not his wife, I mean.'

'Very good, sir,' agreed Osley, to avoid an argument.

'Yes . . . well . . . now, this is my idea: first, you go and see this Bessie Furle. She was the dead woman's confidante, and she'll give us the background so that we can get a stronger line on the motive, see? There were probably quarrels, if the truth's known, and then there's that first illness – a very fishy business, if you ask me. She was there, nursing the woman.' As he spoke, Osley took a sheet of foolscap and made some notes. 'And, above all, she knows everything about the girl – his little piece, I mean – and she'll put you on the track of other friends and associates. Yes, Bessie's our first step.' Pacing up and down, Boltro seemed delighted with his grasp of the campaign.

'Right, sir.'

Boltro consulted a paper of notes in his hand. 'Then there's the Briscolls. Go and tackle them, will you? She's more important than him, because she worked in the house and may know of any tiffs or threats, and what happened before that first illness. And she probably knows where this little Annie can be got at. We want to hear from Annie all about that time the wife was away and the girl is supposed to have come to the house, and all about Annie's dismissal, which may be rather illuminating, I fancy – yes, *quite* illuminating' – and here he nodded significantly, with a tight mouth. 'Briscoll himself can tell us about the weed-killer, but apart from that, I don't think he'll give us much else. No, I don't think he's very important,' concluded Boltro sagely.

'Right, sir.'

'And meantime I'm going to call on his bank manager. They're sometimes a bit shy, and refuse to act without the authority of their head office. But I think I'll work him.' He nodded truculently. 'I want to know all about our account before we lost our missus, and how much we'd been giving our young lady, and how far we were in need of a nice little bequest. Then I want to find the solicitor, and see the doctor again. The bank manager and the solicitor'll hold their tongues, and I rather fancy the old doctor will. I've a notion he's not altogether happy about having upset the beehive. And, Pincer' – he turned to Sergeant 'Pincer' Doyle – 'you've got to get this young woman, Bawne's address.'

'That's oughtn't to be difficult,' suggested Osley.

'How?' demanded Boltro, not too pleased.

'We can get her first address from the school and then ask her landlady where she moved to, and so on. Her letters have had to follow her.'

'Yes, but' – Boltro paused, while he thought how to justify himself – 'she may not have had any letters . . . and what's more, I don't want that school put wise yet awhile – I've been thinking a lot about that – we don't want to spring a wasps' nest there – so, if you go, pretend it's nothing of any importance. See, Pincer?'

'Yes, sir.'

'And I tell you what, Frank, set one of your chaps to watch the school and check this Presset's movements, when he comes out tonight. He may go straight to her. Yes, that's an idea. I believe in having two strings to my bow. That's what we'll do, Frank!'

'Very good, sir.'

'And now we've got enough for a start, I fancy. With any luck we'll be able to see him and the girl within the next forty-eight hours. I believe in pouncing quick.'

Chapter Eight

The brief May glory was in the Elm Tree Road, when the two men came slowly along its pavement. The house-fronts were hidden behind the fresh young green of the trees, the domes of the trees were thickly dusted with the pink and white of May or hung with the pink of chestnut, the mauve of lilac and the yellow laburnum, and the golden privets and laurels along the garden railings were really gold. And the strange sweet fragrance came down the pavement, resting on the warm air.

The two men were glancing at the numbers on the house doors. They were the only two people in sight, for Sunday morning had emptied the street. One of them was a big man in a blue suit and bowler hat, and the other a slighter and younger man in a grey suit and felt hat, with a light coat over his arm. They were Chief Inspector Boltro and Detective-Sergeant Doyle.

Inspector Boltro did not notice the glory. His head beneath the bowler was full of confidence and excitement. Confidence because of the gleanings of Inspector Osley, Pincer Doyle and himself. They had learned from Bessie Furle, poor, frightened little Bessie Furle, that Elinor Presset had thought of changing her will and that she knew things which Paul Presset did not want divulged. They had learned new facts about that first illness: for example, that Mr Presset, in what Bessie had imagined to be his kindness, had refused to have her stay the night; that Elinor's illness had got much worse after she had gone; and that he had not sent for the doctor, ostensibly because 'he had had such a rotten time of late'. They had learned from reception clerks in Bloomsbury hotels about the furtive visits of a 'Mr and Mrs Presset' in the months before Elinor died. They had learned from Annie Mavis – Annie who had broken down when told that she might get into trouble if she didn't speak – that the master himself had come into the kitchen to tell her that she must go, and that the mistress had confessed that it was *his* idea. They had learned from Mrs Bohntree, Myra's landlady, of the girl's distress at times, and of the strange visit of a man who came asking her address on an evening which she believed to be a few evenings before the material date they gave her – anyhow, it was an October day. From the undertaker they had heard of Mr Presset's immediate questions about cremation, and from the neighbours of Myra's stealthy visits to his house, so soon after the death of his wife. Inspector Boltro felt that he was on the best thing of his life.

That was his confidence. His excitement was the old boyish desire to see the house, where the murder had been committed, the room where it had been done, and the man who had done it. 'The gentleman murderer' – he had never had such a one before. He looked up with great interest at the numbers on the doors.

'Twenty-three. Here it is Pincer.'

'Yes, sir. That's it. Hope our friend is in.'

'He'll be in all right. People who live alone are always in at nine o'clock on a Sunday.'

They passed through the gate which creaked a protest at their entry. They walked slowly up the steps and rang the bell.

Paul was in. He was down in his kitchen washing up his few breakfast things. The window was open, and the warm scents of May were blowing in from his garden, to stir and heighten his happiness. Seven months had gone now, and the past seemed buried; seven months, and soon he would be able to marry. Paradise then. Yesterday he had walked with Myra round the curve of the New River in Clissold Park, on purpose to see the pink chestnut blossom that had drifted to both banks on the still green water, and to compare these happy, hopeful days with the sadder ones of the year before. And he had said to her 'Come to my house in the afternoon tomorrow. Yes, I'm no longer afraid. And soon we shall have done with that house, and be gone from all these people for ever.' But Myra had said No, she hadn't the courage to come before dark; so he was going to meet her in an hour's time, and they would make their way into the country to find the best of the spring.

The bell rang in the kitchen. Automatically he looked up at the electric indicator and saw that it was the front door bell. Who could it be? Who would call on him at this hour? Could it be Myra? Yes, surely it could only be she. For some reason she had come frankly and openly to his front door. He straightened his hair and tie, dusted his coat, and ran up the few stairs, eager to see through the leaded panes of the hall door if it was the shadow of her head and hat. It was not. He saw the shadows of two tall men, one in a bowler and one in a trilby; and his disappointment was sharp. Some damned peddlers or beggars, and on a Sunday morning, too!

He opened the door and saw the broad blue front of a strange man and looked up into a round face that plainly desired to be ingratiating. A step behind was a slighter man in grey who seemed like a subordinate.

'Yes?' he inquired.

Inspector Boltro, on the other side of the threshold, saw a small man in a Sunday suit of blue, with stiff collar and cuffs, who looked up at him with wistful and inquiring eyes. For a second his surprise took a strong colour of disappointment. His citadel of proof shook.

'Are you Mr Presset, sir?' he asked, thinking, as he said it, that he was showing young Pincer how the experts worked.

'I am.' The little man stared up, perplexed.

'We must apologise for coming at this hour, sir, but we are engaged on certain inquiries and are most anxious for your help. We are police officers.'

'Police officers!'

'Yes. I'm Chief Inspector Boltro of Scotland Yard, and this is Detective-Sergeant Doyle.'

Inspector Boltro saw the little man's face turn grey, and his hand shoot to the nape of his neck. The citadel of proof stabilised; nay, it stood stronger than before, and his satisfaction returned.

'What do you. . . . Well, if I can help you in any way, of course I . . .' But he still stood there, on the doormat, with the threshold between them.

'Might we come in, sir, and explain?'

'Oh, yes . . . yes, certainly. . . . Come in here.'

And Paul, with a shaking heart and confused head, led them into the dining-room, whose door was nearest. Inspector Boltro glanced quickly round at the brown mahogany furniture and the red walls with the woodland frieze, till his eye rested on the enlarged portrait of Elinor.

'Do sit down,' said Paul. 'Take these comfortable chairs.'

'Thank you.'

'How can I help you?' And he sat down himself, but rather dizzily, on the edge of a hard chair.

'Well, to put it frankly, Mr Presset, we must tell you that, from certain information received, we are not wholly satisfied that your wife's death was due to natural causes. There may have been some accident, of course, but in such a case we always pursue a few inquiries. On the other hand, she might have – had you reason to suppose she had any enemies, Mr Presset?'

'Enemies?' repeated Paul, stupidly. If he had been pale before, he was livid now; and Inspector Boltro had not a trace of doubt left in him.

'Yes. Naturally our first duty – that is, *one* of our first duties – was to come to you and ask your help. I may say we have made a few inquiries already, and they leave us far from satisfied.'

Paul stared but did not answer. His brain was racing like an engine in the effort to mint out words. He tried to speak, but at first his voice wouldn't come. He cleared his throat; and then his brain threw from his lips a blunt, 'Why didn't you come to me first? What do you mean by making inquiries behind my back? That can only mean one thing. I'm not quite a fool, officer. Are you – do I understand that you suspect me of having had something to do with my wife's death. Is that what you are suggesting?'

'We are suggesting nothing, Mr Presset. We don't even know that there was any foul play. We think there is a case for inquiries, that's all.'

'Well, why didn't you come to me first? That's what I want to know. Why have you been making inquiries behind my back?'

Inspector Boltro did not at once answer. To tell the truth, he was at a loss for an answer; and he had a nasty moment when he feared he might not be impressing Sergeant Doyle. 'We thought . . .' he began.

But his hesitation had convinced Paul, terrified him, and driven him to cloak his terror in fury. He leapt up. 'Obviously you've been making inquiries because you suspect *me*. I tell you I'm not quite a fool, Inspector. This is monstrous. Who started the wicked suggestion? What is this "information" you have received? I have a right to know that, haven't I? My wife died a perfectly natural death. Ask her doctor. He's Dr Waterhall, just round the corner here. He was perfectly satisfied . . . perfectly satisfied. Who started this lying tale? I insist upon knowing, that I may proceed against them for slander. Criminal slander. I shall see my solicitor today.'

Inspector Boltro spoke gently. 'Mr Presset, I'd like to be frank with you. There have been gossip and rumours, and they came to our ears. You know what people are.'

'Well, why listen to them? Such criminal nonsense! I shall proceed against them at once.'

'Wait, please. They have seen you about with a young lady very soon after your wife's funeral' – Boltro saw the rush of blood to Paul's face, and the gulp – 'and that naturally caused talk. That alone is nothing, perhaps, but, coupled with the fact that your wife's symptoms were all consistent with poisoning and that, for some time before her death, you and the young lady had been – er – keeping company, well, naturally there were those who started suspicions.'

'This villainous, filthy neighbourhood!' interjected Paul, his eyes flashing.

'And naturally it was our duty to inquire into and, if possible, remove such a fearful suspicion. You say that you are entirely innocent: very good, sir; then we are your best friends, come to work on your behalf. And quite the best thing you can do is to help us all you can.' The Inspector felt pleased with this speech, and satisfied again, before Pincer Doyle.

Paul still stared. 'Seen with Myra' – this had overthrown his wits, and he couldn't collect them again; he couldn't decide what answers to give; now one idea came, and now another. He stayed mute while the ideas cancelled out. Then the pleasant voice of the Inspector broke in. 'I should tell us all you know.'

'Of course I will tell you all I know. . . .' Paul slowly sat down again.

'Yes, that's best.'

'It's simple enough. . . . It's perfectly simple. . . . The doctor will tell you that she was taken ill while I was away from home. I'll take you to him now, if you like—'

'Just a minute, sir. You know that it is our duty to do what is called "caution" a witness, if he's likely to be – if there's some suspicion against him. We quite understand that you indignantly deny the suspicion, but these formalities have to be gone through. It's my duty to tell you that, if you are good enough to – er – make a statement of all you know, it must be a perfectly voluntary statement, given of your own free will, and not as the result of any promise or threat, and of course that it may be taken down in writing and used in evidence; but that's just a formality; so now, Mr Presset' – quickly he became cheerful and ingratiating – 'what I suggest is that we first of all talk the whole matter over and see what light you can throw on things, and then, if you like, we'll have it made into a written statement. Sergeant Doyle will take it down, and you can sign it. Will that do?'

'Certainly . . . certainly . . . of course. I've nothing to be afraid of.'

'Exactly. Well, then, please—'

And with a few questions from the Inspector and much wordy exposition from Paul, the facts of Elinor's death were set forth as Paul desired the world to read them. 'She died of valvular disease of the heart,' he concluded. 'Yes, valvular disease after gastro-enteritis, as the doctor's certificate will show. You can see it at any time. There's absolutely no doubt about it.'

But Boltro, watching narrowly, played a high card. 'Doctors sometimes make mistakes,' he suggested quietly. 'But no doubt his diagnosis will be confirmed at the exhumation.'

'Exhumation? Will there be an exhumation?'

'I think so,' said the Inspector, though he had no authority whatever for such a statement.

Paul, his heart a sickly blob of terror, could not – dared not believe this. He had to believe it a trick of the Inspector's to frighten him; and at once his twisting ingenuity instructed him to meet it with a bold bluff – but too late: the watching eyes had seen his first alarm. 'I'm glad to hear it,' he said. 'I hope they will. It's obviously the only thing to do. Exhume the body, of course! and then these lies will be laid once and for all. I *wish* it. Can *I* get an order for exhumation? What is the method, and how long will it take? I want my name cleared of this foul suspicion.'

'The body is exhumed on the order of the coroner.'

'Good! Then the sooner the better. They'll find nothing – nothing at all.'

'I'm sure you're right, sir, but we have to do these things.'

'Unless, of course, there's something she took in her patent medicines. There might be that, but nothing else.'

'Yes, well . . . perhaps it won't come to that. . . . And now would you care to tell us anything about your life together and about this Miss Bawne?'

Paul jumped up and began to walk to and fro. 'I beg you will leave Miss Bawne out of this. She has nothing to do with it at all. She was just the kindergarten mistress at my school, and we were good friends – that was all. It is perfectly true we did go for walks together sometimes, as any two colleagues might, but nothing more than that. And now, since my wife's death, I don't mind telling you that I've been a very lonely man, and I *have* asked her to marry me; but only when decency permits.' His heart sank into a terrible emptiness of despair as he spoke of his marriage. 'That's all there is to that. Please don't bring her into it any more.'

'I see, sir. Well, that's all right. . . .' And with studied carelessness Boltro played his highest card. 'And no doubt she will confirm all this, and that will settle that.'

'But you're not going to question *her*?' demanded Paul, stopping in his walk.

'Oh, yes, we shall have to,' said the Inspector. 'As a matter of fact, she is being questioned now.' He glanced at his watch. 'Yes, Detective-Inspector Osley and Sergeant Brett are with her now.'

'Oh, my God! It's intolerable.' There was that in Paul's face which, had he been a child, would have broken into defeated, defiant and furious tears. 'It's wicked. What will she think? How *dare* you spring it on her like this? Surely you could have let me – oh, merciful God!'

He walked to the window and gazed out. The two officers said nothing, but sat there, waiting.

Over the sunlit roofs the first church bells were ringing; a sparrow flew from a laburnum in his neighbour's garden to the may tree in his own; the warm scents washed into the room through the partly opened window; and from the sabbath calm in the distances came occasionally the voices of children. Everywhere around the four walls of this room there seemed to be quiet and happiness, he alone palpitating like a beast in a trap. He gazed out at the sunlight on the road.

'May I think a bit?' he asked.

'Certainly. Take your time, by all means. We're anxious to help in every way we can.'

'Thank you. . . . Thank you very much. . . .'

And after a few minutes at the window he turned to them with a drawn, despairing face. 'I think I had better tell you the truth about Miss Bawne. I was very naturally trying to protect her honour all I could. She was – she was my mistress even before my wife died.'

'I see,' nodded the Inspector. 'Tell us everything. It is best for you and for her, too.'

'Yes, but I want you to understand that it was my fault entirely. Every bit of it. . . . She never wanted to do wrong, but I persuaded her to. And even before my wife's death, she left me because she couldn't bear what she was doing. I didn't see her for six months at least before Mrs Presset died, nor for some two months afterwards. Then it was I who went to look her up. because I was so lonely. That may seem wrong to other people, but it is very natural to the one who has been through it.'

'Quite so,' agreed the Inspector sympathetically. 'We quite

see. Now if you would tell us in just a little more detail. . . .'

Helplessly shrugging, Paul sat down and told them all: about the cheques he had given her, the hotels, and her visits to this house. 'That is the whole truth, absolutely,' he concluded. 'And if in a desire to shield me she has told your officers anything else, I will tell her to change it. I think it is just possible she has. She is very loyal. And then you can leave her out of it altogether, can't you?'

'I hope we may be able to. I hope we may be able to rule you both out of it, if it comes to that. And now, sir, it is your assured conviction, you say, that your wife died of heart trouble brought on by a gastric attack?'

'Of course! What else? I am as sure of it as I can be of anything in this world . . . unless, maybe, there was something in the patent medicines she took, but I can't believe—'

'Very good,' interrupted the Inspector. 'Then – I am sorry to mention this but you will appreciate that we have to ask everything – would you like to tell us all you can about what became of a tin of weed-killer that a gardener, Alfred Briscoll, left here?'

'Pardon?'

Again Paul was staring at him with terror in his eyes, so that both the Sergeant and the Inspector thought, 'If ever a man was guilty, this one is.'

Boltro repeated his question. The weed-killer tin?

'That? Why, what about it. What's that got to do with it?'

'It's dangerous stuff, and it might in some way or other—'

'It's nonsense. I threw it away ages ago. There was nothing left in it after Briscoll had gone. I think the dustmen took it the next day. . . . There was nothing in it . . .'

'I see. Then that's about all we want to know. Perhaps you could now help us to get it all into a written statement. I'll give you all the assistance I can.'

'Certainly. Write it all down. I'm only too glad to write it down. The truth can't hurt me.'

'That's right. Are you ready, Doyle?'

'Yes, sir.'

'Well, shall we begin it like this? "I," – what are your names, sir?'

Paul cleared his throat, and the names came huskily. 'Paul Arthur Presset.'

' "I, Paul Arthur Presset, after having been cautioned by Chief Inspector Boltro that anything I say may be used in evidence hereafter, wish to make the following statement" – do you agree to that, sir?'

'I – I suppose so.'

'Good. Well, get it down, Sergeant. "I, Paul Arthur Presset. . . ." '

Chapter Nine

Paul saw them down the steps and shut the front door. Absently, mechanically, he trod the few stairs to the kitchen whence he had come. He had longed for the time when he could be alone with his sickness, and he went to the room he knew, as a dog creeps behind the hedge with his wound.

He stood with the fingers of one hand in the fist of the other, both trembling. Sometimes they jerked spasmodically.

Suddenly, without warning, his security had been gutted around him. Suddenly – so suddenly that he could not yet see it distinctly – menace was everywhere. This morning all was hope; now all was horror. Exposure . . . and exposure, not to a few, but to an execrating world. Arrest, and the reporters racing to the news; his friends reading it, and his parents – his mother with her pride in him! The castle of grandeur that he had erected before them blown into the air, in a cloud of shame! The boys at the school reading all about it! Norman Sandys who had despised him saying with dilated nostrils, 'I told you so. I always thought there was something wrong about that fellow!' Then a cold stone cell and a locked iron door; and long sleepless nights behind the locked iron door that pressed in upon one till one could shriek; a dock before a staring crowd; and – how long before the end? Had he perhaps only a few more months of life?

His hands shook; his body jerked.

No, it wouldn't come to that. He was frightening himself unnecessarily. Such things happened to other people, not to oneself. They wouldn't find enough evidence to justify exhumation; and even if they did, and found poison in her body, they couldn't prove that he had given it to her. It might be accident, or suicide, or it might have percolated into the body from the soil around; they could prove nothing against him; and, after the trial, he would escape into some green hiding place with Myra who loved him.

Myra. In the first flush of terror he had had no room for love, because love is partly unselfish; he had forgotten the existence of Myra. And even now, as he remembered her, he could have said, 'Only save me from this shame, and I will do without her.'

Nor did he recover love at once. He was only wanting to know what they had said to her, and what she had answered. He could see her face, white, staring, horrified, when they told their business. What had she said? Ah, he must go and find out at once. Action would be relief. He could continue this thinking, this ceaseless revolution of thoughts, on the top of a tram.

Oh, yes! And as he moved to run to Myra, he remembered the great comfort of her; and he was then little different from a hurt child that runs for the caress of its mother. But Myra – was that all over? Was that happiness to be struck from his out-stretched hand? O God, what a trick of fate – but no, he couldn't blame fate; even in this disorder of his thoughts he could see that it was no malignant trick of fate, but just the unremitting law that you reaped what you had sown. But God might surely have been pitiful. His position had been so unbearable. Surely God at least had understood that, though guilty, he had been driven, driven, driven . . . and that he wanted to be better. Was God no more pitiful than men? Was there no mercy in the universe anywhere, from sky to sky? No pity among the stars but only payment?

But Myra – O God, had he, who wanted only to be good to her, brought her this misery and shame? 'Myra, I didn't want to do this to you. I wanted to make you happy.' He must go to her at once and comfort her. Neither could he know any rest till they had talked it over, and discussed what to do, what to say.

He ran upstairs to his room, the same round of thought and argument recommencing as he ran: they could prove nothing; they wouldn't even exhume; if they did exhume, they could prove nothing against *him*; even if they arrested him, they'd have to set him free in the end, and then – yes, it was not the end of the world; it was a terrible blow, that was all, a bad period that he had not expected, but it would pass, and then. . . .

Now he felt calmer as he put on his shoes; but he knew that soon the awful round of thought would begin again.

As he descended the stairs, the bell rang; his fright leapt; but it was stilled – or, rather, it was changed into nervousness – by the shadow he saw through the glass of the front door. Myra was standing there; he saw her hand go to her hat, and knew that her face was turned to the road.

He caught his breath, ran his finger round his collar, swallowed once, and opened the door.

'Oh, Paul, let me come in. . . . Shut the door; shut it! . . . There have been men round to see me, they said they were detectives. They've been with me all the morning, asking questions about you. Oh, my dear, what does it mean? They seem to suspect. . . .'

'Come in here, my dear.' Now a sense of protectiveness and strength overlaid his panic, and he took her by the hand and led her into the dining-room. 'I know all about it. They've been here too.'

'Here too?'

'Yes, yes, but don't get worried. There. Give me a kiss, and sit down and tell me all about it.'

Dazed, she removed her hat and laid it on the table.

'But Paul, it's so awful. They seem to think that Elinor – that she didn't die as the doctor said she did—'

He was astonished at his new feeling of strength. His eyes were almost smiling as he said, 'It's very simple, dearest. It's horrid, of course, but I can quite see how it has come about. The plain truth is that they suspect I murdered Elinor.'

'Paul! How *dare* they? Who has dared to suggest such a wicked thing? How *could* they?'

'That's what they think, I'm sure,' said he, shaking his head and smiling sadly. Wonderful how easily his part had slipped over him, cloaking the trembles of ten minutes before: now, before Myra, he was the strong protector, able to treat with grim humour so stupid a threat. 'They tried to cover it up, but I wasn't such a fool as not to see what was at the back of their minds. I charged them with it, and they admitted that there had been suspicion and gossip.'

'Gossip? But who can have gossiped?'

'That I know no more than you, but sit down and tell me all they asked you, and all that you said. Did you tell them the truth?'

'Yes . . . yes, I had to . . . I didn't at first, but he was a very nice man, the one who did the questioning, a Mr Osley, and he persuaded me that it would be best for everybody to tell the truth quite simply. And he told me frankly that someone had suggested that I had stayed in your house that time that Elinor was away—'

Paul had not heard of this; and beneath the strong man's clothes the trembler stirred. 'They know that, do they? What is there they don't know?'

'They seem to know everything. They've been to Mrs Bohntree, and to those people at Chiswick.'

Paul's jaw fell, and then came forward, set with hopelessness – a hopelessness so complete that for the present it did not hurt. 'Damn them.'

'But what are they doing it for?'

'I've told you. They think I murdered Elinor.'

'But how can they think such a thing. Everyone knows that she died quite naturally.'

'She died of symptoms that might be poisoning, and just because they've learned we were lovers before she died, they suspect I killed Elinor to get you.'

'Oh, Paul!'

'Yes; and if it comes to that, I inherited all her money. And once upon a time I had a fraction of weed-killer for my garden, and that's enough: they'll exhume her body, and for all I know they'll find something in it – God knows what she may not have taken by accident! – and not a living soul will believe anything but that I killed her. A jury will cheerfully say so, and they'll make an end of me.'

She jumped up and put her arms around him, as he sat there, gaping glumly. 'No, no! They shan't! Don't talk of such things! I shan't let them.' Hysterically she held him tight to her, now stroking his head, now pressing her lips on his brow. 'How *can* they? Oh, let's go away – far away – to somewhere where people don't say such things. Let's go right away. I don't want anybody in the world but you. You and I'll be happy somewhere.'

Once more he was the strong protector, calming her, strengthening her. 'We can't do that. It would look like guilt. Perhaps it'll all blow over. Come, sit here.' He placed the footstool for her at his feet, and when she had sunk to it, drew her against his knees. 'I'm so terribly sorry I've dragged you into all this.'

'How could *you* help it, if people are so wicked? It's not your fault.'

'It *is* my fault. I should have waited. I shouldn't have run the risk of compromising you.'

'If it comes to that, I compromised you. Give me a little of the blame to bear, I shall be happier then.'

'Myra. . . .'

So they talked, or fell into long silences, she sitting on the footstool, he holding her against his knees and sometimes feeling the shudder that ran up her frame. They discussed who could have started the rumour – who could first have believed it – and one by one ruled out all their friends. They debated what would happen next, and decided what he must do. He must walk among people with head high. He must go to the school, like a man who had nothing to fear. The school! Were they making their inquiries at the school? Oh, how wicked it was, carelessly blasting a man's career, just because a few evil tongues had wagged! In one of their silences he asked, 'Do you want some food? Shall I get you something to eat?' and she answered, 'Eat? I don't want to eat. Do you?' 'No,' he said. 'I seem to want only to hold on to you. I want you close. I just want to feel that I am keeping hold of you.' She rested a hand on his knee, and they dropped back into the silence.

Paul's eyes strayed to the window. What was happening out there? Were detectives abroad everywhere, taking their statements from people? At this moment were they writing them down? 'Tick-tick-tick,' went the marble clock on the mantelpiece: were they building up with every tick a stronger case against him? Was his life ticking away?

'Myra,' he began, 'if they – if they made a case against me, you would never, never believe?'

Her eyes turned up to him. 'How can you ask such a thing?'

And since he did not reply, she went on, 'But they won't – they can't – it's impossible.'

But he, gazing out of the window to where his enemies were forming rank, shook his head and answered, 'I don't know. I hope it'll all blow over, but I know only too well that clever lawyers can twist everything into proof, even the most innocent things. . . .'

'No . . . they mustn't!'

'But they will, if they want to. It's possible the time will come when nobody in the world believes in me but you.'

Her answer was to take his hand.

'And do you realise, Myra dear, that if – if there's a trial – it'll all come out about you? Have you thought about that?'

She turned and stared into the empty grate.

'Every . . . every paper in the land,' he continued, forcing himself to state the worst, though it sent the shiver through her. . . . 'Will you be able to forgive me for having brought you into that?'

After a pause she murmured her answer to the grate. 'If it has to be, it has to be.' Then she swung round and seized both his hands, pressing them at quick intervals, and all her tired face took on the beauty of solicitude and sympathy. 'But you're not to worry about that. Don't you see, it'd probably hurt me less than it'd hurt you. You've always cared about people's praise and love. I don't think I have. Perhaps I did once, but I no longer seem to mind. I want only one person, and now that mother's dead – oh, thank God she died before this, poor dear mother – I've no one whose opinion I care about except yours. Don't you *see* this? It *is* so, truly; *truly*! And when it's all over – when they've acquitted you – as they will – they *must* – because the world can't be as unjust as that – we'll go away together – ever so far away, to some place where no one knows us, and I'll try to make up to you for all you've suffered. We'll go to Cumberland, shall we, to some tiny place among the mountains, and we'll change our names, and perhaps I'll take a few guests in holiday times, and you can work quietly in the garden, which you've always loved, and nobody'll know who you are. . . . Oh, it'll be happy!' Her eyes brightened, for she meant what she had said; something in her had always wanted to run from the world, and it was glad to be driven where it wanted to go -- and yet she was breaking into tears. 'Oh, I don't think it's going to be bad, if we can only endure. Don't you *see*: things'll come all right in any case, if we only wait? What do we mind what people say? I'll wait for you till they've done their worst, and then we'll be terribly happy somewhere, quite alone. It'll be all right, my dear; it'll be all right.'

Chapter Ten

A summer month, and more, went by; and out of the menacing stillness around the house – not a word. Inspector Boltro came no more. The May blossom fell and lay on the pavements in mats of pink and white; the young leaves darkened; tulip and iris withered, their sabre-leaves blackening at tip and edge; and the grass grew tall, with the weeds for company. But Paul did no work with his trowel or his shears; if he came into the garden at all, it was to wander around, or stand still, while he bit at a nail or pulled at a finger, his face drawn, his hands shaking, and fright in his eyes. Islington's month of flowers and colour was past, and he didn't observe it, except to wonder sometimes if he would ever see the iris again.

His brain was working; always working. Round and round the old questions – what they would find out, why they must abandon an inadequate case, what he could answer to their charges, why he was perfectly safe – round and round it went, all day and everywhere; and at night in bed, and in the morning on waking. Why had he not cremated? It was his kindness that had stopped him, and now they were going to get him through his one deed that was good. If so, God was cruel. But they wouldn't exhume – why all this worry; don't worry, don't worry. He was making himself ill with worry; and things always looked blacker to a sick man. What was happening out there in the world, just beyond what his eye could see? Out there in the golden light of summer, and behind the silence? Was Inspector

Boltro even now discussing him with someone? Were they even now collating in some police office the evidence against him? But what evidence? Again the old round began: first he built up a damning case against himself till deathly horror gripped him and he longed to run, or to kill himself; then brick by brick he undid the building for his own peace.

None of his friends had said a word to him about the suspicion – but then he had not dared to go near them. Still, they greeted him if he passed in the street – but only with a bow or a lift of the hand, and were not those gestures perfunctory and unwilling? No, he imagined it; and always his own were lively in return. Certainly the doctor cut him, but that was for an old offence. Tosh Johnson had told him that: the doctor was cold to him because he had called him a 'second-class brain'. The doctor didn't suspect him of anything; he must long ago have told the police that their theory was nonsense.

At school for a while all was as usual. Evidently Heasman, Inglewood, and Sandys, living far enough away, knew nothing; he could have guessed at once if they were hiding something. Each morning his eyes swung for the symptoms of knowledge in Heasman and Inglewood, or, worse still, in the boys; but he did not see it; and before his colleagues and in his classroom, he acted serenity and liveliness, though, at every release of his mind, it went back to the lodestone thoughts.

And then he saw what he was looking for. There was discomfort in the atmosphere as he came in. In the passage Heasman saw him, and hastily disappeared. In the Common Room Inglewood's eyes at once fell on him with a new interest; his 'Hallo, Bertrand,' though kindly, was uncomfortable; and all his subsequent heartiness was forced. As for Sandys, he was just silent – alarmingly silent. At prayers the new mistress kept looking up at him. And he was hardly in his classroom before a boy entered with the message that Mr Heasman would like to see him in his study.

'Oh, certainly,' said he, with studied cheerfulness.

Heasman in his threadbare little study with the busts of the musicians was polite, uncomfortable, distressed, anxious to be kind, but resentful and angry – angry with whom he did not quite know. 'I feel I ought to tell you, Presset, there've been some people here making inquiries about you – police, in fact – it's ludicrous, of course! – and they've been asking Inglewood and Sandys, too. It's very distressing. You know something about it, of course?'

And Paul acted his indignation and ridicule: 'Haven't they got that bee out of their bonnet yet? Yes, they came to me about it, and I thought I'd settled 'em. Idiotic gossip. How they can take it seriously beats me—'

'Yes, yes, but it's very unfortunate for the school, I must say. You will see that. Supposing it gets about? To have a master even suspected of anything is enough to damn a school. I'm very worried: very worried indeed.'

'I understand,' said Paul. 'Well, I'm prepared to stay away.' And he thought, 'How much have the police withheld about Myra? Have they been acting generously here?'

'It's so difficult,' worried Mr Heasman. 'I don't want people to say that I got rid of you because I believed this absurd suggestion. Let me tell you I told the police they were idiots, but. . . .'

'I thank you for saying that, sir, but let me keep away, for all your sakes. I'm not quite dependent on my earnings.' Even in these extreme hours, he, who had been poor so long, could feel a pride in such a statement. 'You must see that it is not my fault if I am vilified like this, but I'm extremely sorry if it should in any way injure the school. I won't have *that*. I'll keep away. And if it all blows over and reaches no ears but our own, I can come back again. If not, I – I can provide for myself.'

'No, but I don't want you to think – I don't want to do anything unfair.'

'It's not unfair. I've seen all along that if this intolerable suggestion gained ground I should have to stop away. But I hoped I'd scotched it. But naturally if it got to the ears of the boys, I knew I couldn't face them. Oh, yes' – his imagination showed him the curious, fascinated eyes of the boys – 'I'd rather be away.'

Heasman looked relieved; also, perhaps, a little ashamed, and anxious to be kind. It was plain that he knew nothing about Myra yet. 'But will it do you any harm to leave the school suddenly like this? Will it add to the suspicion?'

'It may,' said Paul. 'But it can't be helped. It's all I can do. Don't worry, because I know I couldn't stay.'

Heasman's relief was very obvious. 'I don't think it need harm you. I can say – in fact, I shall make it my business to say – that you were run down and needed a holiday. I shall let people see that I did not dismiss you, or lose faith in you. And if this rumour reaches me, be sure that I shall say it's too ridiculous.'

'Thank you.'

'Not at all.' And his next words showed where his real thoughts lay. 'I should have had to do it, if only for the sake of the school.'

So Paul was permanently at home, with all time on his hands and nothing to do but think; nothing to do but go round and round old comforting arguments, as he walked round and round a room, or round and round the garden. He had days with Myra, who now, at his earnest request, gave up her work that she might be with him whenever he needed her. Matters were too serious now for her to worry any more about accepting money from him; and, as he said, he would have gone mad, if he had not been able to escape with her into the country sometimes. She even found a room nearer to him, in a quiet street off the Euston Road. Often on their walks together he was silent and abstracted, and she quiet and understanding. When alone he wanted to be with her, but sometimes when with her he wanted to be alone. Alone with his thoughts. And as the weeks passed, 'I must know something,' he told himself; 'I must know something'; and he thought of writing an indignant demand for information. But he dared not.

Sometimes he would imagine a letter of apology from the police, and, playing with the dream, he would vividly experience the exquisite relief that would follow, and the old excited planning for the future. Sunk in his dreams, he would have lost the day-long nightmare; then, coming up from the dream, he would find it awaiting him.

Or his thoughts would take the other road, and he would imagine a letter announcing the exhumation (for so he supposed they informed you). What then? He stopped his pacing and stood still as he tried, with thumping heart, to determine what then. Flight? He played with the idea of flight. Run at his own chosen moment, some time between the exhumation and the publication of the expert's analysis. Act quick as lightning. Outwit them all and lose himself on the Continent, where Myra would join him as soon as she could – and as he imagined himself and her safely hidden on the Continent, perhaps in some village on a southern slope of the Pyrenees, he would experience again the exquisite peace.

This flight thought became relief like an unguent. Planning had a face like action; and action was always relief. The ever-working brain now played round and round every facet of this thought, and soon he was not without vanity in the subtlety of his brain and the perfection of his plans. It should be easy for him, a very ordinary-looking man of moderate height, without scar or birth-mark, to get lost in the multitude. He was just like a million other small, spare men of fifty. And consider: if only they delayed a little longer, the holiday period would set the whole world travelling and he'd slip easily along with the crowds at station or port. A new portmanteau, new unmarked clothes, money – he must convert all his stock into bearer securities, he must cash cheques to the tune of five hundred pounds till he had, say, fifty ten-pound notes, and gradually he must change these notes one by one at shops and restaurants all over London, till he had accumulated a large supply of gold. He was amazed and flattered by the fine working of his brain: it was thinking of everything, it was burrowing into every cranny and hole, it was finding the smallest crack or flaw and correcting them. The peasant in him liked to think of that bag of gold, and that he would carry all his fortune on his person, leaving none behind. He was impatient to begin these quiet financial operations; and soon he was engaged upon them; and every new sheaf of notes and every new pile of sovereigns was comfort. The second month was passing, and still there was nothing but silence around him. He continued his accumulation of portable money, but began to tell himself that he had panicked too soon. All was happening as he had foreseen: they had not found enough to justify further steps and were throwing up the game. Just as a man cannot 'argue against his income', so necessity compelled him to believe that all that fog of horror was clearing away. He was still far from easy, but he was very much easier; the headache did not hold him all day, he ate his food with more relish, he pottered in the garden with increasing interest, he slept better at nights, and there were times when the old happiness which had been slain rose on its arm to hope again.

And then one day, as he plied the rake in his narrow front garden, he saw a uniformed policeman coming up the pavement from the direction of the Caledonian Road. The policeman was not walking fast, but there is something different in the walk of a policeman approaching a destination from the walk of a policeman patrolling his beat; and this man, surely, was going straight to a goal. Paul rested on his rake, quite certain the man was coming to his gate. He came, opened it, and stood within the garden.

'Are you Mr Presset, sir?' he asked politely.

'Yes.'

'I am Sergeant Davidson from the local division acting on the instructions of the coroner for West Essex.' The Sergeant spoke unemotionally and deliberately, like a policeman in the witness-box who has learned his evidence by heart.

'Yes?'

'I have to give you notice, sir, that the coroner has ordered the exhumation of your wife's body from its grave in Trusted churchyard, which lies within his jurisdiction.'

'I see,' said Paul. 'I understand. . . . Yes, I expected that. I'm glad.'

Chapter Eleven

The great pile of Trusted Church dreamed on its low hill. Even as its spire gazed over the green miles, and far away to the sea, so its spirit seemed to ponder on the centuries, and not on any momentary or transient activity at its foot.

But there was movement about the churchyard wall this sunny evening in July: a small movement and unobtrusive; almost stealthy. Three gates led through the wall into the churchyard: one at the westward corner, opening towards the great porch, one at the north, and one at the south-east, at the top of a tilted alley that ran its cobbles and gutters between the whitewashed cottages and the overhanging half-timbered houses. At each of these gates a policeman of the West Essex Constabulary quietly took up his stance, or quietly paced to and fro. The gates were sufficiently out of one another's sight for the policemen, at first, to excite but little attention. And their faces gave nothing away: from their expressions you might have thought them as little occupied with this present time, and as lost in the centuries, as the high spire above them. The house windows that looked upon the northern face of the church gave no heed to the two in their view; a tip-cart clattered past, and its driver did not turn his head; labourers turned into the bar of the Dun Horse Inn without a glance at the constable who paced before the western gate immediately opposite the bar door. The children of the village played farther down the hill, where the main street broadened into a wide market place; and from them the constable at the top of the cobbled alley was hidden. They went on with their play; and their voices, mingling with the birdsong in the churchyard trees, the clatter of a wagon round the corner, and the whistle of a far-off train, wove a texture that was more like silence than sound.

Nobody had noticed two very ordinary-looking men who had arrived in a car some time before, gone into the tobacconist's shop, come out again in about five minutes' time, and driven on to the rectory. There was no reason to notice them unless you remembered that Mr Neal, the tobacconist, was also the People's Warden up at the church. The two men had spent about a quarter of an hour in the rectory and then come out and gone into the churchyard, just before the three constables walked up with their sergeant and diverged to their stations. They had walked through the gravestones to a white marble angel, the most conspicuous headstone of all, whose hand, stretched over her grave, seemed to be pointing whither to come. They stopped at the marble kerb about the grave and looked at the inscription. One of them drew the other's attention to the concluding text, as if he found it ironic in view of what they had come to do: 'Grant her Thy peace'. The other looked up to the battlemented wall of the church screening them on the right, and down to the row of lime trees at the foot of the slope, shutting out the meadows, and murmured, 'Good job it's on the south side and hidden from the houses. We shan't be disturbed here, I reckon.'

'Yes,' agreed his companion; 'and I tell you what, Clem; that angel's going to take some shifting.'

'You're right,' said the other. 'I'm glad they've got to do it, and not me.'

And both, since it didn't seem an occasion on which to talk much, lit up cigarettes and stood about with their hands in their pockets. Both were more interested than they pretended, for such a task as theirs this evening didn't come to them every day. The one addressed as Clem took from his pocket a typewritten sheet and read it again, his cigarette drooping from his lips. It was headed 'West Essex to wit' and proceeded:

'Whereas I, Arnold Enfield Clarke, Coroner for the County of West Essex, have been informed that on the 15th day of October, 19– the body of one Elinor Presset was buried in the churchyard of your parish of Trusted in the said County and that there is reasonable ground to suspect that the said Elinor Presset died an unnatural death; and whereas I am of opinion that an inquest should be held upon the dead body: These are, therefore, by virtue of my office in His Majesty's name, to charge and command you that you forthwith cause the body of the said Elinor Presset to be taken up; And whereas I am satisfied that it is expedient to order the said body to be removed into the jurisdiction of Mr David Austen Home, Coroner for North Central London, who has consented to such removal: Now I hereby order that the said body shall be conveyed to the mortuary in the parish of Islington Vale in the County of London. . . Hereof, Fail not, as you will answer the contrary at your peril. Given under my hand and seal the –th day of July, One thousand and nine hundred and —

(*Signed*) Arnold Enfield Clarke.

To the Minister and Church wardens of the said Parish of Trusted. . . . To the Constables of the Metropolis and of the said County of West Essex.'

Meantime a small blue motor van, coming from the direction of London, had stopped at the foot of the cobbled alley that led between its cottages to the churchyard gate. A large car following the van had not stopped but gone on, right round the bend of the street and past the north wall of the church and round into Battle Street, as if it had no part with the blue van nor interest in the church. A hundred yards up Battle Street it also stopped, and its doors swung open and four men stepped out.

The first was Dr Waterhall, in a suit darker and a hat at a less lively angle than usual. His manner was subdued and his voice low, to match a solemn occasion; but within he was thrilled and – well, 'happy' is perhaps an unfair word, but certainly he would rather have been in Battle Street, Trusted, this evening than anywhere else in England. No boredom tonight. In all his forty years of doctoring he had never had such an experience as was now to be his, and he was looking forward to it with deep interest. And how could he help hoping that they would ultimately find in the body that which they suspected: he *had* to hope it, both for his own justification and for the drama and excitement that would follow. These weighed more in the balance than the life of little Presset, because, dammit, if Presset had done the deed, he deserved all he'd get. One wasn't a sentimentalist about cold-blooded murderers.

He turned to murmur something to a thin, distinguished-looking, grey-moustached man who had stepped out after him, carrying a mackintosh on his arm. This man bore a very famous name; and he was plainly less impressed and less interested than Dr Waterhall, because he had attended at such a business many times before. With this man, in the journey from London, Dr Waterhall had been rather talkative, in a mixture of self-assertive equality and patent respect for a successful and well-known member of his own profession; and the grey-moustached man had been rather silent, for he was not deceived. He nodded now, as Dr Waterhall, feeling the church very close, spoke to him in a lowered tone; but he gave no other reply.

From the other door of the car Inspector Boltro had stepped out. He, like the doctor, was feeling his importance, and savouring to the full the interest of the hour. The word 'happy' must be given fearlessly to the Inspector's mood: he was engaged, he believed, on his greatest case and bringing it to a successful and ringing issue. Tomorrow the whole country would read of his activity in Trusted village this evening; his name would pass under the lintel of every house in the land. The old people in Wildean would be proud of their son and show the papers to their friends. And in the meantime he was enjoying all this secrecy which he himself had designed: it was spice in the hunter's game. He too hoped – hoped with all his heart – that the hunt would find what it sought; and the hope was as near a certainty as hope could be. It held only just enough of anxiety to make the moment thrilling.

After Inspector Boltro the undertaker stepped out; the same undertaker as we saw in this place before; keen-featured, clean-shaven and well-tailored; moving on soft, considerate feet and speaking in low, reverent tones. He, perhaps, was more impressed with the evening's solemnity than they all; or, perhaps, he alone felt it incumbent on him to gather the solemnity between his folded hands and express it for them all in voice and movement and word.

'Well, gentlemen,' said the Inspector, who seemed to be in charge. 'We may as well go straight there, I think.'

'Right, Inspector,' agreed Dr Waterhall, who considered that, from his different professional angle, he also might be held to be in charge.

The grey-moustached analyst from the Home Office said nothing.

And the four men walked back down Battle Street towards the church: Dr Waterhall and the analyst in front, Inspector Boltro following, with the undertaker a respectful half-pace behind. They entered the churchyard by the western gate, the policeman on duty there saluting; and they walked round the great headland of the church till they saw the white angel in the midst of the tombs, with a little company of men about her.

'That is it,' said Dr Waterhall, pleased to take the lead. 'I was at the funeral'; and he went a few steps ahead, the analyst treading silently after him.

Through the untidy grass they picked their way towards

the little company of people, which now contained, in addition to the two men from the Home Office, a party of gravediggers with planks and shovels and picks, a couple of stonemason's men, and the sergeant of the West Essex police. The four gentlemen took up positions at the grave's foot, and Inspector Boltro exchanged a few sentences with the sergeant, who then nodded to the stonemason's men and muttered, 'Right. Carry on.'

And the stonemason's men began. They separated the white kerbs and removed them to one side; they placed blocks of wood and rollers behind the statue and then, with mallet and chisel, they disconnected the statue from its brick foundation, prized it up, lowered it carefully on its back, and rolled it to a little distance away. There it lay, overthrown, its hand now pointing steadily and stupidly to the sky. They removed the brick foundations and stood back, leaving the diggers to continue the work.

The diggers went about their work with the quiet, whispering reverence of rough men. While the birds sang in the limes, fluttering the leaves as they hopped from branch to branch, and the voices of the children came up from the market place, and the flawless sky of a summer evening arched over their work, they opened the grave. The rest of the company stood watching without speaking, their eyes tranced into thought. So silent was it that one noticed many things which else had gone unremarked: the strong scent of carnations from a neighbouring grave, the overpowering scent of privet from a hedge to windward, and the scuttle of a rabbit down in the hollow under the limes. There was hardly a sound except the plat of the uplifted earth on to the mounting heap, and sometimes the rattle of a shovel on to a recumbent haft as the diggers tossed it down and took up a pick instead. The undertaker stood a yard or two behind the watching gentlemen, his hat in his hand and held against his breast. All were as reverent as if they were at a funeral; and indeed it was the scent of nine months before, reversed.

The operation was long, for the men had to excavate to a depth of nearly six feet. They paused often to wipe their brows with handkerchief or arm. The evening cooled, especially when a soft white cloud began to pass across the sun; and the grey-moustached gentleman put on the mackintosh which he had brought from London. Some of the watchers thought to themselves that 'they'd give anything to smoke', but none liked to be the first to do so; so they just stood, gazing in silence; or perhaps one of them walked a little way and looked at the other graves, their headstones and bright or faded flowers. But at length a spade's edge grated on the top of the coffin, and the digger, intending to refer only to the coffin, muttered, 'Here she is.'

Several heads craned forward, and the undertaker came with whispered apologies through the others to superintend the raising of the coffin; but suddenly the grey-moustached gentleman said 'Hold!' and instantly Inspector Boltro repeated, 'Hold a minute!' and all waited while the expert came and looked down. Dr Waterhall also, as one with a right to do so, stepped forward and looked down. The analyst asked for some earth from the top of the coffin, and it was given him; and he walked away.

The diggers resumed their work; a spade scratched on the nameplate; and soon all was ready for the undertaker to instruct them how to get the webbing straps under the coffin. This was a task that gave them much difficulty, and for a time the quiet reverence was shattered by voices, and the birds seemed to chirrup louder, as if excited or alarmed by this new move. But after a while all was in order; and two men on each side of the grave stood on planks with the webbings in their hands.

'Right,' whispered the undertaker. 'Together now.'

The men pulled on the webbings, but the coffin came only an inch or two and stopped; and one of the men swung himself down into the grave and dislodged some more earth. His spade scraping along the lid of the coffin chafed the nerves. A fairway cleared, he swung himself above ground like a gymnast, and again the four men pulled on the webbings.

Slowly – ill-balanced at first, then truly – the coffin came up . . . up . . . All the watchers bared their heads to salute this return of Elinor.

Its top rose above the lips of the grave; and Dr Waterhall watched with chin dropped. Elinor rising again.

The coffin was now above ground, and all saw that the wood was in good condition but the metal fittings were rusted. The bearers were about to slide it on to the rollers, when the analyst said, 'Wait.'

'Wait!' repeated Inspector Boltro; and the men held it suspended.

Bending down and scraping with the edge of his hand, the analyst dislodged some earth from its side into a jar and took it away. The coffin slid on to the rollers.

Turning round, Dr Waterhall saw that the old verger of the church had wheeled up a trolley-bier. The men lifted the coffin on to this, covered it with a pall, and, at a nod from the Inspector and the undertaker, wheeled the trolley towards the western gate of the churchyard. Dr Waterhall and the analyst followed, leaving behind them a mound of upturned earth, a few men putting planks over a grave, and an overthrown angel whose guardianship had been violated.

At the western gate they saw the small blue van backed against the kerb, with a group of children and loafers standing by and gaping at the policeman. Across the road another little crowd had come to the door of the Dun Horse Inn. There was a movement of heads and a murmur of voices as the people saw another policeman, the sergeant, following behind the trolley.

'Keep back now; keep back,' begged the young policeman, as the trolley came through the gate and halted near the tailboard of the van.

'What is it? What's up?' demanded the people of one another.

'Looks as if the per-leace had been digging for trouble,' grunted one of the men.

'What's that? What's that you say?'

'Look's like an exhumation.'

'Will it be in the papers tomorrow?'

' 'Spect so.'

Inspector Boltro walked forward. Even before a little crowd of villagers he could not refrain from showing that he was really the man in authority. He issued directions, pointing with his arm; he talked importantly to the analyst and Dr Waterhall; he lifted his voice a little as he spoke to the sergeant. Here was the first ripple of that widening publicity. Tomorrow they would read of it, and say, 'That must have been Chief Inspector Boltro'; and for many months to come they would tell their friends that they had seen him. He stood there, the tallest figure of them all, watching the men as they slid the coffin, foot first, into the van.

'Right,' he said authoritatively as the door banged to.

He said a rather loud goodbye to the sergeant; and he, Dr Waterhall and the analyst, lighting up cigarettes, moved off to Battle Street, where their car waited – the undertaker staying behind with the van. A few curious children followed them and stood to gape, as they stepped into the car. The car which had been turned about drove off down Battle Street and Cutlers' Street, and, leaving the town behind, found the road to London. In a very little while Dr Waterhall, leaning back in his seat, saw the blue van ahead of them. They drew closer to it, but could not easily overtake and pass it by, because the road was winding and hilly. So for a time he sat staring at it, as it ran before them; and he thought, 'Thus Elinor returns to London.' On past the green verges where the grass was high and the white of the cow-parsley lay like sea-spume; on between the hedgerows festooned and tangled with bind-weed and tufted vetch, and aflower with dog-rose and bramble; down into a hollow where the bat willows stood silver-leaved and feathery, and then up again on to high ground where the fields of wheat and barley and winter oats stretched to either side; on beneath the chestnut, beech, and sycamore trees; on and on to London.

PART III

Chapter One

It was a quarter to seven in the morning, and Paul, in bare feet and dressing-gown, came from his bedroom to the top of the stairs and looked down to the hall mat. No, the newspaper had not yet arrived.

He went back, and dressed and shaved with fingers that fumbled. All the time he was listening for the click of the letterflap and the fall of the newspaper on the mat. He heard it; and the hearing stopped his heart for a beat. Hurriedly he completed his dressing and came to the stairs. Yes, it was on the mat. Terror gripped him as he descended. His breath shortened and his fingers shook as he picked it up. He opened it at the middle page – and Oh, God, it was the lead story! 'Schoolmaster's Wife Exhumed, Uncanny Churchyard Scene', ran the headlines. 'Excitement in Essex Village, Mr and Mrs Presset's Life in London.' Mr and Mrs Presset – there was the suggestion to all the world.

He read on wildly. The reporters, unable to describe the churchyard scene, had made their bricks without straw. They had made a fine story which doubtless had rejoiced the whole length of Fleet Street last night. They must have swooped down on the village, and interrogated the children, the verger, and the loungers in the Dun Horse bar. They described how the policemen had guarded the gates of the churchyard; they described what they imagined had happened within the gates;

they described the grave as it now was, opened and empty, with the piled earth beside it and the angel recumbent on the grass; they gave the inscription on the stone and pointed out the irony of 'Grant her Thy peace'. They had even published a facsimile of Elinor's death certificate. There it was across the bottom of two columns: 'Death in the Sub-district of Islington Vale in the County of London.' His eye swung at once to his own name, 'Wife of Paul Arthur Presset, Schoolmaster. . . . Signature, Description and Residence of Informant: Paul Arthur Presset. . . .'

Complete despair was almost like rest; and he could take no new pain when he saw that the second column was headed simply, 'Mr Presset.' But he felt the wickedness of this column. He had done the deed, of course, but say he hadn't, they would have published just the same this foul suggestion that here was the man to watch: keeping just within the law, they would have hanged an innocent man before he was tried. A man's life was nothing compared with a little excitement to sell in the market place. The column described the house in which he was now standing; it described the lonely life of Mr and Mrs Presset since Miss Annie Mavis left them; it carefully stated that Elinor's will had bequeathed all her real and personal estate to her husband absolutely; to heighten the news value it showed Elinor forth as a 'woman of means', previously the wife of a well-known city man highly placed in the insurance world, and Paul as a 'classical master in a well-known London school and a member of London University'. This last it had used as a fine piece of garnishing, giving it the crown of a cross-heading, 'University Man'. Thus they had turned his wretched little struggle through matriculation into a heavy and conspicuous burden to bear.

Oh, they had written it up well. 'Neighbours describe Mrs Presset as a gracious and pleasant woman,' they wrote, 'and Mr Presset as a scholarly man, very quiet and reserved. They have been very popular in Islington, though Mrs Presset is said to have been rather the more sociable of the two. In the early part of last year, we understand, she suffered and nearly died from an illness very similar to that which brought about her demise. The doctors are not wholly satisfied as to what may have caused these attacks, and very properly the Home Office has decided on further inquiries. The final result of their expert's analysts will probably not be known for some weeks.'

They must have been round with their notebooks to the neighbours, the tradespeople and the police, for they had not been to him yet. True, a bell had rung last night, and he, seeing the shadow of a strange hat through the front door panes, had slipped into the dining-room, to crouch there like a cornered animal.

Well, every paper in the land would have this story this morning. Think of the excitement at the school, the boys chattering in noisy groups, Inglewood and Sandys exchanging their excitement in the Common Room, and the servants with their 'Oh, I say!' and 'Did you ever hear the like of it?' in the kitchen parts! Think of his father and mother reading it, and his mother's inability to walk down the High Street of Petfield today. And all Petfield would be standing at cottage and shop doors to speak of it to one another. And Elm Tree Road, and all Islington Vale! How was he to go along the pavement when every head would turn to look at him? He dropped the paper to his side, lifted his shoulders, and spread a hand to the empty hall in a gesture of despair.

Flight? The familiar flight-thought leapt into possession, well panoplied with arguments. Always the arguments come for what one longs to do. He had the money . . . why not get away at once before they moved? . . . why not lose himself on the Continent tomorrow? For think: if he got away all would be well; if he was caught, he could always say that, though innocent, he had seen how black a case they could bring against him, and he had run from the suspicion and the shame;

whereas, if he just stayed and did nothing, there was no hope at all.

But not yet. Today wasn't the time. They were waiting for him at the Coroner's inquest, which he had been summoned to attend, and fail not, at his peril. He must show them an unworried face, and disarm suspicion. Yes, something of courage rose up and stood on its feet. 'I will face them. I will give my evidence clearly and simply. They shall see no fear in my face. I'll let them suppose that the thought of flight has never crossed my mind, and throw them off their guard, in case I decide to go. I don't think they've got me beaten yet.' His vanity was now on its feet. 'The fight has begun, but it has not ended. You have a subtler opponent to deal with than you know, my friends.' And, pleased with this image of himself, he went to dress in his best for the inquest.

This was less of an ordeal than he had supposed. The proceedings were quiet, quick, and businesslike, and the Coroner treated him courteously. He asked from him only evidence of identification and of the nature of Elinor's death, and, this given, adjourned the proceedings for a month. They had lasted but a quarter of an hour. And there had been only a sprinkling of people in the court, among whom he had noticed Inspector Boltro, Sergeant Doyle and one or two reporters. He had given his evidence with a quiet dignity, he thought, though his voice had played him one or two tricks, and he had felt the eyes of Inspector Boltro on him all the time. When he had finished, the Coroner had read over his evidence and asked, 'Is that your statement?'

'Yes.'

'Will you sign it?'

'Yes. Yes, certainly I will.'

He had signed it, and the Coroner had said, 'I shall adjourn the inquest until August –th, and bind Mr Presset over to appear at that time.'

But would he appear at that time, Paul had wondered. He simply didn't know. His chief feeling when it was over had been a longing for a cigarette. At the door of the court the reporters had gathered around him; and he had smiled patiently and said, 'Of course I shall be delighted to give you all the help I can, but not just now. Not today. All this has been a great strain, as you will appreciate, won't you?' And with another smile he hurried from them.

He went straight off to fulfil a resolve that had been shaping itself as he sat in the courtroom waiting to be called, or stood to give his evidence. It pleased him because it had about it something of drama and heroism. It was the very small but only pleasing thing in the heavy air around him. He was going to Myra to suggest that she had no more to do with him till this scandal had blown over.

He found her in her room, frightened, staring, angry, the paper on the table before her. It was a bed-sitting room of pleasant proportions in an eighteenth-century house in the street off the Euston Road. In the daytime the bed became a divan; and the large square table was pulled back into the centre of the carpet. Myra sat at it now, with some work in her hands which she had let fall to her lap.

'Yes, that's what I've come about,' he said, glancing at the newspaper. 'I'm not going to drag you into all this. I won't even have your name mentioned in connection with it. I think you had better see me no more till they've found out their mistake and apologised; or if they – if they persist in their idiocy and it comes to a trial – then, Myra, you must break with me altogether. God knows where it'll all lead.'

She had kept her eyes on him as he spoke, and did not remove them now. All she did was to shake her head and say, 'How little you understand!'

'I understand that you've got to be entirely out of this, that's all.'

'And I'm never to see you again after this morning. Is that it?' She was almost smiling.

'Yes. That's what I think.'

'Don't be so ridiculous, Paul. Good heavens, can't you *see*? If it were not so terrible, I should be almost glad of this chance to show you whether I love you or not. Who else have you got to be with you now, and do you think I'm going to desert you at the first piece of trouble that comes our way?'

'No, I've no one else,' agreed Paul, not guiltless of self-pity.

'Don't you *know* by this time that I care little enough for what the world says,' Myra continued, without heeding him. 'I've always been rather bitter against it, and now I hate it because it's being cruel to you – you who're the only good thing in it for me. I shall almost enjoy defying it now. Listen, my dear: this'll pass over, and we'll be more than everything to each other after it. I'll make up to you for it. I *will*, I promise you! And in the meantime, do whatever you think best. If it's any consolation to you, I'll be with you all day and every day. If it's better for you that I should keep away, I'll keep away; but know that I'm with you all the time. Whether I'm beside you or not, my thoughts are with you.'

'I'm so worried I don't know what to say,' he confessed.

'Of course you are. Shall we talk it over and see what's best to do?'

And while he tramped her room like a caged animal, and she sat with her hands folded on her lap, they discussed what manner of case the blundering police could build up against him. Partly to prepare her, and partly in the pride of martyrdom, he made it as bad as it could be; and she protested again and again, 'No, no, they can't say *that*.'

'Oh, can't they?' he retorted with a knowledgeable shake of the head.

'No, no. They'll find nothing in her remains, and they'll see what a ghastly blunder they've made, and you'll be vindicated before all the world. Not that I care any longer very much what the world thinks. I tell you, I'm too bitter against it for that.'

'I don't think I want to be bitter against the world,' said he in a low voice. It was a remark inapt to the hour, but true.

'But then you are more forgiving than I,' she answered musingly. 'I should have thought that was obvious.'

'That may be; but, anyhow, I wouldn't like to say for certain that they'd find nothing in Elinor's remains,' he insisted, refusing to be comforted. 'I wouldn't like to say it at all. It's a well-known fact that arsenic can get into the body in a number of ways before death, and after death. And there's arsenic or other poison in every medicine. No, I'm ready to wager they'll say they've found something, and then all the world'll be satisfied.'

She could not answer this, but stared, defeated; and for a moment he wondered whether to spread before her the idea of flight – but not yet, he decided, not yet.

Restless, he soon wanted to go, even from her. He wanted to walk alone. He wanted to walk south, away from the streets that knew him, and to wander with his thoughts. And as soon as possible he wanted to buy a midday paper, but not to be seen buying it. It was midday, and the first editions should be out now, so, making an excuse, he got himself from her room and out into the street. He turned southward, without looking round.

Had he looked round, he might have seen that a man, idling at the corner as a man might who was waiting for a friend or a bus, slightly turned his head so that the side of his eye could watch him as he went, and that, suddenly, this man glanced at his watch, as if deciding to wait no more, and followed him a hundred and fifty yards behind. Paul turned into Tavistock Place, and instantly the man quickened his steps – nay, almost ran to the corner, where he slowed again, for he saw Paul a little way ahead and did not want to get too close to him. Paul turned into Gower Street, and again the man hurried to the corner to keep him in view, and slowed – even halted a moment – for the vista of Gower Street was long. But when Paul was two hundred yards ahead, he followed at Paul's pace, though looking up at the numbers on the doors as if looking for the home of a friend in Gower Street. At the corner of Bloomsbury and New Oxford Streets Paul bought a paper from a news vendor and stood still to glance at its contents. The man following slowed down and stopped, apparently that he might take out his pouch and fill up his pipe. He pressed the tobacco into the bowl and slowly lit it, watching Paul over the match-flame. And as Paul had folded the paper again and walked on, the man carelessly tossed his match into the gutter and walked on too.

He was a man of about five feet ten inches in height, and of about twenty-six years of age. He had reddish hair and a full youthful face, and was dressed in a neat grey suit. At present his head was bare, though he had worn a cap when waiting at the corner of Myra's road. Capless and smoking, he might well have been a student from the Bloomsbury quarter. In point of fact he was Detective Riseholme, recently transferred from the uniformed police to the C.I.D., like John Boltro of twenty-five years before. This was one of his first jobs, and he was anxious to do well in it and earn distinction. He was sharing with Detective Crewe the task of keeping Mr Presset under unobtrusive observation, and he felt he was doing it rather well: certainly his bird hadn't tumbled him yet. It had been a neat idea to doff his cap when he came out of Islington into Bloomsbury, and so to turn himself into a student. Now he would put the cap on again. Inspector Osley had taught him that half the art of shadowing was to 'dress to the locality' one was in.

Paul, having read in his paper this sentence, 'While the Coroner for North Central London was conducting the inquest, a preliminary examination of the body was being undertaken by Dr Boyes Allan, the Home Office Analyst', had dropped the paper to his side and was walking across New Oxford Street towards Shaftesbury Avenue, with a pain behind his eyes. He wandered on staring ahead of him. Detective Riseholme also crossed the street and, putting on his cap, wandered along Shaftesbury Avenue so lazily, now looking at the photographs hung on the theatres, now dawdling at a shop window, that women stepped out from their lairs to wink at him as he passed.

Chapter Two

That was the first day. Next day the papers were full of the inquest, and Paul, loafing and idling about his rooms, saw from the windows people coming past the house to throw their covert glances at it, or small boys lingering on the opposite pavement and shamelessly gaping at its front. All day they passed, these covert gapers. Then that day was gone, and its night; and next day the papers were empty of allusion to him, and the relief was like the ease after sickness. But it was only momentary; the ache returned as he knew it for spurious relief. This was only a pause: 'it is seventy hours now since the analyst began his examination,' ran his thought. 'How much does he know now? Time is passing; that clock is ticking away my chances of escape. Why don't I do something?' But darkness came down on another day.

Impossible to settle to anything. His only ease was when he sat in a chair or paced a room, debating flight.

Why not? So simple; and any minute it might be too late. He might regret for the rest of a short doomed life that he had not taken the courageous step. So simple. A quiet walk to the station, a couple of hours on the train, a trip from Brighton or Eastbourne to the Continent – and surely it would be beyond the powers of the best to track him there. And the time was with him. In a few days the holiday season would reach its height, with crowds to cover him at the stations, and probably fine dry weather overhead so that he could walk and sleep, if necessary, beneath the stars. This surely was Fate offering him a chance, and he would be a fool not to take it.

He would stroll out of the house quite naturally – without a bag, in case anyone was looking from opposite windows. He would have all day in London, to buy a bag here, a hat there, and new unmarked clothes in twenty different shops. And they could be holiday garments – flannels, light undervests, a straw hat – all so natural to buy and to wear. Oh, he could outwit them! He would walk to some London terminus and take a train to some south coast town, and walk across country to – Southampton? No, the route from Southampton to Havre was too long. He wanted to be there quickly. Once on the quay at Calais or Dieppe he'd be safe – and there came a glow of relief and happiness at the thought. Newhaven to Dieppe by the night boat? Yes, Newhaven was a natural holiday port, where his presence would cause no remark. And Dieppe was a natural place to be going to, in the holiday rush. Next Friday would be the day to go, the Friday before Bank Holiday. Could he safely delay till then? If only he knew how long he could delay!

And Myra? She could come too. Why not? Had she not said, 'What do I care for the world?' What more natural than that she should go off for a holiday at this time? They could go by different routes to the boat, speak but little aboard, and meet on the other side. Then Paris – Madrid – anywhere. Who could find them?

The more perfect the plan, the more inevitable it seemed, when set against the case they could raise against him. This flight-thought was now a longing; and the longing was knowledge that, despite all deliberations, he would act on it. And every day, and every night in his bed, he made it more perfect, and more certain.

Each morning he scanned his paper with a fear so fascinated that it was almost disappointed when it found nothing. Wait long enough for a blow, and you will want it to come; and when it comes relief will mingle with the pain. But it did not come, and now – now it was Friday. Today and tomorrow were the chances Fate was offering him. Was he not a fool to hesitate? Any day now might be too late. He walked the floor, one hand grasping a wrist behind his back. Yes, think of the impotent anger that would gnaw him in a cell, if he knew that he had funked the splendid bid for life. Yes, now, *now*; this morning. Good God, why had he not told Myra before? See, the day was fine and dry, the sky cloudless, and the weather set for a warm dry spell! It looked as if he were meant to escape, the gods being with him.

He dressed impatiently, choosing a lounge suit of 'pepper and salt' whose jacket might well be worn with flannels. He put all his money into his pockets, gold and notes and bearer bonds; and the comfort of them was like the comfort of armour. He came downstairs, his brain racing like an engine when accelerated. He would wander casually into the street, no hat on his head, his hands in his pockets, and a cigarette at his lips. Anyone seeing him would think that he was strolling to the corner to buy a paper. He would even halt in his front garden and pick up odd weeds or odd bits of paper – a stroke of genius that! Then, sauntering carelessly along the Caledonian Road, he would mount a tram, and go to Myra – and from Myra to shops far separated, to buy a bag and a hat and clothes. He felt better than for days, because he was moving – doing something.

But wait! To be hatless was to be remarkable. Fool that he had been! Why not put a cap into his pocket? Why had he not thought of that before? Was his brain, after all, working less well than he had thought? Was it really letting him down, by forgetting important things?

He had a moment of still horror.

No. It *was* working well. The very fact that it had found this little detail of the cap showed that it was missing nothing: it was reaching to and finding out the tiniest flaws. Besides, if he was stopped by every moment of sick doubt, he'd do nothing. He took a cap, rolled it up, and put it in his pocket.

He stood in the hall. 'Have I forgotten anything?' No, he could think of nothing. He glanced up at the stairs and around the hall, probably for the last time. Strange: he'd been unhappy enough in this house, but it was always sad to take a last leave of anything. Goodbye, 23 Elm Tree Road.

Well, move on. Despite the fears that were with him he felt a quickening of excitement, a swell of something that, in a happier day, would have been the thrill of adventure.

He lit a cigarette and strolled out on to his step. He smoked there for a little; then gently pulled the door to, and dawdled down the steps. He picked up odd trifles in the garden while smoking. He strolled through the gate, leaving it ajar. Hands in his pockets, he strolled towards the Caledonian Road and turned the corner.

But he had not turned the corner before a door nearly opposite No. 23 opened, and a young man in a grey suit and straw 'boater' came on to the pavement and turned likewise towards the Caledonian Road. Detective Riseholme did not suspect anything: Mr Presset's action had been too natural, and he could only suppose that he was going to buy a paper or cigarettes. But it was his duty to keep him in view: for this purpose the tenant of the house opposite No. 23, pledged to secrecy, had placed a window and a curtain at his and Billy Crewe's disposal. So Jack Riseholme walked quickly at first, for Mr Presset had a start; and when Mr Presset went from sight, Jack looked at his watch and broke into a run, as if, by the powers, he'd miss his train. He came quickly to the corner where he halted and looked about, apparently wanting a tram. Then he looked at his watch again, and, changing his mind, you would say, dropped into an easy walk, southwards towards the city.

Mr Presset had not stopped at tobacconist or paper shop. He had walked on and on. He had turned into a side door near a public house as if for a natural purpose, and now – Jack's heart jumped – he was coming out *with a cloth cap on his head!* Hello, hello! The bird was flitting, was he? Splendid! Almost too good to be true. How he had hoped for this, that he might do a fine bit of tailing and earn the praise of his Chief! And here, unless he was mistaken, it was happening before his eyes! Yes, Mr Presset had halted at a tram stop. Jack Riseholme looked in at a shop window where some lurid magazine covers had suddenly captured his attention. A tram grated along, and Mr Presset was mounting it. Jack Riseholme looked at his watch, swore loudly to find it so late, and ran and leapt on to the footboard of the tram just as it started. He sat down on a seat near the conductor, breathed heavily, and fanned himself with the straw hat. Mr Presset was in the middle of the opposite seat, sitting rather dumpily and sometimes beating a toe on the floor. He bought a penny ticket from the conductor, which made Jack glad that he had bought a penny ticket too.

The tram rumbled on to its halt near the King's Cross, and here Mr Presset descended, with many others, including Jack Riseholme. And of these quite a few went along the Euston Road, Mr Presset and Detective Riseholme among them. 'Yes, you'll cross here,' thought Jack; and he was right. Mr Presset did cross. 'Quite so. Now round that corner . . . I told you so. We're going to see the young lady, are we? Now what exactly is the game? Is he going to do a guy, or is it only a love visit? But that cap? Eh, what was that dodge for? My, but he's a cute fish, our Mr Presset. There are no flies on Paul. Lummy, I hope it's a first-class flit, but I'm afraid it's only love. . . . There you are! I thought so. Up the young lady's steps. This is where we pause for a quiet smoke, and watch the cats go by.'

* * * * *

'Myra, I'm worried to death,' began Paul. 'I can stand it no longer.'

'I know. I know.'

'It's driving me mad. The more I think of it, the more I feel sure they will arrest me, and why should I—'

'That's nonsense, dear. They can't.'

'But they will, they will.' He beat his foot impatiently. 'That's what's so ridiculous. The more I go over it, the more I see – don't you understand – don't you grasp it – I was the only person near her when she died—'

'But they won't find anything in the body.'

'I'm not sure. I've told you I'm not confident of it at all. I've a fancy they'll find enough to justify arrest. After all, her death looked as if she'd picked up some poison somewhere, and perhaps she did.'

'Paul . . . my dear!' Her frightened eyes fixed on him.

He sat down. 'I can't stand it. I'm worried to death,' he repeated weakly. And he wondered how to tell her of his plan.

'I know,' she sympathised again, touching his hand.

Paul lit another cigarette with maladroit fingers; and after a silence spoke. 'Listen, Myra,' he said; and, watching her anxiously, unfolded his plan for 'going from it all', without, however, mentioning his hope that she would come too.

She listened, silent, frightened, staring. And he, because she did not answer, spoke on and on, guiltily verbose, pouring in a broken and passionate stream the arguments and phrases that had been forming in his head for weeks. It was the passion of the convinced who dare not be unconvinced. But when he paused and she answered him, it was only to say, 'Oh, I don't know. Do you really think it's best?'

'Of course it's best,' he retorted; and all the pent-up eagerness to be gone was gushing again in more explanations and arguments.

'But it makes you seem guilty.'

'Oh, I've been into all that,' he protested, irritated. 'Do you think I haven't been over and over it all? Do you think I've come lightly to a decision like this? If they find nothing, and there's no talk of arrest, I can come back if I want to. If they do find something, well, they're not going to find *me*. Why the devil should I let them? An imprisonment and a trial would be the finishing of me, whatever the result. And I'm just not going to stay for it. Not without a fight, thank you! Do they think I'm going to walk into prison and sit there for months, just to please *them*? If they want me, they can come and look for me.' He was working himself up. 'And look at it this way. If the police choose to charge a man with murder, he's got to pay thousands of pounds to prove that they've made a blunder. Why should anyone do it? I'm not going to. I want to keep my money for you. I'm not going to sit down and wait for them to come and take me, like a terrified rat, and then have to pay a few thousand pounds to get out again. Not a bit of it! I flatter myself they're going to have their work cut out to find me. They haven't got one of their half-educated criminals in me, whom they can bully easily. They've got someone who's their equal in resource. And a shade better, perhaps! We shall see!'

'Oh, it's all so awful,' breathed Myra.

'Awful? Of course it's awful. Awful enough for me to decide to be done with it. And, Myra . . . what I want to know is . . . will you come with me?'

She could only stare.

'Listen, my dear. Are you prepared for something desperate – at least it's not desperate, it's simple really.' And he told her his plan for getting by gradual stages to Newhaven, in time for the night boat, while she, if – *if* she cared to come with him – was to travel openly and simply by the evening train, and see him on the quay, from which they would go up the gangway separately, like unconnected travellers. Then she to her saloon, and he to his; and they wouldn't really link their journeys till they were safe on the other side. It was all so simple. What more natural than that she should go off for a holiday at such a time?

'But when?' she asked.

'Today,' he answered, dramatically.

'Today?' She repeated, brows knit in confusion.

'Yes. Are you frightened of it?'

'Not frightened of going anywhere with you – but only because it's so sudden. Must it be today?'

'Yes . . . and if you don't come with me, I'm going alone. I have made up my mind. If I haven't made it clear to you how necessary it is, I'll do that as we go. Unless, of course, you don't want to come.'

'Oh, no, don't go without me. No, I couldn't bear to be left alone.'

'I wouldn't ask this of you, my dear, if you hadn't said that the world meant nothing to you and I meant everything.'

'It's true,' she said.

'Well, come. . . .'

'But we might never come back?'

'Yes, that is so. On the other hand, we may soon be back. If it all blows over, we can return quite naturally. If not—'

'Wouldn't it be better if I followed you later?'

'No, I've thought of all that. I thought of saying we'd meet in a month's time in Paris – oh, I've been over it and over it – but I can't say where I shall have to be, and I don't want to lose you. You may never be able to find me, any more than they will. I might not be able to communicate with you without giving myself away. But one dash – one dash over the water, and we're safe together.'

'I am so confused. . . .'

'There's no need to be confused.' With her he always felt the manly and courageous one. 'You say this woman here suspects nothing. Tell her you've had a sudden invitation to join some friends on a holiday and that you'll probably be back in a few days – you *may* be back quite soon – who knows? – It *is* only a holiday, unless. . . . And look here, dear, start early and with only a small bag, so that, if after they learn that I've gone they come here to make inquiries, they won't think at once of boat trains' – how wonderfully his brain was serving him! – 'and leave the house before lunch; it'll look more natural to the woman here. And remember this: if they do want me in a day or two, it'll all have to come out, and how will you face her then?'

'Oh, how?' she echoed.

'So you will be much better with me; and we can be so happy together somewhere far away—'

It was not in refusal but in sadness that Myra's head shook. 'I said I hated the world, but I love England.'

'Ah, so do I,' said he with feeling. 'You cannot love it more than I.'

'Never to see England again!'

'But it may not come to that. And it won't, with *you*. You can come back one day. I don't suppose I have more than ten or fifteen years to live—'

'Ach, don't talk like that. I shan't want to live after you're dead. But it's all so terrible. Can't you give me longer to get used to it?'

'No.' By now he had so worked himself up that he could bear the thought of her delay no more than his. 'No, *I* must go. You can have ten hours to think about it. If I don't see you at Newhaven, I shan't, that's all.'

Myra sat thinking. 'Paul?'

'Yes.'

'Are you perfectly certain that it's the only way?'

'Perfectly.'

'Then I'll come. Of course I will! I just couldn't get used to the idea at first.' She looked up and smiled. 'I am your "wife", am I not, and I must go with you . . . of course.'

Detective Riseholme, standing at the corner, saw his man come out of the house and turn towards him, making for the Euston Road. Promptly, but innocently, Jack turned and looked into the shop window behind him. The sun falling strong on the opposite side of the road, the window would be an adequate mirror. He was making some notes of prices in a notebook, as Mr Presset passed, frowning, abstracted, and completely unconscious of *him*. Mr Presset crossed the road diagonally and went east; and when he was a little way along the pavement, Jack followed. 'Is it Islington and home again, or is it by any luck Euston for Liverpool, or, perhaps, Waterloo for Southampton, or Victoria for Folkestone? Have we just said goodbye to the lady? The station is what we must know, sir, and I'm sure the Chief'll be very glad to have you met the other end. 'That'll be rather a nasty jar, Mr Presset: a couple of 'tecs waiting for you at the barrier. But that's what you'll get, unless I'm a balmy. I can't fancy C.O. letting you walk out of the country. No, we're not such fools as that. Hello! Waiting for a bus, are you? A westbound bus? Looks like Paddington. Well, we shall know when you choose your bus, but do oblige me by going on top, this lovely day, because we've ridden together inside a tram once already, and I'd much rather sit inside and have you on top, than sit on top and have you inside. Ah, "Tottenham Court Road, Oxford Street, Marble Arch" – looks like Paddington or Victoria. Good!' This exclamation was because Mr Presset was swinging himself on to the top of the bus. Jack Riseholme ran up and got inside, seating himself next the door and training his eyes on the stairway and footboard.

Along the Euston Road and down Tottenham Court Road the bus rumbled and swung, with Paul above and Jack Riseholm within. It pulled up near the junction of Tottenham Court Road and Oxford Street; and among the many who descended here Jack Riseholme saw Mr Presset; so he descended too. Mr Presset crossed to the south side of Oxford Street and walked along with the stream of shoppers, Jack about seventy yards behind. Now Mr Presset paused outside a shop, a leather-goods shop, as Jack could see even from his distance. Jack did not pause; he came up slowly and was still some yards from Mr Presset when the latter went into the shop. Jack walked right past to a position some sixty yards farther on, where a convenient bus stop enabled him to halt. He took out a notebook, wrote something down, and replaced it in a hip pocket.

Perhaps it was all a wild-goose chase. Perhaps the good man was doing some perfectly innocent shopping. After all, one would hardly start on one's travels without so much as a coat or a – *Golly!* Detective Riseholme gasped. Mr Presset had come out of the shop with a bright new suitcase of brown compressed fibre, leatherbound at the corners. This was magnificent! This was wonderful! No huntsman when he is ahead of the rest of the field could be more delighted than Jack. Not that he didn't at the same time curse himself for a fool, and feel disappointed that he was a detective less brilliant than he had supposed, because it had never occurred to him that Presset had gone in to buy a bag. Gosh, the man had nearly outwitted him! He was an even cuter fish than he had thought. What now? Already the figure in the cloth cap and the pepper-and-salt suit with the bag in hand had gone some distance – should he run into the shop and get what information he could? – no, that would be to lose sight of his man – he had the name and number of the shop, and next time he'd move very much quicker. He ran till he was within forty yards of the figure with the suitcase, and then accommodated his step to the other's. One thing was sure: Presset hadn't tumbled him at all.

'I thought so. Yes, that's the game.' Presset, after pausing at a hosier's window, had gone in with his bag. Jack whipped out the notebook and jotted down the name of the shop, and stood very close to the door. It might be all-important to find out what he was buying in there. It might be the certain way to identify him, if he were really doing the flit – as strike me if he wasn't! Should he dash in after Presset came out and make these inquiries, or content himself with following? Which would his Chief praise him for most? If he went in, he might lose his man; if he contented himself with the name of the shop, the assistant might forget, in the multitude of cash transactions, which was Presset's. No, he had it! He'd run in, say, 'I'm a police officer. That man may be wanted on a serious charge. Note his purchases,' and run out again, leaving the shop assistant with an expression on his face that it'd be a pity to miss. Yes, that was the ticket. 'A smart bit of work,' the Chief would say.

Soon – a good deal sooner than he expected – Presset came out of the shop, quite unsuspecting. Jack ran in; said his words; ran out, leaving the shop assistant staggered but greatly enchanted, and heading straight for his boss; and hurried along Oxford Street after his man, who, thank Heaven, was still there, walking along slowly and looking into shops.

For a quarter of a mile they went on, threading their way, one behind the other, through the thronging shoppers of a gracious summer day. Then Paul stopped before a new window, and after a minute went through the shop door. Jack came abreast of the shop. A hosier's and outfitter's again. H'm . . . he noted the name, nodded, and resolved on the same steps as before. Walking across the door of the shop, he looked in. It was much bigger than the other, but there were only two assistants, and several men stood in its comparative darkness, waiting to be served. Mr Presset stood with the suitcase at rest on a chair by the counter, waiting like the others. Jack did not linger, but walked up the road and returned. When he passed the door again, Mr Presset was being served.

He was a long time within, and other customers came and went. The detective, peeping, saw several waiting while Mr Presset made many purchases. One of the two assistants called a name into the back parts, and a third hurried in. But still there were customers waiting. . . . One of the assistants came to the window and took out a shirt with collar to match. Jack noted it well, and glanced through the door to see if it went before Mr Presset. It did not: it was interesting another customer.

Twenty minutes had gone. Damn the man! Was he buying the shop? For a time he lost himself in contemplating the eddies of shouldering women on the pavement and the mill-race of buses, carts, taxis and lorries behind. He was sinking into a reverie, but it was disturbed by Presset's voice. 'No, that's all right. Leave it to me. Thank you very much. . . . Thank you. . . . I can manage quite well.' And there was Mr Presset, emerging with his suitcase, doubtless heavier now.

'Good morning, sir,' said the assistant, who had come to the door.

'Good morning,' nodded Mr Presset; and turning west, walked off.

'Hi!' called Jack to the assistant – but he was too late. The man had hurried within to the pressure of business. Jack rushed after him, but he went quickly behind the counter and addressed another customer.

'Excuse me. May I speak to you a tick?'

'One minute, sir.'

'No, I must speak to you now.'

'Just one minute, sir. I won't keep you one moment,' said he, firm but exquisitely deferential; and he was walking to the back of the shop. Jack raced after him, feeling in his breast pocket for his warrant card. 'Confound it, man, I'm a police officer, and I want you to make a careful note of all that man's purchases, whom you were serving just now. That's all.' And he ran out again and turned west, as Presset had done.

But he could not see the figure in the pepper-and-salt suit with the bag. His head swung left and right, and up and down, but nowhere could he discern him. For a second he twisted on his heel and looked behind; then ran on to the first cross-roads and looked up and down the side streets. No sign of Presset anywhere. And before him a chain of buses was streaming towards Marble Arch, getting farther and farther away, as he stood in angry doubt. And the other buses were streaming towards Oxford Circus. And taxis were bowling both ways. They were gone round corners and out of sight, while he hesitated.

He had lost him. Now he wouldn't know if he was making for a station today, and if so, what station it might be. He did not even know if he had turned west or east.

Still, he had done well; he had exciting information for headquarters, and they never expected 'detective's luck' to last for ever. Now for a telephone.

Chapter Three

The comfort of the crowds at Victoria Station! Among these pushing and sweating people, all with handbags, some with golfbags, many with straw hats like the one he now wore: women with eyes strained on their goals, children returning from school, city men hastening home to begin the holiday, and jocose fathers leading their families (with buckets and spades) to the happy barriers; among all these crossing and interweaving people who would worry about him, who was like a thousand other small, spare men of fifty? The porters were busy crying over their trolleys, 'By your leave, please! By your leave!' The women were flustered, the children confused, the young persons merry, and all had forgotten that there existed such a matter as the Presset Case. A railway policeman walked past him without a glance; the stationmaster in his top hat hurried towards No. 13 platform, intent on more important traffic; foremen and guards crossed his view, strolling through the turmoil `with professional unconcern; and the medley of noises – the panting of engines, the rolling of wheels, the ringing of buffers, and all the woven voices – seemed to enfold him with a haze of sound. With a lane of people he passed the barrier to the 'Brighton Fast', showing his return ticket to an indifferent collector – a *return* ticket – genius again! Skirmishing with the best, he stumbled into a third-class carriage, and sat in a middle seat with ten other passengers. The more, the better!

The train started with a jerk. He was away! It curved out of the station; and the peace of movement and action was his.

When it was rumbling over the bridge across the river, he opened his paper. Nothing about the Presset Case; no, not on any page. The chief story was 'The Great Exodus from London', and the arrangements of the railways and the hotels to cope with it. It described the crowded stations one by one, the special trains following quick on each other's heels and steaming over the countryside 'with their happy human freight', the overflowing hotels, and the packed sea-margins of all the holiday towns. It thanked the sun for its smiling, holiday face – to be sure, the special correspondent had interviewed the sun who, somewhat above himself, had cried in high, rhetorical humour: 'Come, my millions. I'm in a mood of blazing benevolence, and my toady, the barometer, dare not shift from "set fair"; so away with all worry and work, strap up your bags, and come down to my court by the sea.'

Paul laughed. How infinitesimal one really was – a grain of the sea sand! Who was even thinking about him in this holiday hour? And what a master-stroke of generalship to leave today! Dammit, he was going to prove one too many for them!

The train gathered speed. Good! The houses were dwindling and the green places conquering them. Now all was meadow and hedgerow and wood. The whistle screamed, the smoke clouded past the windows in the rush of the headwind, the telegraph wires switchbacked from pole to pole. One could almost smell the sea. Before you could believe it he was in the Hillgarth country, and yonder was the tilted meadow up which he had walked with Myra to the wood; no fear that anyone would recognise him on the station platform, with the train going through like the offspring of thunder and lightning. It thundered past the platforms with a shriek of its whistle. Now past the high chalk downs, browned by the hot sun; there, on the left, was the pack of them marching into Lewes; and it was over these that he would soon be walking, along familiar paths, to Newhaven. Now with a whistle and a roar into the tunnel, and all the chalk mass was above him. Out into the sunlight again, and they were slowing into Brighton.

He bundled from the train with a hundred others, shook his head at the porter who, quite unsuspicious, inquired, 'Porter, sir?' flowed with the crowd through the barrier, and gave up the half of his return ticket to the collector who took it without interest, turning to a man at his side. It was all absurdly easy. He could just put the bag in the cloakroom and wander for a while in the Brighton streets. He had a long time to kill, and he might buy a few more odd garments at this shop and that. There was such happiness in making these purchases: each seemed a new rivet in his security.

Free of his bag, he went out into the street and down the hill, drawn like all men to the sea. It was about half-past two, and the people on the pavements, many of them mothers shepherding their children, tended to flow with him, back towards the sea.

A shop window halted him. It was dressed with toys and sporting goods, and his eyes were wandering fascinated over the toy locomotives and ships and forts and soldiers when, swinging towards the sporting goods, they fell on a rucksack (a haversack, as he had been used to call such things), and at once it fertilised his brain. 'The New Popular Rucksack,' said the card. 'The Craze of the Moment. For the Picnic, the Walking Tour, and the Weekend Trip. No More Heavy Bags.' Ah, he would buy a rucksack. It would dress him right for his walk over the downs – yes, and another for Myra – with rucksacks slung, he and she, in France perhaps, would look like a hundred others on a walking holiday. Yes, and he could buy more holiday clothes to put into it, such as no one would even know that he possessed, for who in the world knew that he had visited Brighton? He bought a rucksack, and another 'for his young son', putting it inside the first; and he came out of the shop, uplifted, all such actions inflating his confidence.

And still the brain worked splendidly. At one shop he bought with a casual air a light grey mackintosh, at another a panama hat, at another a blue blazer with brass buttons – oh, his brain was one too many for Mr Boltro! – and he brought them out in brown paper parcels and walked down to the beach, where, in a private place, he transferred them to the rucksack. Slinging the rucksack, he stood and looked at the sea. Smooth and friendly and bejewelled by the sun, it was all that lay between him and safety. There, beyond the pleasure craft and the sailing boats, beyond the distant steamer, beyond and below the horizon, were the lands where he would walk in peace.

Well, best get moving. Probably it would take him half an hour to get to Rottingdean in the bus; then he could take his time wandering over the downland summit, by easy stages and deserted paths to Newhaven. Three-thirty. In less than a dozen hours he'd be in France, and defy Mr Boltro to track him there.

Back up the hill to the station, the shops suggesting their purchases: buns and fruit and chocolate for supper, and a rug – yes, a rug would be useful on the boat. Into the station to withdraw the bag – and not a query from the man who gave it him, not a look, only prompt and indifferent delivery!

A new crowd was pouring from a London train, and many, he now observed, were wearing the 'new popular' rucksack – good, he slung his own, picked up the suitcase and went out among them.

He mounted the Rottingdean bus. Here too he was quite in the manner: many were going for the afternoon, or for a stay, to the picturesque village of Rottingdean. He sat himself on the top, with the rucksack on his lap and the bag behind him. And soon the bus was on the high cliff road, with the level sea to the right, and the heaving downs to the left, and the wind rushing past the people's faces, so that they screamed and laughed, and had no thought for the small, middle-aged man in the straw hat, who smiled gently with them. Nor did they notice him, when he slipped from their company at Rottingdean and took to the hills. He was glad to be walking this stretch, even though the stations had shown him so little to fear. It was the fugitive's instinct to keep to the open.

He knew his way well. Over the first crown and down into the valley of Newlands Barn; then up to the hill above Telscombe. He topped the first crown, and dipped down into the valley; and was now a lonely figure, with rucksack on back and suitcase in hand, among the infolding hills. It was warm work, toiling up the second hillside. Not that either bag was heavy, for, save for the rug, they held only light clothing, but even without them today the sweat must have dripped from his brow, beneath the uncurtained sun. There was plenty of time, so he sat on the hillside with the bags at his feet, transferring clothes from one to the other, and pressing the straw hat into the roomy places of the suitcase. Then he wiped his brow, picked up his burden, and went on. Skirting the shoulder of Telscombe Hill, he came to a view of the rust-red village, nestling below in its foliage; and here, before the vast loneliness was broken, he sat down and took out his buns and chocolate, and fruit. He bit alternately at the buns and the chocolate, chewing them slowly and looking right and left over the rolling landscape, like one of the cattle on the slopes.

It was wonderful up here – aye, wonderful was the word. Always it thrilled him with the same wonder and delight. The round hills rolled away, one crown lifting behind another, each a new tint in watercolour, till the last range of all was a wash of pale mauve against the sky. The slopes near the village below were brown with corn, and on one, far across a valley, some labourers with a wagon were harvesting the wheat. Many of the other slopes were green pastures, on which the cattle moved from mouthful to mouthful. At his feet sprang the wild flowers: clover and cat's ear and daisy, poppy and knapweed and yarrow.

The sun was warm on his neck, and the south-west wind, coming from behind him and sweeping on, turned the long grasses to grey on their bed of summer green, so that a silver tremor ran over the hills, like a happy sigh made visible. And the cloud shadows followed, over wheatfield and pasture, away to the wind's end.

He leaned back to take the warmth on his skin and the breeze on his cheek; and behind his shut eyes the sounds made themselves heard, a lark singing high, the voices of the labourers across the valley, and the cows munching far away.

It was after six when he awoke. Only four hours now, and he would be on the boat, cast off from England. Refreshed by sleep, and invigorated by the beauty around him, he felt more than easy, more than confident – he felt exalted. Why ever had he panicked so?

Down into the village of white homesteads, on whose tiled roofs the salt-laden winds had turned the lichen yellow; and up along the ridge of Southease Hill, to a sight of Lewes in the haze. Here he turned sharply eastward by a wood of sycamore and beech, and dipped down towards the valley of the Ouse and the spire of Piddinghoe church which rose from its low hill by the side of the stream. And where the valley widened to meet the sea, there in the mist were the toy-like buildings and cranes of Newhaven.

An ugly little harbour town, smoke-grey, but it held the masts of ships.

He stumbled down the springy turf, through patches of bramble and gorse, and down natural steps in the chalk, pausing often to rest the bag and un-sling the rucksack; and then through the fields of wheat and oats on the lower slopes, till he came to the high road to Newhaven, with the flint village of Piddinghoe on the right, and the water meadows of the Ouse beyond.

It was still too early. Barely eight, and the boat train from Victoria didn't arrive at the harbour till nearly ten. So he dawdled in the flint-walled streets of Piddinghoe, admiring the barges with their furled sails on the winding Ouse, and the little church on the hill with its spire of silver shingle, guarding its parish of water meadows. Through these green levels ran the railway line that would bring Myra from London. The dusk gathered; a light sprang up in the Royal Oak; and he went into its sanded bar to fritter away a half-hour over a mug of ale.

The darkness was nearly full when he came out and set forth on the last easy mile into Newhaven. Twenty minutes later he was trudging through the lamplit streets, rucksack on back, rug on arm, and case in hand. The streets were populous, so warm was the night; people stood in groups at corners, holiday-makers in flannels strolled arm-in-arm along the pavements, lads loafed by the kerbs and ogled the girls, and lovers walked, arm about waist, perhaps towards the quiet of field or down. No one noticed his passing. He passed right through the town, and over the Ouse bridge, from where, looking down the estuary, he saw the funnels of his steamer, berthed against the quay.

It still wanted half an hour before he need go on to the harbour station, so he turned into a little tavern, thinking that perhaps a peg of brandy would be a preventive against sea-sickness. He ordered it from the fat baggage of a landlady who was in easy gossip with two porters in blue jerseys; and when she handed it to him with barely a glance, he took it to a Windsor chair against the wall. Lying slantwise on the next chair was a late edition of a London evening paper, still unfolded, as if the man delivering it had tossed it through the door but a few minutes earlier. His eye, falling on it, caught part of a headline in the *Stop Press* column, 'Sensational Turn . . .' and immediately he knew – one seems to get this knowledge from the moment *after* reading instead of the moment before –

that it was an allusion to himself. Heart thumping and fluttering, he turned the paper and read, 'Sensational Turn in Presset Case, Reported Disappearance of Mr Presset, Warrant for his Arrest, Charge of Murder.' And he read on, 'There has been a sensational development in the case of Mrs Elinor Presset whose body was exhumed some time ago from the churchyard at Trusted, Essex. Late this afternoon a warrant was obtained for the arrest, on the capital charge, of her husband, Mr Paul Arthur Presset, the well-known London schoolmaster, whose evidence was the chief feature at the inquest. Mr Presset left his house at Elm Tree Road, Islington, early this morning, and the police have reason to believe he is attempting to leave the country. Scotland Yard has issued a full description of the wanted man to every police station in the kingdom, and ordered observation to be kept at all main line terminuses, ports and docks, and a search to be made of all outgoing ships by experienced C.I.D. officers. Special inquiries are being prosecuted at shipping offices, railway stations, and hotels. Presset is described as fifty years of age, about five feet four inches in height, sparely built; with pale blue eyes and thin, greying hair; cleanshaven, and of a gentle, serious demeanour; probably wearing a pepper-and-salt suit with cloth cap, and carrying a new suitcase of brown compressed fibre, bound with leather at the corners. Or he may be wearing grey flannel trousers, tennis shirt, and straw hat. . . .'

Chapter Four

As the driver's foot races a motor engine, so terror raced his brain. In a few seconds his decision was made, and the brain was driving him through the tavern door into the night. The tavern was on the outskirts of the town; and he went speedily along the road across the meadows, and up on to the empty hill. Behind a gorse brake he opened rucksack and bag, and changed into the white flannel trousers, striped shirt, blue blazer and panama hat. What had staggered him, so that he still shook under the blow, was the rapidity of the police action, and their amazing knowledge of the clothes he had bought in London. Had they interrogated every shop in London between morning and afternoon? How could he hope to fight such power? Oh, it was hopeless, hopeless. But even here there was a glimmer of comfort. They knew nothing of his purchases in Brighton, or they would certainly have put them in the description. Perhaps, after all, one man, his brain good at any time and now quickened by desperation, could beat even their vast forces. Now he was dressed quite differently from the description, and thank God his face and figure were utterly ordinary – no scar, no limp, no high or rounded shoulder – the description might fit ten thousand men on holiday. Good, he thought; for one is compelled to hope. As he dressed, he was tempted to leave Myra unmet – she would understand – but at once he knew that he could not do this: he must venture a little way into the harbour station to find her. To the last, one emotion at least would be stronger than his selfishness, and that was his loyalty to her. Not that the decision was wholly free from selfishness now, for he could not bear to lose the good opinion of the one person who admired and loved him; death was no worse than that.

Far off in the water meadows, winding by the winding Ouse, he saw the lights of Myra's train, with a plume of firelit smoke flying from the engine. He left his bags behind the brake and walked down the hillside to the road. As he walked towards the danger of the station, he tried to still his heart by telling himself that his present clothes and his empty hands driven into his pockets must make recognition impossible, he would look like some lazy Newhaven visitor meeting the train; but he could not get the full comfort of the thought; one is compelled to hope, but one is also compelled to fear.

Unchallenged, he went on to the station as soon as the train had come to rest, and quickly he mingled with the flow of people who had come from its doors. Splendid! Middle-aged men with brown bags everywhere, and many with cloth caps for the boat! There was Myra, slim and frail and buffeted. And splendid again: her bag was a cheap black feminine thing. He ran towards her, and immediately learned from her white, scared face that she knew all. Her eyes stared into his, as she said breathlessly, 'You've seen the papers, of course? I didn't know what to do. I thought it right to come along. Oh, what are we to do. It's so wicked. How *dare* they?'

'It's all right, my dear. I've thought it all out. Your coming is my salvation. They're looking for a single man, not two people on holiday. Thank you for coming. Alone they might have noticed me; with you we shall pass them by.'

'Oh, do you think so. Oh, I'm glad. . . . But what are we to do? Are we going on the boat?'

'No, we daren't do that. Not yet. We must get out of here. Come . . . come quickly.' As always, her weakness made him feel strong.

'But where?'

'I don't know, I don't know. Let's get out of here to somewhere where we can think. Give me your bag. Now then, come . . . this way.'

There was no one to stop them: the tickets had been examined on the train. They went out of the station into grey side streets, and the relief when the station lay behind was like pain. If anyone watched them go, which is doubtful, for all life seemed blown, like a drift of leaves, to the ship's side, he must have decided in the darkness that the fellow with the girl was certainly not his man. Walking with feigned carelessness, a cigarette at his lips, one hand in his pocket and the other holding the black bag, Paul guided Myra to the road over the meadows. 'We mustn't take a room here,' he said. 'If only we can get to some crowded place like Eastbourne we shall create no suspicion. I haven't yet decided what to do, but come up on the hill for a little. Do you mind? It's warm enough, isn't it?'

'Oh, yes. Let's get away from people . . . anywhere.'

'Yes.'

And he led her up the hill to the gorse brake. Not a figure was in sight anywhere: it was still as midnight and warm as noon, and only the dark hills rolled beneath the stars. He flung himself down on the soft turf, drawing her down too. She curled her legs beneath her, and gazed into his eyes, her brain too disorganised to find words.

And he, after thinking, asked, 'First, do you think you had better go back?'

Still gazing at him, she pondered the question and answered, 'Not if I can be of any use to you.'

He compressed his lips and nodded, as he thought; and she spoke again. 'You said something about my being your salvation?'

'Yes,' he nodded. 'I see that. I'm safer with you than alone; of that I am certain; but oh, my darling, I don't want to drag you into this.'

She touched his hand. 'If I'm of the least use to you, that settles it. I only wish I could help more, but my brain won't work. Besides, I should be much happier with you. But are you sure it wouldn't be better for you to go back and face it?'

'Oh, no, my dear, don't worry me with that. I've thought it all over again and again, and I've made my decision. Try to trust me.'

'But now that you've failed to get away?'

'I'm not at all sure that I've failed. I don't at all see why we shouldn't slip with the holiday crowd on to one of the excursion steamers to Boulogne from Eastbourne or Hastings. Especially with you at my side. It ought to be simple.'

'Oh, do you think so? Then let me be with you.'

'My dear, you're wonderful.'

'Oh, no, I'm not. I'm burning to help you, of course, but it's partly selfish. I've no one else in the world, and I want to hold on to you.'

'Ah, if only we get out!' he exclaimed. 'If only this all passes over!'

'It will, I believe. I feel sure we shall one day be happy together. Something seems to tell me that we were meant to be together. . . .' She looked happier, and her brain seemed to be clearing. 'So now let's plan it all out.'

Quickly they formed their plan, improving it with every minute. Tomorrow evening they would mingle with the holiday crowds pouring into Eastbourne. Eastbourne was some twelve miles over the downs, but down in a hollow on this side of Beachy Head was Birling Gap, to which people came from Eastbourne for a day's picnic. They would move slowly towards Birling Gap during the night – neither wanted to sleep, nor could have done – and in the morning they would drop down on to its pleasant beach, idle there during the day among the other picnickers and return with them to Eastbourne in the evening. There, with their rucksacks they would search for a room, which would raise no remark on this eve of bank holiday. Her black bag should be harmless enough, and they might get rid of the incriminating brown one, hiding it deep in some lonely thicket – 'Oh, yes, get rid of it,' pleaded Myra. In their room they would live as husband and wife. All his clothes were unmarked – how clever he had been! – and she would mark them with some name – what name? 'Wilson.' 'Mr and Mrs Evan Wilson.' She would get new clothes for herself in Eastbourne, and mark them too. And she could wash the newness from the clothes – oh, he couldn't have done without her, and she was glad!

When midnight was a deep blue canopy over a void world, they stood up and moved on. They walked by Heighton Hill to the southern slope of the Furle range, resting often, because they had long hours in hand. In the loneliest spot of all those desolate crowns, in a dense clump of gorse and bramble and sloe, they hid the brown bag, so that not a rabbit, it seemed, could find it, and certainly no lark descry it from the upper air. They dropped into the Cuckmere valley, and crossed the narrow stream by a lonely bridge, and so worked their way up to Fore Down and round the higher slopes to the Friston valley and Willingdon Hill, where they had a view of Birling Gap in the grey before the dawn. Here they lay down, with the rucksacks for pillows, and waited for full day. They tried to sleep but could not, their lids lifting ever and again, to watch the rosy tints of morning flush the hilltops and the sea.

For many it was a dawn bright with the promise of holiday happiness; for them heavy with – what?

Not till the morning deepened did they walk down through Eastdean to Birling Gap. It was nearly eleven o'clock when they walked past the coastguard's cottages on to the beach, and already many picnickers were there, sitting with their bags of lunch and tea. Paul and Myra, their rucksacks slung and the black bag well in the fashion, trudged past them to a quieter part beneath the white cliffs, where they threw themselves down. Here they sat, or reclined, for the rest of the day, Myra revisiting once the green approach to the beach, where there were hawkers from whom she could buy food and drink. They felt no fear of exposure here and sometimes she held his hand to comfort him. The nearest group to them was a man with his wife and four children; and often the man turned his glance their way; but it was not in suspicion; like many married men he had failed to find the love he wanted, and he was looking at them in envy.

In the evening they toiled with the stream of happy and tired picknickers towards Eastdean and the bus. The bus carried them over the green summits into Eastbourne, where the jostling crowds on the pavements, showing every variety of holiday attire, were a quick draught of comfort to them both. Myra, thinking this at the same time as he, squeezed his hand.

And they were but one group of many who went from door to door asking for a room. 'You're about the tenth lot I've turned away already,' said the landladies proudly, and did not know that these words held comfort for them, as well as disappointment. At last, at the door of a cheap boarding-house near Seaside Road, they were taken in. A flaxen and blowzy woman, whom they rightly guessed to have been a barmaid once, greeted them with, 'Yuss. That's just what I can do. I can let you have a room, because a couple that was coming has just failed me unexpected-like. You're lucky in that. But it'll only be for a day or two; it's let again after the Bank Holiday I'm afraid. Yuss.'

'Oh, that'll do,' laughed Paul. 'Thank you very much. We began to think we should have to sleep in a bathing machine.'

'And you wouldn't be the only ones neither,' said the flaxen lady, leading them up the narrow stairs. 'No, that you wouldn't, I'll be bound. How'll this do for you? It's on the small side, but it's sunny – one of the sunniest rooms in the house – and beggars can't be choosers, as the saying is.'

'It's splendid,' said Paul. 'Isn't it my – my dear?'

'Yes,' agreed Myra. 'I'm sure we're lucky to get it.'

'Well, strictly speaking, you *are*,' said the landlady, 'though I say it myself. Supper can be 'ad from seven to nine. It's cold. I find that my people like something cold better than a set-up meal in the evenings. Yuss. And they can have it any time within reason, you see, and dressed as they like. It's a holiday they've come for, I always say, not ceremony. It's the same with breakfast, though I like to be done with breakfast by ten. It's only fair on the gurl, if you take my meaning. Would you like a drop of hot water now?'

'Well . . . yes . . . thank you,' agreed Myra, nervously.

'Yuss; it *is* refreshing,' said the landlady; and she turned and went downstairs.

They shut the door. All that they had seen of the crowds in Eastbourne, and all that they now heard of the separate meals in the boarding-house added to their peace; but Paul could know no real rest till he had slipped down to the empty drawing-room and rummaged on the side-table for the morning's newspaper. Here it was. Yes, 'The Presset Sensation' was the chief news. It was splashed all over the main news page, and his heart took a sickening fall as he saw the large portrait of himself. But then, partly because one must always hope, and partly because the hope was justified, he began to wonder whether the portrait wasn't pleasing him more than alarming him: it had been taken more than ten years before and even then the photographer had been kind and made him look younger than he was. And now it looked as if some Yard photographers had tried to add the necessary years to the face, and, in so doing, had not increased the likeness. Going to the mantelpiece, and looking from the portrait to the reflection in the gold-framed mirror, he decided to think that this portrait would help him rather than hinder him. And, as he remembered with a leap of satisfaction, there was no later one in existence.

He turned to the letterpress. Oh, how they had written it up! What a godsend it had been to them in the silly season! The holiday which had been his best friend in many ways was here his enemy. 'Great Man Hunt Begins, Presset still at Large, Great Activity at Scotland Yard, Inspector Boltro in Conference with his Chiefs . . . As the police suspected, Mr Presset did not return to his house last night, and they are confident he is attempting to fly the country. They are inclined to believe that he did not succeed in passing the police net at the ports last night and must still be in England somewhere. All the resources of Scotland Yard and of the County and Borough Forces throughout the land are to be directed towards finding him; and the Press has been invited to give all the assistance it can; for the authorities are under no illusion that he will be an easy man to trace. Small and commonplace in appearance, he is without distinguishing marks of any kind, and it is significant that reports are pouring in of his having been seen at places as far apart as Liverpool, London Docks, Bristol and Edinburgh. The report to which the police are inclined to give the greatest credence is the one which says that he got off the train at Edinburgh, probably making for Leith or Glasgow. All the other reports they now regard as groundless, but they beg the public not to discontinue but rather to double their efforts at cooperation, and not to hesitate to take to the nearest police station any information that may seem to throw light on the mystery.' And the *Later News* column had a paragraph, 'Presset. This afternoon Inspector Boltro and Dective-Sergeant Doyle visited 23 Elm Tree Road and made a thorough search of the house. They took possession of many letters.'

On the whole, though the palpitating fear must be always there, he was comforted. He ran upstairs to tell it all to Myra and she tried to look as if she agreed that it was comforting, but actually she could not keep from her face the fright that mention of the newspapers and of police activity always started in her. Restless now to see the evening paper, he persuaded her to come out into the town. It was Saturday, and the shops would be open till a late hour and she could strengthen their position by buying more clothes and marking ink. The bustling streets seemed as safe a place as any in the world, and they went out together and walked into Terminus Road. Here the news-bills before the shops, or those flying from the knees of the street-sellers, said nothing of the Presset sensation; and hope, so eager to grow, lifted within them. Nor was is disheartened when, buying a paper, they opened it on the pavement's edge, the crowds jostling them as they passed. 'No News of Presset', the headline ran: and they read what was obviously the attempt of a reporter to make an exciting story out of nothing. 'Up to the time of going to press the police, we understand, have no hint as to the whereabouts of Paul Arthur Presset, but they are confident that they will find him. The police activity over the whole country is immense, and reports of his having been recognised continue to flow into almost every station. It is probable that many hundreds of statements have been taken, but none so far have led to an arrest. Great secrecy prevails at the Yard, but it is whispered that a startling new development may be expected at any moment. When this is published the case, it is believed, will assume a new and even more interesting complexion, but certain formalities have to be gone through, before the final step can be taken.'

'All of which means precisely nothing,' commented Paul. 'Eyewash, that's what it is; pure eyewash. What new development can there be, except an arrest?' and the rational side of him believed this, though the irrational quivered.

'Oh, do you think so?' said Myra, doubtfully. 'I hope so.'

'Of course I do! If that paragraph means anything, it means that the reporters know nothing, and the police know little more. If you ask me, I think they are all at sixes and sevens at the Yard, and don't like to say so. Oh, damn, what's this?'

'What?' demanded Myra, in instant panic.

He pointed to a headline, 'At the Home of Presset's Parents, A Mother's Faith'; and, with angry tears mounting, he read:

'There is a shattered home in the little country town of Petfield in Sussex. Mr and Mrs Presset, the parents of the wanted man, are both over seventy, and live in a pretty little cottage off the high road, where, being people of some small private means, they hoped to spend in quiet the evening of their days. Its front garden is gay with summer flowers, but this festive decoration belies the sorrow within. Mrs Presset has been prostrate with grief since she heard the charge against her son, and has persisted in her refusal to see anyone. It was only when a representative of this journal suggested that her words might be of help to him that she consented to speak. In a little parlour, full of pictures of Paul Presset as a boy, the frail old lady, supported on her husband's arm, said, "My son is innocent. Of that there can be no doubt at all. He was the best boy in all the world. For many years he has contributed to the upkeep of this home. He lived in happiness with his wife, and could not possibly have desired her death. If he has run away, it is because he has been wrongfully accused; and I for one can understand this. It is a terrible thing to have said of one. I have not the least idea where he has gone, but if these words can reach him, I should like him to know that his mother's faith in him is unshaken, and that both his father and I are confident that his complete innocence will be established." Mr Presset was more communicative—'

That the reporter had re-shaped his mother's sentences into his own words Paul could well believe, but what followed rang with the true flamboyance of his father—

'He is a short but dignified figure, with a grey pointed beard and velvet coat, like the subject of some Old Master's painting, and there was nobility in his bearing as he escorted our representative to his gate, and in his refusal to show before the world the distress that must be his. Mr Aubrey Presset was at one time, he gave us to understand, the proprietor of a publishing and printing business in the neighbourhood and the editor of a local journal, now defunct. "Let there be no mistake," he said. "If my boy is arrested and made to stand his trial, we shall leave no stone unturned to prove his complete innocence. Neither he nor we are without means; my income is now small, but all that I have is at his service in this tragic hour. Moreover, assurances of sympathy and help are pouring in upon us, for we are well known in these parts. We have lived here seventy years, and so far never a breath has tarnished our name; and all those here who knew Paul as a boy refuse to believe for a moment this ludicrous charge against him. If this should meet his eye, let him know that his father's trust is complete, and, old though I am, I shall move heaven and earth on my son's behalf." '

Savage though this 'writing up' made him, and heart-sickening though his shame and pity were, the paper as a whole satisfied his hope. He was confident the police had no notion where he was, confident that Myra and he, as Mr and Mrs Wilson, would stir no suspicion. The hope was strengthened with every purchase she made, at this shop or that, while he strolled the footpath outside. They returned to the boarding-house at half-past eight when they conjectured that its diningroom would be deserted, all the visitors having gone on a Saturday night to theatre or music hall or military band on the esplanade. They were right. They had their supper at a little table by themselves, and later went out and mingled with the throng on the parades. No one gave them a second glance.

In the morning they came down early to breakfast, sure that the dining-room would again be empty, on a Sunday morning. It was. Paul picked up a Sunday paper which lay unfolded on the sideboard; and it was a prick of pleasure to read, 'Man Hunt Temporarily Baffled. . . . Up to a late hour last night, the police were still without trace of Mr Presset. They incline to the view, I understand, that he may, after all have slipped through the police net on Friday night before it could be thrown wide enough. They realise that they are not dealing with an ordinary runaway, but with a man of high education and exceptional ingenuity. It has come to my knowledge that he was under observation before he left Elm Tree Road and that he managed by skilful ruses to slip through the fingers of the shadowing police. Indeed, I suspect that there is some admiration for him at the Yard. Not that they have the least doubt of being able to secure him. They have telegraphed his description to all parts of the world, and asked the New York Police to watch the passengers from incoming boats. Provisional warrants are to be issued for his arrest and extradition in France, Spain and Portugal. The C.I.D. realise that this is an occasion for the widest possible appeal to the public, and desire it to be known that every communication, containing even the slightest relevant information, will be carefully considered. There is still much whispered talk of a sensational new development soon, but so far its nature has not been divulged. All that can be definitely stated is that there was a long conference of Scotland Yard Chiefs yesterday, and much coming and going between the Yard and the office, or the private residence, of the Director of Public Prosecutions.'

'H'm,' said Paul, and pushed the paper across to Myra. 'They are just flummoxed, if you ask me. It's bluff. And as for that about the shadowing, I simply don't believe it. It's the invention of some bright young pressman.'

Most of that day they spent reclining on the beach, openly with the multitude, and discussing their plans. At the first opportunity they would slip in a holiday steamer over to Boulogne. And then they would be free. Don't tell him that, once on the soil of France, the French police who'd got troubles enough of their own, would outwit him. And were there not places like Spain where the police arrangements were poor enough? Ultimately they might get to Italy, where they could be as happy as hundreds of other exiles who had sought its sunny skies. Free! And it might be tomorrow! No, not tomorrow. Best to leave the boarding-house naturally, saying they were returning to London, and go instead to Brighton, and sail the next day. 'You are my salavation, my dear. With you they will not suspect me at all.'

There were no evening papers that day, and they returned with quieter minds to the landlady's 'cold' supper, which seemed to consist always of slices of ham and tomatoes. This being Sunday, there were other guests in the dining-room, but these ate their ham and applied their mustard without suspicion.

After three days of undisturbed liberty Paul and Myra slept almost peacefully that night.

And in the morning they were down early to an empty dining-room. The sunlight blazed through the lace curtains on to their table. What a Bank Holiday it promised! Already the open window let in the sound of merry voices and quick footsteps hurrying to beach and sea. Paul, looking through the window, saw that the sky was a steely blue, untouched by wisp or veil of cloud. The smoke from the chimneys went up straight as a white chalk line.

Drought. The weather was set for drought, he murmured to Myra, as they sat themselves at the table. And, the servant gone, his hand went to what it had been trembling to do; it drew the newspaper towards him, and opened it.

Myra watched him, always afraid to open the paper herself. And he had hardly found the centre page before she saw his face sicken to white, his eyes start in horror, and his limbs shake.

'What is it?' she demanded. 'What is it?'

But he did not answer. He was reading, 'New Sensation in Great Man Hunt, Warrant Issued for Woman's Arrest, Young

Schoolmistress at Presset's School, Believed to have Flown with Him, Arsenic found in Mrs Presset's Remains. . . . A most sensational and dramatic turn was given to the Presset case last night, when it was announced that a warrant had been obtained for the arrest of a certain Miss Myra Bawne, also on the charge of murder.'

'Oh, my God!' gasped Paul.

'What—' began Myra.

But he read on, 'It was at the earnest insistence of Inspector Boltro, we understand, that this course was pursued. Miss Bawne is a pretty young woman, engaged till recently as a mistress at Mr Presset's school. He is known to have been very friendly with her, both before and after the death of his wife, and she is believed to have accompanied him on his flight. She left her home about the same time as he, and nothing has been heard of her since.' The rest was guesswork descriptions of her past life, interviews with her landladies, and guarded hints as to her visits to the house in Elm Tree Road. And side by side there were large photographs of them both, with the caption beneath, 'Have you seen this man and this woman?' Paul, scraping for some comfort in the disaster, could find only the unlikeness of one photograph to his present appearance, and the complete ordinariness of the girl's face in the other. That, and a report at the foot of the column, 'A Reuter telegram from Marseilles says that information has been received leading them to suspect that a man strongly resembling Presset, arrived here early on Sunday morning. It is thought that he will easily be traced. . . .'

'Paul, what is it?' repeated Myra.

He handed her the paper without a word.

'Me?' she cried. '*Me!*'

But he, trembling and overthrown, could answer only, 'We must get out.'

'But why should they want *me*?' she wailed.

'I don't know. I know nothing. I can't think. We must get away at once.'

Fortunately the shock was too great for either of them to worry much about the words, 'Arsenic found. . . .' Staring at the stunned, imbecile face of Paul, Myra felt a sudden access of strength: for the present he was clearly helpless, and she would have to get him out.

'What are we to do?' she asked.

'I don't know. . . . We must slip away before they see these papers, and never return.'

'No,' she said, after thought. 'That would make them certain who we were. Leave it to me. I'll tell this woman that we've decided to go to – to Hastings for the day, and that we will go home from there. Thank Heaven we said we were going today in any case. Yes, that will do. Then we can take our things, and they may not suspect anything. Yes, leave it to me.' She got up and put a hand on his shaking shoulder. 'Fold up the paper, my dear, and go and pack. It may be all right. I'll see this woman.'

'Yes,' he said, helpless and speechless.

Twenty minutes later they left the house. When in Terminus Road, they walked towards the station, though why, neither knew. They buffeted through the people streaming towards the sea; and it was some comfort to notice fathers and daughters, or husbands and younger wives, who had almost as much resemblance to the wanted couple as they. No one took any notice of them, though the newspaper placards were screaming, 'The New Presset Sensation'. One bill had a life-size picture of his face with the words, 'Have you seen this man?' He stopped before another such, and stared stupidly at it. 'This man must be found'. And there he was, facing his own picture across the pavement, with a heedless multitude brushing past his shoulder. She touched his elbow, and hastened him on. 'This man must be found' – the words rang in her head. Oh, why were people so dull and brutal. Was there no pity or imagination anywhere? This lust to punish, was it not always the sign of undergrown minds?

When the station was in sight, she asked, 'Where are we going?'

'I don't know,' he answered.

'Let's get somewhere where we can think,' she suggested. 'Let's get on to the downs to some lonely spot, where we can get over this shock and think everything out. Could we go separately to the downs?'

'Yes,' he remembered. 'This way. You can get buses to Beachy Head up here.'

So they turned up Grove Road, saying nothing; but she, turning to look at his grey, drawn face, touched his hand.

He knew the way, but he had forgotten that it passed the Central Police Station at the side of the Town Hall. He stopped abruptly as he saw his face, and Myra's too, looking out from a shining new notice on the board, pasted over old scratched and rain-washed ones of 'Police Sports', 'Foot and Mouth Disease', 'Wild Birds Protection Act', and other such.

'Metropolitan Police,' said the notice, and then 'MURDER' in heavy type. 'Wanted for the wilful murder of Elinor Presset. . . . Paul Arthur Presset and Myra Bawne. Description of Presset. . . . Description of Bawne. . . . Any person having knowledge of their whereabouts is requested to inform the nearest police station at once. A. R. Warne, the Commissioner of Police for the Metropolis.'

He looked at it, defeated, the odds too great. Myra, turning her eyes to him, saw his lower lip quiver and his mouth square, like a child's before tears. His eyes were wide with the last despair. He was dumb, empty, exhausted; for the most wasting emotion of all is fear. His head shook from side to side as he held back the tears. And in that second she went forward to something larger than she had been. All her motherliness poured out to protect him. Savagely, she defied the world. Defiantly, she cared nothing that her portrait was there too. She forgot herself, as all mother-beasts do, when they have the world to fight. Her mood might not stay at this height, but it would not sink again to the pitiful panics of yesterday. Strong with anger, she was larger than she had been.

'Come, dear,' she whispered. 'People are passing.'

They crossed the road to the bus stop. 'You go on the first,' she said, 'and I'll follow on the next.'

'Yes. . . .'

'Yes dear. And see: I'll buy some food and bring it along. No one will recognise me as long as I'm alone. Where could we meet?'

'What?'

'Where can we meet? On the downs somewhere.'

'Meet?'

'Yes, isn't there some isolated place that you know?'

'There's an old flint barn . . . if you go straight on after the path ends. . . .'

'That'll do, if it's lonely enough.'

'Oh, it's lonely enough. All the people go to Belle Tout lightihouse.'

'Very well. I'll join you there. And in the meantime I'll think out what we can do. Now you go alone for the present. I'm going back to the shops.'

When she joined him near the old flint barn in the desolation of the downs, she found him somewhat recovered. His first words, as they sat down in the shelter of the gorse, were 'Myra, you do know, don't you, that I'd have given myself up rather than that they should have done this to you?'

'Of course I do.'

'And I'd surrender tomorrow, but it seems too late to be of any use to you.'

'You're not going to surrender yourself. I've made up my mind about that. And if it's humanly possible to beat them, we're going to do it. I don't feel frightened for myself somehow. I never felt less so. I don't know what's come over me. And in any case they can't do anything to me, can they?'

'No, of course not. *I'll* see to that.'

'Not to you, either. They can't, in the end.'

'Perhaps not.'

'Oh, how did it all come about? Only a few weeks ago, and we were so happy. I can't get my bearings yet. What's been worrying me in the bus is that you said yesterday that my being with you was your salvation, but now it's your danger.'

'And I'm a danger to you, too. If only I'd never induced you to come, I believe you'd have been safe. They'd have used you for their own purposes, but they'd never have committed this crime against you.'

'Ah, well,' said she. 'It's too late now.'

'But couldn't you give yourself up, and explain your innocence?'

'What good would that do? I should have to stand some sort of trial just the same—'

'Oh, don't talk of it.'

'Besides, I haven't the least intention of giving myself up, or you either. I'll fight them to the last minute now. How dare they? How *dare* they? If I gave myself up, I should have to tell them where I left you and how you escaped; and do you think I'm going to do that? Not likely! I happen to be on your side, you see, and not on theirs. And I don't care what they do. I never cared less. The beasts! The beasts!'

Paul, only just recovering from a sickness of utter despair, studied her face. He was amazed at her courage. Was it the courage of innocence, such as he could not know?

'We shall have to separate,' he said. 'You ought to be quite safe alone, in this holiday season. That photograph is something like you, but it's like a thousand others. You'll be all right alone.'

'I know that,' she laughed, with the same defiant conquering note. 'But what about you?'

'Oh, I'll go to some big town and lie low and take my chance.'

'No, I don't think that's the way. I've a better idea than that. We must keep together, but not be seen together. And I'm not saying it because I'm afraid of being alone, but because I'm sure it's best. I can see so many ways in which I can still be of help to you. Think: I can go into shops and buy things, where I'm much less likely to be recognised than you. I'm sure of it. I saw it in the shops just now: no one worried about me in the least, though they must have read their papers an hour before. And if I don't look enough like that photograph to make people wonder today, I promise you I'll look less than ever like it tomorrow. So you see I shall often be able to buy food or clothes or railway tickets, where you can't – or where you'd better not. The face they're really looking for is yours, not mine. And look, if you had to run from some town and hide in the open, I could bring you food, couldn't I? And as long as we keep in touch, we may yet be able to slip away one day on a day trip to Boulogne or somewhere. What do you think?'

As he did not answer, she continued, 'Or am I imagining all this because I'm frightened of going alone. I don't *think* I am, but if you feel I'd be a source of danger to you—'

'Oh, no, I wasn't thinking that,' he interrupted. 'You're right in what you say, but I was wondering if I ought to let you do it.'

'Oh, I'm so glad you were thinking that! Then you really believe I might be of help to you?'

'Yes. . . . I was thinking we might hide in some crowded holiday place like Brighton. We could wait there till it blows over, and then perhaps our chance would come. These summer excursions to France'll go on for a long time yet. We couldn't live or travel together, but we could fix up a meeting place—'

'Oh, yes!' she cried, laying a palm over his hand. 'Let's do it. Brighton is the place, I'm sure. There must be thousands upon thousands of men and women together there. We ought to walk up and accost each other quite naturally, in front of them all, I think. I'll find some perfectly safe place in some old maid's boarding-house, and you'll go somewhere else. Look: we'll go back separately into Eastbourne and take different trains to Brighton. It's Bank Holiday, after all; and all the stations'll be crowded. God has been good to us in that.'

Chapter Five

Inspector Boltro sat at his desk in his room at Scotland Yard, with a pile of statements before him. The downward set of his mouth suggested anger and determination. And he *was* angry and determined. When he first saw Presset he had felt contemptuous for such a mild little man, and even sorry for him; and certainly disappointed, because such an ordinary little specimen seemed unlikely to stir a wide interest and inspire a story in which Inspector Boltro would be the conquering figure. But when the newspapers, hungry for a summer-time sensation, wrote Presset up as a well-known, very able, and rather sinister schoolmaster, he had smiled and let them be. It had suited his book so well. But now this mild little person had apparently outwitted them. He'd admit it to no one else, but Presset had won the first round against them. Got clean out of sight, with God knew what clothes! They had blundered perhaps in only setting a watch on the girl's house, and not entering it to make inquiries till the next morning – but why should they have done this, till they were finally satisfied that Presset had flown? And then they had learned that she had gone too. His Chief had said nothing when he reported, but Boltro, with the nervousness of a conceited and ambitious man, had imagined that he looked dissatisfied. Devil take it! He'd felt merciful to Presset at first, but not a pennyworth more of that now!

The same nervousness read into the newspaper accounts – though in fact it wasn't there – some criticism of Inspector Boltro. By God! . . . But he'd show them yet! He'd got to now!

Presset by his tom-fool flight with the girl had made it a bigger noise than ever; he'd put the romance and the 'human appeal' into the story, to the delight of Fleet Street – it was now a case of almost world-wide interest, the French papers giving it especial prominence after their amorous habit – and all this meant that it'd either be a world-resounding success for Inspector Boltro or a – but he wasn't going to think of that. He wasn't going to be beaten by a slippery little rat like Presset. The man had asked for war, and he should have it! The girl, too. At one time he had felt almost sentimental about her, and had resolved not to proceed against her, partly out of pity, and partly on the police principle that the woman in the case was generally too useful to them, if managed properly. But not now. She'd asked for it, and she was going to get it. Reckon that charge of murder had set them both thinking a bit! Eh, Mr Presset, that was something of a 'Check!' wasn't it?

His telephone buzzed. 'Long distance call from Eastbourne, sir. Chief Inspector Lake, of Eastbourne Borough Police.'

'Right. Chief Inspector Boltro speaking. Yes, Mr Lake?'

A voice spoke of a possible clue in the Presset case. Two persons very like Presset and the girl Bawne had been in Eastbourne as late as eight-thirty this morning.

Inspector Boltro laughed. In his irritability this morning he couldn't for the life of him prevent a little of his contempt for these provincial police from filtering into the phone. 'They've been seen in Eastbourne, have they? Well, so they have in Newcastle, Bristol, Harrogate, and God knows where – France even.'

'Well, here's the story for what it's worth,' said the voice, and immediately he knew that he had created some offence.

'Righto!' he said, more pleasantly, and taking up a pencil. 'Let's have it.'

And the story came through. A man of about fifty and a much younger woman arrived at a cheapish boarding-house in the seaside district of Eastbourne on Saturday evening and stayed two nights. The landlady stated that they both resembled the portraits, but both seemed a good deal older. They left early and rather unexpectedly this morning, saying they were going first to Hastings and then to London. No letters arrived for them while they were there, and they left no home address.'

'Any bag with them?'

'Yes.'

'New?'

'No. Old-fashioned sort of bag – black, and a couple of rucksacks.'

'H'm. Presset has a new bag – a brown one.'

'It's conceivable that he's got rid of that one,' said the voice, with some sarcasm. 'He's not quite a fool.'

'That had occurred to me, too. I'm not quite a fool either, old boy. Go on, what have you done?'

The voice said they'd got the full descriptions, and made inquiries at the station, but no such couple had been noticed.

'They may have gone singly. Were any persons with rucksacks noticed?'

'About four hundred of them.'

'What?'

'About four hundred. All the lads are sporting them this year. Perhaps the fashion hasn't got to London yet.'

'Ha, ha, ha! One to you. One to you, old boy. Well, I'll have the Eastbourne trains met at this end, but if it's Presset and Bawne, I shan't expect to see them in London. They wouldn't say they were going to London if they really were—'

'No, it may be a mere paper-chase, but—'

'Yes.' Boltro nodded into his receiver. As the clue wasn't his, and Lake sounded cocksure, he was inclined to believe it was a mere paper-chase. 'Sounds a bit dubious, on the whole. Still, I tell you what: what time do the evening papers arrive in Eastbourne?'

'Soon after midday.'

'Fine. Then I'll get a headline, "Presset suspected in Eastbourne," and you can bet your sammy it'll be on every placard in the place. Then if anyone has seen anyone like 'em, you'll get the information fast enough. Too much of it, if it's anything like up here. Meantime, what else are you doing?'

'Got some of my chaps on the station, and—'

'Say.' Boltro, being a vain person, was always quick to interrupt. 'Any pleasure trips to Boulogne your way?'

'Yes, and I've—'

'What I'm thinking is, Why Eastbourne? They didn't go to Eastbourne to hear the band, or just to come back again. Got some chaps on the pier?'

'You bet.'

'Informed Brighton and Hastings and all the other places?'

'Certainly.'

'What else have you down there besides Brighton and Hastings?'

'There's Newhaven and—'

'Ah, Newhaven, of course. Well, we've got that watched. Say, I shan't be coming down unless you've got something more definite' – 'No,' thought he, 'too much to do up here without chasing after every will o' the wisp' – 'but let me know if anything more comes in.'

He was still in his room when something came in about four hours later. Eastbourne ringing again; Inspector Lake speaking. Some information had just come in. Two persons, exactly answering the descriptions in the afternoon newspapers, had been seen walking together in one of the loneliest parts of the downs behind Beachy Head. Time, about nine o'clock, which would be just after they'd left the boarding-house, saying they were going to Hastings. Fishy, what? And undoubtedly it was the same two because they'd rucksacks, and a black bag—

'Good, good! But where would they be going behind Beachy Head?'

'Newhaven, do you think?'

'Is Newhaven within walking distance of you?'

'It's not above twelve miles.'

'Well, they'll walk into trouble if they walk into Newhaven. No, I'm not inclined to think that it would be Newhaven.' The simple fact was that he was inclined to disagree with Eastbourne. 'Presset's no fool. More likely Brighton. Could they walk to Brighton from you?'

'If they're prepared to walk about twenty-five miles. They'd be a bit footsore—'

'I wonder if it *is* Presset and Bawne.'

'I think it is. Who else'd say they were going to Hastings and London, and then deliberately take the opposite direction?'

'Absolutely. Quite. Exactly. Just what I was thinking,' said Boltro, who had really failed to give the point its full significance. 'Great Moses, if it only is! What are you doing now? Combing the downs?'

'Not half. Got every available man working from this end, and some of the public helping as well. And Newhaven and Brighton are coming in.'

'Splendid! Great! I'm coming down at once. What trains are there – dammit, the trains'll be all to blazes today. I'll come in a fast car—'

'Yes, but one minute. A Major Fogerty, of Elstone Court, about five miles from here, has rung us up offering his bloodhounds at a moment's notice. A fierce old party, I should say, who's seen the evening papers. He seems eager to be off – straining at the leash, so to speak—'

'Right. Keep him quiet till I come down, if it's agreeable to you. Let him stand by. He may be quite useful. So long, old man; and thanks.' Boltro was disposed to treat Mr Lake very differently now. 'I'll be with you in a brace of shakes.'

He was excited. He had a vision of an arrest that night. He saw the headlines tomorrow: 'Quick Work by Scotland Yard,

Presset Not Long at Large, Smart Arrest at Eastbourne, Inspector Boltro's Net too Wide. . . . The meshes of the net thrown by Chief Inspector Boltro have proved too fine for Mr Presset and his companion to slip through. Yesterday he and Inspector Lake of the Eastbourne Borough Police. . . .' But he must be there before Lake got them. For the story to be perfect he must be in at the death, and bring them back in triumph to London. He rang the bell and bade the messenger find Sergeant Doyle immediately, and when Doyle came running, he exclaimed, 'I've got 'em, Pincer! I think I've got 'em! Come along, my boy, and I'll tell you all about it as we go. Come along, my shining light.'

When, two hours later, Inspector Boltro drove up to the main police station of Eastbourne, at the side of the Town Hall, he saw against the kerb two cars which his practised eye knew at once to be police cars. At the entrance to the yard, talking to a uniformed sergeant, stood a tall, sturdy, grey-haired man in mufti, and as this man immediately came with a grin towards him, he knew him for Inspector Lake.

'Mr Boltro, is it?' said Lake. 'Thank the Lord. We thought you'd never turn up.'

'We've travelled fast enough, I reckon,' said Boltro, ever sensitive to criticism.

'Yes, but everything's happened since we got on to you. It's them all right. It's Presset and Bawne. Not a doubt of it. We've found this bag. The original brown one!'

'What?' cried Boltro, delighted, and jumping out of the car, a big, burly figure in a blue suit and a bowler hat. 'Say it again, old boy. Say that once more. You've found his bag?'

'Aye, we've found his brown bag miles away hidden in the gorse, not far from Alfriston. He must have known we were after him, and got shut of it up there.'

'But I thought he only had a black bag, when seen?'

'So did I, but either he disguised it, or perhaps he'd already got rid of the brown one when the folks saw him. Or perhaps they couldn't see straight. You know what their evidence is worth, at any time. Some chaps working from Newhaven and beating the gorse clumps found it. I've ordered that it's not to be moved till you've seen it.'

'Well, I'm damned. Now's the chance to use those dogs you mentioned, I guess.'

'Yes, that's my idea, too—'

'Of course!' interrupted Boltro, for now that his idea, tentative at first, was reinforced by Lake's agreement, he chose to represent it as a conviction. 'The sooner the better.'

'We'll go right away. Fowler, tell the Sergeant to ring up Major Fogerty and say we're on the way. No time to report to the Chief, Mr Boltro, but he knows you're coming.'

'That's right. Every second's of importance. Pop in, old son. Pop in. You haven't a car that'll beat this one, for all you think we came slowly from London. This is Sergeant Doyle. Right away, Crab. Tell him the road, Lake. Where does this old gaffer live?'

Lake called to another car to follow, and, leaning forward, told the driver of Boltro's car the route to Elstone Court and Major Fogerty's dogs. And the driver, a youngish lad, infected by the general enthusiasm, drove as fiercely as the holiday traffic would allow, secretly imagining himself a fire engine, an ambulance, and Dick Turpin riding to York. Behind him Lake was explaining Major Fogerty to the man from London. 'A fiery old cuss, I should say. Said he'd stand by with the animals till the middle of next year, if necessary. Said we could take him and them anywhen and anywhere: to Jerusalem, if we cared. He's red in the gills about it, I can tell you, and frothing to be off. Probably thinks the women and children aren't safe with a murderer at large on the downs. The women and children, by gad, sir! Or else this is the first chance he's had of using his dogs, and he's feeling like a lad with a new gun. He rather thinks, I gather, that there were never such dogs as his. He gave me the whole of their pedigree over the phone, and then some.'

'Well, we can let him loose now, and he'll probably go faster than the dogs,' laughed Boltro. 'D'you think we'll keep him in sight?'

'What sort of condition are you in?'

'Oh, *I'm* all right,' Boltro hastily answered, not insensitive to a certain filling up of his figure, nor happy about allusions to it. 'I can keep up with most men. I've never believed in letting myself get slack. And I used to be a bit of an athlete in my day. I've won a pot or two in my time.'

'That's good. Then you can keep liaison between me and the Major. *I'm* not going at the double all the way. He'll go like a bullet from a gun, I fancy. He's got a down on your Mr Presset, and no mistake.'

'Well, I don't wonder,' said Boltro vindictively.

A very short drive along country roads brought them to the gates of Elstone Court; and they swung in on to a semicircular drive sweeping before a grey stucco mansion. At the foot of the white steps leading to the front door stood Major Fogerty, tall and lean as a telegraph pole, and holding his two stately hounds on their leads. On that high angular frame his knickerbocker suit hung straight and loose. His face peered at the approaching cars from under a brown peaked cap – a pleasant face on the whole, with a big nose overhanging a lank grey moustache, and pale sea-blue eyes that were full of a simple kindliness – or would be full of it, when not angered by mention of an enemy.

It is sometimes remarked that people tend to grow like the pets they live with; and it would not be too fanciful to see a resemblance between Major Fogerty and the tall hounds, who stood at his side with their red-brown pendulous ears, their full muzzles, their long muscular legs, and gentle, pathetic eyes. They seemed made only for kindness and simple humour, but soon they would be straining on the leads, the haws of their eyes showing red, their voices deep and sonorous, and their muzzles low to the ground.

Major Fogerty raised a hand as the cars came to a standstill. Inspector Lake stepped from the car on to the drive. 'I'm Inspector Lake, sir, who was speaking to you; and this is Inspector Boltro of the Yard.'

'Yes, yes,' said the Major. 'Good afternoon. I'm all ready if you are, but I wish to God you could have come sooner. When was this damned bag dropped?'

'We don't know, sir. About nine this morning, I suppose. We imagine he went up there this morning to hide it.'

'Well, but hell, that's what? Seven hours. We shall be hunting a cold line, and hunting bloodhounds is not at all plain sailing, I can promise you unless the scent is frightfully good. A seven hours cold line! Hell!'

'Perhaps you'd care to get in with Mr Boltro, sir, and I'll go in the other car and lead the way. He's really in charge of the case.'

'Certainly, Inspector. Anything you like. We can only do our best, late though it is. I'm at your service – at your service entirely. There's room for the hounds in here, what? Come on, Wilful. Hop in, Huntress. Gently now, don't get excited! By George, I hope we catch the blighter, though I haven't much hope. I've always wanted to give these hounds a chance to hunt a criminal, what?'

'We don't know that he's done it yet,' laughed Lake.

'Oh, he's done it all right,' the Major assured them as he sat down. 'Never saw a more obvious case in my life. Get your bottom out of the way, Wilful; shift along, what? That's right, good boy, *good* boy. Steady, Huntress. Beautiful bitch, that. Oh, he's done it all right; but I'm sorry for the girl. She's probably been hypnotised by him, don't you think? I hope you won't hang her. I don't like women to be hanged. Not as a rule, that is.'

'I don't think there's much fear of that, sir,' said Boltro, as Lake retired to the car behind.

'Good,' said the Major. 'I'm not so keen on chasing women, on the whole; but look here; this weather's the devil. Dry weather's no good to anybody; if we'd had some rain, I'd be more hopeful. And up on the downs everything'll be about as bad as it can be. The grass is usually short and wind-swept and won't hold the scent. And if these damned men of yours who found the bag have been mucking about with it, it'll be their scent the hounds'll hunt; the latest, you see. We can open the damned bag, of course, and give the hounds a smell inside it, but if it's got nothing in it, well, *I* don't know. You see if you can't give 'em a garment of the person to be found, then you must know that he was the last to pass over that particular piece of land, or to touch the damned bag. The cleaner the start is for some way the more hope there is of 'em sticking to their line. But we'll hope for the best; we'll hope for the best.' And he settled down to an afternoon's enjoyment.

The cars drove at a fine pace over the downland roads to the Cuckmere valley and Alfriston, while the hounds, with panting jaws and pendulous tongues, gazed over the car doors at the passing scene; and the Major gave Boltro their pedigree. And then they were high on the hills above Alfriston, as far as cars could go; and a plainclothes man came to meet them, and led them a mile or more over the turf to a clump of gorse, about which stood several men in a variety of hats – caps, bowlers, and trilbies. 'Oh, deuce take 'em all!' exclaimed the Major. 'Do you expect us to pick up a scent after *that* football crowd's been tramping around? We may pick up one, but whose, God knows.' The men touched their hats to the inspectors as they came up, and the younger of them who had no experience of a Yard visitor, looked with interest at Boltro. All made a passage for the inspectors, that they might go forward to a sight of the bag where it lay, still in the heart of the thicket, but uncovered and exposed by the beaters. Inspector Boltro looked at it and nodded, as if in profound thought. Major Fogerty peered at it, gaping somewhat, like one of his own hounds; and the hounds stood with him, panting. All waited for Boltro to speak. 'Now then, Major,' he said, 'the rest is with you. You take command, will you, sir?'

'Well, open the damned bag,' commanded the Major. 'That's about all we can do now. These fellows of yours'll have obliterated any other scent. Empty. Damn! I thought as much. Well, give 'em a smell at the bag, and let's see what happens. Come on, Wilful. Come on, Huntress.'

At first the hounds were but moderately interested, but then Wilful took the line and pulled off at once, baying excitedly, while Huntress followed him, less enthusiastically, rather flustered.

'Got something!' cried the Major. 'God knows what line it is! But we'll see, we'll see! After him, Wilful. Follow, Huntress.'

And away went these three, the police running after. So hard did Wilful pull that the Major handed Huntress to an eager young detective, thereby making him the happiest man in Sussex, and padded ahead with the straining Wilful. For a few seconds Wilful lost the scent, but Huntress brought him back to it, and together they strained over the bossy turf, quivering with excitement, while the police, no less interested if more bewildered, padded behind. All with their panting jaws and eager, following eyes, looked kin to the animals. Exulting, the just to punish went across the vast loveliness of the downs.

Chapter Six

Paul, coming through the crowds on the Brighton sea-wall, approached the statue of Peace, at the junction of the Brighton and Hove boundaries, many minutes too soon. Always nervousness drives you to your meeting-place too soon. But if his heart was tricky, the indifference of the crowds was a comfort. And there were hundreds, perhaps thousands, of men and women in couples together, the men often twenty years older than their companions. To appear at ease, he lit a cigarette. Fearing somebody had turned to look at him, he glanced round; but it was a mistake; no one was in the least interested him. He walked on, by the Hove lawns, wishing Myra would come, for he shrank from the awful publicity of the sunlight. It was safest to walk like this, but it was a strain: he longed for the shelter of a wall; he did not like to be seen from behind; he felt like a man who fears a shot in the back. As soon as Myra came he would ask her to come to the beach, where he could rest his back against the sea-wall or his shoulder against a groyne.

He returned to the statue at three o'clock, but she was not there. Irritation with her rose in him, and his head began to ache.

Ah, there she was, coming from the Hove direction. She saw him, but pretended not to, and passed. He ran up to her through the people, and touched her on the arm. 'Hallo!'

'Hallo!' she answered. 'Well! . . .' but it was anxious acting, empty of humour and full of strain.

He whispered to her to come and sit on the beach, but she said, 'Not yet. Let's walk on and talk a bit. . . . Then we'll wander on to the beach together. Have you got a room?'

He told her that he had secured a room in a small bow-windowed commercial hotel in the Old Steyne, and how he had feared his stumbling words and husky voice would betray him, but no, the girl in the bureau had laughed with him.

And she reported that she had been lucky too: she had gone to a small boarding-house in Tisbury Road, but it was full up and had passed her on to an old lady who let them have bedrooms for their overflowing guests. Just what she had wanted! And not an eyelid had lifted in suspicion anywhere.

'Why should it?' he asked. 'It's only beside me that you might occasion remarks. Let's go and lie on the beach where we shall be less conspicuous. There are hundreds of other men and women sitting there side by side.'

They went on to the beach. From sea-wall to rippling wave, it seemed almost as packed with people as with pebbles. The light clothes of the women, the gay blazers and white flannels of the men, the straw hats and panamas, the tents and towels and parasols, gave it something of the appearance of a carpet garden massed with flowers, when many of the blooms are blown. Discarded newspapers fluttered like fallen petals. It was his desire to walk on and on to where the crowds thinned – if they ever did – but he found he could not pass the multitude of eyes. And perhaps it was safest to recline in the thick of the press. There was no hope of leaning back against sea-wall or groyne, so they sank into a couple of hammock chairs just vacated, and the canvas of the chair seemed a protection to one's back as strong as concrete. With all eyes on the glistening sea, the bathers, the boats, the canoes and the catamarans, they felt safe. A peddler of chocolates and sweets offered them his wares, and they bought some; a tramping photographer begged leave to take their picture and, on refusal, went smiling; a dog came up and sniffed at their legs, and they stroked and fondled him. The blending of ten thousand voices, men's and women's, children's and dogs', for a mile to the right of them and a mile to the left of them, seemed to surround them with a system of defence that none could carry. The waves sighed peacefully below.

'If it were not for you, I should do away with myself,' said Paul. 'It's only you who hold me to life, because you would suffer so if I went.'

'No, you mustn't talk of death. Either we shall escape – anywhere – I don't care where – or we shall be caught, and you will clear your name.'

'But will I? I don't see how I can. I've been over it again and again, and I can make a damning case against myself, especially as Elinor probably did get poisoned. And there's you. You in prison! My God, I never foresaw that.'

'Don't worry about that. It's strange how one can get used to anything. I'm getting used to it already. Not quite, but nearly.'

'But there's one thing you can be certain of: there is no danger for you. I'll see to that. I don't think they'll keep you long, my dear.'

She patted his hand, and turned her eyes to the left. And immediately she became conscious again of the blended voices: the shrill laughter of women whose gallants tossed pebbles at them, the happy screams of children, the mock-terrified shrieks of bathers, and the barks of dogs who entered wholeheartedly into the fun. She saw again the gaily coloured throng receding away along the shelving beach for miles. All their differing colours were like the uncounted spots on a cotton gown. Bodies moved restlessly, arms waved, faces scintillated, shining surfaces flashed back the sun, and flags and towels and tents thundered in the breeze. And it was in the midst of this massed and pulsing life, flickering and astir, that she made her offer to him.

'Listen,' she said. 'I've been thinking ever since I left you at Eastbourne that, if . . . if by any chance they should convict you and . . . well, you know what I mean' – here she put her fingers over his hand and pressed it tight – 'that then, at the very moment it happens, I'll manage to die myself, so that you won't have to go alone.'

'No, no,' he protested; but she went on, 'I don't see why not. That would beat them in the end, because you would almost look forward to it, wouldn't you, instead of dreading it. You would think that either you were going to meet me in a few seconds, or that we were both going to rest forever together.'

'No, Myra—'

'But the idea pleases me. I *want* to do it. If I can beat them no other way, I can rob them of victory like that.'

'No, my dear, you're not to do that. Promise me you'll not do that. I couldn't bear it. I've wronged you enough already, and if I've got to go, I'd rather take *some* decent memories with me. You have forty years of life before you. One way or the other this will pass over, and you will pick up your life again. If it comes to – to *that*, I shall want you to think always that my last wish was that you should set about life again and try to be happy. Yes, if it comes to *that* – please – I'm going alone.'

Her jaw came angrily forward. 'But they win like that.'

'Nobody wins if you die defying them,' he murmured; and wished then with all his heart that he were innocent. They were grand words, and he would have liked them justified.

They said no more of her offer; but lay back in their chairs, talking sometimes, but more often watching the people and the sea. The evening drew towards sunset, but the crowds had hardly dwindled at all. In the still, warm peace of the evening, both sea and sky were the colours of mother-of-pearl, and there was no marking where they met. Near the beach the sea was silken, and so calm that each isolated swimmer spread a halo of rings around him. An ordinary rowing boat, propelled by a forward thrust of the oars, became a gondola on a wide lagoon. And voices seemed clearer against the background of peace.

One of them was that of a news vendor crying 'Latest Cricket and Racing' as he ran with his fluttering newsbill among the deck chairs and recumbent people. The newsbill flew like a flag in the wind, so that Paul, with his startled heart and uplifted body, could not see what its bold letters spelt. In his fear he thought its first word was 'Presset'. He prayed with irritable anger that it would come to rest. The man drew nearer, and they heard better his cry. 'Latest Cricket and Racing. Pyper. Presset in Sussex, Pyper. *Brighton Argus*. Thank you, sir. Latest Cricket and Racing.' The bill settled for a moment, and they read 'Presset in Sussex, Bloodhounds Out.'

Paul gripped the frame of his chair.

'You must buy one,' whispered Myra.

'I can't.'

'You must. We must know.'

The man was passing as she spoke, and she turned her face to the stones. He had almost passed, and Paul tried to call after him, but his voice stuck in his throat.

'Get it,' she whispered. 'I feel a little sick.'

He called to the man, 'Paper, please'; and the man, turning about, held one towards him, 'Here y'are, sir.' He took it with his fingers so clumsy and vibrating that they frightened him, and he felt bound to act ease and humour. 'Thanks. Must read about the man hunt.'

'Yessir. Presset seen at Eastbourne with his little bit of fluff. Thank you, sir. Pyper. *Brighton Argus*. Latest Cricket and Racing.' And his voice went diminishing away.

Myra's face was still towards the stones; and he opened the paper and read, 'Presset and Bawne, Important New Clue, Bloodhounds on the Scent. . . . Presset and his companion, Miss Myra Bawne, are almost certainly in Sussex; that is the latest news in the most sensational murder case for many years. A couple believed to be them left Eastbourne early this morning and was last seen on Beachy Head walking towards

Newhaven or Brighton. Later the brown suitcase which has figured so prominently in the descriptions of Presset was found hidden in the gorse on the Furle range. This suggests that they were travelling westward, perhaps to Lewes, Seaford, Newhaven or Brighton. Chief Inspector Boltro hurried to Eastbourne and was in conference with the heads of police in Eastbourne, with whom he motored later to a secret destination. Later it was officially announced that bloodhounds belonging to Major Fogerty of Elstone Court were being employed on a scent picked up from the bag. At present it is not known whether a capture has been made. But as a precaution all pleasure steamers are to be watched, and a comb-out will be begun of all the hotels and boarding-houses in the neighbouring south coast towns, though the police realise that the Bank Holiday has made their task an almost impossible one. . . .'

'We must go at once,' he said, passing the paper to her; and all around them the voices and the laughter were as before. The sea whispered peacefully below, and a man in a boat shouted to his friends on the beach.

She read it with her face bent over it, and, after dropping it despairingly to her lap and thinking long, said, 'No. We must stay where we are at least for tonight. That will allay suspicion instead of creating it. After all, you are alone, and they are looking for two of us—'

'I *can't* stay,' he protested irritably, and a bead of sweat fell from his forehead. 'I can't. I can't. The strain's too awful. It's easier for you. You're less easily recognised . . . and you've less to fear. I've all . . . and my nerve's going. I don't seem to be able to do anything: I can't stay indoors, and I can't stand these crowds. I'm shaken, Myra. I want to go right away from people and hide somewhere . . . alone.'

Myra saw his hunted look and realised much. She realised that the strain *was* worse for him, for on him the fierce beam of the world's hostility was really beating; she realised that he was very near to a breaking point and that the power was still with her. She must strengthen and guide him. Almost happily she rose to the task.

'Of course it's wearying you,' she agreed, giving him her comforting hand. 'But I'm so sure that if you can only face your hotel people tonight, it'll be so much better. You needn't go back to dinner, and it's a hundred thousand to one that the police won't visit your place for a day or two. And tomorrow we'll slip away quite naturally with the crowds to London. We won't go by the same train, but I'll see you on the platform in the distance. I'll stay behind and buy more clothes and a new bag and other things. And we'll meet in London and think out where to go. To the other end of England, perhaps. Oh, yes, my dear: we're not beaten yet. Plainly it isn't easy to find us. And if nothing happens tonight, all may be well. But you must go back to the hotel quite naturally, I'm sure.'

'I'm not going back,' he said. 'I can't. It isn't possible to escape; I can't think how I ever supposed it was. I was a fool to run. I've made things worse than ever now. I'd rather give up and be done with the strain. I'm tired. You can escape, dear. You could get away unnoticed, I believe. You take all the money and go.'

'No, that's nonsense,' she rebuked him gently. 'I can't leave you. Should I ever know a minute's happiness if I did? And it's your duty not to give in, too, for my sake. Only last out for tonight, and tomorrow everything may seem quite different.'

Helpless, he agreed. 'Very well. Very well, I'll chance it,' he said, somewhat theatrically. 'I'll put all to the touch at the hotel tonight. And we'll get out of here tomorrow.'

'Yes, tomorrow. And now let's consider our plans. Oh, we won't be beaten easily! Come now, where shall we meet in London tomorrow?'

Chapter Seven

An early train stood against a platform of Brighton Station, and in a middle seat of one of its crowded compartments Paul sat uncomfortably. His relief was sharp as the train pulled out. In the flurry of the day after Bank Holiday he had got from his hotel without question asked, and had passed the station barriers unnoticed among the shoving crowds. And now he felt better – better and better as the train roared on. Through the windows he could see the sunlight spread over the fields; and the air that blew in was warm and caressing. His companions never lifted their eyes to him. Four were evidently city men of some substance; three were a father, mother and grown-up daughter returning from their week-end by the sea; one was a youth in flannels; and one was a spare and mild-faced little clergyman with a bristly beard cut close to his chin. This last was dressed in a clerical pepper-and-salt lounge suit, and an imitation panama hat yellow with age. His gentle eyes were bent over a small black manual, and he was apparently reading his office for the day. All the others, except the elder woman, were reading their papers, and probably about him, who sat in their midst.

Paul had two papers with him, his usual English choice and a French one which had caught his eye on the Brighton bookstall with its headline, 'Le Crime de Londres'. He opened and read the French one first: little had he thought when he laboured to master French for his class at school that he would one day put his knowledge to such a use as this. It was amazing the difference between the English papers and the French. The English, whatever damning suggestions their words might carry, did not dare to speak openly of Myra and him as other than 'the wanted pair'; the French paper called them without hesitation 'les empoisonneurs'. It said joyously that 'M. Presset, un professeur de littérature, et Mlle. Bawne, sa maitresse' had brutally poisoned Mme. Presset and eloped together. It spoke with high relish of the extraordinary cunning with which they had prepared the murder and the flight, their finesse 'tout-a-fait remarquable', with which they had outwitted the whole police force of la Grande Bretagne, and the delicious possibility that they were now in France; but, continued the article, 'la police française est aux aguets. Elle ne manquera pas d'atteindre cet homme, si brutalement inhumain, et de le livrer à la justice et à la guillotine.' Myra, the young and beautiful 'institutrice', it did not consign to the 'guillotine', for French gallantry would not tolerate that; it consigned her only to a long term of imprisonment because 'il parait que cette jeune femme est complètement sous la domination de cette brute.'

'Si brutalement inhumain . . . cette brute. . . .'

The words were a stab of pain, and the paper fell to his knees. A whole world was calling him an inhuman brute, and the knowledge left a set despair; for he had always been of those weaker ones who crave the liking of the world. That he had murdered was possibly true; that he was an inhuman brute was surely not so true, not really; not quite. For once, as the train rumbled on, he allowed himself to think of his crime; usually when realisation of its terrible nature visited him in a blinding flash, he instantly shut off the light and left the thought; even as financiers, and those who force up the price of food, must shut off the realisation that their hand has sent starvation, mental agony, and slow death into a hundred homes. They instantly, thought Paul, slew the realisation and left it behind them; and went off to their honourable clubs, where they sat and condemned the Pressets of this world. Was he any worse than they? He, like them, allowed a callosity to form over an intolerable memory, and went on with his life. And he was ready to understand their temptations and forgive them, but they couldn't forgive him.

Thinking of forgiveness and Christianity, he let his eye stray to the little old clergyman in the corner. It fixed there. At first he supposed him about sixty-five years old: the face, a little simple, perhaps, but gentle and pious, was deeply lined; the stiff, cropped beard had more grey bristles in it than brown; the neck was hollow and stringy like a chicken's. He wore a clerical collar of rubber or celluloid, yellow and cracked at the fold, and a stock of black silk, one corner of which broke from the waist-coat and showed its white lining. The pepper-and-salt jacket was worn and shapeless, and the trousers were turned up at the ends over crumpling grey socks and square-toed shoes. He had two bags on the rack above him, one a basketwork bag held together by straps, and the other a black bag, as befitted his calling. And as Paul looked, three things struck him: first, that when you looked behind the stubbly beard and imagined it gone, you saw that he was not more than fifty or fifty-five; secondly, that a beard seemed natural and in place on a middle-aged parson; and thirdly, that, though he had doubtless worn his for twenty years, that short but adequate stubble could probably be grown in a week or ten days.

In the first days of his flight he had assured Myra that he wasn't going to grow a moustache for disguise; it would be too obvious a trick, and all would be on the lookout for it; the subtler thing was to stay clean-shaven and so discourage suspicion. But now when the strain had become so awful, the emotional need for cover was stronger than cold thought; he ached for a beard on his chin, as he had ached for a wall against his back. And the more he studied the parson the more he found arguments for what he longed to do.

His hand went to his chin and cheek. He had not shaved this morning, telling himself that there was too great a hurry, but really, as he knew, because he wanted even this much of a disguise at the station barriers. And now he had a day's growth there. And it was stiff (it had always been stiff, to his pride) and it was speckled with grey stubble. If he looked ten years older than the photograph, a stiff, greying beard would add another ten years at least. And it would look in place on a parson. And a parson's disguise was no more than a rubber collar and a black stock, which Myra could easily get for him in London. And the pepper-and-salt suit which had been a curse might now be a blessing: he could wear it with the grey flannel trousers and look the typical parson on holiday. And Heavens! even Myra's black bag came perfectly into the picture – ah, was God going to be good to him after all? Perhaps, even, Myra could come openly with him as a daughter – 'the Rev. J. Coulsdon and daughter' – he was then passing Coulsdon station – for soon the hunters would expect them to separate, and it might be safer, less suspicious, to be together. Thinking this, he lifted up the English paper; yes, 'the police are inclined to believe that, if still in England, they will at once part company, in which case the girl will be very difficult to find, in these days when so many young women live in lodgings or take their holidays alone. They will probably concentrate most of their forces on the search for Presset'. Of course that might be a deliberate blind on Boltro's part, who was probably using the Press for his own purposes, but it sounded sensible.

Where to grow a beard? He must be alone somewhere; quite alone, or the growing would excite suspicion. But how alone? How away from every eye? And again a longing that had been swelling in him found overwhelming arguments to support it. If he could hide in some woods for a few days, completely out of sight of the world, with no need to go back in fear to a room at night; if he could hide till his face was changed, and hope was strong again; if Myra would bring him food as she had once suggested. . . . Some nights in the woods to give the beard a start, and while the pursuit wasted itself elsewhere and died down. Then he might emerge with courage again, and every day the naturalness of the beard would improve, and his cover increase. He would face with more ease the stations and the lodgings. . . . Only a few days of it at first, and the weather should hold up for many days yet. He glanced through the window at the stable and burnished sky; he lifted up his paper and read, 'This magnificent spell of dry weather will doubtless be of great aid to the fugitives, who can keep to the open for most if not all of the twenty-four hours. And it is likely to endure. The meteorologists report that a fine weather area is spread over Britain, nor is it likely to give way for many days. Holidaymakers, *and* Mr Presset, may look forward to many days of brilliant sunshine and warm dry nights.'

Was God helping him? Where were there woods in which a man might hide? Immediately his inward eye saw the tall pines and the dense undergrowth where he had walked with Myra on the Lower Greensand Hills. Yes, those miles of wooded country around Pitch Hill, into which he had often penetrated deep when he wanted to be undisturbed with her; there were places in the heart of them where no human foot had broken the branches and disturbed their peace, even on a public holiday. One might be happy, solitary beneath the sky, with a pipe and a book and one's thoughts, and the knowledge that every hour added its quota of disguise.

But then his imagination, working vividly, showed him the long, lonely nights from dusk to dawn, and the stars overhead in the small hours; he remembered a frightening stillness when, an hour before dawn, he had led his friends up the sloping woods to hear the bird chorus – could he wake to that? But the alternative: this slinking into inhabited houses, to the abandonment of the saving disguise; this fear of all watching eyes; the probability of capture and – death – no, no, what will a man not do for his life?

Courage, to face those lonely nights! Courage, if safety lay that way! And it *was* a fine bold move, whereby he might defeat them yet. He called his vanity into play. He was being one too many for them again, and he was going to do it! It was only for a few nights and other men did it; the tramps did it in the summer time. Tramps. If by unlucky and unlikely chance he were seen, he would pass for a tramp with a beard of two or three days' growth. Oh, yes, the idea was sound, and he was going to act upon it . . . if only because there was nothing else he dared to do.

He met Myra, as arranged, in Battersea Park, and immediately noticed that there was something different about her. Smiling, she led him to a seat, and there, when they had sat down, removed her hat; and he saw that her hair which had always been brushed up from her forehead was now parted in the middle and drawn tight on her head and coiled in plaits over her ears.

'Magnificent!' he began.

'But do I look forty?' she interrupted. 'I hope I look forty.'

'I don't know about that, but it makes you different.'

'It makes me look forty,' she persisted, with laughing eyes. 'All this nonsense in the papers about a "girl"! If they'd said a "worn-out old maid", somebody might have spotted me.'

'Well, I'm going to look twenty years older than *my* picture,' said he, smiling sadly.

And he outlined his plan. Her first reaction was the old fright and recoil, but when he had put all the eager arguments – that he *could* not go back into the terror of landladies' eyes – that he longed to be alone – that it was no more than others had done in the summer months – that as far as he could see, it was his only, but at the same time his very bright chance of beating them – she saw that his heart was set on it and she must show, for his sake, not fear but hope. She accepted it. And suddenly, having accepted it, she became more than satisfied with it.

'Oh, yes, and I tell you what! I've been thinking of it all night! When you're ready to face the trains and lodgings again, we'll get right away to the other end of England. There are little remote villages in the mountains where I'm sure we can lie low till the pursuit dies down. I've been seeing them all night, as if God were putting them in my head. I know them so well, and they'll never think we've gone there. Yes, you do this, if it's the only way, and I'll bring you everything you need. Oh, shall we beat them? I begin to believe so.'

This morning she seemed full of hope. Her easy movement among people had built up her confidence.

'I bear a charmed life,' she laughed. 'Nobody pays me the compliment of taking the smallest interest in me. I'm sure I can go wherever I like and buy anything and everything everywhere. Whatever wickedness I may have done, Paul my dear, nobody seems to think of me as a wicked and wanted woman.'

'And I don't wonder,' said he, looking at her simple and kindly face not free from melancholy lines about the eyes and forehead, but lit just now with the desire to live and laugh again.

'And it means we can do this. It means I can really help you, and I'm so glad. I'll come and put up somewhere close, Dorking, say, and we'll arrange a secret meeting-place. I'll stay one day in London to buy lots of things I've thought of, but I shall be glad to get out of it, because, though there are few enough people who know me, it's in London that they are. Tomorrow I'll come out with a new trunk and new clothes – and oh, Paul, supposing everything should yet come all right! Do they go on with these searches forever? Supposing they decided in the end that we must have escaped in the holiday rush, and gave up the search! It might happen so, my dear. And it will, if anything I can do can make it. I believe it will, because if there's a God in Heaven, he must be on our side.

I'm praying to him again, Paul. I'm praying hard, and if he's there, I believe he must hear. After all, he's saved us so far, hasn't he?'

They must not stay long together, so they filled in the details of their plan, and parted: she to go from shop to shop in South London where she was not known, and he to make his new bid for life. He mounted a bus for the first stage of his journey towards the open highlands of Surrey.

Chapter Eight

With a waterproof over his arm, and the rucksack hung fearlessly on his back, somewhat footsore, for he had tramped a great part of the way, Paul limped along a leafy road towards Holmbury St. Mary, the little red village that lies within the lap of the greensand hills. It was early evening, and he had eaten his last meal at a roadside inn, and was coming this way to find a bedchamber in the bracken. A mile this side of the village he turned from the road and took a steep, sandy path twisting between heather and bracken, bramble and thorn, up towards the blown pines that stood against the sky. It was good to get behind the cover of the trees; and to feel that the worst part of his journey was encompassed without alarm, and that now, if he could endure but for a few days, all might be well. Every moment was on his side now. Higher and higher he climbed, the path always tempting him onward to the next hill-top and the farther pines. The path became smaller and rougher, and the woodlands, stretching on either side of him – dwarf oaks, pale birches and dark firs, with the undergrowth tangled about their feet – were filled with silence. He was high enough now to see, when he turned his head, a long sweep of the woody northern heights, from Clandon Down to Box Hill. Narrowing and narrowing, the path seemed little more than a squirrel's track beneath the mantles of bell-heather, ling, and whortleberry, and he had to paddle and brush his way onward. He broke at last into the trees and plunged deeper and deeper, till the bush became impenetrable and it seemed beyond belief that anyone could know of him here.

He chose a place to lie in, where the tall bracken made curtains for his bed, and a young oak threw out an arm for an awning. Collecting dead bracken and piling it for a mattress, he sat down with his back to the tree. His pipe lit, he opened a book and tried to read, while the daylight held; then, after a last pipe before sleep, set his rucksack for a pillow and lay down. He shut his eyes, and lay for a long time in thought.

The night was warm, even hot; and every fragment of sky between the branches was twinkling with stars. The air was heavy with the resinous scent of the pines and the crushed scent of the bracken. It was loneliness, intense and hidden, but he did not think that he would mind it; though sleep was shy of visiting him in so strange a bed. If only he could sleep and get rid of the first night! Come, sleep; but gradually, and instead, his thoughts behind his dropped lids began to prick him with alarms. If thirsty, how would he drink? He should have gone nearer water. But when one is hunted, one goes to the place one knows. Was his brain not working as well as he had believed? Would it fail him in some small but imperative detail, so that he lost the battle? Supposing someone had suspected him on the road, and already they were combing the woods! He lifted his ear to listen. Silence – except that some small animal moved in the underbrush. Supposing he caught a chill, and fever gripped him, and delirium! Would Myra be able to get him to some safe room, and hide him, and nurse him? What would he have done without Myra? Was he putting too great a strain on her, and would she weary and hate him? No, he didn't feel that. He felt as certain of her as of a rock. But it was she alone who held him back from suicide. Were she not there, he would put an end to himself, when the strain became too much, or when he saw Boltro and his men approaching. But now he could never do this. He must keep on the fight, because he couldn't slip from life and leave her to anguish. . . . And if he won! If he won! If God, when He had punished him enough (for surely he was being punished now, and Myra was being punished for his sake), if God extended mercy and covered the rear of their escape, they might yet reach such happiness together as those alone knew who had blent themselves in unity. Perhaps it would be so. Let him hope it would be so. He tried to think it; but if you are alone with nature, in a complete stillness, sometimes you will feel that she is strange, alien, faintly hostile, busy with her own life and indifferent to the interests of men. It was a long time before he dropped into a fitful sleep.

About ten o'clock next morning he was standing well back in the wood, away from a path that led up from Peaslake, on the other side of Holmbury Hill; for it was here that he had arranged to meet Myra. He had wandered to the meeting-place some hours too soon, but had lain out of sight of the path till ten o'clock, when he had come nearer, so that he could peep down the path in the hope that she would arrive before her time. But eleven passed, and noon approached and she did not appear. Noon passed, leaving anxiety behind; and anxiety, in his exhausted condition, became a dull hopelessness that he wrapped around him like a garment, letting time drift by, his jaw slightly falling, but otherwise indifferent to it. All he knew was that if by any chance she had been taken, he'd give himself up straight away and get her off; and perhaps, after all, such action would be a relief.

Then his tautened hearing caught the sound of movement; and, peering again, he saw a figure moving behind a bend in the path. It was she, and since no one was near, he went forward to greet her. As she saw him, she gave him the incomplete smile, quickly corrected, that used to mark her recognition of him in Clissold Park. It was a courageous smile, for her face was worried and white. She was carrying a light bag with what looked like a folded easel and artist's stool strapped to its side.

'I'm so sorry I'm late,' she said, 'but it's farther than I thought – ever so much farther.'

'There's nothing wrong, is there, dear?'

'No, what makes you ask that?'

'I thought you looked worried.'

'Oh, I hope I don't look anxious. I'm trying not to. I don't think I do when people are about. I only let my face go when I'm alone. I'd have put on a better one if I'd known you were looking.'

'I was beginning to think they might have found you.'

'Oh, no. No one's interested in me at all. Listen: I'm staying at a hotel in Dorking, and I pretended that I'd come on a painting holiday for a few days. What do you think of that? Is that clever or not? I got the idea from a shop in Brixton. Behold my easel and my stool. And oh, my dear, I think the best thing I can do is to sketch you with that beard.'

He felt his chin. 'It's growing, isn't it. I always had a stiff growth.'

'My dear, I've come through some lovely scenery, but it's quite the most picturesque thing I've seen so far.'

'It won't make you hate me, will it?'

'*Hate* you?'

'Yes, how can you love anyone with an unshaven chin?'

'Don't be stupid. I should have thought we'd got to a point beyond that. And anyhow I think the beard's rather sweet. How long will it take to grow at this rate?'

'Only a few days,' laughed he, cheered by the good spirits she was showing him. 'I think it grows faster in this weather.'

'Well, it's the most perfect disguise. Oh, Paul, I believe we shall do it! And let me tell you I've decided not to worry about myself any more. I've done nothing, and I don't believe they can do very much to me in the end. They can make a show of me, but they've done that already, and I can survive it, thank you. And now, for goodness' sake, eat. I'm sure you've had nothing to eat. Where shall we go?'

'Come in here,' he ordered, more hopeful than he had been for hours.

They penetrated deep into the wood beneath the glimpses of the sun; deeper and deeper into the inviolate bracken and the secret assembly of the trees. Then they sat down, and Myra, maintaining for his sake the lively manner, unstrapped her bag and unfolded the three-legged stool and set it up.

'There!' said she. 'That lends us a most innocent character, I think. I'm very proud of my easel and stool. It'll explain my movements everywhere. Now see what I've got. I'm sure there's enough here for a dozen.' And she produced sandwiches, rolls, cheese, eggs, pork pies, fruit and chocolate and a cake. And best of all, a large bottle of lime juice and a large bottle of water.

'Ah, good!' he exclaimed, 'but how on earth did you carry all this?'

'Oh, it wasn't very heavy. And I changed it from hand to hand. Tomorrow I shall bring the old knapsack into use. I don't see why not; I've seen heaps about, and I'm not going to be afraid of anything any more.'

'Myra,' said he. 'If you've done any sins in your life, don't worry, because you'll certainly be forgiven for this.'

'Which is nonsense. There's no credit in doing things that you want to do—'

'And if we get out of this safely, I'm going to make up to you for it, during the rest of my life. I vowed last night while I couldn't sleep.'

'How did you get on?'

'A bit lonely,' he smiled. 'Especially about four in the morning.'

'Well, I'll stay with you all day. I'd stay all night too, only it might start the hotel people talking. Now eat.'

She watched him eat, delighting in his appetite and declaring that, if necessary, she could go and buy more. She took nothing herself, except a sandwich to keep him company, saying that she could eat when she got back.

When he had finished, he turned with one arm feeling for her and said, 'Come close to me. I've been so lonely. If anyone sees as, they'll only think we're lovers.'

'Which is what we are, aren't we? At least, I always imagined so,' said she softly, as she came into his arms.

And holding her, neither speaking, he had a sense that life had poised him most strangely between supreme happiness and a great terror. On the one side were Myra and such fulfilment as few men could enjoy; on the other Inspector Boltro and his men. Perhaps all life, he thought, was beauty threatened by danger; perhaps that was God's statement for us all; but for him both terms in the statement had been intensified to the utmost.

But the threat was to come first from elsewhere than Inspector Boltro. Boltro, if he appeared, might be able to break the outward body of their union, but he could hardly touch its heart; and the threat was to aim first at the heart of the matter. Next morning Paul stood waiting for Myra in the woods of beech and birch and pine that flank the tilted track from Farley Green to the summit of Pitch Hill. They had put the whole of Pitch Hill between yesterday's meeting-place and today's, because they did not want her to be seen twice on the same road. And this was surely one of the most secluded tracks leading to the hill-tops and the great views; they had found and adopted it years before, in the misanthropy of new lovers. Not a soul had come along it today, as Paul stood and peered. Not a woodlander broke its privacy; still less a visitor from the towns. Myra was the first person on the sloping footway that morning; he saw her soon after ten o'clock, toiling up the hill, with her face to the ground, a woman with a rucksack and a folded easel and stool. She was early, strangely early; and even at this distance he discerned, or thought he discerned, something agitated in her walk. It was slow and tired, and once she paused and put her hand to her brow. God, was she ill? Had something happened? As she bent her back to the slope, he knew, with sure presentiment, that ill news was coming up the slope with her. His heart deadened.

Now she lifted her face and saw him. She did not smile today, but only stared. Her eyes were red with weeping, and dark with sleeplessness; and she continued to stare at him, almost as at a stranger. Indeed, she looked a little mad.

'Myra!' he exclaimed when she was close.

Then she attempted her smile, but it was sickly.

'What has happened? You look so bad.' He laid a soothing hand on her arm; but she quickly drew it away, and shivered.

'Myra! What has happened?'

'Oh, I don't know. I've had awful thoughts,' she said, putting up the back of her hand in a helpless gesture to her forehead. 'Come; let's find somewhere where we can sit.'

As they plunged into the depths, he turned his head and saw that she was still looking at him, so strangely. Bewildered, he paused at a suitable place, but they did not sit down. He stood to look at her, and she, without a word or even a sigh, threw off her rucksack, opened it, and brought out the food. She spread it, but with none of the affection and playfulness of yesterday.

He watched, terrified.

At last, as she had spoken not a word, he asked again, 'What is it, Myra?'

'I have such terrible thoughts. I – I don't know what I'm thinking.'

'But why? What has happened since yesterday?'

She did not answer, but looked down at the carpet of pine needles and old leaves. Suddenly she looked straight up at him.

'I got a paper last night. The placards were saying, "New Discovery at Presset's House"; and I read it, and it said that the police had been digging in the garden and had found an old tin which had once contained arsenic, buried out of sight. It said that the man, Briscoll, had identified it as the one he had left behind and had come back for, but which you had said the dustmen had taken away. Of course the papers couldn't say straight out all that they implied, but in their cowardly way they left the impression they wanted. And I began to have such terrible thoughts. . . .'

Paul continued to stare at her, but he was not thinking of her now. He had forgotten her. It was true that he had buried that tin deep, not liking to put it on the dustbin so soon after Elinor's death or to leave it lying in the shed. Here was a point where his brain had failed him: he should have dug it up and brought it away, but who would have thought that the police would have had the pertinacity to dig the whole garden over. (He did not know that the police had their own methods of reading the surface of a garden, and knowing where or when it had been disturbed.) And now his brain was twisting and burrowing, to find the lie that should explain this action. He must say that he had found the tin soon after his wife's death and been frightened, remembering the tale he had told to Briscoll, so he had put it out of sight – yes, that would do – perhaps the discovery needn't be as damning as he had thought.

But he had paid his price for finding this excuse: his white alarm, his snatched-away thought, his guilty look at her now, had given his secret to Myra.

Her face went whiter than his, her body shivered, and she gasped, 'Oh!'

He put out his hand to touch her, and she drew away, 'No . . . please . . . don't,' she said; and then, to the woods about her, 'I see . . . I see. . . .'

'Myra,' he began, in a futile attempt to lie. 'Are you suggesting that I murdered Elinor?'

Her staring silence refused to deny it.

'Oh, well,' he said, turning his face away. 'Then I've no one now.'

This stirred her pity. 'Oh, tell me you didn't,' she pleaded. 'Tell me you didn't. I'd give my soul to know that you didn't.'

'Of course I didn't.'

'Paul!' The single word held all her disbelief. 'No, tell me the truth. I must know it. I will try to get used to it. I will try to get back to where we were, but I must know, I must know.'

'If I had done it, would it make all that difference?'

'It does make a difference. I can't help it. It . . . when I think of it, I find it difficult to love as I did.'

He opened a hand, held it open, closed it, and dropped it to his side.

'Paul, what is the truth?'

What was the use of lying? He had told her already, by his white face and his silence. She knew, whether he spoke or not. And yet he couldn't bring the words past his lips. They stood staring at each other.

'I will still do all I can for you,' she said, 'even if I can no longer – even if it's all different.'

He lifted his shoulders and said nothing. But why not speak when this silence was answering her all the time?

'Yes, I did it,' he said at length. 'I don't know how it happened. I've forgotten how it happened. It just – did itself. I couldn't bear to lose you, and. . . .'

'Oh!' She could only stare at him as at a stranger or a changeling.

'I'll try to explain some time how it happened. I think I could make you understand.'

'Oh, it's too awful!' Hopelessly, the back of her hand went to her brow again. 'I can't get my thoughts in order. . . . Paul, I must go away. I'll come back to you tomorrow, to this place, and bring you the food, but I must be alone . . . quite alone. I think I'll go now. I seem to want to get away. Do you mind?'

'No,' he answered, with a shrug. 'I've no one now.'

'I'll do what I can for you still – I'll come back here tomorrow, but – oh, God, God, God!'

This cry did not mean that she was on the verge of tears, but far beyond them. She snatched up the empty rucksack, and went quickly away. His eyes followed her, and his hand stretched out to the departing figure. Turning for a second, she saw this action, and his dropped jaw and beaten eyes, and a great pity went through her, – but no love. The Paul that she had loved had never existed, but someone different, someone different. Oh, God, God, God! Her body blundered on through the undergrowth, but her spirit was moving in an infinite waste. There is no other such waste in the whole journey of life, for while the death of the loved one leaves a desolation not empty of beauty, the sudden destruction of the love is wilderness complete.

Chapter Nine

Her head stunned, her thoughts a racing, disorderly mob, her feet alone commanding her movements, she found the path and hurried up the hill. She went on and on, and up and up, careless of direction, but dimly aware that only the top of the hill could put a term to her distraught climbing. Ling and heather and whortleberry, lying in clumps on the hillside, drove her feet in the way they must go; a grey squirrel, frightened by her advance, scurried along the russet path before her and dived into the thyme. Losing the path at one place, her body brushed through bramble and gorse, till she came to a carpet of moss, and the twigs and cones protested beneath her feet no more. 'Oh, how could he have done it? Oh, how could he have done it?' And the long lying, the easy, consistent deceiving of her! The Paul that she had loved, so gentle and kind, had never existed. In his stead there had been this shifty liar and a man of selfishness so complete that he could put another person out of – oh, but it wouldn't bear thinking of! Therefore all the past which had been sweet in memory – the evenings in Clissold Park, the days in the woods, the stolen nights – were now a sickly fraud. This blow struck the past as well as the present: memory itself was poisoned and slain. Surely there could be no experience so awful as this destruction of the past. The muscles of her face tautened with the pain of it, and her head was of wood that ached.

Evidently she was coming near the top, for the pines were tall and isolated now, and the fronds of the bracken held the sunlight on their hands, and a broad red path ran forward to a breadth of sky. The larches standing among the pines, and a rowan in the bracken told her that she had come to a familiar part; her feet, left to themselves, had obeyed unconscious memory. She was coming to that crown of Pitch Hill which was known as the 'Judge's Seat'.

Yes, here was the vast spread of southern England lying like a picture map below, that gracious parkland of woods and meadows and farm-steadings before whose beauty Paul and she had so often stood in silence. Here was the seat which the judge had placed so that men who came after him could enjoy the view that he had loved. Near it was a tormented pine, and she flung herself beneath it, drawing her feet under her and resting the weight of her body on one hand.

'Oh, God help me. . . . Oh, God, show me what to do. . . .'

For a long time, for hours it seemed, she could only sit there and say this. 'Oh, God help me.' She was glad that she had been praying to him of late, so that her approach to him now was not too insolently sudden. And after a while some little healing did seem to visit her. Right over the expanse of England, and away behind the grey South Downs to the sea, was a summer glory of uninterrupted light. There was no sky anywhere but only light. And somehow the stillness, the one-ness, the wholeness of the light spoke to her untrained spirit of an order lying somewhere behind the riot and disorder of this present world. It made her feel a little better. It hinted at a harmony where all things merged into one, and that one was light.

Very faintly, as she gazed at the far horizon, there came to her a hint of that perception which had come in full to far greater souls than she, out of intolerable pain. In her it took the form of an ache to love – and not only to love Paul again, but to love all. 'Oh, God, show me what to do.' Around her was the mid-week quiet of these hills, and below her a god's-eye view of the world. And she sat there, as it seemed, for hours, hardly thinking, only staring; but it is out of such stillness, and not from disputation, that man's poor vision sometimes stirs and peeps. Dimly, palely, she saw that there had been a violent change in the pattern of her life, while *she* stayed the same as yesterday; but that, if she changed herself to meet the pattern, she would make it a harmony again. A sword had fallen across her life, and if she stayed this side of it, she was a cowering, defeated creature; if she could pass to the other side of it, she walked erect again.

Paul had been changed into something worse and weaker; could she turn into something better and stronger, so as to meet and enfold him again? Then she could love him as before and so recover the sweetness of the past. But how could one feel love for a man who had been able to?—? Pity, yes, but a complete love like yesterday's – how was this possible?

Then it was that, palely, her portion of light came to her: she could go forward and love this weaker, worser Paul without recoil, only if she was prepared to go forward and love all without recoil. If she continued to hate the world, she could not love Paul. But if she began to understand and forgive and pity all, she could struggle back to him. Words leapt up to shape these glimpses – leapt up, ready-made in that rhythm which seems to belong to all thoughts that come less from our heads than from some abyss: 'Boundless understanding and bottomless forgiveness. . . . Forgive all men, and you can still love the one, though his actions slay your love. . . . Hate the deeds, but not the doers; forgive, forgive, forgive;' and they gave a leap of joy to the heart, a tiny touch of the mystic's ecstasy, so that her hand went to her heart, as if to control a pain. '*Real* forgiveness that could not recoil, even from the worst of murderers. Overwhelming tenderness, even for him . . . A mother would not recoil, but would take him in her arms, even with his bloodstained hands. Nay, she would give far, far greater tenderness to him than to others of her sons, because he needed it most of all' – oh, her eyes widened and lit, as she saw, as never before, the meaning of the parables and sayings of the wise.

And Paul was far from the worst. 'He's not *bad*, he's not *bad*,' she found herself repeating. 'I *know* he isn't, even if he has done this awful thing. I must try to understand how he came to do it. . . . It means an inconceivable self-centredness, but I am selfish too, though I would not do *that* to anyone. . . . And *I* was the temptation. . . . Oh, Elinor, forgive me. . . . I helped, I helped, I helped. . . . But therefore what I can do, I must do. . . . And he's not *bad*. How that can be I don't know, but everything in me knows that it's a lie to say he is bad. There is too much gentleness and kindness in him as well, and there's his love of nature, and his hunger for affection – oh, Paul, how could I have been so cruel?'

She saw him as he must be now, wandering deserted in the woods, with the hopeless sorrow in his eyes; and she cried, 'Oh! Oh!' her head falling, as the love rushed back in the shaking pain of relief. She threw up her face, her lips parted, as it might be in the torments of delivery. She saw him fixing a few days ago a rubber heel to his boot to add that little height to his disguise; she saw his white unhappy fingers feeling ever and again the dark stubble of his chin which was his only hope; she saw him coming out of the trees in his waterproof and rucksack, with his hunted eyes, the most friendless man in the world – and the uprush of pity nearly sprang her to her feet and drove her back to him.

But she wanted to be sure of herself: in full possession of this new and larger love. She leaned forward now, her hands clasped over her knees, as she tried, by concentrating, to understand and possess it for ever. And she saw much. She saw that her love for him, so far from dying, must have been there all the time, hidden, but forcing her to this new growth; she saw too that it was partly her need of him, her fear of desolation, that had driven her on, so that the move was not wholly selfless; but what of that? It was through our needs that God forced us forward. She saw that the Myra of only a few days ago had been a poor thing, anxious only to fly from the world, but that she had gone a little way forward when, outside Eastbourne Police Station, she had seen the despair in his eyes and wanted to fight the world for his sake; and that now, when she had learned that she must forgive him an unspeakable crime, she had gone quite a long way forward, so that she had no longer a sense of fighting the world, but only of loving and pitying it, and of ministering to the one nearest at hand. Then she had loved him because he suffered; now she loved him because he sinned; and that was a great advance.

It was joy. Yes, joy. In her present exalted mood Myra, with the world against her, rejoiced as no one else that day. She had what she wanted, saw her way, and felt, for a while, towards all that the world could do to her the high indifference of the consecrated. She sprang to her feet and hurried back down the wide red path, often breaking into a run. With something like ecstasy in her heart, she told herself again and again, as she ran through the bracken, 'I know that I am doing right. And I know that I shall never look back now.' She had a moment of dismay when she wondered if she would find him where she had left him; she stood stock still with her hand to her mouth, as she asked, Had he wandered miserably away, so that there would be no hope of finding him till tomorrow; the dismay was changing into frantic despair when suddenly she remembered that she had left behind her the folded easel and stool, and it was probable he would wait near them till she returned; she broke into a run again, fearful now of losing him; she recognised the path up which she had come and the place where she had left the wood; she turned into it and saw with a blistering pity the remains of the meal he had eaten, and the easel and stool lying on the ground – but there was no Paul near them. Had he, then, gone? Was he wandering somewhere in his loneliness? Would she have to leave him in his misery till tomorrow? Oh, no – and then she heard a twig break as if someone moved in the distance, and, turning her face to the sound, she saw above the breast-high bracken his face peering through the trees. With his four days' growth of beard, his ravelled hair, and his world-weary eyes fixed on her, he looked like some primaeval man scenting danger in the undergrowth. She went towards him and, drawing him against her and passing her hand over his head, murmured, 'Forgive me.'

Chapter Ten

All over England, a few days after this, those who opened their papers in the morning read such headlines as 'Presset. Hunt Hot in Surrey Hills, New Theory of Police', or 'Presset. Scene Changes, The Hunt Flares up in Surrey, Early Arrest Expected'. And as the men went to their offices, the women to their household work, the children to their schools, and ancient men to their seats by the workhouse walls, the story ran in their heads in the very language of the newspaper correspondents.

'The drama of the great man hunt underwent a sudden change last night. After a comb-out of the south coast hotels and apartment houses such as has never been attempted before, the police are confident that Presset is no longer to be looked for there. Wide though the net was thrown by Chief Inspector Boltro, who is in charge of the investigations, and by the Chief Constables of the several boroughs, who gave him every assistance, and small though its meshes were, they realise that in a holiday time like this it was impossible to ensure that he would not slip through. Aware of the concentration of detectives in the neighbourhood, and of the huge force of voluntary helpers at their disposal, he would almost certainly have left the district. And it now transpires that a man who may have been Presset spent a night alone at a small commercial hotel in the Old Steyne, Brighton, and left hurriedly after the news was published that Inspector Boltro was in the vicinity. In age, height, and manner he resembled the descriptions of Presset, and it is strongly suspected that he returned at once to London. He was alone, and the police are now confident that when he is found, Miss Bawne will not be found with him. They hold that these two have long ago separated; and the police, for the time being, are concentrating on finding the man.

'Yesterday an important new clue came to light. Working on the theory that Presset might have taken advantage of the exceptional weather to hide in the open at night, Inspector Boltro prosecuted inquiries as to the woodland places that he knew well, and information received from those who knew him showed that he was a lover of the pine-clad sandhills of Surrey, of which his chosen favourite was Pitch Hill. A man of wide and scholarly interests, he had often in the past conducted his friends on nature rambles among the birches and the firs. The underbrush is almost impenetrable in places and would provide an excellent concealment for a fugitive. Pursuing this theory, Inspector Boltro instituted inquiries in the district, and it soon transpired that a man resembling Presset was seen some days ago, apparently very footsore and weary, walking at sundown along the road to the little village of Holmbury St. Mary, which nestles peacefully under the lee of Holmbury Hill and the veritable pine-forest of Hurt Wood. On publication of this news in the early editions of yesterday's evening paper information reached Scotland Yard that a man who might well have been Presset had gone the same night to the inn at Ewhurst, which lies under Pitch Hill, and after drinking ravenously, had bought bread and cheese and taken it away in a paper. Before departing, he discussed the murder with the people in the bar, but this of course may have been only a blind. All describe him as looking very dirty and almost starved, and as wearing a full moustache over a clean-shaven chin. In this connection it is interesting to learn that, a few days earlier, a strange man of about Presset's height bought a safety razor and blades in a little shop at Gomshall on the northern side of the hills. It also transpires that on the day Presset is supposed to have returned to London a man in an exceedingly nervous condition bought a revolver at a gunsmith's in St. James's Street, London; and the police think it not improbable that the wanted man will not allow himself to be taken alive. During the evening further information was received that a man, exactly answering Presset's description, but also wearing a moustache, slouched up to a coffee-stall in Dorking a few evenings ago, and that early this morning a similar figure passed a shopkeeper who was standing at her doorway in Abinger Hammer, and quickened his step when the woman looked at him. If this was Presset, it seems possible that he is sleeping in the woods at night, and mingling with the crowds in the daytime to buy food.

'Immediately on receipt of this information the whole district was invested in such a manner as to render escape impossible. Inspector Boltro made a dramatic swoop upon the little village of Sherrol and established his quarters at a small hotel there. As soon as he supposed that Presset would have retired to the woods, he put a complete cordon of uniformed police and detectives round the whole area. Many hundred detectives were drafted there from the Yard and the Metropolitan Divisions. Not a lane but had its detective, and all pedestrians and cyclists were stopped, and all cars questioned. In addition the news quickly swept over this usually quiet neighbourhood, creating indescribable excitement, and thousand of willing helpers offered their assistance to the police. Many were accepted, and under the generalship of Inspector Boltro a ring of searchers round an area of some twenty miles began to beat the woods inward. Nothing like it has been seen in living memory. It was as if an army was beleaguering a citadel, but the citadel was held by only one man.

'The night was warm and still, and illuminated by a brilliant moon, but some of the searchers lit torches to aid them in the dimmer tracts of woodland. It made an eerie spectacle, enhanced by the voices echoing among the hills. Not a yard was overlooked, lest some article of the man's clothing should be found or some other clue to his whereabouts. Immense enthusiasm prevailed, both among the police and the volunteers, for all believed that they had cornered their quarry at last. An arrest is expected hourly. Up to the time of going to press there is no news of any capture, but the search will continue all today and tonight. Let eager sightseers take note, however, that approach to the district is discouraged by the police, and only those who can satisfy them that their business is imperative will be allowed to pass the outer cordon. Half the Press photographers in England, it was said last night, were waiting against this outer cordon with much badinage and merry-making, till the police should give them the word to go through.

'A point of interest is that this great co-ordinated search for Presset has now involved the county and borough forces of no less than five counties, Sussex, Surrey, Middlesex, London, and *Kent;* for today, on representations received from Inspector Boltro, who is leaving no single clue unexamined, there will be a conference at Maidstone, attended by the Chief Constables of the Kent County Constabulary, and of Canterbury, Dover, Folkestone, Gravesend, Margate, Ramsgate and Rochester.'

Among those who had this story, in its very phrases, running in their heads were a silent man and woman walking along the lonely road over Birker Moor, in the Cumberland fells. The lofty moor, a thousand feet above the sea, rolled away to left and right of them. On the spaces immediately at their side the heather had not begun, but they could see it on the slopes before them, and on the shoulders of the mountains, lying in shawls of dark brown or pale mauve. The rough road lay ahead of them like a thrown rope on the wilderness of browning grass. The man had a close-cropped iron-grey beard, the cheek-bones and cheek-sides shaved to delimit and emphasise the bristles. He wore a clerical collar, a jacket of pepper-and-salt, and grey flannel trousers, crumpled and stained. The woman, being younger, was smarter: she wore a neat blouse and walking skirt, and carried a light coat over her arm. Both carried the rucksacks proper to the neighbourhood, and tramped forward with stout ash sticks in their hands. They looked a quiet, untidy old parson and his more modern and energetic daughter, enjoying a walking tour in the Lake District of England.

Not another figure was on the moor. Bleakly it stretched away for many a heavy mile, its grass browned by the sun, except for the green patches where the dampness lay. It was furnished only with the outcrops of lead-hued rocks that lay about everywhere on the grass. A few were large enough to be called boulders, and these, steely grey, looked like the fallen monoliths of prehistoric men. The slopes of the moor were easy here, but northward towered the mountains. Far off were Red Pike, Haycock, and the Pillar; nearer on their right, the pikes of Scafell, and the point of the Great Gable stood between. Under the Gable was Wastdale Head with its lonely inn, which they would reach tomorrow, spending tonight in the nearer village of Eskdale Green.

They walked on and on into the afternoon. As they passed through the heather, the noise of their feet put up a brace of grouse, who flew away in a long low flight, whirring and rapid. They heard the quick sharp call of the kestrel, and the wail of the curlew flying overhead with legs thrown back. The red ribbon of road tilted downward to leave the moor behind. On their left was a thunderous headland of upended crags, with the coarse scree lying on its flanks; but ahead were pleasant fields and larch woods and the habitations of men. A stream, prattling over its stones and miniature falls, went with them down the incline. Soon they were between the lichen-spotted walls of piled grey slates that fence the pastures of Cumberland, and walking unremarked along the road to Eskdale Green.

Chapter Eleven

Next day the same two figures were crossing Irton Fell. They had set out in the morning with the intention of reaching by leisurely steps the foot of Wast Water, where they would take a picnic lunch, and then go on through the afternoon to the head of the dale. There the road ended, and the paths into the mountains began, and a little white inn, beloved of walkers and climbers, stood among its ash trees in the last of the fields. In Myra's memory it seemed as safe and natural a retreat as any within the barriers of England. She hoped to find room there for a night or more, and then, if the hunt died down, to go over the passes into Borrowdale and civilization again. If the inn were full, they would return to the little hotel at Eskdale which, lying off the climbers' track, promised to house them for the rest of the holiday season.

To go up and over Irton Fell is to go over a curve like the summit of a world. At its highest point Myra and Paul saw the vast view of the mountains that ring round Wastdale Head. In the foreground the Screes, like an arrested avalanche, pitched down to the silver dish that was Wast Water. Beyond, ringed about the green dale at the water's head, stood the peaks of Yewbarrow, Kirk Fell, and Great Gable, and the spurs and pikes of the Scafell range.

The two solitary figures stood at gaze, for the magnificent prospect was not void of terror. In the overwrought mind of Paul it caused a quick qualm: it seemed to symbolise the terror that surrounded and threatened them. Massive, overwhelming, the dark mountains suggested forces too great for the strength of two puny creatures: to fly or to fight were alike useless. He saw Boltro's men, hundreds of them, closing in upon his lair in the Surrey woods, which he had left only a few hours before Boltro bade them march; he heard the noise of their feet crashing through the bracken. Yonder was Wastdale: a narrow green dale ending in a dark ravine: it was like the little place of love and sweetness which he had found, only in time for it to be threatened by death and the dark. At the same time there was something of comfort in the immensity of mountains; they affected one like the stars; 'what matters the life or death or reputation of one so small as I?'

He said what others have often said. 'I don't think I can live among your mountains, Myra. They're too oppressive by far.'

'Oh, no,' she insisted. 'You'd love them in time, because you're like me: you like solitariness. One feels alone and safe in them, somehow.'

Moving on, they dropped from the heights and came upon a rough country road – the road, said Myra, that meandered as far as the Wastdale Inn and then perished among the foothills. She guided him along it as far as a gate through which they passed, and then she ran with feigned gaiety down a steep meadow towards a fast-flowing stream. Together they walked up the course of the stream, by hazel and alder and willow; and for a time there was no sound anywhere but the sibilant chatter of the water, hastening over whitened stones. Then – it made the hearts of both jump – there was an angry break in the ash wood on the farther bank, and something flew past them up the stream with a whirring and diminishing of wings.

'A dipper,' said Paul, as she quickly turned to him. He said it with a smile, to conceal his own alarm; but he had the fanciful idea that it had run before them to give notice of their coming. 'Chit, chit,' it called from in front.

The stream led them round the curve of the wood to the foot of the lake and a view of the mountains again. But now they were at the foot of that arrested avalanche of stones, three miles wide, the Screes. It, or they (for perhaps they are best thought of as a series of avalanches) hung suspended on the steep face of the mountain, with the water bathing their feet. On a pile of fallen stones Paul and Myra sat to eat the lunch they had brought from the hotel. They sat there for a long time, not talking much but happier than they had been; for the warmth of the sun came off the stones, and a coolness off the water; and the quiet seemed far indeed from that multitudinous activity at the other end of England.

'We'd better go on,' said Myra at last. 'It's a good three miles to the head of the lake.'

'Must we?' he asked. 'Will there be many people at the inn?'

'Only a few walkers and climbers looking just like ourselves.'

'Right,' he agreed, and clambered to his feet.

They retraced their path along the stream and up to the road. A mile along the road, and they had left the trees and meadows behind and entered upon the wildness of the Wast Water bank. On their left the granite boulders lay tossed among the gorse, and an occasional grey-black sheep nibbled the turf on the slopes behind. On their right, ever accompanying them, lay the lake, slate-grey now and fluted by a breeze that brushed its surface like a bird's wing; for a cloud was over the sun. On the far side of the lake were the walls of the Screes, pointing to the sky, as if a sea beach had changed places with a cliff. In this moment of shadow they were leaden instead of multi-coloured, and above them the bracken seemed greener for their darkness.

Suddenly Paul began to limp. 'Damn!' he exclaimed. After two days of walking, a blister had formed on his right heel, and every step was a sting.

'Is it very bad?' asked Myra gently. 'Can you manage a few miles to the inn? Then you can rest.'

'Oh, yes,' he agreed. 'But I pray heaven we shall be able to stop there tonight. I don't want to walk any more today.'

'Oh, I think that'll be all right,' she comforted him.

And they walked on. Their road skirted the lake all the way. Beyond the boulders they heard the roar of the Nether Beck rushing to meet the lake. Ahead of them Yewbarrow reared its knife-edge to the sky; and away to the right the southern face of Lingmell smiled in the sunlight, except when a shadow hastened across it.

A half an hour of walking or limping, and the lake fell behind; and they entered upon Upper Wastdale. It is but a small green floor of meadows intersected by stone walls, but towards it England's greatest mountains turn their feet. There is no other such vale in England. It is the end of a road, and it looks like an edge of the inhabitable world. A white inn, a tiny church among its firs, a few outhouses, and a few sheep cropping the pasture are the last of civilization to face the threat of the mountains. To those who walk on it for the first time it seems as if civilisation, dwindling for miles past, peters out here. It seemed so to Paul, who suddenly felt very far away from Inspector Boltro.

This feeling changed a little when they passed into the entrance lobby of the inn. It was hot with the breath of young men who stood about drinking, in their climbing or walking kit. The rucksacks and the coiled ropes of the climbers were flung against the wall, and the stout sticks of the walkers stacked in the corners. Just round the corner, in a narrow passage, was a bar window where a fat and very hoarse man, in shirt sleeves and apron, was wiping the glasses and serving drinks. The steamy heat of a kitchen range, coming from a door nearby, mingled with the smell of vigorous male bodies that had lately sweated on rock-face or fell.

Paul and Myra, sidling and insinuating themselves through the congestion – though the young men, seeing a parson and a lady, were politeness itself pressing back against the wall – made their way into the coffee room, a spacious oblong room hung round with enlarged portraits of famous rock climbers, the place of honour being kept for the picture of Will Ritson, one time proprietor of this celebrated inn. This room was nearly full, and twice as noisy as the passage outside; and though spacious and ventilated by three good windows, it was not empty of the smell of heated bodies. At the large main table and the small tables climbers, walkers, or fell-runners, men and women, sat before white cloths spread with tea cups, Cumberland cake, rum butter, and dishes of blackcurrant jam. Some of the young men, wearied from their climbs, sat with rounded backs and elbows on the table, sipping their tea. Older men in Norfolk jackets who had tired themselves less, sat back with their arms over the backs of their chairs. The women, in skirts and blouses or knickerbockers and shirts, looked hot and blown and bedraggled, but happy. And they ate and sat with no more elegance than the young men. The rucksacks of many lay dumped on the floor at their sides. All looked up as a clergyman and a woman entered, stared at them, and forgot them.

'It doesn't look as though we should get house-room here,' murmured Paul.

'Ah, they're only passing through, most of them,' said Myra.

'Well, let's sit down somewhere. My foot hurts.'

'It's all right, sir,' said a middle-aged man getting up. 'My boy and I are going now. You have our places.'

'Thank you. Thank you so much,' said Paul, ever inclined to be effusive; and they took these two chairs at the main table, and Paul, sitting down, loosened his shoe.

A servant girl – one could hardly call her a waitress – came up to Myra and inquired, 'Yes, miss?'

'Some tea, please, for two,' said Myra.

'Yes, miss. Thank you.'

They sat in silence till the girl had brought it on a jingling tray. Myra served the tea, and they drank it, and ate their bread and jam, studying the people at the tables rather than talking to each other. They had been seated thus for about a quarter of an hour when two young men burst into the room, to be greeted at once by jeers and laughter from another group in a far corner. 'Ha, ha, ha! Well, I'm blowed! Pete and Sandy back again! I thought we weren't going to see you again tonight, Pete? Don't give 'em any tea, Sarah. They haven't earned it. What's happened, Pete?'

'Too hot,' said Pete, laconically, as he tossed his rucksack into a corner and laid an ash stick against the wall. He was the taller of the two, and when he flung himself into a chair at a corner of the big table, it was like the collapse of a jackknife. The other, Sandy, was a shorter lad, ginger-haired: and he found a seat two places away from his friend.

'Tea, please, Sarah,' called Pete, 'and buckets of it. Don't listen to those idiots.'

'Crikey!' laughed the others, who had heard this from their end of the room. 'Where have you really been, Pete?'

'We only went over the fell as far as Dalegarth Force, if you want to know. Too hot, so we decided to come back at the slow. And it may or may not interest you to know that there's a murderer at large on the fells.'

'What?' shouted his friends.

And the noise of chattering groups and jingling crockery stopped, as if a needle had left a gramophone disc.

'Even so,' said Pete; and proffered no more.

'Yes, that's why we've come back quickly,' said the ginger-haired lad with a laugh. 'I could scarcely hold Pete in. It's lonely up there, and we'd no fancy to meet a desperate man.'

'That's the idea,' agreed Pete. 'It's warm and safe in here, and between us all we ought to be able to put up a fight.'

'But wha'd'you mean? Who is it?'

'The excellent Mr Presset.'

'But that's tripe. He's nowhere this way.'

'Like hell he is,' said Pete, tersely. And then, 'Excuse me, sir,' he apologised to an old parson sitting opposite.

'But I thought he was somewhere in Sussex – or Surrey, was it?' shouted his friend. 'I saw it in yesterday's paper. They'd raised about half a million men there to run him to earth.'

'That may or may not be,' answered Pete patiently, deliberately, and very well pleased to have the whole room for his audience, 'but all I can say is, they've changed their minds since then. . . . Thank you, Sarah; just put it down, and some more bread and butter, please, bless you. . . . After we'd gone over the moor we fetched up at the King Harry for a spot of lunch, and there the landlord was full of it. The bobbies had been in making inquiries only a few minutes before. They admitted it was Presset they were after, but they wouldn't say another word. They've got some deep game on. Have they blown in here yet?'

'No. We've heard nothing of it here.'

'Well, they'll be along soon enough. They're dead certain he's somewhere about.'

'Stuff! They were dead certain he was in Surrey yesterday.'

'Exactly; but you know what police are. They've probably trampled down about twenty miles of national beauty spots in Surrey, and he was never there at all.' Pete sipped his tea as if it were wisdom's cup. 'I mean, as you know, their feet are not small. And it's all rather a pity, because I come from there, and we were proud of our woods.'

'How did they learn he was here?'

'Don't ask me. Haven't I told you that they refused to say a word?'

'Has he got his fancy piece with him?'

'No, he's alone. They did tell the landlord that. Besides, you can bet she hopped it long ago. They'd hardly be such doubldyed imbeciles as to go about together.'

'Have some more tea.' It was Myra's voice, speaking as naturally as she could make it, in the ear of Paul.

'Er – thanks,' he stuttered; and he alone noticed the shaking of her hand as she poured it out. 'Thanks. Some cake?'

'Y-yes. Yes. I'll have a small piece. Thank you.'

'It's probably nothing,' one of the young men in the far corner was saying. 'They're probably just making inquiries everywhere.'

'Darned thorough inquiries, then,' scoffed the lad called Sandy. 'We decided to come home round the foot of the lake, and just as we came down off Irton Fell on to the road, two coves in civvies appeared from nowhere and stopped us.'

'They probably thought Pete was Presset. And p'raps he is!'

'Such wit!' said Pete.

'And they asked us if we'd passed anybody, and if so, who. They were 'tecs. A little farther on we saw a car being stopped and its passengers scrutinized. It's fun, I can tell you!'

Paul touched Myra's thigh beneath the table. Her hand found his and gripped it for a second. God be merciful, the police were as near as that! They must have sprung up within a few yards of a point they had passed, and less than an hour later. He drew on his shoe again.

'What's he got up like?' asked a mild father of a family.

'I don't know, sir,' said Pete, more politely. 'We asked these fellows for information and offered to join in the hunt like one o'clock, but they said their instructions were to ask descriptions of everyone who had passed and to say nothing. My friend said he didn't believe they really knew anything, and they were good enough to wink and say, "We've got him all right this time. He's none so far off." '

'Crikey! I hope he turns up here.'

'Well, if he doesn't, the 'tecs will, soon enough. They're drafting an army into the district . . . More tea, please, Sarah; Sandy's drunk all this. . . . There's hundreds coming, hundreds and hundreds of 'em, my lad, because he's bound to take to the hills when he gets wind of it; and then we shall all be roped in; and I sincerely hope so.'

'Yes, I'll shin up the Gable after him, you bet! Let's go out and meet the cops. *Come* on! This is Life, my lucky lads!'

'Come,' said Paul to Myra. 'We'd better be going now, if we're going to get back.'

'Yes,' she murmured, and rose. Her eyes were terror-fixed, but would anyone notice it? Hardly knowing what she did, she called feebly to the waitress.

Paul interrupted her. 'Our bill, please.'

'Yes, sir.'

He took it, and thrust money into the girl's hand; and doubtless she thought him an old man whose palsied hand was always tremulous like this.

Then he and Myra pushed their way through the chairs and the large sideboard to the door. Imminent danger gave him power to act his part. He looked at the pictures of famous climbers as if in no hurry, and dawdled before one of them. He pointed out something in it to Myra. He lingered at a rack of picture postcards, while Myra went out before him. The voices in the room behind continued their talk; and half a minute later, he went out limping. He passed along the narrow passage, empty now, and into the entrance lobby, where Myra stood waiting. And the first thing on which his eye fell was a coil of climber's rope flung against the wall.

It was a rope made thick enough to bear the weight of a man.

Myra went quickly out into the yard before the hotel, and he followed her, giving a guilty look round. No; no intent and purposeful men were yet approaching the inn door.

'Which way?' he asked.

'This way,' said Myra. 'There's no other way.' And she turned towards the Great Gable and the Sty Head Pass.

Chapter Twelve

Chief Inspector Boltro, sitting in his room in the Bull's Head, Sherrol, behind the Surrey woods, was exceedingly annoyed when, on the morning after an all-night search of the woods and a six o'clock a.m. conference of the police chiefs, the morning of a daylight drive that must round up Presset before dark, the morning when every paper in Britain was 'starring' the tale of his operations in Surrey, a message should come through from the Yard that the Lancashire police thought Presset was in Lancashire.

In Lancashire! Strong suspicion that he was either in Lancashire, or had passed through it the previous day! Boltro expressed his contempt in a vigorous if inelegant syllable. How many more places was he to be seen at? These borough and county police thought themselves very clever, but, being at the other end of nowhere, they didn't seem to realise that the Yard was receiving a hundred such messages a day. Presset was no more in Lancashire than he was in Tennessee or Pekin. He was within a few miles of where Boltro was sitting now.

All men, thrilled with their work, have the artist's jealous love for the creation in hand; and love is an emotion that disables criticism. Inspector Boltro loved, like a painter or a poet or a boy, his cordon of men round the greensand hills, his beaters crashing through the bracken, his generalship of a major operation from an hotel room, the thoroughness, co-ordination and relentlessness of his plans, his picture of a desperate Presset run to earth like a terrified rabbit in the spinney, and the chorus of praise that would be his tomorrow;

and he resented this hint that his creation might be less than perfect. As excited as a young athlete who is confident of winning the cup, he could only – he *must* – ridicule this breath of doubt from far away. It was almost an insult. Faugh! These provincial police! They should be at the Yard for a month.

This was the story that had come through from his Chief at the Yard; and to him, Boltro, it didn't even suggest Presset. A young man, a Mr Alan Stevens, B.A., of Oxford (who doubtless imagined himself an amateur detective and despised the professionals) had been on a train yesterday going home to his father's rectory in Lancashire, and he found himself sitting opposite to a middle-aged clergyman with a cropped iron-grey beard. He had been reading in his paper about the Surrey man hunt, and, having exhausted the news and wearied of reading, he fell, as people do, to studying his fellow travellers. His eye rested on the little clergyman with the cropped beard. And, his mind still full of the hunt, he thought, half humorously, that the beard might have been kept close-mown like that for twenty years but looked much more like a ten days' growth. The cheekbones seemed to have been clipped to heighten its effect, and the cheeks shaved. The parson was just about the height and build of Presset, but he looked older, though that might have been the effect of the beard. Certainly he looked pale and haggard enough. Amused at his idea, he turned again to the paper which had a picture of the hunted man, and over its top he glanced from picture to parson. The beard removed, there was an undoubted likeness between the two. This set him studying the parson's clothes; and he saw that the clerical effect resided in the collar and stock, and no more: for the rest there were the grey flannel trousers, the pepper-and-salt jacket, and the rain-coat mentioned in the descriptions. He studied his baggage: a very new case and a rucksack. He studied his hands: they were most extraordinarily scratched. So he got into conversation with him, and at once he received the impression that this approach frightened him. The little parson was very polite, but he volunteered no information on where he was going and seemed anxious to discourage the talk. But the young man, a rector's son, learned enough to suspect that the parson didn't know as much about the Church as his collar suggested. And, strangest of all, while the young man was in the dining car, the parson changed his compartment. It was now impossible to keep an eye on him without being ridiculous or impertinent, and Mr Alan Stevens contrived to lose sight of him. But it was his idea that he must have got out at Wigan or Preston. When the young man reached his father's country rectory, he was inclined, as he put it, to 'give the sportsman a chance', but his father, whom he told in the morning, wouldn't hear of it and, insisting that they must do their duty as citizens, got into touch with the Preston police.

Boltro, wanting to disbelieve it, found it easy to do so. Probably this was some perfectly inoffensive reverend gentleman who resented the loquacity of a young Oxford swell. Who might not change his carriage if a young man opposite refused to stop talking? All parsons were courteous, and would take the opportunity of the young man's absence to make the move. All parsons wore grey flannel trousers on holiday. All parsons were great walkers, and this one was probably going to walk across the half of England with his rucksack on his back.

Nevertheless, no reasonable clue must ever be neglected, and Boltro agreed with his Chief that the Lancashire police had best make their inquiries at stations, hotels, and apartment houses, while avoiding press publicity.

No more news came from Lancashire that day, and Boltro was pretty sure that he had heard the last of it. Less satisfying was it that the men beating the woods had so far come upon no trace of Presset. All day they had pursued their search, but never did they come upon an unkempt and horrified man, staring out of the thicket. Nor upon a body with a revolver by its side. The chill breath of doubt touched the Inspector's optimism, but he drew away from it. It spelt too sickening a disappointment. Impossible that the championship was going to elude him after all! At dark, after a conference, they called off the work till the morning; and he sat down and wrote a report, and turned into bed to get his first sleep for forty hours.

Next morning he was busy with a huge breakfast when the landlady herself bustled in.

The proprietress of the Bull's Head, at Sherrol, a big, rustling talkative widow, was not a little uplifted by the fact that the famous man had chosen her house for his headquarters, and by the custom it was bringing to the bar. While retaining her dignity, or fondly hoping that she retained it, she had fussed around him, insisting that he must have everything he needed. She had given him her private sitting-room, bustling certain garments, ledgers papers, and a sewing machine from its table or chairs to the cold inhospitality of the passage. 'Yes. You'll be having your hands pretty full, I expect, and will be wanting a little privacy, I haven't a doubt. And you'll need somewhere quiet-like to interview people, I expect. Yes. I only wish I could put you a telephone here, but I'll tell you what I'll do: there's the telephone in the office and you can have it to yourself any time, quite private-like. Yes, any time you want it. And there'll be somebody near at hand all day in case they ring you up, and I'll see that they drop whatever they're doing, and attend to that first. What I mean to say is, we must all do our best to help you catch that villain.'

So now she bustled in with a message of such dignity that the proprietress herself might honourably carry it.

'You're wanted on the phone, Inspector. Yes. It's a long distance call from Scotland Yard. Yes. And it's urgent, they say. I'll see that you're left to yourself.'

The Inspector always pretended a greater indifference than he felt. He laid down his table napkin, and, still chewing his bacon and eggs, walked down the narrow stairs to the office. The proprietress most obligingly shut the door on him.

'Yes, Chief Inspector Boltro speaking?'

And the new story came through. A parson or pseudo-parson answering the young man's description had stayed the same night at a hotel in Stretton-in-Furness *with a daughter*. The daughter in many ways answered the description of Bawne. They had given the names of the Rev. Coulsdon and Miss Coulsdon, and there was no such name in *Crockford's* or the *Clergy List*. They had left in the morning without saying where they were going, but a waitress serving them at breakfast saw them poring over a map, and rather gathered that they would take the road to Ulpha. Bawne knew those parts well, having lived there as a child. There seemed no doubt whatever that this was Presset. The Lancashire police were prosecuting their inquiries with every available man in the district, and the Chief Constable of the Cumberland and Westmorland police was arranging that every available man should be detailed to the search on his ground. For the present they were making inquiries only, under strict orders to publish no details. It was their view that if Presset learned that they knew of his disguise and his companion, he would get shut of both, and the capture would be delayed.

'God's truth!' muttered Boltro into the receiver. Dumbfounded, he could only answer in monosyllables or question unimpressively. Right, he would go down at once, and when was there a train to these benighted parts? Ten-thirty-five, fast. Right, he'd get it or perish.

' 'Struth!'

As he hung up the receiver, a new thought leapt out of the confusion. Supposing the Cumberland police got him before he could get there, and Inspector Boltro was not on the spot!

Inspector Boltro still engaged on beating the bracken over twenty square miles of Surrey. The devil! Supposing he became a laughing stock instead of a hero! The centre of an uproarious jest! No, he must be there when they collared him. Pray the lord they didn't get him at once! Give him ten hours and he'd be in Cumberland with them. So long as his was the chief name connected with the arrest, the world would quickly forget the majestic campaign in Surrey. Or they would say that Boltro, subtle devil, had been keeping more than one kettle on the fire, and knew which to make sing on the hot-plate and which to leave quiet on the side.

Eight-thirty. He must make Euston in a couple of hours. Dammit, Sergeant Doyle was out with the police car. Well, Doyle would have to follow as best he could.

'Mrs Baddeley, Mrs Baddeley!' He was about to enjoy the drama of the scene with the landlady.

'Yes, Inspector.' Mrs Baddeley was at no distance. She was, in fact, standing in the passage, dusting a table-wagon but hoping to hear his explanation of the call. The door of the office opened.

'There's a garage in this place, isn't there?'

'Yes, Inspector. Sayers's.'

'And have they got any fast cars?'

'Oh, yes. They've got fast cars enough. And I'm sure Mr Sayers'd drive you himself if it's urgent. I'm sure he would. I mean, he'd like to.'

'It's very urgent. Would you be good enough to get in touch with Mr Sayers while I do a little packing? I must get to Euston by half-past ten without fail.'

'He'll get you there if it's possible.'

'He's *got* to get me there. Tell him so. Tell him he can undertake to do that or let the job alone.'

'I'll tell him, sir. And may I ask, have you found Presset?'

Boltro nodded knowingly. 'I *think* so, Mrs Baddeley. I think we've got him this time. In a spot we've had our eye on for the last two days. It was always a question of here or there. *And* we've got the woman, too!'

'That Bawne creature? Well, I do congratulate you. I'm sure I'd no fancy for *her* getting off. She's every bit as bad as him, if you arst me.'

'Well, we've got 'em both now. But I shouldn't know anything about it just yet, see?'

'That's all right, Mr Boltro. You can rely on me not breathing a word,' assured Mrs Baddeley, with undue optimism.

Fifteen minutes later he was sitting beside a delighted Mr Sayers in a fast open car, holding on to his bowler hat and gazing ahead of him when it raced; stuttering with impatience when it was compelled to slow; fuming and beating a foot when it was stopped at crossroads; execrating the car in front that refused to yield to their imperious horn; contemptuous of petty constables who stared angrily at their speed; sullen, preoccupied, uncommunicative, and glancing tormented at the street clocks.

For a while Paul and Myra, hastening towards the mountains, said nothing. They kept the path through the grey stone walls and by the larch wood, anxious to get on to the pony track that would up through the bracken over the knee of the Great Gable towards the Sty Head Pass. They must get from sight of Wastdale as soon as possible. Paul, limping beside Myra, glanced at her face and saw that it was pale and dulled and defeated. She was staring ahead of her like a somnambulist.

'Where are we going?' he asked.

'I don't know,' she answered with despairing accent. 'I don't know.'

'But you know the way? You know where it leads?'

'Oh, yes. . . .'

'Where?'

'Over the pass and down into Seathwaite and Seatoller. Let's get up there; let's first get out of their view and think. But I don't know where we can go now. Nowhere's safe.'

Paul, limping, dropped a pace behind. The track was little more than a shelf tilted up the slope of the Great Gable.

'Look here, dear,' he said to the figure in front. 'You must leave me. As far as we know, they're only looking for me, and I'm not going to have you taken with me. You could get right away.'

'No, I'm not going,' she said irritably. 'Not while there's still hope. But I think we'd better keep apart – though, I don't know, you're perhaps less suspicious with me. Oh, I'll think as soon as we get to the top of the pass. Can you come faster?'

'I'll try.' And he limped faster. 'We've only got about three hours of daylight, Myra.'

'Oh, that'll be all right. . . .'

'You can find your way in the dark?'

'We'll be down at Seathwaite by then, and it may be as well to pass through it in the dark. It's downhill all the way after we get over the saddle.'

'Where are we going to spend the night?'

'Oh, I don't know, *I don't know*, I tell you! I'm thinking that perhaps we could go on to Honister Hause where there are slate quarries at the top. It'll be deserted at night, and we might get shelter in one of the huts.' She sighed wearily. 'I don't think we dare stay in any house if they're making inquiries everywhere. Then if my plan's any good, we might drop down to Buttermere Fell. There are woods there, and it's about as lonely a valley as any. You might keep in the woods, and I could get some food and bring it to you.'

'You'd much better go, and leave me to my fate.'

'Oh, don't be silly!' she snapped rudely. 'How can I do that? It'd be impossible.'

Paul looked behind. They were now high up, and Wastdale was a patchwork valley below, with its beck winding and whispering through the meadows to the silver spread of the lake. He no longer felt that they could be seen from down there. The path before them was now steeper and stonier, with boulders at its side, and cairns to mark it – a chamois path; and Myra breathed heavily as she climbed it. The mountains were closing in upon them; the walls of the pass narrowing. Great End seemed very close, as if one could hurl a stone across the narrowing valley and hit it. The Gable frowned darkly above them, for the sun was off it and lighting the cheek of Lingmell. Soon this twisting track would turn the corner by the crags; and Wastdale, with its memory of a ghastly moment, would be left behind. 'Forever,' he thought; and the word reminded him that he was probably gazing for the last time on all things that he passed. He looked up at the peaks of Scafell, and the deep crack of Piers Gill, to say a goodbye to them. Now they were very near the cairn that marked the turn of the track, and involuntarily Myra, though breathless and sighing, quickened her pace. She turned the bend.

He halted. Just here the fall from the pass was precipitous and rocky. One might throw oneself down. He looked back at Wastdale. Miles behind and fifteen hundred feet lower down, it looked like a jigsaw puzzle in green, the stone fences making a crazy pattern of its few meadows. That was the past. If he followed Myra and turned the corner by the cairn, he would see other valleys ahead of him, and the future – and what a future! Myra was out of sight. Should he throw himself down . . . or go on into the world? He shook his head as he decided: loyalty to Myra meant that he must struggle on in life even to the gallows' foot. Strange, if you came to think it out, how she held him to the gallows! He was not a good man, nor a hero; and he would certainly lie when he was caught; but one thing was perfectly clear: he would go to the gallows rather than hurt her. Not a doubt about that. The temptation had lasted for three quick breaths, and he limped after her.

He rounded the corner, and immediately the wind assaulted his face. It was blowing up the Sty Head valley and funnelling through the mountains. In the saddle he saw a green basin with a lonely tarn in it, rippled by the wind. Myra was going off the stony ground on to the level green turf at its side, and he limped behind her, mending his pace to lessen the distance between them. They looked like a pair who had quarrelled.

He had not gone far before he came to a signpost pointing the way with a single arm. In this grim desolation it looked very like a gibbet.

Now he came abreast of Myra, and they walked side by side in silence, till the path narrowed again and obliged him to fall behind. Tilting downwards, it was now a tortuous track of red granite chips and white boulders, with the Sty Head Gill gabbling over its round-washed stones to the valley of the Derwent far below. If they left the stony track, they trod in spongy turf, and the water bubbled over their shoes. But the larger stones, bullying his blistered foot, made every step a wound, so that he limped and stumbled worse than before and fell farther behind.

Suddenly Myra, who had been abstracted and irritable, looked back; and the sight of him struggling along over the splintered stones lifted an overwhelming pity in her and sent her back to him.

'Is it very bad?'

'It does hurt a bit.'

'Rest it for a little and take the shoe off.'

'I think I will, if you don't mind.' And he struggled to a big boulder and sat on it. 'Are you decided where we are going?'

'Yes, I'm sure we can't do better than I suggested. We'll make for Honister Hause and the quarry. We can do it. I'm not very tired, are you?'

'No, it's only this foot.'

He bared it, and both saw the torn blisters on the heel and the ball of the foot.

'Oh, my dear!' said Myra. 'What can we do for it? See, I'll bathe it. That'll ease it.'

And she kneeled on a rounded stone, and, dipping her handkerchief in the water of the gill, bathed and cleaned the blisters. Then, after stopping and thinking, with her hand dropped, she opened the rucksack and drew out another handkerchief, which she tore into strips and bound about the painful place.

'There. That'll stop the rubbing, and we'll go slowly.' Gently she got the unlaced shoe over the thickened foot. 'Is that better?'

'Yes. Much better.'

So they walked on. When the longest stretch of the path was in view, they saw, in the far distance, a lively party of young people, men and women, late like themselves on the pass and hurrying with laughter home. They went slower to let these people get out of sight, and soon their voices could be heard no more. It was easy to keep to the path, because its stones were scratched white by the nailed boots of travellers, and besides, the cairns were built up at every few yards to draw you back if you strayed.

These piled-up cairns! He was just thinking that they were monuments to the friendliness of men, when they came upon the carcass of a sheep, killed no doubt by the ravens, and visited by the buzzards who wheeled about it, rejoicing. Ah, well: the old insoluble riddle: the mercy in nature and the savagery; ineffable beauty, and the dismaying, self-centred rapacity. . .

The track by the Sty Head Gill drops steeply and roughly towards Stockley Bridge, even passing at places through the tumbling gill itself; and here Myra, with a hand at his elbow, helped him down.

It was twilight as they passed between the slate barns and the grey rough-cast cottages of Seathwaite. Their passing started a chorus of dogs imprisoned in one of the barns, and terror started in both their hearts. A child, with unwiped nose, came to the listing gate of a cottage, and a woman's face appeared at a window, and her eyes followed them.

They were glad to be through the village and on the road among the trees. They dawdled the two miles to Seatoller, and only a labourer passed them. But he certainly turned and looked back. Had he heard?

It was dark as they went up the hill through Seatoller, a larger village with well-built cottages of Honister slate and a high wood behind. Not a figure was in the street: only a woolly sheepdog prowled about the stone steps up to the cottage doors. Lights were behind the windows, whose curtains were drawn; and in one room a piano was jingling and a woman singing. The wind whispered in a ring of trees; and they looked that way, thinking someone had moved. But no one saw them go through Seatoller; though, far away back, the dogs were still yelping in Seathwaite.

Very weary now, they staggered up through the oak and larch wood till they were on the open fell by Honister Hause. It was too dark to see what they were treading in, but their feet seemed to be in spongy ground. They could hear the noise of a waterfall. It grew louder as they approached the top of the hause, and now, in the starlit dark, they saw rough buildings and knew them for the hutments of the quarries. Finding one that was not only deserted but derelict, they threw themselves down in it to rest. They had no food so they had best try to sleep till daybreak. They lay close for warmth, and, as the minds of each gave entrance to the thought that this was probably their last night together, they clasped each other close. Once Myra felt him grasp her convulsively, and knew that this thought had shot through him. And she passed her hand over his head and down his arm caressingly. And suddenly she remembered that this was the body they would hurt and slay. Oh, Paul, Paul. . . . A tawny owl hooted in the wood through which they had come, and the churring note of a nightjar tore the stillness of the moor.

And as, very wakeful, she held him thus, she thought, 'I must get this right.' If the end was at hand, and everything in her said that it was, then she must be ready to meet it. Since that hour of exultation on the summit of Pitch Hill her days had been an oscillating between illumination and darkness. She had had moments of irritability, moments when the memory of what he had done threatened the destruction of her love and all the illumination with it, and she had had to fight back to the vision. But always she fought back to it, alone, because it had been too lovely to lose. Whether or not the mystic's experience seems valid to other men, it is certainly valid to him; and Myra, in a very small way, had glimpsed the mystic's knowledge, who perceives that he must change his whole character if he is to attain again, and hold fast, the blissful vision that for a moment was granted him. 'Let me get it right,' she thought again and again that night, holding Paul against her. 'God, give me back my sight, and keep it steady and clear. I love and pity him. I love and pity all. Only by loving and pitying all can I keep my love for him, without which I am so miserable. I must deny all knowledge of his crime – always – even though it is a lie' – strangely enough, this lie would not have troubled her greatly in any case, for her conscience was a curious one, but now she had no other course, or she incriminated him – 'Yes, I shall deny all knowledge. I shall do everything I can for him, right up to the last minute; and as for the others, I have no malice towards any of them, and I will go quietly when they come for me.'

While Paul and Myra were toiling down the Sty Head Pass, Inspector Boltro arrived at Stretton-in-Furness. His hand was opening the door of his compartment before the train came to a standstill. He was a-tremble to learn if they had caught Presset, or if there was still a hope that he might play a part in the arrest. No youth awaiting the result of an examination and fearing the worst could have felt more discomfort in the heart and below it than he. He saw two men standing on the platform, of whom one was in a superintendent's uniform, and the other was very obviously a police inspector in mufti; and he knew with an inner emptiness that, in a few seconds, they would tell him his fate. The train had carried him some way past them, and he hurried out with his bag and walked down the platform towards them. In the half minute before he presented himself he had, as he put it, 'weighed them up': the uniformed superintendent, grey-haired and slim, was a dutiful and competent, but unremarkable, fellow who had arrived at his high rank by seniority rather than brilliance; the fatter man in mufti with his hands thrust deep in his trouser pockets, his jacket thrown back, his felt hat pushed a little way off his forehead, and his general air of ease and self-satisfaction was the younger, more capable, more dominant fellow. Probably a detective-inspector, for the brains, thought Chief Detective-Inspector Boltro, tended to silt up in the detective police.

They recognised him as quickly as he them; and the uniformed senior man presented himself as Superintendent Kerslake of the local police and his companion as Inspector Yarr of the Cumberland-Westmorland force. Boltro took a slight shock at the Superintendent's northern accent, and at the idioms of Yarr who seemed to have come originally from London; and quickly there stirred in him the usual faint pity for the provincial police.

'Have you got him, sir?' he asked, trying to appear indifferent.

'Not yet,' said the Superintendent.

'No, but we ought to have him any moment now,' added Inspector Yarr confidently. 'If you'll come this way, we'll explain where we are. Come on, sir.'

He led them to the stationmaster's office. The stationmaster, with that deep psychological satisfaction that seems to come to many when they can give impressive aid to authoritative men engaged on exciting and sadistic war, was standing near the doorway, ready to usher them into his little office and to be presented to the great man from London.

'The latest is that they have traced him to Wastdale Head,' explained Inspector Yarr who, though junior to all, had quickly achieved an ascendancy. 'But from there he's disappeared into the blue. He's still travelling with Bawne and in his minister's disguise, which shows that even if he knows we're after him, he doesn't know how much we know. All our men have been instructed to ask questions only, and to keep absolutely mum.'

'Quite right. I think you're absolutely right,' said Boltro, anxious not to sound patronising – but not succeeding. 'But where is this Wastdale?'

'We'll show you,' put in the Superintendent, who felt he ought to say something. 'Show him the map, Mr Yarr.'

Inspector Yarr spread an Ordnance Survey map over the stationmaster's desk and pointed with the butt of a pencil at the green Wastdale valley curving into the mountains.

'One thing's pretty certain,' he said: 'He didn't come back by the road along the lakeside. He'd have walked into our arms if he'd done that. But there are several things he may have done: he's at just about the best centre for doubling and twisting. He could have turned left up Mosedale, you see' – he tapped the map with the pencil's butt – 'and gone over Black Sail Pass which would bring him down into Ennerdale. Or he could have gone straight on over Sty Head Pass and either have turned left and come down towards Seathwaite or gone right over Esk Hause here towards Langdale Fells. Or again—'

'But do you mean to say that he and the girl can walk over these mountains?' interrupted Boltro.

Inspector Yarr turned towards him. It was his turn now to pity. 'Do it on their heads,' he said. 'Why on earth not?'

'I imagined they had to be climbed, with ropes and axes or something.'

'Nah, no.' Inspector Yarr dismissed the absurd notion. 'Why, ponies go over the passes. This here's a pony track – though I'm not sure that you don't have to carry the pony part of the way!'

'I see.'

'Or again, as I was saying, he might have turned south at Esk Hause and come down into Eskdale. But I don't think that's likely if he knows we're after him.'

'No,' agreed the Superintendent, feeling that it was time he was heard again.

'No.' Inspector Yarr agreed both with the Superintendent and himself. 'Then it amounts to saying he's probably in the vicinity of Ennerdale, Borrowdale, or Langdale.'

'Well, we can surely block his exit from all these valleys,' said Boltro, pointing to the green places on the map with the long blue lakes.

'We can block 'em as easy as basting butter, but what's to stop him breaking away across any of these fells?'

'But you can't get over this stuff, can you?' asked Boltro, drawing a thick forefinger over a brown and purple patch.

'Do it with your feet in your pocket,' scoffed Yarr. 'Them dotted lines mark the footways.' He knocked first the dotted lines with his pencil, then his teeth. 'But it only brings him down to the road again. No, if you ask me, he'll keep to the tracks of the walking parties, and, as like as not, send the girl along with them to get food. He's got to get food somehow, hasn't he? No, he's somewhere here.' And with a flick he put a girdle round the Gable.

'Yes, I feel you're right,' the Superintendent slipped into the pause. 'But does he know the lie of the land as well as all that?'

'Oh, we know all about that,' said Boltro glad to know something at last. 'We've got that point taped. Bawne knows it. She had an auntie here, and used to spend all her holidays with her.'

'H'm,' grunted the Superintendent. 'That explains a lot, doesn't it? Where was the auntie?'

'Let's see,' Boltro cogitated. ' "Grange"? Is there a place called Grange?'

'Is there a place called Hell?' said Yarr, knocking the spot on the map a dozen times.

'Well, it was somewhere near there,' explained Boltro, a trifle disconcerted.

'Good! Good!' Yarr was delighted. 'Then she'll make towards that way. A thousand to one on it. She'll make towards the part she knows.'

'Yes, I think that's right,' said the Superintendent.

'I bet you an even tanner they went over Sty Head and down towards Seatoller. That's where they are.' He hit the Seatoller district three times triumphantly.

Boltro studied the map. This easy talk of hunting Presset over the mountains was making him nervous and anxious. He had no experience of mountains, and knew only that he couldn't look over the cliff at Eastbourne without turning dizzy and sick. A heavy man, he saw himself stuck halfway up a mountain, afraid to move up or down, afraid to lift his eyes from the rockface, and suffering the agony of the damned; for this Yarr, a conceited and overbearing fellow, was probably representing as child's play what was really a nightmare climb. And he had no use for hanging before the provincial police in a ridiculous position; he wanted to stand before them in places of distinction. Pray Heaven they arrested Presset on the pale brown fells and up some easy incline.

'Well, all the roads,' said he, 'seem to converge upon the town of Randall. I should think the best plan would be to go there.

Then I – er, *we* can bear down upon any point.'

'Absolutely!' agreed Yarr. 'Got it right first time.'

'How long will it take?'

'Randall's the best part of forty miles. I've got a car out there that moves. It shouldn't take above an hour.'

'No, it shouldn't take more than that,' said the Superintendent.

'Then let's put off at once.'

'Right.' Inspector Yarr folded up the paper and straightened his hat.

'Yes, that's it,' said the Superintendent; and he came into the station yard to see them off. 'Good luck.'

So it happened that while Myra was helping the lamed Paul down the steep and rocky stairs above Stockley Bridge, Inspectors Boltro and Yarr were racing along the good straight road by Thirlmere, under the frown of Helvellyn.

Boltro, after sitting dumped in thought for a while, said, 'Strikes me the girl'll lead us to him.'

'If she comes to buy food, you mean?'

'Yes.'

'That's right. That's what *I* think.'

'We can have a man at every likely place where she can buy food, I suppose?'

'Oh, yes. The Super at Randall'll fix that up for you. Disguise them as walkers or young London gents on holiday.'

'Are there any telephones in these mountain villages?'

'Oh, yes. We're quite civilized up here, you know. You're still in England. And what's more, we've got motorbikes too, if need be.'

'Because' – Boltro spoke a little anxiously – 'I feel I should like – I feel I ought, if possible, to be there when they're arrested. I can identify them both, you see. I'm the only one who's ever seen them, and I feel I ought to be there,' he added, almost appealingly.

'Naturally,' agreed Yarr. 'But the Super or one of us'll want to be there too, I expect.'

'Oh, of course, of course. Oh, quite. Oh, definitely.' Relieved and happy, Boltro was enthusiastic over the idea that the Super or one of them should be there too.

Daybreak, and the call of the blackcock, awoke Paul to memory. He saw across the hollow a rim of orange light on the dark face of Honister crag. The top of the crag was a black precipice, but, below, the scree fell in a thousand feet of green slate-chips, with the downward sweep of a lady's train. And there is that about the green of Honister slate which is dark and hostile. A quarryman's track slanted across the face of the precipice and cut through the scree, and a sledway ran up at a seemingly impossible gradient into the heart of the mountain. This reminded him at once of the quarrymen; and, not knowing if or when they would return, he went back into the hut and touched Myra's shoulder. Her eyes opened, and he knew that she too was recovering memory.

There was no food, so with few words they left the hut and began to descend. Their path at first was sinuous, steep and rough, but soon the walls of the pass opened wide, and they saw Buttermere and Crummock Water in the grassy vale below. The path, now a winding river of shale, led them on to more level and greener ground, with rushes marking the dampness, and a population of sleeping rocks and boulders spread everywhere on the thick turf. A spumy and chattering streamlet went with them down to the lakes. Except for its gossip and the far-off roar of a waterfall, all was a world of silence, filled with the morning scent of bracken and heather. As the weight of their bodies helped them down, a solitary philosophical sheep lifted its head to watch them go by.

Before them was a narrow floor of meadows, and then the lake, with the mountains dropping sheer to its western marge.

A wood mantled their lower slopes, and it was to the shelter of these trees that Myra was hastening. But a farmhouse flanked the bridle-path to the wood; and this they must pass unseen. Fortune favoured them: not a sound came from Gatesgarth Farm, and quickly they were hidden in the larches and the oaks. They breathed more freely, and went slower. Indeed, they could do little else, for the trees were closely congregated, and the floor upended and rough, and sometimes wet with a runnel.

'Listen,' said Myra. 'On the other side of the lake I know there's a valley with a beck in it. It's Sail Beck, I think. I remember distinctly it had stone-walled sheep-pens in it, and in one place a ruined stone hut that must have been a shepherd's hut. That hut's been fixing itself in my mind all night. Do you think it's guidance? It might be. I keep seeing it so clearly. It stood at the foot of some of the steepest scree I've ever known. My idea is that we should only use the hut at night, and find some place among the boulders to hide in during the day. If we can get you there, then about midday I can come back to Buttermere village and buy the food. That oughtn't to surprise anybody, because at this time of the year walkers must often be working their way back to Randall through Buttermere. Can you wait so long for food?'

'Of course. But you eat while you have the chance. And why shouldn't you fix up a room in an hotel? They're not looking for you.'

'Perhaps . . . but we'll see. If it's no worse than last night, I shan't mind the hut.'

'But supposing the hut's no longer there?'

'It's sure to be. It used to look as if it had stood there hundreds of years, so it's hardly likely to have blown down since. But if not, there'll be some shelter in the pens – shelter from the wind at least.'

'Ah, well,' he commented significantly, 'perhaps we shan't sleep there tonight at all.'

'Oh, I don't know about that,' encouraged Myra. 'We've eluded them so far. It's evidently more difficult to run people to earth than I ever imagined. And I've great faith in this hut. I can't help thinking we're being guided towards it. It fixes in my mind so.'

'Well, if the worst happens, remember that *you'll* have nothing to fear.'

To which she answered nothing.

The wood covered them as far as the strath between Buttermere and Crummock lakes, but now they had to cross the flat meadows and pass through the few houses of Buttermere village, if they were to reach the Sail Beck valley on the other side. People were moving now, and there were sounds of voices and traffic. The throb of a motor cycle came nearer and nearer, and stopped in the village itself. They glanced at each other. Still, useless to take fright at every sound; nothing for it but to cross quickly, and the sooner the better. Quickly, and with as innocent an air as they could assume, they crossed the open space and the village street, and reached again a welcome wood. No one had troubled about them, so they believed, because the only people to turn their eyes on them were a couple standing together, one an obvious holiday-maker, early afoot with rucksack slung, and the other a motorcyclist, still astride his machine, who appeared to be asking his road.

Soon they were walking on the lonely fell-side, treading the springy and spongy turf, thickened with stag and sphagnum moss; and nowhere a soul to see them. Far away across the vale, high on the hill, ran the ribbon of road over Buttermere Hause. A cart went slowly along it, as if the driver slept. And later, a motorcyclist, probably the one they had seen in the village, raced along it towards Randall. He went with a succession of reports, like a machine-gun firing, that reverberated in the hills; and doubtless, being a young man, he was far more interested in his speed than in the landscape around him.

They went on till the high headland of Knott Rigg stood between them and the road over the hause, and they were on empty fells, unwatched by human eye. A pair of ravens flew in the upper spaces of the sky, leaving their hoarse call behind them. On, round the foothills, Myra ever gazing up the new slopes that came into view.

'It should be here somewhere,' she claimed. 'It stood under some almost perpendicular scree beneath Sail. I'm sure it did.'

'Childhood memory can play funny tricks.'

'No, it's too vivid. . . . Ah, there it is! Yes, that's it, only it's placed rather differently from what I thought. And there's the scree beyond it.'

She pointed to a hut on the green slope. It was like a shepherd's hut in the alps, only built of piled stones.

'No, we won't go into it yet,' she said. 'We can do better than that. See those boulders? We'll climb up and hide among them. From there we'll be able to see without being seen. I don't believe anybody'd climb up that scree, or think we would, but we will. You'd never believe it holds, but it does. It slides under you a little way, and then stops. Look.'

She climbed the scree in front of him, showing him how much better it was to walk erect than to swarm up it on all-fours as he wanted to do. It was a breath-taking climb, and Paul's foot stung him with protests; and often they sat on the stones or on clumps of heather at their side. About halfway up there were crags and boulders, some of a child's height, some more massive and tall; and they went in among them, and sat down in a place where their peeping eyes could command the valley.

After a long rest, Myra said, 'Now I'll go,' and squeezed his hand. 'I'll come back as soon as I can, but I think I'd better dawdle till the late afternoon, when it'll be more natural to be coming back this way. So don't be anxious. Foot all right?'

'Yes; and you – are you sure you'll be safe?'

'Quite. They're not worrying about me. I don't believe that

anybody suspects I'm here with you. Those men at Wastdale said they didn't.'

And to show that she was cheerful, she ran and leapt down the moving scree, turning once to wave a hand.

It was very lonely, once she had gone from sight round a cape of fell. Hardly daring to move, he watched the slow hours go by. Hunger stirred, in spite of the gnawing anxiety. The hills were silent. Only twice people passed along the valley, once a man and a woman going towards Buttermere, and then a party who, since they had children running with them, could not be searchers. He added up his chances, because his only relief was to play with hope. Perhaps he could still hope. He did not believe that any hostile eye had seen them since they left Wastdale; and the country around him now suggested illimitable wilds. If only they abandoned this search as they had abandoned the one at the other end of England! He would owe everything to Myra. Without her he must have been caught. Who would have believed that their early friendship was to enlarge into such dark, astounding happenings as these?

His hunger increased; and he chewed the grass at his hand and counted the minutes that brought Myra nearer. He watched the sun work round the hills and fall over the mountain at his side. Thirst constricted his throat; and he wondered if he dare venture out to the tiny stream that tumbled down the stones to the beck below. It seemed safe enough. Nothing but emptiness and silence everywhere – and he dragged himself in a sit-ting posture across the steep scree towards the water. Cupping his hands, he conveyed the cold water to his mouth; and so refreshing was it that he stooped and drew it up with his mouth like an animal.

He crept back to his hiding place. It was nearly five o'clock now; and in his exhausted, starving and nervous condition, he began to be irritable with Myra, that she delayed so long. And with every minute that passed, more and more irritable.

And then, suddenly, anxious. Supposing she had been taken! The idea was dreadful enough to make him want to descend to the bottom and look round the cape of fell down the long stretch of vale. Ten minutes more of it, and he was half rising to his feet. Should he do it? It seemed perfectly safe: left and right, before, behind, and above, not a movement anywhere; wherever else they might be hunting, they had left this place out of their reckoning. He scrambled down, and walked hurriedly, anxiously, fretfully, to the point of the cape. The first thing he saw was the sun again, halfway down the sky; and then the figure of Myra with its light behind her. The sight of that lonely and loyal figure coming towards him destroyed the irritability and drew an outflow of gratitude and love; and he went to meet her.

Her look at first was one of doubt and alarm, but after a glance at the hills around it became the familiar incomplete smile.

'Has it been all right?' she asked, as they drew together. 'No one been near the place?'

'I don't think so.'

'I'm sorry I'm so late. Are you starving? But I didn't like to leave Buttermere much before three o'clock; and at one time I had the stupid idea that someone was following me, so I wandered off towards Grassmoor till I was sure I was alone. Now eat. Do get somewhere reasonably out of sight, and eat. I'll keep watch, though I don't think there's anything to fear now.'

They wandered on, round the bend, till they came to a deep cup in the heaving grass, and there they sat, hidden from all except the heights. Paul bent over the 'picnic lunch' that she had brought, and began to eat ravenously, while she sat so that her eyes were above the lip of the cup and could command the surrounding scene. He was tearing at the bread and fighting down an irritability that she had not thought to bring him brandy – surely she might have thought of that – when he heard her low, frightened murmur, 'Paul!'

Looking up, he saw her eyes fixed in alarm on the direction from which she had come. He rose a little and looked the same way. A man had come round the cape of fell, followed by two more. High above them, on the sky-line, two more appeared and began to descend a grass-slope at a run. Of the three coming towards them over the grass, one was in the knicker-bockers of a holiday visitor, but the other two were in the trousers and hats of the cities. And one—

'Oh, my God!' This was Paul's voice. In the taller one with the bowler hat he had recognised Inspector Boltro. His hand shot to the nape of his neck. It was over. . . . Boltro bringing death.

Both remained quite still. There was nothing else to do. Somewhere in Paul's agony the thought lifted that it was all very different from what he had imagined. He had imagined that some of the police would be in uniform.

The tall figure took the lead, and Paul noticed that one hand was in his jacket pocket. A revolver? He came over the lip of the cup, just as Paul rose to his feet; and Myra too.

'It's no good, Mr Presset. Game's up. You know me, I think. I'm Chief Inspector Boltro, and these are police officers; and it's my duty to arrest you and charge you with the murder of Elinor Presset.'

'What—' began Paul.

'Stop. And I have also to caution you that anything you say will be written down and may be used in evidence at your trial.'

Boltro caught one of his wrists, and the other big officer was about to take the other, when Paul, stunned, disorganised, hardly aware of his actions, dragged his hand away and exclaimed 'What do you mean? How dare you? I don't know what –'

'No more of that,' said Boltro, and seized with both hands the lapel of his coat. 'Don't pretend you don't know me.'

'Leave me alone, I tell you!' Instinctively Paul's hands went to Boltro's to remove them forcibly; and at once Boltro whipped something from his pocket and clicked it on his left wrist. At first Paul thought they were handcuffs, but then he saw that they were a pair of steel 'grips' shaped like a figure of eight, one ring of which was round his wrist and the other in the fist of Boltro. Now let Boltro twist them one way and he must fall on his face; the other, and he must fall on his back.

A sob like a child's stormed up in him; then sank, perished, and gave place to a long sigh.

'All right,' he said. 'Don't do that. I'm sorry. I'll give you no trouble.' Strange, but, the shock over, he had a sense of relief . . . rest. 'But you don't want Miss Bawne, do you?'

(No more need to struggle and strain; and perhaps they'd give him food and brandy – or hot tea.)

'Yes, we want her,' said Boltro. 'On the same charge.'

'It's ridiculous,' muttered Paul.

'That's all right, Paul,' murmured Myra. 'I understand.'

'Now I shouldn't talk, either of you,' said Boltro, his voice quite kind again. 'Remember my caution. Just come quietly. You'll only have to walk a little way with us to where we've got a car waiting.'

'We shan't have to pass anyone, shall we?'

'No, I don't suppose so. But, anyhow, I'll remove these grips. That's right. I trust you, see?'

The other officer was now holding him by the left arm, and Boltro pressed a hand against each of his pockets in turn, feeling for the shape of a revolver.

'That's all serene,' he said. 'Let him go.'

The two men from above had joined them now; and the little group of seven persons moved over the grass, back towards Buttermere Hause, Paul silent between two of them, Myra silent between two more. As they crossed the hollow and the lower slopes of Knott Rigg, they came in sight of the sun again, which was dropping into Crummock Water.

In parting it threw a glamour on every hill, so wonderful that Boltro, turning to an officer, jerked his head towards the setting sun. 'Pretty lovely, eh?'

'Yes,' said Inspector Yarr. 'We can do you that sort of thing here. We can do you those two a penny.'

'Oh, and *we* can do a pretty good sunset over London, too, sometimes,' countered Boltro. 'You wouldn't believe!'

'You forget I came from that little township once upon a time,' objected Yarr, with a laugh.

Paul looked over his shoulder at the sunset, too. The sun was a golden moon, surrounded with a yellow-green light; and it was so low now as to bear a man's gaze. To either side of it the hills were turning a deeper and deeper purple as it sank. The lake was a sheet of silver. The sun's rim dipped beneath the hill, and you could see the disc go. It was that moment in the day when you could actually see the sun moving, and perceive the upward over-roll of the earth, with its millions of little travellers on it.

Was it the last sunset he would see, Paul wondered listlessly.

The fiery rim disappeared even as they looked, and the red of the sky was reflected at first only on the extreme edge of the lake and along a ribbon of stream that wound through the meadows. Then a tenuous cloud-wraith passed over the hidden bed of the sun and turned to crimson, so that it looked like the motionless smoke of a conflagration far away; and gradually its crimson reflection spread over the surface of the lake. One more sun forever lost. Everything seemed hushed by the first presage of the dark; and the few sheep that they passed were crouched on their hooves, as if in readiness for the night. Held in silence by the stillness of the evening, the little group of people walked on.

PART IV

Chapter One

The car spun down from Buttermere Hause to a level road by the lake. Inspector Boltro sat in a front seat by the driver; Paul in the back between two officers. And it is possible that only in such a situation as this could the thoughts of two men, who sat within touching distance of each other, offer so complete a contrast.

Boltro was exultant. He felt like an aviator who had just broken a record, or like Wellington after Waterloo; the feat was accomplished; nothing now but to sit in a glow and think of the triumph in the newspapers tomorrow. He was impatient to get to the police station, that the news might be published to the world. Towards Presset in the seat behind he now felt only kindness. He sat in the exquisite rest of accomplishment.

Paul looked out at the trees visiting the lake's verge, and the islands sleeping on the still water, and the mountains grey behind, and wondered if this were a part of his punishment, to be given a last look at some of the loveliest country in the world. What – eight weeks? – twelve weeks – twenty weeks, and he would know what was on the other side of death? He wasn't going to be such a fool as to hope any more. Of course he would have to make up some story; he couldn't stand before the world as a confessed murderer; he would have to suggest that the death was an accident; but this would be the last lie he would tell. With nothing to hope for, and nothing to struggle for, he would try to achieve an integrity before the end, for his own peace; yes, there was a speck of comfort now, even though his limbs were trembling and his heart misbeating, in thinking that he would go with dignity. An accident. An accident, not a suicide; because he would wrong Elinor no more. But an accident he *must* say – and he was comforted in this inability not to lie a little by thinking that the lie was necessary for Myra's sake. If there was no murder, surely there was no case against her. The car passed an old labourer toiling home, and Paul remembered that he would never grow old.

'Mr Boltro,' he said suddenly.

'Yes?' The Inspector turned his face.

'Shall I see Miss Bawne again?'

'Oh, yes,' said Boltro consolingly. 'Not at the station perhaps, but at any rate on the train. We'll all be together in a compartment, see? You leave it to me. I'll do all I can for you. And nobody on the train'll know who we are, so don't worry about that. No handcuffs or any of that nonsense. I always know when I've got someone I can trust.'

'Thank you. It's very kind of you.'

'Yes, I'll do all I can for you. You leave it to me,' repeated Boltro, well pleased with both his kindness and his power. 'I'll see to that.' And he turned his face again to the road before him.

They ran into a grey and populous town and stopped before a grey stone building. The Police Station.

Boltro clambered out and straightened himself like a man in good heart. He waited a few moments for Paul and his two guards, and then led the way happily up the steps. Paul followed, trying to show dignity. He was conscious of a dark passage, and then of a large dull room, with windows in one wall looking out onto a yard, and a wide glass screen in the other looking into an office. The boards were bare, the walls were painted with a dark green dado up to a height of about four feet, and with light green paint above. Some way in front of the fireplace, and towards the middle of the room, was a high sloping desk; against one wall was a long bench without a back, and against another an old square table It was rather like a big dusty schoolroom emptied of all furniture except the master's desk, a single form, and an odd table.

The Station Officer, a tall, corpulent fellow apparently only of sergeant's rank, stood before the high desk, and Boltro went up to him to speak in a lowered voice, just as a uniformed policeman, with keys rattling on a chain, bustled through a door and came and stood near by.

From his newspaper knowledge Paul supposed that he was now to be 'charged', and he was resolving to stand before the desk in an attitude of dignity, erect, head up, and one hand holding the other behind his back, and to answer nothing to the charge. There was something he was going to say one day, but not now. This was not the moment. He knew the moment when he was going to say it. He had been thinking it out in the car, and decided that there was one moment when its effect would be most striking, and its publicity widest. He must gather courage to utter it then, in a clear voice.

But this plan of proud silence tonight was wasted. Apparently they were not going to charge him here in Randall. Instead the Station Officer, finishing his whispers with Boltro, nodded to the gaoler with the rattling keys, and said, 'All right. Search him'; and the gaoler said promptly, 'Come on'; and led him out of the Charge Room into a dark passage – Boltro, the Station Officer and a policeman following. The gaoler pushed open a door and led them all into a room small and square but very lofty, with one high oblong window of opaque and grimy glass, through which the shadow of bars could be seen.

'Right. Strip,' said the gaoler, while the others stood looking on.

Paul removed his jacket, vest and shirt, and stood holding his trousers at his hips, as if he had done enough, and anything more would be indecent.

'No; we must have your trousers,' explained the gaoler, but not urgently.

So Paul dropped his trousers, stepped out of them, and stood before his captors in vest and pants, the unlovely figure of a small thin man in the fifties. This was his worst humiliation so far. He felt acutely conscious of his worn underclothes, his scraggy neck, scrawny legs, and thin, unworthy arms. And now while one of them was emptying the pockets of his clothes, taking out penknife, handkerchief, pocket case, papers, and scrutinizing every seam, another was feeling over the whole of his body. It was hard to keep dignity so. An uncomplaining silence was the best he could do.

'OK,' said the gaoler; and they returned him his clothes, but without the braces. 'You can dress again.'

He dressed, fixing the trousers as best he could; and the gaoler, saying, 'This way,' led him through a door into a long white-tiled passage with cell doors opening on to it. Into Cell No. 2, whose door was open, the gaoler gently guided him, a hand pressing lightly on his elbow.

And the door slammed. He stood in his cell and realised that he was behind a locked door for evermore.

He looked about him. The narrow cell was white-tiled to a height of about eight feet; there was a long form built into the wall with a rug folded upon it and a pillow; at the foot of the form, beyond an elbow-high partition, was a w.c. pan, but without chain or cistern, and flushed by means of a bolt near the door; the door itself was faced with iron and had a spy-hole opened from without; the electric light, encased in thick glass, was over the door, so that it lit both cell and passage. There was nothing to break the cold, white, shiny, immovable walls, but a notice to prisoners hanging by the door.

For the first time he knew what prisoner's claustrophobia was. The walls seemed overpoweringly close; that iron door, unopenable from within, and the soundless air in the confined space, threatened terror and madness. It was like being locked in a safe. He felt ready to choke; ready to beat fists on the iron plates of the door; and a wild-eyed, witless creature inside him began repeating, 'You can't get out; you can't get out; you can't get out.'

He felt he *would* have gone mad if it hadn't been for a man's footsteps which now began to move up and down the passage outside, and, strangely enough, for the opening of the eyelet hole and the sight of an eye looking in. Sometimes the steps stopped at his door, sometimes they moved away; but always they returned in a few minutes, and a hand lifted the slide from the observation hole and an eye looked at him. Clearly he was to be examined every few minutes, even if he lay asleep, even if he sat on the closet seat. Dulled, defeated, blunted like an edgeless knife, he sat on the wooden form, with elbows on knees and hands clasped.

Tired of sitting, he walked up and down. Ten feet is not far to pace, and already he had begun the eternal sentry-go of the prisoner – one, two, three, four, five, six – six steps to the end, and five back. How was this, six one way and five the other? He worked it out. Now it was five this way and six the other: it must have something to do with his turning. Up to the iron door, and he touched it. A few hours ago he was free. What was it like to be free? He would never know again.

Tired of pacing, he lay down with the rug over him, shut his eyes, and tried to sleep.

Almost at once he was disturbed by someone bringing him tea and bread and butter, and at the same time the Station Officer visited him.

'You can have something better than that in the morning, if you like to pay for it,' he said.

'Thank you. Thank you very much,' answered Paul, nervously. 'Yes, I *should* like something.'

'Very good. We'll see to it. Everything all right?'

'Yes. Yes, thank you.'

'Well, good night.'

'Good night.'

A good night! Still, the man meant well.

It was better, lying down with closed eyes. And after a while he dozed. He was awakened by a noise in the passage. They were bringing in a 'drunk'. Very lively and quarrelsome he was, as they bundled him into the cell next door; where he sang to himself and stamped up and down, apparently on a floor of wood unlike the stone floor of his own cell. That drunk would be set free tomorrow to see the woods and the sun on the lake, and to pick up his life again.

Police-Constable Neville Birdett, a lanky lad with his shoulders yet to come, and the chin and complexion of a sixteen-year-old boy, was to go on duty at the station from eight at night to four in the morning. It was not often that he looked forward to this stretch of night duty, but he did so this evening. He looked forward to it eagerly, and rather breathlessly, from five o'clock onwards. They were bringing Presset in some time in the evening – *and* his young lady – and it was a thousand to one against them taking the prisoners to London tonight. He would see Presset. With luck he'd get a glimpse of Bawne. Probably he would have to take his share in keeping Presset under observation. Too good to be true. They never had a really exciting crime – not a really *famous* one – in this slow old town, and now, by a terrific slab of luck, they'd got Presset. A murderer. He'd never seen a murderer before; and now, to the end of his life, he'd be able to say that he'd had charge of Presset, one of the most famous murderers of modern times. P.C. Neville Birdett hoped with a great hope that they'd bring him after eight, when he was there. He even hoped, if the truth is to be told, that Presset would have shot one of the arresting officers. The man was said to be desperate and in possession of firearms, and it would be an excitement to see old Inspector

Yarr brought in on a stretcher – not dead, of course, but on a wheeled stretcher. And possibly, if the bird was violent in the Charge Room, they'd summon him to help subdue him. And he'd do it with a will. Some criminals he liked, but he'd no use for a dirty poisoner, and he'd let him feel in his grip what all decent people thought of him. 'The filthy swine! Hanging's too good for him, I reckon.'

He arrived at the station to learn that Presset and Bawne were already in. To his joy, though his face showed nothing, the Station Officer detailed him to watch in the passage outside the man's cell, and to look in on him every few minutes.

'Yes, sir.'

'You've got a responsibility, my lad,' said the Station Officer. 'I'll come along every now and then, but it's your job in the meantime, and you'll be *for* it, if anything happens to him.'

'Yes, sir.'

'Personally, I shall be glad when I'm shut of the responsibility for him, so, for God's sake, keep your ears open and your eyes skinned.'

'I see, sir.'

'There's a drunk in the next cell, but he's asleep and snoring like an elephant with a cold in his nose. He won't worry you till he wakes up in the morning, wishing he were dead.'

'I see, sir.'

And Neville Birdett, as interested and entertained as any young man in any theatre in England that night, went to the white-tiled passage and took up a position by the door of Cell No. 2, at which he stared fascinated. He did not at once look through the spy-hole. Guiltily he waited till no one should be near. Then, with an emotion little different from that with which a boy looks at a caged animal at the zoo, he peeped in. It was a disappointing – a disturbing surprise. Presset, pacing up and down the cell, looked utterly ordinary; he might have been some small shopkeeper of church-going habit. The eyes that looked straight into his were the most pained that Neville had ever seen. They hurt.

'Crikey!' exclaimed Neville, and immediately drew his face away.

A normal and raw young man, he disliked a sudden revelation and turned his thoughts to other things. How on earth could a young lady have given herself to *him*? Girls were quaint things, not a doubt of it; they didn't seem to care much about youth or looks, whereas a man had a job to get going without both. How could she put up with, and even perhaps like – and being a normal young man, he gave a few minutes to picturing the embraces of Presset and Bawne. This caused him to look through the peep-hole again. Up and down; up and down. Still pacing, poor b—! Fascinated, Neville imagined that figure walking to the scaffold in the early morning – going down the drop. He glanced at the neck. Then he caught those helpless eyes full in his own, and drew away.

He also began to walk up and down, thinking he would look in at Presset now and again as he passed his door; and the next time he looked in, he saw him lying down with the rug over him.

'Well, I hope he gets some sleep. I wouldn't be him for anything.'

And for the next hour or so he appeared to be sleeping. Each time Neville looked in he saw him lying flat on his back with the pillow under him and his hands clasped on his breast. And all was in order; one could see his breaths lifting the rug.

'Well, he's no trouble anyway,' thought Neville.

There was no sound now in the cell passage except the rhythmic snores of the drunk which were sometimes like a deep organ note and sometimes like a saw cutting through an iron door. Neville, killing time, thought of all that he'd have to tell the dad and the young lady. He saw himself a centre of interest in the pub or the clubroom tomorrow night. He heard himself telling shopkeepers over their counters all about Presset, while their wives and assistants came up to listen.

It was nearly midnight when, looking into the cell again, he saw Presset sitting up with his feet on the ground, his back rounded, the rug about his shoulders, and his eyes staring before him. Neville Burdet took the sharpest stab of pity that had come to him in his life. And the pity was not less when, half an hour later, Presset was still sitting there, with the blanket about his shoulders.

'All right?' asked Neville.

'Yes, only I can't sleep.'

'No, it's difficult at first, isn't it?'

'Yes.'

'Would you like anything?'

'It wouldn't be possible to have a cup of tea, I suppose?'

'Yes. Yes, I think so. I'll make you one, shall I? It'll be something to do.'

'Thanks very much. It's very kind of you.'

'Don't mention it. You're very welcome.'

And seldom had a job given Neville more satisfaction. He ran to the telegraph room and said to the reserve, 'Just keep an eye on this bloke, will you, while I make him a cup of tea?' He ran – he couldn't just walk – into the Inspector's office where a kettle was simmering on a gas ring; and with eager, rapid and fumbling fingers, he made the tea for Presset. It gave him quite extraordinary pleasure to take it in to him.

'Thank you. It's exceedingly kind of you,' said Presset.

'Oh, no; that's nothing,' demurred Neville. 'We often do that.'

'It's refreshing when you can't sleep. Could you tell me, where is Miss Bawne?'

'She's being looked after all right. Don't you fret.'

'She's quite all right, I suppose?'

'Oh, yes. She was a bit upset at first, I was told, a bit faint like, but they did everything for her, and she's quite comfortable now. That's why you're here really. The bloke from London was for taking you there straight away, but the police surgeon thought she wasn't up to it.'

'Are you sure she's all right?'

'Oh, yes, it was a little faintness, that's all. Don't you worry. I should try to get some sleep. They'll call you at six o'clock and give you some grub. I don't think I shall be here then, as my relief comes on at four. So I'll say goodbye and' – he added this, almost ashamed – 'good luck, I mean.'

Chapter Two

Inspector Boltro sat in a corner seat with his back to the engine, and opposite him, Presset. In the corner seat sat Bawne, and opposite her, the wife of the Randall inspector. In the middle seats sat Sergeant Doyle and a detective from the Randall station. None were in uniform, and people passing the door of the reserved compartment did not turn their heads.

Inspector Boltro had some task to hide his excellent spirits. He felt like a champion taking the cup back to London. He had woken up that morning to remember joy. He'd gone early to the station to collect his prisoners, and had enjoyed telling the Inspector that he'd want a woman to accompany Bawne, and had laughed merrily when the Inspector said, 'What about my missus? She'd enjoy a trip to London at your expense. She likes a bit of an outing.' 'Send her along!' Boltro had ordered, and enjoyed the sharp decisiveness. Would one lad be enough to go with them? the Inspector had asked; and 'Lord bless you, yes!' Boltro had replied. 'I never have any trouble with prisoners. I fancy I've learnt the trick of humouring them. D'you know, I've never had a single case of assault? Not one. I remember one time' – and, very talkative in his happiness, he had poured his tale over the Inspector: 'It was when I was a Detective-Sergeant, and the Chief said to me, "Boltro," he said, "Corker Miles comes out of Wilton Gaol tomorrow, and you've got to go and get him. We want him on another charge," and he suggested that I should go off that night so as to be outside the prison in the morning. But I said, No, we'd ask the Wilton police to collar him at the prison gates, and I'd go down first thing in the morning and collect him at their station. Well, they said they would, and it'd be a pleasure and all that, and the next morning about nine o'clock I walked into their station, to see – ha, ha, ha! – one of their P.C.'s brushing down one of their sergeants – cleaning the mud off his arms and his legs and his backside. And the Sergeant turns to me and says, "Have you come for Corker?" and when I said yes, he says, "Well, he's just rolled the two of us down Stone Hill, but he's here all right. He's in the Detention Room with his missus, who'd come to welcome him, poor thing. If you think you're going to take him back, you'd better have a couple of our chaps to help you. He's a rough customer, I can promise you." But I said, "That's all right, Sergeant. You leave him to me," and I went into the Detention Room, and there was poor old Corker looking as sour as Saturday's milk on Wednesday. I just said, "Hallo, Corker, old man," because he knew me well, but he wasn't showing any friendliness this morning; he was as surly as the devil, and his missus was wiping her eyes and blowing her nose. So I just said, "Had any breakfast, Corker?" and he said, "No," and I said, "Your missus had any?" and he said, "No, nothing to speak of," and I said, "Well, come along, old man, and I'll get you some," and, would you believe it we walked out of that station, all three of us, while the Sergeant stared. I took him to an eating house and said, "What are you having, Corker? Tea? Coffee?" and he said he liked "cawfee", and I said, "Your missus have the same?" and she said, Yes, she would; so I got 'em two walloping cups of coffee and a huge plate of bread and butter, and when they'd finished that, I said, "Like some more?" and they said, Yes, they would, so I got it for them all over again; and then we strolled out into the street. "Got any smokes?" I asked him, and he said, No, guv'nor, he hadn't, so into the first tobacconist's we went, and I got him a half ounce of plug and a twopenny cherry-wood pipe, and out we marched. We walked back to the station to collect a few things, and the Sergeant said to me, "Hadn't you better have at least one of our chaps to go with you, in case he gives trouble?" but I said, "No, thanks. I appreciate that, Sergeant, but just you send a man to shadow us as far as the station, and I'll look after him after that." Then I went to Corker and said, "Come along, Corker. We'd better be moving now"; and he came like a lamb, his missus following. He kissed her goodbye at the station, and stepped onto the train with me as easy as winking. And when we were alone in the carriage and the train had started, I lit up his pipe for him and said, "Now see here, Corker, old boy: it's no good playing up. You don't want me to put the handcuffs on you, do you?" And' – Boltro's voice became quite rich and tearful as he reached the moving close to his tale – 'he just said, "Guv'nor," he said, "I couldn't play up with you now if I wanted to. And that's not because the fust thing you said when you saw me was, 'Had any breakfast?' but because you turned to the missus and asked her if she'd had any. You can do what you like with me now." That's a true story; as true as I stand here.'

In the spirit of this tale he had enjoyed granting Presset's request for a shave, and taking him out to a barber's and explaining on the way that the police always helped prisoners to look their best when they came up before the magistrate, so as to give them every help in their defence. He had enjoyed going up to the guard on the railway platform and saying with a wink, 'We're police officers. Get us a reserved compartment, old chap. Somewhere in front, see?' and observing the stare of the guard and his prompt and interested compliance, for the morning papers had been bright with the news of Presset's capture. And now the guard had shut the door on them and left, after another interested stare.

Boltro felt kind and compassionate. His pity was real, as he saw Presset, defeated, bewildered and emptied, looking this way and that, or gazing out at the busy station, or sometimes swallowing with difficulty. And Bawne: her face was ashen after a night of faintness and sickness, and her voice was low and husky as she said 'Thank you' and took the smelling salts from the woman; after which she too turned and gazed sadly at the platform. His pity stirred him to action.

'You'll be wanting something to read, won't you?' he said to Presset.

'Thank you. If I may. . . .'

'And you too, miss?'

'Thank you . . . yes.'

'Right you are!' And he leaned out of the window and made a selection from the newsboy's basket: serious papers and magazines for Presset, and women's journals and illustrated stuff for the lighter mind of Bawne.

'There,' said he, and felt better.

As the train moved out, he looked at his unspeaking captive.

'Smoke?' he asked.

'Thanks. Yes, I should like to. . . . Yes.'

'Well, here you are.' And he offered him one of his own cigarettes, and struck a match and lit it for him.'

'You like a pipe, too, don't you?'

'Sometimes. But don't trouble. . . .'

'Have we got his pipe, Doyle?'

'No, sir,' said Doyle; and Presset explained that it had got lost on the fell-side.

'Never mind. I'll get you one at the next station. May as well smoke while you can.'

Boltro sank back in his seat and watched Doyle and the other detective reading in the local paper of the capture on the fellside at sundown. For his own part he had hastened to read the paper in the morning, and he knew its phrases by heart: 'Brilliant detective work . . . careful strategy of Chief Inspector Boltro and Inspector Yarr . . . Presset outwitted . . . climax to great search.' Sergeant Doyle, looking up from the paper, caught his eye and smiled. 'They're giving you a good show, sir.'

'Yes. Awful lot of rot they write, don't they?' laughed Boltro, delighted with the rot.

And when they arrived at a big station about lunch time, he greatly enjoyed getting out on to the platform and buying food for his prisoners: undoubtedly mercy had a sweet savour, and he bought sandwiches, rolls, pork pies, fruit and a packet of milk chocolate for Bawne. 'I know you ladies like sweets,' he said. And when the train had steamed far south enough to meet the London papers, he was out on the platform buying them with an assumed carelessness, as if really they didn't interest him. He bought them all and distributed them among his officers, and one by one, as the train bore on, borrowed them to read himself. 'Arrest of Presset and Bawne, Sunset Drama on Lakeland Fell, Inspector Boltro's "I think you know me, Mr Presset", Return to Euston Today.' It was all supremely satisfying.

Paul read the papers, too, with a dull, glum interest that stirred to pleasure only when he came upon the statement, 'Presset, after the first shock, offered no resistance. Indeed Inspector Boltro assures us that he met his fate with dignity and seemed to care little for himself but only for the comfort of Miss Bawne.' Sometimes he looked along the seat at Myra, and she turned to smile back at him bravely. They did not talk to each other; in fact they spoke only when the police addressed them. It was simple and more restful to watch from the windows the country speeding by. To Paul it would have been a sharp experience, had his feelings not been stunned and stilled, to see as they approached the station platforms the advertisements of a world that was receding from him forever: theatres, cinemas, Stephen's Ink, furniture, tours abroad: as it was, he just gazed at them with a weariness behind his eyes. The bustle of the free people on the platform raised thoughts that lived a moment, and died.

It was not till the train began to get near to London that fear struck him. More than once the London papers had named the train in which he would return from Randall and the time it would arrive at Euston: would there be a crowd to see him? Were the newsboys with the evening papers even now shouting his arrival along the gutters? Were the idle and curious hurrying to the sordid streets by Euston, and the crowd creating a crowd? At one of the big stations Boltro had been summoned by the stationmaster and stayed away for some time. What for?

As, slowing down, the train rolled into Euston, his heart sped.

The train slowed against the platform and stopped; and he saw that in front of their compartment a broad space had been barricaded off. Beyond it against the kerb three taxis were waiting with their blinds drawn. People were trying to halt near the barricades but were being moved on by the railway police. All eyes were trained on this empty lane across the populous platform: eyes from other platforms, from other taxis, from train windows, and from platform barriers. Hurrying passengers were craning their heads, taxi-men climbing to their roofs, and porters halting their trolleys to gape. 'Quick!' ordered Boltro. 'Get it over. We'll go first. Bring her after, Pincer.'

And Paul was being hustled across the barricaded space towards the foremost taxi. He heard a few hisses and boos and bent his head to hide his face. He was in the taxi, Boltro following, within five seconds, but he had time to see a surging crowd beyond the ticket barriers. A turn of his head had shown him Myra being run through the hisses into the taxi behind. 'Right away! Get on with it for the love of Mike,' said Boltro in a low voice to the driver. 'Never mind the others.'

The cab ran out towards the station yard, and Paul's darting eyes saw through the chinks a dense, shoving mob, and police holding a lane through it for the procession of cabs. A roar of hate and execration, a spray of hisses, beat up against the windows. 'Yah, swine! Go and hang! You and your bitch! Serve yer right! Good ole Boltro! Put him where you can find him. Best job *you've* ever done! Good ole Boltro!'

As this front car approached in sight of the thickest mass there was a surge forward that drove the police against the cab, and one of them leapt on to the running board.

'Damn!' swore Boltro.

This movement stayed the cab; and for a few seconds, while the police opened a lane again, all the cars were at a standstill, and Paul heard the hisses and jeers directed not only to himself but to Myra in the cab behind. Women's voices shrieked at her: 'Gah! Nice thing you are! You dirty poisoner! Hanging's too good for the likes of you.' Paul rose, but Boltro drew him down. Some hooligans at the back of the crowd, where the police couldn't find them, eager for mischief, shouted half seriously, half jestingly, ' 'Ave 'em out! Lynch 'em, the b—s! Get 'em out, boys! Yah, thought you'd get away with it, did yer? Well, yer didn't! Not on yer lucky. And we shall soon have seen the last of you, thank Gawd!' Boltro muttered his impatience and strained forward, to see when they could get on – nor was he averse from showing himself to the crowd. 'Good ole Boltro! One too many for you, wa'n't he? Three cheers for ole Boltro.' Then long organised groans, sustained hisses, and an eddy of excitement round a woman who had fainted, a policeman elbowing his way towards her, and cries of 'Stand back. Give her a chance, mate. Let the copper get to her. Use yer sense, chappie. Give the lady a chanst' – and the cab moved on again, followed by a roar in unison, to speed the prisoners on their way to judgment. The street dwindled behind, and they ran into the peace of the Euston Road.

'Hell!' exclaimed Boltro, in duty bound, and fetched a sigh of relief, though he had enjoyed every moment of it.

They drove on in quiet, Paul quick with dread lest there should be another such screaming crowd at the North Central Police Station, Boltro hoping for it, and the cheers.

'Is there – do we have to cross the pavement at the police station?' asked Paul.

'No. We shall run into the yard, thank God,' said Boltro.

There *was* another crowd about the station, but the car ran through the police lane in a twinkling, and the gates immediately closed behind them.

A policeman called Paul about six o'clock the next morning; and he came out of his cell and washed in a basin in the cell passage. He washed and tidied himself with care, because this morning he would make a public appearance. He must stand before the magistrate for the first police court hearing – the first revolution of the wheels of justice – and he was resolved that the public should remark, and the newspapers report, his refined appearance and decorous bearing. Besides he had another thing to do at this police court hearing – something known only to himself – and he wanted to give it the emphasis of dignity.

He had a bright young lawyer to defend him. As he returned into his cell, he was thinking of Mr Forrest, who had appeared last night. On arrival last evening he had been charged by Boltro, cautioned by the Station Officer, searched again, and put into a cell very like the one at Randall except that it was older and yellower and more worn and scratched. He had not been long in the cell, sitting on the wooden form, when an officer of high rank came in and said that a Mr Forrest, a lawyer, had asked to interview him, and he could go and see him or not, as he liked. Paul said, Thank you, he might as well see him; and the officer led him to the Detention Room, again a room very like the one in which he had been searched at Randall, and shut the door on him and Mr Forrest who was waiting there. But he, or some other officer remained outside: Paul knew that by the occasional appearance of an eye at the spyhole. Mr Forrest was a tall, youthful figure, with a manner jaunty and confident. He was already dressed for dinner, and the interview was hurried, Mr Forrest doing most of the talking, since he usually talked Paul down directly that bewildered prisoner began to speak. He was the lawyer who had defended So-and-so and So-and-so, he said, naming some very famous murderers of recent years; and if Paul liked, he was willing to take on his case. Money? Pooh! that'd be all right. He'd never had any difficulty about money yet, once a case had created sufficient stir. There were newspapers, weren't there? And counsel'd always do it on the cheap for the sake of the publicity. Would Paul like him to take it on? He'd guarantee a fight for him, with nothing spared – nothing at all. Some of the finest brains in the country on his side. He would? Excellent. Excellent! Well, say nothing in the court tomorrow. Leave it all to him. That was the line for the present. And then when Paul got to South London Prison they'd really look into the matter. Remember, not a word! And Paul had answered him confusedly, because the man's dress suit had been a shock, reminding him of life outside prison walls, and things that he would see no more. He had been inclined to stare dazed, and not to hear all that Mr Forrest was saying; which worried him afterwards, lest he had created a poor impression in the mind of this brisk young lawyer. He saw him going off to his dinner or dance, and there, surrounded by beautifully dressed women and prosperous men, who all wanted to hear what Presset was like, telling them that he was a poor soul without a word in his mouth, who would certainly crumple up in the witness-box. . . . Well, against all Mr Forrest's noisy instructions, he was going to say a word in court today, and say it with a coolness that would startle that young gentleman.

He was thinking this, on the bench in his cell, when a friendly and talkative policeman brought him a good breakfast arranged for by Mr Forrest, and seized the chance for a brief chat.

'I should be ready to come along at any moment if I was you,' said he. 'After breakfast they'll transfer you to the police court.'

'But isn't this the police court?'

'Naow!' laughed the policeman. 'This is the sty-tion.'

'Oh, I see.'

'The court's acrost the yard. They transfer you there, so as to be ready for the Mag. when he blows in. There are other cells there, see?'

'Yes.'

'But, like as not, they'll put you in the waiting-room. It depends on how many prisoners there are, see?'

'The magistrate comes about ten, doesn't he?'

'Abah't hah'–past. But your case won't come on for half an hour or more. He hears the applications for summonses first – then last night's charges. The drunks first, and ladies first too, ha, ha, ha! Then the prawstitutes and beggars and suspects, and then Crime Proper. That's you. But your case won't last long today. Jest evidence of arrest and a remand for eight days. It'll be over as soon as it's begun. It's not really worth the crah'd that's forming outside – my columbus, what it'll be like by ten o'clock, I dunno. They're reinforcing the police out there. What it is to be a famous man!' added the policeman, as crude as he was kindly. 'Got all you want? That's right. You've got a better breakfast than I've had. Well, so long. And remember, the Mag's not a bad ole cove.'

It happened just as the policeman had said. A brisk sergeant came to his cell, told him to come along of him, and led him, without further comment, through the Charge Room, out of a side door, across a yard, and in at the side entrance of the police court. Here he was put in a cell again, and the door shut on him with a bang. He could hear quick footsteps, voices, shouted orders, cell doors banging, and the jangling of the gaoler's keys. At the end of the passage a discussion was going on, in which he heard again and again his own name and Myra's. 'Presset and Bawne . . . Presset and Bawne. . . .' Cabs or vans came rattling into the yard, a horse stamped, a motor left. New policemen came in, perhaps with prisoners, and were greeted with chaff and good cheer by their friends in the passages. 'Mornin', Dick.' ' 'Mornin', Sergeant.' 'How's life, Jumbo? Got your part off properly?' 'Presset and Bawne. . . .' It was all very like the preparation behind the wings for the performance on a stage. It came upon Paul that he was the central figure, the big 'draw', in this play, and nervousness assaulted his heart and damped his brow. He wiped moist hands on his knees and began to rehearse his few words. His 'lines'. He said them aloud to the walls of his cell, and, dissatisfied with his husky tones, cleared his throat and said them again.

Now by the loud calling of names he guessed that the morning's business had begun. One name after another was called, and he was astonished at the speed with which the cases were dispatched. Very suddenly his cell door was thrown open, and yet another policeman said, 'Come on,' and escorted him along a corridor where a string of men and women prisoners stood against a wall waiting their turn, while the policemen watched them. All heads turned as he appeared, and a hum of excited talk arose.

'Silence!' roared someone.

They ushered him into a waiting-room: a square room with a bench round its four white walls, a radiator in the centre, and a skylight in the roof. Here he sat alone till a policeman summoned him into the corridor again, and now he saw Myra standing there, white as death, and he smiled encouragement as the policeman led him past her and placed him just in front of her in the line. He saw that he was near a door marked 'Prisoners Only'. Two prisoners were before him in the line, and the first was now called and went through the door. The opening door released a murmur of voices, and nervousness beat on him again. He cleared his throat, wiped his hands, and steadied his knee. The next prisoner went through; and Paul, to escape the shattering nervousness, stared at the brown dado along the passage wall and hot pipes running under the windows. The door opened again, and the prisoner came out looking sullen; but there was no time to notice him, for the gaoler came to the door and roared, 'Presset and Bawne.'

'Come on,' said the officers at their side.

His heart leaping and scuttling, he passed from the quiet of the passage into the court room humming with voices and hot with human breath.

Too dazed to see much at first, he was just conscious of a large square hall, lit from above, and packed with people to all four of its cream-coloured walls. On two sides it was as if the people rose in tiers; at the back as if they were massed on the floor; at the other end as if the friends of the magistrates were crowded on his dais behind a brown partition. And the people about the magistrate were as 'fashionable' as those at the back were vulgar. Behind the magistrates, framing him and his desk, was a handsomely carved door, surmounted by the Royal arms. Acutely self-conscious, he was aware of a swaying of heads and a shuffling of feet as all tried to see Myra and him, and of a sighing murmur of surprise, as they saw two such ordinary persons; and he had time to hope that they didn't think him small. Immediately before the prisoners' door, almost in the centre of the floor, was the dock, a narrow, oblong pen, raised and railed; and the gaoler was just guiding him into this when Paul remembered Myra and, by force of habit, stood aside to let her enter the room first. At once he heard that sighing murmur again. He bowed slightly as she went past, followed her up into the dock, and gave a little bow to the white-haired magistrate. A policeman followed him, and the three stood before the magistrate, lifted up above the people.

In that moment he experienced the pillory: shame shuddered through him, and his sympathy for Myra was like a sickness.

And the people stared; some blatantly, some furtively. On the whole the women were the more brazen, putting up spectacles and lorgnettes, and turning to their neighbours to speak, and staring again; the men had the kindness to be furtive. The court officials did not look: the magistrate and his clerk occupied themselves with papers – they would have a good view later on; the police walked about, indifferent and formal. Overflowing their usual box, the pressmen glanced up and scribbled busily. Just beneath the dock Mr Forrest leaned carelessly on a desk with his cheek in his palm, perfectly at ease and afraid of no one.

Paul stood as smartly as possible, forcing his agitated knee to stay still. When, of a sudden, he felt the trembling of Myra's whole frame in the dock and saw her hand shake on the rail, he slid his own hand along so that it touched hers. A smart young pressman observed this, and wrote hastily.

Now Inspector Boltro had gone round to the witness-box on the left of the magistrate, and was standing behind it. Some business passed between usher, magistrate and clerk; and then the clerk rose from his desk immediately under the magistrate's, and said:

'Paul Arthur Presset and Myra Bawne are charged for that they did on the sixteenth day of October, 19–, at 23 Elm Tree Road, Islington Vale, feloniously, wilfully, and of malice aforethought, murder Elinor Presset against the peace of Our Lord the King, His Crown and Dignity.'

'Myra Bawne is further charged' – here Paul looked up – 'for that she, well knowing that the said defendant Presset had committed the said felony, did receive, comfort, assist and maintain him—'

At this Myra broke down, and was seen to be weeping; and Paul, understanding little of the law, repeated the words to himself in amazement: 'did receive, comfort, assist and maintain him'. Why, it was the perfect description of Myra's goodness to him, and here was the law seeking to punish her for it. Surely the law was condemning itself in the very beauty of its own language.

The clerk seemed to be asking them if they pleaded guilty or not guilty, and before they could answer, the magistrate lifted his face and told them in a soft voice to plead not guilty.

'Not guilty,' said Paul, but his voice did not come as clearly as he wished.

'Not guilty,' said Myra, who was hardly to be heard.

Then a well-dressed man with winged collar, black coat, and striped trousers, rose from the desk below and beginning, 'May it please your worship', said that the two prisoners were jointly charged with murder and that the female prisoner was also charged with being an accessory after the fact. He paused, while Paul listened with straining ears. The well-dressed man straightened his tie and continued in stilted language that, with reference to the female prisoner, the facts, so far as they were at present revealed to the Director of Public Prosecutions, pointed to the second charge as the only one that would be preferred against her.

Again a stir and sigh among the people: of which Paul took advantage to slide his hand along the rail and touch Myra's and whisper for her hearing only, 'Oh, good, *good*!'

Inspector Boltro stood in the witness-box. He took a little book from the usher's hand and repeated the words of the oath. In response to soft and friendly questions from the well-dressed man he told the court the whole story of the arrest on the fellside and the charging and cautioning of the prisoners at the police station, repeating, as if he had been a dictaphone, every chance word they had spoken on the fellside or in the charge room. 'The male prisoner said, "It's ridiculous"; the female prisoner said, "That's all right, Paul. I understand." ' As the story went on, the reporters wrote hard, and the people, very silent, swung their eyes from Boltro to Presset or to Bawne, as either was mentioned.

Boltro's story told, Mr Forrest rose rather lackadaisically to question him.

'Inspector. Apart from the natural desire to resist arrest, has Mr Presset given you the slightest trouble since his apprehension?'

'No, sir,' said Boltro.

'Has he been a most amenable prisoner?'

'Yes, sir. Certainly.'

'And done all he could to assist you?'

'Yes. I think so.'

'Thank you, Inspector.' And Mr Forrest turned to the magistrate. 'I hope your worship will allow me to reserve any other questions I may wish to ask?'

The magistrate nodded, Mr Forrest sat down, and the well-dressed gentleman rose again and began, 'On that evidence I—'

But here Paul coughed, cleared his throat, and interrupted. It was his last chance, his only moment. For the last few minutes, while Mr Forrest spoke, he had been fighting against his terror of public utterance. The fight had shaken his body, reminding him of happier days when he had suffered thus because obliged to 'say a word' at some wedding or dinner. For a second he had wondered if he could do it less publicly, but at once decided that this was the coward's path. His heart had thundered as Mr Forrest sat down; he had quickly rehearsed his words for the fortieth time; and now he spoke.

'I—' he began. 'May I say—'

It fluttered the court. The reporters who had been chatting together left their gossip and gaped. They seized their pencils. Mr Forrest jumped up and, turning on Paul with an exasperated grimace, motioned to him to keep quiet. The women put up their lorgnettes and spectacles, and rustled to get a nearer view of him. His cheeks flared and steamed. The magistrate, magnificently unperturbed, said, 'I think there's no occasion for you to speak now. If you take my advice, you will say nothing, and leave all in the hands of your legal adviser'; and he turned from the interrupter to hear what the prosecutor had been about to say.

But Paul was not to be thus pushed aside. 'I desire only to say, your worship,' he continued; and his voice was clear enough now to enforce a silence, 'I desire only to say, and with all the emphasis at my command, that Miss Bawne is entirely innocent of all the charges brought against her. She knew nothing about anything.'

That was all. He saw the magistrate lift his eyebrows; he saw Mr Forrest bring his fist down angrily on his desk; he saw the reporters scribbling fast; he heard the rustling and whispering of the audience; he felt the policeman in the dock touch his shoulder warningly – but Myra's hand also touched his, deliberately, gratefully; and he was rewarded.

'On that evidence,' said the prosecutor, 'I ask for remand of eight days.'

Chapter Three

When Paul was bundled from the court by the gaoler, he made an attempt to go forward and say goodbye to Myra, who had gone out in front of him. But the gaoler stopped him, and Myra went from sight. Knowing nothing of criminal procedure, but supposing that her case would now be heard separately from his, he took a shock as he wondered if he had seen her for the last time. She would be taken to Holloway Gaol, and he to South London Goal; and, say both were convicted on their different charges, how could she see him then – before the end? What? No goodbye ever? But she wouldn't be convicted as an accessory. How *could* they convict her? Then, when she was released, she would be able to come and see him in the – in his last prison. And tonight he would write to her. He would write to her at great length when he reached South London Gaol. It would occupy his lonely hours.

He was held at the police station for some hours, first in a cell and then in a waiting-room; and the time hung so heavy that at last, as a man in a dentist's waiting-room begins to long for the chair and the drill, so he longed to be taken and pushed into the prison. About four o'clock, a policeman came and led him out to the station yard, where a car waited against the kerb. Its driver was in plain clothes, and so were two burly men who stood near it; but Paul's eye, by this time, was trained to know policemen when he saw them. They put him into a back seat, and a plain-clothes officer sat on either side of him, without mention made of handcuffs; and the car moved out of the yard into the free open streets. No crowd here now; no waiting eyes;

just the ordinary people going about their business. The car crossed all London from north to south, winding its way at a good speed through buses and vans and taxis; and not a face turned to look at it. Paul did not speak much, but watched for the places and buildings he knew.

One of the burly policemen talked. An indulgent, compassionate fellow, he was at pains to tell his charge that South London Prison wasn't really at all 'a bad sort of shop'; in fact, it was hardly what you might call a prison at all, except for the buildings and warders and the like of that. 'Being as how it's a trial and remand prison, with a few debtors thrown in, it's really made up of chaps who are still unconvicted or who haven't committed a criminal offence at all – not but what there aren't a few star prisoners – aren't there, Harry? And only the debtors and stars are treated like real convicted prisoners – given the prison grub, and made to work on mailbags or cleaning the prison or what all. The others can have what grub they like to pay for, and all the newspapers they can buy; and they needn't work from dawn till dark unless they've a mind to. And they can pay other prisoners to clean their cells, and just set down and live like lords. That's right, isn't it, Harry?'

'That's right,' Harry agreed, and winked at Paul. 'I think he's been *in*, don't you – he knows too much.'

'I shouldn't mind a week or two there, at all I shouldn't,' said the other. 'Not if I had the necessary brass, that is.'

But however pleasantly the men who had not to go into it might paint the prison, fear gripped Paul's heart like a fist when he got his first glimpse of South London Gaol. The car, turning into a side-street and slowing suspiciously, had started the nervousness; and yes, here was the high grey cliff of curtain-wall, and behind it the towering dark halls, massive and merciless, with row upon row of grimy barred windows. Here was the main gate building, twin-towered and castellated like a fortress, with the spiked gates below, black, impenetrable and forbidding. Men said that mercy had invaded the prison system; that might be, but this fearful building was the true descendant and distillation of the old donjon, keep, bastille, and oubliette. The car stopped before the black doors, and the driver sounded his horn carelessly: he had not to go in for more than a minute. A face looked out through the wicket; and noisily the gates were unlocked from within; and one swung open. The car passed through, but only to face, in the darkness under the arch, a second pair of gates. The outer gates closed behind them, but the inner ones were not yet opened: never might both pair of gates stand open at one time. The gatekeeper first looked into the car and 'checked' the officers and their prisoner; for every living soul, including the Governor himself, had to be booked in or booked out. Then he opened for them the inner gate. The car went on, and this gate in its turn shut noisily behind them. The clanging of the gate jarred on Paul's nerves: a second barrier had swung into place between him and the world.

They alighted at the doors of the entrance building. Paul had barely time to notice that there was some attempt at cheerfulness between the main gate and the main building – some shrubs and flowerbeds – before he was following the two policemen and a warder along a corridor to the reception room, and the oppressive weight of a dark and rigid system was closing on him again. If he had time to notice anything in that quick walk it was the premature twilight and chill draughtiness of the corridor, the spotless, ruthless cleanliness of colour-washed walls, scrubbed stone floors and polished metal, and an insistent smell of gas. The reception room was just an oblong room with a long table down its centre. The reception officer took his seat at the head of the table, and scanned the remand warrant handed to him by one of the policemen. He checked and listed Paul's personal property brought by the police in a cloth bag, and ordered Paul to sign for it. This done, he signed a receipt for the 'body' of Paul and handed it to the policemen who promptly departed. Paul, now a 'body' to be carefully preserved for judgement, stood alone with the reception officer and some warders. Appropriate that the reception officer should say, 'Strip.' He stripped, and stood before them, a naked, unpropertied, disinherited body. As at Randall he felt painfully conscious of unshapely limbs, protuberant bones, white flaccid skin, private parts, and the hairs where they were thick on his body. And the search here was even more thorough and intimate than at Randall. They ran their fingers in his every fold and cranny, and in his mouth and through his hair. Then they ordered him into the adjoining room. Naked still and carrying his clothes, he passed into it, to see that it was a large stonefloored room, divided into cubicles, each of which housed a clean, white bath. He went into one of the cubicles and, finding no chair or stool, laid his clothes on a strip of matting on the floor. A bath attendant, one of the debtors in prison clothes of blue, turned on the water, which steamed to the ceiling.

When bathed, and dressed again in his own clothes, he followed a warder to another room where he was given a night-shirt, a brush and comb, a tooth brush, and a china mug and plate; then on again, he following a warder and supposing that they must now come to his cell. At the thought of the cell, terror knocked at his heart again; he dreaded that maddening claustrophobia behind the thick immovable walls and the heavy iron-bound door. Passing on, he caught a glimpse of one of the halls with its spidery galleries around, and the wire suicide nets slung taut between the lower galleries, to catch those who flung themselves from the higher landings to the stone floor. The same chill draughtiness seemed to blow at him from the clean walls and the shining metal of the landing rails. They went on, and while he was wondering where he was being taken to, the warder unlocked a door and ushered him into a large room exactly like the ward of a rather grim hospital.

It was, in fact, a ward in the prison hospital; and he could not imagine why he was brought here. Perhaps, as a 'murder case', he was to be kept under special observation. About twenty beds stood back against the walls, and a highly polished floor reflected the light from the windows. A long table occupied the centre of the floor, and in the distant wall was a fireplace with a high guard around it. Near the fireplace was a large bookcase, with regimented ranks of books, mostly in a dark uniform, well drilled on its shelves. The windows were oblong and lofty, reaching almost to the ceiling: and he could see that they had iron bars outside and that only their upper parts opened. Many prisoners were in the ward, some sitting on their beds beside their lockers, some at the long table reading or writing, some in chairs about the fireplace. That they were of every class was clear from their dress: most wore their own clothes, either dark suits and clean collars or labouring clothes and mufflers, but a few were in prison garments like the debtors, these being they whose own clothes were unfit to wear. They appeared to be talking freely among themselves, but a silence struck them as he entered; they turned to look at him; and exchanged a low and fascinated murmur as they guessed who he was.

Seated near the door was an officer in the ordinary blue uniform, not a special hospital one; and this officer received him from his escort. 'Come on,' he ordered; and led him to the end bed against the left wall. It was already made up, and its linen was fresh for a new occupant. 'That'll be your bed,' said he; and added with the same mixture of good cheer and crudity as Paul had found among the police, 'It's a famous bed, that. It was —'s bed.' He had given the name of the most notorious murderer of the century, who had died in the gallows shed.

Had it not been for the anxiety which sat like a lead weight in his head, and the ever-present but slowly deadening bruise of shame, Paul's life in the remand ward would have been a good deal more bearable than he was imagining when the heavy gates closed behind him and he was walking along the cold, clean, heartless corridors. Brooding often on his chair, he saw (with his dim perceptions) that he sat, as it were, in the midst of a transition. The English prison system was slowly and heavily changing from the facile brutality of the old tormentors' days, still expressed so clearly in the dun and dingy buildings and the sharp and rigid discipline, into something more intelligent and compassionate and worthy of grown men; though the chains and the gyves and the vengeful voice still rang more loudly than the accents of pity. The high windows were barred, the doors were locked, the silence of the prison yards surrounded the walls, the timetable was enforced by brusque commands like those of a drill sergeant to a defaulters' squad, the prisoners (though legally 'innocent' until convicted) were clearly 'prisoners' in the minds of the officers, which is to say they were mere units for rough movements instead of individual men, but, none the less, the place was a hospital ward as well as a guardroom. Beyond warning the men not to discuss their own cases (which they thereupon did very freely) the warders made no attempt to enforce the Silence Rule – except during the brief regular visit of Governor, Deputy-Governor, or Chief Warder. Of the warders who came to take their turn of duty some were of the old tradition, satisfied that all prisoners were the scum of the earth best treated by bullying voices and sarcastic words; but others were friendly and talkative fellows (against the letter of the law) with a clear idea that their charges, if sometimes incorrigible rogues, were often very little different from the people outside, and sometimes much more generous and amiable souls; and that even the incorrigibles had generally a good-hearted and 'sporting' side. And they did not forget that far worse men, who had kept on the right side of the law, sat outside in places of freedom, wealth and honour.

It might seem amusing (were amusement possible here) that Paul who was 'in' on the gravest charge of all should have been so surprised to find that the criminal classes were made up, on the whole, of very decent men, much like himself. Most of these men were probably guilty – he learned that they were in on all charges from forging and manslaughter to indecent exposure and spitting at a policeman – but there were no 'criminal types' here. They were no herd of similar sub-human creatures. They were just Jack and Harry and Mr Goodwin and Major Crewe. True that, except for the forger type, they were often physically undeveloped and mentally unproduced, but, even so, they only reminded him of Alfred Briscoll. And most of them, like himself, were suffering more tortures than they showed. Only those who had done a stretch or a lagging before were cheerful; the rest, if smiling sometimes, were really shocked and shaky and despondent.

Paul, as the only one in on the capital charge, was the aristocrat of the ward, to whom they liked to chat; and he, when not stunned by memory, liked to hear their talk and read their lives. One was a weedy youth with a pitiful expression of misery that settled often into a vacuous stare: his charge was one of indecent assault, and Paul's pity for him was as full and urgent as Dr Waterhall's condemnation would have been. Another was an old man, always grumbling, who, in his pains, limped and shuffled about the room, except in his moods of complete abstraction and forgetfulness, when he 'got off' from his starting point with the celerity of a runner and walked around the room with the ease of a youth. The warders declared he was malingering; but the doctor probably kept him in hospital on account of his age. And there, day after day, he sloped about the ward or in the bathroom, spitting on the floor with clocklike regularity, to the disgust of the debtor-cleaner. Another was a little man of about fifty, with fresh skin, tip-tilted nose, neat moustache and silver hair, who would have kept himself dapper if despair hadn't disabled his hands. He was charged with larceny; and often he spoke to Paul, threatening suicide. One of the old lags, a thick-faced, unprepossessing burglar with heavy body and short legs was perhaps the jolliest citizen of the ward. He seemed proud of having spent eighteen of his forty-three years in prison. 'It's the luck of the torse,' he explained to Paul. 'I've no particular down on the busies when they cop us, nor for these 'ere screws (warders) when they starts chivvying us arah'nd. It's their business, arter all, just as mine is to dodge 'em. I tell 'em so; honest I do. I shall get a stiff lot this time, but I shan't whine. I shall know it's my record that's done it. It's the luck of the torse, that's all. There's lads outside as 'ave never been carpeted once, and they've done much more jobs than me. That's all that ever sticks in me gullet. Time? Gaw! Do it on me 'ead. It's only the missus I worry abaht.' He could be extraordinarily sentimental about the missus. 'Yeah, I'm always sorry for 'er. That lil gurl's stuck to me through thick and thin, guv'nor; through thick and thin, she 'as. No man livin' as ever 'ad a better pal. She's a synte; a synte as good as any of 'em; and I don't care who hears me say so. She'll be there at the prison gytes when I come aht, waitin' for me' – but by this time his eyes were full of tears, and he could not safely continue.

When not chatting, they could read books and newspapers, write letters (one letter a day) or prepare long notes for their solicitors, expounding the impossibility of their guilt; or, bored with these activities and very melancholy, they could sit and watch the debtor-cleaner polishing the wood floor of the ward.

So ran the days. At six-fifteen they were called by the officer in charge. They washed in the bathroom adjoining and made their own beds. At seven-thirty breakfast: one debtor brought a dixie full of tea into the ward, another a dixie of porridge, and the first debtor served the tea into their mugs, but the officer issued the correct amount of porridge: one pint per man. For the rest, bread and margarine. On Paul's first morning, soon after nine, the doctor, accompanied by a principal officer, came round for his examination of the new arrivals. Paul was told to undress and lie naked on his bed; and the M.O came and examined him very thoroughly, sounding heart and lungs, peering into his eyes and teeth and throat, and demanding of him his medical history. When a little way from his bed, he made some comment to the principal officer, who jotted down some notes in a book. Paul got the impression that he was the most precious object in the ward, and that the care of his body was somehow of higher importance than the care of any other. It was of royal importance.

On most mornings they all shuffled out for exercise; and now the ancient brutality took command again. Joined by other remand prisoners from wards or cells, they were formed up by brusque warders on a ground-floor landing and marched out into an exercise yard. This was a rectangular yard of gravel and tar, with the high grey hospital wall on one side, a 'hall' wall pierced with rows of cell windows on the other, and high bounding walls at either end. Against the outer wall was a penthouse of eight W.C.'s to remind them of those prisoners for whom the exercise hour was the official and very cold time for the performance of natural duties. In the centre of the yard the new mercy peeped in an oval patch of grass and flowers; but round this was an oval path of paving stones, then another strip of grass, and another oval path of paving stones. The prisoners, in single file, three yards or five paces apart, marched round and round the two oval paths – round and round, round and round – for an hour on end, among the grass and the flowers. The younger and more active trod the outer 'ring', and the sick and old and slow the inner, and the warders stood on stone blocks like ringmasters, to watch the well-trained animals keep their direction and their pace. They shuffled round and round till weary with the monotony of it; and in their ill-assorted garments, the sunlight making deeper the hollows beneath their eyebrows and their cheek bones, they looked a sad little circus of derelict men.

At noon, dinner, with good food and perhaps a special dish ordered by the doctor. At two-thirty, more exercise, or a 'visit', when Paul went into a special room and sat at a table with a low glass screen across it to prevent contact between him and his visitor, and a warder sitting at the screen's end. Inglewood came to see him once, but Paul's shame was too great for him to get any pleasure from the visit. Inglewood, good fellow, tried to be breezily cheerful and told him that not a soul at the school, not even Sandys, believed he was guilty and that they were all doing their best to tell the whole damned world so, and that he was to keep his pecker up because he was bound to get off; but he did not tell him that Heasman, sure that the scandal had ruined his school and perhaps glad of it, was selling the place for what he could get at the end of the next term, and retiring from headmastership forever. Neither Inglewood nor Paul mentioned a singular, because too apt, conversation in the brown common-room, on a winter morning many months before; though each knew that it moved in the back of the other's mind, like a spectral mystery.

'Well, all the luck in the world, old boy,' said Inglewood, as he went, 'We're all dead certain you're going to get off. Keep smiling.'

'Thank you. Thank you very much,' said Paul. 'Good – goodbye.'

When Mr Forrest, his solicitor, came to see him, which might be at any hour he liked, they met in a different room: this room was a cold, bare chamber of colour-washed brick, with a table and chairs, and he and Mr Forrest sat opposite each other with the table between. No warder was present here, and the door was shut, but it had a pane of glass about two foot square, through which the watching warder could see all, but hear nothing.

Of course there were the days when he was taken back to the police court for the resumed hearing of his case. On these mornings he was taken to the reception room, and all his property was handed back to him, and he was crossed off the prison's books (though everyone knew that he would be back again in the evening) and he was handed over to two police officers who had come for him in a police car. He was 'washed out' of the prison and in the charge of the police – till his return to the prison in the evening, when the whole business of his reception was gone through again, and his body was resumed from the police into the hands of the Keeper of H.M. Gaol. Only after the end of the hearing before the magistrate and his committal for trial to the Old Bailey would the police be done with charge of him and finally hand over his body to the prison authorities for safe keeping.

Tea-supper was at about four o'clock in the prison; and after it, they were free to read and write and talk till eight o'clock, when half a pint of milk was served to each man. Again a debtor brought it, and the officer rationed it. Then nine o'clock, and the night officer came on duty, and the lights went out, one only burning near the officer's chair. No more talking was allowed now; but one whispered to one's neighbour in the next bed. Paul would lie awake long after the others, because he alone wondered if his life were ticking away with the minutes. Of course it was; and in the darkness of his despair there was but a single glimmer, like a star now seen, now lost: all his resolution at all costs to save Myra. This had a touch of sweetness, and was his comfort. But there was nothing else, and the knowledge was a lead weight in his head. He must tell his last few lies and, when these failed, make his peace with God, and die. In twelve weeks, say; or ten? Nine? He turned and tossed for hours, till from utter weariness he sank into sleep. From this warm sleep, and perhaps from a dream of childhood, it was his stab to wake and see the barred windows, and remember all.

Chapter Four

Six o'clock in the evening; and Sir Hayman Drewer left his chambers in Creed Buildings, Temple, and emerged into the Strand. Young barristers and old clerks pointed him out as he passed.

Sir Hayman was easy to recognise, with his tall, heavy body, full face, his small, unlaughing eyes, and his thin-lipped, firmly-set mouth which turned down at the corners. Not that his was a typical lawyer's face: the nostrils were too wide and the chaps too pendulous for that; and the whole moon-face was less stern than humourless. The collar, very stiff and white, seemed to match it; and so did the full black cravat with the gold pin, the formal black coat and silk hat, and the black portfolio in his hand.

He walked at his usual unhurried pace, his eyes turning neither to right nor to left, though he knew that faces had swung to recognize him. The recognition flattered him, but his face showed no emotion: it never did, in court, in chambers, or in street; a fact of which he was very proud. So no passer who saw Sir Hayman go by knew that he was eager, jubilant, impatient to be home that he might study certain papers in his bag. From the fact that Sir Hayman, one of the hardest workers in the Temple, was leaving at six instead of at seven a brilliant young lawyer might have guessed something: the flippant youth might have exclaimed, 'Lord have mercy!' and inquired what was up. But no such youth was there.

Sir Hayman summoned a taxi with an unexcited lift of his arm; and the driver, recognising him, supposed that he was taking into his cab Sir Hayman Drewer, the impassive and cold: and he did not know that he was taking home a boy warm with exultation because a prize over which he had been abominably anxious for weeks was now definitely his. The prize was in the portfolio at his feet: a brief; the papers of the Presset Case.

The taximan, we say, knew that Sir Hayman was sitting in his cab, but did not know that this excited schoolboy was sitting in Sir Hayman; and it is certain that Sir Hayman himself did not know, for, outside his craft in which his competence was immense, he was as simple and unsophisticated, as insensitive and commonplace, as most great legal minds. He did not know that at fifty-eight, with a bull neck, grim-set mouth and ageing eyes, he was still a boy playing a part that he loved and very happy in it. A man who, secretly to his own surprise, has achieved the whole of his ambition is always as healthy and happy as a child at play: we have seen the same high condition in Inspector Boltro. Sprung from a lowland manse, the lad Hayman had dreamed of becoming a great advocate, famous and wealthy, before whom the criminals trembled; but in that straitened home he had hardly dared to hope. He had nothing on his side but his dour Scots will. Still, the will had set his mouth, emptied his eyes of gaiety, and driven him to London. In his early days of devilling in London, when he watched the great men come and go, and endured their ill-temper and their snubs, he had often been near to despair; but the good Scots will had clenched his fists and advanced his jaw in a vow to be one of the great men himself in a dozen years, with the privilege of being short with the clerks and snubbing the juniors. Frustration fanned a fire of determination, and he worked as no one else; and the work did not tire him, because his ambition was driving him; nay, the work kept him well, because it was release. He outdid all other juniors in his preparation of a case. 'Not a loop-hole' was his motto; 'not a weak link'. And soon one of the great men perceived this, and was glad to have him as his junior. The great man stretched down a hand and pulled him on to the first step. He was well begun. True, he made more reputation than money at the criminal bar, but he preferred fame of the two; and, anyhow, his acute mind saw that this was best at the beginning.

He worked; how he worked! He sought no social life and made few friends, for he grudged the time; he went to few theatres, less concerts, and never an art gallery, for, if he returned from his chambers at seven o'clock, it was with plenty of work in his hands to fill the hours from dinner to bed. And gradually his well-known thoroughness secured him briefs that involved a mastery of detail; and the money came with them, and more and more thrilling labour into the small hours, but less songs and less friends. And he counted himself a happy man! He pitied others! He did not know that the criminals in the dock were often more alive, and certainly more interesting, than he. He supposed himself an ornament at a public dinner party, an object of interest to all eyes; he did not know that the woman at his side, who was interested in other things than law, was sometimes more impressed by his dullness than his fame.

He had arrived; but the white walls of the manse were still about him, and the smell of cheap eating-houses in London, so that, even now, he could hardly believe that he was famous, wealthy, titled, expensively dressed and grandly housed, and a man before whom the criminals trembled.

Oh, he was happy. The silent man sitting in a taxi with a black portfolio at his feet was happy. He prided himself on the character they gave him at the bar. He affected to pooh-pooh it, but he loved it, and did his best to fill it. 'Cold . . . ruthless as a machine . . . thorough as a telephone directory . . . able to do the work of ten men, and expecting others to do it too . . . as unsparing with the police in conference as with the criminals in the dock, so that the coppers begin to wonder if they'll get off with less than three years. . . .' Such was the character in the gossip of the bar messes. And, strange to say, he did not think it other than admirable: it would have shocked him to hear that some might think it the choice of a fifth-form schoolboy, and a heavy lad at that. He enjoyed hearing that prisoners in South London Gaol, when told that Sir Hayman Drewer was to prosecute them, grimaced, and mentioned the Redeemer's name; he was flattered to hear that Presset, when given the same information, had said sorrowfully, 'I could wish it were anyone else.' What a tribute! He liked to be told the latest jokes about him. 'Is it true that Old Drewer is going to prosecute Presset? Good! No one'll hang him as high as Hayman.' 'Is it true that Old Drewer's had a breakdown at last and been ordered a year's rest? Yes, he was prosecuting Godenstein, and the man was acquitted.' Sir Hayman laughed, for he prided himself on his sense of humour, and often mentioned it, as men do in whom it is not strong. He enjoyed the contrast which hard-headed lawyers – generally a romantic and uncritical race – loved to point between him and Sir Kennedy Eddy, whose taste ran to defending. 'Old Drewer is monumental; Ken Eddy is small and restless and perky; Old Drewer is a grim black bull; Ken Eddy is a genial and good-natured cockatoo, with a hell of a bite; Drewer's all logic, Eddy all sentiment; Drewer all head, Eddy all heart; Drewer steel, Eddy a pinch of gunpowder; Drewer is always unruffled, calm and relentless, but Eddy may be anything from suave as a shop-walker to frenzied as a Goth with a battle-axe; tears have been known to break Ken Eddy's voice, but Old Drewer is always level and cold as a sword, and kills quite as effectively.'

Yes, this man, kind in his home, tender with the dog, compassionate with the sick, was proud of his ruthlessness in the courts; than which, surely, there is no clearer proof of a limited vision. That men as a result of his ruthlessness languished in gaol for years; that some were turned into criminals for life; that others – three weeks later – stood on a platform with sick terror in their hearts and went down with a shriek did not lose him (as he often said) one hour of sleep. 'That's not my business,' he would maintain. 'My duty is to work the law as I find it; it's others' job to alter it.' And, in any case, he was pretty content with it as it stood; if he desired to change it at all, it was in the direction of greater severity; he believed in 'exemplary punishments' and would be annoyed when the prerogative of mercy was used in favour of a man whose condemnation he had secured – 'it's nothing more than arbitrary interference with jury trial by a politician,' said he. 'It's maudlin sentimentality,' he declared; and felt very superior, strange to say, instead of very commonplace. He believed in the 'cat' and advocated it in all cases of cruelty to animals; he really did. He believed that the 'strong man' and the 'hard man' were one; and thought that virility meant freedom from the weakness of pity. It had never entered his head that true strength and true virility deal always in patience, understanding and mercy; and that anything less is merely adolescence. 'My clerks or my devils make only one mistake,' he would say, grimly smiling; and imagine it was a strong man's remark. He thought it was virility. Poor boy.

From the moment a brief for the prosecution reached him he had but one objective – a conviction. Without his noticing it, the possibility of the man's innocence usually dropped from his view. If by chance a doubt remained he was always scrupulously fair – he prided himself on this as a good British lawyer should – but the doubt very seldom remained, because he *had* to win the game; he *had* to maintain his fame as 'the greatest prosecuting counsel in the land'. 'Not a loop-hole; not a weak link', said he to clerks and devils and police. Napoleonic, he made it clear that he would suffer no will to be paramount but his own (and what a nuisance Napoleon still is, ravaging the weaker states!). 'Either I have complete control of the police engaged in the case or I decline to conduct it.' He summoned the police to long and gruelling conferences in his chambers, and at the end of the conference issued his orders coldly. He was coldly sarcastic with them if they were dull. By a lift of the eyebrows he made them feel their incompetence. Inspector Boltro was not half such a great man in Drewer's chambers as in Randall police station. Sir Hayman did not hide his impatience with Boltro. Some of the police chiefs he admired very heartily, and was generous, not to say sentimental, in his extolling of them; but not Boltro. He thought Boltro ambitious and vain; and Sir Hayman found it hard to forgive a man ambitious and vain.

And the police, with half their minds, hated him for his slave driving and sarcasm; but with the other half they wanted him, because he was the best crown upon their work. 'Whatever you may say against him, he's a strong man,' they said; for police too are simple souls.

So tonight he sat in his cab in a warm glow. That miserable anxiety lest the Presset case, since it was a poisoning case, should go to one of the Law Officers of the Crown was over. It had come to him: the most famous case for years. From the minute he had read the story of Presset and the girl Bawne – and he had read it with enthusiasm – he had known that if only they gave it to him, he could secure a conviction of the man. It would be a fascinating case to work – one that lent itself to his talent for slow merciless exposure. He knew that there would be nothing left of Presset when he had done with him. And it would give him real pleasure to bring *that* man low – obviously a vain, ambitious and pushing little creature. He'd do it; do it easily. And it would be the *cause célèbre* of the hour. What fame! What publicity!

The cab stopped before his house in Ennismore Gardens. The butler saw it from the window and opened the door before Sir Hayman could use his key.

'Her ladyship out?' asked the master.

'Yes, Sir Hayman.'

Thank Heaven. 'Then will you send me some dinner on a tray into the library. I've a great deal of work to do.'

'Very good, Sir Hayman.'

Having given the man his hat, he walked straight into the library, a fine room with oak bookcases, heavily carved, all round the walls, and a massive carved desk in the centre, and a thick-piled red carpet. A massive and commonplace room.

Alone. Good! Not that he disliked his wife. He believed that he loved her. He did not know that his only real love was his ambition. Next to this, however, he was very fond of his wife and his daughters. And they loved him, for Sir Hayman, the terror of criminals, was very indulgent to those near him. And not only to his family. He was always moved to relieve pain so long as he saw it with his own eyes; but he could not see without his eyes. This evening he seized his portfolio happily, and settled down to a delightful night's work.

Chapter Five

The police having done with him, it was prison officers who conveyed Paul to the Old Bailey for his trial. Two warders in uniform took him to an ordinary taxi that waited between the inner and the outer gates. He went handcuffed. In the taxi one warder sat at his side, and the other on the tip-up seat before him. All the way they were visible to the people in the streets, so he kept his face down. One of the warders told him with pride that, according to the papers, sixty additional police had been told off for duty in and around the Old Bailey, and the Under-Sheriff, unable to cope with the demand for tickets of admission to the court, had issued cards available for half a day only, to ensure that as many as possible got a taste of the trial; so he was not surprised, when they pulled up to the high stone building, to see a swaying crowd at each of the public doors, and the city policemen forcing them back. Before the crowd could recognise him and surge towards the cab, it had gone out of the noise into the yard of the Old Bailey; and a minute later he was walking in the marble silence of corridors to a waiting-room beneath the dock. This was a plain, distempered room with one small window high up. It had no furniture except a table, and a bench built into three of its walls. Here his warders removed his handcuffs and waited with him till it should be time to go up to the dock. They waited a long time, hearing many footsteps and voices and an occasional bell, and last of all a voice calling, 'Fetch him along'; and the officer in charge of cells looked in to say, 'Ready now, mate.'

'Come along then,' said the warders; and Paul walked between them along a narrow passage to the foot of the stairway that led to the dock.

Now he could hear the woven texture of subdued voices in the court room above; and suddenly three loud raps and a cry of 'Silence!' Then the sound of many people rising, the murmur of a voice, and a call: 'Put up Paul Arthur Presset.'

'Come,' whispered the leading warder.

Paul braced his shoulders, set his face, and followed him. Strange, this little lost focus of pleasure in his resolve to show no emotion. He walked up and straight forward to the front ledge of the dock; and the first thing he noticed was a pleasant scent: the front of the dock was sprinkled with sweet herbs.

The scene before him was the police court over again, but on a larger and grander scale. The dock was not a narrow pen, but a large compartment with plate-glass windows at the sides and behind. The serried faces sloped up to the panelled walls, but there were far more of them, to say nothing of the cloud of witnesses in the public gallery above. The barristers in the well of the court wore gowns and wigs; and in the place of a single unrobed magistrate, on the high bench of honour before him, there was the Lord Chief Justice in scarlet and wig – the central jewel of the whole setting – and an array of figures in aldermanic and other imposing attire. These included, he was to learn later, the Lord Mayor, three city aldermen, the Sheriff and an Under-Sheriff. Not for many prisoners did such distinguished persons take their privileged places on either side of the judge.

Now the arraignment. From his seat beneath the judge the Clerk of Arraigns rose, called Paul by name, read the indictment to him, and asked, 'How say you? Are you guilty or not guilty?'

Paul cleared his throat for the lie. 'Not guilty.'

Then followed the swearing of the jury, one by one, where they sat in their two-tiered box on his left. 'You shall well and truly try, and true deliverance make, between our sovereign lord the King and the prisoner at the bar whom you shall have in charge, and a true verdict give according to the evidence' – Paul, hearing the oft-repeated words had time to mark their beauty, and he was reminded of other lovely words, '. . . for that she, well knowing that the said defendant had committed the said felony, did receive, comfort, assist and maintain him.' For which she lay in Holloway Gaol, her trial as an accessory delayed till they should know the result of his. He was thinking this when there broke on his wool-gathering the loveliest words of all. He was being given in charge to the jury. 'Gentlemen of the jury . . . upon this indictment he has been arraigned, and upon arraignment has pleaded that he is not guilty, and has put himself upon God and his country, whose country you are. . . .'

He looked at the twelve men of the jury who would send him to his death. He wondered what their little shops or their homes were like. He thought how strange it was that they and he should have converged along their several life-journeys to this meeting, to this terrible intimate relationship; and that in a very little while they and he would part again, they to life and he to death.

But the trial had begun. A warder motioned to him to sit down, and a tall, heavy man in wig and gown rose from the well of the court. So that was Sir Hayman Drewer. 'May it please your lordship' – he was saying – 'gentlemen of the jury' – and in his celebrated low and level tones he opened the story of the life of Paul and Elinor Presset in the house in Elm Tree Road. A large house, and perhaps a rather gloomy one, as houses were that had known better days; and therein a woman, older than her husband, and past her attractive days and unable to minister to his desires – an invalid indeed – but possessed of desirable means; and a middle-aged man, poor, earning but little money at a private school in the neighbourhood, worried about his future and deeply entangled in an intrigue with a young woman whom he desired with all that lamentable – they might think rather despicable – infatuation to which middle-aged men of a weak, flaccid and romantic type so frequently succumbed – a man somewhat sly, since it would be shown that he had steadily misrepresented his age, upbringing, and scholastic attainments to those who had employed him—

At this point one of the counsel, sitting nearer the dock, moved impatiently in his seat. Much smaller than Sir Hayman, he had a ruddy face, a long nose, darting eyes, and a little greying wig perched on the top of his head, so that he really did look something like 'a genial and good-natured cockatoo, with a hell of a bite'. It was Sir Kenneth Eddy, Paul's defending counsel, of whom people all over England were saying dramatically, 'If anyone can save him, it'll be he. He'll fight every inch of the way'; Ken Eddy, and he was beginning to simmer.

But Sir Hayman went on with his story, soft-voiced, unimpassioned, unperturbed. He was building up the 'motive'. The prisoner had practised a long course of deception, some of which the dead woman had known, and, if angered, might have revealed. It was not unimportant to emphasise the deceitfulness that was so marked a characteristic of the accused: it had a strong bearing, in the submission of the prosecution, on his actions both before and after the death of his wife. For example, he had concealed from all, except the very nearest, that their life together was anything but a happy one – was, indeed, full of frictions and quarrels and violent recrimination. Seldom, in his submission, had the Crown been in the position to show a stronger motive. Consider –

And bit by bit, in a tale like the fireside story of no mean artist, he built the motive for them: lust and avarice and fear. And ambition. 'Vaulting ambition, which o'erleaps itself, and falls on the other side.'

From his uplifted dock Paul saw the piles of notes which Sir

Hayman had amassed to make his death and agony sure. Line by line the quiet artist enlarged them to power. The jury, the audience, the young barristers who stood crowded by the dock's side, the robed and grey-haired figures by the judge – children all, for the time – listened in silence with gazing eyes. Away to the right the newspaper men scribbled and scribbled the story of that grey house, eager to extend the walls of the court to the outer margins of the world, so that all could hear.

And if much of it was true, much, very much of it, was so mistaken. Paul grew restive with indignation. Not only the truly incriminating facts but other quite innocent ones were being built into the proof of his guilt. Some of his simplest and most natural utterances were being twisted, by honest misconception perhaps, into the rope that would hang him. He was guilty, he knew; but with an appalling shock he realized that if by chance Elinor's death *had* been an accident, he, at any rate, must have hanged just the same. 'No, no!' he wanted to rise and cry, as one of these errors was given the same weight, in that even, measured voice, as the truly guilty deeds. To have to sit there silent while such lethal mistakes were made! Tears of anger spurted to his eyes, but he only kept his head down and muttered to himself, 'All over. All over.'

These were honest errors perhaps; but the misrepresenting of his relations with Myra seemed coldly dishonest and wicked. Or perhaps Sir Hayman was unaware of his own motives. For now, with every artifice and every subtly chosen adjective, he seemed out to use Myra for all she was worth as a trump card to inflame the jury's hate; and so to take his trick. That morning, in a court of the Old Bailey, the bent head of a prisoner shook from side to side in denial, and an agonised cry: 'Oh, no. *No!*' stayed unuttered. A young and simple girl, young enough to be his daughter, who had come from a poor but God-fearing home to a humble position in the same employment – a figure who should surely have stirred a man's chivalry and protection – this girl he had quickly seduced and turned into his paid mistress. He had taken her from her home and paid for a room elsewhere. Gradually he had acquired, it would seem, a complete domination over her – as every subsequent event showed. And this intrigue he had concealed by every trickery from his sick wife at home and from the school where he – and she – were engaged on the responsible task of teaching the nation's children.

And now let them consider this. The jury might think it not without significance that during the great influenza epidemic of that year the wife became very ill and, while many of her symptoms were the same as those of other unfortunate victims of the disease, others were peculiar to herself and resembled those which, several months later, accompanied her death.

Immediately Sir Kenneth Eddy was on his feet, protesting. He leapt up, as if he had been waiting for this opportunity for a long time and was glad to be presented with it. He began a baffling argument with the judge, garnished at every point with 'With great respect, me lord', and 'Certainly, me lord', and 'If your lordship pleases'; while Sir Hayman watched the give-and-take sorrowfully, with turned head and lowered notes. They tossed 'admissibility' about; they mentioned this case and that; Sir Kenneth spread his hands as if his great respect hampered him in telling 'me lord' what he thought of him; the judge, a little bright-eyed old man, made his points very slowly and quietly in an old man's voice and with the aid of his forefinger on his desk; Sir Kenneth lifted up his little wig and rearranged it on his head, and said, 'If your lordship pleases,' but not without a look at the jury that seemed to say, 'You at any rate are fair-minded men and can see how I am hampered'; Sir Hayman, invited to argue, contended that it was entirely necessary for him to mention this for reasons that would soon be clear, if his learned friend would exercise his patience; Sir Kenneth shrugged and spread his hands and sighed; and the upshot seemed to be that the judge ruled there was no justification for Sir Kenneth's outburst and every reason why Sir Hayman should be allowed to continue.

But Sir Hayman did not for the present avail himself of this consent. 'Perhaps,' thought Paul, 'he has achieved his effect and desires no more, unless it be an impression of great fairness.'

'Well,' proceeded Sir Hayman, 'the woman recovered, and these two people continued to live in the grey house, alone, unhappy, quarrelling. And so it remained till that happened which altered the whole complexion of the tale. By an accident Mrs Presset discovered the intrigue with the woman Bawne, and rightly insisted that he should see her no more. The accused gave her a promise that he would not do so – a promise which, as you shall hear, he did not honour.

'That was the situation. . . .'

He paused impressively. Then, having built up the motive he came to the means. 'The accused had a patch of garden. . .' Oh, how was it fair to suggest, as Sir Hayman was doing now: 'You may wish to ask yourselves whether this conversation with the jobbing gardener about the properties of weed-killer was or was not evidence of his state of mind at the time?' That talk with Briscoll had been quite innocent. But what matter? Fair or unfair this opening, the rest of the weed-killer story, his lies about the tin and his burying of it were going to convict him, he knew, as he listened with bent head. And yet all these actions *could* have been innocent. Terror *might* have explained them.

From means to opportunity. Sir Hayman was not hesitating to suggest that he had deliberately got rid of the maid, Annie Mavis, that he might be alone with Elinor for the crime. Great God, was there not enough to hang him without all these lying hints? And that it was soon after Annie's departure that Elinor's first illness occurred! O God!

So by true hints and false hints the terrible weaving went on. Not a man within the four walls of that court but believed him guilty now – and spurned him. 'Elinor Presset fell violently sick and died in a few hours, after suffering great agony.' Sir Hayman appeared to pause that the picture of her agony might not be wasted. Paul felt a wave of hate come towards him – and yet the agony had horrified him as much as any of them. 'Elinor Presset was buried in a grave in Trusted churchyard where there was a space already bought and paid for' – was he hinting that Paul – but no sooner had he said this than he added, with his scrupulous fairness, 'the accused asserts that this was in accordance with her last wishes.' Thank you for nothing, Sir Hayman. 'The doctor will tell you how he had no hesitation at first in signing a certificate of death from valvular disease of the heart, but that later, after hearing that the accused, with unseemly haste and, as you may think, incredible heartlessness, had resumed his intrigue with the woman Bawne, and after an illuminating talk with the jobbing gardener, grave doubts arose in him – so grave that at length, with a high sense of public duty, and even though the prisoner was his friend, he carried them to the proper authorities.'

Then the story of the flight. 'Why flight? What had he to fear? When he fled and tried to escape from the country, there had been no announcement made of poison found in the body. You will surely have to ask yourselves whether anything but guilty knowledge could have caused that flight. And in this connection you will bear in mind that at the police court he made use of the phrase, "Miss Bawne knew nothing about anything". If you are prepared to believe that, on that occasion, he had braced himself to speak the truth, however vaguely, and save his partner, you will, I submit, find it hard to resist the conclusion that there was matter of which guilty knowledge could be had.'

So he came to his peroration. 'It is now my duty to call evidence to prove all these facts in the proper manner. I suggest that, as in the familiar jig-saw puzzle, all the facts will, at the last, be seen to create a complete picture – the picture of the accused preparing and executing the murder of his sick wife that he might secure himself from her embarrassing knowledge, enjoy her money, and, above all, possess his mistress. If you are satisfied that this is so, then you, a jury of the great city of London, will not shrink from your task. You will fearlessly, and with a clear conscience, do justice by the dead and your duty to Society.'

Sir Hayman sat down and began to consult some papers, as if he were giving no thought to whether his speech had been good; when, as a matter of fact, he was doing nothing else. In the court there was rustle and movement as at the end of an act; in Paul's mind despair, and the words, 'All over . . . it's all over'; in Sir Hayman's a complete satisfaction, and that glow of success which all know who have spoken well.

Then, after formal evidence proving documents and plans, there followed a procession of the friends Paul had met on his pilgrimage, all going into the box to play their part in ending his life. First, Bessie Furle, pale and flurried, her voice hardly above a whisper, with evidence of Elinor's illness, her will, Paul's resentments and their quarrels – Bessie looked relieved when Sir Kenneth Eddy, in his turn, rose to cross-examine her and answering his question, 'Were those quarrels such as might be found in many married couples?' with a 'Yes. Oh, yes, certainly,' as if she were glad to say a word in Paul's favour, and responding quickly to a further question, 'If this terrible suspicion had never risen against him, would you have described him as a kind man?' with an eager emphasis, 'One of the kindest men I know.'

Sir Kenneth, his hands behind his gown, turned his long nose towards the jury, and, looking at them, said 'Thank you, Mrs Furle; *thank you*': to underline her words; and sat down.

Then Mrs Briscoll, who manifestly had long ago lost all

sympathy for Mr Presset – Mrs Briscoll, fluent, talkative, flattered by her notoriety, but revealing all the way a bias in her evidence – to the grim satisfaction of little Sir Kenneth, who moved this way and that in his seat, talked to his two juniors and to the solicitors instructing him, and finally put on a pair of tortoiseshell-rimmed spectacles the better to study her. He rose to cross-examine, touching the spectacles with two fingers, and putting his hands beneath his gown. He began in a manner more suave than any travelling salesman, 'Now I only want your assistance, Mrs Briscoll – only in one or two little matters'; but those who knew him sat up to listen. He drew from her first, with gentle questions, that Mrs Presset was much given to the sampling of patent medicines and that 'the house was always full of old bottles'; and then shot at her abruptly, angrily, 'Was Mr Presset ever anything but kind to you?' and Mrs Briscoll, taken by surprise, thought with her head on one side and answered, 'No, sir, I can't say as he was ever unkind,' but grudgingly, which was just what Sir Kenneth wanted. He looked at her long; he turned his bird-like nose towards the jury and looked at them long; and trusted that this look would convey to them all that he could not say. At last he spoke again. 'Mrs Briscoll: apart from these quarrels, have you ever seen Mr Presset do an unkind thing to anyone?' And Mrs Briscoll, after a hesitation, answered, 'No, I don't think I have – but then I wasn't there always.' Sir Kenneth shook his head sadly, and turned and looked at the jury again, to emphasise for them her grudging qualification; he adjusted his spectacles and lifted up his papers, to leave time for it to sink in. And when this damning pause had lasted an uncomfortable time, he asked quietly, 'Was he always considerate to you and the maid Annie?'

'Yes, I suppose so,' admitted Mrs Briscoll. 'Yes, he was considerate; that I *will* say.'

Sir Kenneth had trouble with his spectacles again. The court waited. 'You make use of the expression, "That I *will* say!" This suggests a slight hostility to the prisoner. *Do* you feel that hostility?'

'Well, who wouldn't?' exclaimed Mrs Briscoll, trapped.

'I see,' commented Sir Kenneth, and sat down with an amazing promptness. His bump on to his seat was the most perfect discrediting of the witness he could have contrived.

Then Briscoll, his hair plastered down, his celluloid collar cleaned up, his manner perky – Briscoll, ready to talk to the Lord Mayor, if necessary, about gardens and weed-killing; and with no apparent feeling about the prisoner, one way or the other. He agreed very pleasantly with Sir Kenneth that Paul's garden was his hobby, that he was always weeding and caring for it, and that his questions about the properties of weed-killer were capable of a perfectly innocent interpretation. 'Yuss, I've always said *that*,' he affirmed. 'I've always said that anyone might have asked them questions.'

'Thank you, Mr Briscoll. I am *very* much obliged to you,' said Sir Kenneth effusively. And his effusiveness pointed the contrast between this witness and all hostile ones who had gone before, or should come after.

Then the lawyer with evidence about the will; and the bank manager with evidence about Paul's cheques payable to Myra in Elinor's lifetime, and his financial transactions after her death; and the receptionists of the Bloomsbury hotels, with evidence of his and Myra's daytime visits; to all of whom, after Sir Hayman had finished his examination-in-chief, Sir Kenneth fired the remark 'No questions', with a kind of glorious, airy confidence, as if to say that none of this evidence could damage his case in the least. Not a word of it. He knew how he was going to deal with it.

And then Annie.

Annie stood in the witness-box, her cheeks rosy as ever

because they could not be anything else, but terribly frightened, all the same. Her gloved hands trembled, her eyes darted this way and that. Her glance met Paul's for a second, and her skin flushed from under her hat to the fur of her coat collar. And she had not answered six of Sir Hayman's questions before Paul knew that, though she had been called for the prosecution, and despite her terror, she was going to do her best to save him; and his heart went out to her in love. When asked about the quarrels, she added her comment, 'But if I may say so, sir, he weren't to blame; not altogether, by no means.' When asked if he had ever used violent words, she replied, 'Well, he'd fire up like, sometimes, like anyone might, but that isn't to say—'; and here the judge told her rather tenderly to confine herself to answering the questions and not to add comments of her own; and she blinked and apologised, 'Yes, sir, I beg pardon, sir'; while no doubt at the back of her Cockney mind she was thinking, 'Well, I said what I thought, all the same.' When asked if he had any part in her dismissal, she admitted, Yes, but – and the shrug of her shoulders conveyed most of the comment that the gentleman had forbidden her to offer. By this time Sir Kenneth was leaning back and watching her with a pleased interest. Apparently he expressed his pleasure to both his juniors and to the solicitors instructing him; and sat back touching the spectacles, to enjoy a little more of it. Much of it was defeating Sir Hayman; but when he came to that evidence which suggested that Myra – or someone – had slept in Paul's room during Elinor's absence, Annie bowed her head, and said, 'Well, it certainly seemed like there'd been scent on the pillow,' in a voice very low, as if she hoped the jury would not hear.

Skilfully Sir Hayman chose this for his climax, and sat down. And Sir Kenneth rose – slowly. His juniors sat back. In his gentlest voice – a voice whose soft tones were enough to suggest to her the kindest answers, he asked, 'Was Mr Presset always kind to you?'

'Oh, yes, sir,' she answered, her eyes brightening.

'And he would help you when you were tired?'

'Yes, sir. Orfen and orfen.'

'Go out of his way to help you?'

'Yes, sir. He – he was always a gentleman to me.' And she began to break down.

'I see,' soothed Sir Kenneth, very well satisfied. 'Now I don't want to put too great a burden on you. Just one or two more questions, Miss Mavis. Just one or two. What do you mean by what you've just said?'

'By what, sir?'

'By those words. "He was always a gentleman"?'

'I dunno, sir. . . . Simply that he was always the nicest gentleman . . . to *me*.'

'I see. Thank you. Thank you, Miss Mavis. And when you were dismissed, there was not the least suggestion that he was anything but sorry to lose you?'

'No, sir, not in the least. He was ever so kind about it – he always was' – and at that she lifted her face, her eyes bright with tears, and defied the judge and the court with a hysterical cry, 'Oh, he never done it, sir! He never done it!' and buried her face in her hands.

'Yes, yes,' said Sir Kenneth soothingly, and sat down, not without a glance at the reporters, who were writing hard. And gently the usher led the sobbing girl away.

'Dr Waterhall.'

There was some stir round the court at this name. Dr Waterhall came briskly past the reporters and the police officers' table, and stepped into the witness-box. This was the moment he had looked forward to. He had read often of doctors speaking authoritatively at a famous trial, while judge, jury, and audience listened respectfully, and the reporters scribbled down this essential evidence for a waiting world. And now he was going to fill this honourable position. Ceremoniously dressed for the occasion, in morning coat and white waistcoat slip, he faced Sir Hayman. Impossible not to think that, after all these well-meaning but uneducated witnesses, the court would be relieved to hear the testimony of a cultivated man, and an expert. His answers during his examination-in-chief were crisp and unembroidered. It was, 'Yes, that is so, Sir Hayman. . . . Yes, Sir Hayman', spoken as by an equal to an equal. He was pleased when he could speak learnedly of the symptoms of gastro-enteritis and arsenical poisoning and knew that neither judge nor jury understood some of his more technical terms. Mitral disease, stenosis, tricuspid and aortic and pulmonary valves – it gave him pleasure to use these high-sounding words and explain them with helpful hands to a wondering court. And when his evidence-in-chief was over, he felt that he had been a good witness and stood before the world as a public-spirited man, and a learned one.

It was nearly five when Sir Hayman Drewer sat down, and the judge looked first at the clock and then at Sir Kenneth Eddy. 'Will your cross-examination of this witness be long, Sir Kenneth?'

Sir Kenneth rose. 'Very long, I hope, me lord,' he said significantly, but with a pleasant smile.

'Very well. Then I think this would be a good point at which to adjourn.' And he bowed to the whole room and went out.

A warder touched Paul on the shoulder, and he saw no more. He went down the steps to the waiting-room beneath. Almost at once the doctor from the prison came to visit him and inquired in a friendly voice, 'All right, old chap?'

'Yes, quite,' said Paul with a smile, anxious to give no trouble.

'Right,' said the doctor. 'Good.'

The warders replaced the handcuffs and led him out to a taxi and conveyed him back to the prison. Here there was no reception or searching, because he had never been out of the prison's hands. He went straight to the hospital ward, where they gave him for supper a mug of cocoa, eight ounces of bread, margarine, and a small piece of cheese.

Chapter Six

Next morning the court reassembled, abuzz with interest. From the corridors of the Old Bailey the happy young barristers in their wigs and gowns crowded against the right wall of the dock. They wanted to hear Old Ken Eddy cross-examine the old doctor man. Every since that sinister remark, 'Very long, I hope, me lord', the rumour had been hauling among them that he had got his knife into this witness and would go to the very edge of the law in attacking him. There should be fun. Three raps; the judge's entry; and in a trice the court room was exactly as it had been eighteen hours before: the prisoner in the dock, the doctor in the witness-box, the lines of faces, tier upon tier, staring at the witness, and Sir Kenneth standing at his desk, with his hands beneath his gown and his wig perched high on his head.

He waited a long time while he arranged his notes and his spectacles; and a silence waited for him. Then, lifting his face, he looked at the witness and addressed him with a strangely quiet politeness, 'Now, Doctor, I want with your kind assistance, to arrive at one or two facts . . .' but the young barristers nudged one another. 'You attended Mrs Presset, I understand, in that first illness of which we have heard so much?'

'I did.'

'You had not the smallest doubt then that it was an ordinary gastric condition?'

'No.'

'Have you any doubt now?'

Dr Waterhall did not answer, but pursed up his mouth as one who thinks.

'I beg you to answer. Either you have, or you haven't; is it not so?'

'I have.'

'I see. I see. You have no faith left in your diagnosis on that first occasion?'

The doctor flushed. 'One can make mistakes . . . especially when symptoms are so alike. . . . The best of doctors claim no infallibility.'

'Exactly. Precisely. The best of doctors can make mistakes. . . .' Dreamily, forgetfully, he murmured to his notes, but carefully loud enough for the jury to hear, 'Great and terrible mistakes. . . . Now, sir, I want to consider this earlier illness further. I am sure you will help me all you can.'

And straightaway, with gunfire regularity, he shot at the doctor question after question on gastric influenza, acute gastritis, gastro-enteritis, aortic disease, disease of the mitral valve, hypertrophied heart muscles, and the collapse under strain of a condition of compensation; about arsenic and its distribution in, say, realgar, orpiment, and sulphide of iron; about its medical use in the organic compound cacodylate of soda in cases of leuchaemia, trypanosomiasis, psoriasis and eczema. With some dismay Dr Waterhall perceived that his opponent knew as much as he, or more, about the relevant diseases and poisons – or that he was singularly well primed up for the battle. Incomprehensible terms flashed between them – some of them incomprehensible, unhappily and most obviously, to the doctor – and the jury listened with knitted brows like twelve schoolboys when the teacher's subject matter has soared beyond their ken; the reporters abandoned their pencils and the effort to cope with it; and the judge, not knowing how to stop them because he could not disclose his complete bewilderment, pretended to write more notes than he was actually putting down. In the dazzling mist of words one thing only was clear to him: that the doctor was no great shakes at his job.

'And this distrust of your own diagnosis applies equally to the second illness, the one of which this unfortunate lady died?'

'I do not quite see what you mean.'

'Let me put it plainer. I desire only to get at the truth. You were perfectly satisfied that it was gastro-enteritis, and you had no suspicion till long afterwards that it might be something else?'

'I – er – I had some doubt at the time, I think. Yes.'

'What? You had some doubt, and yet you had no hesitation in giving a death certificate? Come, sir, you had some suspicion of foul play, and yet you did not do your "public duty"?'

'I did not say anything about foul play.'

'Ah! You did not suspect foul play. You did not suspect foul play. What did you doubt, then? Not your own medicines, I take it?'

'Certainly not.'

'Some accident, perhaps?'

'There might have been an accident . . . certainly.'

Sir Kenneth's pause here was astonishing: it resulted in everybody hearing himself repeat, 'There might have been an accident . . . certainly.' When he resumed, his voice was as ingratiating as a shopwalker's, as apologetic as a dentist's. 'Now I am sure you will help me all you can, Doctor. You must forgive me if I seem to press you in this matter, but I only want to get everything absolutely clear and above board – absolutely clear and above board. Let us have it plainly for me lord and the jury: you had no suspicion of Mr Presset at the time?'

'No.'

'Why not?'

'It never entered my head that he could be that type.'

'Exactly. Now when did you change your view of him? When,

if I may so put it, did this sense of public duty develop?'

'I heard from the man Briscoll about the weed-killer.'

'Oh, I see.' Sir Kenneth's voice was still perfectly sweet. 'Then it comes to this: that if my wife dies of some gastric trouble, I must let weeds grow in my garden, or the doctor will be going to Scotland Yard.'

'But there was the previous illness to consider.'

'My dear sir' – now his eyes flashed and his voice rose – 'just now you told me learned friend – just give me those papers, Mr Swann – you told me lord and the jury that the previous illness formed part of the patient's "history" which justified you in thinking the second illness an ordinary gastric attack like the first: you really cannot have it both ways. It amounts, I suggest, to twisting the facts to suit your theories. This is a serious matter, sir, and when a man is standing his trial on the capital charge, it seems to me – with me lord's permission – a dastardly thing to gossip and theorise a man out of his life—'

But his lordship was not prepared to grant permission for this. 'Please do not comment, Sir Kenneth,' said he. 'I cannot have the witness bullied.'

'I am not bullying him. With great respect, I am simply suggesting what is the inference from his answer.'

'Well, there's no need to be so vehement about it.'

Sir Kenneth tossed down his papers. 'With great respect, me lord, there is every need to be vehement. It is my duty. My client is fighting for his life. The witness has done his "public duty", and I now propose to do mine.'

'And I am sure you are doing it with great eloquence, Sir Kenneth,' smiled the judge, conciliatory and persuasive; 'but I will not have the witnesses upset.'

Sir Kenneth bowed. 'If your lordship pleases.' He picked up the papers again, and left his lordship victor – technically, anyhow. He addressed himself again to Dr Waterhall, in a voice smooth and friendly and pleasant, as if there had never been a trace of ill-feeling between them. 'Now, Doctor, as far as I can understand you, you say that these two facts, that Mrs Presset was twice ill with certain symptoms, and that between the first and second ills her husband weeded his garden, justified you in going to Scotland Yard?'

'No – that, and the fact that immediately after her death, he was associating with his mistress.'

'Associating with his mistress. Very well. *Very* well,' sang Sir Kenneth, dangerously obliging. 'Be it so. Be it so. Associating with his mistress. But unfortunately in this wicked world there are many men with a mistress as well as a wife, and you say that if the wife dies of gastric trouble, and the husband cares for his garden and does not cast off his mistress, it is a case for Scotland Yard?'

'But I was proved right! The poison was found.'

'Please keep to the question. What right have you to say, sir, that because poison was found in the body, you were proved right in your suggestion that her husband put it there? That is for the jury alone to say, sir, as me lord will tell you; and I suspect that a jury of intelligent men will not jump so easily, so glibly to such a damning conclusion. You say that these two facts justified you in going to the Yard?'

Dr Waterhall did not answer. How could he?

'Please answer. I want you to help me about this. There must have been sufficient justification, or manifestly your sense of public duty would not have allowed you to take such a step. Is that not so?'

'I – er – I thought there was a case for inquiry.'

'Quite so – and at this rate, Scotland Yard will be kept very busy. Now, is it true to say that before your suspicion developed – and – er – your sense of public duty – you had quarrelled with Mr Presset?'

'Yes.'

'It is so, is it not, that he had called you "a second class brain"?'

There was laughter at this – laughter that, to a conceited man, sounded like delighted endorsement. Dr Waterhall flushed angrily. 'Yes.'

'With the result that you were no longer on speaking terms?' (More laughter.)

'We had quarrelled, certainly.'

'And you felt vindictive against him?'

'No, certainly not.'

'Oh, come, sir. *I* should be. Come, come, Doctor, you have sworn to speak the whole truth. Do you seriously tell me lord and the jury that you felt no vindictiveness against Mr Presset after he had called you a second-class brain?'

'I felt annoyed with him, certainly.'

'Annoyed. Very well. Very well. Be it so,' sang Sir Kenneth again. 'Just one or two more matters. One or two only. You are a bachelor, I think?'

'Yes.'

'And you have many friends?'

'I think so.'

'And you like, when the day's work is done, to put on your hat and wander round, have a chat with them and bring them the day's news?'

'Perhaps.'

'And is it so that you went round retailing your suspicion to all your friends? You do not, I suppose, deny that?'

'I may have discussed it with them.'

'May have! Do you not remember?'

'I think I did discuss it with a good many people. Yes.'

'And was this after your quarrel with Mr Presset or before?'

'After.'

'Immediately after?'

'It may have been immediately after, but may I point out that the suspicion was hinted to me before I passed it on – er – discussed it with anyone else.'

'Quite so. Quite so. But you, if I may so put it, thereupon promptly delivered it?'

'I don't know what you mean.'

'My dear sir, where is the difficulty? I make myself clear, do I not? You immediately delivered this suspicion that had been handed to you, and you added to it your new suspicion about the first illness. You delivered this information to everybody. Perhaps I can make my question clearer by asking this: are you known in your neighbourhood as "the postman"?'

'Most certainly not! I' – but Dr Waterhall, red with wrath, his ears burning with the laugh of a crowded court, could speak no more.

Sir Hayman had risen to protest, but on the judge saying sorrowfully, 'Really, Sir Kenneth!' he sat down again, as if to leave the matter to his lordship.

'But I am instructed to that effect,' objected Sir Kenneth, innocently.

'I cannot see what is gained by such a question.'

'With great respect, me lord, if you will permit me to continue, the gain will emerge.'

'Continue by all means, but I will not have the witness unfairly attacked.'

Sir Kenneth bowed. 'I apologise, me lord. The fault is mine entirely. I am grateful to your lordship for these frequent corrections. I would only point out – with great respect – that I do not know if your lordship, in your distinguished career, has been called upon to defend a man on a charge of murder and to feel that his life depends on your success or failure. I have had some little experience of such advocacy, and I have always understood that it is legitimate for the defence to suggest that the accused has been the subject of cruel and unfair suspicion. Here is a man who has been most cruelly attacked and condemned by public opinion before ever—'

The judge's eyes twinkled. 'If you have finished addressing me, Sir Kenneth, I will repeat my insistence that you treat the witness fairly.'

Sir Kenneth threw down his papers. 'Very well. Be it so. If I am not allowed to conduct the cross-examination of a most important witness in the way that seems best to me, I will continue it no farther. I bow to your lordship's ruling. No doubt I shall have an opportunity of expressing to the jury my view of this witness later.' And he bowed to the judge, to the jury, to Sir Hayman at his side – very emphatically to Sir Hayman at his side – and sat down, well satisfied that he had achieved the whole of his design. He leaned back, lifted his wig, and settled it more comfortably on his head. Crossing his legs, he removed his spectacles and beat them patiently on the documents before him.

Sir Hayman saw what his adversary had achieved, and his wrath far exceeded that of the judge, because the judge was not fighting to win. To be cheated of his prize by such methods! To have *his* witness treated like this! A friend of Eddy's out of court, he at this moment hated him. But it was part of his studied 'character' to show no emotion – rather, to slay his adversary by its absence – and very coldly he asked Dr Waterhall those few questions which would rehabilitate him, as far as possible, in the eyes of the jury. But it was a hopeless task, and he did not pursue it long. Instead his mind was playing with those barbed phrases with which he would attack Eddy's methods in his closing speech. He let Dr Waterhall go.

And that gentleman went from the box, red, palpitating, muttering, contemplating letters to the papers and questions in Parliament. He tried to walk right out of the court, but a policeman sent him to the seats at the back. He went as far back as he could. He could not endure the eyes of the people, and wanted to be alone with his fury. So far from having made an honourable name for himself, he had been pilloried, and his pillorying would be broadcast to the world. The injustice of it! The only thanks he had got for his public spirit was to be made a cockshy. He hoped that Presset would hang. The vainer the man the greater the torment when his self-love is wounded. After Paul, perhaps the most miserable man in England that day was Dr Waterhall.

'Chief Inspector Boltro.'

Inspector Boltro gave his evidence with the soldierly smartness of all police witnesses. He flattered himself that he would not crumple up as the doctor had done. Nor did he. Sir Hayman thought him a conceited fellow but had no intention of revealing him in anything but the best light to the jury; Sir Kenneth sought evidence only of Presset's orderliness and helpfulness since his arrest, which Boltro, the victor, was most pleased to give, secretly thinking himself a generous and sportsmanlike figure. And when Sir Kenneth said 'Thank you, Inspector; I'm much obliged to you'; and Sir Hayman indicated that he would not re-examine, Boltro stepped from the box in a very good conceit with himself, and with an eye on the reporters. Let us be glad that this history contains the unmitigated triumph of at least one man.

After Boltro some of the interest went from the trial, as in a play that is sagging. The tedious evidence of the experts quickly bewildered the jury and left the judge more fogged than it was his business to admit. Very soon in the course of it members of the audience yawned, jurymen examined their finger-nails, reporters sat back inactive, the young barristers filed from the court, and the judge's eyes undoubtedly closed for a brief minute. Paul, looking down from his ledge on to the solid block of the 'defence' – barristers, solicitors, solicitor's clerks, specialists, with their piles of papers, plans and books before them – saw suddenly a gleam of beauty in this phalanx of grey-haired and substantial men fighting inch by inch and line by line for him, one of the world's failures. His last friends this side of the condemned cell. It was a gleam of human decency and justice, an earnest of man's high destiny, in that hot and headachy court. For the court was now heavy with the breath and smell of crowded human bodies. Women, he noticed, were fanning their faces or rubbing their brows with cubes of menthol drawn from their handbags. Men exhaled heavily and sat forward in attitudes relaxed and hunched. And the evidence of the experts dragged on.

Then, somewhat unexpectedly, after the last of the experts had gone, Sir Hayman said, 'That is the case for the crown, my lord'; and the court came astir again. The people stopped yawning, the jurymen rustled in their box, the judge took new paper and pretended he had not missed a word, and the young barristers came hurrying back to hear Ken Eddy's opening speech. But almost before all this had happened, almost before Sir Hayman's voice had died away, Sir Kenneth had jumped up with alacrity and enthusiasm, as if there were really no case to fight and the contest was as good as over and the victory won. Indeed, he was saying as much to the jury. Here and now, said he, and before a single witness was called for the defence, he contended that the prosecution, though conducted with the conspicuous ability (and, if he might say so, the well-known fairness) of his learned friend, had entirely failed to *prove* that it was the prisoner's hand which had administered the poison. There was doubt – doubt at every point – and if there was one trace of reasonable doubt in their minds, he was entitled to a verdict of 'not guilty'. Not for him to prove the innocence of any man – that was the proud boast of English law – it was the onus of the prosecution to establish his guilt. And this, in his submission, they had signally failed to do. Point by point he emphasised the doubt, and then, abruptly, triumphantly, surprisingly, after a speech of less than thirty minutes, he put his spectacles on to his nose, touched them into position, and said, 'Me lord, I call the prisoner.'

Some of the young barristers who loved superlatives declared that it was a 'master stroke'. It suggested, 'Why should I weary you with a long speech? I have but to call the prisoner, and the case is answered.' Others, more cynical, said, 'Ken's going to keep his ammunition to the end,' or 'He hasn't enough to fill two speeches, so he turns even that to his advantage'; and they stood there, waiting to see what would happen now.

Chapter Seven

It was late afternoon when Paul went into the witness-box, and he was there for the rest of that day and most of the next. He followed a warder through the side door of the dock and along a gangway in front of the jury box and stepped up into the witness-box and faced the throng. His heart might be thudding, but his resolve to speak in a quiet voice and show no fear was master. It made him throw back his shoulders, moisten his lips, rest his hands upon the ledge of the box, and then, observing their vibration, withdraw them behind his back so that he stood like a private soldier 'at ease'. Since his counsel's speech he had felt almost hopeful.

With gentle and courteous questions, as though to a man much wronged, Sir Kenneth drew from him the story of his life with Elinor. These quarrels, did he admit them? 'Yes. Sometimes. And no doubt the fault was largely mine.' Quite so, quite so, nodded Sir Kenneth, most approvingly. And the medicines, was it so that she – but Sir Kenneth corrected himself from 'leading' – what had he to say about them? 'She certainly took patent medicines . . . sometimes.' And why, Mr Presset, did the doctor not know of it? 'Because she concealed it from him, thinking he wouldn't approve.' Exactly, exactly, nobody could be more pleased with this simple answer than Sir Kenneth. And his association with Miss Bawne, did he admit all that had been alleged? 'Yes. Absolutely. But any sin there may have been is mine.' Sir Kenneth nodded many times, understandingly, compassionately. And did he admit the visits to the hotels? 'Yes. All of them.' This first illness: it had been plainly suggested that he was poisoning her then: did he, in fact, do so? 'Most certainly not!' – and oh! the relief of being able to speak the truth with conviction.

'Before that illness, had you bought any weed-killer?'

'No.'

'When did you buy any?'

'Never.'

'How did it come into your possession?'

'Quite unsolicited.'

Exactly, exactly. Defending counsel did a lot of this musing between his questions; with his eyes staring into his own thoughts before him, and his hands clasped – or 'washing each other' – in front of his watch-chain. That burying of the tin, would he please tell me lord and the jury, in his own words, why he did this strange thing. Because, said Paul, he had told Inspector Boltro that he had thrown it away, and then, finding it immediately afterwards, was afraid to put it in the dust-bin. Exactly, *exactly*. (What simpler?) And his flight, what had he to say about that? He admitted every word of it. But why – *why* did he fly? 'Because I was frightened of being arrested and being unable to prove my innocence.'

'But, Mr Presset, you didn't know, when you fled, that they had found arsenic in the body?'

'No, sir. But I think I believed they had found something. I thought the medicines might have contained something, or even the weed-killer since it had been left lying about. The rumour was all over the place that they had found it, and everybody was turning their faces from me. And I remembered a conversation at the school that they always did find something and it was usually impossible to prove one's innocence.'

'I quite see; I quite see,' commented Sir Kenneth, most sympathetically; and turning sharply to him, he came to the great question: did he, in fact, poison his wife? And Paul, steeled for the lie, spoke it in a firm voice, 'I did not.'

'And you are now ready to answer any and all questions that my learned friend may want to ask you?'

'I am ready.' But he spoiled it by adding, with the overstatement of the insecure, 'Absolutely ready.'

Sir Kenneth sat down and put his hands in his trouser pockets with the air of a man who has won his case. He crossed his legs and leaned back to watch the duel between his client and his learned friend, as if there were nothing left now but to enjoy the consolidation of the victory.

Sir Hayman got slowly to his feet; while Paul, his hands behind his back, grasped a wrist tightly, to stay any trembling. If this was to be his last appearance before the world, let it have dignity; let Myra read that he showed courage. And, as Sir Hayman arranged his papers, all remarked the contrast between the tall, imperturbable advocate, and the little, staring, weak-chinned man. Conscious success faced conscious failure; a man from the top of the world faced a man who had plunged to the bottom.

Sir Hayman's first questions were plainly intended to suggest that Paul had got rid of his maid so as to have an empty home in which to murder his wife. 'You persist that it was your wife's idea that the maid should go, on the score of economy?'

'Certainly.'

'H'm. . . . Do you suggest that your wife was a mean woman?'

Paul hesitated. 'No.' Sir Hayman raised an eyebrow and let that be his comment; and Paul, angered by the unfairness, added 'My wife is dead, and I do not wish to say anything against her.'

'I see. But if you had not needed money for the support of your mistress, surely you could have afforded domestic help for your wife?'

Paul stared. 'I didn't support Miss Bawne. I only helped her.'

'I see. How did you account to your wife for the money you were spending?'

'I – I'm afraid I invented excuses.'

'Lies?'

'I suppose so.' Then, defiantly: 'Yes, lies.'

'H'm,' muttered Sir Hayman.

'I was in a very difficult position,' pleaded Paul.

'You certainly were. . . . And you did not wish your wife to die?'

'Pardon? . . . No. . . . No, certainly not.'

Perceiving the hesitation, Sir Hayman pushed the advantage home 'You mean you wished your unhappy home life to continue and all chance of happiness with your mistress to be lost?'

Paul hesitated again, unable to cope with this. 'I did not want her to die,' he replied weakly.

'Wouldn't the noblest thing have been to break with your mistress and to use the money you gave her in providing help for your sick wife?'

'I – I suppose it would have been.' And he added, more brightly, 'I did that later.'

'After she had found out and insisted on it?'

'No, no. It was *before* she found out.'

'But when she did find out, you promised never to see Miss Bawne again, and broke your promise?'

Paul saw that his foil had been turned. 'Yes,' he allowed. 'That is so.'

So they fenced; Sir Hayman winning point by point, because he was at ease and happy, and his mind worked well; Paul losing, because his brain was disorganized by nervousness, insecurity and anger. Sir Hayman was interpreting a hundred things in his life so unfairly. Any stick seemed good enough to beat him with – and it wasn't fair. But keep dignity, keep control, keep the steady eyes and the firm voice that belied the shaking heart. . . . The reporters were looking up at him and taking notes.

Sir Hayman made great play with the weed-killer tin. Of what was he frightened when he buried it after the Inspector's visit? It was just possible, suggested Paul, that some accident *might* have occurred with it. 'What sort of accident?' He could not say. 'But hadn't you the slightest idea what the accident might be?' His wife might have been handling it and got some on her fingers. 'What? A few hours before she died?' Paul saw his meaning. 'You seem to forget that I knew nothing about the time arsenic took to work.' It was a point to Paul; Sir Kenneth Eddy, moving this way and that on his seat, and talking to the solicitor and his nearest junior, and nodding vigorously, saw to it that the jury realized the point; Sir Hayman perceived that Paul had scored, and he was annoyed: one doesn't like to be pricked by one's inferior; and he hastened to counter it. 'I am forgetting nothing, Mr Presset. I was about to ask you, do you really ask the jury to believe that you imagined a poison like arsenic could lie in the body for days without working?'

'I don't think I gave it any thought.'

'And yet you were thinking hard enough when you buried the tin?'

'I don't think I was thinking at all. I was just terrified.'

'Oh, come, Mr Presset. You had no reason then to fear that she would be exhumed?'

'But I *wanted* her to be exhumed. I *asked* them to exhume her. I wanted to be cleared.'

'Then why bury the tin?'

'Pardon?' began Paul, frightened lest he had made a slip, and trying to gain time.

'One minute you say that you thought there might have been an accident with the poison, and the next you say that you wanted her exhumed in order that the world might see there was no poison in her.'

'I thought there might have been an accident – yes.'

'Then were you lying when you told the police Inspector that you wanted her exhumed?'

Paul felt trapped, and could not quite see how: his brain was whirling and he could see nothing clearly. He did not see that a simple answer would have been, 'But I did not find the tin and think of an accident until *after* the Inspector's visit.'

'I – I believed that innocent men had been hanged on less evidence than they could scrape up against me – and I still believe it!' he said angrily.

'That is a dubious compliment to my lord and the jury,' smiled Sir Hayman; and gave himself another point.

So round and round the weed-killer tin, till all hearers were confused where they had got to, and knew only that Presset 'was getting himself badly tied up'.

Then to the flight. Where had he heard these rumours that they had found arsenic in the body? Silence. 'Who would be likely to mention them to *you*?' He couldn't remember. 'But didn't you say that no one was speaking to you at the time?' That was so – more or less. 'Then surely you can remember some one isolated person who told you?' Paul pretended to think, and lied, Yes, he remembered overhearing talk in a public house. 'What public house?' The 'Maid's Head'. 'Where was that?' In the Caledonian Road, quite near his home. 'Were you then sitting in a public house while the whole neighbourhood was talking about you?'

Oh, trapped again. His heart sickened and sank. He stammered, 'Pardon? . . . Yes, I did go in once. Yes. . . . I went in to see how they would receive me.'

'And they actually discussed you in your presence?'

His brain worked desperately. 'They did not see me at once. They were talking about me as I came in. Everybody was talking about me at that time.'

Sir Hayman spread a hand as much as to say, 'How can one deal with a man who piles lie upon lie?' and worried the topic no more. He came to Paul's words in the police court proceedings, 'Miss Bawne knew nothing about anything.' Knew nothing about what?

'Anything.'

'You had told her, I suppose, that your fear of arrest was your reason for flight?'

'Yes.'

'She knew there was a warrant out?'

'Yes.'

'She knew later that there was arsenic found in the body?'

'Yes.'

Sir Hayman lifted his voice angrily. 'Well, what was the thing she did not know?'

Paul shrugged his shoulders. He was able to deal with this question confidently. The conviction of rightness here, the sweet feeling of goodness after all his lies, gave him security and power. Everyone noticed the change from the culprit, trapped and twisting, to the lover, simple and secure.

'It is difficult to know what one's words mean. I think at the time I was thinking that the evidence was pretty black against me, and that if everybody believed that I had murdered my wife, nobody should believe anything of Miss Bawne. Nobody should think that she was a party to it, or knew anything about it. She knew nothing about my secret thoughts, my lies, my stupid and cowardly actions. And I think I was thinking that if they used these words against me, they must, in fairness, use them in favour of her.'

Sir Hayman realised that Paul, by the simple dignity of this statement, had swung the whole court round to a sympathy with him – a sympathy that ever after hung around the name of Presset, together with the infamy. Thoroughly sentimental at the bottom, as all these people are who play the stern, cold 'strong man', Sir Hayman was not without a sympathy for him himself. But sentiment must not impede justice, and he went on, 'I suggest that they are strange words to use, "nothing about anything"?'

'But what else could I say? If I said simply "Miss Bawne is absolutely innocent," it was equally incriminating for me. I fully believed that things would go badly for me – as they have – and I had to say something.'

Something like a sigh of pity went round the court. It annoyed Sir Hayman. At this rate the watery sentimentality of audiences and juries would dissolve his majestic case to nothing. Justice must be protected against pity. Like some other advocates he was fond of saying with a laugh, 'One must know when to stop cross-examining on a certain point, for fear of eliciting unwanted answers'; and did not perceive that, to a plain man, this suggested playing for one's side instead of playing for truth. He fumbled among his papers for the question he had kept to the last, as the most damaging against the prisoner.

'I see. Now I want to go back to one or two questions I omitted to ask earlier. You say that it might have been some accident that killed your wife – something in the medicines she took or some handling of the weed-killer. Did you, at the time of your wife's death, make any such suggestion to the doctor?'

'No, I don't think so.'

'Did you say anything that might cause him to examine the bottles?'

'No. . . . No, I hadn't thought of it then.'

'Have you ever mentioned it to him since then?'

'No.'

'To any living soul – ever?'

'No – er – at least—'

'Not till there was a warrant out for your arrest?'

'No. . . . I suppose not. . . .' Hope was flying away from Paul again; though he felt there was some simple answer to these questions that his terrified brain would remember when he was back in the dock.

'You say you decided on flight directly you heard the rumour of poison having been found: will you explain why, long before that, long before the exhumation even, you were realising your assets and accumulating money in a portable form, foreign bonds and gold?'

Paul had forgotten the possibility of this question, and shook beneath it.

'I – I thought from the first that flight might be necessary.'

'From the *first*? What do you mean by that?'

'From the moment Inspector Boltro called on me.'

'What? Before there was anything more than a vague suspicion?'

Paul stared, and struggled for an answer. 'Yes. . . . Yes, there was suspicion enough: Miss Bawne, and the weed-killer, and – and—'

'And what?'

His brain refused to work. He stared and gave no answer. 'That is all,' said Sir Hayman, 'Thank you.'

Without a trace of hope left, Paul turned to go; but the warder touched him to show that his counsel had risen to re-examine. 'Oh, yes,' he acknowledged. 'Thank you.'

There were not many questions in the re-examination, and he answered them as well as he could, but without hope. He bowed to the judge, left the witness-box, and walked through the people, erect. But that lifted head and still face hid a dull certainty that this was his last walk before the world. And the door of the dock shut on him with a bang.

Chapter Eight

The last stages of the Presset trial were remarkable only for the speech of Sir Kenneth Eddy. Interest remained only in this. The case had gone plainly against the prisoner; and the closing speech for the prosecution, and the judge's charge to the jury, could be little more than re-statements of fact and statements of law. But Ken Eddy – what would he say. How would he, redoubtable little fighter, strive to extricate his client?

He jumped up, his mien confident as ever. There was even a smile at his lips, a rather insolent smile, as though the fewest possible words from him would suffice to show how ridiculous was the whole case against Mr Presset. It was not the plucky, swaggering rise of a boxer from his corner, who has taken cruel punishment and must soon take the final count; it was the rise of the gentleman from the opposite corner, confident, smiling, unshaken, ready to give the knock-out in this very round. He lifted the little wig an inch, and re-set it on his head. He put on the tortoise-shell spectacles enthusiastically, and began.

His opening was more sensational than sensible. He attacked the audience who, day after day, had sat there to gloat upon the sufferings of this poor man, and the distinguished writers especially employed by the newspapers to convey these sufferings in the most attractive form to the outer world, and sell them in the market place. If these people, 'whom some of us must surely despise', expected any eloquence or sensational copy from him, they would be disappointed.

And, with this exordium, he gave them ninety minutes of astounding eloquence and superb copy.

The last piece of evidence had been given, the last word spoken in the box; and dare any man say that the prosecution had *proved* that the prisoner had played any part whatsoever in bringing about his wife's death. Not for the prisoner, he repeated – not for the prisoner, under an English sky, to say how, among the thousand changes and chances of this mortal life, poison had got into his wife's body. It was to his honour that he had refused to accept the possibility of suicide as a defence. He had told his legal advisers that he did not – *could* not – believe this of her, and, now that she was dead, he would not allow anything to besmirch her memory.

'He admits all that the prosecution contend – every word of it – they are beating the air – save only' – and he beat his fingers on the desk – 'that he was guilty of the inconceivable crime of dismissing his wife from the world. And every scrap of the evidence is consistent with his story. He admits that he had been deceitful, mendacious, immoral, and cowardly. But neither deceit, nor mendacity, nor cowardice, nor immorality even, are crimes in law; and we are not trying him for them. The policeman cannot arrest us for lies; my friend, the Clerk of Arraigns, cannot arraign us for timidity and terror; me lord himself cannot sentence us to imprisonment for fornication or adultery. These things are between ourselves and God. We are trying him on no other count whatsoever than deliberate and intentional murder. He has, on his own admission, done many things whose publication to an interested world must have been torment far in excess of the punishment they deserved, however wrong; but how true they seem, how perfectly "in character"; how consistently they fit into the story he has told!

'The lies and deceit? Well, members of the jury, he is not the first man to have had a mistress and to be involved thereby in mendacity and chicanery. Gentlemen – *gentlemen* – will you say of yourselves that you have never been guilty of something underhand, and been deceitful and lied about it. I think not. I will not say it of myself. The immorality? Far be it from me to excuse it; I will not justify it, but I *will* pity him. I *will* suggest that he is not the first man who, hungry, lonely, unloved, and unsatisfied, has turned aside from the straight path to find somewhere, if possible, a little sweetness and love. The cowardice? You and I, gentlemen, in our comfortable security, may find it difficult to imagine the cowardice that led to a flight as foolish as it was futile. Please, *please* hearken to me on this point very carefully, for this poor man's sake, for your own sake, for your oath's sake. *Put yourself in his place.* It seems to him that, by a sinister combination of circumstances, enough suspicion, enough evidence even, has gathered around him to justify an arrest. Arrest on such a charge is the end of everything, *even though he be acquitted*! Oh, I know that you and I, comfortable and unthreatened, are tempted to say glibly, "he should have stayed like a man and faced the fire." But which of you does not know that, if he were wrongfully charged with murder and then acquitted, not only would he have spent torturing months in prison, not only would his life's savings be gone in establishing his innocence and himself be left a beggar, but his whole future would be laid waste before him? Which of you might not, in your anger and indignation, as well as in your fear, say "I am not staying for this. Why should I? I am going to preserve my little capital from this unwarrantable attack. I am not going to spend months in prison for anybody. I am going while the going is good. I will escape into a foreign land with my little property, and there, under an assumed name, enjoy what happiness I can with the woman I love"?

'Gentlemen, to me it is all so intelligible; it is all so consistent – the hand that gathered in terror his money about him, and the hand that buried in terror the weed-killer tin. Consider what he must have felt when he found that ghastly tin, so soon after Inspector Boltro had visited him and inquired about it and he, all unwittingly, had told an untruth about it? It must have seemed that the gods themselves were making a mock of him. In an agony of confusion, despair and dismay, he puts the new piece of evidence far out of sight and makes ready to fly.

'Gentlemen, he pleads guilty to terror; but, if there were a court in this land where such an offence could be tried, I can imagine a verdict of "justifiable terror" or, at least, a strong recommendation to mercy.

'He has frankly told us of his lies, his irregular life and his cowardice. He has spoken of his irascibility. It has been for others – and they witnesses for the prosecution – to tell us of his kindness, consideration, and amiability. One after another as I questioned them, they testified to his unvarying gentleness, mounting to a climax when a little maid, moved beyond endurance by the sight of him whom she had known and loved sitting there in a dock accused of so incredible a crime, was guilty of the impropriety – for which me lord and you all forgave her – of crying out, "He never done it! He never done it!" In different and better phrasing perhaps, but with less power to move you, I am restating her claim. I say it is not consistent with the gentle character, to which all have testified, that he should have done so monstrous a thing. There is a terrible inconsistence in the prosecution's case; and all the consistence is in the story of the accused.'

And, having taken the evidence point by point, and emphasised its perfect consistence with the prisoner's story or the element of doubt that, in this view, invalidated it, he paused, he faced the jury squarely, he gazed at them for a long ten seconds, forcing by this silence an expectant stillness on the court, he removed the spectacles and abandoned them to the desk, he put his hands on his hips and in a voice very low but very distinct, began, 'Gentlemen, I ask you to look at the accused. Look. Imprint his figure on your mind, and all his story. Remember that on your verdict his life depends. There sits a man who has suffered unbearable things for offences of which we all, if we are honest, are sometimes guilty. Whatever your verdict, he will suffer now to the end of his days. He is irretrievably ruined. On the brink of old age he will have to begin life anew, and he will be fortunate if fingers do not point at him and faces turn from him, in this Christian world, till he goes before One who will not turn from any man, however sinful, nor speak the unkind word. Will you now send him from here to freedom and such peace, such quiet, such healing as may still be possible for him; or will you send him to a locked box where he will be reserved and preserved for a ghastly death in twenty days? If there is a flicker of doubt in your minds, which of you will be able to bear the thought of that cold slaughter three weeks hence? Gentlemen – gentle and understanding men – the responsibility of a dread decision is yours.'

Sir Kenneth dropped down to his seat, for the first time exhausted, white and shaking. His junior expressed his congratulation by a pat on the shoulder. The audience was silent, thrilled, confused, as if the pattern of things had been changed. Standing by the dock, a young and flippant barrister whispered to his neighbour, 'Christ! I believe he's saved him!'

Slowly Sir Hayman rose. He was angry, but his face showed nothing. Emotion and slush! Maudlin sentimentality! By heaven, he wasn't going to be robbed of the game, and the only fair verdict, by methods like these, and after he had held all the trumps! His tactics were to erase the memory of that speech. He must be slow and quiet and prolonged, so that it went back and back into the past. By coldness, by quiet, by a weariness even, he would show that the case was so obvious as to need no eloquence from him. 'My learned friend has pleaded inconsistency. But it is a commonplace, I have always imagined that this so-called inconsistence has appeared in every convicted poisoner. Always we have heard that, in their private life, they have manifested a gentleness and a piety even.

Besides, on his own admission, the prisoner has led a life of chronic deceit such as now leaves his friends bewildered. None of them at first found it "consistent" with his character that he should be cohabitating with a mistress. And throughout this trial, in dock and in witness-box, this so-called gentle, weak, and terrified man has manifested an iron calm, an astonishing self-control, a power to hide his feeling from all' – oh, the unfairness of it, thought Paul: thus they turned his one nobility against him! 'His manner in the dock must either imply an insensitiveness or a capacity to present to the world what face he will. If he is capable, as the prosecution has suggested, of coldly planning the death of his wife, he is surely also capable of hiding his guilty thoughts beneath a gentle manner even as, in the view of the prosecution, he hid his weapon beneath the earth of the garden—'

'Old Hayman wins, I think,' whispered the flippant barrister by the dock's side.

'Yes, no one'll hang him as high as Hayman,' jested his friend.

'Sh!' warned the other.

In level accents Sir Hayman's words were falling on the silence. 'Counsel for the defence has again and again worked on your feelings by reminding you that this is a case of life and death. I agree; but of more than one death. A weak and ailing woman has her appeal to your pity. You are gentle and understanding men, he says – rightly, I am sure; and therefore, before your pitying and angry eyes there appears the figure of a woman, lying dead and done for, sent from the sunlight and from the enjoyment of her many friends, a white and pitiable figure, surely, lying on the bed of her agony, in a house where no one was present except the man whom she was trusting to care for her. There is no more vivacity in that white face; the light has gone out in the dulled eyes. Who extinguished it? Who had anything to gain by extinguishing it—?'

'Yes, old Hayman wins,' murmured the barrister.

'I submit to you, gentlemen, that it could have been no other than the accused. I suggest that the evidence is convincing and capable of no other interpretation. Let us glance at it once more.' And, twisting a piece of tape that had come from some of the documents, he, in his turn, went through the evidence, but grimly and unemotionally. 'If, after hearing all this, you have any reasonable doubt left, then of course it is your duty to acquit the accused, and I am happy to stand by my learned friend in urging you to this; but if you can feel no reasonable doubt at all, then you have but one duty – as you are understanding, as you are gentle – to bring in a verdict of "Guilty". You are asked to think, in my friend's eloquence, that the life of this man is on your shoulders. Maybe; but English Justice is also there. It is bound to your shoulders by the bands of your oath. And you must not fail it. You alone uphold it now, or let it fall. In considering this man, let not pity derange and confuse you. Consider also the victim and all those who cry for protection. Consider not only 'that morning of cold slaughter', as my friend has described it, but other slaughters that may result if men think that murderers can go free. Remember that you are the wall, the dyke, against the waters of crime which are ever ready to flow in and engulf the land, if you, the defenders, grow soft and weaken. Remember that, and be content with nothing less, and nothing more, than your stern duty.'

And Sir Hayman, no more heated than when he rose, sat down and folded his arms, as if there were nothing now but to wait for this duty to be done.

All faces turned to the judge, to learn, if possible, in which scale his Charge to the Jury would fall. He began with a suave rebuke to Sir Kenneth. 'In the opening of his supremely eloquent speech – and we must all be glad, to feel that the prisoner has had the advantage of some of the ablest brains in the land – he was guilty, I think, of a somewhat dangerous attack on the members of the public and on certain distinguished writers who had been retained by the Press to describe this trial. I must record my view that the public has every right to be here, for it is an established principle of English justice that it is open and public – else what is the public gallery for? – and that it is highly improper to suggest that they have come to gloat over the sufferings of the prisoners. It may well be that they think, with other sane and healthy-minded men, that the working of the laws of their land is a matter for their interest and study. The laws, after all, are their laws, not solely mine and Sir Kenneth's. And as to the distinguished writers retained by the Press, I must suggest that they are here in the way of their profession and in the discharge of their duty, precisely as Sir Kenneth is here; and that, if they are, in his words, "selling their copy in the market-place", well, unless all that I have heard is untrue, Sir Kenneth's earnest and eloquent labours in these courts do not often go unremunerated.'

This pleasant sally at Sir Kenneth drew a general laugh – and with that laugh – though the judge would have been the last to wish this – went a little more of Paul's chance of life.

This matter disposed of, he came to the main business of his summing up; and its first words hinted that it would go against the prisoner.

'Counsel for the defence has made an appeal to your pity. He has asked if you will care to have the life of this man on your consciences. Now, while fully admiring the fine qualities of heart that have prompted this appeal, I must ask you to put it from your minds. Be very clear that the question as to what follows upon your verdict – whatever punishment or whatever release – is *not* your responsibility in your character as jurymen. It is the responsibility of the State. Divest yourselves then of all sense of responsibility for the *consequences* of your verdict. Then alone can your minds be clear for the discharge of your solemn duty, which is to be loyal to your oath and to give a true verdict according to the evidence. In this hour, as jurymen, you have no other responsibility whatever—'

'That's pricked old Eddy's bladder,' whispered the flippant young barrister.

'I'm afraid so,' said the other.

'Afraid? Why afraid? The lad did it all right.'

'Sh!'

The judge's voice went on, calmly weighing every part of the evidence, and with perfect fairness suggesting in which scale it lay – but the pile in the scale of death was mounting and mounting. He spoke for an hour, and then quietly finished and rose and left the court.

'Well, that's the whole packet,' laughed the young barrister signficantly, as the jury retired through their door and the silence was shattered into a hundred chattering voices. 'I'll give you five to one it's "Guilty".'

And in the waiting-room below Paul sat with legs crossed and eyes gazing into emptiness, while the two warders said nothing or spoke in low voices, with the respect of coarse men, not for guilt but for pain. Paul had no hope, and in the woodenness of his despair he found a dull strength. When free of hope one can stiffen with acceptance: on the rock-bottom one can stand erect. His chief thought was what to do when he heard his sentence: stand erect and flinch not – be seen as a man the last time the world looked on him. Say nothing? No. 'He nothing common did, nor mean, Upon that memorable scene. . . .' 'Nothing, my lord,' with fearless eyes. Yes, there was always a faint pleasure in this resolve.

Lifting his eyes, he saw the skylight of the waiting-room. Light! In twenty days he would see it no more. Myra. He would never see her again, after twenty days . . . unless people did meet again beyond the grave; but she would be an old woman before she died, and how, and in what guise, did people meet? And if there were nothing but extinction for everybody? . . . He passed a little while stringing loving and heroic phrases of farewell.

The doctor from the prison entered. 'Well, feeling all right, old son?' he asked with much pity. (Paul had learned now that, the nearer men stood to the prisoner, the greater the understanding and pity.)

'Yes, perfectly, thank you.'

'That's good. . . . Well, good luck. . . .'

'Thank you.'

'Yes . . .' murmured the doctor; and, defeated, he drifted out.

And Paul went back to the subjects of his thoughts: his deportment in the dock for his last two minutes . . . the passing of the minutes and life with them . . . the words of his letter to Myra: 'It has gone against me as I feared, and the only thing is to accept it bravely. . . . All that I care about now is that you should have as little pain as possible. . . . Sir Kenneth Eddy was wonderful, and I have nothing but gratitude to him and to all who worked so splendidly for me, but they could not conquer against impossible odds. . . .'

After about an hour there was movement outside, and an officer looked in and murmured something, and his two warders led him out to the passage and to the foot of the stairway to the dock. But either it was a false alarm or they had informed the cells long before the jury actually filed back into their box, because he and his warders stood here for twenty minutes or more, one warder leaning against the wall and the other constantly going up one or two stairs and peeping into the court. Down the shaft of the stairway, Paul could hear the buzz and hum and sibilance of many prattling voices, punctuated at times by coughs, the blowing of a nose, the drumming of feet or hands, or even a suppressed titter. His warders chatted together, or occasionally spoke in friendly tones to him, as, hands in pockets, he stood, first on the right foot, to swing the left across it, and then on the left foot, to swing the right across it, for twenty dragging minutes. Sometimes he sighed. Sometimes he drew the hands from his pockets and fiddled with his fingers or passed a hand over his forehead and hair. Then against a sudden silence there was the noise of many feet crowding from both directions into the court – jury doubtless from one end and counsel and excited young barristers from the other – the jury seemed to be answering to their names, a warder from the top of the stairs said 'Fetch him up', and with his own two warders he went up the treads, bracing his shoulders and straightening his tie. Once more he stood at the front of the dock, with a warder on either side of him.

Except for the charged atmosphere, mute, waiting, and frightened, the court was just as he had left it: judge, jury and people in their place. Only the crowd of young barristers, standing to the right of the dock, was larger than it had ever been. All eyes were on the jury, except those that swung furtively to Paul to see how he faced this moment. The jurymen, embarrassed and strained, gazed ahead of them at no one in particular; and Sir Hayman Drewer seemed to be watching them a little anxiously. Sir Kenneth kept his eyes down. The Clerk of the Court, who was standing, turned towards their foreman. 'Do you find the prisoner – stand up, please, the foreman – guilty or not guilty of wilful murder?'

The foreman, corpulent and grey, drummed his knuckles nervously on the desk.

'Guilty.'

A sigh passed over the people like a sharp shudder of wind in the wheat; and with it all eyes turned to Paul. Though they saw no movement, he had stiffened within his clothes. The word had been like a blow on a dead place; that was all.

A deathly silence; and the Clerk was facing Paul. 'Prisoner at the bar, you stand convicted of the crime of wilful murder; have you anything to say why the Court should not give you judgment of death according to law?'

He lifted his head and said in a clear voice, 'Nothing.'

Immediately, and completely unappreciative of his attitude, damaging it, the Usher cried with rapid perfunctoriness, 'Oyez! Oyez! Oyez!' and commanded all persons to keep silence while sentence of death was passed upon the prisoner at the bar. The judge's marshal put a square of black material on the judge's head – and the untimely thought ran through Paul, 'Oh, is that the black cap? I always imagined it was a kind of skull-cap.' It hung on his wig rather stupidly. A chaplain in a black gown seemed to have appeared from nowhere, and was standing near the judge.

And the judge, still seated while all the rest stood, as if a great Figure had come into the court, said, 'Paul Arthur Presset, after a long and careful investigation of this charge, you have been convicted on indubitable evidence that you poisoned your wife, possessed yourself of her property, and attempted flight from justice. On the ghastly and wicked nature of your crime I will not dwell. I only tell you that you must entertain no expectation or hope that you will escape the consequences of your crime, and I implore you to make your peace with Almighty God. I have now to pass upon you the sentence of the Court which is that you be taken from hence to a lawful prison, and from thence to a place of execution, and that you be there hanged by the neck till you are dead, and that your body—'

His body! Surely, thought Paul, it was cruel to talk to a living man about his lifeless body. Might they not, without loss to justice, have left this out – or did people really prefer old ceremonies to present mercy?

'– your body be buried in the precincts of the prison where you shall have last been confined after your conviction. And may the Lord have mercy on your soul.'

'Amen,' murmured the chaplain with bowed head; and almost before he could realize all that had happened, the warders were guiding him below. Before he could realize his own sentence of death, it was over. He had not even had time to remember his dignified bow to the judge, as he had wished to do. He was going down the stairs to the waiting-room; having done with life. All the people he was seeing as he passed on – warders, policemen, the prison doctor standing in the passage, and the cell officer – and all the people whose voices he could hear – the judge thanking the jury and the crowds filing from the court – and all the people in the dense multitude outside the Old Bailey – all these had their expectation of life and no thought of death. He alone, in twenty days. . . .

PART V

Chapter One

In top hat and black coat, with his ebony stick in his hand, Sir Hayman Drewer walked out of the Old Bailey. He had not gone many steps before the loitering crowd recognised him, raised a cheer, and moved towards him. 'Well done sir!' they shouted. 'Best day's work you've ever done, I reckon! You've put 'im where 'e ought to be, awl right!' Some press photographers ran up and snapped him, holding their cameras near their eyes. Two policemen hurried forward to secure a passage for him, and Sir Hayman passed on, much pleased, though his face showed nothing. He provided the crowd with the cold, impassive figure they wanted to see.

Actually he was aglow within; and he decided to walk part of the way home, so that, after the habit of many orators, he could repeat to himself the more successful portions of his speech. He walked down Ludgate Hill to the Circus, but here he was forced to stop. The policeman on point duty had signed to the cross-wise traffic to move on; and no one for a while could cross the road and enter Fleet Street. Sir Hayman stood on the pavement's edge, waiting his chance.

Before him was a cart with a frightened horse, that tossed its head and reared, while the driver cursed and hit it. In response to the blows the horse did not move but only tossed its head in greater terror. Leaping down from his seat, the driver pulled savagely at the horse's reins, and struck him on the flank with the butt of his whip. 'Come on, will yer!' The animal's eyes started.

A spasm of pity and indignation shot through Sir Hayman.

'Here! Stop that!' he called, and stepped off the kerb, 'Stop that bullying, or I'll give you in charge.'

The driver turned on him sourly. 'You bloody well mind your own business.'

'It *is* my business. It's everybody's business. I don't stand by and see cruelty done to a dumb animal. Perhaps you don't know who I am. . .'

'I don't care if you're Jesus Christ. . . . Come on, you barsted, will yer!'

Instantly Sir Hayman pulled out pencil and note-book, and jotted down the name of the firm that owned the cart. 'I shall lodge a complaint against you with your employers. I think you'll find my name will carry weight.'

Something frightened, for this cove was obviously a swell, the driver tried humour.

'All right, guv'nor! You aren't the King of England, I suppose?'

'Don't add insolence to your other offence.'

But this was too much for a high-spirited Cockney. 'Insolence your arse!' he exclamed. 'Can't a chap defend hisself? Who do you think *you* are?'

'Never mind who I am. You'll soon know that.'

'All right! Get a chap into trouble if you want to. I shall lose me job, and the nippers'll go hungry, but that don't matter. Nah, not a bit. Nah, we like it.'

'You should have thought of that before,' said Sir Hayman. 'I am not going to stand by and see a horse ill-treated. It's un-English, and the sooner you understand that, the better.'

'All right!' shouted the man, mounting angrily to his seat. 'Report me! Report me to the King! 'Atchett's me name. I'll give it to yer! Fred 'Atchett, 15 Staple Street, 'Oxton, see? I ain't going to be bullied by you, not if you're a dook. He reckons he's the Lord Mayor of London,' he explained with a wink to a group of gapers. 'Git on, Steve, git on. Tootaloo, old cock!'

Still showing the cold, unemotional face to the gapers, though within he was boiling – 'old cock!' – he crossed the road and went on towards his home. And soon he had forgotten the horse and its driver, and was thinking only of his triumphs in the court. He paid a brief visit to his chambers, and then took a taxi to his door.

The butler opened. 'Well, I hear you won, sir,' said he, taking hat and stick.

'Yes, we won, Berridge.'

'Well, I reckon he deserved all he got, sir.'

'Not a doubt about it. Her ladyship in?'

'She's in the drawing-room.'

'No one with her?'

'No, Sir Hayman.'

'Right, then. I'll go up.'

Lady Drewer, sitting on a sofa, a slender and gracious figure, gave a gasp of pleased surprise as he entered. 'It's over earlier than I thought. Sit down, you must be tired. Did you do well? Did you do justice to yourself?'

'I don't know.'

'Of course you know. Don't pretend to be modest.'

'Well, the jury were not absent very long.'

'And that means that you were overwhelming, I'm sure.'

'Or the judge was.'

'Pooh! Silly old Hayman. I can always tell when you come home pleased with yourself. . . . There was the usual awful scene, I suppose? I rather wish they'd get rid of that stupid pomposity.'

'It's not pomposity at all, my dear,' corrected Sir Hayman, unperturbed, as became a person quietly conscious of his superior wisdom. 'I think it's rather magnificent. The majesty of the law. . . .'

'I suppose it *is* that?' queried Lady Drewer, dropping her clasped hands thoughtfully to her knees; and then her eyes became mischievous. 'If it's not a lot of boys unconsciously dressing up and playing a pretty grim game? . . . But there! don't think I don't like it sometimes, but not when it's telling a man that he's to be done to death. Not then, somehow. . . .'

Sir Hayman smiled on her with the kindly contemptuousness of the learned.

'It's then that it's more than ever necessary, my dear, to emphasise the sanctity of human life.'

'Oh! . . .' Lady Drewer could have argued this further, but refrained. 'And now what about the girl?'

'She'll get off, I'm afraid. I don't see where we can really *get* her. She's guilty enough, but—' he shrugged, and left it.

'You think so?'

He nodded his head knowingly. '*She* knew all about it; perhaps not before, but certainly after. But I don't see how we can get a conviction. At least, that's how *I* read it,' he added with a wise lift of his eyebrows. 'Who did you say we were having to dinner tonight?'

'The Goodwins and Lord Meldorf and Mabel. . . . How did he take it?'

'Who?'

'Presset.'

'He didn't seem to mind. He never moved a muscle.'

'Let's hope he didn't mind. I must say, I always hope they *are* callous. He'll hang, of course?'

'Oh, he'll hang right enough. Could I have a cup of tea?'

'Yes, it's coming. . . . When – when will it happen?'

'Oh, in about three weeks' time, I suppose.'

'Poor brute – though I don't know – but it's all rather terrible, isn't it? Three weeks' waiting, and then. . . .'

'I'm afraid it won't disturb *my* sleep,' murmured Sir Hayman, settling himself comfortably on the sofa. 'If ever a rat was guilty, he was. And the girl too; though full justice will never be done in her case, I very much fear. Do you know, I think I'll have sherry, not tea, after all.'

With his two warders Paul sat in the waiting-room. He asked them what they waited for; and they told him that the Old Bailey authorities had sent for the prison van that should take him to Gunterbury Gaol; and as they said 'Gunterbury' he remembered hearing it described in South London Gaol as 'a hanging prison'. He sat there, and said nothing, and the two warders respected his silence. Perhaps a half hour dwindled away and then a policeman opened the door and muttered to the warders. They got up.

'It's here,' said one of them to Paul.

So Paul rose too, staring at them as if for information what to do.

And just then two strange warders came into the room. Officers from Gunterbury, no doubt.

'These two gentlemen'll look after you now,' said one of his old warders. 'They have to take you to Gunterbury.'

'I see,' said Paul.

'Well . . . goodbye . . .' and the warder put out his hand.

Paul took it, and the warder said all he could with a strong pressure. That pressure forced up the tears towards Paul's eyes, but he kept them down. 'Goodbye, and thank you for all your kindness.'

'Don't mention it,' said the man awkwardly. 'You're welcome, I'm sure.'

The other warder followed the example of his friend. 'Goodbye, old chap,' he said, pressing Paul's hand hard. 'Never say die. Goodbye, and good luck.'

'Goodbye. Remember me to some of the others at South London.'

'You bet. . . .'

And they turned about uncomfortably and went.

'Well, come along,' said one of the Gunterbury warders, as cheerfully as he could. And they led him to a van waiting in the yard. Paul had time only to see that it was a small motor van, square and blue, before they guided him into it. Within, it was a mere oblong room with a cushioned bench all round and windows above the level of his head, and one behind the driver's back and a very small one in the back of the van. One warder sat himself beside him, and the other in front; the door slammed, and the van moved off. Sitting in that small room with his two big warders, he suddenly remembered that never again in his few weeks of life would he elude the watching of eyes. Eyes. No privacy in the twenty days, even though he must get ready to die. Twenty days – four hundred and eighty hours – how many minutes? – about twenty-eight thousand – and one of them had gone even as he thought – and another – and another – and another. Through the very small window in the back of the van he could get a peep at the streets falling behind. His last view of streets.

Like the warders from South London these two men respected his dazed silence, and did not speak themselves, or, if they spoke to each other, did so in lowered voices.

He felt the van swinging round the corners, halting in a traffic block, then moving ruthlessly on, shedding the world behind it. He felt it run quickly and smoothly in a road where the way was straight and the traffic easy. He wondered if people on the pavements were turning their heads, as he used to do, when he saw a Black Maria pass and considered the unfortunates within. Bending forward on his bench, he could see little but the backs of motor vans, the tail-boards of lorries, and the footboards and steps of buses, with a receding vista of traffic and pavements behind. So the world, as he had known it, fell away from him. The van was slowing, and now through his window he saw the high grey curtain-wall of a prison. In a second they were running alongside it, so that it seemed extraordinarily high, blocking out the world with its cliff of grey brick. The van stopped; the driver's back disappeared from the window; a bell rang; and heavy gates opened. The driver returned to his place, and the van turned and passed through the great gates, which clanged behind it. It halted in the darkness between the outer and the inner gate, and the gatekeeper looked in to speak to one of the warders and gave a quick, interested glance at Paul. Then the inner gate opened, the van went through, and the second gate closed behind it with a heartless bang.

'Well, here we are,' said one of the warders, as the van stopped.

'Yes,' said Paul; and rose obediently.

He got out, and saw the great entrance building towering above him.

A warder opened to them, and they led him into a corridor strikingly empty. At once the powerful associations of smell brought South London prison before him. It was exactly the same smell: scrubbed floors, polished wood, gas, damp cold – something like the smell of a clean cellar. There was the same chill draughtiness as in South London, blowing from long, scrubbed corridors and lofty halls, and the same premature darkness of an old-fashioned and ill-lit building – indeed, one or two dim electric lamps were already burning. They led him into the reception room, and the reception officer studied his committal warrant, entered all the details in a book, took the little bag of his property which the warders of South London had handed over to his new guards, and then said, 'Well, search him.' He was moved behind a screen and told to strip. 'Naked, please.' He stripped naked, and there before the reception officer and the other two was the flaccid and scrawny body for the slaughter shed.

That he might get away with no means of suicide they searched in his hair, felt in his mouth, and fingered his crutch. The doctor came and examined him, eyes, teeth, tongue, chest, abdomen, knees, with especial attention to his heart and lungs, which in a few days they were going to choke and still for ever. Now he supposed that the bath would follow; but no, they sent for prison clothes and told him to get into them. For the first time he drew on the uniform of the convicted: vests and pants which were too large for him and coarsely patched and darned by the unwilling hands of prisoners; socks, black, with red at the top and the toes; a shirt of ill-laundered white with blue stripes; trousers and jacket of pale grey, the trousers so long that he had to turn up half a foot of them. No braces or belt: he had to fix his trousers by straining the first button-hole across his stomach to the brace button. No collar and no tie; boots, but no laces. And lastly, a grey cap like a forage cap. He wondered whether to put the hat on indoors; tentatively he did so, and no one commented. And now he was dressed. Dressed in grotesque garments, and done with the brotherhood of man.

A principal officer appeared; and he and the two warders led him into one of the halls and along its ground floor. Again he saw the galleries above and the spidery stairways to them and the nets stretched from rail to rail to catch the would-be suicides and the great arched window at the end of the hall. The principal officer stopped at a door, selected a key from his bunch, and opened it. The two warders and Paul entered and he saw the condemned cell.

Before he could take it in, the door clicked behind him, so that all three were locked in, with no means of opening the door except by ringing for an officer without.

He looked round on his last home. It was two ordinary cells knocked into one, so that there were two barred windows high up and two doors both now locked. Under the right window he saw a table with three plain wooden chairs about it; under the left a black iron bed like a hospital cot, a strip of matting, and a shelf-like table in the wall. A bell-push was between the two doors. In the side wall on his right, to his surprise, a door stood ajar.

'There's a bathroom and double-u in there,' said one of the warders. 'If you want to use it, let us know, see?'

'I see . . . well, perhaps I will'; and Paul passed in and was about to shut the door when the warder stopped him.

'No, just leave it ajar, old man. You have to do that, you see.'

'Oh . . . I beg your pardon,' stuttered Paul, and obeyed.

While in here he looked about him. It was a third ordinary cell, converted into a bathroom. There was a good bath against the wall, a wash basin next to it, a gas-ring beyond it, and a closet pan in the corner.

Returning to the main cell, he tried to show courage by being facetious. 'Quite a nice little flat,' he said.

'Yes,' said the warder, who seemed relieved that he had spoken at last. 'Not too bad, all said and done. And good company all the time,' he added, to keep up the cheer. 'Me and George for a little, and then the other boys.'

'What other boys?'

'The lads from the other prisons. Six of 'em.'

'How do you mean? I don't quite—'

'It's like this, see. Directly you was – directly they knew the result of the trial, they sent off for a couple of warders from Dartmoor, two from Maidstone, one from Oxford and one from Chelmsford. You see, they'll look after you – they'll be with you, two at a time, in three goes of eight hours each. See?'

'Yes.'

'Yes. They're coming along as fast as they can.'

'I see.' Six of them from all parts hurrying to Gunterbury! So precious was a sinner reserved for sacrifice.

'Yes. Officers from here aren't supposed to have anything to do with the C.C. I think that's the idea.'

'The C.C.?'

The warder coughed awkwardly. 'Yes, that's what we call it – this place . . .' and he quietly switched off that explanation. 'So George and I are holding the fort till they arrive.'

'They're always here, aren't they?'

'Yes, two of them along with you – but they're decent lads – always are, and you won't mind 'em. They'll do all they can for you.'

'I'm allowed to talk to them, aren't I?'

'Talk? Bless your heart, yes. Talk your head off. And play games with 'em. Anything you like.'

The conversation was now well started, Paul sitting on the edge of the bed, and the warders on chairs by the side of the table.

'I can get letters, I suppose?'

'Oh, yes.'

'When?'

'Any time. Whenever they come. The principal officer'll bring 'em.'

'I'd get a letter from Holloway all right? There wouldn't be any delay about that, would there?'

'No, I shouldn't think so. But you talk to the Governor. He'll do anything he can for you. Sure to.'

'If it's written today, I shall get it in the morning?'

'Yes. . . .' His 'yes' was rich and comforting. 'Not a doubt of it, I shouldn't think.'

For a minute Paul sank into thought, but the kindly fellow seemed to think it wise to keep him talking. 'It's from *her*, I suppose.' A natural good sense told him that Paul would be eased by talking of her.

'Yes.'

'Her trial comes on any day now, I'm told.'

'Does it?'

'Yes. They were only waiting for the result of yours. And do you want to know what we all think?'

'Yes.'

'It's a crash. Isn't it, Fred?'

The other warder nodded.

'A crash?' asked Paul, seeking explanation of the word.

'Yes: a wash-out. She'll get awf.' He said it with smiling, triumphant eyes. 'If that's any comfort to you, take my word for it. She'll get awf. Bound to.'

'It's about the best comfort you could give me.'

'Is it? I'm glad. I'll tell you what one of our fellows says,' pursued the man, encouraged to carry on with the comfort. 'He's a chap who reckons he knows a dickens of a lot about the law, and he does – not as much as he thinks he does, because the Lord Chancellor doesn't know all that – but a tidy lot. He says the police were justified in arresting her, but they won't be enthusiastic about this accessory-after-the-fact business. Not now that they've – er – not now that your trial is over. He says the charge is "well knowing that you – well knowing all there was to know about it". They've got to prove guilty knowledge, he says, and they just can't do it; and are probably not all that anxious to do it, either. He says that if they've taken your statement that she knew nothing, and used it against you, they can't, in common fairness, do anything but use it *for* her. That's what we all think too. Juries are mugs, but they won't fall for anything else than that, and a good K.C.'ll keep it staring them in the eyes. . . . No, she's as good as awf, if you arst me.'

'But she knew that there was a warrant out for me. That's the point that worries me.'

'Yes. We put that to him, and he says they might get a conviction for obstruction or something, but they won't bother to bring that against her, after she's got away on the first charge. Not after she's been in prison, and all.'

'Good. I'm glad you told me that.'

'Yes. I thought I'd just tell you that. Of course, I don't *know,* mind you! I'm only telling you what he says. He's not a real educated man, and he may have been talking through his hat; but it sounds convincing enough.'

'*It's* all right,' said 'Fred', the other and less talkative warder. 'Stands to reason it is. I wouldn't mind betting what you like on it.'

'Thanks,' said Paul. 'I only hope you're right'; and as the conversation lapsed, he lay back on the bed.

'Yes, you lay down a bit, if you're tired,' said Fred.

Lying back with the pillow under his head, he looked round again upon the 'C.C.' He saw that the walls were lime-washed from the roof to within four feet of the floor, where a line of green paint bordered a cream dado. He saw that the peep-hole in the two doors was blocked up: presumably because there was no need for the landing officer to look in, since the prisoner was under the ceaseless observation of two men, and others must in no circumstances be allowed to do so. Turning up his eyes, he saw an electric lamp in the ceiling; turning them farther back he saw the blue sky through the thick dirty glass of the window; dropping them, he saw the stone floor. A clean place within, but bare of comfort. Comforts! Never again would he know a sofa or a cushioned chair. Or pictures. Never again sit on a soft seat with a hand in Myra's. All that was over, as if he were already dead – with only his mind still awake. And – his heart missed a beat as he remembered it – the awful hour had come many minutes nearer while he talked to the friendly warders – his body moved upon the bed – God send him strength not to play the coward.

His thoughts were disturbed by the jangle of keys outside and the door opening. An officer in a white jacket and apron entered, bringing him tea in a metal can and bread and butter on a thick china plate. He noticed the man's quick sharp interest in him.

'You'll be able to get better food tomorrow,' encouraged the chatty warder, 'after the M.O.'s seen you.'

After his meal he washed up the plate in the bathroom, and then, with the passing of time – this terrible passing of time – longed to get into bed. Longed to cover himself up and close his eyes. The warders told him that there was no objection to his going to bed when he liked. So he made up his bed, undressed – and wondered what to do about a night-shirt. Not liking to ask, he slipped beneath the sheets in his day-shirt, and the warders made no comment. He lay and thought. The warders remained seated at the table. Sometimes the smell of smoke came to him, and he knew that one, or both, had lit their pipes. Through his closed lids he was conscious of the dim light burning in the ceiling. It kept sleep at a distance, as a light in the forest keeps an animal at bay in the dark. And it must burn there all night, they had told him. Of course it must, else how could they see that he was not doing something to deprive the law of its satisfaction in killing him? Unable to sleep, he opened his eyes once or twice, to see each time the limewashed walls of the condemned cell, the two iron-bound doors, and the dim light.

Sixty more minutes gone. . . .

Apparently he dozed, for he awoke to an unlocking door, several voices, a light switched on – and to that missed heartbeat as he remembered where he was. Oh, yes, it must be the warders from the other prisons: two of them taking over. He pretended to be asleep, for he did not want to talk; but he listened to the new men speaking, and the old ones going. The door banged; and suddenly he remembered that he would never see those two good fellows any more. He would ask the Governor or someone to say goodbye to them, and thank you.

Chapter Two

Three Sundays would pass before the end. Nearly three weeks; and minute by minute they wasted away. 'There can be no such place as hell,' someone has said, 'because in ten days you would get used to it.' Paul did not get used to it – he had flashes of awful realisation that left him a jaw-dropping dull-wit – but a kind of leaden resignation did blunt the pain for most of the day. Thought became passive, nearly comatose – active at two points only: one, Myra, and the other, the last two minutes. In that last two minutes would he be strong enough to do as he longed to do – go with head up, lips still, and firm tread? God help him to set his teeth, clench his fist, and hold himself together for just long enough. One ghastly second, and then all would be over.

These wasting hours, how to fill them? Take a man in perfect health, keep him with the utmost care in perfect health so that he can really suffer, remove the future from him – cut out, that is to say, all aspiration, all hope of achievement, all necessity to earn, all desire to make the body fine and the mind strong, all pleasure in creative work – and how will he spend the hours?

Drift from one unrecoverable minute to the next. Drift, with a stupid, dropping jaw. Talk for a minute, play for a minute, and then remember, and gape, and drift again.

According to the Governor, a simple, well-meaning man whose mind obeyed stock phrases as obediently as he himself, when a subaltern, obeyed the word of command, Gunterbury Gaol was a 'hive of industry'. 'Nothing like work,' said the

Governor, 'for rebuilding a poor fellow who's gone to pieces, steadying his character, restoring his self-respect, and making a useful citizen of him again'; and he did not perceive that, while this is perfectly true of free and willing labour, it is perfectly untrue of regimented and loveless work, which will invariably be done by sullen men, to the souring of their characters. Forced labour never yet ennobled anybody, thanks, indeed, to a noble spirit of independence in men. And when it is obvious to the dullest prisoner that most of the work would be much better done by machinery and is only done by hand so as to provide labour for so many men and so many hours, it is certain that he will regard it, not as a pleasant occupation, but as a stupid, punitive and hated task.

Let us be simple, then, and say that, all around the condemned cell, Gunterbury Gaol was a hive of slave labour. As Paul learned from his warders, the six hundred prisoners in the shops or in the cells were sewing mailbags, cutting firewood, baking bread, plaiting baskets for the Office of Works, making engine-room mats, clews, fenders and lashings for the Admiralty, making birches and cat-o'-nine tails for use on other prisoners somewhere, washing clothes in the laundry, printing and binding books for the Prison Service – doing, in fact, everything that the trade unions would allow them to do – and in the midst of this industry was a little locked box of hopelessness, idleness, and separate pain.

It was almost a sound-proof box. Footsteps might be heard, or the clang of a door, or the voices of men returning from the shops, but few other sounds: the boxed-in man was shut off from further hope of sounds he had loved: birdsong, the knocking of a green woodpecker on the bark of a tree, the sigh of the wind along the top of the woods, and the voices and laughter of friends. So too from the smell of green things, and from all dear sights: the flirting movement of the wagtail in the grass, the scuttle of the grey squirrel into the brush, the falling of the sunset down the sky, and the visit of the stars. Curious to be alive and know that one would never see them again! Through the high barred windows came a golden light, and he guessed the autumn glory on Pitch Hill, and among the trees of Clissold Park, and along the track from Hillgarth to Petfield, where he had walked with Myra just two years before. In his mind he saw the trees russet and apple and gold against the purple distance and under a luminous sky.

And, seeing it, he cleaned and tidied up his box. He made his bed and swept the floor. And he got some small pleasure from doing this, for, if a man has nothing else to do, he can enjoy a sweep round and a general clean and tidy up. Paul especially.

He ate his meals, but what for? Each meal was a reminder that another big portion of a day had gone, and what was the sense of strengthening the body? They were good meals: good food, perfectly cooked. On his first morning the doctor had come in, embarrassed but kind, and asked, 'Well, how's things? Feeling pretty fit?'

'Oh, yes, thank you.'

'Quite comfortable?'

'Yes.'

Then he had told him that he could have more or less what he liked for his meals. 'Tell me what you fancy, and I'll see that you have it. Like something extra for breakfast?'

Paul said he didn't want to be a nuisance, but he wouldn't mind a little bacon.

'Yes, bacon. And something for dinner?'

Well, could he have a pudding – but not if it was any trouble.

'Oh, yes, we'll see to that. And tea? Something special for tea?'

Well, he didn't know . . . a little jam, perhaps?

'Oh, jam. That's easy, but what about an egg now and then?'

'Oh, thank you very much. Yes, it would be nice.'

'I'll see that you get all that. And some cigarettes, eh?'

'Oh, thank you very much. It's most kind.'

And now these more inviting meals were brought to him by the officer from the kitchen in his white coat and apron. Everything came ready cut up for him, so that he could eat it with a spoon. And once the bread came up from the kitchen with its destination chalked on the crust, 'C.C.'

The warders, whatever they might be outside the condemned cell, were compassionate men within it – as was everybody. The two who spent the best part of the day with him were Mr Plaistow and Mr Evans. Mr Plaistow was a long, straggling, powerful man, and Mr Evans was a few inches shorter and a few inches wider, but a tall fellow too. These, and the two who succeeded them before the night shift, were now, as near as might be, his merry friends. His last friends. They chatted easily, kept up his spirits with tales, played cards with him, and dominoes and draughts. They even taught him card tricks – what for, God knows. And he taught them some, rather sadly, since they would use them in the outer world and tell everybody, 'That was taught me by Presset.' Sometimes they gave him some of their cigarettes. Since the doctor's first visit, the prison had issued to him ten cigarettes a day, but often this supply ran out, and then one of the warders would always say, 'Here, have one of my fags.' He suspected that this was not legitimate, and would try to keep, therefore, to his allowance of ten. 'Thank you,' he would demur, 'but I don't like taking yours.' 'Gahn, that's nothing,' laughed either Mr Plaistow or Mr Evans. 'Help yourself. Here you are, take this one.' And they lit the fag for him, since he was allowed no matches of his own. And some of their talk, was it strictly legitimate? If not, it was kind. In answer to one of his questions Mr Plaistow assured him, with averted eyes, that it was 'only twenty seconds, old man,' from the cell door to death.

With Mr Plaistow and Mr Evans he would take his morning exercise. He had probably awakened early to the limewashed walls, the two locked doors, and the two drowsy nightwarders at the table. Perhaps it was half-past six, and his sleep was disturbed by Mr Plaistow and Mr Evans coming in to relieve their colleagues of the night. He got up – why not? It was something to do – and his breakfast would come in at seven-thirty. And after breakfast, exercise. At eight – eight on the dot – the officer on duty outside opened the door and asked, 'Ready?'

'Yes,' said Mr Plaistow.

And the three officers led him along a passage out into a yard. Here he saw that he was somewhere near the front of the prison, and in a part where buildings obscured him from all the windows of the great halls. The boundary or curtain wall rose on one side of him; twenty feet of grey stock bricks with hoop iron between their courses, that none might batter through it, from inside or without. Beyond it he could hear the traffic of the street and the voices of those who still had their life before them. On the other side of him was the basket-maker's shop, but it was always empty when he came out for his walk. If he had passed beyond the shop, he could have seen the high walls of one wing with its rows and rows of cell windows, but his guards never let him get into view of these. There was a day, however, when a noise broke upon them of many feet, some voices, and crunching wheels. It was a working party of prisoners approaching, pulling a barrow. Instantly the warders pushed him into the empty basket-makers' shop and hid him there till the working party was gone from hearing. But not before he had caught some of their words, and had known that, though in theory they must speak of nothing but their labour, they were speaking of him. 'In about a fortnight . . .' he heard; and 'Poor b—,' and 'You're right.'

The six hundred prisoners knew all about him, though not one of them had seen him. A man under sentence of death is no sooner within the prison walls, no sooner approaching them even, than he becomes the chief subject of illicit talk. Soon they would know the date of his execution, the time of the executioner's arrival, the names of the executioner and his assistant, and the preparations going on in the execution shed. The passage from man to man of such grim but oddly exalting news is simpler than it seems. Both at associated labour when the warder's head is turned and at exercise in the few paces between warder and warder all expert prisoners practise the art of talking through motionless lips; the barber, himself a prisoner, operating in hall and shop and exercise yard, though a warder watches over him, bends his head to cut the hair close to his client's ear, and the tale is told, without his lips having moved – told in hall and shop and exercise yard; prisoners climb on their stools to their high cell windows, and the tale goes through ventilating pane to ventilating pane; what is sanitary paper for if not to pass a message to a friend; and what cannot an ingenious man say, with closed eyes and pious voice, in chapel during the responses of the litany?

After exercise Paul might receive a visit from the Governor, who was always friendly and considerate and ready to give him the 'letter' for which he always applied. Or, more interesting still, since now and now only the warders left him, going out but leaving the cell door ajar, the chaplain might sit and talk with him. As a priest, or a man of God, the chaplain did not impress him at all. He had the thick neck, red face and full flesh of the fundamentally sensual man. He had the untidiness of a lazy one. And the lines about his eyes and mouth were those of selfishness rather than of piety and love. Never a fool, and with all his perceptions heightened by the nearness of death, Paul could not but see this man for what he was: an overworked functionary who discharged his tasks less in the fear of God than in the fear of the Governor and the Prison Commissioners; but the condemned cell seemed to make Christians of everybody who came into it, and the Rev. Wilfred Forder, who was probably short and hurried and uninspiring enough to the other prisoners, did try to give of his best to him.

They argued long and often, and Paul would be amazed to learn that, even with death so close, he could still care to show off to this man his wide reading, his intellectual and up-to-date ideas, the logical strength of his mind, and his generous sympathies with the under-dog. He could want the man to know that he was not like his other illiterate prisoners. They argued theology, morals, and the problems of social punishment; and very soon Paul felt, as he had felt with Dr Waterhall, that he was the cleverer and more imaginative of the two. With gentle approach, so as not to wound Mr Forder, Paul submitted to him a certain inconsistency in the bringing of Christianity into prison cells, where, no matter how well the punitive and revengeful treatment could be justified on practical grounds, it was plainly the reverse of Christianity. And if this was true of every cell in Gunterbury Gaol, how much truer was it of the C.C.? And he knew a small gratification when the chaplain sat somewhat 'flummoxed' for an answer.

But, however he might appraise Mr Forder as a man who had retired from clear thinking many years ago (if, indeed, he had ever begun it) it did not follow that the ideas which he put forward professionally were wrong; and Paul liked to hear what he had to say on God and forgiveness and Holy Communion and the hope of reunion with a loved one hereafter. The chaplain believed firmly in such reunion. 'Don't *you*?' he asked.

'I don't know,' said Paul. 'I'd like to. With all my heart I'd like to.'

'Well, it's my task to assure you of it,' said the chaplain.

At this Paul gazed into a vacancy between his chair and the cell wall. 'One thing I'm sure of,' he answered, 'and that is, that it is as purely dogmatic to deny these things as it is to affirm them. One may at least *hope* that they're true, or that the truth is something like them.'

'Exactly!' agreed the chaplain, almost triumphantly. 'One must have faith. If one *knew*, there'd be no faith.'

'I can go so far as a blind faith like that,' said Paul. 'I have always been able to.'

Yes, it was an interest to talk to him, and a relief to tell him everything about his home life and Myra, except the one unspeakable truth. He would hope that he would not quickly go away – and then, when he was gone, would remember that thirty or forty more minutes had passed.

Sometimes he read a book. A principal officer brought him a selection from the library – he had, as a matter of fact, gone to the library and said to the red-band prisoner on duty there, 'What shall we give him, Wittaker? Something light and bright, I think, don't you? Short stories are the best, we usually find, these poor devils can't concentrate long. And nothing educational,' he laughed. 'Reckon his education's over' – but Paul, anxious to show off before him, as before the chaplain, pretended to despise the bound-up volumes of magazines and asked for something with more intellectual body to it. He even showed off to the extent of asking if they had any French books in the original. De Maupassant, perhaps? Because short stories would be the best; he quite agreed that short stories would be the best. And a confused principal officer returned to the redband prisoner and inquired if they had anything in Greek or Persian or Hebrew, because plain English didn't seem good enough for the cove in the C.C. All he could find was a volume of translated short stories from the French, and these he brought with apologies to Paul. Paul thanked him; and now for a few minutes – never longer – he would forget his position in the fortunes of some hero or heroine.

But, almost always after reading, the dark mood got him, and he found he was pacing to and fro the twelvefoot breadth of his cell, while the warders sat silent, observing his distress. If it was evening, when the dark mood was on him, he got into bed, since there was nothing else he cared to do. He tried to sleep, but tossed for hours, hearing faintly the noise of prison doors, or feet passing, or voices of men in the yard. Also the lowered voices and shuffling feet of the two warders seated at the table. Sleep came at last, as it does to all, even in the C.C.; and he escaped apprehension of his surroundings, only to wake again to the limewashed walls, the two locked doors, and another day.

As the days passed he noticed an increasing kindness in the Governor.

The Governor was a tall grey colonel, grey-moustached, with a military air and a cane under his arm. He was generally, thanks to his wife's eye for a colour scheme and her affectionate teasing in their house on the prison wall, dressed in neat grey. Like Inspector Boltro he was often hostile to prisoners when he read about them in the papers, and sympathetic with them when they were before his eyes. Like Sir Hayman Drewer, if he saw pain, he ministered to it, but he did not see it easily without his eyes. A retired colonel, duty-loving, obedient rather than critical, unsophisticated, preferring order to thought, a disciplinarian by creed and a sentimentalist at heart, he was perpetually discovering, with simple, surprised eyes, that criminals were often much better than their deeds suggested. As he loved to say over his wine, 'There's a soft spot in the worst of them, if you can get at 'em in the right way, sort of thing'; and he did not know as he said it, that he was uncovering a soft spot of his own.

On his first visit to Presset in the C.C. he was struck with surprise, as the two warders came to attention and the prisoner nervously copied them, to see a small, sad-eyed, and apparently harmless man. A few minutes conversation, and he was surprised to find him courteous, considerate, and uncomplaining. And with the days this surprise became distress, a distress that could find relief only in little services to him.

On the third day, learning from the warders that 'he was worrying about his young lady', he went to see him, and said,

'Well, what's worrying you, old man? About Miss Bawne, is it, what? Tell me, and perhaps there's something I can do, sort of thing.'

'When is her trial?'

'The day after tomorrow, and I'm told she'll get off.'

Paul looked at him with worried brow. 'But supposing she doesn't? Is there anything I can possibly do or say that would help to get her off? I really know nothing about the law.'

'I'm afraid I don't know much about it, either.' The Governor laughed awkwardly. 'I never could make head or tail of most of it, and left it to wiser heads, what? I don't suppose you can do more than you've done already; but if it's any comfort to you, I'll put anything you want to say to the proper quarters.'

'I should like to say that it'd be a terrible miscarriage of justice if they do anything but acquit her.'

'I'll do what I can. Be sure of that.'

'Thank you, sir.' Paul dropped his eyes to the stone floor, thought for a space, and lifted them again. 'And could you say this, sir? Could you say that I *know*, and that I'm the only person in the world who can know. I'm dying and done for now, and I shall be before God in a few days, and knowing that, I should like to say that, if there've been any faults anywhere, they've all been mine.'

'I'll do all I can,' repeated the Governor.

'You see, sir, what I mean is: won't my life be enough? . . . Isn't that a fair price to pay for – for whatever's happened. Need they make her pay, too?'

The Governor's eyes warmed, and he swallowed with difficulty. Paul's eyes, too, swelled and moistened at his own words.

'She's innocent, sir, absolutely innocent of all wilful wrong. She ought to be rewarded for all she's done, not punished. As I was saying to the chaplain, it's quite certain whether Christ would praise or blame her. Certain as the day, because she just did what He said—'

'My dear chap—' The Governor had command of his voice now – 'you can be sure that I'll do everything that's legally possible.'

'Thank you, sir. She's—' Paul, having worked on his worn emotions, was near to breaking down, and he turned his face away towards the high barred window – 'she's been the one lovely thing in my life.'

'I'm sure she has,' murmured the Governor, hardly knowing what he was saying. 'Yes. And – er – you've everything you want in here, sort of thing?'

'Yes, thank you. Everyone's been most kind.'

'That's great. Well, I'll try and bring you some news tonight.'

Late that evening he returned and said brightly, 'I don't think you need worry. I've been talking all the evening to a lawyer-chap – the very devil of a clever fellow, and what he doesn't know about the law isn't worth knowing, sort of thing – and he says she's bound to get off. He says that they can't possibly prove that she had guilty knowledge, and a good counsel won't even put her in the box or call witnesses.'

'Oh, good! And what happens then? Is she set free at once?'

'Absolutely. Of course. Discharged at once, sort of thing.'

'And then will she be able to come and see me?'

'Oh, yes. Absolutely. Good lord, yes! No difficulty about that.'

'Thank you. I should like to see her before the end.'

'Oh, we'll fix that up for you all right. Not a spot of difficulty about that, what? No. Well. . . good night.'

'Good night, sir.'

And from that moment no one in all England awaited the result of the Bawne trial with greater interest than the Governor. He had set his heart on being the first to take to Presset the news of her acquittal. And at about tea-time two days later, he hurried along to the door of the C.C. as pleased as a boy with good news. He went into the cell, and with a smile about his eyes, stretched forth his hand to the prisoner.

Paul took it, understanding; and his upper teeth shot over his lip.

'Yes,' said the Governor. 'It's just as everyone said. The old judge practically told the jury that there was insufficient evidence and that if your words about her "not knowing anything" had been used against you, they couldn't very well be used now except in her favour, whatever they might think about – ahem, about you, so to speak. His summing up was as good as a speech for the defence, they say. And her counsel was great, too, by all accounts; absolutely great. Declined to put her in the box, or call a word of evidence, so she didn't have to go through the ordeal of cross-examination. And the jury weren't out more than ten minutes. I'm so glad, old chap; I'm so glad. And now she's free, and we'll get her along to see you, eh?'

'Thank you, sir. Thank you for coming to tell me.' For a moment or two Paul could only wring his hand. 'And do you know where she's gone?'

'No. Hasn't she some home?'

Paul shook his head. 'She had no home at all, except with me.'

'But she's got some friends, or something, hasn't she?'

'No. I don't think so. . . . I can't think of any. . . . She gave them all up for me. . . . She wrote saying that some minister or other had offered her a temporary home, but I don't know whether she's going to it . . .'

'Well, that's easily found out. And I don't suppose there's anything to worry about. The lawyer-fellow, what's-his-name, Forrest, is sure to have looked after all that. I'll get in touch with him, shall I, and let you know?'

'Yes, thank you, sir. I should like to know where she is.'

Chapter Three

In the corridor outside No. 1 at the Old Bailey a strange figure moved up and down. Solicitors, barristers, clerks, men and women visitors, hurrying along, turned to give it a second look, and a third. Especially the women. It was a figure not much over five feet tall; and since it was rounded at the shoulders and protuberant at the stomach, and was clad in an old cassock and leather belt, with a black overcoat over all, into the pockets of which the hands were thrust as it wandered up and down, and since the face was rubicund, the hair greying, the eyes dreamy and the nose long, it looked remarkably like a figure of Punch in Holy Orders. Up and down it wandered, a hand sometimes leaving a pocket that the thumb-nail might knock against the teeth. Sometimes the lips moved as of a man talking to himself. Or perhaps, since often when the lips moved, the eyes shot abruptly to the roof of the corridor, he was talking in some anxiety to his God. Once or twice he fetched a sigh.

A young man came quickly out of the court room, looked up and down the corridor for this figure, and ran towards it.

'Mr Hanks!'

The figure stopped and turned.

'Mr Hanks – the jury have just gone out, but Mr Forrest doesn't think they'll be long.'

'What?'

The young man repeated the information to eyes that seemed to have difficulty in coming back to the world.

'Oh, yes,' said Mr Hanks. 'The jury. Of course. Quite. I see. Yes, thank you very much. It's over, then, is it?' And Mr Hanks noticed for the first time that in the court room, where there had been a single voice speaking, there was now a buzz of many voices, and a coming and going through the doors.

'Yes; all except the verdict. I'll let you know when they return, shall I, sir, and you can come and hear their decision?'

'Yes, thank you very much. . . . No, no. . . . No, I'd rather you came out and told me the result. Yes, I'd rather that. I'll be here, somewhere.'

'Very good, sir.' And the young man went back.

And the strange little figure resumed its pacing. No one in the Old Bailey corridor knew who he was, but in his hill village of Hoelane, where he walked the roads and the meadows in the same garb, all would have greeted him: women with a pleased smile, carters with a lift of a friendly whip, labourers with a finger to their caps and a 'Morning, sir'; and children with a race up to his absent-minded figure and screams of 'Mr Hanks! Mr Hanks! Mr Hanks! Mr Hanks!' as if his were company to be enjoyed. And in the streets of Widdering, the cathedral city near by, the burgesses pointed him out and told tales of him. They said that he was a familiar figure on their pavements, generally to be seen with a string of his village children running and skipping behind him, and racing up to his side, because he was leading them to the cinema-show in the Corn Exchange, and travelling rather faster than they, in a reasonable excitement to see the newest film of Mr Chaplin. They told tales of the services in his church on the hill. They said it was worth going to see. They said that his choir of surpliced urchins, oafs and greybeards, in a long psalm, would rashly attempt the change from the first chant to the second, and there would be a period of transition enduring through four or five verses, at which point Mr Hanks would wake up and realise that two chants were being sung more or less contemporaneously in his church and promptly roar the correct tune for three or four more chaotic verses, till the last laggard in the choir had successfully crossed the points and the congregation, which so far had been loyal to the first tune, now out of sheer respect accepted the changed conditions and followed their pastor's lead; whereupon Mr Hanks ceased to roar, and fell back into thought again, satisfied that his children walked in truth.

He was still wandering up and down the corridor when suddenly his abstraction was broken by a noise in the court room: the jury were returning. Then silence. Mr Hanks stood stock still, and his lips moved violently. He seemed to be breathing quickly. A lip-reader might have seen on his lips, 'God in thy mercy . . . in thy mercy . . . in thy mercy . . .'

Then all was bustle and hum in the court, and people began to pour out of it into the corridor. He stopped a young barrister in wig and bands. 'Excuse me. Would you tell me the verdict?'

'Oh, "Acquitted", sir.'

'What? Acquitted? Thank God. Thank you, sir; thank you so much'; and he smiled at the young barrister as if somehow he was responsible for this happy result. 'Acquitted? Yes. That's splendid, splendid!' and, nodding goodbye to the young man, he turned to resume his pacing. To resume his pacing, and to lift, unseen, his eyes to the roof.

Soon all the people had gone, and he was alone in the corridor, except for a policeman who passed him now and again. The best of fifteen minutes went by, and then the young clerk who had first come out to him appeared from the direction of the great staircase and looked up and down the corridor.

'Ah . . . Mr Hanks. She's downstairs and ready now, sir. If you'll come.'

'Yes, of course. Downstairs. Yes, yes, I didn't realise that. Thought she'd come this way. Is she all right?'

'She collapsed in the dock when she heard the verdict, but she's quite recovered now.'

'Poor child, poor child.'

Together they went down the staircase, and at the foot the young clerk said, 'It's this way, sir'; but Mr Hanks interrupted, 'No, I'll wait here. I'll be by the door. I don't want to meet all those people. I don't understand all that kind of thing, really. Bring her out to me here, would you?'

'Yes, sir. Certainly.'

So Mr Hanks was now left to pace the lower corridor. Presently a door opened, steps echoed in the lofty emptiness about the great staircase, and Mr Hanks, turning about, saw Mr Forrest approaching him with Myra Bawne. He waited shyly, and when the brisk young solicitor said, 'This is Mr Hanks, Miss Bawne,' he put out both his hands, took both of hers, and said only, 'My *dear*, my *dear*.'

Myra, white, trembling, ready to weep at the least word of kindness, controlled her shaking lips and began, 'It's so good of you—'

'Not a bit, not a bit,' said he, patting her hand. 'Now come along. Is it all over in there, Mr Forrest? All over? Splendid. Then come along, my dear. I've a car waiting – yes, it's a hired thing – it's just here, and there's nothing to be afraid of; there's no crowd or anything. I've had a look. Nobody'll know who we are. Nobody knows me, and nobody'll know you. . . .' And he led her from the Old Bailey to the waiting cab, and helped her in. 'Liverpool Street Station,' he said to the driver. 'And Liverpool Street entrance, see? Not the other one.' And he bundled in after her.

'This isn't *my* car, you understand,' he said as he sat beside her. 'It's only a hired one. You'll – er – we shall never see it again, though I'm sure he doesn't know who we are, really. But just in case . . . I'm afraid I've arranged a rather neat little trick. I hope you'll forgive me. I thought it all out, and thought it best. I've a comfortable car waiting near the Bishopsgate entrance to take you down to Hoelane, but I thought, you see – I thought that perhaps it would be better if the chauffeur supposed that I'd met you at Liverpool Street station – in fact, I've told a lie or two lately, God forgive me.' He laughed nervously. 'So we'll take this car to one door, get rid of it, and nip through the station and out at the other, ha, ha! And I'll bring the new car along. How's that?'

'I think you're wonderful,' said Myra.

'Good heavens, no. What's wonderful in that? But I'm glad you don't mind that little trick. You see – but I'll explain it all in the other car.'

They ran into the station yard, and, the first car dismissed, he led her, almost running and pretending all the time to laugh at the trick, first to the baggage counter, where he drew out a bag, and said with a most knowing wink, 'Here's your bag – yes, you didn't expect that, did you? – but there'd best be a strange bag – no, I'll carry it – and it's got one or two little things in it for you. I believe – yes, the wife looked after that, and quite enjoyed it, she did, ha, ha!' and thence right through the station to the Bishopsgate entrance. Here he said, 'Wait just a minute,' and went off, really running now lest she should be kept waiting too long, to where the other car stood in a side street. He signalled to it, and it came round to the station entrance, a large and comfortable limousine.

'Well, jump in,' said he to Myra; and 'Hoelane Rectory,' to the chauffeur; and he climbed in after her. 'That's better,' he murmured, as he sank into the cushions.

'Is this your car?' asked Myra, for something to say.

Mr Hanks laughed. 'Mine? Lord, no. I don't run a car. I've just hired it for a week or two; in fact, if it's anyone's, it's yours; that's to say, it's entirely for your use as long as you stay with us; yours to see the country in – and it's lovely country – and I expect you'll want to come up to London sometimes' – he said this quickly and looked out of the window, thinking of a man in a condemned cell – 'and it'll be in the stable ready for you. It can do the journey in two hours. Don't worry about it; I've often had it for guests before. And of course, if you'd rather tramp about the country, you shall tramp about. You see, my dear' – he touched her gloved hand – 'not a soul'll know anything about you in my little village – if you see what I mean – after all that publicity – and it's my idea that you should walk our lanes in peace.'

She turned her sad eyes on him.

'Why do you do all this for me?'

'How can I do enough for you, my dear?'

Myra continued to gaze at him. 'How do you mean?'

'How can any of us do enough for you? If you would make me happy, please accept all that we can do for you without any questions. The more you'll take the easier we shall be, because, after all, there's a wrong to be righted, yes, surely – *surely*.'

'A wrong?' echoed Myra.

'Why, yes. We – er – Society's done you a wrong – I'm as convinced of that as of anything in the world; and my wife and I are rather inclined to feel that sort of responsibility . . . My God, *yes!*' This he said with a sudden, hissing anger. 'So please let us do all we can, and help us to feel less – less unhappy about it. You are to do exactly what you like. You can have your meals with my wife and me, or you can have 'em alone, or you needn't have 'em at all, ha, ha! If you want to talk, you shall talk to me all day; if you don't want to talk, you shall keep silence. The least trace of politeness, and we shall all be quite miserable.'

'But,' stuttered Myra, 'I don't like to put you to all this trouble and expense.'

'And that's the last time you'll say that!' smiled Mr Hanks. 'My wife – I – we – I'm rather well off, and, as a matter of fact, we don't feel that sort of thing – and perhaps there are others in it. Perhaps you have many unknown friends anxious to help you – but you must just trust me, I'm afraid. The world isn't altogether bad, you see? Perhaps there are many that love you.'

But Myra knew more about Mr Hanks than he supposed. Mr Forrest had told her all about him when laying his invitation before her. Mr Hanks, said the solicitor, was a man of considerable wealth, most of which came from coal royalties, and as he had his doubts ('being an extraordinarily conscientious old chap,' said Mr Forrest, implying that he himself wasn't troubled in like manner) about this levying of a personal tax on the people's warmth, he gave back to the world all that came to him from the coal. Strange, but so, said Mr Forrest. Usually he gave in secret, but sometimes his gifts had to be known, because a very favourite trick of his was to buy up the advowson of a living and present the benefice to some poor parson who in his selfless and unadvertised labour had been sufficiently like his Master to be neglected by the bishops, the colleges and the patrons. Mr Forrest had got to know him because, for many years now, he had contributed to the defence of some indigent prisoner or provided the money, on his release, that would start him again in the world. And directly he heard that Mr Forrest was defending Myra he had come to him and said, 'This is too awful, Forrest: what can we do? What can we do?' And when later he heard that her acquittal was almost a certainty, he had come with his diffident suggestion that if she liked – if it was true that she had nowhere else to go – nothing would give him more happiness than that she should come to him. With him she would at least be at peace, and unknown.

So much Mr Forrest had told her; but he did not tell her that Mr Hanks had sat in his office and said, 'Too awful! Too awful! Just think, Forrest. She's done nothing but help a broken man, and we've tortured her for it. And now she's got to endure those days before they hang the only person she loves. Think of her at two minutes to nine on the fatal morning! Think of it, Forrest! She must be surrounded with love. Yes. And if you send her to us, we'll try – by heaven, we'll try!'

Myra's first response to the idea had been a recoil. If she were released, she wanted to run away by herself somewhere. She wanted to be alone – absolutely alone. But as Mr Forrest urged her to accept, speaking much of Mr Hanks's goodness, she had remembered how, in her long thoughts in the prison, she had known that this overthrow of her life must result either in sour mutiny and an aggravation of her old hostility to the world or in the acceptance of that way of love which she had seen in her exalted hour on the summit of Pitch Hill. Sometimes anger and a revulsion from all goodness had triumphed, but at other times she had recalled the serenity, the feeling of wholeness and the exultation which had been hers when she loved all and condemned none, and then the vision had brightened within her again. So much sweeter and happier this! And the legacy of that hour on the hill was too strong to be long defected, and more and more her soul had longed for the peace of goodness and giving; so that now, listening to the lawyer's description of Mr Hanks, she had begun to wonder if this were not the one person to help, encourage, and establish her in it – a pleasing thought which was soon strengthened by another, that there would be seclusion at Hoelane Rectory, and secrecy. She so longed for cover. In the end she had sent her deep gratitude to Mr Hanks and accepted; and Mr Forrest had returned to tell her that Mr Hanks, on hearing this, had seemed as excited and exuberant as a boy, and impatient to run off and get everything ready for her.

Remembering all this in the car with him, she broke down and cried quietly; perceiving which Mr Hanks said cheerfully – the word slipping from him, either in an excess of feeling or in an absent-minded impression that he was talking to his daughter – 'That's right, my darling. That'll do you good'; and he took her gloved hand and held it. The car drove on into the peace of the country, Myra keeping her face towards the window, and Mr Hanks saying nothing but occasionally patting her hand.

And at length the car was climbing a low hill and passing a mossy wall, behind which the trees stood densely congregated like a barrier against the world. 'Here's the Rectory,' said Mr Hanks; and the car swung through a gate and along a drive to the front of a large, square house. 'Come along,' he said, and helped her down, and led her into the porch, where he turned the handle of the door, said, 'Tut, tut,' on finding the latch caught, and began to fumble for a key. In this moment of hesitation, Myra, very nervous and casting her eyes anywhere, saw an illuminated writing framed in oak and hanging by the side of the door, as might be a church notice. It was mottled and crimped with the damp, but she read in the fading script:

> 'I saw a stranger yestreen;
> I put food in the eating place,
> Drink in the drinking place;
> Music in the listening place;
>   And in the sacred name of the Triune
> He blessed myself and my house,
> My cattle and my dear ones;
> And the lark sang in her song,
>   Often, often, often
> Goes the Christ in stranger guise;'

and just then the door was opened by a neat maid, even as Mr Hanks produced his key; so that he said, 'Ah, yes. Splendid!' and put the key back in his pocket.

Behind the maid came a smiling matronly woman who took Myra's hands and kissed her on the forehead; while Mr Hanks watched the kiss absent-mindedly and said, 'Yes. Quite.'

'We're so glad you've been able to come,' smiled the lady. 'And did you have a nice journey?'

'Yes . . . very . . .' stuttered Myra.

'Yes,' repeated Mr Hanks, to no one at all, but very cheerfully. One felt that he ought to have rubbed his hands together, but he didn't; he just stood there as if not certain what they all did next.

'Well, now come up and see your room,' invited Mrs Hanks.

'Ah, yes. The room,' exclaimed her husband, sharply illuminated. 'I'm going to show her the room too. This way. No, no' – this was to the maid as he took the bag from her hand – 'that's all right, Emma dear. I'll look after that. You go and see about the chauffeur chap. Give him some tea. The mistress and I'll see to Miss – Miss Vera's things. . . . Splendid. . . . Come along, Mrs Hanks. Come along, dear. . . .'

And he hurried ahead of both up a wide staircase and along a narrow, carpeted passage, often looking back at them as a terrier does who is more anxious to get on with the journey than his human companions. Standing by an open door, he ushered them into a room at the back. It was no more than a young girl's room, but a leaping fire burned in its grate and flowers brightened mantel-shelf and dressing-table. The flames threw a rosy glow on the flounce of a chintz-covered easy chair and the folds of the chintz curtains. A little writing desk stood in the window corner, with a shelf of books beside it. Round the walls were framed photographs of Mr Hanks, Mrs Hanks, schoolgirl friends, school groups, some parsons, and a church. A crucifix hung over the small oak bed, with a holy water stoup beneath it, and a dried palm, folded into the form of a cross, hanging on a nail at its side. The Blessed Virgin was also extensively reproduced about the room, in coloured statuettes, framed pictures and neat little lace-edged cards.

'Oh, what a sweet room!' exclaimed Myra.

'As you perceive: my daughter's room,' said Mr Hanks. 'Yes, Millie's. She's at school, thank God, ha, ha! You'd like Millie, I think; she's two-thirds a papist as a rule, but she varies, she varies. We've a guest-room somewhere, but we thought you'd prefer this – less formal and more one of the family, eh? Come and see the view.'

He had gone to the window, and Myra turned to his wife to say, 'Oh, I think it's all so lovely'; at which Mrs Hanks somewhat surprisingly, whispered with a smile, 'Let him hear you say that. It *will* please him so. He's been fussing about this room for the past two days.'

So Myra, joining him at the window, said, 'I think it's all perfectly lovely, Mr Hanks' – and then looked down upon drooping lawns and solitary yews, with the country stretching for miles behind, like an extension of the garden. On a leafless branch, in the empty October evening, a single thrush was setting forth a song so multiple and various as to shame the nightingale.

'Listen to the old thrush,' said Mr Hanks. 'Yes . . . well . . . I'm glad you like it.'

Chapter Four

Paul walked to and fro in the cell, his heart irregular. It was nearly two o'clock, and Myra was coming to visit him at two; and this nervousness had possessed him for hours. He longed to see her, and yet the interview would be so blent with distress that he could almost wish he wasn't going to. Better perhaps to have died without seeing her any more. This restlessness demanded action, and he went into the bathroom, washed, and brushed his hair with a damp brush, so as to look his best even in these grey prison clothes. But it was difficult to brush one's hair with a wet brush and no mirror – for there was no mirror of any kind in the condemned cell. He felt with his finger to see if the parting was straight, and with his palm to know if the hair lay smooth and glossy behind.

A principal officer opened the cell and said, 'You can come now'; and the two warders and he went out, Paul as nervous as if about to speak on a public platform, or to be interviewed by a prospective employer. Not many steps away the principal officer threw open the door of another cell, and Paul and his warders entered, to be immediately locked in.

He found himself in an ordinary cell, a side wall of which was broken by a plate-glass window that looked into the next cell. Framing this square of glass was a grating, or grille, through which the voices could pass. Immediately opposite the window, on his side of it, there was a small backless form, fixed to the floor. When he sat on this, as told to do by the warders, he saw through the glass a couple of course wooden chairs in the cell beyond. The two warders took up a standing position behind him. Thus Myra would see, framed by the grille, a picture of him sitting on his bench in the grey prison clothes, with two warders in blue behind.

He felt a chill of disappointment. The glass window seemed a cold screen between him and Myra, symbolising something that was between them now forever – and even while he was thinking this, the principal officer brought Myra into the cell before him and put a chair for her and, drawing back the other chair, sat as far as might be behind her.

And Paul and Myra stared at each other with frustrated eyes, the glass partition between them. She was in a blue costume that he had never seen before, and she looked quite smart and well cared for, but her face was very pale – probably paler than his, her eyes were deeply shadowed, her cheeks seemed thinner and older, and her arms, thinner too, were trembling from the narrow shoulders to the fingers fiddling together on her lap.

'Well? . . .' he began.

'Well, dear. . . .'

'You don't look too well. Have you suffered very much?'

'Ach, don't talk about that. What are my sufferings compared with –' but Myra, her eyes roaming over his grey clothes, his drawn, white face, and his carefully irregularly parted hair, could only shake her head with sympathy and love, and tighten her lips as she tried not to cry.

'It's good to see you. . . .' she stuttered, but could not continue.

And he, so drained and drawn was he now, and so threadbare his nervous control, he too, at the sight of her tears, had to tighten his lips if he was not to cry. But he made the effort: he gulped, and conquered the weakness, because he wanted to show courage. He must speak. He must say something quickly, but what? What could he say that he hadn't said in his letters. Oh, what was he to say?

'It's wonderful to see you,' he began – but evidently she had been thinking the same as he, for she broke in, 'Paul, dear, you do believe that everything I've written in my letters is true, don't you?'

'Of course.'

'I mean: it's a little difficult to say everything before these gentlemen.' She blushed, and turned to smile at the principal officer.

'That's all right, miss,' he encouraged. 'You go right ahead. We aren't listening.'

'Oh, thanks,' stuttered Myra, and turned again to Paul. 'It's good to see you again, even if it's difficult to speak.'

Paul tried to help her. 'Well, tell me all about the place where you're staying.'

Relieved to have something to say, she told him all about Mr Hanks and her little room overlooking the garden and her walks in the beautiful country around – but all the time he could see by her eyes that she was thinking of something else. She was wishing for something better to say; and her actual words, unfollowed by her mind, were forced and unreal.

'That's good,' he said. 'I'm so glad you're happy.'

'Yes, they're awfully kind. . . .'

'Good. . . .'

And, to his dismay, the talk sank into a silence – sank deeper and deeper with every wordless second – and was drowned. The principal officer looked at his finger-nails. One of the officers behind Paul turned and studied the barred window. The other, his hands behind his back like a soldier standing at ease, began to swing from heel to toe, from heel to toe, his eyes considering the floor. Passionately Paul cast about for words, and the more he cast about, the less he could find any. Myra was staring at him, and he knew that she was struggling to come up from the silence, too. And it was she who contrived to break the menacing spell with words. 'Tell me what I can tell you about anything you want to know.'

'I think all that I want to know is that you're happy, really.'

'You know all about the petition for your reprieve?'

'Yes, but there's nothing in it. I know *that*.'

'Oh, I don't know,' she objected; and began to speak hopefully of it, but he could see through her words, as clearly as he could see through the glass window, that her expressions of hope came from a desire to comfort him, and not from belief. And because of this her words were again unreal; and, because unreal, they would not glow. And they were followed by another of the awful silences. Staring at her through the glass, he thought desperately that the thirty minutes of her visit – one of the last they would have – were passing away, and they could only gaze at each other with unhappy, defeated eyes. The interview was a failure. 'Myra! Myra!' his thought cried out to her, but not to be heard. He was sitting in silence.

Then both spoke at the same moment, in an effort to save the conversation, and Paul apologised, 'Pardon,' and yielded place to her; but she said, No, it didn't matter; it wasn't very important.

And it was at this moment, though they had not been talking fifteen minutes, that he began to want her to go. No, no, not want her to go, but want this interview ended. Yes, though: it was the truth, he wanted her to go . . . wanted to end the strain and to be alone. Perhaps he would do better next time. And he could write to her; it would be easier to write; already while he ought to be talking to her he was inventing explanatory and loving phrases for his letter after she had gone.

But this was awful. He *must* speak.

'Oh, by the way, thank you so much for the photograph.'

'You are able to have it?'

'Oh, yes. It's on the table by my bed. I like it so much.'

'I'm so glad, my dear.'

And both dropped into silence to think of the photograph. Each was seeing it, a postcard portrait of Myra with her words across one corner, 'Yours always, always, always. . . .'

'Yes, I look at it when I want a little comfort,' said Paul, with a deprecatory smile.

'That's right. That's what I want you to do. And those words on it are absolutely true, my dear. I can't say more.'

What else? What else could they talk about? It stood in the eyes of both that they were twisting and turning this question. There were fifteen more minutes to fill up, and Paul, for his part, was wishing there were only three.

How they filled up those fifteen minutes he could not afterwards remember. Some of the minutes were better than others, running easily, but most of them dragged and floundered and stuck. There was more than one of those baffled and heart-slaying silences. And it was with relief that he heard the principal officer say, 'I'm afraid it's time now, miss.' Relief!

'Oh, is it?' said Myra, and rose nervously. 'Goodbye, Paul. I'm afraid I haven't been able to say much. It'll be better next time, when I'm more used to it. . . . But you *do* know that my thoughts are with you every minute of the day?'

'Yes. And it's the same with me. I'll write. I'll write all that I haven't been able to say. Goodbye, my dearest.'

She took one last long look at him, putting all the love she could in her eyes, and went out with the principal officer.

Gone. And the visit had been a failure. His head shaking from side to side and his lips quivering as he did battle with his tears, Paul went out of the visiting-room with his warders, and along the stone-paved floor to his cell. In a passion of disappointment he would have liked to hurl himself on to his bed and sob into his pillow like a child; but he could not do this before his warders' eyes. There was no more privacy in his life, not even for the relief of tears.

Chapter Five

It was three o'clock in the afternoon, and the Governor left his office in the entrance building and, turning inwards, passed through the central hall, from which the four wings or 'halls' of the prison radiated away, like four great draughty churches, open from floor to roof and surrounded by spidery galleries. The whole place was quiet: all the prisoners were in their cells or at associated labour in the shops. With a sigh, and a despairing throw-forward of his jaw, he walked along the ground floor of one of the halls, passed the tight-shut doors of the condemned cell, and went out through a door beside it. This brought him into a yard and immediately opposite a small square building whose door, some dozen paces away, faced the exit through which he had come. A small building, with its four low brick walls and its hipped roof, it looked like a one-room cottage, or perhaps an outhouse – but when did an outhouse stand so lonely in a wide yard as this? With other buildings round, it might have been a tool-shed or machine-room or private carpentering shop; and in a sense it *was* a tool-shed and machine-room, but for a curious piece of work on living human tissue and sentient human nerves; and there were those among warders and prisoners who in grim humour referred to it as 'the butcher's shop'.

The Governor opened its door and walked into the one square room that its walls contained. Its brick walls were white washed, its floor was planked, and in the midst of the floor was a square trap closed at the moment, but one could see where its two doors met in the middle, and how, when released, they would fall downwards and apart. Above this trap, at right angles to it, say eight or nine feet from the ground, was a large stout beam from wall to wall. From a hook in the beam hung a hempen rope of finely selected quality. The rope's end was turned back into a noose which slipped up and down by means of a spliced-on ring, called by sailors and hangmen a 'thimble'. Under the beam and by the side of the trap was a lever not unlike a lever in a signal box. In a corner near the door there were steps leading down to a pit beneath the floor.

This machine-room was not empty today. A tall officer with enough gold on his cap to show that he was of high rank – he was, in fact, Mr Wrexham, the Chief Engineer – was fumbling with a part of the rope and a shapeless sack that lay on the trap, its slack neck tied securely to the rope. He came erect as the Governor entered, and each greeted the other. Each was expecting the other, because the Governor had said yesterday, 'I want you to see how the shed works, Mr Wrexham. I'll come in tomorrow at three o'clock'; and Mr Wrexham accordingly had caused a sack to be filled with sand up to the same weight as the condemned man, and seen that it was properly in place for the Governor's inspection.

'It doesn't seem a very big sack,' said the Governor, with an apologetic kind of laugh. 'Not very big, what?'

'No, sir. Nine stone something.'

'Is that all? I should have thought he weighed more than that, small though he is.'

'No, he's lost weight. Lost a good deal since he was at South London.'

'Not while he's been here, I hope.'

'No, it must have been there. He's gained here, if anything.'

'Gained, what? Funny. Looks a long drop. What is it?'

'About seven and a half foot, sir.'

'God!' exclaimed the Governor. 'That's kind of tall, isn't it?'

'Well, I reckon Crompton'll give him seven-foot-nine.'

'The devil he will! I thought seven foot killed anyone.'

'That may be, but Crompton never takes any risks, and especially not with a small man.'

'Well. . . .' The Governor made a sound of distress behind his teeth – but what was the good? He had his duty to do. Must obey orders, and leave the responsibility elsewhere. 'Well, carry on, Mr Wrexham.'

Mr Wrexham stepped away from the rope, and the sack hung shapeless and dead over the crack in the trap. Mr Wrexham pulled the lever, and at once the trap-doors fell inward, the sack went from sight, and the rope tautened and swayed and began to twist. It had strained on its fastening, and now swung to and fro, and round and back, easily and stupidly. The Governor stepped forward and looked down into the pit. The sack was swinging down there quietly enough.

'All right,' he said, and sighed, and came out of the building rather quickly.

This was the first rehearsal. It was only a week before the execution, and the Governor, a conscientious and anxious man, would probably see the sack hanged again in the course of the next few days.

Wednesday – the last Wednesday of one's life, for on Tuesday at two minutes past nine in the morning, one will not be alive. A minute or so earlier one existed; then one will just be no longer. One will be among the things that were. And the last Wednesday pales and darkens, and the light comes again into the prison cell: and it is the last Thursday. Then Friday; and the chaplain asks him if he wouldn't like to take Holy Communion on the Sunday morning. Why not make the great gamble of faith and come? He used to go as a boy, and he had agreed that all these things *might* be true, so why not come, if only with the faith of 'Lord, I believe; help thou mine unbelief'? And Paul, after long thought with elbows on knees and hands clasped before him, says, Yes, he will come. If God will take him on those terms, he will come. He will try to believe.

He had been before to ordinary services in the big prison chapel. Attendance at morning service was compulsory for the other prisoners and optional for Paul; attendance at afternoon service was optional for all; but Paul had chosen to go to both, for the sake of something to do. And so, before any of the other prisoners had left their cells, his two warders had escorted him to his special screened pew near the altar wall, where, boxed in, he could not see the other six hundred prisoners, nor be seen by them. This pew was a kind of horse-box or pen at the angle of the east and south walls, its floor space perhaps six feet long by four wide. It held one wooden form large enough to hold himself and his two guards in comfort. The screening walls were of wooden panels and rose about eight feet from the ground – the work, so Mr Plaistow and Mr Evans told him, of one of the prisoners. A curtain could be pulled back from the altar wall to the woodwork, and through this opening he could see the altar, the organ, and the Governor's seat by the altar's side. Let us liken it to an anchorite's cell with a 'leper squint' to the altar, or a king's secluded pew, where Paul Presset sat in the royalty of death.

Once safely deposited in this pew for morning or afternoon service, he could hear the other prisoners being admitted to the chapel. They filed in rather noisily, and he felt – it seemed something stronger than imagination – he *felt* the fascinated interest of six hundred pairs of eyes on the walls of his enclosed pew. He heard their voices perfunctory and low in the Amens but loud and hearty enough in the hymns. He heard their titter if the chaplain made something like a joke in the sermon, or if by chance he made a mistake. The service over, he heard them filing out, for he was kept in his pew till the last man had gone.

Then his two warders motioned to him to come, and all three went out through a door in the wall and down some stairs to the ground floor and the C. C.

Saturday and Sunday were regarded by the whole prison population as the worst days of the week. Even the isolated Paul could feel the gloom and the hush which settled upon the buildings and the yards from noon on Saturday to the rising bell on Monday morning. There might, perhaps, be a noise of cleaning at some time on the Saturday afternoon: a clatter of pails, a scrubbing of brushes, a jingling of keys, a banging of doors and shouting of orders; but thereafter the hush was the greater for the passing of this noise. All the prisoners, except the few employed on household duties, must spend the whole weekend in the solitude of their cells, except for the two separate hours in the chapel and a brief exercise round the rings on Sunday morning. Their library book was probably finished, or already boring them; their cell task, which they were allowed to work on during Saturday and Sunday lest the empty hours maddened them, was soon a weariness and a nausea; and they began to be conscious of the iron-bound doors – those doors that were locked on them, and would remain locked for hours on end. If there was a hammering on the doors, it throbbed through the prison, as likely as not, in the hush of the week's end.

And now it was Paul's last Sunday, with just such a gloom in the buildings and the yards. The other six hundred might dread the day, but at least they were better off than he, who must think that he would never hear this Sunday silence again. When next it invaded the prison he would be as if he had never been. It was about half-past eight in the morning – after the breakfast hour, but the chaplain had asked the Chief Officer that Paul's food might be kept warm for him. Mr Plaistow and Mr Evans, having straightened and dusted their coats and smoothed their hair for divine service, stood waiting for the principal officer to fling open the cell door and let them all out. This was done, and they accompanied him through a completely empty and echoing hall, up the stairs and through the small door into his private pew. Its curtain was drawn back, and he saw the altar with its 'fair linen cloth' upon it, ready for the Master's hospitality. The two candles, one on either side of the cross, burned yellow and cold in the full morning light. And Paul, thinking hard with a fold in his brow, suddenly remembered that this was indeed a 'last supper' for him. Next Sunday those candles would burn there too. . . . When he had been seated a little while, with a warder on each side, he heard some movement in the body of the chapel; but from the echoes under the high arched roof he judged that not many were coming to this service. Just before the service started, the Governor came through the small door of the condemned pew, passed right through it, and knelt in his special seat by the altar's side.

Did he come always, with the simple piety and conscientiousness of a soldier, Paul wondered, or had he come this morning for *his* sake? In either case it showed him as a likeable man and Paul did in fact like him and count him one of his last friends. He remembered how, late last night, he had come in person to the C. C., to say, 'I'm terribly, terribly sorry, but the reprieve has been refused,' and Paul had answered, 'Never mind, sir, I didn't expect anything else. Thank you for coming to tell me'; and then the Governor had turned his eyes adrift and told him the day and hour of the execution and Paul had answered simply, 'I see, sir'; whereupon the Governor had put out his hand and taken Paul's, and said, 'God bless you'. And now he had come to be with him in his last communion.

The chaplain in surplice and stole came through a door on the far side of the altar, went to the midst of it, and began the service.

And Paul, kneeling and listening, noticed how word after word held a stab for him who had forty-eight hours to live.

He began to look for these stabs. The Commandments – they seemed hardly appropriate to him any more. The Prayer for the King – but he was done with the kingdoms of this world. Besides, 'Rex *v.* Presset. The King against Paul Arthur Presset' – that was what they had called his trial, and now they asked him to pray for the King. Well, he had confessed his crime to God and asked forgiveness, and if he was to receive this communion worthily, he must be at peace with all. So 'Amen' to the Prayer for the King. The Epistle for the Nineteenth Sunday after Trinity – 'Let all bitterness and wrath and anger and clamour and evil speaking be put away from you, with all malice. And be ye kind one to another, tender-hearted, forgiving one another, even as God, for Christ's sake, hath forgiven you' – was it a blasphemy, or merely inapt, for such words to be echoing under a prison roof and over a condemned pew, like frightened and unhappy birds that beat their wings to escape into an air they could breathe? 'Ye that . . . intend to lead a new life. . . .' Life! But the Confession was over and the chaplain had turned to pronounce the Absolution. 'Almighty God, our Heavenly Father, who of his great mercy hath promised forgiveness of sins to all them that with hearty repentance and true faith turn to him, pardon and deliver you from all your sins . . .' and here Paul bowed his head.

Now the Consecration was done, and if the chaplain's doctrine were true, Christ was in the prison, not twenty paces away. The chaplain was partaking of the consecrated elements, and kneeling and bowing before the altar, as if to thank a God thereon for his touch upon his lips. And now he had risen and was coming towards Paul with the paten held breast-high – to him first of all. Paul heard a slight shuffle and movement in the echoing chapel, and knew that the congregation had moved their bodies and lifted their heads, fascinated to watch what the chaplain was doing. So *he* was there, thought they; and their eyes pierced like gimlets his high screening walls. The shuffle was followed by a marked silence. Paul tried to hold himself in prayer, but nervously clearing his throat to prepare for the coming of the Sacrament, he coughed, and instantly knew that his cough had stirred an audience near enough to hear much that they might not see. They seemed now to be coughing too, many of them, as if in nervous sympathy. He strove his way back into prayer, for the chaplain was now within the curtain and bending with the paten over his head. 'The body of our Lord Jesus Christ, which was given for you, preserve thy body and soul unto everlasting life. . . .' ('Preserve thy body'! 'And your body shall be buried within the precincts of the prison. . . .') 'Take and eat this in remembrance that Christ died for thee. . . .'

'Lord, I believe; help thou mine unbelief. Forgive me my great and terrible sin, and, if it be Thy will, take me to Thyself. But, above all, watch over Myra and give her happiness. If by any suffering of mine, I can purchase her peace, grant that I may suffer, O Lord. Help me to die bravely when the time comes. Oh, help me to die bravely. Be with me that I may not tremble or show fear. . . .'

Chapter Six

On Monday, in the morning, a small man of middle years, forty-five perhaps, in a suit of decent black and a bowler hat, and carrying a small black bag, came to the outer gate of Gunterbury Gaol and rang the bell. The gatekeeper opened to him and, not having seen him before, inquired with lifted eyebrows, 'Yes, sir?'

The small man explained in a soft voice, 'My name is Crompton. I am the executioner.'

'Oh, yes. I see.' The gatekeeper's respect dropped several points; but the drop was social rather than moral.

'Mr Griffin is reporting a little later.'

'Mr Who?'

'Mr Griffin, my assistant.'

'I see. Good. Well, come along.' And he admitted him through the wicket.

Shutting the wicket so that the small, bowler-hatted figure stood locked between the outer and the inner gate, the porter went back into the entrance lodge and telephoned through to the Chief Officer in the main building. 'Crompton is here, sir.' And the Chief Officer's voice answered, 'Oh, is he? Right. Well, keep him till I come.'

'Very good, sir,' said the gatekeeper; and came out again to the little dark-clad visitor, to explain, 'the Chief Officer will be here in a minute.'

'Quite so. Thank you. Thank you very much,' replied the visitor, somewhat diffidently, as if anxious to be a trouble to no one. Precisely, in fact, as Paul Presset would have answered;

whom Mr Crompton in many ways resembled. He ran his finger round his collar as he acknowledged the services of the gatekeeper, just as Presset might have shot his palm to the back of his neck. He coughed nervously after speaking. And now he stood there in the dimmed light between the two gates, holding his bag all the time, as a mild man does, instead of putting it to the ground and loafing about with the ease of the self-assured. He started slightly as the Chief Officer appeared behind the bars of the inner gate, knocked with a key in his hand on its wicket, and shouted, 'Gate!' And he stepped quickly aside as the gatekeeper hurried out to open to the Chief.

'Good day, Crompton,' said the Chief, coming through the wicket.

'Good day, sir.'

'Your assistant not with you?'

'No, sir. He'll be coming along a little later. He – er—'

'Oh, well, that's all right.' The Chief Officer interrupted the apologetic explanation. 'Come along, and I'll show you your quarters.'

'Yes, sir. Thank you, sir.'

And Mr Crompton followed the Chief Officer through the wicket of the inner gate, across the forecourt, and up into the main building. They walked along a corridor, Mr Crompton a diffident pace behind, till they came to a door which the Chief Officer opened, going ahead of him into the room, like a host.

'These'll be your quarters. I think you'll be quite comfortable here.'

'Yes, sir. Thank you, sir.'

It was a spare warder's room, Mr Crompton saw, rigged up as a simple bed-sitting room for him, with a bed borrowed from the hospital, a table from one of the offices, a plain wooden chair, a Windsor armchair – and a bible.

'Is that all right?' asked the host pleasantly.

'Yes, sir. That's fine,' said the little man, dumping his bag on the chair. 'Fine,' he repeated nervously, for he could not bear to be a nuisance to anyone, or to hurt anyone's feelings.

'Right . . . well . . . good day for the present.'

'Good day, sir.'

And the Chief Officer left him. Mr Crompton unpacked his bag, set his toilet articles and a book on the table, placed his sleeping suit on the cot, and pushed his bag beneath it. This done, he sat himself in the armchair and opened the book.

He was now a prisoner, if a courteously treated one, till after nine tomorrow, when his work would be done. They would not let him out of the prison till then because they wanted to control his food and drink. Two pints of beer they would allow him today, but no more: his brain must be clear and his hand steady for his work in the morning. Nine o'clock in the morning – he let fall his book to think. He was always a little anxious on these vigils; nothing must go wrong. Seven-foot-nine – yes, he always gave the full drop for fear of accidents – sometimes even a little more than was recommended by the table of drops. Seven-foot-nine was what he gave Vostand, the Liverpool murderer, who was a small man. He remembered the Governor of Cannonstone Prison asking, 'What are you going to give him, Crompton?' and when he replied, 'Seven-foot-nine, sir'; the Governor whistling and exclaiming, 'Good God, man! You'll have his head off!' but of course leaving it in confidence to him, who knew his business, had gone through his course in hanging, and was well known to be as humane as possible; and whom he himself had recommended to the Sheriff. Off-hand he couldn't remember what he had given Elsie Merrileys, who had been a little thing – poor child! – but it had certainly been an inch or two more than the figure assigned by the table of drops, so as to make absolutely safe. 'No accidents' had always been his motto; and it was a merciful one, surely. Besides, one accident, and he'd be done: not a governor would recommend him again to his High Sheriff, and there could be no denying that the fees for his work coming in every now and then made a satisfying addition to a working man's income. Ten guineas and all expenses was a pleasant sum. He'd be able to buy now that new bed and its linen that Mrs Crompton wanted so badly: he and Mrs Crompton'd go into Wivelsdale and choose it next week. And, of course, if he got that other job – if the man wasn't reprieved, though of course for *his* sake he hoped the poor fellow would be, he'd be able to get some more furniture for the room. But *one* accident, and his reputation would be gone. And his reputation was pleasing in its way. He knew very well that the Governors recommended him more than any other, declaring, one and all, that Crompton was a 'thoroughly decent little chap, expeditious and humane'. He knew that they told each other that he was a deeply religious man in his private life. He knew that it was a grim joke among the warders that 'his gallows-side manner was perfect'. Not that he approved of joking in this serious connection, but they meant it, in their crude way, as a tribute to his humanity.

Ah, well . . . all would go off all right . . . no sense in worrying . . . nothing had ever gone wrong yet. Mr Crompton took up his novel again and continued reading where he had left off.

He had a lot of time to kill between now and tomorrow, when he would kill a man.

Monday afternoon, and Mr Crompton was still in his Windsor chair reading, though much further on in his book, while Paul sat in his cell with hands clasped in front of him waiting to be taken to his last meeting with Myra. He had sat thus for most of the day. What else was there to do? One didn't want to play dominoes or draughts. And what sense was there in eating? Sometimes he had got up and walked about and dropped a sigh, but not such a sigh as Mr Plaistow and Mr Evans could hear. He had arrested the sigh before it became noticeable. Once he had opened a book, but after reading a few lines he had laid it down again. He could not get on with it as Mr

Crompton was getting on with his. He just sat and thought. There was only one thing to look forward to now, and it was this last visit of Myra's; but could one really look forward to it? How about her last look as they escorted her from the room? Did he really want the interview, or dread it? He didn't know. That last sight of her, that last word – Oh, God, it would be better to be dead, and done with these questions. The Governor, in his sympathy and helpfulness, had advised him not to see her. 'Let it alone, I should,' he had stuttered. 'Such interviews are always too painful, really, what? It's bad luck on her, isn't it, what?' and, after thinking on his advice, Paul had resolved to see neither Mother nor Father but only to write to them in love, and had written to Myra suggesting that she did not come; but she had replied, as he knew she would, that of course she was coming. And the Governor, hearing this, had promised him that his last visit should be in a special room with only a table between him and Myra, and that, before she went, if he gave his word of honour that nothing illicit should pass from hand to hand or mouth to mouth, they might kiss each other goodbye.

A principal officer opened the cell and told them to come along now; and he and his warders went through the empty hall and along empty passages in the direction (as he imagined) of the main entrance. They went into a fairly large room which he judged to be a committee room. Its walls were as bare as all others in the prison, limewashed and painted with a cream dado like his cell; but it had a large polished table, with a dozen or so plain wooden chairs about it, and a large fireplace with a plain chimney piece of stone. Almost before he could apprehend the room, an officer, with the celerity of prisons, gently guided Myra through the door.

They put her, white, haggard, shaking and speechless, at one end of the long table, and Paul at the other, his escort standing one on either side of him; and the officer who had brought Myra went quickly away.

He and Myra faced each other – and neither knew that Mr Crompton was sitting within his four walls, reading a tale, not a great many paces from them.

Myra could say nothing. Only with an agonised sympathy in her eyes she breathed, 'Paul!'

And it was he who said the words he had prepared and rehearsed. 'I want you to be brave tomorrow when the time comes. Will you think that I am trying to be brave, and you must be also?'

'Yes, dear.'

'And of course my last thoughts will be with you. You know that, don't you?'

'Yes.'

'I want you to say to yourself, "If he thinks that I am suffering too much, it'll be all the more difficult, so I must bear up", see?'

'I'll try.'

'You see, dear, you can almost be happy really. You can think that you have been the one bright and lovely thing in my life' – and here his own words played upon his overwrought emotions so that the tears welled up – 'and that I wouldn't have missed living, or I'd have missed you.'

Myra buried her face in the handkerchief that she had been crumpling in her lap. The warders looked away, and one of them set his lips tight.

'I'm sorry,' she said. 'I didn't want to break down.'

'That's all right,' Paul encouraged. 'And what else did I want to say? Oh – tomorrow – don't think it worse than it is. The doctor tells me that it's all over very quickly. He's been extraordinarily kind like everyone else. The Governor has promised that your photograph and your letters may be buried with me. He says he'll do anything I ask. I want you to thank him before you go, if you can – or to write to him – because he's been so good. And you can thank these two gentlemen, too, if you like,' he added with a smile. 'No one could have been kinder. And tell them to thank the other four warders.'

Myra lifted her eyes to them and said, 'Thank you so much'; and they murmured something and nodded, for a prisoner's visitor should not, in strictness, talk to the warders.

Paul replaced his crooked smile and said, 'Well, I've said most that I'd made up my mind to say. Is there anything you want to tell me?'

She thought; but half shook her head and said, 'Only that I shall be with you all the time, right up to the last moment, and beyond.'

Paul nodded and smiled; and Myra, encouraged, went on, 'I shall be with you as much as I am now.'

'Bless you.'

'You'll think that all the time, won't you?'

'Yes. . . . And now I want you to say something else, Myra.' There was a curious, diffident smile at his lips.

'What is it, dear?'

'I want you to say that you forgive me for all the wrong that I've brought into your life.'

'That's not necessary to say—'

'And that you know I never meant it – I never wanted it to happen – I only wanted to bring you all the happiness I could—'

'Of course, of course. . . . And that reminds me, dear, there's one thing I wanted to say. I wanted to say – we all do wrong – terrible wrong sometimes – but' – her lips trembled and she began to break down.

'But what, Myra?'

'But what matters is – what we are as a whole, and I know – whatever people say – that I've been loved by a good man.'

She brought her handkerchief to her eyes and mouth, affected by her own words; and her voice was not in control but broke and gulped as it went on, 'Yes – *good* – not bad. To the end of my life I shall think that, and I know better than anyone else . . . so much more good than bad. . . .'

'You've made me happy by saying that,' said Paul. 'I'm not good. I know *that* well enough, but I don't think I'm quite as bad as people say. And as long as you think it, that's all that seems to matter.'

'I *know* it. I know that, ever since your arrest – whatever you were before – you have been good, and all they can do is to – but there!' and she bit her lip to get control. 'And I wanted to say this, dear: to the last day of my life I'm going to say a prayer for you, "God be good to him, and give him happiness and peace." Mr Hanks said I might, and that it would be all right. He's been so kind.'

'I'm so glad. Will you give him my thanks?'

'Yes.'

'My deepest thanks. Don't forget.'

'No. And, by the way, he sent you his "love".'

'What?'

'Yes. Just that.'

Paul stared at her, and after thought, added with dropped eyes, 'Is he convinced, then, of my innocence?'

'I don't know. . . .'

'Tell him the truth, won't you?' said Paul; and his eyes, gazing into hers, conveyed his meaning.

Myra hesitated, trying to find the right words. 'I don't believe it would matter with him, whatever he thought.'

'Wouldn't it? Then I suppose he believes in Christ.'

'Oh, yes.'

'I should like to, too. I hope I do, but I don't know.' And he told her all about yesterday's Communion Service. And she told him something of the movements in her own thoughts: of her growing desire to serve, and how Mr Hanks was tending and strengthening the desire, and of many projects he was suggesting for her future. For the time this meeting was going so much better, so much more naturally, than any other; if not happy, he was at least at ease. He did not want this one to end. Down below memory there was an anguish ready to rise, but for the time it was overlaid.

It was grey in the room, as if the first of winter darkened the afternoon without. A light must have been switched on in the corridor outside, because he could see a ribbon of yellow radiance along the bottom of the door. Artificial light before the day is done is always saddening; and the sight of it this afternoon raised memories of lamplight in the little parlour behind the stationer's shop at Petfield, of gas flames burning on winter afternoons in his classroom at Bishop Abercorn College, and of electric light switched on in the dusk of hotel rooms where he sat with Myra. And it reminded him that much of the time granted for this interview had passed; and the anguish stirred and lifted.

'How much longer have we got?' he asked one of the warders.

'Not much, I'm afraid,' the man answered. 'Half an hour's the usual time, though I don't think it'll matter if you go on for a little. You go on,' he encouraged.

But at his words the ease had flown from both. The knowledge that there were but a few minutes more stood in the room, disordering their thoughts and disabling speech. They sat staring at each other numbly. Their lips started words which their voices did not support. Once Myra began a phrase, but coughed and killed it; and a sickly smile appeared at her lips. Paul longed to stretch a hand across the table and say by a touch what his voice would not say; but the table was too long, and besides, it wouldn't have been allowed. And then that terrible feeling that he could wish it were over and she gone peeped up and threatened to possess him. This, and it was their last few minutes together! He sat and glared at her, his heart thudding with hopeless despair – a kind of despair which felt it could not cope with life but desired only to lay his head on the block and cry to the headsman, 'Strike! For God's sake, strike! I am defeated.'

And then – before he had got out a word – the officer who had brought Myra opened the door and looked in, somewhat perfunctorily, to see if the interview were over. Perhaps the warders behind signalled to him to keep away for a little longer, because he nodded and went out. But his visit was enough to force Paul to speech. He cleared his throat and said, 'It's about over now, dear. . . . Don't worry. . . . Don't be too unhappy tonight . . . and look here: when it's over – tomorrow, I mean – I want you to begin life again cheerfully. Do you see? I really mean it. I want to *know* that you're going to make the best of the life before you. I want you to forget the past and go and find happiness. . . . If I know you're going to do that, it'll make it all much easier for me. I don't want you to forget me – if you understand – but I want you to begin again, determined to be happy see?'

'Yes.'

'Will you do it?'

'I'll try.'

'Promise me.'

'Yes.'

Paul turned a head to one of the warders. 'The Governor said—'

The warder nodded. 'That's all right,' he said.

And Paul rose. 'You may give me a last kiss. The Governor said you might.' He moved to the side of the table, the warders keeping on either side of him. One of them, by an inclination of the head, signed to Myra to come. She came, and they embraced – tightly – Myra pouring into her kiss all that she had failed to say. Loath to let each other go, they remained in each other's arms for a long half-minute; and the warders did not disturb them. It was Paul who gently broke from her, and, turning to the warder on his right said, 'Let her go now.' And the warder touched a bell which rang in the corridor. Myra's officer came in; and Paul, with a last, lingering hold of her hand, said, 'Goodbye, my dearest.'

'Goodbye. . . .'

'God bless you.'

'And you. . . . Oh, Paul. . . .'

'Take her away,' said Paul. 'Goodbye, my love.'

And with her head shaking from side to side, her face in her handkerchief, Myra was led away by her officer, who put an arm behind her back.

Chapter Seven

And the day wore down into the night, but not before two warders had completed a work on which they had been busy with shovels and pick, in a green plot against the prison wall. On the bricks of the wall, at intervals, certain initials were cut; but nothing else marked the use of the earth beneath the green grass. The eye saw nothing but a green patch lying under the twenty-foot wall.

The two warders had brought little enthusiasm to their task, and little talk. For the most part they had driven the spade into the earth, or wielded the pick, in silence. And when, just before his lunch, the Governor had walked up, in his grey suit and with his cane under his arm, he had barely spoken to them, either. He had looked at the deepening grave, and walked away. The man standing in the grave, a big, square-shouldered fellow with magnificent muscles, had gone on with his quiet work till he chose to say, 'He's here, isn't he?'

'Aye,' said the other, who stood idle above the grave; 'he's coom.' This man was a shorter fellow, but tough and sinewy, with legs a trifle bowed, merry eyes, and an accent from the north.

'Where've they put him?'

'In one of t'warders' rooms. Aye, and with a bible and all!'

'Well,' sighed the first, spitting on his palms and taking up the pick. 'I hope it keeps fine for him. Funny job, his.'

'Aye, that's reet. . . . But Ah doan't know that Ah reckon so much to this job, neither. It's noan so much to write home aboot when tha cooms to look at it. Nooa, Ah reckon Ah've done better jobs nor this, tha' knows.'

The first man did not answer the witticism. He exchanged pick for shovel, as if it were best not discussed. But no one likes to leave a thesis unfinished, and the man from the north continued, 'Diggin' a grave for a chap that's as sound as meself. Wey, he's probably talkin' nineteen to doozen, at moment, to them two lads fra Dartmoor! Chattin' away like a two-year-owd!'

'Seems silly,' agreed the taciturn one from the grave.

'Aye, and him not aboov a hundred yards away, while we're doin' it!'

'Well, someone's got to do it,' grumbled the one from the grave. 'And, anyhow, it seems to me I'm doing it, not you.'

'And tha'rt doin' very nicely, lad,' grinned the other.

'Well, suppose you give us a lift.' The toiler tossed the pick on one side, put a hand on either rim of the grave, and vaulted up out of it.

'But tha wer doin' it champion!' objected his friend.

'Never mind that,' said the other, shaking his trousers into place, and dusting them. 'You do your share of the dirty work.'

'Aw reet!' And the other leapt down into the grave. 'Keep cool. Allus keep cool. Give us t'shovel. I never wor one to shirk, tha knows. Nah then, lads, heave it oop!' And he was working with a will, while the other stood above the grave, idle and gazing at the wall. For some time he said nothing, this one, but sucked his teeth and contemplated the bricks in the wall. Then, observing the initials cut in this brick and that, he drew one more sibilant suck and muttered, 'Well, he'll be in good company.'

'Aye, that's reet.' The man from the north gave his glance at the wall. 'That ought to be summat to comfort 'im, any road.'

'Though I daresay some of 'em weren't such bad fellows, after all,' suggested the first.

'Nooa; that's reet. They're never so bad when you know them. And no one can say what brought them to it. Happen there was more to it than any of us knows. Happen they didn't have much chance. But toss us the pick, lad, and let's get on with it, any road. He's waitin'.'

And the Governor, on leaving them and returning to his office, had felt no more ease about his task of signing the notice to the coroner to hold an inquest on a man with whom he had just been in conversation, and with whom, after the notice was sent, he would soon be in conversation with again. He had been to Presset that morning, and Presset had laid a little proposition before him. He had suggested that some small piece of his personal property – or say a sovereign or two – should be given to each of the six warders who had looked after him, because they had all been so kind. And the Governor had told him that this would never be allowed, but he was sure that the men would be grateful and touched that he had thought of it. And he had come away from this talk to sign this notice to the coroner. He hesitated before signing it; he sighed as he wrote his name; and then he pushed it a little way to the right and sat over it pondering, with his elbow on the desk and his penholder knocking his teeth. Then he sighed again, and got up, and looked out of the window at the prison yard.

The day wore down into night, and darkness gathered over England. In the living-room of their cottage at Petfield, an old couple, nearing eighty, sat opposite one another in front of a fire. The leaping flames of the fire were the only light that fought with the falling dark. The old lady's face was a greenish white; her knit-up mouth moved out and in; her eyes protruded in a set horror, somewhat as a fish's eyes protrude when it finds itself on the horror of dry land. The clock ticked on the mantelpiece – ticked away the last minutes of a day – and sometimes the old lady's eyes, almost mad, glanced up at it. Then a shiver rent her. The old man twisted his long grey moustaches or stroked the neat pointed beard of which once he had been so proud. He said little; he just sat there in a mood that was wooden and dull, because helpless. Once or twice he looked anxiously at his wife's face. He lit a pipe, but it was a long time before the shaking hand that held the match could fire the tobacco in the bowl. And in a few minutes the pipe was partly ashes, and completely out.

'I'd better get the lamp,' he said.

The old woman glanced at the clock. Yes, it was doing its duty mercilessly: it was ten minutes later than when last she looked at it. Now, suddenly, her face had the greenish hue of someone whose stomach has overturned; and she got up quickly to stagger to privacy. Her husband jumped up and held her by the armpits and aided her from the room. For a while he supported her, while she vomited and groaned and vomited again. When she was better he led her into the kitchen, her head swaying as she groaned, 'My boy! my boy!' or even gave a mad shriek, 'Paul!'

He put her – or let her fall – into a basket chair; and without a word, tried to light his pipe again.

'Why don't you go to bed?' he suggested at last.

'Go to bed?' She stared at him. 'Go to bed? Don't be a fool. Do you think I shall sleep? Are *you* going to sleep while Paul is . . . oh, my boy! Oh, Paul! . . . It's a wicked suggestion, and I wonder that you have the heart to make it.'

'It's no good attacking me,' said the old man, but not ungently. 'I don't see what's gained by that. I only meant "lie down". You can't sit about from now till – for another dozen hours. There's no sense in it. If you liked, I might go to the doctor's and get you something that'd give you a little sleep. Anything's better than this. Just sitting about and waiting. Upon my soul, I wish it were over.'

'How can you *say* such a thing? How can you *say* such a thing? *Paul* – and you wish it were over! Paul, your only son!'

'Well, you know what I mean,' grumbled the old man. 'I want what's best for you. I want you to try to sleep.'

'I don't want to try to sleep. Sleep while he is suffering! Sleep through his last night on earth! I'm going to do all I can to keep awake. I told him in my letter my thoughts would be supporting him all the time – and you want me to sleep! I said, "If you wake up in the night, just think, Mother is with me, thinking of me and praying for me." And I said, "When the time comes, remember that I'm nearly eighty and I shall be coming to you very soon, and God will let me comfort you for all that they are doing to you." And I'm going to do what I promised him. I'm saying over and over again, "I'm with you, Paul; your mother is with you." If I doze off even for a moment, I shall never forgive myself.'

'Well, I think you're making yourself ill like this.'

'I hope I do make myself ill. I hope I make myself ill and die and go to my boy.'

The egotist in Aubrey Presset was tempted to inquire, 'And what about me?' but pity conquered, and he said nothing.

Jane Presset looked at him and shook her head, her despair being too complete for tears. It was a despair that could issue only in physical sickness. 'I'm sorry, Aubrey. I don't know what I'm saying. I'm going mad, I think. You're being very good to me, and I don't know what I would do without you.'

'That's all right, old lady. Come back to the parlour fire.'

'Supposing I had been alone!' suggested Jane, rising to follow him. 'Supposing I'd had to go through this alone!'

'Someone'd have come and sat with you,' he explained, helping her along. 'People do.'

'Yes, but it wouldn't have been you. Not his father – oh!' – the word reminded her of all, and she glanced again at the clock, as they came stumbling into the parlour together. 'Oh, what am I to do? I can't bear this much longer. Half-past five.' And her head began to roll in an agony of realisation, as she sank into her chair by the fire. Aubrey, looking at her falling jaw and starting eyes, got up with an oath and took the clock from the room.

'Better put the damned thing away,' he said.

Jane did not answer. Probably she had not heard.

He returned with the lamp and set it on the table, and resumed his place in the chair opposite her. And here they both sat for a long time without speaking. Now and then Aubrey kicked the fire with his heel or put on a piece of coal. He lit his pipe again and held the bowl meditatively, playing a tattoo with the mouthpiece on his teeth and gazing into the fire.

Jane spoke suddenly, 'Thank God we shall never see this room again, or this home. Thank God we're going soon. I thought I should live and die in Petfield, but I never want to see it again. I never want to come near it. Thank God we're going somewhere where every field will look different. I thought this home was going to be the place we should both die in; I never thought we should have to begin all over again – begin from the beginning somewhere else. . . .'

'I daresay it won't be so bad,' he comforted. 'Things never are. One gets used to things.'

'I shall never get used to it. I shall never get used to what I have to remember. I'm too old. It'll – oh, but I'm thinking about myself instead of about him – "I'm with you, Paul. Mother is with you. I'm with you. I'm at your side. I'm thinking of you" ' – and her lips fell to framing such sentences over and over again. Her eyes and thoughts had gone from her husband, and she looked to be gibbering.

So they sat on. Aubrey Presset, not knowing what to do and disliking his thoughts, picked up at one time a newspaper that lay unopened on the table. He glanced at some of the headlines and cross-headings, and thought of Paul: 'New Play opens at His Majesty's Tomorrow . . . Football . . . Great Day of Sport on Thursday . . . Curtain goes up on a Brilliant Winter Season . . . First Preparations for Christmas. . . .' He closed the paper again, absent-mindedly folding and refolding it, as if shaping it for an envelope. Then he got up and went to the window. He put the blind to one side and looked out. Instantly he heard a scamper of feet which ran down the hill to the High Street. Hardly once in these last few days had he looked from the window but he saw somebody walking furtively past to look up at the house of two old people whose son was soon to be hanged. Nor gone down the High Street to the shops without people turning their heads and whispering together. And for half a century he had been vain of the figure he showed to Petfield! He had thought himself intellectually a cut above the rest, an artist, a man of birth and gifts! He dropped the blind and came back into the room.

Jane was still sitting in her chair, leaning uncomfortably forward and gazing ahead of her, like a stone statue of despair. He went and put a hand on her shoulder.

'Come along, old lady. Come and lie down. You needn't sleep, but you can rest your body if not your mind. And I'll be sitting beside you. Come on, to please me. I'd rather you did.'

At first he thought she had not heard. But after a prolonged silence she stood up on tottering feet and consented to be led upstairs. But as she passed the room that had been Paul's her head rolled and swayed. Her husband steadied her, and got her to the bed in their room, where he laid her down, putting a second pillow under her head and an eiderdown over her. And she lay there, staring up at the ceiling, while he sat beside her, with a hand on each knee.

In her little bedroom at Hoelane Rectory Myra sat also with lost eyes. She sat on a hard chair, leaning forward, both arms extended together at the side of the knee, the fingers clasped. She sat still; she did not sway or moan. Sometimes her breast heaved and sank in a long sigh that caught itself before completing; sometimes a great shiver ran through her. Her eyes were dry and fixed, for her pain, like Jane Presset's, was too complete to move in tears.

It was dark now, and eight o'clock; Jane Presset had long been lying on her bed gazing at the ceiling; Aubrey Presset had sat for an hour at her bedside; and Mr Crompton, in his room, had nearly finished his novel. Myra wanted to be alone: from now to the morning she had got to go through with it. Later she would lie down perhaps; lie down and stare at the darkness. A teapot and empty cup stood on the dressing-table, and some aspirin for her head when it throbbed and throbbed. Mr Hanks had brought these up for her, and kissed her before leaving her alone. And Mrs Hanks had brought her up some brandy, begging her not to put too great a strain on herself.

Mr Hanks, before she left him in his study downstairs, had offered to be with her all through her long vigil, but she had said, 'I'd rather be alone. I'd rather not be seen. You do understand, don't you?'

'Of course,' he said, with a sympathy that she could feel like a supporting arm. 'Of course. And you won't really be quite alone. Our Blessed Lord will be with you, if ever He has stood by anyone. Yes. Think of that sometimes. He is with you, both. *Both*. Yes, surely, surely.'

'I think of it. . . . I try to believe it.'

'It is so,' said Mr Hanks, with his simple, uncriticising faith.

And he, knowing all, had tried to comfort her by pointing out that, although there had been a great and terrible evil in the past, God had wrought good from it. Grandeur even. He had lifted her, said Mr Hanks, to heights that otherwise she might never even have glimpsed, and beyond question – beyond question – He had carried Paul, the sinner, to something better than he had been. 'And remember, my dear, he goes to the scaffold in good company.'

'You mean . . .' asked Myra.

'I mean that, even though he's guilty, there's One on the scaffold with him who's been there before, by the side of the guilty. Isn't it so? Yes. Of course. . . .'

'And there is forgiveness for him?'

'There is forgiveness for all.'

'Even for *that*?'

'There is forgiveness in full measure, pressed down and flowing over. Yes. Don't doubt it. God is so much kinder than men, isn't He? So very much kinder, till God wakes in them.'

'But *she*, Mr Hanks? . . .'

Mr Hanks shook his head, but in affirmation, not in doubt. 'Don't you think, my dear, that if God has worked so much good out of it all for you and him, He has worked also for her?'

'Oh, I do try to believe it so. I hope it so. If one only *knew*. . . . And oh, Mr Hanks, what is he suffering now? What is he thinking – there? What will the night be like for him – and the dawn? Oh, God, oh, God, how can we torture people so, whatever they've done? And his mother. It'll kill her.'

'She knows that I have a chain of good people praying for her throughout the night, and I think she'll feel their support. Dear, good, faithful, understanding souls, each praying for an hour or so in their own homes. For you, too, and for *him*. Think of it sometimes. He will go to his God, wrapped round with the prayers of good people—'

'Ah, you have been so good! What should we have done without you?'

'There, there! Never mind that—'

'And you will come to me in the morning, won't you? Be with me then. I think I shall want someone then.'

'I shall be with you. Of course. Of course.'

He touched her shoulder and she gave him one look of gratitude, and went slowly up the stairs to her long vigil.

That was two hours ago. Two hours had gone, and there were thirteen more to go. The shiver passed through her again: 'Paul! Paul!' her fingers clenched; her lips pressed together; and she raised her eyebrows patiently. 'I must bear it.'

In his house on the prison wall the Governor sat in his study with his eyes on the fire and a book dropped to his knees. After dinner he had sat for a time in the drawing-room with his wife, speaking not at all, while she bent her head over her needlework, respecting his silence. Then he had decided that he must be alone, and had gone to his study and walked up and down it with jaw thrown out. He had tried to write some letters but, his mind astray, he had made every mistake. A bad taste had formed in his mouth and an ache settled across his brows, so that he had got up, helped himself to some brandy, and gone out for a walk, to get the night air on his forehead. But his return towards the high grey curtain wall and the gloomy halls behind, silhouetted against the night sky, had set that brown taste in his mouth again and renewed the throbbing in his head. In his study he had taken another tot of brandy and thrown himself into the easy chair with a book. But, unable to make sense of more than two paragraphs at once, he had let the book fall and fixed his eyes on the fire. 'I shall be damned glad when it's all over,' he had told himself a dozen times. 'Damned glad.'

Within the walls of the prison, behind the cell doors, the six hundred prisoners had worked since tea at their cellular labour, or lain on their beds and read, or sat on their stools and drawn on their slates. Or they had passed the time, in the fashion of prisoners, with some stealthy and forbidden occupation. This man made patterns and buildings with the furnishings of his cell: many quaint patterns, and oriental palaces even, can be made with a bible, a prayer book, two library books, a mug, a salt jar, a water can, a plate, a tin basin, and a chamber. Another man carved an Eastern dagger out of the bone handle of a toothbrush. Another moulded little men out of a fingerful of soap or cobbler's wax, or shaped the private parts of women, to give some futile ministration to his hunger. Others twisted and twisted a length of mailbag thread, or wove to their fancy with the ravellings of blankets, or made a mandoline and some music by stretching threads across the wash-bowl and plucking them gently when sure that the landing officer was out of hearing. It was cold in the cells – it always was – and they kept warm as they worked, with blankets round their shoulders and their feet.

But, whatever their occupation, it was pierced through by the thought of a man in a cell down below. The absence of all vocational or domestic interests in their lives, and the consequent vacuity of their minds, together with the depressed condition inseparable from the imprisoned and the driven, rendered them abnormally responsive to any emotional stimulus, so that they laughed more loudly than other men at humour in a sermon, wept more quickly at pathos in a song, fired up more fiercely at what they conceived to be unjust treatment, and certainly thrilled more tensely at the thought of a man in their midst who would have his neck broken for him tomorrow. Some dropped their work to pace between door and wall and think about it. Some left off drawing obscene pictures on their slates for their comfort, and drew instead a body swinging below a gallows, with head insanely fallen. Others mounted on their stools to the high window frames of cast iron, glazed with fluted glass, and peered through, in the dead hope of seeing some homicidal activity in the yard. They saw nothing and heard nothing, and were the more unhealthily disturbed for that. In some their vindictiveness against society was heightened, so that their lips and jaws set in ugly lines, and their eyes were sullen. A few shrugged and were indifferent to the death of a fellow prisoner, but not unexcited by it. No one was unexcited by it. A very few who had 'found religion' prayed for the man down below. The rest just thought about him, and, while pitying the 'poor b—', were probably glad of this interest and excitement. And in the silence, in their inability to allay in any way the curious emotions and cravings within them, till they were called in ten hours' time, they began to feel the maddening pressure of the thirteen-foot box that housed them – the heavy, arched ceiling, the massive, iron-sheeted door with its strong spring lock inaccessible from within, and the limewashed walls of which the outer one was plastered that one might not interfere with the bricks. The pressure began to choke them and to force their eyes forward from their sockets.

The prison was strangely quiet. The warders went listlessly about their tasks, since there was nothing else to do, but their thoughts were held by one part of the prison only – one locked door. And none of their looks were quite the same tonight; when spoken to suddenly, they seemed to be wool gathering, and their movements, in response to commands, were uneasily brisk; their laughter was uncomfortable and quickly over. Many were conscious of a feeling of alarm, no more analysable than that which visits us when a storm lowers; but there was a still, frightened, lowering atmosphere in the whole prison, in every wing and gallery and corridor, every ward and office and store. It was an unnatural hush in which you heard more clearly than usual the restless prisoners pacing up and down. The bang of a door made you start, and you noticed the clocks ticking. Such a quiet fills any house where a man is dying, but it is not heavy and dank with a feeling of guilt. Irrational, inexplicable, and unjustifiable perhaps, but every man in the building felt worse tonight, and more capable of dark deeds. And especially those who denied the feeling most vigorously. They protested too much and too loud.

Mr Crompton prepared for sleep. The chaplain, the doctor, and the Governor reminded their servants to call them punctually in the morning. Somewhere in the outer world the Under-Sheriff bade his servant call him early.

And in his cell Paul lay on his bed; and his two warders sat at the table, silent, unhappy, blunted by perplexity, and stunned from thought. Paul thought of his childhood, and of his father and mother whom he would never see again, and of the river in Clissold Park and the dead leaves and the blossom, and of Myra – 'goodbye, my beloved'. And he thought often and often, 'It is done quickly. Probably one second of excruciating pain, and it's all over. I can hold myself together for that.' He tried to picture what he would see in the execution room, his last view of the world; and he rehearsed his last words. He turned in his bed, but not too often, because he wanted the warders to think him 'a good patient, who bore up well'. Sometimes he waited a long time before allowing himself to turn. Sweat formed on his brow and slipped to the pillow, as if the cell, with its dim light burning, were unusually warm, but he waited before brushing it away or throwing back the clothes; because dignity sat ill with restlessness. But why, he asked himself, did he worry any more about what people thought of him? Soon he would be done forever with the world. One moment of excruciating pain, and he would be done with it. Done with it, and what then? He had made his effort of faith, asked forgiveness for his fearful sin, and if all the chaplain said was true, he would pass into God's peace. In a few hours. Peace. Why, if this were true, surely he ought to be almost happy! And if it were not true, well, he must just shrug his shoulders, and then square them to the senseless burden of life. A burden and a blow, and all would be over. Peace in either event. And in either event he must finish well – oh, yes, yes! This vanity, or this pride, was with one to the last, stepping like a faithful friend on to the execution platform at one's side, and standing under the beam. He must show a straight back, a lifted head, and a steady lip. 'It is done quickly. Twenty seconds from cell door to scaffold; and one second of pain. I can hold myself in control for that half minute. I'll not show fear. I'll not show fear.' To steady himself for the great moment he repeated it a thousand times as the night wore away. 'I'll not show fear.'

Chapter Eight

Paul opened his eyes to see the cell grey with morning. The grey light brightened so that the dim lamp burning in the roof lost all its power. One of the warders uncrossed his legs and stretched them before him. A sparrow chirruped and chattered in welcome to the day. Paul's heart began an irregular and rapid hammering; and he tried to steady it by repeating, 'One moment of pain – that's all. . . .' He lifted his hand off the bedclothes to see if it was shaking. It was, and he clenched his fist to master it, but could not. 'Oh, God, give me strength. . . .' The light brightened. How much longer? – but he dared not ask the time. 'Get it over . . . get it over . . . get it over. . . . God, give me strength. One moment of pain and all will be over. Oh, Myra . . . Mother . . . Dad. . . .' It was lonely with nobody near him in his last moments, but there! All men died alone. The moment had to come when they went alone, and for him that moment had come some time before his death: that was all. It was as if he were dead while yet alive. How quickly the light was brightening. He might as well get up, for something to do. He lifted his body and put a foot to the cold floor, leaving his bed for the last time. Some instability in his limbs caused him to stumble; and the nearest warder put out a hand to help him, and then patted him encouragingly on the back.

'It's all right,' said Paul. 'I'm not afraid. I missed my footing, that's all.'

The prison awoke. The prisoners rose, washed, and cleaned their cells, thinking of one thing only. Sometimes they stopped their work to imagine the scene more vividly. At twenty-five minutes past seven breakfast was served to them in their cells; bread, margarine, tea and skilly; and they wondered what *he* was having. They saw in their imagination a kitchen officer in his white coat taking him eggs and bacon and coffee. Having eaten their breakfast, they wondered what the time was, for the prison clock was not striking today: it had been purposely stopped that none might know when the hour was nine. An unearthly silence had settled on the prison. The great halls were soundless as tombs. Not the most fractious of prisoners made a noise in his cell this morning. Associated labour did not begin till nine-forty; and behind their locked doors, six hundred men either sat thinking in their cells, thirteen feet by seven, or paced them, five steps this way and six back.

The Governor, who had tossed most of the night, rose from his bed, warm-eyed and heavy-limbed for want of sleep. At his dining-room table he sipped some coffee but left his breakfast untouched. He glanced at the headlines of his paper, but took none of them in. His thoughts running to the duty ahead, he began to feel rather sick, and, muttering 'Damn!' he got up and mixed himself a strong brandy at the sideboard and drank it quickly. His brow felt like wood. After a quick, almost frightened glance at the clock on the mantelpiece he left his room in his house on the prison wall, crossed the forecourt, and went to his office in the main building, to await the Under-Sheriff. Except for the large writing table, littered with official forms, and a few book shelves and cupboards, the room was as plain as any other in the prison: it had the same limewashed walls and low ceiling, and its window, looking on to one of the yards, was barred. A huge plan of the prison, browning and freckled with damp, was nailed to the wall, like a schoolroom map. This showed, near to the ground-plan of one of the halls, the ground-plan of a very small square building, which the architect, long dead, had designed for the business of today.

The Governor did not look at the plan; he stood by the window and looked out at the prison yard. He was thinking of Presset. How on earth could that decent little fellow, considerate for all, have done so shocking a deed? It defeated the imagination. Last night when he went to say goodbye to him, Presset, considerate to the last, had said: 'I can never thank you enough, sir, for all your kindness. And these gentlemen, too, and the others; I'm sure they've all been kindness itself. I don't want anyone to be upset about me. I dare say I deserve it, and anyhow, I'm not sorry to go. So please don't let anybody worry.' Whereon the Governor had been moved to say with swelling eyes, 'Goodbye, and God bless you.'

Steps in the corridor. It was the Under-Sheriff. He came in, a silver-haired, clean-skinned, trim little gentleman, drawing off his gloves and automatically smoothing and folding them, as if he had come to tea.

'Good morning, Governor.'

'Good morning.'

The Under-Sheriff looked at his watch. 'I thought I should have a job to get in,' said he. 'There's the usual crowd of loiterers about the gate. Or rather, it's six times as big a crowd as usual, and they rushed towards my car to peer at me. What satisfaction they get from seeing me I don't know.'

'Gaping idiots!' snapped the Governor.

And neither of them said much more. Waiting there was a little like the assembling of mourners before a funeral. The Governor continued to stare out of the window. The Under-Sheriff rose up and down upon his toes. The M.O. joined them, and the Chief Officer, but after nods of greeting, did nothing to open a conversation. They too stood about waiting.

At last the Governor, looking at his watch, mumbled with a bitterness that surprised him, 'Well . . . now for murder number two, what?' and strolled towards the door. The Under-Sheriff passed out before him, and the Chief Officer and the doctor after him. In silence the four men walked through the corridor and down the long hall to the condemned cell; and about them was the silence of six hundred persons straining their ears for sinister sounds. Though they walked as quietly as in a church, their footsteps echoed under the high roof; and nervously the Under-Sheriff coughed. Immediately they felt that the six hundred prisoners had heard.

At the door of the condemned cell stood Mr Crompton and his assistant, both in suits of a decent sombreness. Mr Crompton's collar was celluloid and very white, his tie black and thin, and one felt that the shirt-front beneath was false. He held in his hand something that looked like a leather belt; and his assistant, a slightly taller man than Mr Crompton, held a narrower strap.

Once again the Governor looked at his watch. He waited a little, and then nodded. The Chief Officer opened the cell door; and Mr Crompton entered, the Governor following him. Presset was standing there, dressed now in his own clothes, with his two warders and the chaplain. His suit was the pepper-and-salt suit in which he had hoped to escape from Elm Tree Road and the police. His shirt was open at the throat and had no collar, for a new, strange collar awaited him in the execution shed. His face was grey with foretasted death, and his eyes started, like the eyes of a mouse in the jaws of a cat. The Governor dropped his eyes, but he knew that he would see that face ever and again, forever – a face holding terror at bay, its texture grey, its eyes starting, and its nerves twitching, as it looked for the first time at Crompton. And Crompton's quiet and celerity and efficiency – Crompton who, in his smallness and soft-voiced consideration, was so like Presset!

'Good morning, old chap,' Crompton said. (Yes, good morning was what he said.) 'Just put your hands behind your back will you? That's right. Thank you.' And he pinioned him with the leather strap. 'That's right. Thank you,' he repeated to the trussed figure, and turned and glanced at the Governor.

Automatically the Governor nodded, and immediately the chaplain led the way out of the cell at a quick pace. The executioner and his assistant slipped in front of him, like two children or two cats, so as to be first at the door of the execution shed. Behind the chaplain came the Governor, and the Deputy-Governor who had since appeared, and the Chief Officer after him. Then Paul himself between his two warders – his lips moving. 'Oh, God, strengthen me,' and his eyes starting, but his steps firm and his head erect. Last of all came the doctor. With no formality this little procession passed very quickly out of the building into the bright day, and Paul saw in front of him the execution shed—

It was a minute to nine. In her bedroom at Petfield, Jane Presset stared up at the clock which she insisted should be there. Supported by the arm of her husband who was stroking her hand, she sat on the bed, jaw fallen, eyes staring, face twitching, grey-haired and ashen and old. Quick short gasps came from her; her body and limbs quivered and shuddered; and Aubrey Presset was saved from thinking of his son by fear that she might die. The clock ticked on to the hour, and Jane Presset shrieked madly, 'Paul! Paul! Paul'! She tore from her husband's hands and beat her head with her fists. She hurled herself face downward on the bed, clutched at the pillow, and shook her head from side to side. Mercilessly the church clock of Petfield struck nine, and in madness she beat her fist on the pillow, 'Oh! Oh! Oh!' Nine times the clock struck, without hurry; and she stopped, deadly still, madly still, to listen. *Paul!* What are they doing to you?' Aubrey Presset tried to lift her, but she cried, 'No, no, no . . .' and he sat helpless by the prostrate and quivering figure, with an arm across her shoulder. She would be better when the paroxysm was over.

The head of another lay pressed in agony on the counterpane of a bed. But Myra was kneeling. She knelt in the little bedroom at Hoelane Rectory. For an hour or more she and Mr Hanks had sat side by side, not saying much, but he holding her hand in a strong grip as the hour passed. 'It's those last few minutes that'll be so awful,' she had said, shivering.

'We'll kneel together, my dear,' he had answered. 'Yes . . .' and he patted her hand.

He had watched the clock, and at five minutes to nine he had gently drawn her to her knees and knelt beside her. 'Let me keep your hand,' he had said. And Myra, burying her head in the crook of her arm, had left her hand in his. And he began to pray aloud, 'O Blessed Lord, the Father of all mercies and the God of all comforts, we beseech Thee look down in pity and compassion upon Thy afflicted servant. Thou writest bitter things against him, and makest him to possess his former sin, but, O God our Father, in Thy dear mercy, strengthen and support him; break not the bruised reed nor quench the smoking flax; speak to him of Thy forgiveness and take him to Thyself, that the bones which Thou has broken may rejoice. Deliver him from fear of the enemy, and show him the light of Thy countenance—'

But the clock clicked and prepared to strike nine, and a shiver like a rigor rushed through Myra, and she tore her hand from his. He saw that she was not listening to him nor praying for Paul. She was crying to God, 'Take me too . . . take me . . . oh, take me. . . .' And he knew that she was gone from him into some blinding desolation where he could not reach her. Like Aubrey Presset, miles away, he rose and laid his hand on her shoulder that she might feel, if possible, the comfort of a friend. And he waited till she could find her way back to him; waited on duty, as he had waited at the Old Bailey doors.

The clock struck, and Myra became stiller than stone, Nine times it beat upon them.

Meanwhile, far away in Gunterbury Gaol, Mr Crompton and his assistant had passed into the execution shed, quickly followed by the two warders and Paul, while the Governor and other officers stood halted to let them pass. As they too followed and stood bunched about the door, Paul was making his last great effort of his life. He had stepped briskly on to the trap, half a step ahead of his warders, and now he stood beneath the beam, squared his shoulders, and said aloud to them all, 'Well, goodbye everybody, and thank you. . . .' and to himself, 'Goodbye, Myra, my dear; goodbye, dear Mum and Dad. . . .' Crompton's assistant quickly strapped his feet together; the two warders stepped quickly off the trap to the platform on either side of it and took hold of the two short ropes to steady themselves when the trap-doors collapsed; Crompton quickly produced and fitted a white cap over his head and face, making of him a grotesque, hooded figure, slipped the rope's noose over his head, drew it close round his neck so that the 'thimble' came just under the ear, and fixed it there with the little leather washer. The slack of the rope was held together by a piece of black thread which must snap at the first pull; and Crompton gave a glance at this slack, took one of Paul's pinioned hands and pressed it in farewell, stepped off the trap to the lever, and pulled it briskly. The Governor gasped, as the two doors of the trap fell inward, striking the walls of the pit with a thud muffled by their pads, and Paul went from sight. The rope tautened and began to sway.

Instantly the doctor, very white, went down into the pit, while the others wandered silently out into the bright sunlight and lingered by the door, the chaplain interlocking his fingers and pulling them apart, and the Under-Sheriff fiddling automatically in his waistcoat pocket, as if he would like to take out a cigarette and light it. The shadow of the execution shed lay long on the prison yard. The great wings of the prison were silent, but the far-away rumble and rumour of traffic came over the boundary walls. The doctor joined them in a little while, and assured them that he was dead and must have died instantaneously. And Crompton, who had followed and heard this, looked up at the Governor and asked, 'Was everything satisfactory, sir?'

'What?' inquired the Governor, who was thinking of other things.

'Was everything satisfactory, sir?'

'Oh, yes, yes. Quite. Thank you, Crompton.

'Very good, sir.'

And Crompton went back to his room to collect his bag, and get ready to return to his home. And all the others went away also, leaving Paul alone. They must leave him there, in his last room, for an hour. Crompton's assistant followed his senior, aching for a cigarette. The Governor and the Under-Sheriff made their way into the prison towards the Governor's office, to sign the declaration for the outer gate, where the crowds awaited it. The chaplain went with them. The doctor and the Chief Officer wandered back to their houses. The Deputy-Governor strolled off into the prison yards, where he could be alone.

And in the silent pit, the pinioned and wrecked body, with its hooded head at a foolish angle, swung perceptibly no more, but sometimes twisted round and back again; round and back again; the body of a man who had foundered.

The dead leaves lay on the New River where it curved between the trees of Clissold Park, and the children ran in play along the railings that guarded its green banks. The wren sang in the woods that mantle the Lower Greensand Hills, while the linnet hopped amid the furze and the rabbit scuttled beneath the bracken. In a garden in Elm Tree Road its particular robin sang above the unkempt grasses and the weeds. On the meadows and hills around Petfield the sunlight threw long shadows into a silence disturbed only by the noise of cows cropping the rich, hale grass, and the twitter of the goldfinch on his perch, and the song of the skylark on the wing. And down in the hollows of the South Downs the copses of bare thorn were a purple cloud of berries, with the rooks and magpies rising above them, at the sound of happy riders cantering up the hill.

THE END

also available from
CAPUCHIN CLASSICS

You Shall Know Them
Vercors. Introduced by Ann Atkins
From its opening with a suspicious death, Vercors' controversial and chilling masterpiece wrangles with the uncomfortable question 'What is man?' And, consequently, 'What is murder?'

An Error of Judgement
Pamela Hansford Johnson. Introduced by Ann Widdecombe
An Error of Judgement is a subtle study of human weakness and conflict. Partly a wry social comedy and partly a study in good and evil, it is brilliantly written and observed, assured and skilful, a truly modern work by one of the most underrated novelists of the last century.
'One of the best novels in English since 1939.' Anthony Burgess

The Voyage
Charles Morgan. Introduced by Valentine Cunningham
First published in 1940, *The Voyage* is a story warm with Morgan's love of France. Set in the Charente country and the Paris music-halls.
'As one reads one forgets everything, enchanted by the beauty of the setting, fascinated by the subtlety of the spiritual reasoning, the provisional speculations, the ethereal love-story.' *Daily Telegraph*

Silas Marner
George Eliot. Introduced by Jane Feaver
Set in the early 19th century, *Silas Marner* tells the story of a weaver expelled from a small religious community for a theft he did not commit. Living as a recluse in the village of Raveloe, Silas exists only for work and his precious hoard of money – until that money is stolen and an orphaned child wanders into his house.

Silas Marner is a classic and exceptionally powerful tale of familial love and loyalty, reward and punishment, and above all humble friendships.